THE CAGE OF DARK HOURS

TOR BOOKS BY MARINA LOSTETTER

THE FIVE PENALTIES

The Helm of Midnight
The Cage of Dark Hours

THE
CAGE
OF
DARK
HOURS

MARINA LOSTETTER

TOR

TOR PUBLISHING GROUP
NEW YORK

THE CAGE OF DARK HOURS

Copyright © 2023 by Little Lost Stories LLC

Map by Jennifer Hanover

A Tor Book
Published by Tom Doherty Associates/Tor Publishing Group
120 Broadway
New York, NY 10271

www.tor-forge.com

Tor® is a registered trademark of Macmillan Publishing Group, LLC.

Library of Congress Cataloging-in-Publication Data

Names: Lostetter, Marina J., author.
Title: The cage of dark hours / Marina Lostetter.
Description: First edition. | New York : Tor, a Tom Doherty Associates Book, 2023. |
Series: The Five Penalties ; 2
Identifiers: LCCN 2022040595 (print) | LCCN 2022040596 (ebook) |
ISBN 9781250757470 (hardcover) | ISBN 9781250258755 (ebook)
Classification: LCC PS3612.O7745 C34 2023 (print) | LCC PS3612.O7745 (ebook) |
DDC 813/.6—dc23
LC record available at https://lccn.loc.gov/2022040595
LC ebook record available at https://lccn.loc.gov/2022040596

Our books may be purchased in bulk for promotional, educational, or business use.
Please contact your local bookseller or the Macmillan Corporate and Premium Sales Department at
1-800-221-7945, extension 5442, or by email at MacmillanSpecialMarkets@macmillan.com.

First Edition: 2023

Printed in the United States of America

0 9 8 7 6 5 4 3 2 1

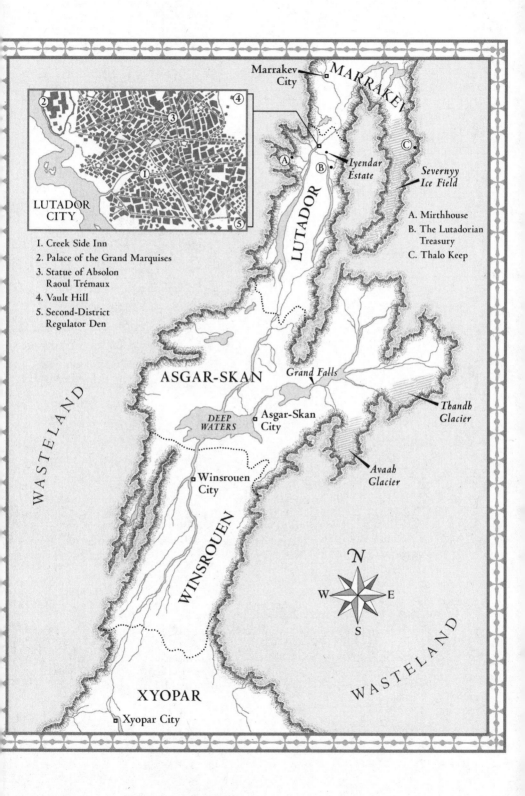

LUTADOR
CITY

1. Creek Side Inn
2. Palace of the Grand Marquises
3. Statue of Absolon
   Raoul Trémaux
4. Vault Hill
5. Second-District
   Regulator Den

Marrakev
City

MARRAKEV

Iyendar
Estate

Severnyy
Ice Field

A. Mirthhouse
B. The Lutadorian
   Treasury
C. Thalo Keep

LUTADOR

ASGAR-SKAN

Grand Falls

Thandh
Glacier

DEEP
WATERS

Asgar-Skan
City

Avaah
Glacier

Winsrouen
City

WINSROUEN

WASTELAND

N
W E
S

XYOPAR

Xyopar City

WASTELAND

THE CAGE OF DARK HOURS

ARKENSYRE MAGIC

You can't enchant a person.

Or so everyone says.

Magic comes from the Valley rim, where eons ago the five gods poured out their divine force to erect a protective barrier. Their essence seeped into the stone and soil, the trees and sand. These materials can be harvested and engineered into enchantments—sacred objects that allow people to wield the gods' power in strict, specific ways.

This is how magic works.

Or so everyone says.

DAYS PAST

The Helm of Midnight:
The Five Penalties, Book One

Melanie DuPont was unwittingly—*impossibly*—enchanted. It was an accident, one Sebastian Leiwood, her fiancé, inadvertently committed when he saved her from a monstrous echo trapped in a death mask. This chance event starts the couple down a dangerous path that entwines their fates with the echo of a decade-dead serial killer, Louis Charbon; as well as a mad enchanter turned valet, Horace Gatwood; and two Regulator sisters in charge of keeping banned enchantments off the streets, De-Lia and Krona Hirvath.

Ten years previous, Gatwood's wife, Fiona, helped Charbon commit his murders under the direction of Thalo puppets—ancient monsters wielded by a cruel creator deity, the Thalo. The puppets take the shape of humans, can erase memories, and make themselves invisible. Most of the unwitting populace believes these beings to be little more than bedtime stories.

They are dead wrong.

Charbon's murders were, in the Thalo's words, meant to reveal the truth about Arkensyre magic: that it is not harvested from the divinely touched natural materials on the Valley rim but is instead stolen from people themselves, at birth, by their oppressive governments. The only way to prove this, the puppets insisted, is to locate evidence of a fifth humor, pneuma, present it to the public, and convince them to rise up.

And the only way to look for the humor is to tear a living person apart. Bit by bit.

Fiona's obsession with this "truth" ultimately led her to search for the humor in her own child. Grief-stricken, Gatwood murdered her in return. But when he encounters Melanie years later and sees the truth of her enchantment, he takes up his wife's gruesome cause. If Melanie can be enchanted, the proof must lie within her . . . and her unborn child.

He steals Charbon's death mask in order to utilize the dead killer's knowledge of anatomy and performs a series of test murders to be sure he can properly cut out Melanie's magic when the time is right.

Hot on his trail, with the aid of her criminal friend Thibaut, Krona Hirvath battles her varger phobia and contends with the phantoms of her family's past in order to decipher who the intended target is and keep them safe. But danger is brewing close to home. Using enchantments with capabilities Krona has never heard of, the Thalo puppets beguile Krona's sister, De-Lia, into aiding the new killer against her will.

All parties clash at Melanie and Sebastian's wedding, where the bride is saved but Krona's sister is lost. There, Krona sees a Thalo puppet kill Gatwood with her own eyes. This glimpse into the realm of myth, along with these new enchantments—ones that can control people, ones that use blood to identify people—force her to question her entire worldview.

After the fight, fearing they will be discovered and hunted once more, Melanie and Sebastian hatch a plan to leave Lutador for the northern city-state of Marrakev. There they hope to learn the truth about Sebastian's childhood memories . . . memories of magic he could do with his own hands, without an enchanted object. Before the time tax was taken.

THE THALO

The Thalo created the world. It created the sun and the moons and the stars and the land that lies beneath it all. It created great beasts to populate the land, creatures that revel in bloodshed and delight in carnage.

When its children, the gods, made for themselves their own animals—fragile things called human beings—it laughed at their folly and sent its monsters to devour the soft flesh and brittle bones of the strange little sentients.

THE VALLEY

The gods desired to protect their creations, and so when a man, Absolon Raoul Trémaux, found a valley—a great crack in the land—with high walls and good soil and beautiful rivers, they sent all humans on a Great Introdus. When the people arrived after a long and harrowing journey, the gods realized there was only one way to prevent the Thalo from finding and killing all of their humans.

The gods gave of themselves. They took all of their magic, all of their power, and built a barrier on the Valley rim, to keep the Thalo and its creatures at bay. All they ask in return is that the humans comply with their five directives or face their five penalties.

For the most part, the gods' efforts prevailed. For the most part, they were successful. But the Thalo can still make its puppets appear within the Valley—false humans who spread misfortune and steal secrets. And one monster can crawl over the rim to feast on the people: the varger.

And yet, life goes on. Humans persist.

The natural materials that touch this god-barrier are subtly infused with magic. The wood, the sand, the gemstones, and the metals are all mined and made by careful, skilled craftspeople into items of power known as enchantments.

THE VARGER

Unkillable monsters from beyond the Valley, varger all have one goal—to devour humanity. There are five types, each with their own strengths and vulnerabilities to enchanted metal:

Gold for the love-eaters that sniff out couples who are dearly in love, or those who are filled with hate—preferring to rip those with great passions apart to the exclusion of all other potential meals.

Silver for the jumpers, which can disappear and reappear at will, making them the most difficult to shoot.

Iron for the mirrors, the hardest to evade; they can copy a victim's every move, anticipating where they will run to next.

Bronze for the mimics, masters of camouflage. These can twist their bodies to blend into their natural surroundings, hiding perfectly within a grouping of stones or the shadows of an orchard.

And nickel for the pack leaders. Twice the size of their fellow monsters, they can orchestrate attacks with an almost human-like level of intelligence.

THE FIVE PENALTIES

The Rules of the Valley are as harsh as they are pure.

The gods sacrificed much for humanity, and require us to sacrifice for each other in return. Beware the Five Penalties.

Zhe is the Minder of Emotion, and emotion is the basis of all human bonds. Emotion must be shared through an emote tax. The penalty for hoarding emotion is the numbing of feeling.

He is the Guardian of Nature, and there is a natural order. That order must be respected and maintained. The penalty for subverting the natural order is toiling for the benefit of others.

Fey are the Vessel of Knowledge, and too much knowledge without preparation is dangerous. New knowledge must only be sought when the time is right. The penalty for invention without preparation is the removal of offending hands.

She is Nature's twin, and the Purveyor of Time. Time treats all things equally. Time must be shared through the time tax. The penalty for hoarding time is an early death.

They are the Unknown, pure and utter. One day they may choose to reveal themself and to gift magic unto the Valley. Until then, they demand only fealty and the promise that their future penalties will be paid.

—Scroll 318, writ by Absolon Raoul Trémaux
after the Great Introdus

I

THALO CHILD

Three Years Ago

Thalo Child, not yet age twelve, One Who Belongs to the Eye of Gerome, took his place in line behind the three Thalo children, age six.

The members of the procession, only a dozen of them in all, walked in careful, halting steps through the darkened hall that lead to the door of Ritual Way. Blue-gray incense smoke curled upward from small crucibles set atop iron braziers, which lit and warmed the hall. The scent of moldering spices and dried leaves made Thalo Child's head fuzzy and his eyes watery. The slippers on his feet were thin, and the cold of the stone floor aggressively seeped into the pads of his feet with each step.

Before him, at the front of the procession, two adults in black hoods chanted, "I am one with the dark; the dark is one with me," and the three six-year-olds echoed the chant back in a small, high lilt.

Each smaller child wore a purple robe, and around their neck a choker of blue flowers set on a tight, black ribbon of satin. The ends of the ribbons trailed down to the floor, and Thalo Child hoped no one would misstep.

With a pit growing in his stomach the closer they came to the door—the door that was half a dozen persons tall, but as narrow as any leading to the cot rooms—Thalo Child looked into the chalice cupped stiffly between his hands. The sickly yellow paste he'd mixed for the ritual was already beginning to separate, the edges of it wetter and the center a half-congealed blob. He longed to sneak a finger over the edge, to swirl the paste, make sure it was the correct consistency so that Gerome would not look upon him with his Eye and find reason for . . . disappointment.

But such a slip while they marched would draw the ire of the priest behind him. And their ire would draw Gerome.

The thin door seemed to stretch as they approached, disappearing into the opaque gloom of the ceiling. It loomed, lorded. Felt as watchful as any of the priests or Possessors. It seemed an agent of the Savior in and of itself.

Black, red, and purple inverted triangles covered its polished surface. A long, golden crossbar, set vertically in the wood, running the length of it from floor to ceiling, was the only means of moving the great door.

The lead priest brought out a key—a small disk of the same metal as the crossbar.

Metals were the means of transition. They shifted the nature of things. They were the keys of the soil, the padlocks of stone, the passwords for leaves.

If one had tried to open this door without the proper key, the crossbar would reject them, would channel great sparks from the sky and focus a spiteful, painful—at one time, lethal—bolt of righteous lightning into the offending body.

No other lock was needed. No mere mechanical means worked half as well as enchantment.

As the crossbar accepted the key, the priest pulled open the door.

Thalo Child involuntarily took a step in reverse as the great hinges creaked, treading on the robes of the priest behind him.

They *hissed*—a terrible sound, inhuman in its rage.

Thalo Child skipped forward; a graze of sharpened nails graced the back of his neck, snagging at the collar of his deep-blue robe.

"Keeper, desist," came another priest's voice from behind. "Decorum in Ritual Way. Lest a Possessor take offense."

The nails did not return.

The six-year-olds continued to chant as they passed over the threshold and into Ritual Way, though the priests leading them went quiet. Tiny voices bounced between the crags of sharply hewn black granite. Flecks of quartz made the walls sparkle as though with stars, even as real stars shone overhead.

The Way was a borderland of existence. Between annihilation and invigoration. Undiluted God Power undulated overhead, keeping the sky in perpetual, aurora-filled night. One could not remain in Ritual Way for more than an hour before absorbing a lethal dose of that Power. And yet to serve the Savior meant one needed to be exposed to the searing of God Power, needed to have their body strengthened and their being set alight.

It was how they were able to excavate the secrets of others—of those they kept safe and ordered, on the Valley floor far below.

Like a small replica of the Valley, the Way was widest at its middle, narrowest at the far end, where a crack perhaps wide enough for someone to squeeze through zigzagged off. There was no way to know what lay beyond that, what lay immediately beyond the walls, or down the mountainside beneath the Savior's Keep.

Not for one such as Thalo Child, anyway.

Five black stone altars lined the center of the Way. Inlaid atop them were uncut rapturestones. One bore the chalk-white blast pattern of a person who lay too long atop the altar. Someone who had overstayed their time in Ritual Way, absorbed too much. Their body had burned to ash from the inside out.

A few feet in, another ugly swath of ash made a crescent against the base of the left wall, as though a supplicant had huddled there. A few feet after that, more ash a story up, where someone had climbed and then expired. And the crack—the crack was caked in many layers.

The ash would never be cleaned.

The ash was a reminder.

Greed for too much God Power carried only one penalty: self-destruction.

Each six-year-old was led to an altar. Thalo Child cringed as one was given the ash-stained stone.

The children lay faceup on the flat of the altars and the priests arranged the ribbons of their chokers so that they flowed down over the black rock, the ends curling around the base of the pillars.

The little ones looked so small on the slabs. Delicate, with chubby fingers and cheeks—baby fat Thalo Child was only beginning to lose himself. They had only just received their first needle's worth of color a year earlier. Each sported a tattooed swirl of blue—each a different shade against their different skin tones—on the back of their neck. The pattern was particular to their cohort. Marked them as Thalo of a certain generation.

Thalo Child looked at his chalice again, at his hands, the way the tattoos curved between his thumbs and forefingers, allowing him to form a perfect, unbroken circle of robin's-egg blue around the mouth of the cup.

A circle, round and round. When one Thalo ended, another began. The Savior brought each back, began them over again from birth. Raised them. Taught them to find their magic once more.

And when they were ready, He would look upon each, search their past, their death, and bestow their true name upon them.

Thalo Child startled when the leader of the procession, the one with the key, let out a great shout.

It had begun.

The eight adults, keepers and priests, raised their arms, lifting their palms toward the flairs of God Power. An incantation—seemingly wordless, in a language Thalo Child was not yet privileged to learn—slowly seeped from them. Low at first, quiet. So soft—and their lips barely moved. But the fervor rose. The crescendo built.

A bolt of lightning erupted over the edge of Ritual Way, striking a long metal spike set high in the rock, and Thalo Child shrank from it. An unsettling scent fell over the Way, like something both burnt and frosted.

Thalo Child hurried to his place: two shallow grooves set in the path of the Way near the base of the center altar. They were the footprints of ages; for centuries, Thalo children his age had stood in this exact spot, waiting to perform this exact rite.

The six-year-olds shivered on their slabs. With fear or anticipation, rapture from the stones or simple chill, he could not say. The trio's eyes were wide, unblinking. They focused on the flashing overhead—one of the last things they would see in a long while.

"Be brave," Thalo Child whispered. Mostly to them. Partially to himself.

He reached out lightly with his mind, hoping not to draw the priests' attention. He was not yet permitted to use his magic outside of lessons. If they caught him . . .

His role in this ritual was a great honor. Out of all of his peers, Gerome had chosen *him*, had put away the Eye and touched his shoulder and told him how proud he was. How, soon, Thalo Child would earn his naming.

Using his magic put that in jeopardy.

But he remembered, starkly, this moment from before. When he was the young one on the rock.

Six was so small. Six years were so few.

He'd been so scared. So terrified, despite the enchanted stones working their emotive magic on him.

So, he sent out the smallest tendril of intrusion, letting the mouth of it seek the small ones' secrets. Happy secrets. Things they loved that they kept only for themselves.

One, fey loved insects. Especially the glittering beetles that shone green and gold. He filled feir mind with a false memory—a flash that would not stay, that would disappear the moment he stopped pushing the image, for he was not yet skilled enough to make the untrue become permanent—where the beetle sat on feir knee and revealed its rice-paper-thin wings.

Feir shivering momentarily ceased. Fey became calm.

He moved on to the next. She loved the smell of corn cakes—a love intimately tied to the memory of her first tasting—and he filled her mind with the scent.

The third, the one in the ash, kept a buried memory of a smile. And it *was* buried—deep. A remarkable achievement for one of his age. But Thalo Child's skills were stronger; he'd trained twice as long. He pried at the memory, attempting to pull the smile out of obscurity and resolve it into a full face.

Many Thalo children treasured the smiles of the ones who'd guarded them when but babes. It was not typically treated by the mind as a secret, not typically a retrievable notion by Thalo magic.

But as he forced the information to come forth, he realized why this boy had kept the smile so close, pushed it so deep.

The face appeared to be a woman's. But it was strange. Dark, unblemished skin covered her entire face. Not a single tattoo. Not one mark of the Savior. Nothing in which to absorb and channel the God Power to ensure one's magic was strong.

Only the Savior Himself could walk out onto the brim of the world and not need the tattoos to give Him strength and stealth and substance.

Who was she?

Before he could pry further, before he even had a chance to falsify the smile in the boy's consciousness, the door to Ritual Way opened once more.

Through it, carried by two of the lowly Mindless on a narrow, open litter, came Gerome.

He sat with his legs crossed akimbo and tied, the two of them woven over and knotted in gold- and milk-colored silks. His feet were propped on top of his legs, each heel in a hard-soled sandal with iron spikes attached. The points of the spikes dug into his sides, bloodying the silk, splattering his finery—a sacrifice required of him for the rite. Four small, round scars framed the top and bottom of his blue-painted lips. Similar scars flanked his cheeks, his jaw. His hair—long and black against his pale skin—was plaited down his back and stuck through with spikes of different blessed metals. He wore a copper headdress that fell low over his forehead. It had a high, curving crest that spanned from ear to ear, and small, sharp horns that jutted out just above his eyes. Small strings of diamonds hung from its edge, obscuring his gaze behind their glitter. Each took on a red sheen as it reflected the sky above and the blood on his torso.

Long cerulean stripes, each a finger wide, trailed down his cheeks and his chin. His expression was blank. No obvious pain from the spikes. No irritation. No frustration.

In each cupped, clawed hand he held a small pile of salt.

Thalo Child did not see the Eye, but it was never far.

"Thalo Child," Gerome said stiffly, his voice always deeper than Thalo Child expected, always grander, even, than his countenance. "Thalo Child, One Who Belongs to the Eye of Gerome, aged nearly twelve years beneath the roof of our Savior, have you prepared for this day?"

"Yes," he replied, trying to keep the quiver in his throat from snaking its way onto his tongue.

"Will you do well for these, those beneath you? Have you mixed the cement soundly, to ensure the closure, to ensure you protect their sight?"

"Yes," he said, fearing another glance at the separated paste.

"Then bestow upon them their years-long darkening, so that they too may carry the honor of One Who Belongs to the Eye of Gerome."

Thalo Child took steps on wobbly legs toward the first child. Fey had already closed feir eyes, were at ease, ready. "I welcome you," he said, dipping two fingers into the chalice, swirling them quickly, shielding the movement with his body, to be sure the cement was the proper consistency. "We are proud of you this day," he told fer. Gently, he caked the mixture over feir delicate eyelids. "When this dries and your lashes cannot be lifted, you will belong to the Eye of Gerome. You will be our family. You will walk in the darkened way and learn to trust in that family. Learn to trust your other senses. Learn to trust Gerome."

He packed the cement generously, smoothed it out, so that beautiful, circular disks of it covered feir eyes.

It would harden within minutes. Become stone within the hour. Eventually, it would fall free of the small child's face, but not for many, many moons.

It had taken nearly two years for Thalo Child to regain his own sight.

"You are one with the dark," he said as he finished.

"I am one with the dark," fey said, voice so small, so light.

He moved on to the next six-year-old. She squirmed as he repeated the words of the rite, and her eyelids almost fluttered, but she held on.

"You are one with the dark," he repeated when finished.

"I am one with the dark," she said firmly.

Finally, the boy. As Thalo Child leaned over him, the six-year-old met his gaze. He did not look away, did not blink. His mouth was a thin line, and his chest rose and fell with alarming rapidity. Thalo Child wetted his fingers in the paste once more, but the boy remained wide-eyed.

"Close your eyes," he whispered.

The boy shook his head.

"Close your eyes. Gerome will take care of you," he promised, glancing over his shoulder, unsure if Gerome had seen the hesitation, if the Eye had come out of hiding. "*I* will take care of you," he said. "But you must give trust to your family."

"Family?" the little boy gasped.

"That's right. Now close your eyes. Close your eyes and . . . think of *her*."

The boy's lip trembled. Though Thalo Child still didn't understand who the woman was or where she could have come from, it seemed he'd found the right thing to say. The boy took a deep breath—like he was going under water, like he didn't know when he would breathe again—and warily closed his eyes.

Thalo Child performed his work, doing his best to ignore the way the boy's cheeks trembled beneath his fingers. "You are one with the dark."

"I am one . . . with the dark."

Thalo Child spun away, holding his chalice high.

Seeing the task was done, Gerome took both mounds of salt and, with a great cry, smashed them into the jagged wounds the spikes had bored in his sides.

The two Mindless set the litter down, and each brought forth a small rame-kin and scraper from their robes. After Gerome thoroughly rubbed the salt into his wounds—making it all a bloody, pasty pink—they scraped it away into the small bowls.

Hastily, they brought the stained salt to Thalo Child, exchanging it for his chalice.

Now was his real test. Gerome watched him intently from beneath the diamonds.

Returning to each child, he made a ring of bloody salt around the cement disks.

Had he sealed their eyes correctly? Had he protected them from the sting of the sacred salt?

All three endured silently. No salt seeped beneath the brim, and no tears streaked out.

"The blood of your family, the salt of the divine," he said when finished. "Let it protect you. Let it stick to your skin and seep into your body. May the magic you take in here today empower you and us and we and all. Gerome sacrifices for you so that you may learn to appreciate the Eye."

Gerome made a small gesture with one hand, and the Mindless unbound his legs. He stood, slipping from the litter with the slightest of limps, to take powerful steps toward Thalo Child, who knelt.

Gerome was tall. So tall.

"You have done well," the Possessor said, surveying his work. "Your charges are protected. You have made me proud."

Thalo Child let out a deep breath, as though his breath and the boy's breath had been the same and he'd just now broken the surface to gasp again. He made a circle with his hands, forming the blue ring between his fingers once more, dipping his forehead to touch the tattoo.

"Small one, rise," Gerome continued, digging his thumbs into his sides, into the open wounds. "Let me anoint you."

Thalo Child looked up sharply from his supplicating posture, surprised. When he saw the openness in Gerome's body language and the red on his hands, his heart swelled. This—Was he worthy of this? Such a blessing of blood and salt was not part of the ritual. He might expect to receive it four times before receiving his name, but this would be an extra. This was not only unexpected but a great, great gift.

Finding it difficult to draw a proper breath, he stood. He dared to look up into Gerome's face, to try to see into his eyes.

The diamonds continued to obscure.

The Possessor of the Eye grabbed both sides of his head roughly, and Thalo Child instinctually took hold of Gerome's wrists, hesitant. The man's thumbs dug into the base of his eye sockets and scraped down the front of his cheeks, leaving blood that quickly cooled.

And still, when he'd finished drawing, he did not let go. He pressed against Thalo Child's skull. The pressure mounted, slipping into uncomfortable, then painful. Thalo Child tried to tug away, to slip down into a kneel once more, but Gerome would not let go. He pressed harder, harder, clearly daring the child to cry out, to indicate discomfort or pain.

You think you can keep their secrets? Gerome said, though his mouth did not move. *Child, you cannot keep your own secrets from me, let alone another's.*

A spike of realization and fear gutted Thalo Child just as surely as the iron spikes had gutted Gerome.

He *knew*.

Of course he knew.

You are right to be afraid. When we lie to our family, we should fear.

"I—I didn't—"

Nothing in your training could teach you to obscure thought from me. You are still such a child, with a child's ways and child's thinking. You need this blood, for you may yet be a child *for a long while to come.*

Then he chuckled. *I sense the notion of the Eye in you. No. The Eye is not for something so petty. But I will pluck from them their secrets, take them forever, so that you understand that using your magic without guidance is not a kindness. It can only hurt the ones for which you are responsible.*

With that, he released Thalo Child, who hadn't realized his knees had gone weak. He fell to the hard stone, and none of the priests moved to help him up. None gasped. None were surprised.

Likely they *all* knew what Thalo Child had done.

The Possessor of the Eye took a large, swirling step around him, as one might sidestep a puddle or a bit of animal foul. He approached the six-year-olds slowly, making sure Thalo Child was watching. He needed him to remember every punishing movement.

Thalo Child longed to cry out for Gerome to stop. A simple denial. A single plea.

But that would scare the little ones. And they were already so scared.

He watched helplessly as Gerome went to each small form and lightly smoothed a palm over their foreheads. It was a parental gesture. Delicate and loving. Each child let out a happy sigh, but then frowned deeply. The kind of frown one makes when a thought has flitted away. When you were about to say something but the words are suddenly gone.

Gerome left his hand on the small boy's forehead for an instant longer than the other two. He himself frowned.

But then it was over. It was done, and Gerome came back to Thalo Child's side.

I do not do this to be cruel, Gerome said in his unmoving way. *I do this because you must learn that actions have consequences. What we do here—in the keep and below—we do for the protection of Arkensyre. That requires order and discipline as much as it requires love.*

And then his hand fell to Thalo Child's forehead, and for an instant he feared the loss of one of his own little delights. But he sensed nothing leaving, no happiness now diminished.

And then the hand was gone and Gerome spun away, lifting his hands high. "Ones Who Belong to the Eye of Gerome, welcome!" he announced. "The priests will help you up, little ones. And then, we feast!"

As Gerome climbed back atop his litter, Thalo Child touched the blood cracking on his cheeks, felt the loss the smaller children could not feel for their memories. Memories he had invaded. Memories his actions had ultimately stolen. Pleasures now gone. Secrets no longer secret but *nonexistent*.

There was no longer love in the smell of corn cakes, for the memory of that first taste was gone.

No longer delight in the shiny shell of an insect, for the instant that had first sparked that delight had been erased.

No longer the hope in . . . in . . .

Thalo Child shook his head, scratched at the tattoos on the back of his hands.

What had been the boy's secret again?

>-+◇-+-O-+◇+-◄

A woman stands watching as the procession reenters the keep—the little ones stumbling, despite how often they'd each shut their eyes and played the Darkness game.

The woman plays her own version of the game now—not to keep from seeing but to keep from being seen. She tugs her pearl-blue cloak around her all the tighter, sinking back into the shadows, against the age-worn stone. Only thin, curling strands of her white hair peek out from beneath her hood, and still, it does not matter. She enjoys a level of power most Thalo cannot muster—not just to slip from the minds and away from the eyes of those who have had their magic taken but also from her fellow Secret wielders.

Only someone as powerful as a Possessor or the Savior Himself can see through her projected invisibility. She's counting on this now. The children cannot see her. The priests cannot see her. Only Gerome. And she wants to stay hidden from him for as long as possible.

Her blue eyes track him as he is carried past her hiding spot. A small pang of remembrance catches her in the side, and she loses her breath for a moment. An image of Gerome—still a Nameless child himself—springs unbidden to the forefront of her mind. Not smiling. But not frowning.

Even.

Passionate, but even.

Even in a . . . *cold* way.

He'd been well trained.

She'd trained him well.

When the procession has passed, she flees her hiding spot. There will be a meal before the next Orchestration—a feast, to honor the small ones' graduation out of the nursery and into the dorms—but she will not attend.

She feels out of place now in the Order of the Thalo. Many here still see her as akin to a queen, despite her newly claimed role as strange wanderer. There is no other Thalo like her, no one given the freedoms she's been given. The trust she's been given—

Which is why she must not miss her chance. Why she must take the advantage while the advantage is given.

>─┼─◆>─○─<◆─┼─<

Hours later—no longer weighed down by nostalgia—she enters the Orchestration Chamber. The high-ceilinged room is dim, the braziers filled with deep-orange embers but absent of flame. The dimness is on purpose, to make the room feel small, intimate. To instill a sense of quiet, closed conspiracy in those about to meet. There are seven seats at the long marble table which occupies most of the chamber's floorspace; it's shaped like an eye, with two pointed corners and two long, bowing edges. Five of the chairs are filled when she enters, trailing behind the Savior—keeping to her place at His side, with her head held high.

The light chatter in the room dies down, and all five of the Grand Orchestrators stand out of respect, ducking their chins. Each Orchestrator is dressed just the same, in deep-blue robes with periwinkle swirls that leave bare the arms and hands, along with a thin black veil over their head that obscures most of their features but stops just short of hiding their identities. The veils are held in place by aged metal circlets and edged with shining black beads of smoky quartz.

The Savior says nothing. Does not acknowledge the Grand Orchestrators or their respects. He Himself wears a hooded, billowing shroud of all black, belted in the middle with a wrapping swath of metallic blue. His face is *truly* hidden, as it will be forever; His countenance cannot be seen. In its place is a mask, one of plain black, flat and expressionless—but it always glints strangely when caught out of the corner of one's eye, as though there might be silver etchings in it. Sigils. But staring at it straight on, one cannot discern any such adornments.

He takes His seat at the head of the table, and the others sit in turn. The woman, however, remains standing, leaving the last chair empty. In truth, it belongs to her. But she abdicated it long ago.

She stands behind the Savior and says nothing.

With a single nod from Him, the Orchestration begins.

They all know what they're here to discuss.

"This is *thrice* now this particular scheme has failed," Valya announces, casting his watery gaze around the gathering. He is frail-looking, hunched and shaky—old in body, not just years. Rare in a Thalo.

"It may not have gone as expected, but that doesn't mean it was a waste of time," comes the smooth, booming voice of Akachi. Fey are tall, dark, and well padded, and carry femself with an infallible dignity. The woman has always been fond of Akachi.

"Gatwood never made his pronouncement to the masses—not even from the gallows," Valya points out. "One of those oh-so-law-abiding Lutadorian Regulators took their revenge against the enchanter before all was said and done, and that was that."

The woman makes no attempt to correct him. She empties her mind of that day, that moment, pretends it was insignificant. She doesn't let herself treat it as a secret, as clandestine. The Orchestrators might not be able to use their magic on her in that way, but the Savior . . .

She's still not sure she knows the full extent of His power.

"I ask you," Valya barrels on, "what good is a play that never reaches the final act? What's the point of proving dough that will never see an oven? From the mouths of the untrustworthy, that's what we've relied on for centuries, and yet—"

"And nothing has changed," Akachi says. "The more unsavory or untrustworthy the source, the more likely the information will be dismissed. Especially if it's an uncomfortable truth. The gods know this, rely on us to execute their plan."

"The best way to keep the populace from believing what's right in front of their noses," a third Orchestrator, Savoya, insists—direct as ever, clearly siding with Akachi, "is to make sure they have to stick their noses through *a pile of shit* to get to it."

"I don't need your vulgarities," Valya chides. "The *gods* don't need them."

The woman is rather amused by them, actually.

Savoya is unfazed by the reproach. "The point is," she continues, "when *murderers* and *thieves* and *conspiracy theorists* speak the truth, no one listens. In fact, they do worse than *not listen*—they dismiss their claims outright. What better place for the truth to hide than in plain sight? What better way to keep a secret than to have the dregs of society shout it from the rooftops? That is why we seek out people like Monsieur Gatwood, like Charbon before him, and *Madame* Gatwood before him. All three can easily be said to have dug their own graves *long* before—"

"Before they could do more than spread our spoon-fed 'theories' to their *small* enclave of followers," Valya insists bitterly.

"The cult members who followed Gatwood were eager to speak," Akachi reminds him. "Papers all across the Valley published their statements. Repeated both our truths and our lies. They've sown *doubt,* which was their very purpose."

The woman pointedly does not react.

Valya, on the other hand . . . "It's not enough. What about the apprentice healer? She escaped, and with that *mark,* which we still don't understand, and—"

"She will be *dealt with,*" the woman says sternly.

Valya pauses, turns his head only slightly in her direction, as though calculating the best response. After a moment, he decides on *no response* and proceeds with his complaints. "And hers is not the only mark of such mystery, *is it*? On top of that, *all* of the city-states are pushing for an age of invention—have you seen what they're building? A railway. That spans from one end of the Valley to the other."

"Rumor," Savoya dismisses.

"No!" Valya snaps. "The Orchestrators under me, in the field, have seen the designs. The iron mines have twice as many workers as they did in the year before. They're already smelting the ties."

"But the calendar, the penalty—Knowledge's penalty—"

"There's this newfangled idea that *extrapolation* of current ideas is not the same as the development of new ideas."

"Of all the weaselly—"

"There's too much peace," comes a calm, even voice.

All of the Grand Orchestrators fall silent.

The Savior has spoken.

"Too much cooperation," He intones softly. "We want them to prosper, and they have. Their needs are met; they have everything they require. And what do people who have everything they require *want*?"

No one dares answer.

"More," He says. "People always want *more*, and therein lies the problem. If we had simply restrained ourselves in the first . . ." He trails off, takes a deep breath. "You are all well aware of the consequences of human want and ambition. They will keep reaching, keep testing their boundaries, until their fingers brush the true power of the gods, and then . . . and *then*."

They all know what "and then" means. It is why they are trapped here, as overseers of exiles, as caretakers of the remnants.

The woman tries not to scoff.

Yes. They all *know*.

Once more, she clears her mind.

He cannot be allowed to know her thoughts. He cannot discover that the walls He's constructed in her mind are crumbling.

Ever the servant, ever the servant, I am ever His servant, she silently reaffirms.

"What we've used to maintain the status quo is no longer as effective as it once was," the Savior announces. "Valya is correct."

The Orchestrator does not preen, but he sets his shoulders all the straighter, his hunch slightly less pronounced.

"We must force them to fall back," the Savior continues. "So that instead of seeking *more*, they put every ounce of energy into protecting what they have."

"How do we do that?" the woman asks—the only one confident enough in her place to speak when He does not go on.

"We lead them to war."

2

KRONA

Krona watched with a pained grimace—well hidden behind her helm—as the crack of the Matron's whip drove the line of prisoners forward, toward the Penalty Block. The noise was sharp, and the gathering crowd jumped at its snap. The prisoners, however, were desensitized to it, plodding onward evenly, approaching Krona and Tray's position at the base of the Penalty Block listlessly.

The lawbreakers had walked there in a processional from the nearest House of Penalty—a place very different from any other jail or prison. It was both coterie and confinement—a place for those who'd earned the gods' wrath to repent before receiving their punishment.

The sky was clear overhead, bright and still—in a way that made the pentagonal shape of the public gathering place seem cheery. But being well lit and the air calm only guaranteed the gore to come would shine all the starker. Sunlight would glint off the fresh blood, and any screams of pain would not be muffled by the wind.

There were six who would pay Knowledge's penalty today. Six with their heads hung low, and their shoulders hunched and their wrists bound—the last time their hands would make a tidy pair. Six who'd fancied themselves deserving of forbidden knowledge.

And one of them Krona had personally apprehended.

His name was Yonder Jamiss. An academic—which was no surprise, really. Those who most often slighted Knowledge's orders were those most enamored of the very thing fey represented: wisdom, intellect, discovery. Knowledge knew hubris often accompanied a keen mind, and that's why fey had tried to temper intellectual hastiness with feir commandment.

Monsieur Jamiss was a bit different from his fellow prisoners today; the forbidden advancements he'd attempted to make weren't in mechanical engineering, nor chemistry, nor medicine, nor enchantment.

No, his crime had been astronomy.

Well, his crime had *also* been stealing an enchanted spyglass, which was why a Regulator had been assigned to the concern in the first place, and why Krona had made the arrest. But that was not the crime for which he'd lose a hand. Optics had been what interested him, and his desire to develop a better telescope by which to see the planets and the stars had so overwhelmed him that it had condemned him.

Krona watched him closely, even as she and Tray mounted the steps at the rear of the Penalty Block to take their place on one side of the raised stage. His brown hair fell ragged and dirty around his ears, over his brow. Uneven stubble covered his cheeks, and he looked at his chained feet as he shuffled forward.

A stark contrast to the tidy, confident man she'd apprehended.

The thickly planked staging area was large enough to accommodate a dozen hangings at once, but today it featured only a half a dozen wooden pedestals. A second pair of Regulators—from a first-district den—flanked the opposite end of the Penalty Block, helms on, visors down, marching together in perfectly stoic synchronicity. Once all four of them were in place, the pair nodded in tandem to Tray and Krona, and the two of them nodded back.

It was the first time Krona had felt the intimidation of the uniform staring back at her. The cherry red of their visors—which she often thought of as a warm splash of color on her own uniform—seemed cold, lifeless, and mildly gruesome. Like dried blood. The horns on their helms, which matched hers perfectly, were fit for goring. Instead of the rich, onyx-colored leather representing duty and strength, for an instant she saw it as the physical incarnation of demanding brutality.

The aura projected by the first-district pair was one of *pressure*. Krona was used to embodying that pressure—to personifying order and control. Putting on the helm and becoming a faceless enforcer was usually a relief. It was where she felt confident and prepared. It was the part of her life that had clear, meetable expectations. There were laws and she upheld them . . .

Until she took off the uniform in the evening and broke them just the same as these poor sods about to lose their limbs.

She suddenly couldn't breathe in her own helmet. Her armor became absurdly claustrophobic. She wanted to tear at its seams, pull down her collar, throw off her bracers, and toss her helm into the crowd.

But she never let her posture change. Though her muscles twinged with the effort, shaking minutely, she held herself steady and projected serenity. She could not let her own inner failings become a concern to the outer world.

Still, Tray knew her well enough to realize something was wrong. "Steady?" he asked via reverb bead.

"I'm fine," she answered flatly.

The line of prisoners arrived at the Penalty Block, and the Matron ordered them to climb the stairs. The crowd began to shift and murmur, knowing what was to come, their collective mood shifting from excited to uneasy in turns. Jamiss was the third onto the stage. There was no way for him to recognize Krona, and though it should have been a comfort, instead it sent cold guilt fluttering through her like a snow flurry.

Each prisoner was shackled to the planks behind a wooden pedestal, and one of their arms at random forcibly placed atop the plinth. A metal cuff was bolted over their forearm, to keep it pinned in place.

Krona looked away as Jemiss turned pleading eyes onto the crowd, knowing no one there could be counted on to save him.

She was the same as these people on the chopping block. She'd spit just as firmly in Knowledge's face, seeking forbidden information. She'd done it over and over.

And she'd do it again without hesitation. This very day, even. As soon as the sun went down.

There were words for the kind of hypocrisy she was engaged in—which was not just the hypocrisy of *do as I say, not as I do* but the sanctimoniousness of one willing to dole out punishment to others for committing the same sins simply because she was in a place of power and they were not.

She recognized all this—rolled it over in her mind and on her tongue and let it boil in her belly until she felt sick—and yet she had no intention to make it right.

She would not call for the executioners to stay the penalty. And she would not turn herself in.

Nor would she stop.

I have my reasons, she told herself, even as she immediately scoffed and thought, *They all have their reasons.*

When each prisoner was locked in place, the jeers started in earnest. The crowd hurled insults at the blasphemers, and their tongues cut Krona just as sharply.

The executioner took up their axe, and the Matron from the House of Penalty began reading off the first prisoner's crimes.

Krona tuned her out, let her hearing go fuzzy.

Only secondary to her guilt in this moment was disgust at her own self-pity. Here she was, protected by her station, nauseated at her own actions, while right beside her, half a dozen people were about to truly suffer.

And for what?

All of the Penalties, save this one, could be seen as attempts to balance the societal scale. For disobeying the gods, they owed their fellow peoples a debt.

Nature demanded one toil for others. The deadening of emotion did not mean those emotions went to waste but that they were added to the state's stockpile, which was purchased by *Emotioteurs* and circulated in their enchanted stones. And Time's penalty—an early death—was exacted in a number of ways. The most societally beneficial was applied to tax dodgers. Extra time was pulled from them, which directly boosted the economy, putting more time vials on the streets to balance out the number drained by old aristocrats cashing out.

But Knowledge's penalty . . .

Krona flinched as the executioner's axe fell the first time, and it did not escape Tray's notice.

. . . Those severed hands would become pig feed, nothing more.

The first prisoner wailed relentlessly as a set of healers pulled her free of her restraints and dragged her off the Penalty Block. Out of sight from the crowd, they'd do what they could to stop the bleeding and bandage what remained of her wrist.

Stepping over the fresh streaks of blood, the Matron—a younger woman than her station evoked, with deep black hair and an equally black dress—read out the second prisoner's crimes.

Krona's eyes caught on the blood, the way it painted the wood and shone in the late-morning sunlight. She'd served as witness to plenty of Penalties in the past three years. She'd seen people hanged—their necks snapped, their eyes unseeing and their bodies limp. She'd seen them robbed not just of limbs but of life. And yet that one hand on the chopping block, the fresh blood flowing freely, pumped by a healthy heart, felt different in ways she could not fully order in her mind.

She was no stranger to blood. But the last time she'd seen it with that particular shimmer, it had stained grass instead of planks. And it had been flowing not from a wrist but from a neck.

Her sister's neck.

Unconsciously, she slapped a palm against the jaguar mask clinging to her belt, letting its presence steady her.

What I do is not blasphemy, she insisted to no one but her inner demons. *I have to right this wrong. Knowledge knows what I search for is just.*

The axe fell again.

Thwack.

This time, it wasn't just the owner of the dismembered limb that cried out, but Monsieur Jemiss next to him as well. Tears began to fall down his cheeks in earnest as the bleeding man was dragged away and the Matron began to list Jemiss's misdeeds.

You could stop this, a part of Krona insisted. *He wanted to look at the stars. He wanted to better see the world as it really is. Does he really deserve to lose his hand?*

Even if she stopped the axe from falling today, it would fall tomorrow instead. She didn't have the power of pardon. She was a cog in the justice system's machine. Its gears turned round and round and round, and she turned round with it.

To stop the penalty today wouldn't save Jemiss's hand. It would only pull Krona into an unnecessary spotlight.

The Matron finished her reading and stepped aside. The executioner approached.

Jemiss squirmed and begged, leaning as far away from the oncoming axe as his restraints would allow. "No, please. No—no, please!"

He clenched and unclenched his doomed fist, and Krona watched his face contort through every possible expression of panic and fear.

He did this to himself. His own actions condemned him, not you.

I should be right there with him, right there beside him.

Her station let her get away with the very thing she condemned others for.

The executioner lifted their heavy blade.

Jemiss's pleas increased.

It was over in the blink of an eye. The heavy *thump* of the blade passing through bone and flesh to catch on the block of wood beneath provided the bass to Jemiss's treble of a scream.

⊱┄◈┄○┄◈┄⊰

The witnessing left Krona shaken but undeterred.

As the crowd dispersed and the amputees were cared for, Krona, Tray, and the other pair of Regulators left the scene to return to their respective duties. She had a difficult time mounting Allium, so wobbly were her legs. So numb were her hands.

Tray didn't hide his concern. "Krona, are you feeling all right? Are you sick?"

"Just fatigued," she dismissed. "Fitful sleep these last few nights."

He didn't press her, but the answer clearly wasn't satisfactory.

Lost in thought as they rode toward their next destination, an asylum, Krona gazed out toward the Valley rim, wondering what the gods truly thought of her.

3

KRONA

Krona hated asylums. *Supposedly,* they were just another type of hospital, but they never felt like places of healing. She'd been a Regulator for over six years now, and she knew a prison when she stepped into one, no matter its name.

In truth, very little felt different here from a House of Penalty.

Even the sounds were similarly anguished.

How could it be medicine when it sounded like torture?

The long ride from the Penalty Block had at least allowed her to regain her composure. She strode stiff-backed and steady.

Empty gazes followed the deep black of her uniform as it swept past. The Regulators moved like living shadows through whitewashed hallways, their capes sweeping elegantly over the stained stone floors, past the rain-rot that warped the molding, and their boots tapped out an echoing rhythm as they strode. Beside Krona, Tray walked with his helm pointed straight ahead, following the asylum's director without hesitation or distraction. Dappled light fell over them as they passed by barred window after barred window.

"He's just this way," the director said as though apologizing for having to lead them from the relatively subdued communal areas into the unseemly depths of the asylum. "Not much farther."

They were directed to a heavy, white door with a palm-sized window concealed behind a small metal shutter, workable only from the outside. Pulling open the shutter, feeling oddly like she was peering into a dollhouse, Krona could just make out a figure draped in yellowing white stretched out atop a cot beyond. No other furniture or accoutrements graced the room, save several bundles of dried lavender that had been hung from the ceiling by rough twine. It only barely obscured the gray-black of a water stain created by a long-unattended leak in the roof somewhere.

High-set, gentle-smelling herbs decorated most of the grounds. Supposedly, the scent had a calming effect on the patients. Scathingly, she wondered what effect fixing the mildewed plaster might have.

"Is he coherent?" Tray asked as an orderly pulled a large key ring off their belt and unlocked the door with a thoroughly scratched brass key.

"Sometimes," the director said with a small shrug, pushing his spectacles up on his pale nose.

The door opened on stiff hinges, and the orderly waved the two Regulators inside. The man on the cot groaned and rolled over. One arm flopped from where it had been clutched to his chest, falling over the side of the cot's thin metal frame to drag on the floor. Krona knelt to examine it, but the director cleared his throat.

"Side of his neck," he said, indicating the position with a tap on his own skin.

The patient was balding, perhaps in his mid-fifties, pale and short. Like this, half-asleep, he could have been anyone, from any walk of life. A baker, a farmer, a lawyer.

Even his residence at this particular asylum would suggest a commoner.

But he was noble-born.

Gently, Krona took him by the jaw, her black leather gloves a stark contrast to both his skin and the insipidness of the starched sheets and white walls. His head lolled to the side with no resistance.

And there it was. A raised, red mark. If she touched the tips of her pointer finger and thumb together, the loop could just about encompass the entire thing. The mark was angry-looking, filled with fine lines like raised scratches, and the skin beneath and around it roiled with welts.

She knew what it was, though how it had gotten there was still anybody's guess.

"Yes, it's another one," she said with a heavy sigh.

"That's *thirty-eight* in the city proper in the last three months," Tray gritted through his teeth. "*That we know of.*"

Not to mention the sixteen in the country and the reports of even more coming in from Marrakev. Since the first marked corpse had shown up a year ago, they'd had accounts of nearly two hundred wounds exactly like this.

And a string of bodies and lost minds connecting each one, like dots, though the trail led who knew where.

"Monsieur?" Krona said softly, patting the patient's cheek. "Monsieur, will you speak with us?"

The nobleman made a series of groggy gargles before his eyelids fluttered open. His pupils fell on her helm and immediately went wide, his mouth gaping open into a startled O.

"Monsieur, can you tell us how this happened to you? How you came by this wound on your neck?"

He moved suddenly, slapping his hands on either side of Krona's helm, drawing her close, looking into the deep red of her faceplate.

No, not looking into, she realized. He seemed to be marveling at his own reflection.

Krona held her ground, made no indication his behavior was alarming. After all, she'd pawed at him first. "Monsieur?" she prompted lightly.

"This face," he said in a distant sort of awe. He released her with one hand, drawing his fingers down his own cheekbone. "This face is all wrong."

"What about the mark? Is the mark wrong? How did you get it?"

His face contorted, as though he'd been struck by a sudden pain. "I can't say where I've been. I can't . . . I don't know who . . . How . . ." With a choked-off sob, he turned away, pushing at her faceplate and covering his mouth as his back bowed.

She let him push her away, rose to her feet. She entreated him to speak several more times, before gesturing for Tray to have a go. Neither Regulator was successful at pulling out more than a handful of nonsense words at a time.

Eventually, Krona had had enough.

Perhaps they should have pushed him harder, questioned him longer. But there was no doubt in her mind: he was the same as the others—the others who hadn't *died*, that is.

They would get no meaningful information from the victim himself.

She turned to the director. "And the family? Did they mention any enchantments in the vicinity when his mind broke?"

"No, nothing. I only sent for you because of the public notice." He dropped his voice. "It *does* look an awful lot like a creator's kiss, doesn't it?"

That's because it is, she silently answered. *It's an enchanter's mark*. Outwardly, she sighed deeply. "We'll need the address for his next of kin, if you please."

"Of course, Mastrex Regulator, anything you need. Anything at all."

As they followed the director back out the maze of halls, Krona's glass shell reverberated in her ear. "You're worried it's spreading, aren't you?" Tray asked.

She licked out for her dangling reverb bead. "Yes. Twice as many victims in the last six months than the previous six. It'll be a proper pandemic soon. And with no clear line of connection between any of the victims. No evidence they knew each other, or had traveled to the same places before developing the marks, or eaten the same foods, or made purchases from the same merchants. Nothing."

"There was a report from Asgar-Skan this morning . . ." He took a deep breath before continuing. "From the sketches of the victim, I think it might be the same phenomenon."

She looked at him sharply. "Why didn't you tell me?"

"Didn't want to distract you until we'd confirmed this case. If only we could identify the epicenter—if we understood what led to that first man's death—then perhaps we'd have a chance of understanding what in the Valley is happening."

Guilt pooled itself like hot lead in Krona's belly. Thwarting Knowledge wasn't the only misdeed she'd have to answer for at some point—she was lying to Tray as well.

Perhaps that was the worst part of this concern. She *knew* who had started it—patient zero, as it were. And it *hadn't* been a now-deceased ginger farmer whose body had been found in some Marrakevian tavern on mount nowhere.

It had been an apprentice healer right here in Lutador. Melanie Dupont.

Three years ago, after glimpsing an enchanter's mark on Melanie's forehead, Krona had told the pregnant young woman and her husband to flee the city-state and never return. At the time, it had been the only thing she could think of to properly repay them for trying to save her sister's life.

Now Krona knew she could be responsible for all of these new injuries and deaths simply because she'd chosen to take pity and let the woman go.

She wished—at the *very least*—that she'd asked more questions before sending the pair on their way. There was so much she didn't know about Melanie and that blasted mark.

What she *did* know was this: Master Belladino's mask was missing its enchanter's mark. And that same mark was on Melanie's forehead. The mark of the enchanter who'd ultimately tried to murder her. Who'd murdered so many . . .

But *how* it had come to scar the young woman's skin, Krona had no idea. Had Gatwood tried to enchant Melanie? Or had he transferred the mark from Belladino's mask to her somehow? And what did it represent, truly?

Melanie couldn't *be* enchanted.

. . . could she?

That didn't make sense.

No, that wasn't right—it *shouldn't* make sense. But Krona had seen too much on the Charbon-Gatwood concern to label anything "impossible" ever again. Sense or no, it was a possibility; Melanie *could* possess magic in some form.

But there was no way to know if that magic was usable, or if she'd consented to the process that had given it to her—if she'd sought it, stumbled upon it, or had it thrust upon her by that madman.

Whatever had happened to Melanie had happened again. And again. And again. That was evident by all the corpses popping up with marks on their bodies and enchantments in their possession, each bauble *seemingly* a forgery of some truly enchanted object—just as she'd thought Belladino's markless mask a forgery.

And then there were the living who appeared in asylums just such as this, with similar wounds, and family members who never had *any idea* what the Regulators were talking about when they asked after enchantments.

"What? Any broken or missing enchantments in the household? No, of course not."

Of course not.

And the wounds on all the victims, both living and dead, didn't look right. They weren't like Melanie's. Melanie's scar had been clean, all of the lines precise. None of this "boils and burns" nonsense. No accompanying odd growths or charred-looking skin.

Perhaps that was because Melanie's was older and those other blemishes had healed.

Or perhaps it was a clue. A clue as to why victims of the marks were turning up dead or deranged.

Which meant the phenomenon could be much broader than Tray or anyone else even suspected.

They could simply be seeing the results of failed enchantment attempts.

So, where were all the successes?

And how did this tie back to Melanie? Because it *had* to. There was no way this was a coincidence.

Krona had tried to abdicate her responsibility for Melanie. She hadn't wanted to know where the couple had run off to, or what their lives were like, or if her mark had disappeared or blossomed into something new.

She'd just wanted her and her family to be safe.

They deserved to be safe and happy.

Alas, she knew they were not.

Whatever we burned, it wasn't our baby.

Krona had read those words thousands of times now.

Whatever we burned, it wasn't our baby.

They were etched in the backs of her eyelids and rattled around inside her ears.

Whatever we burned, it wasn't our baby.

Approximately a year and a half after she'd told the couple to flee, a mysterious letter had arrived at the den, addressed to her but with no information as to its sender. She only knew it had come from Marrakev. And though she knew the contents by heart now, she still pulled it out of her desk every day in the den, looking it over for anything she might have missed, her gaze always darting

around the text, taking in the smooth, looping handwriting, its neatness coun-
terpointed by many ink splatters, scratches, and blotted spots that indicated it
had been drafted only this once and in haste.

> *Our child is* not *dead*, it read. *Whatever died in our care and was given
> Lutadorian rights was not our baby. I don't know how I know. I just know.*
> *When the babe's time tax was taken, the Groom's great-aunt heard voices.
> She is prone to this, I will admit, as well as theatrics, but she would never—*

Here, several lines had been thoroughly scratched out.

> *These voices did not speak directly to her. She overheard them discussing
> how they would steal the baby away.*
> *But there was still a baby in the morning. And the next week. And the
> week after that.*
> *Except we all slowly began to understand it was something else.*
> *And then it died.*
> *I've tended to dead children—you know I have. I do know what death
> feels like. I do. And when my fingers brushed the thing's frigid skin, I knew it
> was gone. I held the tiny, cold form in my hands and had no doubt.*
> *But whatever it was, whatever we burned, it wasn't our baby.*
> *I know this sounds like nothing more than the ravings of a heartbroken
> mother. The invention of a grief-rattled mind. I* know. *Everyone else in this
> village believes we're in denial. Perhaps we are. If anyone else had said it—
> anyone—I would not believe it. But the Groom trusts his great-aunt un-
> equivocally, and I trust my Groom, and my Groom trusts me.*
> *Someone conspired to steal my child. To make us believe the baby had
> passed. I do not know how. Or why. But I know these ashes that hang from
> my neck do not belong to my child.*
> *Please, Mistress Hirvath, help us find our baby. You're the only person I
> can turn to. The only one I know we can trust.*

It was signed simply *The Bride*.

Krona had tried her best. She'd looked into missing-persons cases and the
reports of dead children. But infants were prone to dying suddenly, and of no
apparent cause. This had always been the case. She could find no evidence of it
happening any more frequently now, in Marrakev, than it ever had before.

She'd found several accounts of parents claiming their baby wasn't their baby, however. Unfortunately, the accounts were all so old that there was no one left to interview, no leads to pursue.

Since receiving the letter, she'd made no progress and seen little else from day to day that could connect back to the Bride and her lost babe.

Save for this. These warped marks and warped minds.

After receiving the required information from the director, Tray and Krona retrieved their horses and rode away, toward their den.

"I don't like that this is getting worse right when all of the diplomats are arriving for the Pentaétos summit," Tray said via reverb bead as they rode.

"You think it's related?" Krona asked, hunching low over Allium's neck, patting the beast absently as she tried to turn her thoughts away from her anxiety and guilt to the summit.

Every five years, the leaders of the city-states came together to renegotiate their treaties, to reaffirm peace and cooperation. And to best one another in various arenas—sports, arts, riches, gallantry.

It was Lutador's turn to host the gathering. For weeks, nobles from all over Arkensyre had been arriving in great caravans—enjoying a freedom of movement across the Valley's borders that the common folk could only dream of. It made security a nightmare, even for the Regulators. While Krona and her colleagues might not have to worry about the safety of the nobles themselves, they had to contend with new enchantments crossing into Lutador—unregistered and unlisted.

Tray sighed heavily. "No. I don't see how it could be. But the summit is fraught enough as is—what with Winsrouen suddenly deciding to press its luck and redraw its borders—so if someone simply wanted to increase already-strained tensions? Who knows?"

"Regardless, since social station is clearly no obstacle for whatever this is, I don't relish hearing that next month there's been an outbreak in Xyopar simply because we couldn't track the cause well enough to keep it from spreading. So far, the southernmost city-states seem unaffected. I'd like to keep it that way."

"Same," she agreed.

The day after tomorrow, their detail, along with many other Regulator details from across the city, would head to the palace of the Grand Marquises as part of the security forces overseeing some of the official ceremonies of the summit. That night would mark the opening ceremonies at the Palace Rotunda, and everyone of import would be there—all the dignitaries, Lutadorian high nobility, and famed performers from across the city-state.

Everything had to go right. Arkensyre's future depended on it.

Noting the sun was getting low on the horizon, that it would be night by the time they reached the den, she asked, "Do you need my help with the report?"

There was a long pause before Tray replied. He knew why she was asking and what her evening plans consisted of. "Krona . . ." he began carefully. Though she could not see the direction of his gaze beneath his helm, she knew it had settled on her side—on the mask. "You see De-Lia nearly every night," he said carefully. "Krona, it's not . . ."

Not healthy.

Krona understood these days that she was of two minds. She was two people, really.

By day, she was Regulator Captain De-Krona Hirvath, adjunct professor of teleomachy at the Academy, overseer of Penalties, polished and professional.

By night, she was someone she barely recognized.

Someone Tray disapproved of.

Someone the law disapproved of.

Someone even *Thibaut* disapproved of.

"Do you need my help?" she reiterated, voice stern.

"No," he said with a resigned sigh.

Good. Daylight hours were for concrete concerns; the dark hours were for ghosts.

4

KRONA

It was an obsession, but Krona didn't care.

Perhaps it was better that way.

With measured actions came measured results, and what Krona desired was no measure a sane mind dare inquire after. So, despite the guilt, despite the anxiety, she made her way this evening, like every evening—disregarding sleep, disregarding the pleas of her maman and the warnings of Thibaut—to the catacombs.

Entrances to the various branches were always in the center of joyous and lively places—parks, celebratoriums, theaters, music halls. Locations that embodied the fullness and happiness of *being*. In this way, the placement of the catacombs echoed the hourglasses they housed: time yet to run out atop, spent remnants of the past beneath.

Tonight, she would enter via the State Conservatory, where the horrid concern that had stolen her sister first revealed itself. Where Horace Gatwood's goons had released varger and stolen Charbon's Mayhem Mask and the insidious despairstone.

The gardens around it were well-kempt, and the green-glass windowpanes spotless.

The building gleamed in the moonlight.

It was quiet. Regal.

No signs of the bloodbath that had taken place there three years earlier remained.

She hurried to the observances entrance with her head bowed low, a hood obscuring her face. She'd shed her Regulator uniform for worship skirts and a heavy cloak.

Before mounting the steps that led to the door, she pulled the jaguar mask from her belt and stared at it in the low lamplight. She itched to put it on, to feel De-Lia's echo surging. Her fingertips tingled in her gloves, urging her to discard the delicate cotton gloves she'd donned this evening to feel the grain of the wood and the gloss of the paint with her bare hands. For a moment, she turned it over, staring into the bowed back of it, toying absently with the black leather ties that would secure it to the wearer's face. It looked so inviting. It seemed to call to her—offering comfort and familiarity, especially if she promised not to cage the echo. If she let it run freely, it would be good to her.

An unseen force lifted Krona's hands, bringing the bowl of the mask toward her bare face.

Just a moment. Only for a moment.

At the last second, she flipped the mask over again and settled her forehead against the jaguar's in a simple, grounding touch. She knew if she gave in to the urge and put the mask on, she would lose herself, which wouldn't do.

She had a meeting to get to.

With shaky hands, she lowered the mask and resecured it to her belt.

The observances door was flanked and adorned with stained glass depicting various devices for timekeeping—hourglasses, pocket watches, sundials. Small candles set behind the panes allowed outside observers to see the glowing illustrations. They were meant to entice outsiders to enter, rather than comfort those within.

Double-checking that her cloak covered the death mask at her hip, Krona knocked lightly on the wooden door. A young priest answered, her deep-brown skin and wavy hair a marker of Asgar-Skanian descent. "Five days in a week and five visits from you," she said, though not unkindly. "The goddess does not wish us to spend so much time focusing on the grains that have passed by."

Krona's feelings toward the goddess Time—and her constant march forward—were not kind these days. Indeed, the priest would find Krona's intent here not just unhealthy, or even unseemly, but *unholy.*

Blasphemous.

For if she could, Krona would gladly twist Time's clock hands behind her back and force the goddess to return what had been stolen.

"Time would not deny us our periods of grief," Krona said simply, adjusting the scarf that covered the lower half of her face—the priest may have recognized her, but Krona was certain she did not know her true identity. "For why would we keep the sand if not to see it?"

The young woman bowed in acknowledgment, swept a welcoming hand inside, and held the door open for Krona's passage.

The stone steps leading down in a clockwise spiral lay just off the door, and the priests' alcove sat directly opposite, little more than a shallow nook with a narrow, tall-backed chair where they could rest their feet during their shift.

The scent of warm, sugared mulberries underscored the aroma of old incense in the entryway, and Krona wondered what sort of celebrants would be partaking of berry pie from the conservatory's kitchens come morning.

With one last nod to the priest, she took the stone steps two at a time, her skirt and cloak flapping wildly as she moved. She was late, after all, and did not want the woman calling after her and wasting more of her time, offering a reading from the scrolls or even a lamp to guide her way. The sooner the goddess's watchful ones realized Krona did not seek or desire their company, the better.

In her haste, Krona missed a landing—one she was typically keenly aware of, as it was offset from the others, half a step too low. She stumbled, caught herself on the rounded wall of the narrow well. Her heart leapt into her throat as her time pouch came loose from her belt. The vials within went bouncing down the way, tinkling as they went. The glass would not break—vials that could shatter so easily would not be fit to hold enchantment—but she worried the noise would draw the priest.

Krona cursed at herself—a common occurrence these days—and pulled out a light vial to better see where her money had gone. The dealer she was to meet would not be gracious if she came up short.

Wrapping the enchanted vial in a handkerchief, she smashed it against the wall, then tipped the shards into a sturdy bottle from her pouch as the daylight held within burst into being. Counting to herself, she found every last minute and hurriedly replaced them in her purse.

The catacombs were long and winding, the walls glittering with bulbous hourglasses set in finely wrought metal. In most places the ceiling was low—she would've had to duck if she'd worn her uniform, helm and all. The passages smelled of age. Not of rot or mildew but of history. Mourner after mourner had stalked these ways, beginning with the first to grieve those who'd perished excavating them, back at the beginning, at Lutador's founding.

Corner after corner led her deeper into the city. To the appointed meeting place. Once in a while she heard voices through the walls, in places where the stone separating the catacombs, sewers, and the Dregs was thinnest.

Eventually, she arrived at her destination.

The communal sand pit was ten feet in diameter, and she had no idea how deep. A skylight above let moonlight stream down, giving the sands—the *ashes*—an unearthly gray glow. The pit was sealed under glass and surrounded by a low wall, both of which kept mourners from toppling into the mass grave.

Krona peered over the side. The surface of the ash pile was peaked and rippled, like a model of Xyopar's great dunes in miniature.

Nearby, perpetually burning braziers kept the air dry and the ashes from caking.

Centuries of Lutador's dead shared this pit, along with the hundreds of other pits like it throughout the city. Everyone from bakers to Regulators to artisans to beggars—all but the Dregs and the nobles. The Dregs kept their own, separate customs, while the dead from high society flanked the pit, filling the walls. Thousands of hourglasses lined the twisting paths of the catacombs.

One body, one glass.

Everyone was equal in death . . . except that they weren't.

It seemed both fitting and unfair that De-Lia had been given an hourglass of her own. It was a great honor, and yet it meant she'd always be alone. Secluded in her own glass. Kept from Krona when she too passed and inevitably went into the pit.

Someone behind her cleared their throat, and Krona raised a hand in acknowledgment. She kept close to the moonlight, forcing the broker to come out of the shadows so she could get a good look at him. "Monsieur Brant?"

A figure in a cloak of pale blue stepped into the dim glow. They were tall, broad, held their head high even while their visage was obscured behind the brim of their low hood—nothing like the short, mousy man she'd been told to expect.

Krona was instantly at the ready, her hand twitching toward her dagger. She didn't have her saber, but she'd never be so remiss as to engage in black-market dealings without a blade.

"You're not Brant," she said, voice low. She wanted to cut any attempted trickery off at the quick.

No, the figure acknowledged—the word coming from everywhere and nowhere at once.

As the figure moved to calmly draw back their cowl, revealing snow-white hair, Krona's breath caught. There were blue markings on the person's face—lines on their chin and swirls on their jaw.

It was *her*.

The Thalo puppet.

The one that had revealed herself after killing Gatwood.

She was older than Krona remembered during the DuPont-Leiwood wedding. And yet there was something nebulous about her. Krona wanted to say she was perhaps sixty, but that felt wrong—far too old. And yet . . . Forty? No, too young . . . *and* too old?

She gave off the impression of being well aged and in her prime at exactly the same time.

Perhaps it was her build—like a wrestler—and the way she held herself, coupled with the shock of her snow-white hair.

I didn't come here to harm you, the puppet said evenly, lips perfectly still.

You're real, Krona wanted to reply. There were times she'd speculated—after days and nights of burning the candle at both ends—about whether or not her vision of this woman had been just that: a vision. Insubstantial. A waking dream. Krona had wondered if somehow grief had made her rewrite her own memories, creating figments out of thin air.

But the woman was *here*. She was real, tangible.

Which meant her words had been real. Krona remembered them clearly: "*You are not immune to all our tricks. Don't let on that I've allowed you to see. The others must not know I aided you. Change is on the horizon.*"

"I expected to see you again sooner," Krona said evenly. "Either that or never again."

Which meant something must be happening. She had to be on the cusp of something, or else this apparition would have remained a memory.

You've been busy in my absence, the woman said. She reached for a small satchel on her hip, her cloak fluttering aside to reveal not robes, as the myths described, but leather armor not entirely divorced in design from what Krona wore on duty. Only these were bright cobalt blue, studded through with steel grommets. *I ran into the broker you were to meet.* She held up a small, black velvet pouch.

Krona nearly leapt at her, hands twitching to snatch the pouch away. As it was, she rubbed the pads of her fingers together, itching to touch, to inspect. "What did you do to him?"

The woman shrugged. *He forgot he had a prior engagement, nothing more. Luckily, I relieved him of the spirit beads he was going to sell you.* She tossed the pouch and Krona caught it, grasping it like it held the rarest gems instead of glass charms. *You should know they're fake. All spirit beads are fake. And need I remind you that attempted necromancy is, in fact, illegal?*

"I don't see how that's any of your business," Krona said, tipping the pouch over, letting five pearl-like beads drop into her palm. The glass was milky but not completely opaque, and something seemed to slither deep within. Her hands shook with anticipation. She wanted to get them home now, to use them as soon as possible.

It had been too long since she'd had a new enchantment to try, and her life-line tingled with the need for a fix, for an attempt.

You have her echo, the woman said, nodding at De-Lia's mask. *Be content.*

Krona bit back a retort, leaning into the neutrality of silence though she wanted to argue. Krona knew to maintain her guard. This woman was a Thalo puppet—a supposed manifestation of the cruel creator, imbued with its will, and the Thalo had only one goal inside the Valley: to torment humanity. Anything she said could be a twisted truth or an outright lie.

Despite the fact that she'd appeared to help Krona at the end of the Gatwood concern, Krona knew that didn't mean the woman was automatically an ally.

Just because she *appeared* to be out of sync with the other Thalo puppets didn't mean she was.

The spirit beads *could* be fake. Or this woman could be leading her astray.

I came here to warn you, the woman said, glancing off down one of the catacomb's branching halls, as though a sudden sound had concerned her. Cautiously, she strode to the other side of the sand pit and tilted her head, clearly listening for something more.

"Are you afraid we're being watched?" Krona asked.

Not at the moment. Though I can't say for certain if I've been followed. I must be brief. You cannot *go to the palace of the Grand Marquises night after next, during the celebration of the Pentaétos. Find whatever excuse you can to stay away. There will be a murder, and* they are going to frame you for it. *If they can. Do not let them.*

Krona kept her expression hard and even as she slipped the beads back into their pouch and tied the velvet to her belt, using the moment to turn this warning over in her head before responding outright. There was every reason to doubt this woman—for Krona to doubt her own senses, even—but she could not ignore intel like that. "Who's 'them'?" she demanded.

My people. The Order of the Thalo.

"Who are they set to kill?"

A noble twin who may have great influence over Lutador's future. I can't be more specific than that.

"Can't, or won't?"

The more details I give you, the more likely you are to show up exactly where I don't want you. I may not be able to manipulate you, but I can still see your secrets. The instant I told you to stay away, your intention to attend grew stronger, which you hoped to hide. Believe me, if I could simply invade your mind to keep you away, I would. But you're immune, even to me.

Krona tamped down on the resentment that bubbled up in her throat at the suggestion that her will might be so unfeelingly subverted if she didn't possess said immunity. "You would do me an honor *by staying out of my mind altogether.*"

Speaking directly into your mind is safer for the both of us, came the weary apology.

"Why do you care what happens to me, anyway?" Krona huffed. "Why would anyone want to frame *me*?"

You pose an insufferable risk to the very foundations of Arkensyre. What's worse, you have no idea you're a threat.

"Then why not simply kill me? You killed Gatwood so easily—why not off me as well?" Krona tensed, readied herself for a fight, just in case her suggestion bore fruit.

Believe it or not, I—we—do not murder often or impulsively. You're a Regulator, she offered, tone suggesting Krona could reason this all out for herself, *you deal with conspiracy frequently. Why don't those who seek influence and power simply kill all of their enemies?*

"Because they fear reprisal."

Is that so?

No, Krona knew it wasn't so.

"Because an enemy's image is useful. An adversary cannot simply cease to exist; it's often more advantageous to sully their legacy than to take their life."

Exactly. They aim to use you just as they used the others. Even your sister. She said it with another pointed glance at the jaguar mask on Krona's hip.

A tingle of hatred buzzed through the back of Krona's head, and she gritted her teeth. *Don't you speak of her,* she wanted to shout. You *denied her justice. You denied her murderer a proper punishment and granted him a merciful end.* "What have I done to deserve such consideration?" she asked instead, tempering herself.

Proven less than vulnerable. Uncontrollable.

"And yet here you are, still intent on controlling me."

I'm trying *to* protect *you,* the woman countered, harried. *And the only way I can think to do that is to ensure you are nowhere near the murder when it happens. Be seen—be seen far, far away from the palace. Fake illness, injury. Whatever it takes. If you must alert your brethren to a murder plot, do it, though I doubt they will believe you until it is too late. Just . . . heed me.*

Krona let the silence stretch, watching the woman closely. "Tell me who the target is—who your people intend to kill—and I'll consider it."

The woman sighed, clearly exasperated. *Please remember I can see your secrets. No, you will not consider it.*

"And please recall I told you to keep away from my mind—what is the point of having a conversation if you can simply see my intent? You cannot have seriously come here thinking to alert me to an assassination—because that is what we're talking about, isn't it?—while assuming I would be inclined to be less involved in the summit. *Who is it?* One of the diplomats?" Winsrouen's patron god was Nature, Time's twin. As such, they valued noble twins with the same fervor as Lutador. The woman had at least let slip that a twin was the target, so it could very well be someone in their visiting detail.

Winsrouen's new bout of aggression, their border dispute with Asgar-Skan and their disruption of trade south to Xyopar . . . would this, this *Order* of the Thalo take an interest in such a dispute? If one of Winsrouen's diplomats was killed, would that fuel their antagonism? Their expansion?

How would the other city-states respond?

Krona's mind whirled.

That the Thalo and its puppets would take interest in spiritual affairs made some sense. The Thalo despised the gods' creations, found it amusing to toy with them and their devotion. That it would create a cult and sully the Unknown God made spiritual sense.

But what did it care for politics? For assassinations and intrigues?

The more she considered it, though, the more it fit. *Of course* politics would be of interest to a being who loved disruption and chaos.

Krona couldn't just let the Thalo puppet slip away again, not with an assassination on the line. She needed to bring her in. To the den, for a proper interrogation. Krona had manacles with her. If she could get close to the puppet, perhaps she could move quickly enough to cuff her before she disappeared—she was sure the mist-like quality of her invisibility did not truly make her insubstantial. Once she was bound, she would stay bound.

The woman let out a heavy, theatrical sigh.

It took Krona a moment to realize why. "Saints and swill," she cursed.

Anything your mind treats as clandestine will always be known to me. Even your nursery rhymes about the Thalo teach you that.

"Then come with me, freely, to my den. You don't approve of this scheme, you wish to undermine it, or else you wouldn't be here."

The woman let out a small chuckle. *True enough. But I cannot come with you. I've already been away from my detail for too long. Just—listen to me. That's all you have to do.* She shook her head, ran fingertips over her brow. *Forgive me; I haven't had to deal with such belligerence in a long time. I thought it would be refreshing. It's not.*

With that, she vanished.

"Wait!" Krona stumbled forward, as though the ground had moved beneath her feet. "How are you even doing this? Helping me?" Krona asked, grasping for a way to keep the woman talking, to keep her present. "You're a puppet, a manifestation—"

I'm flesh and blood, she countered. *As human as you are. Every "Thalo puppet" is no more than that. And certainly no less.*

"What enchantments give you your abilities, then? What cloaks you? Allows you to speak inside my mind?"

I carry no enchantments.

"Bullshit," Krona said in half laugh. "If you're human, then you must hold enchantments in order to—"

You cannot be made to grasp all that is unknown to you in this instant, and I do not have time to explain it to you!

"Where do you come from? And why would you serve a creator who wants to harm—?"

Just heed me, the woman insisted, her voice now sounding far off. *I will answer your questions the next time we meet, but you* must *do as I ask.*

Krona turned on her toes, trying to decide which way she'd fled and how best to follow. "Why would I listen to you?" she called, trying to rile her, to bring her back. "As far as I know, you are a phantasm who murders those who should instead be brought to justice by the law. As far as I can tell, you're a co-conspirator with the likes of Gatwood and his cultists—just one who decided to turn on him in the end."

You are not that far from the truth of it, said the quiet voice inside her mind, *but you have to understand: Horace and his cult, Fiona, Louis, Eric—they're all part of a larger picture. I have to go.*

"Wait!" Krona cried, "Do you know anything about a kidnapped baby?"

You'll have to be more specific, said the woman, but she did not show herself again.

"A baby whose parents were made to think the child had died?"

You'll have to be more specific, came the slow reply, each word emphasized to carry weight, to make Krona understand.

It wasn't just Melanie's child, then. There were others.

She wasn't sure how to formulate her next question, to fit the implications into a structure that made sense.

"What's done to them? Why—"

I do not have time.

The words fell like a finality, and urgency made new questions spill from Krona. She shifted the conversation again, trying to find something to keep the woman talking. Krona needed to retain her for as long as possible, unable to otherwise integrate all she'd learned here without furthering their exchange. "Wait, what about markings? Wounds and scars shaped like enchanter's marks? What do you know of those?"

But there were no more answers. No more denials, even. The Thalo woman had faded away, gone into the night.

5

THALO CHILD

Two and a Half Years Ago

"Close your eyes," Gerome bade the group.

Thalo Child lay with the other Thalo children from his cohort, on thin reed mats placed over the cold, black stone of the chapel floor.

Emotion's cloister was small, intimate. The six of them lay elbow to elbow, the proximity comforting. If Thalo Child hadn't been able to feel the occasional jostling from his siblings, he would have been adrift. Lost in the emotions Gerome fed them here.

Of course, losing one's self was the point, and Thalo Child did feel guilty for grounding himself—for not fully giving himself over to the sea of feeling.

But Gerome had yet to punish him for this secret, and so he kept it.

High above them, a small, white light drowned out the chapel's tall ceiling. The rounded, rough-hewn walls tunneled up, *up*, high away from the polished floor. The black stone altar at the children's feet was a blocky pedestal of a thing, placed before a life-size statue of Emotion sitting with zhur legs crossed, cut from the same jet-black rock. Its facets shone, glittering with every slight movement in the room. And while the stone itself was lovely, the statue's form was grotesque.

The god's body in most depictions was nothing more than a sunburst—too bright to look at, too intense to bear. But as Thalo, they must look upon the form beneath. Must see the true manifestations of Emotion. They must know that all the gods were roiling, shifting forms. Not the pale parodies of human bodies that so much of the Valley chose for their depictions.

Here, Emotion had been carved into four sections, its upper right quadrant an illustration of cruelty, with a demon's terrible, distorted face jutting off one shoulder, and slime dripping down and covering the exposed bones of the god's arm—or arms; the form was so distorted, it was difficult to tell what was a limb and what was a knife or a spike. The lower right represented grief, with an anguished woman's face capping off the knee, and the shin of Emotion's leg split wide into a pit into which the woman's tears and various flower petals disappeared. The lower left was apathy, and dozens of faces, round and blank but raised like boils, covered the god's leg and lower body. And the upper left represented mania, with the god's shoulder capped in the upper body of a figure lunging away, mouth opened wide in a sort of terrible glee, the fingers of one of its hands peeling at its own skin, curling it away, the other doing the same to Emotion's forearm.

At the top center of it all, a rudimentary face grinned broadly, as though ecstatic to share these awful feelings with the world.

Thalo Child gazed through his lashes and down his body, past his toes, to the statue, his eyes half-lidded in the dim light.

Gerome walked back and forth just a few inches beyond the children's heads, the enchanted Eye exposed, seated on the top of a long staff that *tap . . . tap . . . tapped* as he walked.

Suddenly, he was directly over Thalo Child, peering down, bending low over him. Gerome's long hair toppled over the ridges of his copper half-mask, the strands straight and smooth—reaching for the Thalo Child like fine, oily fingers.

"Close. Your. Eyes."

Thalo Child screwed them shut. His skin prickled out of fear and anticipation.

He hated this ritual.

Every second of it.

But it was necessary.

If he wanted to earn his name and go out into the world to help people, he had to learn to be strong.

"You're drifting," Gerome said.

The rhythmic tapping had never ceased.

Tap.

Tap.

Tap.

"You're relaxing."

Tap.

Tap.

Tap.

"Folding in on yourself."

Tap.

Tap.

Tap.

"Folding and drifting. Folding and drifting. Over and over. Until you are small and thin, like a wisp of spider silk."

Tap.

"Light."

Tap.

"Airy."

Tap.

"Thin. And free. No feeling, not even calm. Empty. So empty. Just a vessel. Waiting to be filled."

The tapping ceased.

Thalo Child's ears rang with the sudden silence.

"You will feel only what I tell you to feel. And you will feel it wholly. Near bursting with it. You will be *made* of the feeling."

The Eye swung low over their faces, slicing through the air, making a threatening *swish* like a knife in the dark.

The relic—one of seven artifacts from the Before Times—was a large, clear jewel, studded through with inclusions: veins of various minerals and stones. A diamond encasing gemstones of all kinds.

This stone, the Eye, had been manufactured, not found. Where jewels typically budded in the earth, this one had been made in some madman's lab. It was a stone that should not exist—could not exist—in nature. Many emotion stones grown on top of one another, encased in diamond.

But the Eye was not enchanted the same way other emotion stones were enchanted. The ruby inside did not carry despair. The emerald did not carry pride, the amber no hope, and the aquamarine no joy. Instead, they could channel those specific emotions. Straight from the Possessor.

And then that feeling was amplified one hundredfold by the diamond.

Whatever Gerome could make himself feel, he could make *them* feel.

And he always started this ritual the same way.

"Now," he said darkly. "Deep breath—"

Thalo Child filled his lungs, already sensing the foreign emotion, its snaking tendrils both barbed and oozing. His body recoiled. His breath caught.

"—and *suffer.*"

When not under the Eye's gaze, Thalo Child often thought of the word "suffer." He tested its syllables in his mouth, tasting their shape, feeling their depth. Such a small hiss of a word for all the torment it encompassed.

Then he'd imagine the Eye. Imagine Gerome wielding it. He would send himself, mentally, here, to the cold floor in front of the terrible statue. He would make himself feel the suffering, thinking he could stretch his emotions, make them more elastic, make his body more receptive and less vulnerable when he had to face the feeling for real.

He'd sink, of his own accord, into suffering.

Imagine suffering.

The worst suffering.

Take a deep breath.

What's it like, to feel the worst kind of pain?

Ongoing. Unstoppable.

The suffering of the body—long torture. The sharp slice of a paper cut, over and over. The surprising pain of a stubbed toe, extrapolated out to every joint, over and over. Long pins stuffed under fingernails. A razor on the delicate flesh of the corner of one's mouth.

The suffering of the spirit—watching others hurt, watching them die, losing them. Beholding a tragedy one had no power to make right.

The suffering of the mind—reaching for words that are not there. Memories that are gone. Thoughts that are not one's own. Thoughts that turn on you, make you doubt yourself, hurt yourself.

Hurt yourself.

Suffer.

Thalo Child liked to think it helped. Trying to suffer away from Gerome's guided suffering. Outside of the cloister, he convinced himself it worked.

But under the Eye, the truth was always revealed.

He tried to breathe, but every twitch of his lungs hurt. His heart stuttered, his hands clenched, curled into claws. His spine bowed against the reed mat, and his siblings on both sides lashed out with their elbows.

One of Thalo Child's sisters let out a half gasp, half shout. She *always* screamed first.

"Think of the worst suffering you've ever experienced. Feel that. Feel my suffering and your suffering, fused. Sink deeper into that feeling. Deeper into suffering. Suffer. Suffer more. *More.*"

With the pinch of a taut leash suddenly snapping and flicking back, lashing the skin, the suffering was gone. The children all let out a cathartic scream together as Gerome released them.

But he gave them no pause, no chance to bring their own emotions back to level before he was stretching them in the opposite direction.

"Rapture," he said. "Elation. Ecstasy. Be light. Be full and light."

Thalo Child choked, gargled, as his body whipped from one end of the spectrum of feeling to the other. The tension that had filled his muscles released him and he went limp, unable to flex even if he wanted to. His mind felt fuzzy, and for an instant he would have sworn that he was floating. He couldn't feel the floor anymore. Or the sharp elbows jabbing him. There was just a . . . buoyancy. A featheriness. A purity of happiness. A freedom from worry, from stress.

So light.

So happy.

"More. Let that joy consume you. Let it fuel you. Let it command you and take hold of you. You can do so much, be so much. Let the mania creep up. The urge to *do*. There's so much happiness inside you. So much potential. Let it move your fingers, your toes."

Thalo Child's hands began to shake with the need to touch, to create. To do. It felt as though ants were crawling under his skin, urging him to push off the floor, to dance, to jump, to *fly*. Because he could. He could do *anything*.

Another sibling cried out, unable to contain their euphoria.

But in the next instant, that jubilation was torn away.

Gerome didn't have to say it.

They all felt it.

Suffer.

>─◆─○─◆─<

As they stumbled out of the chapel, his cohort all in a line with Gerome following after, Thalo Child's mind felt hazy. His limbs were too heavy, and yet they felt empty—hollow. His arms hung like dead weights at his sides, dragging him down, bowing his back, and each step was excruciatingly difficult.

He found his gaze dropping, repeatedly, to the floor, though he tried to drag it up again, tried to focus on the back of his sibling's neck in front of him.

They passed several Mindless as they retreated—servants with no consciousness, who moved like automations.

Thalo Child felt like one of the Mindless himself.

"You all did well," Gerome praised. "You will be so strong when you leave the keep. You will be able to endure. To serve and endure."

Thalo Child barely registered the heavy, quick footsteps headed in their direction. Boots. Someone wearing boots.

The keep's halls were all cavernous, and boots always echoed—thus the slippers.

Boots meant a Thalo in service *outside* these walls. They meant an Orchestrator or a Harvester.

He lifted his head a little, peering through the fringe of his corn-colored hair.

A woman in blue leathers and long white hair was striding toward their line, a bundle in her arms.

Behind him, Gerome gasped before he could.

They all knew this woman. All revered this woman.

Hintosep.

The oldest Thalo. The Savior's most beloved.

The one who'd given up her post and authority to return all the way down the line of command to Harvester. She was an ex-Guardian, ex-Possessor, ex-Orchestrator.

And yet, just because she'd formally abdicated her authority, that did not mean she'd lost it.

All of the children tensed, sensing Gerome's fluster. He was never flustered. He was a rock—one who offered his blood without flinching, once who doled out punishments and delights with the same evenness, the same sternness.

There was no one, except the Savior Himself, who could cause such a stir in their Possessor.

"Kneel," he hissed at all of them.

Limbs still wobbly, they all complied as gracefully as they could.

Though Hintosep continued to approach, she kept her gaze locked on the bundle, cradling it with care while a soft smile played across her pale-blue lips.

It took Thalo Child a moment to realize the bundle was gurgling.

"Stand," she ordered as she came close, attention still occupied.

The children followed her direction just as readily as they had Gerome's, and Thalo Child had to put a hand on his sibling's shoulder to keep from falling over.

His head buzzed; his vision dappled. He felt light-headed. Hopefully, neither of them would order the group down again.

No one spoke. Gerome swallowed heavily, as though gulping down questions, waiting instead for her to acknowledge him.

It was unnerving—seeing their guardian so wrong-footed.

Hintosep bounced the bundle in her arms, and the swaddled baby within let out a small, cooing laugh. The lines on her face weren't deep, and though her hair was as white as snowcap, it was impossible to guess her age. Impossible, it seemed, even to place how old she *looked*, compared to the Mindful or the Mindless in the palace, who all aged naturally, without the aid of added time. She was strong, moved with a firmness and precision that no one of such an advanced age typically enjoyed.

How old, exactly, was she? Hundreds of years? Thousands? He didn't know. He wasn't even sure Gerome knew.

Thalo Child had never been this close to her before. He'd only ever noted her from afar. Across a crowd during a feast-holiday, or when she came to pay the blood tithe—when all Thalo returned to the keep at once.

Her proximity sent a tingling across his skin. Her power was palpable.

Suddenly, her gaze snapped up. Her eyes were dark—irises the deepest midnight blue.

Her stare fell directly onto *him*.

She took a step forward, and it took everything Thalo Child had not to take a step *back*.

Ignoring the children at the front of the procession, she swept around to the rear, and for a moment Thalo Child hoped he'd been mistaken. Perhaps she'd been looking at Gerome.

But she stopped next to him.

His siblings all pivoted slowly to watch her, risking Gerome's ire by failing to maintain order.

He wasn't sure where to look—if he should acknowledge the attention or shrink back. He averted his gaze, let it fall to her thick, cobalt-blue boots.

"Eyes up," she said gently.

Thalo Child cursed himself for guessing wrong. He followed her direction, letting himself glance at Gerome for an instant, to gauge his reaction.

His Possessor was inscrutable, mouth in a thin line, gaze partially obscured by his low crown. For a moment, Gerome's lips twitched, pulling at his scars, but he said nothing.

Without a word, Hintosep leaned forward, arms outstretched, *offering him the child*.

He froze. The others openly gasped. One of his sisters covered her mouth in shock.

Thalo Child felt Gerome go rigid next to him.

A beat followed. Then two.

Hintosep waited.

He was making Hintosep *wait*.

"I am not yet old enough," he blurted, words falling panicked and quick from his lips, though he regretted speaking the instant he opened his mouth. One *did not* rebuke a Possessor. Even an ex-Possessor.

But he wasn't trying to be contrary. He was trying to express his unworthiness.

One of his age wasn't allowed to hold an infant.

Being handed one could only mean one thing.

Thalo children were given charges at fifteen. Their final duty before earning their name.

That he would be given this honor, this responsibility . . .

"Take zhim," Hintosep said definitively, still holding the baby out.

The small thing wriggled in her grasp, and he leaned forward a little to get a better look. Zhur brown face was pinched, on the edge of crying.

Thalo Child could not refuse. He lifted his hands, felt his muscles shake, even without any added weight. The ritual had sapped him of his strength, and now he was being handed something so precious, so fragile. His arms tremored as he held out his hands.

He tried not to sob with the worry, the strain, as the baby was placed delicately in the cradle of his arms.

At any moment, his limbs might fail. At any moment, he could drop zhim.

"Zhe is yours now," Hintosep said proudly, voice still soft. "To protect, to guide. The reincarnation of a named one lost to us." She held her hand over the baby's forehead. "Zhe was very powerful in zhur former life. I can feel it."

"A Possessor?" he whispered, trying not to let his voice betray his worry.

"Perhaps."

The idea that *he* was to guide a Thalo so powerful, that he might be so worthy . . .

He felt overwhelmed. His breath caught, and he fought the tremble in his lip and the wet heat rising around his eyes. This task was big, important. And he could fail so easily.

Thalo Child chanced another glance at Gerome, not knowing what he'd see. Gerome could be proud—the Savior's most beloved had chosen one of *his* children for this apparently special task—or he could be furious. This Thalo Child belonged to *him*, after all. Gerome made Thalo Child's choices, guided him, was supposed to be his sole light—the sun, the moons, the stars—until the Child earned his name.

Gerome's expression was still disturbingly neutral. Only the hint of hardness, of speculation and study, pinched the corners of his mouth.

Without looking at Gerome for even a moment, Hintosep turned and walked away. Gerome swayed in her direction, as though fighting the instinct to follow.

They all watched her retreat silently—nothing but her footfalls and the baby's gurgling could be heard—staring after her until she disappeared around the corner of the darkened corridor.

And then, as if a spell had broken, Thalo Child's siblings all swooped around him. They dare not touch his new charge, but they began chattering excitedly and leaning in, trying to get a good look.

Thalo Child was still flabbergasted. He couldn't enjoy their excitement, couldn't share in it.

Only a moment passed before Gerome shook himself, seemingly coming back from someplace deep, deep inside his memory. "Order!" he barked.

Thalo Child startled, and the others squeaked. He grasped the baby more firmly to his chest as his siblings realigned themselves. He openly turned to

Gerome, needing guidance, needing to know what this meant in the grand scheme of his life and his learning.

"Am I—"

Gerome laid a hand on his shoulder, the sharp tips of his filigree-capped fingernails curling claw-like around him. "You are still *my* child," he said firmly.

Relief flooded through Thalo Child, and he nodded, placing himself back in line, glancing down at the baby.

And you, he thought—fear shooting through him, despite his exhaustion, how wrung out his feelings—*are* my *child*.

This was not an exercise. This was not a stretching. This was not sport.

This was real, and weighty, and Thalo Child had no idea what such an unexpected turn meant for him, his naming, and his place in service to the Savior.

6

KRONA

In the moments after the puppet left, Krona remained still, staring off into the darkness of the catacombs. When she was sure she was alone, she moved closer to the sand pit, where the light of the twin moons shone down silvery-blue. Jittery, she pulled a single spirit bead from the pouch, holding it up, looking closely for an enchanter's mark. And—yes!—there it was, tiny, but perfectly formed, magically fused deep within the glass.

She couldn't wait to get them home. To lock herself away in her room of misfortune and attempt the blasphemy that all the gods found most foul. To undo a death slighted both the forward march of Time and the natural order set down by Nature. To subvert grief was to offend Emotion. And to seek such terrible ingenuity when Knowledge strictly forbade it was to risk her hands and her livelihood, for ones who'd received a god's penalty could no longer serve in the constabulary.

She'd just been informed of an assassination plot—one where she herself was supposed to take the fall—and yet all she could think about were the beads, and the patronizing, *condescending* way the woman had said, *Be content.*

It rattled in Krona's brain and between her ribs, plinking hollowly, cruelly, against her bones.

Be content.

Be content.

As though anyone could be content in a world so wrong. Would a fisherman be content if the Deep Waters dried up, or the rivers stopped flowing? Would the traveling caravans in Xyopar be content without the desert oases?

Should one be content with the night if the day had burned away?

"All spirit beads are fake." Ha. *And there are no blood pens, no mythical Thalo puppets, and no enchanted journals.*

The goddess had made a mistake; she'd taken De-Lia before her time had run out. And if she could take someone prematurely, then she could give her *back.*

All existence was a formula. All magic was a formula. There was a recipe for life as there was a recipe for death, and Krona would find what she needed to breathe De-Lia back into being, to set things *right*.

Fingers trembling, Krona slid her hand down to touch the jaguar. She itched to put the mask on, right there. To feel De-Lia's presence, as fragmented as it was.

Her sister's echo was a hollow thing, as all echoes were supposed to be. A remnant, a reverberation of who she'd been, nothing more.

Charbon's echo hadn't been that way. He'd felt strangely conscious. Aware of himself, even as a shadow.

Krona had hoped for the same with De-Lia. Even though she knew masks and echoes like no one else, Krona couldn't help but imagine the mask as a small house where her sister resided. Where Krona could still visit her. She'd imagined putting on the mask would be like opening a door and stepping into their apartment.

But, of course, it was nothing like that. It was like wading into a cold pond, one swirling with thought and feelings and memories, yes, but all without direction. Without purpose or true intent. The mask was just a metaphorical divot in the ground—a place where some wispy essence of De-Lia had pooled, trickling in each time she'd gone to the *Teleoteur* during the enchanting process.

She wasn't there.

Pieces of her were scattered throughout Lutador, but *De-Lia* wasn't anywhere.

Her ashes in the hourglass, her echo and a sliver of her knowledge in the mask, her blood—dried, long crusted—on the blood pen, locked away in the vaults.

But *she* was no more.

And it was devastatingly *unfair*.

Krona yanked her hand away from the jaguar to cover her mouth as a shaking half sob rose in her throat.

She didn't want to feel the sadness, the loss—those emotions had always been immobilizing for her. Stowing the beads once more, she tried to reached for the anticipation, for the relief that came with a new attempt to undo death. It had been weeks since last she'd tried anything new, since she'd had an opportunity as promising as this.

Krona wanted to get home as soon as possible. To begin.

But first, she had to pay someone a visit.

With leaden feet, she picked her way to a familiar hall in the necropolis, the bulbs of its timepieces glimmering in the enchanted glow from her light vial—each reflecting a spot of glare, like watchful eyes moving with her, judging, as she stalked forward to stand before her sister's.

Each hourglass was roughly the same size, and each was set into its own nook. Individual styles varied greatly, depending on the *Kairoteur* who'd enchanted the glass and forged its housing. Some glass had a silver sheen, or an inner layer of quicksilver, or the opacity of leaded glass, depending on the family's priorities in preservation. Like with time vials and varger bottles, the glass could not be broken, and it took an enchanter to open and close the vessels.

There she was.

De-Lia.

The last of her body.

Once power, and beauty, and decisiveness incarnate, now naught but a pile of ash.

The Chief Magistrate had spared no expense in procuring her hourglass. It had been plain when De-Lia's sand had been entombed—the glass framed in no more than black-stained wood. Later, metal Xyoparian desert roses had been added, ringing the top and bottom of the stand, the metal itself painted red as grief. The arms of the stand were thick and curled like the plant's branches and trunk. Bits of opal white threaded through the stand for highlights, and a similar rainbow sheen colored the glass of the bulbs. Bits of griefstone had been fused into the glass, and Krona kept her fingers free. She didn't need enchantments to deepen her emotion.

It had been years, but the pain was still fresh. Every time she stood here, Krona was not comforted. She was reinvigorated—focused in her anger, in her certainty that this was erroneous. The world had gone *wrong*, and she was good and right to want to correct it.

Necromancy might be the blasphemous stuff of fairy tales, but what had killed De-Lia had been just as mythic.

She reached out for the small wheel set into the stone next to De-Lia's nook. With a delicate flick of her finger, she spun it, and the hourglass turned over. Her older sister's ashes flowed through the neck, down into the bottom.

Krona didn't need to count as the sands ran. She knew exactly how many minutes her sister's body tallied.

De-Lia should be here, now, to experience every single one of them.

Her time hadn't run out. It had been stolen.

"Soon, De-Lia," Krona promised. "Soon."

><+>-O-<+>-<

Krona tried to take the most direct route home, eager to test her night's prize, but she found herself lost in thought—lost in obsessing over the words *be content*—and hardly noticed when she took a stray turn onto a rougher street.

She passed two men leaning casually against an alley wall. They pretended not to notice as she went by, but she could feel their gazes—hot and predatory—on her back.

Don't do it, she thought at them. *Don't test me.*

The day's events had already pulled her thin and wrung her out. The last thing she wanted was an altercation.

She breathed deeply, her heart rate picking up as she heard boots behind her. *I won't look back,* she told herself.

"Hey, pretty!" one shouted.

She pretended not to notice, picking up her pace—stomach sinking, blood thrilling—as the boots behind her did the same. Clenching her teeth, steading herself, she took a corner, then another. She would give them every opportunity. She would not start this fight, would not lay the first hand.

Her pulse leapt as the boots caught up, as a hand fell hard on her shoulder and spun her. Her back hit a wall and she let herself go, surprised to find herself reveling in the way the air thumped out of her lungs—in the way it made her extremities tingle.

Irritation spiked in her gut, and she tried to press it down. If she let it, it would bleed into her bones and make ready her hands—but she wasn't looking for a fight. She didn't want to fight.

The scent of stale sweat wafted into her face as the first man leaned in close. "Hand over your time vials and you can prance on your way," the man said.

She looked between them—both tall but not overly bulky. Ragged but not Dregs. Average ruffians.

Both of their faces were inscrutable in the dark.

"Gotta pay the toll," the second one chuckled.

"I don't have any time vials," she lied gruffly. She hadn't meant to use her Regulator voice—she'd meant to play the rabbit to their foxes for longer—but couldn't help it.

"Well, isn't that unfortunate," the first one said. "This cloak is nice," he said, rubbing the edge between his fingers. "Someone dressed like you always has something of value on them." He flung the cloak edge aside, clearly looking for her purse. He saw the mask instead. "Spend all your time on this, did you?"

That got her attention. Anger rose like bile in her throat. "If you *so much as touch it*—" she warned breathlessly. Her entire body was taut against the bricks. She stood on a high wire, poised precariously between doing what she knew was right—arresting them for mugging, dropping them off at the nearest Watch post—and doing what instincts told her to do: cut off their hands for daring to threaten the mask. For threatening what was left of *De-Lia.*

Krona was a wound spring, held by the lightest latch.

The man's fingers moved toward the jaguar, and everything seemed to slow. These were the instances that decided how he would leave here tonight.

"If you *touch* it—" she growled again.

One brush of his fingers against the yellow paint of the jaguar, and Krona snapped.

The latch lifted, the spring uncoiled.

Using the wall for leverage, she brought her boot up into his gut, shoving him away with a pointed kick, a shout breaking from behind her teeth.

He let out a surprised *oof,* stumbled backward.

Both men were caught off guard, but she didn't give them so much as a second to catch up. There was no reason to. She'd given them too many chances already. They'd crossed the line, gone for the mask, and she was well within her duties as a Regulator to incapacitate the threat.

Justification after justification rattled through her skull as she grabbed the second man by the back of the head and bashed his face into the wall.

The first scrambled to his feet. She clutched the second by the rear of his tunic and threw him into the first. They landed in a heap.

With blood thumping through her ears, she took up a fighting stance, fists at the ready.

Their faces hardened, they separated, and each drew thin knives.

Yes, something in her hissed. A buzzing, a thrumming, soared at the chance to draw blood, a reason to pull her own blade.

She twitched toward it but held herself steady.

They were no match for her. Untrained. Likely unaccustomed to their mugging victims putting up a fight of any kind.

The first came at her, blade raised inexpertly. She parried with her left forearm, punching him squarely in the jaw with her right fist.

He stumbled out of the way, and the second was on top of her. His blade drove at her middle, and she caught his wrist, twisting, forcing him to drop the knife. His nose was already bloody from his encounter with the wall. It gave a satisfying second *crunch* as she pushed his head down to meet her upcoming knee.

His blood left a patch on her skirt, and the stain filled her with something akin to satisfaction but with an acidic, bitter edge.

He let out a sob, falling to the ground and staying there.

She spun on the first, pouncing on his back. He hadn't yet recovered from her blow. She shoved him bodily, face-first into the wall and held him there.

"It's not your night, is it?" she said, twisting his knife arm behind his back, tilting his fist so that the blade tip pressed against his spine.

"Fucking—"

She tilted farther, let the knife cut into his clothes, press farther, into his skin, press, press . . .

He cried out.

"Oi!" came a shout from a few stories up as a window was thrown open and a candle thrust out. "Some of us have pressing engagements with Asgar-Skanian nobles in the morning!"

Krona looked up and went cold.

Thibaut.

Gods, of course it was Thibaut.

Where else would her feet have led her but to his very doorstep?

He looked mussed in the candlelight, wore a light linen sleeping shirt, unlaced. Even his gloves were off. She couldn't see the scars from here, but she could still imagine them vividly.

Could imagine his fingers—long, strong. She could imagine them entwined with hers. She could imagine them tracing lightly down her arm, or up her throat, or across the seam of her thighs—

The first mugger groaned beneath her, and she twisted the knife away from him, sliding it into her own hand, removing the bloodied tip from his back. "Be quiet," she whispered harshly.

She was sure Thibaut couldn't make her out in the dark. Was sure he had no idea she was beating men senseless beneath his window.

Her breathing changed. No longer the tight, deep breaths of combat, but high and ragged, as though she'd been caught in an intimate and compromising position.

The mugger tried to say something, and she shoved him harder into the wall, waiting. Waiting for Thibaut to retreat.

"Yes, that's good, thanks," Thibaut said lightly, whisking his light away, back into his apartment.

And with that the spell was broken. She'd spilled all the blood she would spill tonight. Had broken all the noses she would break.

The momentary satisfaction left her. And now she felt another sort of itch, a different sort of longing in her palms.

One that she would never stoop to satisfy.

⊱⊰⊱•◦•⊰⊱

Sore, bloody-knuckled, and tired, she returned to the apartment she shared with her maman.

She told herself she'd done well. Two more brutes were off the street—she'd left them with the Nightswatch—and would pester vulnerable people no more. And she'd kept her dagger sheathed. That was a triumph in itself. Something in her had thrummed for blood, but she would not take that next step. Would not engage in an unnecessary level of violence.

Acel Hirvath was fast asleep in her bed, which settled something inside Krona's chest that she hadn't realized was ill at ease. Walking into the apartment, knowing De-Lia would not be there, was one thing. A ghost of a feeling, like she could lose her mother at any moment as well, hung about her like a haze.

Before she could so much as think about peeling off her clothes and sliding beneath her own covers, Krona went to De-Lia's bedroom to test the spirit beads.

Three heavy magical locks held the door fast, and with the proper enchanted skeleton key, she flicked them open one by one. The door creaked ever so slightly as she shouldered it open. She paused for a moment, to be sure Maman would remain asleep, then hurried inside, eager to shut herself away.

Some people preserved the bedrooms of the dead, kept them exactly as their loved ones had left them. Not Krona.

Acel had begged her to move from her sleeping nook into this, the largest bedroom. After all, Krona was now the captain, now the one keeping this roof over their heads. But Krona knew she would have no restful nights in this room and therefore couldn't claim it as her own, yet she hadn't let it become a shrine, either.

No, it was something much, much more important.

She'd blacked out the window long ago with ink procured from one of the print shops not far down the block. Nary a flicker of light could be seen from outside.

She lit the small candle she kept near the door, and wandered over to the bureau. Flyers littered the top of it—leaflets Krona had been gathering for years now, mostly advertisements by independent music tutors that had been pinned on message boards. De-Lia had urged Krona to learn to play a musical instrument—the cello, specifically—right before she'd died, and while Krona had always wanted to play something, these days all music simply renewed her grief. Now she gathered such advertisements for the future—a future in which she had her sister back and music brought joy to her once again.

The bureau had been stripped of all its drawers—they now littered the bed—and Krona had placed planks in the dresser's bones to make shelves for easy access. The walls of the room were papered with clippings, old and new alike, anything with an inconsistent story involving enchantments. Anything that hinted at the broken world as she knew it.

She'd made a space for the spirit beads between a mummified paw of an unknown creature and a branching chunk of lightning glass. Her collection was still small by collection standards, but even the two dozen or so impossible and illegal enchantments she'd procured these last years were enough to see her hang if anyone above her station ever found out about them.

Consequences be damned. Her life was a small thing to risk to return to De-Lia what was rightfully hers.

Krona had verified that at least half of these enchantments, so far, were indeed fake. Including the first one Thibaut had procured for her—the very candle she now burned. Supposedly, it would let one illuminate the souls of the deceased, let them be seen walking the world of the living. All it managed to do was burn longer than usual and smoke more than was common.

Each failure had simply spurred her desire to keep searching. She sought forbidden knowledge like a drowning man sought air—or perhaps more like a junkie sought their next hit.

She took a moment to glance at the files she'd brought home to study—ones pertaining to the mark epidemic. They contained photographs of each, no matter if the victim had been living or deceased. Soon, they'd have a full file on the man at the Asylum to add to the grim, growing stack.

Each mark was so distorted, Krona had yet to be able to match any of them to their enchanters. A few she'd come close with, but couldn't be certain. Was it telling that all of her close calls had belonged to *Teleoteurs*? Did it suggest perhaps only masks were involved?

Sighing, she shoved the day's worries, and its questions, away.

From one shelf in the bureau she drew forth a large copper funnel, big as a mixing bowl, which the spirit beads needed to function properly.

Supposedly.

With this set, one was supposed to be able to communicate with the dead.

She took the funnel and the pouch to the bed, dumped the beads out on the coverlet. They weren't all identical; each of the five had a subtly different hue to its pearl-like sheen—red, blue, yellow, green, and purple. Plucking one at random from the pile—the yellow one—she set it spinning around the edge of the funnel so that it circled the bowl of it, like the shady antiquities dealer had instructed her. Around and around and around it went, making first a scraping sound, and then . . . Could that be? A voice? A sound both metallic and faint but with a distinct rhythm, like speech.

"Hello?" Krona asked, her heart skipping a beat. "De-Lia, are you here?"

The bead reached the bottom of the funnel and plopped out onto the bedding. The sounds stopped. Hurriedly, she tried again, sending through the purple, then the red. The almost-voice started again, seemingly more distinct this time.

A rush of adrenaline filled her limbs, making her lighter and keener than she'd been in the alleyway during the fight. Maybe this was it, she'd actually found a necromatic enchantment that *worked*. Yes, even if she was hearing the dead, she had no way of knowing if it was De-Lia or some other specter, but it being *possible* and *real* was all that mattered right now. It meant there was hope, a chance that there was something beyond this life, a place De-Lia *was*.

As each bead dropped out, she scooped it up and set it spinning again, pouring them all in faster and faster, listening closely for a clear word. After her dozenth try, she began to notice something, though. A pattern. The sounds were nearly the same every time, made more obvious the more beads she could get to spin through the funnel at once.

Her heart dropped and the wind went out of her. She stopped reinserting the beads and instead dragged the pad of one fingertip lightly over the inside of the funnel, searching.

Yes, there were thin grooves. Extremely faint but there, etched in the copper. There was nothing sentient in the sounds. The trailing of the spinning beads over the grooves in the funnel produced a pitch and tone like a voice, the rhythm like words. The items might have possessed enchanter's marks, but it took very little magic—perhaps no magic—to make the device perform its trick.

And a trick it was, nothing more.

The spike of excitement ebbed, and Krona felt bone-tired, like she couldn't hold herself up another minute. Shaking her head, she carelessly shoved the beads and the funnel off the bed, caring not for the clatter as they bounced to the floor. She felt drained and listless. Empty. She crawled up the bed, pushing the drawers to the side, and lay next to the only other enchantment in this room she knew to be genuine besides the mask: the journal that had so hexed her sister.

Cushioned on De-Lia's old pillow, Krona untied the death mask, holding it out to study it for the umpteenth time, still surprised every time she noticed a new quirk in the paint or grain in the wood.

The spotted jaguar's maw was wide—opened in a snarl or a roar. Vines and leaves and a handful of brightly colored birds framed the face. The face so unlike De-Lia's, but the embodiment of all that was left of her mind.

The man in the asylum had said, *"This face is all wrong."* *This* face. Almost like he was surprised to be in his own skin.

Perhaps he wasn't in his own skin.

If his mangled enchanter's mark had come from a mask, what else could have come from it? Could an echo . . .

The idea spooked her. She shook it off, brushed it aside.

Flipping over the jaguar, she gently laid it against her face.

The first tickles of De-Lia's presence felt soothing. Good. Too good, if she was honest with herself. Whereas trying to cage the echo, to push it into a little box in the back of Krona's mind, felt viscerally *wrong*—always did, no matter when or where she donned it.

She had yet to use the mask for its intended purpose: expert quintbarrel-wielding. Every time she'd taken it to the practice range, fully resolved on suppressing the echo and doing De-Lia the honor of putting her knowledge to good use, Krona had failed. The echo had surged, overwhelmed her, despite her damndest to cage it.

This was Krona's expertise, after all: mask-wielding. She could subdue even the strongest echoes in record time, utilize any mask regardless of magnitude.

Except De-Lia's.

Every time she slipped the jaguar mask on, Krona was burdened by a little voice in the back of her head: *She's your sister. You can't do that to her. You can't lock her away. You can't cage who she was.*

Never mind that an echo wasn't a person. Never mind that she'd only ever met one—Charbon's—that seemed to be aware enough to realize what it was.

Still, that voice made her fumble, made her weak. Made her vulnerable in the daylight.

Nights, however, were different.

Now Krona allowed De-Lia's echo to flood her system, take hold of her limbs. She kept just enough control over her own body to keep herself pinned to the bed, but otherwise let the echo flit through her mind as it pleased.

In a sense, it was Krona who got pushed aside. Diminished, in her own mind. She went to a place where everything was calm and simple. Where there was no grief, because De-Lia was *right there*, with her. It was an easy place. Where she could observe De-Lia's memories if she wished, or turn herself away and let them play out, blurred. She could be intimately aware of the echo's thoughts and desires, or she could let it keep its secrets and its wants.

She gave herself to the echo, and in return, it gave her peace. As long as she let it work, let it think, let it mull over past concerns or dither over a memory of Maman, or share a sweet moment with a past lover, it was gentle, and warm, and did not push too hard to fully claim her form.

These moments, at night in the mask, were Krona's only respite these days. The only place she could sink below the surface of her problems and feel at ease. The world could pass her by without worry or notice.

There was no fear, or anger, or anxiety.

There were no blue faces, or blue robes.

There were no undead murders, or assassination plots.

There was no De-Lia and no De-Krona—only this soft combination of past and present, of the essence of two, mixing, gently, into one.

Sisters reunited, lazily bonded.

Eventually, when Krona felt herself sinking too far, she sluggishly shoved the mask away, letting it flop down onto the journal.

The night's events were catching up with her, tugging at her eyelids, pulling them down. Soon she was slipping off, away. Into blessed, exhausted oblivion.

7

MANDIP

Life was a game, and Mandip Basu intended to win.

All young nobles with a shot at true power and authority understood this.

Those who had access to luxury without responsibility did not. Instead, to them, life was little more than an intellectual exercise muddied through with opportunities for hedonism. All matters of state were simply thought experiments, their actual workings of little consequence, but great fun to discuss with an air of superiority and a veneer of *special insight* while out at the salons or cafés.

As though their philosophizing wasn't just regurgitated nonsense they'd gleaned from some hundred-year-old tome they'd just been assigned by their court tutor.

Mandip *despised* such tittering.

And the damn staging tent was *awash* with it today. It was sweltering beneath the heavy awning, despite the shade it provided—the last two autumns had ben unnaturally warm, in Mandip's opinion—but more so than the heat, it was the conversation that was getting under his skin.

"No, no," Ignace—who was to be Mandip's sparring partner today—insisted, "we should have called in the Borderswatch. Had a *parade*."

"Marrakev has the best Borderswatch," countered Raphaël. "Everybody knows that."

"What do you say, Mandip? Which city-state has the best Borderswatch?"

Mandip glanced away from his assigned lockbox—in which he'd already carefully placed the majority of his court silks—to where the three other youths sat on a long wooden bench, each only half out of their well-pressed clothes and into sporting attire.

They and Mandip had agreed to participate in a set of sparring matches in honor of the Pentaétos summit. It was an assembly of great importance, and along with the hearty helping of inter-city-state politics came an equally hearty helping of entertainments. Peacocking displays put on by the host city-state to boast their artistic prowess and physical might.

Later that evening, he was to play host and escort to one Juliet Maupin, known simply as La Maupin on stage—show her around the palace, the Rotunda, so that when it came time for *her* peacocking, she in turn would do Lutador proud.

His responsibilities had seemingly increased tenfold during the summit. His sparring companions, on the other hand, had bemoaned the introduction of any responsibility at all.

"Depends on how you define *best*," he said, carefully taking his precious silver watch from his pocket and secreting it inside the box, beneath his trousers.

It was special. Enchanted. It didn't tell time. Or, rather, it told *all the time*.

Decorated with archaic geometric symbols and studded through with chips of unenchanted bloodstone and diamonds, it kept track of every time vial that went in and out of the city-state's reserves. The three dials on its face tracked vials in and out of the treasury, the amount depleted by cash-outs, and the number of infantas who had yet to pay their tax.

But the watch itself was so much more than an accounting.

"Supposedly," he continued, "most varger come across Marrakev's rim, so theirs are the most well-tested, having encountered beasts most often. But Xyopar has the most rim territory, and their Borderswatch is far superior if one were to judge by numbers alone."

"Where is your state pride?" Ignace demanded—his thin face pinched beneath his mop of blond hair. "You don't believe Lutador's army the finest?"

"Patriotism has no place in governance," Mandip said frankly. "Patriotism is for the masses, to ensure they back their city's politics. Politicians should deal in the quantifiable, nothing more."

"Nothing more?" asked Aramis incredulously, zhur gaze narrowing in a way it always did when zhe saw a chance at debate.

Mandip smirked. Here came Aramis's bleeding heart. Zhe liked to play at opening a vein for the peasantry, and yet Mandip had never seen zhim interact with someone of lower social standing than zhur own family.

"Nothing more," he reiterated.

"So, I suppose you think that nobles getting to lead longer lives than the peasants is *perfectly quantifiable* and not a state-created problem?"

"It only *makes sense* that the nobles have access to cashing out more time when the peasants do not," said Ignace before Mandip could voice an opinion. "We have more influence, affect more lives. We can do *more good* with extra minutes, whereas an elderly peasant is simply a draw on society's resources."

"Oh, yes, perfectly reasonable," Aramis shot back. "Which is why your family *advertises* that your great-grandfather is one hundred and thirty-seven."

"He is not!" Ignace denied, a little too fervently. "Because—because he's *dead*."

"Your great-grandfather took your grandfather's name when he kicked the bucket to hide how much time he took from your family's coffers. Admit it. Everybody knows it."

"I will admit no such thing!" He sprang from the bench, fumbling for his foil. He flicked its tip in Aramis's direction. "If the exhibition roster wasn't already set, I'd challenge you on a point of honor!"

"Ignace," Mandip said gently, strolling over to place the flat of his palm on the blade, pushing it down.

"Did you hear what zhe said?"

"I heard." He turned to Aramis. "And zhe's one to talk. How old is your great-aunt Astrid?"

Aramis looked away, bit zhur lip.

"That's what I thought," Mandip said.

Raphaël let out a hearty laugh and Aramis immediately stopped looking contrite, pivoting back to the offensive. "I don't know what you're laughing at. You're the one with an uncle in the paupers' asylum."

Raphaël's smug expression slid off his face. "It's not a pauper's—How do you know about that?"

"My sister was at the meeting where he lost his mind. He claimed he was going to become a master orator in moments, slipped into his study with an enchanted mask, then came out again a blubbering imbecile."

Raphaël did not deny the claim.

"And your aunt immediately shoved him away in that *place*," Aramis went on.

"Well, I'd think you'd be *in favor* of *that*," Raphaël shot back. "That's where all of the common nutters go, so why should he be treated any better?"

Aramis's mouth fell open. "He's your *uncle*. How can you—"

Mandip lost interest in their tittering and moved away again.

The others could argue and philosophize all they liked. It was nothing more than hot air and holier-than-thou proclamations. What did any of them know of statecraft? Of governance? None of them were twins. None of them would have the responsibilities of more than a single household thrust upon them.

He was the one truly in the game. With pieces on the board and a chance to win.

The flap of the staging tent was thrown back, and they all turned to mark the newcomer, who was none other than Mandip's twin brother, Adhar.

They were fraternal—easily distinguishable from one another. Both just on the cusp of twenty, Mandip had maintained his soft, boyish charms while Adhar, post-puberty, had barreled full-on into a firm jaw and steely presence. Mandip's chin was narrower, his nose more arched and prominent, and his build was still slight, though athletic, whereas Adhar was broad and projected a hardy sort of strength. Where Mandip's dark hair fell in perfect, loose curls around his ears, Adhar had taken to shaving the sides and keeping his curls shorn short and tight.

"Good luck," Adhar said, "though I'm sure you've already worked out the win between you." He gestured pointedly back and forth between his brother and Ignace.

"We have," Ignace said happily. "Your brother will take the prize and I'll take, well . . ." He winked. "Whatever prize throws herself into my arms after."

"Don't be vulgar," Mandip said, though there was no bite behind his rebuke.

"Oh, come off your high horse," Ignace said with laugh. "As though you aren't vulgar when it suits you."

"Good luck nonetheless," Adhar said to Mandip, smiling and a little breathless—as though he'd rushed there and was about to rush off again.

"You won't be watching, will you?" Mandip asked, trying not to sound crestfallen.

"No, unfortunately not. They have me showing the priests from the Founding Coterie around the palace grounds."

And by "they," Mandip knew he meant their parents had volunteered him.

"I'll find you this evening, yes?" Adhar asked.

"Of course."

This was typical, really. Rarely were they ever in the same place at the same time when it felt like it counted.

Especially when something was about to be won or lost.

Noble twins could not be in competition with one another. It was unseemly—confused and compromised their joint authority. So, Mandip and Adhar had each taken up like-minded but different endeavors. Their parents had pressed a saber into Mandip's hand and a crossbow into Adhar's. They'd each learned to ride but had never raced. Mandip had been given tutors for fiber craft, and Adhar for sculpting. Mandip was allowed to paint, and Adhar allowed to play a sarod. One was never allowed to lay a finger on his brother's activities, lest it spark some malefice.

They had to be united at all times, yet show individual strengths.

This put them in prime position to be nominated for the next Grand Marquises, yet left them very little time for private bonding. Mandip and Adhar had always been good friends, but these days, it felt like the very things that were supposed to be feats of unity did nothing but keep them apart.

"I'll leave you to finish your preparations," Adhar said with a clap on Mandip's shoulder and a bright smile on his lips.

"Don't let the priests try to steal you away," Mandip said good-naturedly. "You're to be a politician, not a proselytizer."

"Same to you. No running off to become a swashbuckler."

Mandip rolled his eyes.

⊱──◈─◦─◈──⊰

The piste was outdoors—better to accommodate the increased number of spectators.

Various countexes and duchexes strolled around the sporting area with fans in hand, and groups huddled beneath the thin blanket of shadow provided by the garden's ornamental trees, whose leaves were just starting to turn red, yellow, and orange. The native Lutadites in more feminine dress still wore high collars and long sleeves, but the garments were made of teasingly thin lace or silk. Some of the more modestly minded masculinely dressed still wore their brocade jackets, but left them unbuttoned and had fully undone the ties on their undershirts, letting them gape open to their navels.

Mandip and Ignace had not only decided to forgo the white gambesons they'd usually don for such a match, but also the netted masks that would typically protect their distinguished faces. The pair of them wore loose chemises, high-waisted breeches, and fine, well-shined boots.

At first, Mandip thought the suggested change to their attire silly, since Ignace had recommended it only because he insisted it would draw so many more desirous looks from eligible bed partners if they were in their smallclothes. Mandip had ultimately gone along with it because of how sweltering the day was.

As they stepped out from the staging area onto the piste proper, the gathered crowd let out little gasps and faint applause—they all seemed to think it quite thrilling, and Mandip warmed to the showmanship of it.

Why not add in an air of danger? A dash of excitement and a little indecency? Perhaps some of the elder nobility would gawp and snipe at their choice to fight in their underthings, but so be it.

The southern wing of the palace of the Grand Marquises loomed over the pitch, providing a small amount of shade to the open lawn. Above, on a bowing balcony, the First Grand Marquis peered down on the event, flanked by two hulking members of his Marchonian Guard who stood stiff and at the ready, each with a ceremonial pike in one hand and a gnarled enchanted eye patch over one eye. They appeared to be sweating in their full plate armor.

Mandip and Ignace both shielded their eyes before bowing to the Grand

Marquis. The white, veined marble of the palace's cladding created a glare that was nearly too bright to look at in places, and the gold-trimmed windows with their yellow panes reflected harsh, stabbing glints at certain angles. The towers were topped with tall, conical spires, and the pink and gold celebration ribbons that had been tied to their peaks hung limply in the absence of wind.

The Grand Marquis waved idly—almost dismissively—back. His usually well-coifed blond-gray ringlets looked uncharacteristically lackluster, and despite the distance, Mandip could tell his brow and cheeks were blotched from the heat.

It was even too warm for most of the birds. Their bright chirping was conspicuously absent. And where Mandip would have expected the lawn to smell of grass and fall flowers, it smelled of hot stone and warm, dead leaves.

As soon as direct sunlight hit his skin, the young lord began to sweat. He tugged lightly at the collar of his chemise and tried to ignore the uncomfortable prickling of his skin.

He drew his epee, gripped it firmly, and winked at the group of young nobles gathered close to the silk rope strung around the match area. They were all somewhere about twelve to fifteen years of age. A few of them giggled, one contessa swooned, and Mandip fought to keep his eyes from rolling. It wasn't that he didn't enjoy the attention, but they were children and decidedly *not* eligible bed partners, despite the openly flirtatious glances.

They'd yet to have their emote tax taken—had yet to focus and temper themselves. Children were full of such *severe* emotions—Mandip wasn't sure how he'd ever survived the roar of feeling that had consumed him before the tax.

He'd always preferred his conquests be older than himself, anyhow. More experienced, more worldly. It wasn't difficult to impress someone on the verge of adulthood. There was no challenge there—no real prize to be won.

At near twenty, he was plenty ready for bigger fish, as it were.

While he took his place on the opposite side of the center line from Ignace and waited for the presiding sword master to introduce them, he glanced farther afield. The visiting parties from the other city-states were all easily distinguishable, from the deep-purple and blood-red banners of the Marrakevian north, to the ambers and jungle-greens of Asgar-Skan, to the purely black-clad visitors from Winsrouen and the indigos of Xyopar that always bled into borders of burnt umber. The fashions and trends in each city-state were unique, each revealing only a touch of influence from the nations they bordered.

The president waved at each of the two young men in turn, shouting their praises, announcing their past fencing accomplishments.

Mandip's gaze searched out the dignitaries from Asgar-Skan. Instantly, his eyes were drawn to his cousin, Gudhal, who'd come up not a day before, accompanying the Kalif's court north for the summit.

Fey were looking . . . well. Fey wore a ruched jama—tangerine, embroidered with gold. A cascade of necklaces studded with emeralds fell down feir torso, matching the golden bangles hanging heavy from feir wrists. A tight turban hid most of feir hair, and a carefully styled goatee adorned feir chin.

On feir arm was a dashing blond man in his mid-thirties, and when Mandip caught sight of him, his stomach immediately clenched in a familiar way—with want, and with jealousy.

Bigger fish, indeed.

It was unseemly for noble twins to have rivalries with one another, sure. Mandip and Adhar had to constantly appear as a united front, as perfectly in sync with one another, lest they lose their chance at the most influential seats of appointment. But that didn't prevent Mandip from having rivalries with other members of his family.

Namely, Gudhal.

Mandip could not remember a time when the two of them had not sought to possess what the other had. Toys, clothes, achievements . . . people. Perhaps it stemmed from how close they were in age, or how rarely they saw one another, given that Gudhal lived in a different city-state.

How had his cousin procured such an attractive date in so little time?

"Salute!" the president ordered, and both Mandip and Ignace snapped to attention.

Both young men crossed swords, then acknowledged the audience.

A faint cheer went up.

"To first blood!" the president announced.

That was followed by a much bigger cheer.

Ignace and Mandip took up their ready stances.

Ignace *winked*.

Mandip did his best to keep his eyes from rolling away and out into their audience.

They'd agreed back in the staging tent, after Adhar left, that Mandip would draw Ignace's blood. A good, shallow swipe across the biceps or the abs—whichever target made itself available.

"You'll get the win," Ignace had told him, "and I'll draw in sweet, sweet sympathies. Find myself a lady with a gentle hand. I always have preferred a healer's touch."

"You have a problem," Mandip had said, unimpressed but still amused.

"I know what I like," he'd said with a shrug, playfully pushing at Mandip's shoulder.

"It's always about sex with you."

"Oh, and it's not for you?"

"Some of us have matters of state to think about. Actual responsibilities to prepare for. Images to uphold."

"Come off it. You're just as much of a letch as I am."

" *'If the exhibition roster wasn't already set, I'd challenge you on point of honor!'* " he mimicked.

"Just for that I ought to make you really beat me."

"As though I couldn't?"

Now, as the presiding swordsman called "En garde," Mandip tried to keep his attention on his opponent and away from Gudhal's guest, but found he couldn't.

He'd seen the blond man before, hadn't he? Yes—several times. Many times. He was sure. Here and there throughout the court. The man was not noble himself, and seemed to flit from arm to arm like a butterfly from flower to flower. Which could only mean one thing—

Ah, yes, that explained it.

The man was for *hire.*

Which meant he could be bought—bought *away* from Gudhal.

Mandip racked his brain for the man's name, sure he must have heard it before.

Thierry? Theobald? Tonrigat?

. . . Thibaut?

Yes, that sounded right.

Ignace thrust forward, and Mandip just barely retreated in time, mind elsewhere as it was. Ignace raised an eyebrow at him, and Mandip tightened his shoulders and clenched his jaw, refocusing on the task at hand.

Their epees were tipped with soft cork nubs—which was distinctly *not* how a bout to first blood was typically managed, but it was better not to poke each other's eyes out. Luckily, the cork did nothing to diminish the clangs of steel meeting steel, or the impressive gritting of teeth and rippling of muscles as each thrust, jabbed, and parried in turn.

It was a rehearsed dance more than a fight, but no less impressive for it. They both worked up a sweat, both put all their force and effort forward.

The closer they came to the agreed-upon climax of their performance, the smugger Mandip started to feel.

Just as this match was rigged, so too was the game Gudhal had unwittingly started.

If Thibaut was for hire, then it was simply a matter of money.

Mandip would "win" the match, and then he would "win" Thibaut away from Gudhal.

He could almost *taste* his cousin's indignation.

Seeing his opening, Mandip slashed at Ignace's shoulder, and the other man leaned in to it. Mandip immediately dropped his guard as Ignace spun away, fingers clutching at the tear in his shirt—probing at the gash, coming away crimson—as he hissed through his teeth.

The slice was clean and shallow, and Ignace's reaction was suitably melodramatic. A fitting drama—a reflection of the entire summit in miniature.

A larger cheer went up this time as the president declared Mandip the winner, and he gave a shout of triumph and a suitable salute with his epee.

Having won, Mandip immediately turned a bright, haughty smile on Gudhal—boasting with his eyes, his airs, his cheers and hollers, in a way Gudhal and no one else would take as a personal affront. He grinned wide as fey looked away and shook feir head.

Curiously, Thibaut stared at Mandip as though scrutinizing him—trying to decipher a puzzle.

Smirking—having seemingly solved the riddle in record time—Thibaut made an obscene gesture and raised a suggestive eyebrow.

Mandip frowned, looked away. Did a double take.

Had that been an insult or a flirtation?

Either way, it was just the sort of thing to get a young man—whose heart was already beating fast, who was already hopped up on the pride of his win—simultaneously confused, irritated, and, to Mandip's mortification, *aroused*.

Mandip found Thibaut's eyes again, narrowing his gaze and holding the older man's stare for a beat too long, hoping Thibaut would yield—that he'd realize how openly and *inappropriately* evocative he'd been toward a high noble *miles* above his station.

Instead, he looked rather pleased with himself.

Perhaps Mandip wasn't the only one here who liked games.

After shaking hands with Ignace and watching him wade off into a crowd of dithering young ladies, Mandip immediately left the piste and made his way toward Gudhal and the intriguing stranger.

"Well done . . . again," Gudhal said, with only the minimum amount of enthusiasm decorum required.

"Well done yourself," Mandip said, indicating, and then bowing to, Thibaut. "Who might you be, monsieur?"

Gudhal gasped and looked around, yanking Mandip upright before one of the elder nobles could catch a glimpse of such indecency.

The bow was heartily inappropriate—just as Thibaut's obscene gesture had been inappropriate. A noble accidentally bowing to another noble below their station was a gaffe. A noble bowing—on purpose—to someone of *no* station or any authority was downright *lewd*.

To Mandip's delight, the blond man grinned wide. "Thibaut," he said, confirming Mandip's suspicions and returning the bow (*his* entirely proper). "Excellent match. That was quite the performance. I especially liked that little backhanded pirouette you did. Very dashing."

Mandip did not miss the rich way *dashing* rolled off his tongue.

"How is it, Gudhal, that you managed to acquire such interesting company so quickly? You've been in Lutador less than two days."

It was no mystery; he just wanted to hear fer say it.

"Monsieur Thibaut came highly recommended as a day's companion."

"Night's, too," Thibaut mumbled under his breath, looking off in the distance.

Mandip narrowed his gaze, trying to discern what Thibaut's endgame was. Was he well versed in the noble family trees? Their branches? Their ties? Did he realize who Mandip was and how deep his pockets were compared to his current employer's?

Sure, he'd been making suggestive overtures, but Mandip highly doubted this man's true goal was to get him into bed.

Not that Mandip would *mind* winding up there . . .

"My dear Gudhal, *you?*" Mandip said, as though scandalized. "*Paying* for company?"

They *all* did it, of course. Paying for company was an open secret and well-established tradition. Was one even truly noble if they'd never forked over time vials in exchange for pleasantries?

But the teasing way Mandip said it put heat on Gudhal's cheeks nonetheless.

"Not all of us have an army of prepubescent girls throwing themselves at our feet," Gudhal shot back, gesturing to where the group Mandip had noted earlier were huddled together, whispering, giggling, and clearly staring at him.

Mandip glared at his cousin. He only realized he was doing it when he caught Thibaut's gaze—when he noted *him* noting *them*.

Thibaut clearly saw the rivalry and was trying to figure out how to use it to his advantage.

So, Mandip decided to cut to the chase. "How much?"

The other two blinked at him.

"How much are fey paying you?" Mandip demanded of Thibaut.

"That's a rather indiscreet question, Lord Basu," Thibaut said flatly.

"I just won a fencing match; I'm in a rather indiscreet mood. How much? Whatever it is, doesn't matter, really." He waved a hand flippantly through the air, as though chasing the specifics away. "I'll pay double."

Gudhal's mouth fell open. "You'll *what*? You can't just go stealing my—"

"Stealing your what? You don't own him; you hired him." He turned a sly smile on Thibaut. "And I can offer better employment, that's all."

"'Better employment' is relative," Gudhal insisted, turning to Thibaut. "He may have more time vials at his disposal, but, but"—Gudhal scrambled for an effective protest—"the hoops he'll make you jump through, the *humiliation*."

Fey pulled Thibaut to the side, voice dropping to a whisper, though notably not actually quiet enough to keep Mandip from listening. "He has odd tastes," Gudhal insisted, "bordering on the dangerous, the deranged, and I—"

Mandip drew a deep breath to defend himself when Thibaut raised a wry eyebrow and said, "My dear, don't threaten me with a good time. I've suffered far worse indignities than whatever *this* particular Lord Basu can dream up, I'm sure."

The skeptical, *patronizing* way he said it made Mandip's blood rush in several different directions at once. He wasn't sure now whether it was more prudent to defend his honor against Gudhal's slights or Thibaut's dismissals.

Both Basus were flustered, and Thibaut was clearly delighted.

"Do you have a counteroffer?" Thibaut asked Gudhal.

Mandip's cousin frowned deeply. How many time vials were fey willing to lose in order to *win*?

"No," fey said begrudgingly.

"Pity. I'll return your time for the unfulfilled hours," Thibaut said solemnly, patting Gudhal's hand. "That is, unless you *both*—"

"*No*," the Basus chimed together.

8

MANDIP

Thibaut's grin remained wide as both Basus glared at one another. The crowd suddenly began clapping, indicating the next sparring match was about to begin, but it did nothing to break the tension between the cousins.

"Right," Thibaut said pleasantly. "Are we finalizing this handoff, then?"

"Fine," Gudhal spat. "Go with him. But don't say I didn't warn you."

Once Thibaut slipped from Gudhal's arm to Mandip's, the visiting Asgar-Skanian left in a huff. Fey didn't go far, of course, just to the other side of the troop of dignitaries, approaching a woman—clearly a friend—who met fer with a sympathetic frown.

"Fey never did take losing well," Mandip said, not bothering to hide his smugness.

Once his cousin was out of sight, he extricated himself from the loop of Thibaut's arm. "Well, that was a spot of fun, wasn't it?" he said casually to Thibaut, who looked confused by the sudden excess space between them. He'd obviously expected Mandip to close the distance.

As the clanging of swords bit sharply through the air anew, the young lord brushed off his chemise and trousers, then strode off in the direction of the nearby staging tent. "Come," he called, "there's some time before the awarding of the laurels, and I'd like to put on proper clothes between now and then."

For a moment, Thibaut failed to follow, but soon those fine boots of his were swishing hurriedly through the grass. "What are our plans, then?"

"Plans?"

"For the afternoon?"

Mandip shrugged. "As I said, there's the ceremony . . ."

"And then?"

Mandip held back the tent's listing flap, waving Thibaut inside. "Then . . . what?"

Instead of entering, Thibaut crossed his arms and leveled a sly look at Mandip. "Is it just me, *milor*, or is it that—now that you have me—you don't rightly know what to do with me?"

"I hired you to annoy my cousin. Nothing more," he insisted, though he couldn't help it when his gaze fell to Thibaut's jaw as the man pursed his lips and set his smile—then down his throat as he swallowed—before quickly flicking back up again.

"Nothing?" Thibaut asked, raising an eyebrow.

"Nothing," Mandip said firmly. So what if Thibaut knew Mandip found him attractive? He clearly knew he was desirable.

In truth, Mandip didn't need the distraction, as appealing as Thibaut was. He needed to be ready, in case he was needed for more important matters during the summit. Just as Adhar had been called on to escort a group of Founding Coterie priests, so too could he be called away in an instant.

It was Ignace who had the luxury of throwing himself into whatever hedonistic fancies he wished, not Mandip.

"As long as keeping you in my employ irritates Gudhal," he said, "that's where you'll stay."

That was the small pleasure he would afford himself.

"I see," Thibaut said thoughtfully, clearly unconvinced.

"I'm not in a position to indulge in diversion right now."

Thibaut threw a thumb over his shoulder to the piste. "And what do you call all that?"

"I'd think you of all people could easily distinguish between providing diversion as a service and engaging in it yourself."

"Touché."

When Thibaut still failed to take a step inside, Mandip ducked in himself. All of the other fighters were gone, and if the noise from the crowd were anything to go by, the current match was quite thrilling.

"So, what am I supposed to do for the rest of the day?" Thibaut asked. "Follow you around like a stray pup?"

"If you wish."

Mandip hurried to his lockbox, loath to put his formal clothes on again but happy to be out of his sweaty underthings. Given the temperature, he could probably get away with just the jacket and no shirt.

He heard the bench squeak as Thibaut plopped himself heavily upon it. "Surely, you didn't pay *double* just to have me stare at you—*longingly*, to be clear—from a distance?"

"Then you can assist me," Mandip said, pulling out his watch.

"With what?" Thibaut asked. "Shall I carry your trophies and any lacy undergarments thrown your way?"

"I believe that's a practice reserved for the peasantry. Nobles don't tend to throw their undergarments around."

"Could have fooled me," Thibaut said under his breath.

Mandip spared a glance over his shoulder as the bench squeaked again. Thibaut had laid himself along it, with one knee pulled up and one arm thrown dramatically over his eyes. "Gudhal said you'd be demanding," he said snidely. "Fey should have warned me you'd be a deathly *bore*."

Mandip spun on him then, pointing firmly—the watch's chain jingling in the open air between them. "Are you going to be a problem for me? Should I call my purser and send you off the palace grounds?"

Thibaut lifted his arm to peer at Mandip with one eye. When he saw the pocket watch, something in his gaze brightened. He immediately righted himself, stood, and pushed into Mandip's space, reaching for the timepiece.

Reacting on instinct, Mandip swept the watch behind his back, took a step away, and drew his epee—now sans its protective cork. In one swift move, he caught Thibaut under the chin with the blade's tip. "Don't," he said warningly.

"I just wanted to have a look at it," Thibaut said innocently, chin raised just off the point. His tone was carefree—that of a man who was used to having swords brandished at him over the smallest offenses. "I have a particular interest in clockwork. Windup curiosities and the like." Shifting slowly, with clear intent, he raised one finger and pushed the blade to the side. "You are certainly uptight for a man your age."

"I'm *not* uptight. I just appreciate my place and my duties." He lowered his epee, sheathed it again. "Wait outside while I finish getting dressed," he ordered.

Thibaut *tsk*ed under his breath but did as he was asked, exiting the tent with a flourish.

Mandip took his time putting on his clothes, enjoying the relative coolness of the shaded space. Normally, right after a bout, he'd seek out a bath or a dip in one of the many swimming ponds scattered about the palace grounds. He didn't think Thibaut would protest such activities, and he struck Mandip as the type to happily act the valet during a bath, but he also struck Mandip as the type to expect payment fast and up front. Best to get to the purser before figuring how to utilize the time he'd purchased.

Securing the ties on his fresh pair of trousers before running a hand through his hair, Mandip took a deep breath and threw his jacket around his shoulders, sliding the watch into his pocket.

With a curt nod to himself, he exited the tent.

"How dashing," Thibaut commented, gesturing grandly at Mandip's new getup.

"You don't need to do that," Mandip said swiftly.

"Do what?"

Mandip waved a less-than-illustrative hand through the air. "The flatteries."

"Oh, but nobles are so *fond* of being flattered."

He said it in that teasing tone that made Mandip's humors clash—made him feel instantly indignant and intrigued at the same time. He could not deny that he was, indeed, fond of being flattered. And he *had* picked this particular jacket because canary yellow always complemented his skin tone in outdoor lighting.

But it irritated him that Thibaut had the audacity to point out his vanity.

All the same, an eager sort of knot balled itself in his lower belly as Thibaut stepped into his personal space and said, in that same voice, "How long until the awarding-of-the-laurels bit?"

"An hour."

Thibaut licked his lips and drew a green-gloved fingertip down the pearl buttons on Mandip's jacket. "Perfect. Just enough time for us to gather my compensation and for you to show me around the ornamental peach orchard."

Mandip swallowed thickly. He intended to remain as outwardly unmoved by this man as possible. There was something about the escort's delight in the tease and the fluster that made Mandip want to resist at all costs. "Why do I get the feeling you know your way around that particular orchard already?"

"Well spotted," Thibaut said, tone low and sly.

"I told you, I'm not interested in being diverted right now."

"Milor, you have a whole *hour*. What could the world possibly demand of you between now and then?"

"I . . ." Mandip didn't have a good answer for that.

Thibaut raised an eyebrow.

"I suppose a stroll wouldn't hurt," he admitted.

"Wonderful," Thibaut declared, pulling away. "A stroll it is."

"But *nothing more*," Mandip reiterated.

Thibaut gave him an over-accentuated bow, throwing one arm out to the side. "Whatever my employer desires."

>-+-◊>-•-O-•-<+-+-<

That was then; this was now.

Now Thibaut had Mandip in a secluded grove in the aforementioned peach garden, pressed up against a tree. The escort's face was hidden in Mandip's neck, and as his knee slid firmly between the lord's legs, Mandip bit his lip and looked toward the sky, doing his best to maintain his composure.

But Thibaut's hands were *wandering* and they were very, *very* talented.

It was incredibly difficult not to squirm and moan just as he had his first time indulging in secret kisses off in the bushes somewhere. *That* had been *ages* ago, and he would *not* revert back to a schoolboy just because some overly cocky, incredibly alluring, *arrogant,* twice-dammed—

Thibaut's hand disappeared inside the front of Mandip's coat, and the young lord *whimpered*.

"When did you say we have to be back for your awards ceremony?" Thibaut asked, his breath rolling hot against Mandip's throat.

"Just past two," he replied, unwinding his arm from around Thibaut's shoulders to fish in his pocket for his watch. "So, we have . . ." He'd meant to count off the minutes they had remaining for their impromptu tryst, but was startled to find nothing but lint in his pocket. "Wait—"

Thibaut pressed him more firmly against the bark.

"Wait," Mandip said again, shoving at his chest. "My watch—"

"What about it?" Thibaut asked, lips grazing the side of his throat.

"I can't—Will you *hang on*?" He stiff-armed the other man away, and Thibaut threw his hands up, taking two steps back in capitulation. "I can't find it," Mandip said, patting himself down.

"We can look for it later," Thibaut said. "No reason to interrupt our perfectly pleasant afternoon."

"No. I need it. Now." Slipping past Thibaut, Mandip scoured the ground, kicking through the dusting of fallen leaves, searching.

"Surely you have plenty of timepieces."

"Not like this," Mandip insisted, worry creeping into his tone. He couldn't have lost it. He *couldn't* have. "It's enchanted. Special. *Important.* I must have dropped it."

"We'll come back to look for it after the ceremony," Thibaut said, still maintaining his pleasant airs. "I promise."

"You don't understand," he snapped. "If anything happens to this watch—" He bit his tongue, pinched his lips together. This—this *hireling* didn't need to know that without this specific timepiece, the *entire economic schema of Lutador* was at risk.

Not to mention, if Mandip failed to recover the watch before someone else, he may well have just destroyed both his *and* his brother's political standing.

He should have left it in the lockbox.

Gods, how could he have been so careless?

Mandip kicked through a few more leaves for good measure, his panic burgeoning. "Help me look!" he demanded.

He began to retrace their steps, hurrying back to the main path. The graveled walkway was lined with tall planters, each sprouting an arrangement of autumn flowers. Mandip dropped swiftly to his knees, searching between them.

Thibaut allowed him to shuffle around in the dirt for a few moments before dipping down to pull him back to his feet. "Milor, don't cause a scene." He nodded to where a pair of ladies were strolling slowly toward them. "Surely there are people trained to locate enchanted items such as your watch, are there not?"

"Regulators, yes," he said absently, eyes still darting along the ground.

"Good. Then after the ceremony, if you still haven't located the trinket, we can—"

Mandip cut him off. "Wait." His brow furrowed, and he took a large step away from Thibaut. "You were eyeing it earlier."

"Eyeing what?"

"My *watch*," he barked. "Of course. How could I be so . . . This is your full gambit, isn't it? I should have known. Good with your hands, aren't you?" He propped one fist against his hip and held the other out. "Come now; give it back."

Thibaut frowned. "Milor?"

"Give it back and we'll call it a bit of fun instead of a criminal scheme. No need to alert the guards or the Watch, or even the Regulators."

"I promise you I would never put my employment in jeopardy for a trinket."

"It is no simple trinket, which you obviously know."

"An heirloom, then. I make my bread and butter putting smiles on noble faces; why in the Valley would I risk—"

Mandip was done playing. "If you do not produce it this instant, I will call the guards and order you strip-searched."

Instead of blanching, as Mandip expected him to, Thibaut paused as though about to say something, but then broke into a sly smile instead. "If all you desire is a strip game, milor, I assure you I've played plenty before and do not need the pretense. Unless the pretense is part of the thrill?"

"This is *not* a *game*!" he shouted, drawing the attention of the strolling ladies.

Not wanting to be of further spectacle, he roughly took Thibaut about the arm and hurried him back to the staging tent, his eyes grazing the ground as they went. No pocket watch lay on the open path back to the piste, and there was no glimmer of silver outside the tent. He hoped Ignace might be pulling some kind of prank, but only for half a moment before realizing not even he would be so bold as to nick this particular enchantment, even for a lark.

Pushing Thibaut under the awning and through the flap—relieved to once more find the tent empty—he gritted his teeth when the escort chuckled, still apparently unaware of how serious this all was. "Stand right there and do not move," he instructed, placing Thibaut nearby but out of arm's reach so that he could keep an eye on the escort while he made doubly sure he hadn't misplaced it prior to exiting the staging area.

He upended his lockbox, went through the pile of sweaty clothes to be laundered, and nearly tore the tent apart at the seams before doubling over, trying to breathe deeply but finding his lungs refused to work.

"Milor, milor—" Thibaut entreated, standing before him and grasping him by both shoulders, hoisting him upright. "We will find it. Who knows it's missing? Just you and me. No one of consequence. Not yet. I've heard that Regulators—especially those at the third-district den—are incredibly discreet. We will whisk ourselves off to the carriages, ride to *that* den, employ their best and brightest, and then the watch is sure to be back in your hands by nightfall without anyone of import being the wiser."

Mandip clutched at his throat—was able to draw a single, shaky breath—and threw off Thibaut's hands. Right now, all of his anxieties were tied up in the missing watch, and there wasn't room for anything else—for diplomacy and steadiness. There was only one place the watch could be. "One last time," he said darkly, "produce the watch or I will call a guard and have it produced."

Thibaut crossed his arms and raised one eyebrow in challenge. "I possess no such item, so do what you feel you must, milor."

If he believed he was calling Mandip's bluff, he was sorely mistaken. The young lord summoned a pair of guards posthaste, and Thibaut's wry expression fell when two people of exceptional bulk entered the tent and fell into regimented attention before him.

"This man has stolen my watch," Mandip said frankly. "It has to be on his person."

The guards both reached for Thibaut and he swiftly held up his hands, as though in contrition.

Mandip was sure he'd won—that Thibaut was caught. The sick feeling in his stomach started to subside.

"Please, gentlefolk, I know how to undress myself," Thibaut said smoothly. "If you'll permit me, that is. You see, I'd rather not have anything torn. My tailor charges a small fortune for even the lightest mending."

One of the guards nodded and Thibaut began divesting himself first of his jacket, then undershirt, before moving on to boots and then trousers.

Mandip refused to see this as evidence he'd been wrong. He'd expected

Thibaut to confess or to resist the search, yes, but surely his compliance didn't point to innocence.

Thibaut continued to undress with an air of certainty and a flair of dignity Mandip was sure he himself had never possessed while changing in front of other people. Each item he folded—neatly—then placed carefully on the nearby bench, only to have one of the guards immediately snatch it up and shake it out before placing it in a pile out of Thibaut's reach.

In his coat pocket there was a long, good-sized jewelry box. The type one might expect to find a necklace in. A guard opened it and flashed the contents at Mandip. A rather petite silver knuckleduster—if a knuckleduster could ever be called petite—sat in a nesting of tissue paper. Mandip waved it off as none of his concern.

When the escort reached for the hem of his underthings, Mandip instantly turned around out of trained politeness—as though he hadn't just summoned two strangers to ogle the man openly.

A light whisp of a sound indicated Thibaut had dropped his drawers. "Happy?" he grumbled.

"Not yet. Everything," one of the guards ordered.

"*These* don't come off in public," Thibaut countered.

"*Everything*," they insisted.

Mandip spared a glance over his shoulder, watching as Thibaut—naked, save for his green leather gloves—held up his hands and flexed his palms. Clearly nothing so bulky as Mandip's watch could be stuffed in there alongside his fingers.

"How in the Valley do you imagine I've hidden a fairly large pocket watch inside one of my—"

"Leave him his gloves," Mandip ordered.

Thibaut had the audacity to look grateful, as though Mandip had come to his rescue and wasn't orchestrating the whole humiliating affair.

It made sour guilt bubble in Mandip's chest, but he gulped it down. Thibaut hadn't been proven innocent yet. *This is necessary,* he told himself.

"Cavity search?" one of the guards suggested.

Mandip blanched. "Good heavens, no. He didn't have opportunity for *that.*"

"There's nothing else on his person," the first guard said.

With a frown, Mandip turned fully around to face the three of them. Thibaut stood perfectly unabashed. Mandip consciously prevented his gaze from drifting *down.* "You're sure? Positive?" His heart sank to the vicinity of his bowels.

"You could take the tie from my hair," Thibaut suggested, tone oddly ireless given the humiliation Mandip had just made him endure.

"There's no watch on him, milor."

"Thank you," Mandip said evenly. "That will be all."

The guards left, stiff-spined and without another glance back.

"Well," Thibaut declared, making no move toward his clothes. "I presumed I'd end up naked sometime today, but I have to admit the particular circumstances are a shock."

"My apologies," Mandip said with sincerity, reaching for Thibaut's jacket, holding it out to him like a peace offering.

Thibaut made no move to take it. "Ah, yes, look how very contrite you are. But that won't make those guards unsee my nethers, now, will it?"

Feeling sick with guilt—remorseful that he'd made such a mortifying error—Mandip averted his eyes, fiddling with a seam on the jacket's shoulder. "I will make amends. You may ask any favor of me—once we've found the watch."

"Explain to me what's so important about it, and you have an accord."

"It's useless in the hands of anyone else but very important to me."

"Ah, yes, everything is clear now."

Mandip shot him a glare. "It—my watch—is the beginning and the end of all of my obligations. It is *the* item on which the sun rises and the moons set. It is the *one thing* in this world that I *cannot* misplace—*and I have misplaced it.* Do you understand?"

Still irritatingly unfazed, Thibaut nodded.

"Get dressed," Mandip ordered. "We're going to the Regulators, as you suggested."

"What about the ceremony?"

"Damn the ceremony."

9

KRONA

When Krona woke the next day, she shot up as though a bucket of ice water had been upended over her head.

There was going to be an assassination. Tomorrow night. During the celebration—the gathering at the Palace Rotunda.

She'd been too wrapped up in herself—almost *inebriated* by her own nonsense, her own grief—the night before for it to sink in.

Someone important was going to die.

She had to stop it.

She needed to *do* something.

But first, she had to think.

There was nothing to do until she could *think*.

A kidnapping, a faked death, a plague of strange scars, and now *this*. An assassination.

All linked, she was sure. That . . . that *Blue Woman*'s appearance had made their interconnectedness abundantly clear.

And yet, the pieces Krona had to work with all seemed to belong to different puzzles. How did all of these unnatural occurrences relate? There was no obvious through line.

Fumbling off the bed, still groggy, she staggered to the bedroom door, bumping the hollowed-out dresser in the dark. The blacked-out window meant she had no way of knowing what time it was, and the candle she'd lit before falling asleep had clearly snuffed itself out some time earlier.

She threw the inner latch open and yanked the door back on creaking hinges. A harsh stab of sunlight hit her sensitive eyes, and she cringed.

The scent of fresh butter croissants and bitter bergamot tea sifted into her awareness before the slight tinkling of porcelain against porcelain.

Krona cracked an eye open and glimpsed her mother at their rickety dining table, sitting up straight and proper, a slight, disappointed smugness pursing her lips.

"Long night?" Acel asked evenly, taking a dainty sip from her teacup.

She didn't look at Krona.

She hardly looked directly at Krona these days. Acel had already lost her husband and her eldest child, and she often behaved as though Krona was already gone too.

Krona didn't blame her. She thought she understood. It was a way for Acel to protect herself. De-Lia and their papa had given their lives to dangerous professions—one of which Krona shared. If Acel ignored her sometimes, pretended she wasn't there, then maybe, in the end, it wouldn't hurt as much if she died, too.

With the way Krona was leading her life these days—burning the candle at both ends—it might not be so long before she ran herself straight into a sand pit.

They both saw that.

"Yeah," Krona answered evenly, stumbling to the mismatched chair opposite her mother.

"Were you drinking?" Acel asked, gaze averted—plastered to the croissant she was diligently slathering with blackberry jam. She tossed her head lightly, repositioning her long, thick plait of gray hair.

"No."

"Oh."

Oh. The way she said it made it sound like having a daughter who liked to waste her evenings getting full as a tick might have been preferable to having a daughter who . . . whatever it was Acel suspected Krona got up to in the dark hours.

"What time is it?" Krona asked. Her mother hadn't set a place for her, but she reached for a croissant nonetheless, still blinking blearily into the sunlight.

"Nearly two in the afternoon."

What?

Krona shot to her feet. "*What?*" *Saints and swill,* she'd wasted too much of the day already. "Why didn't you wake me?"

She'd promised herself she wouldn't let her nights interfere with her days. She'd been so good at seeing to her responsibilities so that she could rationalize her indiscretions. She didn't have a problem if she could balance the two halves of her life. She'd managed to keep that balance for the past three years—she couldn't slip up now.

"You're long past grown," Acel said pointedly. "You can look after your own appointments. Besides—" She lifted her gaze, looked fully at Krona for the first time that morning. "You weren't in your own bed."

De-Lia.

Krona's hand automatically flexed at her side, sensing the empty space at her hip where the mask should be. It was never out of arm's reach if she could help it. Even realizing she'd simply left it in the adjoining room made a cold sweat break out across her neck and her palms itch.

She knew her reaction wasn't normal. Wasn't *healthy*.

She didn't care.

Swiftly, she darted back into De-Lia's bedroom, scooping up the mask and pressing it to her chest. She let out a deep breath, immediately relaxing once more. Pulling herself together, she made ready to ride. Not for her den, but for the offices of the Chief Magistrate of Justice.

>—+—◆>—◇—<◆—+—<

The Chief Magistrate's offices were on the fourth floor of the Council Towers. These municipal buildings were solemn, and the busts sweeping off the top corners of the façade were brutalist—heavy, forlorn-looking figures with square chins and square noses and heavy brows, contrasting sharply with the delicate, organic vines and swirls of the Jugendstil architecture on its flanks and across the street. The building looked like a soldier among dancers or a bear among deer—sturdy and severe in the midst of the recherché and graceful.

Fitting, as it reflected the structure's tenants.

Everyone inside moved with precision and stiffness, shuffling from one chore to the next in even, automated-looking strides. Like little wind-ups set to task. Though most of the people Krona encountered on the first three floors were not noble, they all sported the duller browns, tans, and whites Lutadorian nobles had decided noted *formality* some five years earlier.

Of course, now the Deep Waters tide that had washed in a preference for natural neutrals was washing right out again. Krona had already noticed bright colors popping back into the closets of the higher nobles, just as the peasantry had started to afford the calfskins and undyed cottons that, previously, only the richest Lutadites had had access to.

That was the way of fashion, really: the nobles decreed a favorite style, and then the merchants sought to mimic their panache, and so on and so forth down through the classes until the poorest peasant was scraping out enough time vials to buy a single shawl that might impress the neighbors. But even as that peasant spent their money at the tailors, the nobles were already changing their minds, turning up their noses at the style simply because the poor now sought to claim it as well.

After all, it can't be considered a trend if it's everywhere, now, can it?

What the rich had, the poor wanted, but there was no keeping up. The rich begrudged the poor so much that as soon as a style was mimicked by those the nobility considered lesser than themselves, it had to be discarded.

She'd noticed this with décor as well. The cluttered atmosphere of a peasant's residence was offset by the minimalism of the rich, which was followed by a haste to minimalism by the poor, which was followed by a return to the clutter by the rich.

Round and round they went, chasing each other's tails, like the twin moons chased the sun across the sky.

A bit like Krona had chased De-Lia, once. The older Hirvath had always been moving up, moving on, discarding something as soon as Krona had clasped at it.

Even De-Lia's last station as captain had been filled by Krona once she'd passed.

The only place Krona had left to chase her sister was into death itself.

She shook off that last thought as she stepped off the stairwell and onto the fourth-floor landing.

Unlike in the den, where most Regulators' desks were out in the open hustle and bustle, here the offices were closed off. The halls were narrow and the doors were imposing. A lone man sat at a desk near the stairs, ready to direct persons to their appointment. "Name," he said without looking up from the paperwork in front of him.

"Captain De-Krona Hirvath."

"Appointment?"

"None. But the Chief Magistrate and I have an understanding."

He glanced up. The man's dark hair was graying at his temples, and he had thick wrinkles around his eyes. He was no unseasoned doorman, a mere hireling. He understood that what she said, she meant.

The Chief Magistrate's "understandings" were favors. Emergency meetings he handed out sparingly, only to those he trusted would use them with equal rarity.

"Your coin, please," the man said, holding out his hand expectantly.

Krona undid the ties on the front of her collar, pulling back the top bit of leather to access the hidden pocket that kept her Regulator coin close to her chest.

It always felt strange when the weight of the coin left her breast. It was a constant comfort, a badge telling her who she was and what she did. She didn't like being without it, even for a moment.

But this was its purpose: not to comfort her but to convey the sincerity of her authority to others.

He took it, was quickly satisfied with its authenticity. "Wait here," he said, scurrying out from behind the desk to take quick, sharp strides to the door at the very end of the hall.

Chief Magistrate Iyendar and Krona had reached an "understanding" after the Charbon-Gatwood concern. The plot had taken place in his household, right under his nose, and had ended in a battle right in the middle of his perfectly manicured lawn. He'd been there when Krona saved Melanie. He'd been there when De-Lia had died. He'd been there when Krona had explained about the enchanted blood pen, the mist—the impossible.

. . . And he'd been the one who'd instructed her to keep all of that information *secret*.

Little did he know how many other secrets she kept. About the Blue Woman, about her illegal donning of Charbon's mask, about the journal that had helped enthrall her sister, and about where the woman apprenticed to his family healer—where *Melanie*—had gone.

When the man came back to lead her into the Chief Magistrate's office, Krona wasted no time getting to the point. "There's going to be an assassination attempt," she said as soon as the door had closed behind her, dipping into a perfunctory salute suitable to his station.

He sat at a grand wooden desk with a sheaf of papers between his hands. He peered up at her over the top of a pair of reading glasses—which, Krona noted, were new to his person. He held perfectly still for a beat before saying, "Hello, welcome, and respects to you as well, Captain Hirvath."

"It'll happen tomorrow night," she said, not moving from the doorway.

The light streaming in from the three tall windows behind him was oddly dim, highlighting the dust motes swirling up away from the files in his hands—which appeared to be old. The rectangular room itself wasn't overly large, but there was nothing in it besides his desk, his chair, and a potted, leafy plant in each rear corner.

There wasn't even a guest chair in which to seat herself.

"Take a deep breath, Captain," he instructed, removing his glasses and rubbing at his eyes before standing himself. He was a large man, and oddly jovial for a member of the constabulary, but Krona had always credited that to his upbringing. The seriousness of nobility was characterized firstly by cutting levels of politeness—which bordered on saccharine in tone—until, secondly, all that was swept away in devastating fury and declarations of absolutes when things went bad and push came to shove.

In the common ranks of the constabulary, Krona had most often witnessed the opposite. Much grandstanding and assholery were the hallmarks of day-today interactions with the Watch. But when things got rough, it was sobriety and solemness that ruled.

She hoped her own sobriety shone through now. "An anonymous source informed me it will happen tomorrow. At the Rotunda." Swiftly, she laid out the potential targets and all the details she had—save her own purported framing.

"I think a plot dealing with Winsrouen's border disputes is most likely the cause," she said, "since that's the elephant in the room, the subject the summit members have been tiptoeing around. An assassination that favors a side would force all of the city-states to confront it head-on and would undoubtably deepen the conflict."

"Saints and swill, it would likely spark all-out *war*."

She nodded grimly. "Only trouble is, with the information I have at hand, I can't guess if the assassination is intended to help Winsrouen or strike a blow against them, since Lutador and Winsrouen are the only two city-states in which multiborn nobility is of particular importance."

"Meaning if we can detain the Winsrouen dignitaries, we won't know if we're detaining the possible victims or the possible perpetrators."

"Right. But perhaps it doesn't matter which, not right at the moment. Any action on our part that disrupts the plan is the correct action."

The Chief Magistrate looked into the middle distance for a moment, his gaze tight with thought. "But why here? Why now?"

Krona shrugged. "Easy access. Typically, heads of state are free to refuse an audience. Not during the Pentaétos. They all have to send representatives at the very least. So, it's a matter of closeness and opportunity."

"You don't think it odd that they'd commit to such a crime on foreign soil, though? In a city-state that has thus far not interfered? This brings *all* of the city-states into it."

"I think it was bound to come to a head. It's the train—meant to be a sign of advancement and cooperation, it's just revealed Arkensyre's weak points. Think about it. Winsrouen can't prove it, but they blame saboteurs from Asgar-Skan for blowing up the iron mine in the Altum arm—the mine that was supplying most of the iron to *our* steel factories. Who's our biggest supplier now? Asgar-Skan.

"So, now Winsrouen considers the border expansion their recompense. Asgar-Skan is, understandably, holding their ground, and so Winsrouen has done the only other thing it can to put pressure on them: disrupt their trade down to Xyopar.

"The greater part of the Valley is already neck-deep in this conflict. I'm sure someone's been waiting for us to join the fray. I have no idea if Winsrouen or

Xyopar has asked for our aid, but I'm fairly sure we haven't offered any. Committing such a crime here means we can no longer ignore the dispute. It even brings it to Marrakev's attention, blessedly far away from it all as they are."

He still looked skeptical.

"Have there been recent threats made toward specific nobles?" she asked, hoping to narrow down the list of targets if there were preexisting pressures.

"That I'd take seriously? No."

"What does that mean?"

"Not a day goes by I don't get a report that someone on the street threatened to murder a noble, only to find out the noble in question ran over someone's foot with their carriage, or knocked over a fruit vendor's display, or failed to send a payment on time, and was—in actuality—simply told to go shove their head up their ass." He chuckled, though it lacked real mirth, given the grim subject. "We of a higher station tend to be oversensitive to such talk," he admitted.

"So, no, then?"

"No. I presume you have a course of action in mind regardless?" he pressed.

"Yes." She'd given it a lot of thought on her ride. "I'd like to detain everyone from Winsrouen for the evening. And I mean *everyone*: from the footmen to His Esteemed Excellency, Supplicant of Nature's Higher Virtue."

"And where do you expect me to put them? Not in any jailhouse, I presume?"

"No. That would be too obvious, anyway. Someplace she . . . Someplace no one would anticipate would be best." Krona dreaded the thought of making a predictable move that might play straight into the assassin's expectations. "Perhaps a coterie? I can't imagine any priests would turn you away."

"I suppose you're right."

"We should also put all of the vulnerable Lutadorian noble twins under house arrest for the evening. Those who are related to the conflict in any way—perhaps those who have family embroiled in the tensions. Especially the twins who do not yet hold high office, and therefore don't have their own Marchonian Guards."

He stroked his chin, tallying up all of the families that would touch. "The twins of the Gaia and Fra families have relatives in Winsrouen," he muttered. "And the Kreks and the Basus would have a stake in this, for certain. And the Basu twins are of very high standing—Mandip and Adhar; they're one of the pairs favored to be elected the next Grand Marquises, if rumor is to be trusted."

"It's possible one of them could be the assassin's target. *That* would entrap Lutador in the conflict for certain—presuming ensnaring our city-state is at least part of the goal.

"I don't propose we change anything about the securities at the palace itself," she went on. "Keep the same number of the Watch, of Regulators. This way, the

Marchonian guard will have even fewer distractions and can really focus on the Grand Marquises, and our presumed special targets will get special focus. I think that's the best we can do."

"And what do we tell them?" he asked. "About why we're keeping them from the most important celebration of the Pentaétos?"

"That I leave to your judgment. You know better than I do if telling them about the attempt will help earn their cooperation."

"Seems the heads of the families should know, at the very least," he said to himself. "They can choose to tell their relatives, their children, what they will. I know I wouldn't have . . ." He trailed off, looked away.

But Krona knew what he was going to say.

He wouldn't have told his granddaughters.

She understood; children shouldn't have to worry about being murdered.

"I leave it in your hands, then," she said, turning to leave. She had her own preparations to make for the celebration.

Preparations and protections.

He stopped her. "Before you go," he said, "tell me about this other concern you're working on. The one with the scars."

A cold chill ran up her spine.

He and Krona had never discussed Melanie's scar *or* the young woman's disappearance. She didn't know how he felt about her vanishing, or what he presumed happened to the young healer. Krona didn't even know if he'd ever seen Melanie's bare forehead, if he knew about the mark seared into her skin.

She had to be careful about what she said.

So many mixed-up secrets. So many jumbled lies.

Fuck.

"Not much to tell," she said, voice cracking on "tell" in a way it *never* did. She cleared her throat. "It seems to be a string of similar accidents related to enchantments. There's no single perpetrator, as far as we've been able to ascertain, and no one enchantment source. It's not a case of fraudulent enchantment practices, I mean. No one bad enchanter running around making bad enchantments. It appears to be a series of mishandlings, though we can't say how."

"Does it concern you that the number of these mishandlings is . . . growing?"

"Of course."

"It seems unlikely that these are independent accidents."

"Indeed."

"Have you isolated the reason why some people die and some people . . . What would you call it?"

Lose themselves. Seem to become someone else.

"No, we haven't isolated a reason," she said, not bothering to conceal her sidestepping.

"I've seen the illustrations and the photographs," he said carefully. "I'm not ignorant; I know what the markings look like. And I need to show you something. I've been meaning to summon you about it, but I . . ." He tugged his glasses off, rubbed at his eyes—brows pinching, as though with pain.

He took a small brass key from his pocket and unlocked a drawer low on his desk, retrieving a weathered envelope that sported signs of water damage and ink smears. Gently, he set it on the desk top between them, treating it with the utmost care, like something that was somehow both a fragile gift and a bomb.

Krona didn't reach for it, waiting for an explanation before she made a move.

"A few years ago," he said softly, voice gone rough, "I opened a missing-persons concern. A concern personally important to me."

He went quiet. Krona put her arms behind her back and held herself at parade rest.

After pursing his lips, he tapped the envelope with a harsh jab of his finger. "A month ago, I received this from a contact in Marrakev."

Krona's heart jumped. Had he found her—found Melanie?

Did he know about her missing baby? Perhaps Melanie had reached out to him. Of course, that would make sense. She'd clearly trusted the Chief Magistrate while in his household. If she'd felt comfortable enough contacting Krona, perhaps she'd feel equally comfortable reaching out to her former employer.

"What is it?"

"Proof that they'd found who I was looking for."

She tried not to let her anticipation show. "What *is* it?" she asked again, suddenly suspicious. Why had he hesitated? What *wasn't* he saying?

He scooped up the envelope and hastily drew out its contents, dropping three sepia-toned pictures—one by one—in front of her.

The first was a blurry picture of a body in the snow. Someone in more feminine Lutadorian dress—skirts rather than trousers. The lighting was such that their skin seemed light and their hair perhaps dark. It was impossible to tell more than that.

As the second photograph fluttered down, Krona immediately noticed that it was of an intricate scar—one like those on her concern.

Before her mind could decide for certain if it was Melanie's—after all, she'd only seen it the once—the third photograph was already nestled half on top of the second. And its subject was unmistakable.

There she was. Melanie. A close-up of her face, sans ferronnière. Eyes open, lips parted.

Stare empty.

Dead.

The sudden shock of seeing the healer's face again—and so devoid of life—had Krona reaching out to steady herself. Her hand swiped at the air behind her, looking for a chair that wasn't there, before she swooned forward and braced herself on the Chief Magistrate's desk.

"This is why I'd hoped . . . hoped you had more to go on by now," he said sadly. "Or a working theory, at least. She escaped Gatwood, but she couldn't escape . . . whatever this is."

"What about her family?" she asked—her voice sounding airy and distant. "Her husband?"

"Didn't ask," he said sadly. "I only concerned myself with Mademoise—er, *Madame* Dupont."

Krona's gaze snapped up to meet his, and she did her best to maintain her decorum—to remember who held the authority here. But he'd kept this from her. He'd had this for a month. A month! Which meant any leads she might have been able to track down were long cold. "Why didn't you bring these to me *immediately*?"

"I suppose . . . I was ashamed. I should have protected her while she cared for my granddaughters, and I didn't. I failed to make sure that even the rooms beneath my own roof were safe. *My own roof.*" Clearly unable to meet the healer's dead stare anymore, he flipped the photograph over. "Would it have made a difference if I'd come straight to you?" he asked sadly. "You've learned so little from the other victims, the other crime scenes, and this one—"

As Krona's ire raised, so did her voice. "But I *knew*—" She bit her tongue and took a deep breath, trying again. "I met Dupont. *That* might have made the difference. And you know as well as I do that one crime scene is never like another. Why bother to investigate any at all after this, hmm? Since I've failed so *spectacularly* to divine anything of substance so far?"

"That's not what I meant," he said evenly. "By the time I received these, there was no crime scene left to speak of. This happened nearly a year ago. Her body had already been returned to the sands."

"Who returned her? Who claimed responsibility for the corpse?"

"I don't know."

"Can you at least tell me *where* in Marrakev these were taken?"

"Konasavi."

"Well, that's something."

He reached for the photographs again, and she placed her palm over them first. "Can I keep these?"

The Chief Magistrate hesitated, but eventually nodded, withdrawing his hand. "I will focus on putting the nobles under house arrest, and leave . . . Melanie . . . to you."

"Thank you." She swiped the photos from the desk and turned, staring down at them as she left his office and retraced her steps through the building.

The healer's expression was so . . . cold.

Oh, Melanie, what happened to you?

10

MANDIP

"Are you sure you won't tell me more about this very important timepiece of yours?"

The carriage jolted as it passed though the palace's gilded outer gates, awkwardly jostling Mandip from the striking, brooding pose he'd adopted—with his elbow propped on the frame of the open window, and his head in turn propped on his tight fist.

Across from him, on the opposite bench, a now fully dressed Thibaut leaned forward eagerly, expression open, earnest, and interested.

Mandip tried to keep his gaze locked firmly out the window.

The palace of the Grand Marquises was set atop picturesque bluffs which loomed over the Praan River on one side and sloped swiftly down into Lutador city proper on the other. The road to the palace was winding and well-guarded, and the trees were sparse—which kept the approach clear and allotted anyone leaving the palace a breathtaking, all-encompassing view of the city.

The buildings sparkled in the afternoon sun—their large, stained-glass windows made the city look like it was studded with gems. Various coteries were notable by their high, limed walls, and at this distance, it was easy to spot the way the streets were laid out to pay tribute to the number five.

Five days in a week, and five penalties to tie the citizenry together, and five gods to protect them all.

He let his gaze trail to the high ridges of the Valley's rim. The sky above them was clear, bright. Only a faint haze hung over the peaks. It was easy to imagine there was simply more beyond—more unnatural beauty to match the god-created beauty of the Valley.

But no. Beyond was wasteland. Beyond was a hellscape. Beyond was a desolate expanse fit to match Mandip's grim mood.

"Milor?" Thibaut prompted when Mandip didn't immediately answer.

"You don't need to know," he grumbled at Thibaut.

The escort crossed then uncrossed his legs before reclining into a corner, only to right himself again a moment later—all apparently in an attempt to find a casual position that would offset the tension in Mandip's countenance.

"Need?" Thibaut echoed. "Not in the strictest sense, no. But I didn't even get a good look at the thing back in the tent. How am I supposed to be of any help if I can't even provide the Regulators with a corroborating description?"

"It's not your concern. You won't have any reason to speak to them."

"Oh, so you have a plan for keeping the investigation off the record, do you?"

Mandip's brows pinched together as he turned toward Thibaut. "What do you mean?"

"Well, you and I both know there's the public-facing work done by the Days-watch and the Nightswatch and the like, and then there's the more hush-hush work done to address the crime in *your* circles. But even if your loss won't make the papers, it's still likely to reach the ear of someone you'd rather never heard tell of your . . . mishap."

"The whole point of going to the Regulators now is to find my watch post-haste and get ahead of any rumors."

"Rumors are not reports. The Regulators will make a record, to be sure. And that record may come back to bite you in the arse later. Politically speaking. Unless . . ."

"Unless what?"

"If there's any way for us to pass it off as *my* watch, then perhaps the true nature of the item might never go on record. In which case you'll be protected."

Mandip let out a deep huff. "It's not just any timepiece. It stays out of the public eye, like all enchantments tied to state function. But the Regulators know of such things. They will recognize it."

Thibaut licked his lips, then lifted both of his hands as if to speak sweepingly, but apparently thought better of it. Clearly, he was trying not to appear overeager but was doing a piss-poor job of it. "It sounds," he said carefully, but with subtle trill of excitement, "like this watch is better suited for a vault than a lordling's pocket."

"*It sounds,*" Mandip mocked, "like you don't understand the finer points of city-state security, and I don't really have the energy to explain them to you."

"I suppose we'll just ride in silence, then." Thibaut pouted, crossing his arms and leaning away.

That was fine with Mandip. More than fine. He had half a mind to ask the carriage driver to stop at the first respectable roadside establishment to drop Thibaut off before they ever reached the Regulator den.

Mandip had *known* this man would be a distraction. Had known, deep down, from the moment he laid eyes on him that he would be trouble. And still, he'd let himself get caught in his orbit.

And now . . . and now the watch was *gone.*

He took a shuddering breath, closed his eyes. Anxiety swelled in his chest. He chewed on his lip and tried to reassure himself that everything would turn out all right. The Regulators would find the watch, that was what mattered most, and he could think about the consequences of losing it later. He could think about everyone he'd let down later. He would think about his . . . his *punishment* . . . later.

They would disconnect him from the watch. That wasn't supposed to happen for another eight years. They would take his link away, and—

And not in the usual manner.

There would be no careful extraction of the metal imbedded on his person. No.

They would simply cut. Chop. As they would if he'd offended Knowledge and needed to suffer feir penalty. And it wouldn't be just his hand. It would be everything from the elbow down. They'd take his arm. They'd take his fucking arm and—

Later, he told himself. *Worry about that later. Later, later, later,* he chanted, squeezing his eyes shut all the tighter. *Later, later, later.*

But no matter how he tried to calm himself—to push the feelings away until *later*—his sense of impending doom grew and his lungs stuttered.

How had he let this happen? *How?*

A gentle hand landed on his knee. "Milor?" Thibaut asked softly, sounding genuinely concerned.

He opened his eyes, though they felt too hot and too wet to turn on anyone. He looked to Thibaut anyway, to say something dismissive, but no words came. He pinched his lips together, tightened his jaw.

He was not a *child*. He would not *cry*.

"Surely it can't be as bad as all that," Thibaut said, swallowing thickly. He looked suddenly emotional himself, though Mandip couldn't pinpoint why.

"It is. It *is* as bad as all that; you don't understand."

"No, I don't."

Mandip dropped his hands into his lap and turned away from Thibaut again, refusing to behave like a watery-eyed child in front of this man. After a moment, he found himself subconsciously rubbing a hand over the underside of his left forearm and abruptly stopped, threading his fingers together instead.

Beneath the sleeve where he'd been rubbing was what looked like a perfectly typical stretch of skin.

It was anything but.

Mandip considered telling Thibaut—blurting it all out and showing him exactly what was at stake, *personally* and *bodily*, for him. He'd have to show the Regulators anyhow. The secret would be revealed to Thibaut soon enough if the Regulators insisted he be present.

But, for now, sense made him hold his tongue and keep still.

In a hidden pocket in his jacket lay a special handkerchief—ratty and grayed, as old as the missing watch itself. The fabric was stiff and always smelled oddly—faintly—of salt, as though soaked with fresh tears. It was enchanted in a way that had been lost to time, and Knowledge had not yet seen fit to grant pursuit of its rediscovery, made to temporarily wipe away concealments.

If he were to retrieve said handkerchief and draw it up the length of his arm, he'd reveal a perfectly straight line of what would look like painted silver, running from his wrist to his inner elbow. But it wasn't paint. Nor was it something like the tattoos of Xyopar. It was an imbedded *tongue* of silver, thin and flexible.

And enchanted, of course. The third in the five-part enchantment system that allowed him into the inner vaults of Lutador's time repository, the treasury.

The watch and the silver tongue were kept on his person. The three other corresponding enchantments, which were required to open the locks, were built into the repository.

Mandip, himself, was a Key.

It had been the luck of the draw. Every ten years a new Key was randomly appointed, chosen from the noble twins eligible for the highest offices. *Who* the Key was at any given time was always secret. Past Keys and potential Keys all held similar watches to the enchanted one, to confuse the trail and thwart anyone clever enough to learn about them and bold enough to think they could pull off a heist at the treasury.

The entire system was a secret held closely among the ruling class. Not even Mandip's parents—neither being a twin themselves and therefore of lower political standing—knew about the measures, let alone that their son had been chosen for such a responsibility.

The system was, in part, why body modification was illegal. For the masses, of course, not for one such as Mandip. But the masses didn't need to know that.

He tried to calm himself again, to breathe deeply and cleanly in through his mouth and out through his nose. Still, he continued to feel worse with each passing moment.

Thibaut patted Mandip's knee. "Don't fret. It will turn up, milor," he said firmly. "Soon. Yes, I can feel it."

⊱──⋅◈⋅──⊰

The rest of the journey was spent in companionable silence, and Mandip took the opportunity to recompose himself. It wouldn't do to show up maroon-faced and blubbering. He'd been trained to present himself as neutrally as possible. To make his expression and body language unreadable when necessary. And it was often necessary in courtly environments. He could pull upon that same rigidity—that same stoicism—now.

By the time they approached the flint wall surrounding the complex, he'd smoothed away all signs of distress. There was no dampness to his eyes or heat on his temples. He was simply a noble calling on the constabulary to do their duty. No need to make a scene.

Visible from the road were the rolling knolls of the den's living sod roofs. He noted the majority of the compound appeared to be underground. A guard at the gate checked the driver's credentials before letting them through.

The footman leapt off the rear of the carriage as it drew near the main entrance, running ahead to make sure there were no unexpected potholes or puddles. When the carriage came to a halt, he opened the door for the two passengers, bowing low to Mandip as he alighted. The young lord waved him off with an idle "Thank you" that had Thibaut frowning.

Mandip straightened his jacket and took a deep breath, but before he could make his boots march toward the doors, Thibaut skipped ahead. "Allow me, milor."

Mandip sighed. "You know you don't have to end every sentence with 'milor,' don't you?"

As Thibaut put a hand on the door's clasp, he looked over his shoulder with what was surely a cheeky retort on his tongue but was cut short by the door forcibly swinging outward—bashing into him hard enough to send him to the ground. With an *oof* he landed on his backside, the cobblestones clearly doing a number on his tailbone if his sudden grimace was anything to go by.

Mandip instantly dropped to a knee at his side—startled, then angry on his companion's behalf. He turned, a sharp admonishment on his lips. "Why don't you watch where you're—"

The young woman who'd so firmly interrupted Thibaut's stride peered around the door as though thinking she'd hit some sort of stopper instead of a person. As she caught sight of him, sprawled indignantly, her round face swapped its confusion for concern. "Monsieur, is that my doing? Forgive me."

Thibaut—who'd thus far been nothing but an irritating brand of suave—simply gaped at her like a fish. His lips tried to form words, but his throat barely offered a sound. "Y-you're—"

She smiled brightly at him, nodding encouragingly.

"You're—*You're*—"

Mandip did a double take, realizing who stood before them in all her flamboyant glory. Short and round in every way, she wore a puffy pink dress so rich in color and framed with such an abundance of rouching, it had to have been designed and constructed by the superior court artisans in Asgar-Skan. Her blond hair had been twisted into sleek ringlets and then piled intricately atop her head. Delicate lace gloves covered her small hands, and her eyes were framed in unnaturally thick, dark lashes.

Everything about her carried a performer's air.

"You're *La Maupin*," he offered on Thibaut's behalf.

"Last I checked," she said, cheeks becoming rosy, her smile widening on her bright pink lips.

"The court engineers are trying to invent recorded sound because of you," Thibaut said numbly, mouth still hanging open.

Juliet Maupin, often referred to on the stage simply as *La Maupin,* was— despite her youth—the greatest singer of all time as far as most people were concerned. Voice like wind chimes or a deep kettle drum or the surest, purest flute. Her range was matched by none; her performances were legendary.

Given the way Monsieur Thibaut seemed to be having an out-of-body experience at the moment, Mandip gathered he must be one of her fanatical supporters.

"You *are*; I—I mean—" Thibaut started, but quickly changed course, still stumbling over his words. "That is to say, you are, without a doubt, the most brilliant artist I have ever had the privilege to, um—" He lost his words, looked away, clearly feeling *shy*.

Thibaut, the man who had so openly tried to seduce Mandip only a few hours before, *was shy*.

Mandip chuckled under his breath.

Thibaut had been so quick to spot the game between him and Gudhal—to use it to his advantage and keep Mandip off-balance. It was gratifying to see the tables turned.

"Oh, an admirer," she said, clearly well practiced in dealing with this kind of response. "A true patron of the arts. I thank you, Monsieur; you are too kind."

With his cheeks darkening and his arse covered in dirt, Thibaut seemed to finally realize he was staring like a brain-dead donkey and picked himself up, barely registering Mandip's hand at his elbow.

"Forgive me, Mademoiselle, I didn't mean to—" He gestured at the ground, as though he'd somehow inconvenienced *her*.

Mandip cleared his throat, and Thibaut turned toward him, eyes wide, silently asking, *Can you believe who this is?*

He obviously expected the young lord to be just as flustered.

But no. Mandip traveled in such circles all the time. Meeting a renowned singer was no more a thrill for him than being related to the heads of state. It was, however, a wonder to watch *someone else* thrill up close.

"La Maupin, a pleasure to meet you in person," Mandip said, offering Juliet his hand and kissing hers delicately when given, before exchanging formal introductions. "I am, in fact, scheduled to be your escort around the Palace Rotunda this very evening."

"You *are*?" she asked with what Mandip thought was just a tad too much surprise. "Oh, what a delight. How fortunate to bump into you early." Her cheeks reddened. "If you'll pardon the expression."

"This is Monsieur Thibaut," Mandip said, gesturing at Thibaut, whose mouth was still doing that wonderful impression of a Deep Waters fish. "You'll have to forgive my companion. He's easily excitable."

Thibaut's voice rose and cracked, "No! No, I'm really not."

"What a place to meet such a fine performer," Mandip continued, suddenly in his element. It was amusing to play the *stately gentleman* to Thibaut's *bumbling devotee*. The thrill of it was enough to quash the last few dregs of anxiety he hadn't been able to weasel away deep within himself.

"Is there trouble?" he asked. "Might we help?" He, at least, would adhere to manners and offer aid, especially since such courtesies seemed beyond Thibaut at the moment.

"Oh, I was inquiring after a past concern that held some personal interest for me," she said, as though it were a trivial matter. "Unfortunately, the Regulators were quite resistant to letting any extra information escape. I was pointed toward the papers, but you know how those are."

"Perhaps they might be more forthcoming if we were to—" He gestured into the den.

"That is very kind, but I doubt it'll help. I was unable to meet with the lead Regulator on the Charbon fiasco—a new captain. Seems the former has passed on . . ." She trailed off, clearly lost in thought for a moment, but soon she retrieved herself. "Anyway, she's not here at the moment, by the by, and I doubt any other Regulators would be willing—"

"Charbon?" Thibaut broke in, regaining a bit of his composure. "*Louis* Charbon?"

Her eyes flashed in exactly the same way Thibaut's eyes had flashed when he'd first seen Mandip's watch. "Yes," she confirmed. "His death mask was stolen and used to commit several murders."

"Oh, I know," Thibaut said eagerly. "What I mean is I assisted my friend on that very concern."

"No," she said dramatically, clearly delighted. "What good fortune!"

"Your friend?" Mandip asked, shooting Thibaut a skeptical look. "You never mentioned having a Regulator *friend*. Is that why you insisted on this den specifically?"

A small tingle of suspicion crawled up the back of Mandip's neck.

Thibaut paid him no mind, completely enamored of Juliet.

"You *really* worked with the Regulators?" she asked.

"May Time pull me up short or Nature strike me down," Thibaut swore.

"Well then, gentlemen," she said cheerily, slipping her arms through both of theirs—a feat, given they were both of a height and, in comparison to her, quite tall. There was force and strength in her small frame—she spun them back toward the carriage with ease. "Would the pair of you care to join me for coffee? Or tea? Salt, even?"

"When?" Thibaut asked, eager.

"This instant."

"Good heavens, that is sudden."

She tugged them forward. Mandip noticed a faint, pleasant perfume rolling away from her neck and hair—the scent of refined sugar and luxurious vanilla. It was distinctly expensive, yet in a playful way most noble ladies dare not skirt. Artists were allowed different airs, he supposed.

It was enticing and . . . distracting.

Damn it, distractions *everywhere*.

"Wait!" he said suddenly, planting his feet, dragging the others to a halt. "What about my watch? I'm sorry, Mademoiselle, but our business here is urgent. We—"

"Milor," Thibaut said evenly. The escort now carried himself as he had before—with a slyness and smugness that should have been off-putting but was *maddeningly* alluring. "Are you sure you searched your pockets *thoroughly*?"

Mandip blinked at him, furrowed his brow. "What kind of a question is that?"

"It might behoove you to take a second look."

The young lord untangled himself from the songstress, frantically patting down his person.

It couldn't be that simple.

No.

It couldn't.

A pit opened in his stomach while, at the same time, hope flared in his chest.

It can't be. This damnable bastard can't *have been playing me this whole*—

His fingers slid into his jacket's right outer pocket and landed on familiar, smooth metal. He yanked the object free, turning his prize over and over in his hands, making sure it didn't have any scratches or missing jewels—that not an ounce of harm had come to it in the time they were parted.

Finding no hint of damage, he immediately turned his ire on Thibaut.

How? When?

He'd been strip-searched!

He'd made Mandip feel *contrite* for having him strip-searched.

He'd—

"You—You *used* me," Mandip accused, hating for all the world how petulant he sounded as he said it. "You needed to come here for some reason and *used*—"

"Yes, and you used me first," Thibaut countered. "You *needed* to spite your cousin, in the same way I *needed* someone to drag me along to the Regulators' doorstep. Only, *I* can admit it was less of a *need* and more of a *lark*. I have a gift for a dear friend and thought I'd have a little fun in the process." He let out a heavy, put-upon sigh. "Unfortunately, it seems the very Regulator I'd hoped to see is not at home, and yes, my dear Lord Basu, I've thus far made poor company for you, and now my true nature is revealed. Alas, neither of us is getting what we wanted out of this deal."

Juliet glanced between the two of them, clearly amused. "What *have* I stumbled into?" she asked with a sly lilt.

"Nothing you can't handle, I'm sure. Given the stories," Thibaut said with a wink.

"Monsieur, I like you more and more," she said.

"Well, I, for one, like him less and less," Mandip spat. "I told you. I told you how important—"

"Which is why you have it back," Thibaut snapped. "You would have had it back in the end nonetheless."

"Oh, *horseshit*," Mandip snapped back. "You just didn't want to be sent off to prison or the camps. Once you really thought about how much trouble you'd be in—what kind of *sentence* you'd be facing—you decided to hedge your bets and quit while you were ahead!"

Mandip gritted his teeth and pocketed his watch, feeling every inch the fool. Gods, how had he let this cocky, swine-kissing cutpurse get close enough to—

"What's the matter?" Thibaut taunted. "Not used to your pawns fighting back, having motivations of their own?"

"I'm certainly not used to such insolence from a *commoner*." He had half a mind to demand this boil of a man return his time vials.

"Oh, well, lucky for you," Thibaut said cryptically, "I'm no commoner." He narrowed his gaze. "I'm *much worse*."

Mandip heard the challenge in Thibaut's tone and took a lunge at him, with Juliet still between them.

Instead of standing aside, the trobairitz firmly placed a palm against Mandip's chest. "Lads. *Lads,*" she interjected. "I find the pair of you fantastically intriguing and would very much like to continue observing this strange row, but perhaps from a more comfortable seat, with a slice of cake at my disposal. Let us be off to a wonderful little café I've heard tell of, and *then,* if you must pull at each other's ears and tweak each other's noses, at least you'll have libations to look forward to at the end of your lovers' spat."

"He's *not* my lover," Mandip said with a sort of heavy *finality*. He'd be damned if he'd so much as entertain the idea of taking him to bed now.

She smirked. "Hard to say yet if that's a shame or my gain." With a wink, she began tugging Thibaut away before Mandip had a chance to process the implications. "Come along."

Her fine heels and Thibaut's boots left the cobbled curb and crunched along the gravel drive, the sound receding as the young lord blinked slowly after. He suddenly felt far, *far* out of his element, as though he'd stumbled into a strange ritual integral to a culture he'd never encountered before.

He was the noble here. *He* was the one who should be ordering them about. They should be listening to *him,* not stringing him along like a show dog for their amusement.

"Are you coming, dear Basu?" Juliet called, she and Thibaut having bypassed his waiting carriage and reached a small hansom cab that must have been her own.

Schooling his expression into a look of stern condemnation, he wagged a finger at Thibaut once more, taking steady strides after them. "I expect a refund. You humiliated me. You *swindled* me."

"I did nothing of the sort," the man insisted, waving Juliet's footman back to his place at the rear of the carriage to help Juliet into the cab himself. "Wasn't it you who insisted I was hired to—what was it?—annoy your cousin and *nothing more*? I'd say you're getting far more out of the bargain than you paid for: an afternoon with La Maupin *herself.*"

Mandip reached Thibaut's side with another demand on the tip of his tongue, but before he could let loose, the escort leaned in close to his ear. Mandip refused to shrink, fighting the instinct to jerk away. "Besides," Thibaut whispered, voice silky. "I do believe we've been propositioned."

"What? No. She didn't—"

"I believe she did." Thibaut pulled back with a wink, then climbed up after Juliet.

The driver stared at Mandip. Mandip crossed his arms and glared back.

"Lord Basu?" Juliet asked. "Are you coming?"

"That is a cab built for two," he said, exasperated.

He wasn't sure what was keeping him there. He should have already turned on his heel and stomped away. No—he should have already gone into the den and demanded the Regulators arrest Thibaut for pilfering right off his person.

"I think we can all fit if we get friendly enough," she said, not bothering to hide the flirtation. She curled a finger at him expectantly.

I shouldn't, he told himself, internally putting his foot down. He'd been impulsive in hiring Thibaut, and so far, that impulsiveness had led to nothing but trouble. He should cut ties now while the temporary loss of the pocket watch could be written off as an unfortunate mishap rather than evidence of bad judgment.

Mandip realized he was nervously tapping his toe against the ground. Like an irritated rabbit.

"If you come along," Thibaut said, "I promise I will make it up to you. *And* keep my hands to myself, if that's what you desire."

"You nearly put me in an early *grave*."

"Monsieur Basu," Juliet said sternly, though her smile was still sugary sweet. "Get in the gods-damned cab."

As if compelled by unseen forces, Mandip complied.

She had a way about her.

Just as Thibaut had a way about him.

They were two halves of a Venus flytrap, and Mandip felt like a hapless insect.

With a frustrated huff, he snuggled up to La Maupin's left side, while Thibaut made himself cozy on her right.

As the driver nickered at the horse and the carriage jolted forward, Mandip conceded that at least one good thing could be said of Thibaut's company: it certainly wasn't *boring*.

II

THALO CHILD

Two and a Half Years Ago

Thalo Child knew he should be excited. Usually, he *was* excited when receiving his new blessings—the tattoos that allowed him to grow, to absorb more God Power. Each one was a marker of progress, a signal to everyone in the Savior's palace that he'd earned a new place in their order, that he'd achieved a new level of enlightenment.

They meant Gerome had seen him as *worthy*.

But this time felt different.

"You have a child of your own. It is unseemly for you to walk around in nothing more than your infantile patterns," Gerome said as he led Thalo Child to the line-layers' grotto.

This should be a reward.

So, why did it feel like a punishment?

Gerome carried a scroll tucked beneath his left arm, and he wore tall, stilted sandals, which lengthened his stride and made him tower even higher above Thalo Child than usual, making it difficult to keep up. The sapphires on the half-helm he wore today jingled gaily as they swayed with the rhythm of his steps. "I've drawn up the patterns that will best fit your form, allowing for the most efficient absorption. They are extensive, I must warn you."

"I receive them with gladness," he said, voice sounding small and very young, even to his own ears.

Muffled cries of pain—strangled through gritted teeth—reached Thalo Child even before they turned the corner and found themselves at the entrance to the grotto.

Steam curled from the entrance, pooling on the hallway's dark ceiling.

Beneath the Thalo keep was a spring, and beneath that, the mountain's center was molten. Hot water bubbled up through various cracks in the keep's natural foundation, creating places for warm baths, clothes-cleaning, and sacred rituals.

There were two pools hot enough to scald: one in the Savior's private wing, and one in the line-layers' grotto.

Scalding water was good for sanitation. It kept the needles clean.

The entrance was marked with gossamer-thin curtains of deep eggplant purple and gave the grotto only an illusion of privacy. Inside, line-layers saw to half a dozen Thalo of various ages, prodding and pressing, working a spectrum of blues permanently into their skin. Many small lamps, like fairy lights, hung about the rough-hewn ceiling, and the edge of the grotto dipped away from the tattooist's cots down into the steaming spring. There at the lip, Thalo Child could see a girl about his age—a young apprentice—washing the line-layers' tools.

The Master Line-Layer—a thinning old man whose pale, watery eyes were flanked by strips of deep maroon and his lips dotted with sapphire—drew back the curtain when he saw Gerome approaching. "Possessor," he said, setting a palm against his own chest and bowing deeply as Gerome swept inside. "Who have you brought with you today, Your Magnanimousness?"

As the curtain fell behind him, Thalo Child tried to breathe deeply but found the air too humid and thick for his liking. Most wings in the palace were chilled, and some outright frigid. He was used to crisper, sharper air.

"This One Who Belongs to the Eye is to receive three years' worth of achievement," Gerome said flatly, neither looking at nor physically indicating Thalo Child. He unfurled the scroll. On it were two diagrams, illustrating the front and back of a bare body.

Thalo Child swallowed heavily when he saw them, hot and cold sweeping through his body, creating a storm front of emotion. There were so many lines—and he was so *proud*. Proud to have what no one else in his cohort would have. But he was also afraid. And ashamed.

Thick cobalt-blue bands encircled the figure's forearms and shins. Spirals and dots aligned in sacred patterns filled the gaps between. The tops of his feet would each receive powder-blue double crescents to represent the moons, razor-thin streaks of violet would be set at the base of his fingernails, and a rosette would grace the hollow of his throat.

But there were no designs planned for his face. The first thing people saw, the first thing they looked at, would still be naked. Would still mark him as a child.

Instead, there was a large diamond, filled with swirls, planned for his back, between his shoulder blades. It was unusual to have absorption lines set against the spine or the sternum, as one was rarely so bare on Ritual Way.

He was to be given all of the lines as befitted one with a baby. But they would not all be placed as they should.

The Master Line-Layer was understandably stunned as he took in the drawing. "W-well done, child," he stammered. "I will create a schedule specifically for him, Your Magnificence, and all of his blessings should be fully completed by—"

"No. Now."

"Now?"

"Today. He will receive them all today. In this very session."

Mild horror widened the Master's eyes. "Not to argue, Your Wondrousness, but . . . I would not make the child sit for so long. Once he's old enough for his name, he may be able to stand the needles for six hours or more, but now? It would be cruel. And these designs will take *sixteen* hours at least."

Thalo Child drew in a sharp breath, struggling to keep the worry off his face. It wasn't the pain he found daunting—that he could endure. He was far more concerned about being separated from his charge for so long.

Thalo Child had had to leave the babe with one of the Mindful in the nursery. The Mindful usually did more complicated tasks than the Mindless—having been allowed conscious thought, unlike their counterparts—but were of a similar servitude to the Savior and the rest of the Thalo. It was typical to have them take over basic care and feeding, and Thalo Child left his infant with them whenever his obligations to the Eye and his own training called him away, but that was never more than an hour or two at a time. Usually, he could check in on zhim between tasks.

Even though he'd only had the babe for two weeks, he didn't like the idea of leaving zhim for nearly a full day.

"Then have more than one line-layer work on him," Gerome said dismissively. "That should make it go faster."

"It's not strictly about *time*, sire," the Master said. "His body . . . He may go into shock. He will be ill after. This much ink in such young skin, with that many pricks of the needle . . . not to mention the amount of blood . . ."

Gerome stared stoically at the Master, waiting for his protests to die away before he spoke again. "I will come back for him in eight hours," he stated, brooking no argument.

The Master conceded. "Eight hours," he agreed.

Gerome turned to Thalo Child. "Eight hours."

Thalo Child simply nodded, unable to meet his Possessor's gaze.

Gerome left just as swiftly as they'd arrived, his sandals clopping off into the distance.

Once the Possessor was gone, Thalo Child found he could no long keep his fears hidden. The grotto's air, which had been too thick for his lungs even before he'd seen his designs, now felt stifling. He couldn't draw a full breath. His knees shook, and he instinctually reached out for the Master Line-Layer.

The old man freely took his weight, gabbing his arms, guiding the boy into a hug for support. "You will do fine," he assured him. "You have earned this, have you not? You must have done something extraordinary to achieve these blessings so quickly. He would not commit you to these lines if you could not handle them." The Master snapped his fingers at the apprentice Thalo Child had noted earlier. "Water. Drinking water," he demanded.

A few moments later, a bone cup was held beneath Thalo Child's nose, and he pushed himself away from the Master to take it. "Thank you," he whispered, drowning his gaze in the bottom of the cup.

"Wait outside," the Master said, pushing him toward the entrance. "I need to prepare a cot and my tools. And organize my line-layers. Wait outside, where it's cooler."

Thalo Child nodded and allowed himself to be pushed through the curtain once more.

Outside, he collapsed against the nearest wall, fighting back swell after swell of new emotion.

The shame rose the highest, roared the loudest.

These blessings were being given begrudgingly, he realized. He hadn't made Gerome *proud*; he'd drawn his ire. And through no fault of his own that he could see.

There was no other reason for his lines to be placed somewhere they were unlikely to see the sky. There was no other reason to leave his face so blatantly unmarked.

He took a sip of water, but his hand tremored, sloshing it over his chin, his robes, his slippers.

Wiping his face clean, he attempted to stretch his emotions like he'd been taught—like they'd practiced with the Eye. But the more he focused on the shame, the more rattled he became, the more he feared the needles—which he'd never feared before—and the more he dreaded reentering the grotto.

Suddenly, harsh whispers—hissing voices—erupted from just around the corner.

And one of the voices was unmistakable.

Thalo Child froze, afraid of being seen even though he had every right to be exactly where he was.

"Why one of *my* children?" Gerome demanded.

"I have no children of my own," a woman replied.

"And whose fault is that?" Gerome asked. "It's *you* who gave up your position—you who decided to defile yourself by *descending* the ranks. If you did not have His favor, you would be no more."

"Be careful. That sounded like a threat."

"I would never threaten you," he said, tone cold but sincere. "I *could not*. But answer me: Why him? Why that child? Why not one of age to care for an infant?"

"I looked into his mind and saw that one of his secret prides is his kindness."

"That is a secret at least half the children hold. And the other half hold their cruelty just as closely. That is not a reason—it's not even an excuse," Gerome bit out. "No one is allowed to interfere with my children except the Savior."

"Then why didn't you tell him to reject the babe?"

Silence.

Thalo Child knew he should down his water and plug his ears and pretend he'd never heard this exchange. It was about him—there was no mistake—but it wasn't *for* him. He shouldn't intrude on such a conversation. He should leave the hall, go back into the grotto.

He *should*.

But a feeling more insidious than shame flooded Thalo Child's system: Curiosity.

Instead of retreating, he set the cup down and crossed the hall toward the voices. His slippers kept his steps soft and undetectable, and he moved with great care so as not to rustle his robes.

Carefully, he peeked around the corner.

There stood Gerome, with the great Hintosep.

Gerome was *arguing* with Hintosep.

The two of them stood at a distance—facing off but clearly wary of one another. Gerome's back was turned to him, and Thalo Child could see Hintosep only in profile.

"I can feel you in my mind, Gerome," she said after a moment, a simmering warning in her voice.

"And I cannot feel you in mine!" he countered harshly, hands flinging outward in frustration. "Do you no longer care what goes on in my thoughts? What secrets I keep? In discarding your rank, have you also discarded your children?"

"I keep out of your mind out of *respect*," she said tenderly.

"What are you hiding from me?" he demanded. "Why are you shielding your reasons from one of your own?"

Her expression tightened, then smoothed, demeanor shifting as she strode forward, into Gerome's personal space. "You once belonged to the Cage of Hintosep," she said, strong fingers cupping his cheek. She let her thumb trail up along the edge of his half-helm, then down to touch one of the scars above his lip. "But no more. You are no longer mine."

To Thalo Child's dismay, Gerome leaned—*greedily*—into the touch. The boy bit back a gasp—he'd never seen his Possessor look so vulnerable before.

It made him uneasy.

Queasy, even.

"It's why you insist on wearing all these headdresses, isn't it?" she asked. "Because you miss the familiarity of the Cage. The security. The knowledge. So too will your children miss the Eye when it's gone from their lives."

"They hate it," Gerome said bitterly. "It's not like the Cage."

"You and I both know that's not true. All the artifices have exactly the same purpose. And you did not always love the Cage. Most of my children did not love the Cage."

"Can I . . . Can I see it?" he said, sounding both sheepish and hopeful.

"I put that Possession away for a reason. No one has seen it for a long while, and I will not pass it on."

"I don't want you to pass it. I don't even—I don't want to wear it. Or touch it. Just see it."

She ran the side of her finger over the bridge of the helm's nose. "You've made enough cages for yourself; you don't need that one."

"Everything was simpler in the Cage."

"Only when you finally accepted its wisdom. It drove many of your siblings mad."

"That's why they perished and I remain."

"I think you're right."

She drew him closer, and he leaned down into her chest, spine bowing, crystal beads tinkling when his forehead made contact.

Thalo Child looked away, embarrassed to have caught his Possessor in such a state.

Quietly, he returned to the grotto.

The bitter shame of disappointing Gerome had turned into the sour shame of seeing what he shouldn't have seen. In bearing witness to a private moment.

But it seemed to have calmed his nerves. He no longer wanted to run from the needles.

Thalo Child pushed through the curtain with a purpose. "I'm ready," he declared.

The Master Line-Layer had set out his utensils near a cot at the rear of the grotto: leather gloves, bamboo and metal rods of various lengths—his khem sak and tabori tools, each with a finely honed tip or group of delicate needles for jabbing the ink into the skin—his color pots, and a basin of fresh water.

"Good," the Master said, waving him over. "We will start with two, myself and Cinta." He waved to a woman nearby. "If you can endure, and I see no signs of shock, we will move to three. Then four. No more than four, I promise."

Four. Four line-layers would mark him at once.

Setting his shoulders, determined to see this through—after all, one did not refuse a blessing—Thalo Child took a deep breath and disrobed down to his underthings. He handed his clothes off to the apprentice with nary a tremor in his fingers and took up his place on the cot without hesitation.

"Lie back," said the Master. "Close your eyes, if it helps."

Close your eyes, he says.

Just like I instructed the six-year-olds.

Thalo Child thought of Gerome. Of the curve of his spine and the laxness in his body when he'd allowed himself to fall into Hintosep. She had soothed him, as Thalo Child had soothed the young ones. Their empathy had taken different forms, but it came from the same place.

"I looked into his mind and saw that one of his secret prides is his kindness," she'd said.

And it was true.

Thalo Child was not yet skilled enough to feel someone chasing after his secrets in his head, and he was sure he'd never be able to feel someone as capable as she. But *this* secret, at least, he wasn't embarrassed by.

He *did* wish to be compassionate, to be good to others.

And he coveted every ounce of kindness he received in turn.

But he would find no such succor here. Not because the Master and his line-layers were unkind, but because the very nature of their task was painful. It could not be escaped. There was no way to shield him from the ache that was to come.

>-◦-○-◦-<

For hours, he lay on his back, arms and legs outstretched, spread wide. Slowly, two tattooists became three, became four. The apprentice dabbed the sweat from his brow with a scratchy cloth, and every inch of his skin felt like it was alight with bee stings. The pain was sharp and consistent, the *push push push, jab jab jab* of the needles a rhythm he could track.

He clenched his jaw so tightly, the Master brought him a strip of leather to bite so he would not chip his teeth or chew through his tongue.

The Master was open and free-flowing with his reassurances and praises: "You're doing so well." "One more line here, then we'll move on." "So still; I've never seen a child your age stay so still."

But none of it brought peace to Thalo Child's mind.

The only thing that helped was focusing on a single fairy light above his head—focusing so intently that his vision blurred and all he could see was the glow.

And thinking about emotion stretching. About feeling only what he wanted to feel—about not feeling at all. About leaving the bad emotions behind.

Eventually, he felt his consciousness lift away from his body, felt the pain recede only because he was floating and had no more skin, or bone, or muscle.

Here, in the numbness of soul-flight, one of Gerome's demands reverberated over and over again, as though the question itself was a thrumming in the universe—a pulse in the walls, a tempo tapped out in the thrusting of the needles, a rhythm in the lapping of the spring.

"What are you hiding from me?"

There was anger in the asking.

"What are you hiding from me?"

A sense of betrayal in the phrasing.

"What are you hiding from me?"

It was an accusation, and an entreaty.

And it held implications Thalo Child could not begin to dissect—for him, for his charge.

For his place at his Possessor's side.

12

MANDIP

Mandip *seethed*. Every bump in the road felt like a personal affront, and every glittering laugh from Thibaut felt like a betrayal. Part of Mandip wished for Thibaut's *head*; another simply wished to flee their . . . whatever this strange outing was . . . and yet a third portion—the one he took the most umbrage at—wished he could simply shrug it off and enjoy himself.

Ignace would have no problem waving off Thibaut's thievery as *antics* and a *joke*. Even Adhar might say something like "No harm done" in the end.

But Mandip couldn't bring himself to be so flippant. To simply let it go.

Thibaut did, at least, seem to understand the gravity of what he'd done. Even through his posturing and dismissals, there was clear guilt underneath.

Just not enough for Mandip to find satisfaction in it.

La Maupin, for her part, lived up to her reputation. She was bright and cheery during their ride into the city—a small whirlwind of a person, flitting from subject to subject and leaning half out the cab to wave at those who called to her. Thibaut politely asked if he might hold her around the waist in such moments—to ensure she didn't fall, of course. Juliet batted her eyelashes at him and said, "Oh, of course, Monsieur, for *safety*," and then it was perfectly clear they both knew what kind of game they were playing.

Mandip did his best not to openly grouse but found he couldn't help it. He leaned himself away from them and did his best not to wrinkle his nose when Juliet tipped just a tad too far and her skirts went flying up into his face. But he didn't stop himself from batting away the tulle and silk as though it were a swarm of gnats and not perfectly tailored finery.

After a fit of squeaks and giggles, Thibaut pulled her in and she plopped onto the bench next to Mandip once more, face flushed. "Well, aren't you a sourpuss?" she said to him, all in good fun.

"I don't like being manipulated," he said flatly.

"Well then, you're sure to have a terrific time at court," Thibaut said.

"Politics isn't about having a good time," Mandip snapped. "It's about getting work done."

"My Lord," Juliet said, poking at his shoulder. "Surely, it can be both?"

"Your work is all frivolity," he said dismissively. "I don't expect you to understand the burdens that come with ensuring the entire city-state runs effectively."

Her smile twitched, falling for half a moment. Not in a way that suggested he'd wounded her pride, and not even in a way that suggested he had no concept of what terrible burdens she secretly carried. It clearly wasn't even the words "expect," "understand," or "burden" that had rattled her expression.

It was "effectively."

That made him . . . uneasy, for some strange reason that he couldn't put his finger on. He shifted in his seat, crossing his legs and angling himself away from her farther.

Despite his discomfort, he thought to apologize—it was the gentlemanly thing to do; he'd been too harsh, too hasty—but she was already onto a new subject.

Their destination was a delightful little café, not far from Absolon's Square, which sported outdoor dining instead of an alleyway between itself and the next building. Juliet hurried ahead with her footman (who apparently was also her bodyguard) to make sure the trio would be able to dine semi-privately. This left Mandip and Thibaut awkwardly waiting on the sidewalk, doing all they could not to make eye contact with one another.

Mandip kept his hand in his pocket, clutching the watch in a tight-knuckled grip.

Thibaut attempted to whistle a tune, found he couldn't carry it, and grimaced to himself.

"Come on, lads," Juliet called, eventually popping out of the side door, onto the low-gated, awning-covered patio. "We'll eat out here. I've ordered Asgar-Skan coffee for three."

⊱┈┈◦◦◦┈┈⊰

The afternoon had grown cooler, what with the sun slipping closer to the Valley's rim, and so the small table they were afforded on the patio was quite comfortable.

The café owner had made sure to seat them in the most visible streetside table—clearly to draw in business—but was courteous enough to leave all the adjoining tables empty. Lovely yellow stained-glass lemons filled the space in the delicate wrought-iron fencing that separated them from the street proper, which matched the lemons decorating every piece of dinnerware set before them.

A child in a long smock delivered their coffee and three spiced cakes, then scampered off again.

The table and chairs were dainty, their spokes and legs thin and filigreed. They reminded Mandip of the crocheted doilies that had been the height of table decoration in his childhood. The furniture hardly looked fit for use by anyone heavier than a doll but in actuality were iron painted over in white. Their apparent softness and fragility were a deception . . .

Much like Juliet's.

As they trio sipped their coffee, the songstress regaled the two men with firsthand accounts of stories Mandip had heard a dozen times in gossip. Juliet hardly looked old enough to have been on as many adventures as she had, and Mandip was slightly embarrassed to learn she and he were of similar age. She'd already seen and done so many things, while he, so little.

"Did you really rescue that young woman from a mountainside coterie?" Thibaut asked.

"Rescue her?" she asked, incredulous. Her finely painted nails, each imbedded with a small gem, clicked against the porcelain cup. Mandip wondered if the stones were enchanted. "I *married* her, thank you. One doesn't scale a granite cliff face in nothing but their knickers for anything less than true love."

"You're not married," Mandip stated, matter of fact.

"True love is fleeting," she countered, leaning back in her chair, teetering on its hind two legs for the simple buzz of it. "Doesn't make it any less *true*."

"Hmm," Thibaut acknowledged, glancing away, out toward the statue of Absolon. Her declaration had apparently hit a nerve. Mandip tucked that knowledge away for later.

Street traffic was light this afternoon, but still, once in a while, someone recognized La Maupin, and her footman-cum-bodyguard would intercept. She'd wave at them cheekily; they'd wave back, then be on their way.

"Enough about me," she said eventually. "What outlandish stories might I have missed about you, Mandip?"

Thibaut narrowed his gaze and drew a breath, as though to protest, but ultimately held his tongue. He and Mandip both knew all this pleasant conversation was a diversion. The young lord had been a part of enough tête-à-têtes to know that when someone desperately wanted information, they put off talking about the subject for as long as possible.

Charbon's concern was important enough to Juliet that she wanted it to seem *un*important.

"Oh, I don't know," Mandip said, feigning diffidence. "I've certainly never challenged a head priest to a duel, or jumped the Marrakevian border in a turnip cart, or ended a bloodbath with a ballad."

"It was more of a tavern brawl than a bloodbath," Juliet said modestly, "but I take your point, you poor, sheltered boy. We must figure out how to inject some excitement into your stodgy life of civil service."

"I manage," he said, bringing his coffee cup to his lips, letting the earthy aroma waft over him.

Thibaut suddenly leaned forward, bracing himself on Mandip's arm—clinging to him right over the strip of silver. Mandip froze with the cup halfway to the table and stared at Thibaut's green-gloved hand as though he might burn it away with his gaze alone.

"Did you know," Thibaut began, and Mandip did *not* like the particular pitch of his tone; there was an arrogance to it, "that Lord Basu's family can trace its lineage all the way back to the days of Absolon? Their records are that good."

To hide his nerves, Mandip took another sip of his coffee.

"I mean," Thibaut continued, "we all ended up in the Valley the same way, but apparently, if you've got vellum that says so, that makes you a noble."

Mandip choked on his drink. Juliet threw a hand over her mouth.

"Course," Thibaut went on without skipping a beat, "*how* they came by this piece of vellum—which is a decree from Absolon himself—remains a mystery."

"It is *not* a mystery," Mandip said harshly, yanking himself out of Thibaut's grip and wiping his chin on the back of his hand like a commoner, too agitated for manners. "And it was certified by the heads of all five city-states, so how *dare* you imply—"

"You see," Thibaut spoke over him, "Mandip's great-great-*great*-uncle came to Lutador bearing this document when he was nineteen years old. In Asgar-Skan, the young man had been a painter. A very good one. But not good enough to raise his family out of poverty and into the merchant class, unfortunately. But then he goes and discovers this document submerged with his ancestor's *corpse*.

"Did you know that's how they deal with the dead in Asgar-Skan? They don't return them to the sand; they return them to the water. That's Knowledge's tradition—something about the roots of the present drinking up the information of the past. Anyway, they make these fantastic enchanted boxes they call *coffins*—waterproof, you see—then chain them to huge stones and sink them at the bottom of the Grand Falls. Thousands and thousands and thousands of bodies down there, and no one ever talks about it.

"Once a body is sealed and sunk, it's never supposed to see the surface again. Because that's just a tad unsavory, isn't it? Not to mention rude. Imagine you're dead and someone gets it in their head that they'd like to gawk at your half-naked, mostly decayed body. *Rude.* But that's not the point. The point is that Mandip's great-great-*great*-uncle decides that simply entreating the gods for a better social standing is no good. They don't tend to answer often, so I don't blame him. So, he decides that asking his *ancestors* for a little mystical aid is the way to go. But you see, since they don't have sand pits or hourglass catacombs in Asgar-Skan, they have to go to the Grand Falls with all the tourists and shout at their relatives above the din.

"Have you ever been to the Grand Falls? Of course you have, my dear, forgive me; I forgot who I was speaking to. Loudest sound in the Valley, isn't it? Rivaled only by Mandip when he finishes."

Mandip felt the blood drain from his face, and his mouth fell open.

"Finishes a *tournament*," Thibaut corrected himself, though it had clearly been no slip of the tongue. "You gave quite the mighty shout this afternoon. As I was saying, Great-Great-*Great*-Uncle Basu yells into the roar of the Falls—crying, screaming—and is just *sure* his ancestors can't hear him. So, he dives in. Which is illegal. Very illegal. It's dangerous. The power of the water there is like none elsewhere in the Valley. It can suck a horse under and you'd never see it again. Fish *drown* under the pounding of the Falls.

"So, the Watch is called to retrieve this none-too-bright young man and save him from certain death by brutish waters. Their best swimmers go to pull him out, but the idiot's been caught up in some kind of whirlpool and goes under. Gets his foot hooked in a coffin chain. No one can get him loose, so they pull the dead up with him. Takes ten of the Watch to do it.

"Fate has it that he got caught on one of the oldest boxes in the river. And when they wipe all the algae and grime of ages off it, the Basu family name is carved right into it. Since a funeral needs to be planned in order for anything to be legally sunk, they can't just throw the box back in.

"So, the young man takes it home with him.

"He claims later that the seal breaks—all on its own—the enchantment dissipates, and inside is this perfectly preserved proclamation from Absolon. As Mandip said, authenticators from all over Arkensyre have a look at it. It's legitimized. It says a Basu was one of Absolon's closest confidants, that their family was to be given all the authority and standing that should be imbued upon those who best helped Absolon lead us to the Valley and out of the clutches of the Thalo and its creatures. All well and good. Excellent, seems reasonable. Save one small issue."

Thibaut paused, taking a large bite of his cake, chewing thoughtfully.

What small issue? Mandip had never heard tell of a problem with the documents.

He couldn't help himself—he leaned in. As did Juliet, absolutely taken with the possibility of an intrigue.

Clearly perfectly pleased with the way he'd captivated his audience, Thibaut took his sweet time masticating his way through his mouthful of confection.

"Yes?" Mandip prompted. "Spit it out."

Thibaut swallowed. "Well, one small issue, save the fact that it's strange that in thousands of years, no Basu had tried to claim their birthright, and the writ ended up sunk and nearly useless, of course," he said. "It wasn't the handwriting—that matched the scrolls. The ink was the right type and the right age. The vellum, too, was a fine skin, only eaten a little by mites and such. Everything appeared perfectly in order. Except . . ." He coughed, as though his throat had gone dry, and took a long pull from his coffee.

Mandip gritted his teeth.

Thibaut's theatrics were fooling no one.

"Except," he said, "there was a single boar's bristle from a brush caught in one stroke in the A on Absolon. And one authenticator claimed it was from a kind bred into existence many centuries after the Great Introdus."

"So?" Mandip asked, voice a tad *shriller* than he'd meant it to be. His heart rate ticked up, and his muscles coiled. He knew what Thibaut was getting at.

"So, it was a kind quite common in paint brushes of your great-great-*great*-uncle's time. I'd wager any painter—even a destitute one—would likely have owned such a brush. And if that painter was skilled, and industrious, and dead set on not resigning himself to both obscurity and poverty, well . . ."

Mandip had had enough.

Before he could think better of it, the lordling was on his feet, pushing his filigreed chair back with a harsh grating across the stones. He leaned over the table, jostling the porcelain settings, making the remaining coffee in their cups slosh and splatter onto the fine tablecloth. "I demand you rescind your disparaging accusations," he said through his teeth, pointing a finger sharply at Thibaut. "I did not hire you to slander my family in front of—"

"Slander?" Thibaut said, as though *he* were the one being insulted here. "Why, I'm talking you up." He gestured to Juliet. "The mademoiselle asked for an interesting story about you, and you were content to act an absolute *bore*. What's more interesting than the fact that you will inherit access to a set of high-priority positions based on an exquisite forgery created by your enterprising ancestor?"

"It's *not* a—"

"Come, now. Your family have already been at it for generations—with nary a scandal in any appointments, and that's saying something. The truth of how they got there is no less shady than any story brought to bear by any other noble family—*bless you all*—and no one in their right mind would challenge you at this point."

Juliet's eyes sparkled. Mandip's blazed with righteous indignation.

All it took was a gentle touch from La Maupin to subdue Mandip's newly re-aroused anger. "It was a delightful story," she assured him, gesturing at his chair, clearly indicating he should sit again. "Do you share any of your clever relative's artistic skills? Have you ever forged a highly important document?"

The questions were earnest. Where Thibaut was clearly making fun, she was brimming over with interest and sincerity.

All the heat left Mandip then, like his bellows had been deflated. "I . . . have excellent penmanship," he said weakly, slumping back down into his seat.

"Maybe you could forge a nice bill of sale or certification of death if you really put your mind to it," Thibaut suggested.

"I would never engage in such illicit activity," he spat.

Juliet's eyes changed, only for a moment, as though the suggestion that Mandip might be *useful* was something to tuck away for later. "Marvelous," she said, her voice carrying the slyness of a snake-oil salesman.

And then she turned on her true target. Thibaut. "And what about you?"

Both men knew what she was asking.

The mood at the table shifted considerably. Where Juliet and Thibaut had both been gleeful, now they were suddenly somber.

"I was there," Thibaut said, lowering his voice conspiratorially, "when the Mayhem Mask was used." He paused for dramatic effect.

"And?" she prompted. "What did you learn from it?"

Why was she so interested?

A woman who scaled coterie walls could be interested out of macabre curi-osity or meaningful intent. All the subtle cues of her person implied the latter in Mandip's mind.

"Nothing so terrible as to how to skin a man or where to separate his joints. I didn't don the mask. That would have been a terrible betrayal of our oh-so-generous state," he said, glancing sideways at Mandip. "That mask is as illegal as an item can be. But I was there when someone else put it on. I feared for my life, you know. Some masks carry more than knowledge. I could see the intent of the long-dead killer in my—in this *person's*—eyes. I could sense that intent turning on everyone and everything. I could have died by a familiar hand." He threw in a dramatic shiver that seemed to impress her less than it should have.

"Yes, I know," she said impatiently, "about echoes, I mean. That's what I'm curious about. What did the echo say? Anything? Anything strange? Anything *personal*? Anything about its victims—present or past?"

Her questions came out more like demands, edging on interrogation instead of casual conversation.

Thibaut seemed taken aback by her sudden directness. "When properly controlled . . ." he said carefully, "most echoes are never allowed to say anything at all."

She narrowed her gaze. "Then the Mayhem Mask said nothing? Charbon was contained?"

"Why, exactly, are you so interested?"

"I need to know why he did it," she said frankly. "I don't mean the rubbish they read out in court; I mean—" She leaned forward, overzealous. The gaiety of her person was gone—her personality shifted entirely, to reveal a woman on a mission. Someone with clear purpose behind her actions.

Catching herself, she took a deep breath and smoothed her skirts. She glanced at the tabletop, and when her eyes rose again, the mask of blitheness was back. "Did the echo give you any *names*?"

Thibaut's gaze unfocused, as though he were looking back, into himself, and didn't like what he saw.

"Monsieur?" Juliet prompted.

He'd gone off alone in his mind. He seemed genuinely bothered.

"Forgive me," he said sincerely, "the memory still leaves me raw."

"Perhaps you need time to compose a proper answer?" she suggested. "I understand the trauma of it. Perhaps you will both join me as my guests tomorrow night? As Lord Basu hinted earlier, I'll be performing at the Palace Rotunda, for the delegates of the five city-states. It's time again for their Pentaétos, and I am to be part of the celebratory evening's entertainment. Please, come. I will ease you with comforts and pleasures, and then you will tell me of that horrid man's mind. Agreed?"

Thibaut clearly forced himself to clamp down on his boyish enthusiasm. His cheeks were flushed and his smile broad. But he bit his tongue, said nothing, clearly worried about being overeager. Mandip wondered if Thibaut had ever been able to attend a performance at the Rotunda. Perhaps the level of nobility he'd been able to reach with his charms had never been so lofty.

It would be a terrible offense to decline, and Mandip's upbringing overrode his good sense. "It would be an honor, mademoiselle," he answered for the two of them.

He'd be in attendance regardless. Why not as her special guest?

"Wonderful," she declared, snapping up the remainder of her cake and throwing down her cloth napkin. "I must retire now, to do my afternoon gargling." She patted her throat with the back of her hand. "An instrument such as mine takes a mountain of care. See you soon, my dears."

"This evening," Mandip reminded her. "For your tour."

She smiled sweetly at him. "Of course."

With that, she took her bodyguard's arm, and the two of them sauntered off.

"Why did you tell her that—about my family? How do you *know* any of that?" Mandip demanded as soon as she was out of earshot.

"As though I wouldn't research your cousin before taking feir time vials. The accounting is all in the Hall of Records. It's no secret, but very few people bother with so much reading."

The child in the smock returned, hurriedly clearing their table, though both men still had coffee in their cups and cake on their plates. Thibaut swiped his last morsel as the dish was pulled away. "La Maupin's food patron will be billed," the child assured them, and Thibaut understood this to mean her patron would *not* be paying for a second more of *their* leisure.

"Come, milor," Thibaut said, holding out his arm for Mandip. "The afternoon is bright, and I do believe we've been invited to the most exclusive performance in town. We should *celebrate*," he added coyly.

"We should *part ways*," Mandip countered. "First you manipulate me, then you steal from me, then you insult me. Why would I want to spend one more minute with you?"

"Because you're having fun," Thibaut stated, as though it was obvious.

"*What*, exactly, about you questioning my authority and undermining me at every turn, is supposed to be *fun*?"

"The *novelty* of it all?" he suggested. "You're not being pandered to by the underclasses, for once in your life." Thibaut rounded the table, dodging the boy as he continued to clear away the dishes.

He pressed into Mandip's personal space, bracing once hand on the back of his chair and leaning over him. Mandip held his ground. "You know nothing about my life," he spat.

"I've known a lot of nobles," Thibaut said, voice gone dark, rich. "Know you're all after the same things, in the end."

"I know what you're doing," Mandip said, standing, batting him away. "You're *still* trying to use me. You know you'll never be let on palace grounds without a noble escort, despite a verbal invitation from La Maupin."

"And La Maupin would clearly be cross with you if you took her up on her invitation *without* me."

"Without your *information*," he corrected. "She wants what you know."

"Quite," Thibaut said tightly.

"What do I care if a songstress is upset with me?" Mandip asked, raising an eyebrow.

Thibaut looked at a loss for a moment, and Mandip *thrilled*, chest swelling in victory.

He was starting to feel the ground steady beneath him. He'd found his footing with Thibaut.

Mandip realized he liked this better than if Thibaut had simply capitulated from the beginning. *This* power balance felt right. He was in charge, in control. Thibaut needed something from *him* that he could withhold—*not* the other way around. Thibaut had taken Mandip's control, and now Mandip had wrenched it *back*.

Thibaut was right: there *was* a novelty in having to *win* his dominance.

While Thibaut floundered, eyes darting as he searched for a convincing argument, Mandip grabbed him by the back of the neck and pulled him in, kissing him suddenly and soundly.

Thibaut made a surprised, indignant sound, then melted into it, though his confusion was clear in the hesitant way he kissed back.

Mandip broke the kiss just as suddenly, pushing Thibaut away. *Pressing* and *pulling*, hoping to keep Thibaut just as off-balance as he'd felt all afternoon. "I will meet you tomorrow night, at a place of your choosing, and you will escort me to the performance," he said. "I expect you not to trouble me until then."

Thibaut touched the corner of his mouth, breath quick, expression stunned. "Whatever you wish, milor."

13

KRONA

When Krona finally reached home that evening, after a long day of work and learning of the young healer's death, she fell into her mother's arms with an eagerness of affection she hadn't shown Acel in a long time. Warmth bled through her maman's housecoat, and Krona snuggled into her chest. Acel's scent always carried notes of spiced tea and honey and a specific *depth* that spoke to her age. That scent was everything to Krona—the scent of the only family she had left.

Acel did not ask questions; she simply cooed at Krona and shushed her when a small sob broke free of Krona's chest.

Neither of them had yet settled with their grief for De-Lia—though most often Acel's hurt manifested as despondence and detachment—and so she likely thought Krona's outpouring was one more bubble bursting, one more day of memories that could not be laid to rest.

She wasn't entirely wrong, of course. Melanie and De-Lia's deaths were embroiled together in Krona's heart; she'd known as soon as she'd lost her sister that she had to let the young woman go, despite the implications of an enchanter's mark etched into her skin. Krona had to encourage her to flee, to *live*. Live the life she wanted.

Somehow, knowing Melanie's family escaped had made De-Lia's passing a little easier. De-Lia had been honorable, had wished to save people. She hadn't *traded* her life for theirs—no, such a notion was horrible—but she'd *fought* for them. And their survival meant, to Krona, that such a fight had not been in vain.

But now Melanie was dead. And De-Lia was dead.

So, what had been the point of that whole terrible fiasco?

What had De-Lia died for?

Krona knew it was a petulant thought. Most people didn't get to die *for* anything.

They simply died.

The afternoon before the performances at the Rotunda, before they headed to the palace to begin their duties, Krona briefed her team on their positioning and reminded them to defer to the Marchonian Guard at all times. She and the five other members of her detail—Tray, Sasha, Royu, Tabitha, and Gorvin—would all be stationed at the main entrance of the Rotunda's lobby. A post Krona had purposefully traded for. Originally, they'd been tasked with patrolling the exterior perimeter, but Krona needed to be as close to the attending dignitaries as possible. And, this way, they would each pass before her. She'd see everyone, be able to account for all in attendance.

Not once did she consider heeding the Blue Woman's warning to stay away.

As long as the Chief Magistrate had done his job and kept the most vulnerable home, she was confident she would be able to disrupt the assassination plan. Even with so little to go on.

The Regulators all donned unique armor, reserved especially for those times they fell into direct service of the Grand Marquises. It was slightly heavier and much showier.

They were still mostly shrouded in black, with thick leathers and sweeping umanori for ease of stride, but their bracers—typically brass or copper, with a single emotion stone each—were plated gold and studded up the wrists with several small topaz and garnets for courage and resolve. All of the metal they wore was ornate, decorated with Lutadorian pentagonal seals and human figures, including embossed gold-plated pauldrons, which sat heavily atop their shoulders. The typical cherry red of their visors had been replaced by gold-tinted glass, and their horned helms were all the more imposing, the horns more twisted, with veins of gold running through the black.

The uniforms were flashy in a way that Krona detested, but at least they weren't full plate armor, as many of the Marchonian Guard often wore.

Her detail would arrive at the palace long before the evening's frivolities were set to begin, and everyone had chosen a mask from the den's armory to wear beneath their helms. Tray had given Krona a particularly hard stare when she'd chosen Motomori's half-mask.

"It's been a while since you've touched that one," he'd said, clearly trying to keep his judgmental tone under control but failing.

She'd gently taken it from its cubby, rubbing the pads of her gloved fingers over the carved teeth. The mask would only cover her nose and mouth—an unusual design for an enchanted mask. It was the likeness of a stylized demon's maw, with clear Marrakevian artistic influences, painted in stark neutrals.

In truth, she would have preferred to take Mastrex Pat-Soon's otter mask, which granted the wearer incredible stealth. The ability to blend into the shadows and trail a suspect without being noticed would have been invaluable under the circumstances. But, alas, that mask had disappeared during the Charbon concern, and they had yet to recover it.

Motomori had been a master of persuasion and hypnotism, able to convince nearly anyone of anything in the moment. He could make even the most obvious lie seem a truth, and mesmerize his subjects into the oddest of states, willing them to enact the strangest of behaviors.

"The echo is strong," she'd told Tray dismissively. It wasn't a lie—the mask was Magnitude Nine Point Eight, the most difficult she'd ever encountered, the nearest to Magnitude Ten she'd ever seen—but nor was it the real reason she'd passed over it for years now in favor of possibly less useful masks.

When she'd last used it in an interrogation, she felt she'd gone too far. That she'd been able to use the mask *too* well. It allowed her to press upon a person's will to an uncomfortable degree, to the point where she wasn't sure they'd really ever come back to themself—that the hypnotic influence hadn't penetrated more *permanently* than she'd meant it to.

That had been well before her brush with the Thalo puppets, her encounter with the Blue Woman. But, now, she recognized Motomori's abilities as akin to theirs.

She didn't know what that meant, exactly. Or how it was possible. Enchanted wood only contained knowledge—imbued skill upon the wearer—nothing more. If the Thalo employed strange magics, it should be impossible to find their mirror in a mask.

She'd considered wearing no mask at all, seeing as how the knowledge she needed to rely on at the Rotunda was her own. She wanted to stay sharp, her mind entirely clear, and she certainly couldn't guarantee that with an echo present. Especially Motomori's, which was likely to intrude upon her thoughts even after the initial seclusion. But it felt unnatural to enter into such a situation without every tool at her disposal.

She had De-Lia's mask, of course—*always*—but it would stay at her side, concealed beneath her cape. Even if she *could* suppress De-Lia's echo enough to access her abilities—to shoot the whiskers off a varg at a hundred paces—her particular skill set would, hopefully, be of no use tonight.

Now her team stood before her for inspection, helms tucked beneath one arm, masks in place.

Tray's was bone white, and a series of faux ribs and vertebrae outlined his facial features and topped a set of real human teeth imbedded in the enchanted wood. Mistress Loureda had been a skilled fighter—hand to hand, she'd been able to subdue adversaries twice her size and could near-instantly disarm anyone anywhere of any weapon. A useful mask for anyone of his stature, be they already well trained or no.

Krona—who would not don Motomori until much later—looked him in the eye while giving him an approving nod but quickly glanced away again.

De-Lia's echo had been rather . . . *adamant* . . . about memories of Tray last night. Intimate memories, revealing far more about her sister's relationship with their childhood friend than Krona ever suspected. She couldn't remember specific details without the mask on, but the awareness of it, of what they'd meant to one another, had not been stolen by daylight.

She'd been robbed of a sister, and Tray? Tray had been robbed of a lover.

They'd kept their relationship a secret, and Krona tried not to be offended. Hurt.

Perhaps it had been casual and they hadn't wished to get anyone's hopes up. After all, Acel, especially, would have begun planning their wedding in her mind before so much as an "Oh, that's nice" could fall from her lips.

Shaking off such thoughts, Krona continued down the line, inspecting each Regulator with the same rigor and attention to detail she knew they'd face under the scrutiny of the Marchonian Guard. Sasha wore Leroux's mask—for detecting lies. Royu chose the luna-moth mask of Mastrex Hollen, who'd known how to train and prep feir eyes for clear vision in unlikely places—in thick smoke, pure darkness, and even underwater. And Gorvin, the newest member of their detail, wore the mask of Madame Ka-Diana Imbal, whose keen eye for aesthetic detail meant its wearer could instantly spot things out of place—like the seam of a hidden door or a strange bulge in a pocket.

Pleased with everyone's readiness, they hurried to the stables, mounted their horses, and set off for the palace.

As they rode, Krona's tension mounted. She couldn't help but feel she hadn't done enough in regards to the Blue Woman's plot. There'd been so little time to act, so little information to act *on*, and yet she could not shake the looming sense of *failure* burgeoning in her chest.

Something wasn't right. Something wasn't as it seemed.

But there was no time to investigate. No one to interrogate, and no leads to follow up on. This problem was inside-out and backward. Fundamentally, she knew who the perpetrator was—the very knowledge she usually lacked on a concern. And yet, the thing she always possessed—a concrete victim—was elusive.

After passing through the palace gates, their detail was herded into a courtyard filled to the brim with lawpersons—members of the Dayswatch, Nightswatch, Regulators, private guards, and even Borderswatch. The day was as uncharacteristically warm as the day before, and Krona was thankful for the broad awnings in purple and yellow strung over the area to provide shade.

There they were met by the Captain of the Marchonian Guard, Veratas—a grizzled-looking bear of a person, tall and broad.

Everything on the palace grounds had an aesthetic purpose as well as a practical one, and the Marchonian Guards were no different. Where the orchards were lovely and the walkways serene, the spires grand and the windows awe-inspiring, the Marchonian Guards drew darkness and shadows and fear with them wherever they trod. Their majesty was imposing and off-putting at the same time, even for someone like Krona.

They wore no helms, and all kept their skulls clean-shaven, better to display the scars born of their obedience, and the surgical modification of their eye sockets.

Captain Veratas was particularly gnarled, zhur expression perpetually grim. Zhur breastplate had an anatomically correct pair of hearts etched into the steel—a reminder that each Marchonian was magically tethered to their charge. A set of six metal insect legs—thick and segmented, like those of a scorpion—burst forth from around zhur right eye, as though a creature had burrowed into zhur brain and was clawing its way out again.

Each Marchonian Guard had been fitted with the same enchantment, connecting their humors to the Grand Marquises, letting them feel the very beating of their masters' hearts behind their eyes and in their chests. Imbedded beneath the knotted center of the insect legs was an array of glass, gemstones, metal, and wood, all working in tandem to alert the guards to the mood and health of one of their leaders—whichever twin they'd been assigned to, the First or the Second.

They all knew when a Grand Marquis was in pain. Or happy. Or furious. Or making love. Their own blood would simmer—dulled but noticeable—their own fluids spiking, humors shifting. They were intimately familiar with every arthritic ache and surge of triumph.

Once a Marchonian Guard was initiated and surgically altered, the be-legged enchantment could not be removed without killing its wearer.

To have one's existence tied to someone else's so intimately meant the guards loved them like they loved themselves. They were vested in their moods—their happiness, their safety and serenity.

And when their masters were threatened, the Marchonian Guards were known—expected—to be unreasonable.

Violently unreasonable.

Krona had seen it for herself, once, and the memory still turned her stomach.

The Second Grand Marquis had broken his leg two years back when he'd fallen from a rearing horse. She'd been on palace grounds and had watched from a rampart as the nearest detail of Marchonian Guards had gone into a berserking rage, tearing both the horse and its trainer to bloody shreds in a matter of minutes.

The guards hadn't stopped there, clawing and howling, gouging their own skin until the Second Grand Marquis's leg had been set and plastered and a sleeping draught administered.

Any violence they committed while in such a rage was considered righteous. A Marchonian could do no wrong when reacting to a Grand Marquis's pain. It wasn't so much that their judgment was final—as one is required mindfulness to have judgment—but that their savagery was holy. Virtuous fury, blessed by Time.

Get between a Marchonian and their charge, and you were as good as dead.

The palace guards made Krona uneasy.

They made *most* people uneasy.

But they were guaranteed to protect the palace and its occupants more rabidly than any dog.

Captain Veratas ran the attending constabulary through their paces, as Krona expected, lining them all up to examine their uniforms and their weapons and their attention to detail and formality. Krona was proud of her team, who held themselves as firmly and professionally as the Marchonians themselves.

"My people have been warned of an impending assassination attempt, and the Grand Marquises and attending dignitaries have been alerted in turn," Veratas announced. "Given the already-heightened security and the vagueness of the threat, the members of the summit have agreed to let the night's gaieties proceed. Rest assured, extra action has been taken to protect those considered the most vulnerable."

Having one's humors tied to another's—so that you may feel every press and pull of fluids, emotions, pains, on and on—meant one's preservation was intimately tied to the other's preservation. Many of the guards had been linked to the Marquises for decades. Having that second heart beat ripped away would be instantly maddening, devastating—as it was designed to be, an extra "protective measure." Assassinations were supposed to be more difficult because of it. Who would dare try to take a life when it put everyone within arm's reach of a berserking guard in danger?

. . . Who would dare?

Tension rose in Krona's throat, making her breath tight, short. For half a moment she wondered if she'd been wrong about the likely targets. After all, the Blue Woman hadn't made the *intent* of the assassination clear; Krona had simply drawn her own conclusions. And the Thalo was nothing if not the embodiment of chaos, and what would cause more chaos in Lutador than—

But no. Not the Grand Marquises. The Blue Woman might be supernatural in some way—despite her claims—but she was not a deity; of this, Krona was certain. She did not have a god's reach or a god's invulnerability, and neither did her fellow puppets. The Grand Marquises were the most well-protected twins in the entire Valley—more so now that they had wind of a potential assassin.

After inspection, Captain Veratas led Krona and her team to the front entrance of the Rotunda, where they'd be stationed. None of the invited guests would come or go without Krona's notice.

But what about the uninvited guests?

She requested a tour of the servants' entrances, the stage house, and the attached kitchens—which sported its own specialty wine cellar, accessible only by the head sommelier. Once the Rotunda itself had been exhaustively examined, she insisted on being shown the glass-enclosed "skywalk" that created a bridge three stories up—spanning over the gravel drive that led to the stables—which the Grand Marquises used to alight in the Rotunda from the palace proper when they desired privacy or the weather was considered untenable. She was assured Marchonian Guards would be stationed at all of them, but still, she regretted she could not be everywhere at once.

The Blue Woman had made it clear Krona had unusual invulnerabilities. Which just served to highlight everyone else's weaknesses.

As she followed Veratas over the glass bridge and into the palace, Krona's hand went to De-Lia's mask, petting over the muzzle.

De-Lia had been a better strategist than Krona. She would have known what to do with these vulnerabilities.

Was that true, though? Or just a rosy-colored perception?

Krona could never fault De-Lia for her unwilling role in the Gatwood-Charbon concern, but the older Hirvath hadn't spotted many of the clues the younger had. She hadn't thought Charbon's past important to the present, hadn't seen the long-standing connections between the *then* and the *now*.

Krona had always ascribed a certain level of professional infallibility to De-Lia, and only now, after her death, had she begun to see how that had created a distance between the two of them. How it had only increased Krona's own doubts in herself and built an awkward combination of hero-worship and resentment in her core.

Stop competing with De-Lia, she chided herself. *She's not even here to outperform you.*

A pair of Marchonian Guards were already on the palace end of the bridge, standing statue-still with their hands braced on the pommels of large war hammers, each emblazoned with the seal of the Grand Marquises.

Krona expected to be dismissed then. She'd been shown every inch of the Rotunda, and her duties would not carry her any deeper into the palace. But Veratas guided her into a room some way from the bridge. No one was waiting for them, and the space was mostly taken up by a large-scale model of Arkensyre Valley, its topography incredibly detailed.

Veratas shut the door and turned to her. "The Chief Magistrate indicated you informed him of the assassination plot."

Krona's hands flexed, itching to touch her sword. She couldn't tell by the tone of zhur voice if zhe'd pulled her aside to commend her or accuse her.

Fully helmed as she was, the other captain could not see her expression, and yet she made her lips a thin line and her gaze hard. She tried to focus on zhur uncovered eye, but her attention continuously drifted to the legs bursting from the other socket. "Yes," she replied evenly.

"He also indicated he trusts you with his life."

The tension left her chest. She let out a breath.

Commend it was, then.

"The Chief Magistrate is too kind."

"No, he is not," zhe said frankly, an edge of amusement in zhur voice. "He does not say such things lightly, nor magnanimously."

Veratas turned away, wandering over to the model. With idleness that was clearly purposeful, zhe took a small figure from the Lutador's southern border and examined it. It seemed to represent a battalion of Borderswatch. "Is Regulation your calling?"

Krona strode to zhur side. "My calling?"

Zhe turned to her. "You strike me as someone very duty-bound. Someone who appreciates her responsibility to the people, to the state."

"I also appreciate it when others are *direct* with me," she said, hoping the point would come sooner rather than later.

"The current Grand Marquises have a few years left in their tenure. Five, perhaps, before the Council of Lords decides to hold new elections. Some of my people will be weaned away from their current tethers so they can be tied to the new set, but many will remain connected to the current twins for the rest of their lives."

Ah. "You're recruiting. For when the time comes."

Zhe nodded. "New Grand Marquises means new Marchonians. And you have quite the reputation—for enchantment use, loyalty, determination, professionalism. The Grand Marquexes, whoever they turn out to be—the Basus, the Fras, the Thalésis—would be lucky to have you."

Each compliment hit Krona like a fist. They were all true, and they were all untrue. "I'm flattered."

"Don't be. I'm not a flatterer."

"Are you expecting an answer?"

"Not right at the moment. I simply wanted to plant the possibility in your mind."

"Consider it rooted."

"Thank you. Your consideration is honorable." With a slightly exaggerated sweep of zhur arm, zhe replaced the battalion marker back on the model, clearly drawing Krona's attention to the expansive diorama and its movable pieces. To the *way* they were arranged.

It only took her a moment to matrix the patterns into clear intent.

These were war plans.

The Borderswatch was, as the name implied, responsible for securing the borders. But for the past several hundred years, this had mostly applied to keeping the varger population at bay and seeing that smuggling operations, bandits, and highwaymen were put in their place.

These battalions were placed like an *army*. A mass of them just on the wrong side of the Asgar-Skan border.

Were they invading the larger city-state? Or being loaned to Asgar-Skan in aid?

Were these actual *plans* or just possibilities played out in forethought?

Krona wanted to ask but knew her questions would go unanswered. Veratas had simply drawn her attention to the model as a means of persuasion. If the current Grand Marquises involved Lutador in violent conflict, this could affect not only when the new Grand Marquexes were voted into service, but under what conditions they'd need protecting. Zhe hoped the knowledge of impending conflict might speak to Krona's sense of duty and drive her to enter service at the palace.

It did speak to Krona's sense of duty, but in a very different way. It made the importance of thwarting the Thalo's plans all the starker. She didn't want to see this model of events play out in full scale.

Her anxiety rose. She felt like she was being propelled down a path with many exits, many possible forks and diversions, and yet she could not make her feet take any of them.

This cannot come to pass, she declared to herself. And yet, she felt like there was little she could do to stop it.

Why shouldn't she fail to keep Lutador from war?

She'd failed in so many important tasks.

She'd failed to save De-Lia. Failed to find Melanie's baby. Failed, even, to keep the young healer alive.

14

THALO CHILD

Two Years Ago

"Shh. *Shhh.*" Thalo Child bounced his charge in his arms, walking in circles, alternating between careful coos and harsh hisses, attempting whatever he could to calm the crying infant.

The Thalo Ones around him shot the occasional glance his way—sometimes in irritation, sometimes in sympathy.

It was strange to see a child of his age in the nursery. He knew this. Knew how out of place—how out of his depth—he was. "Please, babe," he bid in hushed tones. "Please, just sleep."

Zhe had now been his for six months. Zhe had said zhur first words—was very adept at applying "no"—and yet, at the moment, was too distressed to utter even that.

He didn't know what was wrong. Didn't know what to do.

He hoisted zhim higher on his shoulder, with zhur chin perched over his neck and zhur soft cheek butting up against his jaw. Zhe whimpered, and he tried rubbing a soothing circle between zhur shoulder blades. The baby's skin smelled powder-clean, but zhur breath was unusually sour.

An older Thalo One—nineteen, maybe twenty, well past the point when one would typically earn their name—watched him with more intensity than the others, who were all focused on their own mewling babes.

Thalo Child had seen fer around—feir hair was long and ashen, pulled back in intricate loops that looked delicate, like they could be pulled free on a careless finger—and fey moved through the nursery with the confidence of one who knows their surroundings intimately.

Fey came over to his side, set a gentle palm over the baby's forehead. "Zhe's warm," fey tutted. "Go to the kitchens. Ask the cooks for some fermenter's syrup. It should help zhim rest."

"What if they won't give it to me? Not everyone knows I . . . What if they don't believe me when I tell them what it's for?"

"You can tell them I sent you, if you need to. I'm the oldest of the Nameless—which is almost a name in and of itself," fey said with a reassuring smile. "Here, give zhim to me. I'll look after zhur needs while you're gone."

Gently, he tipped the baby from his shoulder into feir arms.

>⚬⚬⚬⚬⚬⚬<

It felt strange wandering the halls on his own. One of his age was accompanied almost everywhere they went, save the privy. Whether it was Gerome, or the priests, or the other members of his cohort, he hardly ever found himself roaming so solitarily.

It was . . . unnerving.

The keep was vast but underpopulated for its space. He'd never explicitly thought about it before, but he supposed perhaps five hundred Thalo called the keep home, with perhaps twice that many Mindless and Mindful combined. Which meant he didn't meet more than the occasional servant on his way to the kitchens.

His slippers were quiet on the polished floor, but all around him the keep made sounds. The gentle whistle of mountain winds through the tall corridors seemed louder than usual, and the braziers crackled with more intensity.

Down one set of wide stairs, Thalo Child encountered a Mindless mopping the floor. They raised their gaze to his, mouth slightly slack, eyes milky white and pupilless. Two large, blue circles had been inked on the back of their hands and were faded and slightly distorted. A Thalo's first tattoos.

Even though Mindless were to be mostly ignored, Thalo Child gave this one a nod, suppressing a shiver as he strode past, leaving them to their work.

To become a Mindful was to be a failed Thalo—one brought to serve the Savior but found lacking by the gods. They could not progress through their lessons, could not properly absorb the God Power on Ritual Way.

To become a Mindless was a great punishment. Each had done something terrible. Abused a fellow Thalo. Killed or cheated.

Rebelled.

Only the Savior Himself was powerful enough to create a Mindless. It was His judgment that determined who would be lost to themselves, who would advance, and who would gain a name.

Thalo Child hoped to meet Him one day.

But not too soon.

Not soon at all.

The kitchens were vast, their ovens dark, layered clay domes that roared with fire and seeped curls of smoke from their grates. The cooks' clothes were white and heavy, liberally smeared in fat and blood. Pots and pans hung from racks imbedded in the carved ceiling, and one long corridor led to the ice pit where much of the keep's perishables were stored.

Thalo Child made his request, and while one cook went to find him a vial of the syrup, the child stood idly by, making sure to keep out of the way and his hands to himself.

He realized, for the first time, that he didn't know where all the food came from. He knew it was paid in tribute, but he had no notion of what that entailed or even who provided it. After all, the Thalo protected peoples who did not realize they existed. They were subservient guardians to the outside world, and that world gave them nothing in return.

At least, that was what Gerome always said.

The cook returned with a small bottle of the dark, goopy syrup, and Thalo Child swiftly retreated back the way he'd come.

When he reached the wide staircase again, the Mindless was gone, but instead there was Gerome. Today he wore a simple strip of netting over his eyes. No metal, no gemstones. It was the kind of cage Thalo Child imagined Gerome put himself in at night, to cradle him while he dreamed.

The Eye was with him, glimmering and glassy atop its staff.

"There you are, One Who Belongs to the Eye," Gerome said sternly. Clearly, he'd been looking for him.

Thalo Child instantly dropped his gaze, palms going sweaty around the ampule he'd been given. "I didn't abandon zhim," he explained quickly, fearing he thought him delinquent in his caregiving.

"The eldest explained," Gerome said. "We'll drop off the syrup for your babe. Then you will aid me in my task."

"Yes, Possessor. Thank you, Possessor." He hid his hope, his sudden excitement. Gerome had been looking for *him specifically*, so that Thalo Child might *give him aid*? Thalo Child had been uncertain when receiving his tattoos, but surely this meant Gerome had begun to see him in a new light? Saw him as special—worthy. Worthy enough to help a mighty Possessor with their secret tasks.

Thus, he walked with a lighter gait as he followed Gerome through the keep, as they delivered the syrup and thanked the eldest before moving on.

But Gerome soon led him *up*—up up up. Staircase after staircase spiraled higher through the sprawling wings of the keep. *Down* was where the secrets were. *Down* was where comfort and protection and knowledge lay. The heart of the keep was its most sacred space—where the Savior's own apartments lay. To continue *upward* was to continue *outward*, away from the Thalo sanctuary and toward the world beyond.

The world they protected. A world they secured and watched over.

Thalo Child had not glimpsed that world since he himself was a baby. Since he'd been brought into the safety and service of the keep. And he had no memories of before.

They reached a wing that was outward enough that the heat from the volcanic springs failed to maintain their loving hold on Thalo Child's thin limbs. He began to shiver. His usual robes were meant for inside wear only, and an icy spike shot through the pads of his feet with every step of his silken slippers.

His discomfort did not escape Gerome's notice. "There is a cloakroom, not far," his Possessor reassured him.

Indeed, only a few minutes later they entered into a deep room filled with racks upon racks of furs dyed all possible shades of blue. Gerome selected cloaks for both of them, draping one around Thalo Child's shoulders before stepping back with a frown. It was too long, but that was understandable; children did not leave the keep, or its courtyards, or its warmth. Ever. Ritual Way did not count. Quickly, Gerome located a belt and arranged the fur just so, tightening the sash around Thalo Child's middle so that the hem would not trail across the stones and threaten to trip him.

"We are receiving Sacrifices for Time tonight," Gerome said suddenly.

Thalo Child's blood ran cold. A deep-set chill entered his bones, the kind the furs could not fight. "Am I . . . Am I expected to . . ."

"No, Child, you will not administer the needles. Of course not. The Mindful will take care of that. You will help me prepare the Sacrifices. They often need washing, feeding, soothing. I will use the Eye. You know how to soothe a different way; I've seen you do it."

"I don't know what you . . ."

"A pleasant secret," he explained, without ire. "You will find a pleasant secret and amplify it for them."

Warmly dressed, they continued on.

Finally, they reached an *outer* door, one leading onto the ramparts. Thalo Child had spent many a lovely day in several of the keep's courtyards, and for some reason he expected the ramparts to feel like more of the same. But when they exited onto the top of a long stone wall, with little more than a low parapet—spiked, like a row of jagged teeth—keeping him from toppling over one side and the accompanying sheer cliff that led down into the ice fields, he blanched, felt woozy.

All of this openness—the broadness of the sky—felt unnatural. The young Thalo was a child of walls and narrow passages and sky-glimpses. Out here, in the open, everything felt shifted. Inverted.

He drew close to his Possessor, clutching at Gerome's robes like he used to at a tender age, and Gerome did not begrudge him this closeness, this touchstone.

Thalo Child turned away from the vastness, glancing around Gerome's steadying form over the other side of the wall and into the keep proper, noting where the castle clung to the mountain—like a great, wide hand with its wrist growing out of the weather-worn stone. It looked as though it should crumble and fall, as though it should not be able to cling to the crags and should instead topple down into the ice sheets under the audacity of its own weight.

Perhaps enchantment keeps it in place, he thought.

The aurorae from the gods' border swam and crackled on the ridgeline, where the mountains rose up and stretched out. Thalo Child squinted through the purple-blue-blackness at the point where the castle blended into the unforgiving rockface, trying to identify Ritual Way itself.

Overhead, the moons sat behind a thin, cloudy haze.

A chill wind suddenly whipped around him, stealing his breath and forcing him closer to the warmth and firmness of his Possessor.

The top of this particular rampart stretched out five hundred feet in front of them, leading from the door they'd exited to yet another. What that door might connect to, Thalo Child could not say, and it seemed the pair of them did not mean to walk the rampart and push onward. Instead, they waited. For many minutes, still and quiet.

After a dense silence, Gerome suddenly spoke. "Zhe will be given to another Possessor when the time comes." Thalo Child did not have to ask who he meant, and the cold quickly returned to his veins. "You should prepare yourself."

"Why not you? I thought . . ."

"Already you are too attached to this infant," Gerome said firmly. "The two of you should not belong to the same artifact. You are responsible for zhim, but zhe is not yours."

"I understand."

"Do you?" he accused. "Or have you been prideful? Thought yourself special?"

Thalo Child was suddenly grateful for his physical closeness to Gerome for an entirely different reason: from this angle his Possessor could not see his flush of shame, or his guilty, downcast eyes.

He *had* thought himself special. The great Hintosep had picked him out of all the Thalo his age, out of everyone in his cohort. She'd entrusted him with something as precious as an infant, and Gerome had given him his lines early and asked for his help here, now.

Was taking pride in that really so horrible?

Of course it was. Of course. The Thalo were servants. Beholden to a higher power, closer to the divine than anyone else in the Valley.

He needed to do better. He needed to *be* better.

Just then, the doors at the opposite end of the rampart were heaved open. Two tall, broad Thalo—great, hulking Harvesters—shoved at the doors and secured them open. Behind them, a long line of people—given warm cloaks, just as Gerome had given Thalo Child, but clearly with rags underneath—were flanked by a dozen more Harvesters on either side, guiding them across the rampart, toward the keep's entrance.

Toward Gerome and Thalo Child.

The Sacrifices had arrived.

Their eyes darted about as they took in everything around them. Even to Thalo Child—to whom the keep was familiar, all he'd ever known—the realm of the Thalo was imposing and awe-inspiring. How must it seem to these people, he wondered? These people who truly understood so little about their own Valley, who the Thalo were, and what privileges the existence of the Order of the Thalo afforded them.

Though, as Thalo Child took them in—noted their downtrodden appearance— the word "privileges" was quickly erased from his mind.

"Who are they?" he ventured, hoping not to rankle Gerome with his probing ignorance. "Where do the Sacrifices come from?"

"The undercities," Gerome explained, attention now diverted to the task. "Each city-state has some place they push their unwanted. Into the sewers, the gutters, the most barren parts of the desert. These are the outcasts and the offcasts. Those who would have been missed by very few before the gods chose them. Those who will be missed by none now after, for we have made their loved ones forget.

"They give of themselves for the protection of all the Valley," he continued. "For the protection of what little family they have. For the few they hold dear. They are our preservation. They are why we persist."

Gerome spoke as though they'd had a choice. As though these people had been given an opportunity. A blessing. And he wanted to believe his Possessor. He *did*.

But if these people had been blessed, they did not look as though they understood the blessing. They were harried, frightened—frightened worse than the six-year-olds he'd been able to comfort as they lay on their little altars in Ritual Way.

"But don't we get our time from the time tax? The Valley people use most of it for trade, but . . ."

"But they have no idea how much time they truly give," he said, both finishing

Thalo Child's thought and agreeing with him. "They think it a handful of years when it is decades, and thus we are able to take the excess in tribute without upsetting them—without their discomfort. And their time does come to us, for redistribution, yes. But it is not enough. And these Sacrifices," he said with a nod toward the people, "their time will go directly to the Savior."

"All of it?"

"All of it."

There were twenty Sacrifices in the group, by Thalo Child's count. None of them were especially young, but none were old, either. If they each had thirty years left to them, then that would mean the Savior . . .

Their Sacrifice would extend His life by *six hundred* years.

Gerome could clearly see the child performing the calculations. "The Savior does not accept Sacrifices in this quantity often," he said. "In my time, I have only seen another culling of this size once."

"How old is the Savior? How old is Hintosep?" he blurted.

"Older than the Valley itself," came his Possessor's even reply.

How old is the Valley?

He realized he didn't know.

How old is Gerome?

That question he dared not voice.

Thalo Child knew he himself had not yet received any extra time—from the city-states' taxes or otherwise.

"Why do the Valley people still trade in time?" he ventured. "Why do they not return it all to themselves?"

"They do not understand time, though they think they do. Extra time is a stopgap, extending a period of life as though it were on pause. When one stops inserting extra time into that gap, a life proceeds as normal. The Valley people think time is tacked on, that it is something to be recovered only when one is already on the path toward natural death."

"Why do they think that?"

Gerome looked down at him. "Because we tell them it is so. If they knew the truth, it is as you say: they would selfishly drain their reserves. There would be chaos. The magic upon which all of their economies depend would vanish, and their societies would crumble. We keep the balance. That is our purpose."

The Sacrifices drew nearer, and Gerome put space between himself and Thalo Child, wide enough for the procession to pass through. The Harvesters walked around the two of them, letting them work as the line strode onward.

"You know how to soothe," Gerome reminded him. "Follow my lead."

As the first person approached, Gerome waved his hand over their forehead, openly locating the types of secrets Thalo Child had searched for on Ritual Way. In turn, he approached the second Sacrifice in line—a woman, her expression harried and terrified. He gestured for her to bend down so that he may reach her, and she immediately complied. For some reason, the sight of Thalo Child seemed to soften her, and it only took him a moment in her mind to realize why.

She secretly thought all children to be innocent. Or thought them all *ignorant* and *incapable,* truly—that was the secret part of it: she thought of all children as unformed people rather than people in their own right, and had learned to hide this opinion—but it meant that she thought a child could never be dangerous, as they possessed no true personhood and therefore no capacity for personal motivation.

He could not bring himself to be angry at her for thinking of him this way, as what he was about to do proved her folly.

Just as instructed, as he had instinctually done before, he located a pleasant secret.

Adult secrets, it turned out, were more complex than children's secrets.

This woman hated her spouse but did not hate her neighbor. The two things entwined secretly made her extremely happy.

Thalo Child did not understand it, but he amplified it.

When she let out a pleasant sigh, he moved on. Gerome had already seen to three others, and though Thalo Child knew he could not match his Possessor's efficiency, he still wanted to do his best.

After all twenty had passed beneath their palms, Thalo Child thought their work was over. But not so.

"This is just to keep them calm on their way through the keep," Gerome explained. "Soothing them while they are Sacrificed will take more effort."

"I understand," he said, though he did not.

The Sacrifices could hear them—Gerome made no attempt to keep his voice lowered or his wording obtuse. But now that they had been set inside their favorite secrets, the outside world must have seemed far away and unreal.

The Harvesters nudged the line of people forward, and they dragged their feet in a new way. Theirs was no longer the hesitancy of fear, but the reluctance of relaxation.

Thalo Child was glad he would not have to administer any needles or be responsible for bottling the time, but he'd hoped he wouldn't need to be present for the ritual itself. The thought of having one's essence taken—whether it be magic or time or . . . or anything else he might be too young to know about—had to be horrible. Perhaps even gruesome.

Gerome had mentioned feeding and washing, but it seemed their time was to be taken first. There was no delaying.

The Harvesters led the Sacrifices to a tower Thalo Child had never entered but had always considered benign. There were no enchanted doors to keep wanderers out; there were no strange noises or unnerving auras. It had seemed just another pentagon-shaped tower in a keep full of pentagon-shaped towers—someplace one was likely to find dusty, neglected books or additional bedrolls or a Mindful fast at work, mending robe hems and fighting off moth holes.

Its winding staircase led to three levels. A portion of the Sacrifices were herded onto the first and given comfortable-looking chairs to sit in, while one Harvester kept the rest in waiting at the bottom of the stairs. One Sacrifice was picked at random—the first woman Thalo Child had soothed—and led out again by a single Harvester, with Gerome and Thalo Child trailing behind once more.

The second level was a place of preparation. Time runes had been cut into the walls and in a pentagon on the floor, and a copper basin of water sat next to a set of perfumed candles on a tall table near one wall. Here the Sacrifice was given new robes to replace her sturdy-if-worn leathers, and a changing screen for modesty. Her new clothes were themselves thin and ethereal-looking, and bared her arms. Gerome then gently sponged the dirt from her face and shoulders before she was whisked away once more.

As they continued their ascent toward the topmost floor, the air changed. *Thickened.* The space that moments before had felt inconsequential suddenly seemed oppressive, heavy with deep bass reverberations that Thalo Child could only feel, not hear, and an electric tingle reminiscent of an oncoming storm—not quite as crackling as Ritual Way but strong enough to raise the fine hairs on the back of Thalo Child's neck.

But the bass—the sound that wasn't a sound—was far more concerning.

He reached out, trailing his fingertips along the stone wall, making sure he could feel the vibrations there as well, not just in his chest, not just in his stomach. He had no idea what could create such a sensation.

A loud whirring—inconstant yet rhythmic, as though made by something vaguely metallic and perhaps connected to a bellows, running through a pattern of motion on repetition—slammed into him as the Harvester opened the door at the stairs' terminus.

Beyond, three Mindful scurried about the chamber in light-blue smocks, each with a thick pair of goggles strapped to their faces. In the center of the room lay a large chair-like contraption, though it looked in fact more like an upturned centipede, with the "body" of the invertebrate bowed and flowing in a ripple, and the "legs" all curled inward. Each leg was in actuality a long, multi-hinged set of pipettes tipped with silver needles—poised to plunge into anyone situated in the chair. In the rear of the room lay the contraption making the deep vibrations and strange whirs; it held a giant glass receptacle, like a large preservation jar, and pumps and flaps constantly flooded and unflooded the jar with first a yellow liquid, then a blue liquid, then one faintly fuchsia. The device was connected to the needles on the chair via long tubing.

There was no clear power source for the contraption. No obvious gas, steam, or magical input.

The Sacrifice was led by one hand—daintily, as though she were a highborn lady—over to the chair, where the pipettes momentarily curled aside to allow her to sit.

Gerome immediately hurried behind her, letting each hand hover on either side of her head, just above her temples.

The Mindful went to work strapping her down, and she let them with a smile on her face.

Her glad eyes turned on Thalo Child, and he swallowed harshly and looked away.

In front of the chair lay a stained-glass window. Abstract blues of many hues swirled together, obscuring the view of the ice field and mountains but letting a pleasant, cool glow filter through the room.

Thalo Child understood about blue. Why it was everywhere, why it was their sacred color.

"It is the color most easily forgotten," Gerome had explained when Thalo Child was small. "It is calming and vague. It is unthreatening and easily blended. Once, there were whole societies that had no word for blue. Blue is less important to the human mind than red, and made more organic by yellow. Blue helps the mind unsee and let go. Our order takes its name from a blue, phthalo blue. Copper salts are at the heart of it. Fitting, since salt is the element that corresponds to our magic. If our abilities are taken from us—which is a rare punishment—it can be used to enchant salts."

Thalo Child only had a moment to relive the memory before the Mindful began their work. The centipede's long legs curled toward the woman, thrusting the needles *down*.

In.

There was no attempt to spare the Sacrifice's new clothes; the needles plunged into bare skin and fabric alike.

The Sacrifice jolted slightly, but the unnatural smile never left her face.

And then the machine began to work.

Thalo Child had thought that as her years were drained away into the enchanted jar, the woman might spontaneously age, become shriveled and gray in minutes instead of decades.

But that wasn't how aging or time worked, he realized. Wrinkles were *earned*. They marked years used, years passed. Not years robbed, taken.

He supposed that made sense. He knew the tax was taken from babies, and the process did not magically age them.

As the time was pumped from her body, Thalo Child let his gaze wander to the glass jar. At first, nothing seemed to change. Time itself was typically ephemeral. One could see the effects it left behind, but it was difficult to see time itself.

But as more time filled the space, small flashes of symbols spluttered in and out of sight. Sometimes they appeared to be rolling over, counting up or down, like the beads of an abacus freely sliding back and forth. They moved almost as though liquid, sloshing into reality—shimmering slightly pink or golden—and then dissipating in a spray or sucked away as though in a Deep Waters tide. And yet, overall, the impression was always that the jar was empty. The level of these swift visions rose higher and higher, but nothing else ever denoted changing mass or volume.

After a long few minutes, the extraction was over. The needles collectively retracted and the legs spread away. Small spots of blood seeped from her small wounds, speckling her all over and staining her thin robes in a clear pattern.

Even if she hadn't withered into nothing, still, he'd expected . . . something. That she might even simply expire—die right there in the chair, with no more time left to draw a breath or for her heart to beat—and yet she stepped down from the contraption on steady legs with a smile on her face, despite the many small wounds littered across her skin.

The process was repeated with each Sacrifice, until one man sprang up abruptly at the end of his session, too fast for Gerome. In the split second he was away from the Possessor's hands, Gerome's magic slackened.

Whatever the chair was doing to these people—whatever it felt like to have one's years siphoned away—hadn't been *lessened* because of Gerome's efforts. Just masked.

For a brief moment, the man doubled over, letting out half a scream of despair before Gerome was once more at his side, weaving a wall of pleasantries in front of the pain.

Thalo Child knew firsthand how intense Gerome's magic was. How practiced and perfected. If one split second away from his influence was enough to make the man cry out, that meant the process he was masking had to be excruciating.

After, when all twenty had given of themselves for the Savior, Gerome and

Thalo Child attended to each as though they were their servants. They took the group to the hot springs used for washing, and gently scrubbed each down with soft cloths and sweet oils, then helped them dress and groom their hair.

Disturbingly, Gerome praised and cooed at them in a way he'd never spoken to Those Who Belong to the Eye. He told them how wonderful they were, how pleased the gods were that they'd arrived here at the keep, how the Thalo would be happy to serve them for a long time to come.

And then, once they were all made clean and comfortable, it was time for a meal.

The feast was grand. Thalo Child only got to eat this well once a year, during the Anniversary of the Introdus. There were spiced cakes of all kinds, pickles from Marrakev, and curries from Asgar-Skan and Xyopar. Breads from Wins-rouen and sugared fruits from Lutador. Fish-head stew, lamb pie, pork dumplings, and vegetable tarts. Favorites of each Sacrifice had been carefully prepared and perfectly seasoned.

Everyone, from the Harvesters to the Sacrifices, broke bread and spoke to one another as though they were long-lost companions.

Thalo Child grinned and laughed, though he realized these people's gaiety was not natural. They had forgotten how they'd gotten here. Forgotten why they'd agreed to come—or if they'd even agreed at all. They'd already been made to forget the ordeal in the tower and the tough journey they'd taken.

When the first Sacrifice let out a hearty yawn, the festivities began to wind down, and the Sacrifices were each escorted to a grand room, unique to them, each with a bed the likes of which Thalo Child had never seen. His entire cohort could have fit comfortably on one of these mattresses, and the blankets had a pleasant poof to them, and there were pillows of all kind—from pudding-soft to pleasantly firm.

Perhaps it's not so bad, he thought, *giving over decades, if they're to be treated like this for all their remaining time.*

When Thalo Child shut the last chamber door behind him, he grinned up at Gerome. But the gentle, secret smile his Possessor had worn all evening had already slipped away.

"You will help the Mindless retrieve the bodies in the morning," Gerome said dismissively, striding away without a look back.

Thalo Child tripped over his own feet in an attempt to keep up. "Bodies?"

"What do you think happens when you have no more time left to spend?" he asked, as though Thalo Child were dull-witted. "Yes, bodies."

Nausea swamped into Thalo Child's gut. Of course. He hadn't seen any Sacrifices regularly wandering the keep. He'd heard Gerome promise these people things he knew weren't true. But even so, he'd thought, maybe, that they would be sent home again, or sent . . . just sent someplace else. After the frivolities, he hadn't let himself entertain the idea that the Sacrifices would not *survive* long enough to leave.

Thalo Child stopped walking. His feet refused to carry him farther.

These people, who'd just told amusing stories from their lives or regaled them all with frantic tales of brief adventure, would be dead by morning.

And he had helped kill them.

"They will go to sleep happy, well fed, and filled with hopes," Gerome said, clearly frustrated. He took Thalo Child by the arm, made him take awkward steps down the hall. "Few people would choose a different end."

Thalo Child held his tongue, but the words still rang out in his mind: *But you did not give them a choice.*

He *had* been prideful. In the worst way. Gerome had asked for his help in this because he *knew* it would serve as a humbling lesson. He knew Thalo Child needed to see the harsh realities of balance and progress. Safety often meant manipulation, killing, *sacrificing*. That was the way of the Thalo, the fate of the Thalo.

And he could not escape it.

15

MANDIP

Mandip had just under three hours to prepare before he needed to leave for the Creek Side Inn—Thibaut's chosen meeting place. From there the pair would head to the palace complex and alight at the Rotunda as La Maupin's special guests. What privileges this afforded them, exactly, he did not know.

But it was one more thing he could hold over Gudhal's head. One more thing to flaunt.

He knew it was petty, but he had so few *chances* to be petty, and he simply couldn't be blamed for taking advantage of the opportunity, now, could he?

Juliet had been a delight to escort yesterday evening. Though, oddly, he couldn't quite understand why she'd requested a tour. It was obvious within the first few minutes that she knew the Palace Rotunda like the back of her hand, having both performed there and acted as a stagehand many times before.

Instead, she'd spent an inordinate amount of time asking after *him*—his ambitions, his dreams, and his watch, of course. Though the questions he found most intrusive were about his extended family in Asgar-Skan.

Mandip chalked it up to curiosity sparked by the socially embarrassing story Thibaut had told, and yet, some of her questions were too in-depth to be based on such a simple tale.

The bell at the front door rang, interrupting his musings, but he ignored it as he went about his rooms, having failed just yet to settle on exactly what to wear. La Maupin was always dazzling in her performances, decked out in the extravagant and the impractical. Her costuming was as much a calling card—as much a draw to her productions—as her voice. Mandip would never dream of trying to overshadow her—and surely would fail, even if he made the attempt—but he should dress to at least complement her lavishness.

Typically, his valet would help him with his evening's selections, but the man's tastes had started to become woefully out of style. Frankly, he just couldn't keep up with the times. So, Mandip had dismissed him after he'd drawn the young lord his bath.

Mandip turned the gas up all the way on the lamps in his closet, sending stark shadows across the ceiling, cast from the elaborately carved crown molding. He examined himself in his full-length glass, first sitting on the duvet opposite, then standing and turning. He wasn't sure how he felt about the lace cuffs on this tangerine getup. It was overly long, completely covered his hands. His grandparents wore a lot of lace; he found it difficult to believe it was really coming back into fashion.

What would Thibaut be wearing? He wished he'd sent his escort a letter, so they could coordinate.

He frowned at himself, then shook his head and yanked his jacket off.

Not lace. Thibaut definitely wouldn't be wearing this much lace.

There was the dhoti sherwani Gudhal had brought for him from Asgar-Skan. The fabric was a slick, shiny indigo blue, and the cuffs, collar, and front were all lined with thick, intricate gold embroidery, depicting stylized lizards and fern fronds.

Adhar had been given one in berry and silver to match.

If Mandip wore his tonight, his parents would think it a wonderful gesture of goodwill toward his extended family. But it might just burn Gudhal right up to see Mandip using feir gift to impress the songstress and feir former company.

Yes, it was appropriately flashy, formal, and the obvious diplomatic choice. He pulled it from where it was still tucked in its gift box and quickly pulled on each piece in the set.

As he finished with the last button on the sherwani, a strong knock emanated from his chamber door.

"Coming!"

He strode from the closet across the bedroom to his antechamber, but the door was already opening, a familiar gait tapping across the hexagons of the well-polished wood floor to meet him.

Adhar was not yet dressed for the gathering, still in his housecoat, his facial hair ungroomed. "Ma and Baba need to speak with us." He looked his twin up and down. "It suits you. They'll be pleased."

"You think so?" He straightened his sleeves. "Then hopefully they won't be too scandalized if I stay out late."

Together they left their wing of the mansion, making their way through the opulent halls, passing various servants who stopped working to bow their heads respectfully as the brothers passed. Eventually, they were met by their steward, who guided them to the receiving room—a very strange place for Mandip and Adhar to find themselves if the family wasn't expecting company.

Inside, their parents both stood, speaking in close quarters and hushed tones with the head of the house guard. Baba chewed his lip and shuffled his shoes, while Ma held herself tall and regal, expression tense in a way that Mandip easily recognized; she was about to deliver news her sons would not like.

As the steward bowed and gestured for the twins to enter, she turned to them with her hands cupped together at her diaphragm and her elbows extended in what Mandip always thought of as her ambassadorial posture. Her large copper earrings swayed, dangling down over her shoulders, lying almost like armor plates over the shoulders of her cream-colored dress. "My sons, we will not be attending the performance at the Rotunda this evening."

She was always stoic and formal when those of a lower station were present, but the tremor in her voice revealed how shaken she was, how worried.

"Has something happened?" Adhar asked, his tone even and formal.

She gestured for the guardsman to speak. "We've been informed of a possible threat to the lives of prominent Lutadorian figures."

"So, the performance has been postponed?" Mandip pressed.

"No. But the Chief Magistrate of Justice has asked that certain noble families remain home."

"How many other families are affected?" Adhar asked.

"Eight," the guardsman said.

"Have we been threatened specifically?" Adhar asked.

"It doesn't matter," Madame Basu said, throwing up a hand before the guardsman could answer. "If the Chief Magistrate requests that we stay home, we should."

The brothers shared a look.

The Basus and the Iyendars had a history, one not always rosy. Tensions had been high between them ever since it had been revealed that Chief Magistrate Iyendar's granddaughters had been twins—a fact that had not come to light until after one of the girls had passed away. The secrecy meant the Chief Magistrate had had designs for the girls—had been aiming at the same offices as Adhar and Mandip.

The Iyendars were of a lower social standing than the Basus. The secrecy had allowed them to keep the girls out of the political crosshairs, allowed them to prepare the girls in private, allowed them a strategic place and time of their own choosing to appoint them as candidates. It meant no one had tried to interfere with the political leanings of the girls except their own family.

Mandip and Adhar, on the other hand, had been pursued left and right since they were small, by people either wishing to gain their favor, groom them toward certain ideals, or persuade them away from office.

There could still be a bitterness there, in the Chief Magistrate. A callous reason to interfere with the political opportunities of other households. Mandip's parents would never say so. They would never think such things of someone who'd lost a grandchild, no matter the shift in political positioning. But others were far more ruthless than they were.

"Surely, you can tell us if we've been named. Or what kind of threat has been made."

"Unfortunately, I was given few details myself," said the guardsman. "For security reasons, the specifics of the plot are being kept close to the vest. Better to catch the culprit, if they don't know the Watch is on to them."

"Of course," Adhar said, obviously unconvinced.

Mandip cleared his throat. "Ma, forgive me, but are we sure that our best interests are truly—"

Her eyes went wide; she leveled a look at him that made him bite his tongue.

"Mandip is right to ask," Adhar insisted—he was clearly thinking the same thing. "This evening is important. The cocktail hour may be our only chance to speak to some of the dignitaries. We can begin to make inter-city-state alliances outside the family. An opportunity like this—"

"Will come along again," their mother said firmly. "I will not risk your safety."

"We're not *children* anymore," Mandip countered. "How can you expect us to make decisions for all of Lutador if you won't even let us decide—"

"*I'm* not deciding," she snapped. "*We're* not deciding. This is a special order from the Chief Magistrate, and we will obey it. End of discussion. You are dismissed." With that, she turned her back on them.

There was no arguing. When their mother was finished, she was finished.

The brothers bowed, and the steward opened the door for them to leave. Together, they stomped back to their wing.

"This is nonsense," Mandip grumbled as they went. "Tell me you don't think this is nonsense; I dare you. A credible threat to so many families would get the performance postponed or canceled."

"The state has been planning this night for years; it's not so simple," Adhar said.

"And yet surprisingly simple to get us locked away for the night. Political prisoners, that's what we are."

"Don't be so dramatic."

"I'm hardly ever dramatic. I have a right to be once in a while."

"But why over *this*?" Adhar asked lightly. "You've never been a fan of the opera."

"I've never been a special guest of the opera, either. But now that I have a direct invitation from—"

"Yes? Go on. From who?"

"La Maupin."

"Oh." Adhar did a double take, stopped in his tracks before they'd reached the hall that led to their rooms. "*Oh.* Why didn't you tell me? You and—" He lowered his voice, took Mandip conspiratorially by the elbow. "You and Juliet Maupin?"

"Don't sound so surprised. But it's not . . . it's not like that."

"Like what?"

Mandip waved his hand up and down Adhar, indicating his posture, his clandestine tone. "Like we're secretly betrothed or something. I barely know her, just met her. But if it hadn't been for that infuriating man—"

"The one who tried to fleece you? The escort?"

"Yes. He introduced us, in a sense."

Adhar narrowed his gaze at him, and Mandip found the eye contact difficult to maintain. He looked away.

"Oh, so, *she's* not why you're so keen to go, then? Will he be there too? You were spitting mad with him; why . . ."

He hadn't told Adhar everything. He hadn't told him Thibaut had attempted to steal his *watch*. Hadn't told him about the strange press and pull of giddy emotions that had swamped through him that day—how Thibaut had been both absolutely maddening but utterly intriguing at the same time.

Mandip looked back at his brother to see an uncomfortably soft expression had settled over his brow.

"Don't look at me like that." He brushed him off, hurried toward his chamber door. "I'm not going for *him*. I mean, yes, he was invited as well, but it's—it's the Pentaétos. It's just as you said. We, the two of us"—he gestured between himself and Adhar, who was following close behind—"need to make ourselves known to the people of import." He pulled open the door, gestured for his brother to enter first. "And this is our *best chance* to cultivate cross-state relationships before we'll be counted on to uphold them."

Stepping into the antechamber, he undid the top three buttons on his jacket, casting his gaze about the room as though it might provide him with a solution to his predicament.

"*If* we're counted on," Adhar reminded him, making sure the door was securely latched before continuing. "To be honest, I've got my eye on the Chief Magistrate Iyendar's position myself."

That gave Mandip pause. He whirled. "You want to be Chief Magistrate of Justice?"

"Is that so strange?"

"Yes. It's a *singular* position."

"So?" He said it so casually. So flippantly.

But when their gazes met, Mandip could see the depth of seriousness in his eyes. "So? *So?*" he asked incredulously. "We're . . . we're twins. We could be the *Ministers* of Law; we could be—I know we don't like to say it out loud, but we could be the Grand Marquises, so why would—"

"I don't want to rearrange the justice system; I'd just like to . . . I don't know." Adhar leaned heavily against the door, hands behind his back, and let out a heavy sigh. "In truth, I'd rather remain in the Borderswatch."

Mandip gaped. Like many young nobles, Adhar had enrolled in the Borderswatch expecting to gain some military experience and sense of discipline before moving full-time into political life. Rarely were such individuals ever actually deployed during their brief tenures. Adhar had been through basic training, and Mandip knew it would be easy for his brother to rise in the ranks if he prolonged his service, but—"You would leave me for the Borderswatch? You want to camp day in and day out in the wilds of the rim, near the mines? In the dirt and the rain, with nothing but hardtack and sun-dried meats to keep you full? With the, the insects and the wild animals and—and the *varger*. You've never laid a hand on one of those needled guns—whatever they're called. You'd die of exposure within the first week. Then there's the foot sores and the parasites and—The weather; have I mentioned the weather?"

"You did," Adhar chuckled.

"What has gotten into you? You've never mentioned this before. Do not, for the love of the Five, let Ma and Baba hear you talk this way."

"Would you relax? It's just a notion. An idle one at that. I enjoy the structure, the comradery; that's all. Don't worry; I'd never do anything to threaten your chances at the highest seats."

"*Our* chances," he corrected—half-bewildered that he had to.

"Our chances," Adhar agreed. "But seriously, you never think about doing something other than politicking your life away? Never at all?"

"Only when Ignace suggests we clean out the family coffers and invest in a nightingales' roost."

Adhar leveled a glare at him.

"What?" Mandip asked flatly, as though it hadn't been a joke, then added more seriously, "Honestly, some of them make good money and get to be quite free with their time."

"I wasn't under the impression that you'd become a *nightingale* in that scenario," Adhar said, eyebrow shooting up.

"No, I just . . . Sorry, I was just thinking. About my companion for the evening."

"Oh, so, you're *still* paying him. And for"—he made a rude gesture, not unlike the one Thibaut had first made—"at that."

"No. Not exactly."

"Mm-hmm," Adhar said knowingly. "*Not exactly.*"

"It's—It's complicated."

"No judgment on my part," Adhar reassured him. "On you or him. Especially if he's bringing out this side of you." He made a sweeping, illustrative wave up and down Mandip's pacing form.

"What side is that?"

"The disobeying Ma and Baba side."

"I've simply disagreed with them, not disobeyed them."

"Ah. Not yet. But I can see it in your eyes. You're trying to figure out how to escape."

"And you?" Mandip asked. "You're content to stay here when this could be a ploy? One designed to keep us from those highest seats you mentioned?"

"No, not at all. As you said, they're treating us like children."

"So, what are we going to do about it?"

"*We* are going to get *you* out of here," Adhar said definitively, pushing away from the door, crossing the entryway over to the far window.

"Me? Not both of us?"

"Not both of us," Adhar confirmed, glancing at the bushes outside, studying them in the late-day sun. He tested the molding around the window, examined the latches. "One of us needs to stay behind. You know they'll be looking in on us. I'll cover for you."

"Why me?"

Adhar gave him a wry look. "You have a date. *Two* dates, actually. I won't be disappointing anyone if I'm a no-show."

"We should go together. If I'm to mingle with the dignitaries, it should be with you. A united front."

"Sometimes, being a united front means we each play separate roles," Adhar said firmly. "It'll do us no good to go together only to get caught and brought back to the estate. I'll be the lookout, be your alibi. If they want to talk to you, I'll insist you've locked yourself away in the washroom and refuse to speak to anyone. You know they'll believe me. Have you ever snuck out before?"

"No, never. Why?"

Adhar nodded to himself. "As I thought. You've never even aired out your antechamber—these seals are all painted shut. Come, you'll have to leave via my room."

"Wait, are you suggesting *you've* snuck out?"

"Don't look so scandalized. You were the odd child, not me. This will be easier. I can tell you the best route for getting by the guards. Quickly, fill your pockets—anything you think you might require."

Mandip scurried about his rooms, racking his brain for anything he might need and hastily shoving it into a drawstring purse. Extra time vials and disks, a handful of luststones—it was polite to offer them to one's potential partners, after all—and a small atomizer for breath refreshment all went into the purse. He double-checked the security of his pocket watch, then followed his brother into the adjoining wing.

Adhar's rooms were much like his own, though perhaps tidier. Personal touches—even in one's private rooms—were considered uncouth these days, and so all around there was nothing but cold opulence. One would have to examine the contents of drawers and closets to get a sense of the person who lived there.

Often, Mandip felt his relationship with Adhar was just the same. Exceedingly formal on the outside, with plenty of warmth and personal touches—not to mention secrets—hidden beneath the surface.

"You'll need this, of course," Adhar said, striding to a dresser and sliding his hand behind it before retrieving a small something. He handed Mandip a thin, hinged silver case, like those some of the merchant class had started to use to carry their cigarettes.

Mandip popped it open to find a small set of papers—worn at the edges, old, and pressed with the official high-noble seal administered only by the Grand Marquises themselves. A sepia photo of their father—some years out of date—stared up at him. Small, glittering threads of enchanted glass woven into the equally enchanted paper made this kind of identification impossible to fake.

"What? How did you—"

"He's never missed it," Adhar said. Such things should have been kept under lock and key. "Be prepared for the Watch to note it's out of date, though. Be gracious, apologetic, but insistent. Start jovial, shift to demanding if they press you. You know, act like Baba and everything will work out. *Do not lose these.* I'll want them back."

"But as soon as they try to do a match . . . the enchantment, it'll know I'm not Baba."

"Touch it."

The papers knew their owner. That was the whole point. Should anyone who didn't own them set skin to fibers, nothing would happen. Should the proper Lord Basu lay a hand on them, however . . .

Mandip did as his brother directed and was startled to see the paper shimmer and turn green. "*Impossible.*"

"Improbable," Adhar corrected. "A mistake in the enchantment. I noticed these papers reacted to me same as they react to Baba well before they expired, and I simply nicked the set when the court enchanters made his newest ones. None of his others—before or since—have harbored the same imperfection. These recognize a Basu but are flawed enough not to know *which.*"

Mandip stared for a long moment at the green leaves of paper before snapping the cigarette case shut. "How long have you been doing this?" he demanded. "Sneaking out?"

"Do you remember when we were twelve and I told you we should run away for an afternoon but you were too scared?"

"Yes . . ."

"I've done it about once a fortnight since then."

"You have not," Mandip insisted in disbelief.

"I have so," he said, grinning wide.

"You? Mister *military precision* and *duty* and *dignity*?"

"You never did understand. That's precisely why I can get away with so much. When you don't get your way and behave like a petulant child, they *treat you* like a petulant child. On the other hand, prove you are oh so reasonable and responsible to their liking, and you can get away with anything."

"Except throwing away your potential for the Borderswatch," Mandip said. He meant for it to be a tease.

Adhar's smile faltered. "Quite."

16

MANDIP

The downside of crawling out a window in secret instead of confidently striding out the front door was that Mandip couldn't take a carriage from the family estate to the Creek Side Inn. By the time he arrived at the little inn's stoop, his boots were caked in mud and his three-hour lead time had all but dried up.

Mandip was cold and irritated. His clothes were far too fine for the trudge he'd just endured, and any careful attention he'd paid to his perfumes was surely useless now that he was drenched in the scents of the city.

He drew a kerchief from his sleeve to dab at his brow before approaching the doorperson to be graciously let inside.

When he entered, Thibaut was, surprisingly, behind the front desk instead of simply taking up space in the lobby. His face lit up when he saw the lordling, and he hurried to stand before him.

"My, what a picture you make," Thibaut said warmly, either ignoring the signs of Mandip's struggle or simply not noticing them. He fingered the seams on one of the jacket's cuffs. "Juliet will love it, I'm sure."

Mandip glanced around the place, taking in the warm, polished-wood finishings, small stained-glass fairy windows in the molding, and plush furniture. "Do you work here?" he blurted.

"You could say that."

"But I thought you—"

"And you think correctly." He straightened the fit of the jacket across Mandip's shoulders, fiddling with the lay of it as he spoke. "I know this is a strange, unnatural concept to someone of your station, but many people have multiple avenues of employment. We have to make ends meet somehow. And, really, I'm just keeping an eye on the place. For a friend, while he and his wife are away. The inn practically runs itself." He suddenly took Mandip by the chin, looked him in the eye. "Why do you have a harried look about you?"

"It's nothing," he said dismissively, jerking his chin away, taking a step back. "Stop fussing with my clothes. Shouldn't we be on our way?"

perhaps a nefarious reason, but he decided—for his own peace of mind—that he'd rather not dwell on it.

Luckily, before Thibaut could compose an explanation, Mandip's gaze fell to a bit of green finery hanging right next to the healer's smock. "What about this one?" he asked, pulling the outfit from its nesting. "You said you didn't have anything grand. Velvet, double-breasted, slim-fitted, military cut. And look at this gold embroidery." Gently, he trailed his fingertips over the perfect stitching.

"That's old," Thibaut said dismissively.

"Almost old enough to be considered vintage and therefore quite posh," Mandip insisted. "The coat's tail would just about hit you in the same place as the hem of my sherwani hits me."

"But it's so . . . green."

"To match your gloves."

Thibaut went still, quiet. "Yes. To match them, exactly."

Mandip paused, taking in the stiff line of Thibaut's shoulders, the way he wasn't looking at either Mandip or the ensemble. "This one is special, isn't it?" he asked carefully.

Thibaut crossed to Mandip in a few stiff strides and took the hanger from him, sliding his palm down the crushed-velvet collar. "I wore it once. An age ago."

Mandip chuckled softly. "You speak of it like a widow would a wedding dress," he said, intending a tease.

Thibaut turned sad eyes on him. The young lord quickly realized his mistake.

"Oh. Oh, monsieur, forgive me, I didn't—"

"Just the right shade of green to really offset the aqua of joystones."

"I'll put it back; I'm sorry."

Thibaut pulled it to his chest. "No. You're right; it's perfect. I should wear it this evening."

"You don't have to. The tan ensemble is fine, really—"

But Thibaut was already pulling off his innkeeper's clothes—unbuttoning his cuffs, shrugging out of his jacket.

He produced that same box Mandip had seen him with before—the one meant for a necklace that contained a weapon instead—and tucked it straight away into the green jacket's inner pocket. "Haven't run into my friend yet," Thibaut explained when he caught him looking. "Don't misunderstand; this is a fine establishment, but there are still valuables one should keep quite literally close to the vest while surrounded by people just passing through."

There was no changing screen in the room, so Mandip simply turned his back as Thibaut continued to strip down further, feeling an extra bit of shame since this was twice now it seemed he'd made Thibaut remove his clothes under duress. He held himself stiffly as he looked into one corner of the papered wall; its design was subtle, a vine pattern just a few shades off from the creamy background.

It was Thibaut's turn to laugh lightly. "Always the gentleman," he said to himself.

Once he was dressed—including a sleek green velvet top hat he let sit slightly askew on his brow, like a proper cad—they hurried once more to the ground floor.

They did make quite the pair, Mandip thought. He hoped it would bring a sparkle to Juliet's eye.

"Where's your footman, then?" Thibaut asked as they strode into the lobby.

"No footman."

"Who's to see us into the carriage, then?"

"I haven't got a carriage."

"A lord without a carriage? Next you'll be telling me you haven't got a manor, and oh yes, you're not a Basu after all. How are we to get to the palace, then? Surely, they won't simply let us in if we stride up to the gates just as we are."

"You have no transportation of your own?"

"Milor, the man who *owns* this establishment couldn't afford his own carriage; what in all the Valley makes you think an escort such as myself would have one?"

"Well, whatever are we to do, then?"

Thibaut opened the front door and waved Mandip forward. "When one of my station wants to appear especially posh," he explained as the lordling brushed past, "we rent."

"Well, that sounds *horrid*."

"Says the man who walked here through what appears to be a trough of mud."

"What?" Mandip glanced down but was relieved to find his footwear no more splattered than he remembered. "It's not that bad—"

"Why is it no one of a higher station seems to have the slightest idea when they're being teased?" Thibaut asked, briskly following Mandip out onto the street.

"Teasing, in my experience, is most often hostile."

"I assure you I tease out of nothing but fondness."

The pair was about to turn and walk up the thoroughfare, toward a carriage house Thibaut was familiar with, when the doorman stopped them. "Pardon, messieurs, but your transportation has arrived." He waved to a nearby deep-black brougham carriage, whose horse was tilting its head and lightly stamping at the cobblestones, as though eager to be in motion.

"I didn't order a carriage, Philip," Thibaut insisted. "Are you sure it's not for a patron?"

"No, monsieur. The driver has just given me this." He produced an envelope. "It's addressed to you."

Indeed, it had a bright pink seal depicting a pine tree, and his name had been scrawled in huge, looping letters across the front.

Mandip stood back, intent on giving the man his privacy, but Thibaut turned toward the lordling as he slipped a gloved finger under the wax, clearly expecting to share its contents. The letter was not perfumed, and the paper's color was not audacious. It read simply:

My new dearest friend,

    I've heard news of poor Lord Basu's detainment. As he will not be joining us this evening, and seeing as how you've lost your escort to the palace, I've sent for you myself. I trust you are not the kind of individual who would consider such a gesture too forward or presumptuous.

Yours sincerely,

La Maupin

"You've been detained, have you?" Thibaut asked, raising an eyebrow.

"Delayed," Mandip said quickly. "On account of my carriage. It . . . The wheel . . . A spoke—"

"When a person such as Juliet says *detainment*, she means *detainment*," Thibaut interrupted.

"Yes, all right, fine. For some strange reason, the Watch has declared that my brother and I are not to set foot on the palace grounds this evening."

"And you decided to go anyway? So driven, in fact, as to come here on foot?"

"Yes."

"I don't know whether to be impressed by your gumption—which, if I may be frank, I didn't think you possessed much of—or incensed that you neglected to mention this . . . this *hiccup*. You must realize that as soon as palace security gets sight of you, they'll haul you right back home and we'll never so much as do more than glimpse the roof of the Rotunda over the wall. How exactly did you imagine we'd get inside?"

"I have my ways. I'll pass as my father."

"Oh, you will, will you?" Thibaut asked skeptically. "Looking all of a young sapling, as you do?"

"Enchantment will *confirm* I am my father," he countered.

"Perhaps, but not half so much as your face will confirm *you are not*."

"You don't understand; the palace runs on magic. Enchantment is to be trusted above something so fallible as one's eyes."

"And what happens when we run into a group of your peers and they start openly bandying about with your given name?"

"Well, what do you suggest, then?"

"You saw my wardrobe. Don't pretend you didn't."

"Yes, so?"

"With a bit of false facial hair and a little makeup work around the eyes, we might be able to pass you off as a man of advancing age. Might. Still, probably best if we keep you hidden for as long as possible. Avoid as many probing questions as we can. Lucky for you," Thibaut continued, "as I've been called for by La Maupin herself, it will be easy for me to slip past at least the first few checkpoints without a noble escort."

Mandip's eyes snapped to the carriage, small as it was—meant for two at *most*. Yes, it was not so open as a buggy, but it could hardly be said there was sufficient room for *hiding*. "And where exactly—"

"You'll have to get down on the floor," Thibaut said, then added slyly, "on your knees."

Mandip scowled. "Between your legs, I suppose?" he asked indignantly.

"You said it, milor, not me," Thibaut replied with a wink. "Wait for me in the carriage," he said, turning back toward the inn with a triumphant air about him. "We'll make a true sneak thief of you yet."

17

THALO CHILD

Less Than Two Years Ago

"Nose," Thalo Child said, poking his child lightly on the tip of zhur little button nose.

Zhe giggled raucously, giving him a mostly toothless smile.

He was in the dormitory, which he still shared with the members of his co-hort, getting his infant ready for bed. These days, zhe slept in a bassinet at the foot of his cot and usually dozed peaceably for at least a few hours if he played such a game with zhur before settling down himself.

"Ears," he said, pulling on the tips of zhurs.

Zhe covered zhur eyes with zhur pudgy brown hands, as though pleasantly embarrassed.

He wound a finger in one of zhur soft, black baby curls. "Hair."

Zhe rarely attempted to parrot the words back, but zhur eyes shone with recognition and calculation. He had no idea how old zhe was, exactly, but he guessed perhaps a year now.

There were very specific words zhe liked and used often, and as zhe lifted zhur head to smile at him again, he could see one poised inside zhur chubby cheeks.

"Up," zhe demanded, lifting zhur arms.

"Time for sleep now," he said, shaking his head.

Zhe frowned. "Up," zhe said, with more insistence in zhur tiny voice.

A small tremor of fear went through Thalo Child, as it always did when his babe did not behave.

It was an infant's prerogative; not understanding meant not adhering to the rules. But Thalo Child *did* understand: Gerome only allowed zhim to sleep in the dormitory instead of the nursery because Thalo Child had promised zhe wouldn't disturb the others. Whenever zhe woke up crying or became demand-ing before bed, he feared zhe would be taken away.

There was nothing wrong with the nursery. The Thalo Ones who looked after the babies had an adjoining dormitory, and he had no doubt they would attend to his infant just as readily as their own—and yet their babes would always take priority. If their arms were all occupied with their own charges, zhe would be left alone, without comfort or succor. Those early months, when zhe had slept there, Thalo Child himself had gotten little sleep, picturing zhim awake and distressed and alone.

"Time for sleep now," he said firmly, and this time zhe simply yawned and lowered zhur little arms, acquiescing without protest.

Thalo Child let out a deep breath of relief.

All around them, the others of his cohort readied themselves for bed, some chatting, most nearly asleep on their feet. But none of them acknowledged him. Even those he'd been close to before Hintosep had given him a baby rarely spoke to him these days.

He felt both revered and like a pariah. The others acknowledged the importance of this responsibility, given to one so young, but they did not understand it or want it, and it was as though they thought acknowledging the baby or his caregiving might result in a sudden bouncing burden of their own.

In truth, besides his babe, he felt alone these days. Where he'd known his place in the order before, been comfortable in it, now he felt like an outsider. His feelings on the matter were conflicted, muddled. He was proud, and afraid, and lonely, but never alone. He loved his infant, and Gerome, and Hintosep, but resented all of them for driving a wedge between him and the other Nameless his age.

His was a place of uncertainty and opportunity. And as much as he craved it, sometimes he didn't want any of it at all.

>–I–◆>–O–◆–I–◁

Thalo Child was awoken in the middle of the night. Not by the cries of his charge but by firm fingers grasping him about his biceps and pulling him from his bed. He was startled—sudden terror swelled in his chest—but he did not fight. There was nothing to fight in the keep. Nothing but his own misgivings, his own shortcomings.

His instincts told him it was likely Gerome even before the enchanted light globe dangling from a strap around the person's neck shifted and threw their features into stark relief from below.

Instead of his Possessor, there was Hintosep, dressed for an excursion in the wilds, with a fur collar over her blue armor and a long cape sweeping down behind her. Her white hair was braided in a tight crown around her head, adding a regal frame to her face.

"Up, Child. Come with me."

He pushed himself away from his pillow, obediently got to his feet, despite still being woozy with sleep. Knowing better than to ask where they were going, he only spared a glance for his babe sleeping soundly in the stone bassinet at the foot of his bunk. All around him, members of his cohort snored or tossed restlessly.

"The young one will be fine while we're gone."

"But what if . . . if zhe wakes up and cries? Disturbs the others?"

Hintosep shifted toward the bassinet and waved her hand over the sleeping babe. "Zhe will not wake until you return," she said warmly, turning quickly and striding out of the dormitory.

Thalo Child wanted to ask what she had done—how she could be so sure—but he feared reprisal. It was not yet clear why he'd been roused at such an hour; if it was in punishment, he didn't want to make his circumstances worse, and if it was in reward, he feared having it taken away.

Luckily, as his small strides fell into step behind Hintosep's much-longer ones, she took pity on his ignorance. "I took the secret of wakefulness from zhim. Your babe is too small to understand such a thing, too young for even their body to fully grasp it—the very concept of living is still full of secrets and wonders."

"Why do the eldest children not do the same for their babes?"

She glanced over her shoulder, her steps never faltering. "It's dangerous," she said frankly. "The manipulation of autonomic secrets is far too advanced to be used by those who have not fully Become. Should one of them try it on an infant, the babe may never wake again. Such skills are typically only applied when bringing a new babe into our fold. While transporting them to the keep."

From outside. From beyond. From wherever the keep's babies came from.

"Zhur restfulness is a special gift I give the both of you tonight," she said. "But I would not dare take such secrets from zhim often."

He nodded his understanding and continued to follow, pulling his thin sleeping robes tight around his body. The halls were dark, of course. Nearly pitch-black. But Hintosep made no attempt to light the way with anything more than the pendant dangling from her neck. Thus, Thalo Child kept close, shying away from the shadows and the deep, yawing blackness of branching, echoing halls.

When they reached a familiar staircase, he realized where they must be headed: the antiquarium. What an unusual thing, to visit a library in the middle of the night. It was open to all Thalo during waking hours, after all. He and his cohort had been led there often, and left for hours on their own with instructions simply to read—*read read read.*

At the base of the staircase, Hintosep paused, whirling, holding up her light pendant to peer into the darkness behind them. As though she feared they were being followed.

She stood there for only a few moments, but the darkness made time feel dense and stretched. Thalo Child held his breath, as though one puff of steam from his throat might awaken whatever had made the great Hintosep so wary.

When she lowered the light, seemingly satisfied, he expected her to once again lead, but she waited for him to stride on. Gestured up the stairs for him to go.

That first step in front was uncomfortable. And the next no better. He was made to follow. He always followed a Thalo of a higher station. Always. His shoulders and jaw tightened, and his spine tingled with the *wrongness* of their order.

If Hintosep noticed his unease, she made no indication.

"Why are we going to the antiquarium?" he ventured.

"I need all the scrolls we have on varger," she said, her voice lowered, now barely a whisper.

"V-varger?" A cold tingling ran up his spine and across his scalp. "What for?"

She said nothing, and he let it go. It wasn't his place to know her mind.

Thalo Child had no more than glimpsed Hintosep that first time, before she'd decided to put him in charge of a baby, and it still bothered him—why she'd taken a special interest in *him*, specifically. Perhaps it had been a random choice and not some underlying clue to his true name—to whichever powerful Thalo he might have been in a past life.

But now she'd returned, seeking him again, specifically, for a different task.

Though their footfalls were quiet as they maneuvered through the palace, each one seemed to call out to Thalo Child, echoing a question: *why, why, why?*

He could not ask. Not now, not ever. Not unless he became a Possessor or a Guardian and could match her in authority.

He did not need to glance back to be sure she was keeping close. He could sense her eyes on him, gaze steely. He felt like she could see everything and he could see nothing. Her stare could strip him down to the bone, and he would never have more than an imaginary notion of what might lay behind her eyes.

Perhaps *match* had been the wrong word. No one could ever be her match—in authority or otherwise.

When they reached the antiquarium—its entrance blocked by a wall of faceted clear crystal, revealing the illuminated, blocky rows of tall bookshelves inside—Hintosep moved in front of him, tossed the edge of her cloak aside, rolled up her sleeve, and pulled a bluish-metal pin from a shunt imbedded in her forearm. She inserted it in a nearly invisible lock and twisted, until the magical mechanisms inside the door began to trip and twirl, sending sharp fractures of light and glimpses of rainbows into the hall, despite the low light.

Hintosep put a hand out behind her, gesturing for Thalo Child to take a step back, because this door did not open.

It *melted*.

Starting at the ceiling, the wall dissolved, first running like a fluid curtain—a small waterfall—then evaporating entirely.

The scent of salt filled the corridor.

When every last bit of the sodium crystal was gone, Hintosep stepped through and Thalo Child quickly followed. She paused only to insert the same key in a small crystal dais near the entrance, and the entire process reversed itself, the door coalescing, flowing upward, not so much condensing but un-evaporating, the entire event running backward.

All Thalo, even the very young, were familiar with the antiquarium. It was the home of all scrolls and books in the keep. But no matter how many times Thalo Child witnessed the grandeur of this particular door, he was still fascinated.

It relied on magics he didn't understand. Elements he'd only heard mention of.

Time, nature, and Thalo magic all wound together to make a door that made and unmade itself . . . with the insertion of the right key. He didn't know what would happen if someone inserted the wrong key, but he knew it was *something*. Something bad. The sodium would transmute into some other dangerous form.

At eight years old, he'd asked Gerome why the antiquarium required such a special door. His Possessor had gathered the entire cohort around to listen to the answer.

"There is information here that only the Thalo can comprehend," he'd explained. "Information that could destroy villages and topple their little would-be empires. Knowledge is power, and those who don't know how to apply it must not have it.

"Everything we do is about protection. Everything. If you ever doubt, trust in the Savior. Trust that He has built this land well. Trust that these dealings are well thought out. Trust in these doors, these walls, these measures. You are allowed this information because you can be trusted with it, because you trust *in* it."

Now he trusted in Hintosep, keeping close on her heels as she strode confidently through the tall rows of shelves.

The antiquarium was one large hall, built in the likeness of a horn; the salt-wall entrance was the sharp point, and from there it grew outward, from one story to two to three to four to five. In the back wall was a towering fissure, a concave nook housing the most precious thing in all the keep. The one object every Thalo in existence would die to protect.

Thalo Child glanced up, up, *up* along the angled ceiling, following its mosaic tiles that mirrored the stars, until he glimpsed the top of the mighty casing that held the object in place.

A dark metal cap, spiked and filigreed, clamped over the top of a giant, egg-shaped opal, the glint of it just barely visible past the tops of the tall shelves in Thalo Child's path. Chains of the same metal suspended the cap—held it in place—as did answering chains on its opposite end. They suspended the impossible stone—which nearly filled the whole of the five-story crevasse—keeping it from touching the floor or the ceiling or the wall.

The opal was impressive, to be sure. But it was what lay *inside* the stone that he would set down his life for, if it was asked of him.

A corpse.

Larger than a human—twenty feet tall and three times as broad as any man. With a face like an empty hole. A deep pit.

Thalo Child shivered and looked away, despite not having glimpsed the strange face itself, focusing on the fluttering hem of Hintosep's cape instead.

Still, he knew what lay back there, could picture it precisely. He was forced to see it in all its glory exactly once a year during the Introdus celebration.

It was their most sacred relic.

The body of a god.

For now, he tried to ignore its looming presence, as he always did when brought here to study.

Hintosep suddenly called for the late-night antiquarians, her voice ringing clear across the vast space. Unnaturally loud for the hour.

Three Thalo and two Mindful swiftly came to their aid, obviously having dropped whatever they were doing to see to the former Possessor's needs. She held out her hand, palm up, for one of the antiquarians to take.

The antiquarian hesitated, blinking at her from behind their glasses, clearly understanding what she wanted but very uncomfortable. She flexed her fingers impatiently when they didn't immediately comply.

With a resigned frown, they took her hand and the hand of the antiquarian next to them, who took the hand of the antiquarian next to her, and so on, until all five of them had formed a chain with Hintosep.

Thalo Child watched closely, suspecting but untimely unsure of what was happening. Hintosep said nothing—or, at least, nothing Thalo Child could hear, and her lips did not move. After a few moments, all five workers started to look dreamy, with a far-off gleam in their eyes. Soon, the first antiquarian released Hintosep's hand, but not the others', and led the group away. Out.

They left the antiquarium entirely.

Thalo Child and Hintosep were alone.

He barely stopped himself from asking *Why did you do that?*

It was obvious she desired secrecy, but she did not owe him her reasons.

"This way," she bade him. "We must be thorough. You will look for all mention of varger appearances. Not just encounters—*appearances.*"

"I'm not sure I understand," he said apologetically, heart sinking with the weight of her anticipated disappointment.

But she did not snap at him the way Gerome would have.

"Varger are the only creatures from beyond the Valley that can breach the god-created borders, correct?" she asked.

"Yes."

"How do we know that?"

It felt like a trick question. "Um . . . we've seen them come through? Someone has seen them, I mean." *He'd* never seen more than a painted varg in an illuminated manuscript.

"Have they, though?" she challenged. "Seen it?"

He wasn't sure whether to keep his thoughts on the matter to himself or to press the conversation for clarity's sake. He tried his luck. "Are you . . . Do you . . . I mean . . ."

"Go on," she encouraged, glancing down one row of shelves before shaking her head and moving on.

"If no one's ever seen it, are you suggesting that maybe they *don't* come through the border?"

She said nothing.

The very idea made his throat go tight. He'd never seen one, but that didn't mean he hadn't heard the stories, hadn't been right there to grieve with the others when one of the Guardians had been torn apart—her belly eaten out—last spring.

"Where *else* would they come from?" he asked. "There's more and more of them all the time, and they don't breed in the Valley, right? There aren't any pups or cubs or whatever we'd call them . . . right?"

"Correct," she confirmed, taking an abrupt turn to her left, swooping down a row, forcing Thalo Child to pivot sharply and swing his arms to redirect his momentum. "No pups."

"So, then where would they come from if not outside the Valley?"

"I have my suspicions," she said cryptically, "I've noticed a correlation. Between varger numbers and . . ." She trailed off, scrunching her nose thoughtfully as she scanned the shelf. "Ah-ha," she said lightly, tugging down a book, then another, then a set of scrolls. She handed each to Thalo Child, and soon his arms were weighed down with tome after tome about varger.

"Varger numbers and . . ." he ventured.

"And people numbers," she said frankly.

"I don't understand."

"Neither do I," she admitted. "That's why we're here."

18

MANDIP

Mandip did, in fact, spend half of the carriage ride hunkered down on the floor between Thibaut's knees, hiding. A place he wouldn't have begrudged so much if the other man hadn't spent the entire ride looking *so very smug*.

"There's a story here, and I'll get it out of you," Thibaut insisted, propping his elbows on his spread knees and, in turn, his head in one hand to peer down at the young lord crouched low.

Looking up—batting aside strands of the long, dark wig laced through with silver at the temples, which Thibaut had provided—Mandip found their faces far too close for propriety. He was in no mood for this kind of teasing flirtation, or being interrogated—largely because all he really knew was that there was some supposed "great threat to his personage" at the palace, which was ridiculous because—despite what Adhar had said—if that were truly so, then the proceedings would have been moved or perhaps put off a night.

Wouldn't they?

His sudden frown tugged uncomfortably at the false facial hair around his lips—a styled mustache and a simple goatee—and he could feel the makeup caking in the creases around his eyes where Thibaut had given him false age lines.

The styling of his disguise was nothing like his father's in the official photo, but hopefully the family resemblance and faulty enchantment would be enough to pass.

"I'm much more interested in Juliet's story," he replied. Not entirely truthfully, as Juliet's story was quite public and he'd never been much for the opera, but knowing of *Thibaut's* interest in her, it worked as a deft deflection nonetheless. "And she seemed rather interested in yours as well," he added suggestively.

With a sigh, Thibaut sat back, melting into the stiff seat cushions as though the air had been squeezed from him. "I very much doubt La Maupin's interest in my tale is idle, academic, *or* romantic," he said thoughtfully, a little disappointedly, before adding, "Which means she has *reasons*. I do *like* reasons—there's often blackmail or time vials in them."

"You have absolutely no interest in blackmailing that woman," Mandip countered. "And she's an artist, which means she has patrons, not wealth. There's a difference."

"Ye of little imagination," Thibaut said dismissively, waving his hand through the air, brushing away the conversation.

When they reached the first checkpoint, Mandip ducked his head, hiding his face against the inside of Thibaut's knee, as though he were a small child who believed that if he could not see someone else, then they could not see him. Thibaut, clearly sensing his nerves, took pity on him and dropped a soothing hand into the wig, petting lightly—comfortingly—as he turned his attention to the guard.

The guard who'd just demanded the driver prove he was in La Maupin's service.

A set of Watchpersons trudged up and down the road, examining the coach, poking at its undercarriage and the like, but never mounting the step to peer through the window directly. One asked Thibaut for his invitation, and he smoothly produced the letter, making no indication he was anything but alone in the cab.

"Everything is in order," they eventually announced, handing back the papers. "You may proceed. Know that you will be divested of any and all suspicious or enchanted accoutrements when you alight at the Rotunda, and you may be pressed for a strip search."

"Oh, luckily, I've had one of those lately. At least I know what I'm in for," Thibaut mumbled.

Mandip had no way of knowing what kind of reaction the Watchperson had had to the cheeky statement, nor if they'd actually heard Thibaut at all, and yet his cheeks burned with embarrassment. Thibaut had made him a fool twice over—if not *thrice* over—with that watch business.

Instinctually, his hand fell to his pocket now, where he was sure it was properly stowed.

The carriage jerked forward, and Mandip found himself jolted rather unceremoniously into the apex of Thibaut's velvet-covered thighs. He quickly reeled back, mortified.

Thibaut simply grinned down at him before letting out a hearty laugh and reaching forward to press at the edges of Mandip's new false mustache and goatee, to be sure everything stuck fast. "You know, your virtue—no matter the state of it—really is quite safe with me," he insisted. "I'm here for *your* entertainment, not the other way around."

This was what both attracted and befuddled Mandip. He was unquestionably drawn to Thibaut, but he'd never felt so wrong-footed in the presence of another human being in all his life.

Several checkpoints later, Mandip realized that if his life really were in danger, the Watch was doing a piss-poor job of defending it. Only one of them had bothered to actually yank open the door of the carriage, and he and Thibaut had each put on a good show respectively, with Mandip wiping his mouth and Thibaut hastily pretending to fix up his trousers. The guard chuckled and promptly slammed the door shut again, waving them on without so much as inquiring after Mandip's name.

"A tawdry dalliance is almost as good a disguise as all that false hair you've got on," Thibaut said as the driver nickered at the horse.

It was at the outer gates to the palace proper where Mandip knew hiding would no longer prove a safe strategy. He shoved himself onto the seat beside Thibaut, unconsciously fiddling with his goatee until Thibaut batted his hand away from his face. "Stop that. You said it yourself; the enchantment is more trustworthy than their own eyes—as long as their eyes don't trip up because your mustache has fallen askew."

"Why *do* you have so many . . . costumes?" Mandip asked.

"Would you believe me an actor?" Thibaut asked, faux innocence thick in his voice and written unconvincingly in his overly wide eyes and pursed lips.

"Not the stage kind, no."

The carriage ride grew smoother as they drew nearer to the palace—the road that much better maintained than anywhere else in the city. When they reached the tall, gilded gates, Regulators with scanning spheres swept their carriage, and all weapons and most enchantments were relinquished.

Mandip stiffened when he was asked to take out his pocket watch. The scanning spheres, he knew, could not detect the related metals imbedded on his person, but the watch . . . if they attempted to take it—

But the Regulator he reluctantly handed it to handed it back after only a few moments. "This is a tethered item," they said in low, almost conspiratorial tones.

They knew it denoted his importance.

"It is," he confirmed, doing his best to project an air of certainty and confidence. Like his father.

"Please take extra caution with it tonight."

"I will."

The Regulators continued their search, and Thibaut openly laughed when they made Mandip hand over his small pouch of luststones. "I didn't think one so young as you would need such aids," he said.

Where a few days before, Mandip might have blushed, here he grinned openly, sharing in the witticism. He was beginning to understand when Thibaut was joking with him and when he'd become the joke.

"Everything else about nobility is disingenuous," Thibaut muttered. "Why not your emotions as well?"

"That's unfair," Mandip countered as the carriage drove on, though he wondered, truly, if it was.

"And if I'd offered you herbs instead?"

Mandip wrinkled his nose.

"Exactly. There are herbs that can change one's mood as well. Plants you can burn, minerals you can digest. Common in places like the Dregs but illegal. Considered immoral and a disgrace to society. Oh, but emotion stones, those are posh, now, aren't they? Clean. More importantly, *expensive*. Those are the *proper* way to alter one's mood, aren't they? By experiencing the extracted feelings of others and wearing them in showy finery—rings, necklaces, brooches, et cetera."

"What's your point?"

"That it's one more irony, one more hypocrisy. People are not so different, no matter their stations, but nobles do consider themselves so, so superior. And for the oddest reasons."

"The difference is safety and civility," Mandip countered, hating how much he actually sounded like his father in the moment. "The stones, they can be put away and the wearer returned to their natural state without any undue strain, whereas the plants and minerals make one sick and a layabout."

"Never mind there are plenty of nobles I've never seen without emotion stones. As though magic cannot create dependency and sickness. Please."

Mandip shifted uncomfortably on his seat and looked out the window, away from Thibaut. "I'm sorry to have offended you so."

Thibaut let out a put-upon sigh. "It's not the stones I object to."

"No?" Mandip asked, whipping back around to glare at him. "Could have fooled me."

"It's that two things so similar can be given such different moral weight. Such different stories. Street drugs are a social stain, lab-made stones a petty delight."

"I had no idea you were so civic-minded," Mandip said, trying not to sound condescending. In truth, he'd never looked at this particular topic from Thibaut's angle before, hadn't thought about it that way. The substance-dependent poor ended up in the mines or work camps or the Dregs, usually against their will. The magic-dependent nobles were quietly secreted away in their mansions, perhaps equally against their will, but there was no debating their luxury and excessive enchantment use continued. And if their magic abuse was discovered? They were pitied, not ridiculed. Applauded for attempting recovery, not shoved aside to work off their shame.

Thibaut seemed taken aback. "I'm . . . I'm not. Usually."

"But you speak of the plight as though you've given it great thought. The differences—or similarities, if you will—between the problems of various social circles."

"I have my reasons for comparison, nothing more."

For the first time, Mandip felt like he had the upper hand in the conversation. "Enlighten me."

Something in the other man seemed to harden then, all the tease fell from his voice, and a long-standing hurt was suddenly left bare. "What would you say if you discovered a Dreg among your people at the palace? Touching your finery and eating your food?"

"I don't see how they would make it past the sentries . . ." Mandip said flippantly.

"You sidestep my point," Thibaut groused.

"I'm sure they'd be thrown out in an instant," Mandip said. "Is that what you want to hear? That we'd all be appalled and fall onto the nearest fainting couch, our delicate sensibilities so offended as to send us into a tizzy?"

"You don't care about those people enough to be thrown into a tizzy," Thibaut countered. "You care enough to curl a lip in disdain and have the guards do the dirty work of removing them from your presence. But what if they'd been invited?"

Mandip scoffed.

"Is it really so far-fetched?" Thibaut asked, a slight pang in his tone. "That one of the people you lot have seen fit to throw away might be escorted into your company?"

"Where would I, for instance, meet a Dreg in order to invite them in the first place?"

Thibaut frowned, fell silent. He propped his elbow up in the window and said no more.

Up the winding gravel drive, through groves of ornamental fruit trees, and between the walls of the miniature version of Lutador (about a dozen or so petite buildings that resembled the city's most famous landmarks)—which served as a play-village for the Grand Marquises' children—brought them to the guest entrance on the east side of the sprawling estate. Here the drive was lined with tall gas lamps, and since the sun was just dipping below the Valley rim, they slowly came alight.

This portion of the palace had been renovated recently to match the art and architecture styles in vogue these days, with beautiful, branching swirls, an organic asymmetry, and brilliant panes of stained glass in grape and cranberry colors, which offset beautifully against the gold and white-granite façade.

"Why so morose?" Mandip pressed his companion as they approached the Rotunda. "I thought I was supposed to be the uppity one."

"Oh, I'm sorry, am I failing to entertain?" he asked sarcastically. "Forgive me if the mask drops once in a while. I've become less adept at continuously play-acting in my advanced years."

Drawing closer to the Rotunda meant encountering more nobles walking through the grounds, dressed in all of their theater-appropriate fineries.

Thibaut continued to throw his attention out the carriage window instead of directly at Mandip, observing the counts, countesses, countexes, and the like with a sort of glum fascination. "You all laugh at my amusing stories, gawk at the outlandish ones, but would never entertain something that isn't . . . entertaining," he mumbled. "*I* cannot talk policy or current events with them—they'd pretend they didn't hear, or change the subject, or laugh as though it were another joke before waving it aside like so much pipe smoke. I am allowed among you so long as I remain pleasant, guarded—the embodiment of frivolous frivolity. The moment I reveal an earnest bone in my body, the illusion is shattered. Sincerity and concern have no place in my *place*."

Before Mandip could even begin to form a counterargument, Thibaut waved out of the carriage at the Rotunda itself.

"You want to know my weasliest thoughts, your lordship?" he asked Mandip. "What really eats at me when I'm home, alone, where I belong? Away from such grandeur? Something so magnificent as this theater could never be built without excess, without the hoarding of resources, wealth, and respectability. Which is a crime against humanity. And yet, to have such a thing never exist would be a crime against the gods—its beauty, its splendor, all reflect the glory of this sanctuary, the Valley. And yet further still, did the gods not give the Valley to humanity in equal measure? The scrolls say so.

"How can one building be a monument to the gods—a wonder—and somehow blasphemous and grotesque in its sprawl, all at the same time?"

"I . . ." Mandip was at a loss. Thibaut blew hot and cold in a way he hadn't expected. This was no flirtation, but a dissecting, clawing sort of *sneer* at the wealth distribution of the lands.

Something he'd never received from a man in his employ before. He'd encountered it as a topic for the jawing young nobles to titter over in their tea-and-salt houses—or in the preparation tent before a dueling exhibition, of course—but never as something so serious as Thibaut made it out to be. As though it should be seen as something greater than a relativistic intellectual exercise.

As the carriage stopped and a footman approached, suddenly Thibaut deflated. "And yet I chase after all this just the same. Just as a pet hamster can be aware of the wheel and spin it just the same. I'm sorry; we're here for La Maupin. I beg you to forget my tedious outburst."

"Of course," Mandip said quickly, still trying to process what Thibaut had said. Still trying to figure out what had spurred the spiteful discussion in the first place.

The carriage door creaked as the footman opened it, bowing low. Mandip was allowed to set one foot on the step before two palace guards came sweeping forward, halting the lordling in his tracks.

At first, he thought the jig was up—they'd come at him with such urgency, he was sure they'd seen him for the imposter he was—but then he noticed who had arrived in the carriages right after them: the diplomatic delegation from Xyopar.

Two dozen people poured from the cabs, all dressed in Xyoparian finery, topped with shawls and coats made locally in Lutador. The desert nation was a place of fierce daytime heat and cool-to-frigid nights, and the region's styles were often layered to accommodate the shift.

A large, towering person stepped from the lead carriage, head wrapped in a beautiful, swirling ichafu of bright tangerine, with a masculine isiagu, sweeping skirt, and heavy beaded jewelry to match.

Mandip pulled up short and had to stop himself from staring.

This was Xyopar's Eze—their living head of state who typically deigned to stay home and watch over the city-state's ruling ancestors rather than make the trek northward. It was well known zhe kept to zhimself, and it had been assumed zhe would send an envoy in zhur stead.

The *Eze* of *Xyopar* was here tonight, and Mandip and Adhar had been shut out of the event? This would have been their first opportunity to make inroads as Lutador's potential next Grand Marquises, could have been his first direct contact with the highest leader of another city-state, but instead—

No one could properly introduce him to the Eze. And he certainly wasn't about to approach zhim wearing a false mustache.

Two small boys, sans shirts but in waist-hiding wraps, scurried in front of the Eze, spraying a fruit-and-flower perfume, and Mandip was reminded once more of the unseasonably warm and humid weather.

What he wouldn't *give* to run around so bare. But such scandalous attire would never be acceptable for one such as him at an event such as this. The citizens of Xyopar had more freedom of dress—and what thin clothes these children wore were *fine*. Expensive. Xyopar was a deep bastion of fashion and did not care for regimented personal presentations.

Perhaps that had to do with the fact that their patron god was Emotion, and thus they highly valued expressiveness and emotional personification.

Which was the exact opposite of Winsrouen—whose delegation Mandip could not see anywhere, though he strained to peek past the Rotunda's doors.

Though Winsrouen's patron god was Nature—the very embodiment of evolution and malleability—they were the most rigid in dress and presentation, all blacks with the merest hints of gold and nothing more. Their society was the most uniform, the most regimented in all aspects of life. It was as though they saw the facets of their patron god as something precious and rare, too divine to be trifled with.

Flanking the Eze were loan-guards—Sublime Protectors—part of a custom that helped preserve peace and trust among the city-states. As the leaders of each nation passed through another, they were loaned a guard of that city-state's highest caliber. Thus, as the Xyopar delegation had traveled northward, the Eze had acquired a guard from Winsrouen, a guard from Asgar-Skan, and a guard from Lutador to match their own. If the Eze had traveled all the way to Marrakev, they would have had the complete set of Sublime Protectors.

Of course, as Mandip watched, he observed the Sublime Protectors eyeing each other more than the crowd. It seemed Asgar-Skan and Xyopar's Protectors were united in their scowling at Winsrouen's—sizing him up as though he could turn on them at any moment. In turn, he appeared to grit his teeth as one unduly scrutinized.

The Sublime Protector from Lutador seemed to be the only one more concerned with the Eze than their fellow guards.

The rumors of rising conflict were not rumors, then. The tradition of Sublime Protectors was old and sacred. If the Protectors themselves carried such tension with them, then relations between their city-states were much more strained than certain nobles would have had Mandip believe.

Was that one more piece of information that had been subtly wielded against him and Adhar? If they did not know the depth and breadth of such important foreign goings-on, then they could not be considered fit to lead.

A deep pang of political envy hit him when he saw Contessa Agea come sweeping through the Rotunda doors to greet the Eze as though zhe was an old friend. A few years older than Adhar and Mandip, she and her identical twin still had high aspirations for the ultimate office, even though they were considered outside of the appropriate age range to replace the current aging Grand Marquises.

"I don't think there's any threat here," he whispered to Thibaut, "except, perhaps, to my political career."

"How sad for you, to have your ambitions threatened rather than something so inconsequential as your *bodily integrity*."

"Your sarcasm isn't subtle."

"Is it supposed to be?"

Inside the doors, a single Regulator met the delegation, imposing with their large helm and black cloak. They too held a scanning sphere, and though it whirred and chirped with warning, buzzing around the delegation members like a bee, pointing out the location of each enchanted item, the Xyoparians were only asked to give up a handful of their enchantments.

In truth, many they could *not* give up, regardless.

Like Mandip, many of them had enchanted metals laid under their skin, or bark- and metal-based inks in their tattoos. The ban in Lutador against such body modification save for state necessities was couched in moral and religious terms—the idea that Time should be the only entity to willingly enact change on one's form—but Mandip knew it for what it was: another measure of control.

Piercings and the like meant enchantments could be attached to the body, imbedded in the skin—could become part of one's person and personhood. Which made magic more difficult to contain. More difficult to *remove*. More difficult to regulate if it were allowed amongst the general masses.

Once the delegation had passed through the lobby, sweeping up the grand staircases beyond, Mandip and Thibaut were allowed to enter, as were the other nobles who'd been held back. Their identities were asserted to the doormen—Mandip's false papers checked and *confirmed* once again—and then, miracle upon miracles, they were in.

The Rotunda lobby was glittering and gold in the gaslight. As were many of the attendees. A man in far less finery—a stagehand, by the look of him—approached them hesitantly, work-cap clutched in between his hands like a shield. "Beggin' yer pardon, sirs, might ye be with La Maupin?"

Thibaut was quick with the letter. "We are indeed."

The man nodded. "This way. The mistress has picked out special seats fer ya."

Mandip fell into step behind the stagehand, who was clearly intent on leading them around to the performers' entrance, when a voice called out from behind, "You've got to be joking."

Mandip turned just in time to see a Regulator in full palace regalia step in front of Thibaut.

19

KRONA

Krona had turned Captain Veratas's invitation over and over in her mind all afternoon. She wanted to feel pride—knew she should. Only the most elite were recruited into the Marchonian Guardianship. It was a great honor to be asked and truly should have put any personal doubts and misgivings about her abilities to rest.

But people like Veratas only saw who she wanted them to see. Zhur impression of Krona was one she had spent a long time cultivating specifically to hide her weaknesses and her vices. She was capable and duty-bound, yes; that could not be faked so easily. But these days, she thwarted the law as often as she followed it, and this blurring of her own moral borders had made her understand the relationship between power—or lack thereof—and crime in a new way.

When De-Lia had been alive, sometimes Krona had wanted to be her, be another person. Now that her sister was gone, she often felt like two people. And neither of them were really who she was.

What if she didn't know who she was?

What if she had yet to meet that person?

What if she never did meet her real self?

These were thoughts for another night, she knew. Things to wrestle with in her own bed, in the dark.

Not here, under the bright lamps of the Rotunda's lobby. Not now, when someone's life was at stake.

Beneath her helm she wore Motomori's mask, which felt strange—was *made* strange by the *absence* of pressure over her eyes and brow rather than the strong pressure of the wood over her nose and mouth.

It may have been a half-mask, but it was not half-enchanted. There was nothing of halves about its influence, its echo.

Motomori's echo had attempted to persuade her of its rightful place at the forefront of her mind through negotiation and flattery rather than fight. Most high-magnitude echoes were characterized by *fight*. Krona always had to battle with them, to ease them, to subtly draw all of the struggle out of them until they were drained. But that kind of insistence wasn't part of Motomori's personality. His aptitude for persuasion relied on first setting his subject at peace. It was about making others believe his ideas were in fact their own.

Motomori's echo wasn't aware it was an echo, or in someone else's mind, but it *did* recognize a meeting of wills and was determined to assert its own.

Carefully, slowly, she'd caged it. She'd rebuked the gentleness, met it with violent resistance of her own, throwing more and more ire its way until it vibrated with unease. Until the echo became unsure of its purpose, its place. And then she'd pushed it downward through her mind like pushing an object down through water. And as the depths of herself grew darker, so too the echo grew dimmer, and soon she had subsumed it into a small, warm place, where even the lapping of her thoughts could not reach, and the echo now lay dormant.

Dealing with every echo was different. She wondered if that was why so many young Regulators struggled with them in the academy: they expected patterns, thought that since enchantments were all created through practiced processes and precisely measured ingredients, the results must then be equally calibrated.

But each enchantment was a wonder in and of itself. Magic's strength lay in its variances. In the careful construction of tools formed from the gods' power.

The Rotunda's lobby was shaped like a half-moon and had stairs leading to three levels, which matched the theater's seating around the thrust stage. The outer wall was lined with glass, and three sets of doors welcomed the guests into the lavishly adorned space. Gold-and-green enamel vines wound up from rolling roots at the corners of the floor, up the walls, and to the ceiling, where they wound together to form intricate patterns. From small vine-curl hooks, dangling enchanted lights—each in the shape of a turquoise berry cluster—dotted the array with a twinkling glow. Traffic through the lobby was paused once an hour to swap out the dimming enchantments with fresh examples. A small clockwork bird, perched at the primary entrance to the theater's seating area, kept the attendants on time with its chirping.

Krona had stationed herself at the right-most set of doors so she could watch the entire sea of guests enter. When a dignitary passed before her, she urged them to find their seat quickly, giving them the slightest persuasive push with Motomori's abilities.

She kept her ears perked for any suspicious conversation—anything that sounded coded or secretive. Gossip wound through the lobby like pipe vapors, most of it inconsequential. People had noticed the absence of the Winsrouen delegation, but it didn't seem to be causing much of a stir. However, one line of speculation did draw her attention.

"Do you think it has to do with His Esteemed Excellency disappearing his cousin's entire family?" asked a noble woman.

"*No*," her companion said quickly, scandalized. "That's a vicious rumor, nothing more."

"But I heard he found them all in the midst of some kind of demonic ritual. With marks on their bodies. Broken enchantments all around. Some of the children had gone mad, and his favorite first cousin once removed was dead—"

Marks on their bodies. Krona inched closer, hoping for clarification.

Gods, had the epidemic propagated that far south already? And now *children* were involved.

The noble pair moved on, the woman's companion shushing her into silence, clearly unnerved by the topic.

Krona refocused on the task at hand.

Her plan was as sound as she could make it. Once all of the nobles were in their seats, she would walk the Rotunda's perimeter sans helm, eyes on the lookout for anything unusual—both in the natural and supernatural realms. She would stay connected to her detail by reverb bead, as always, and would not hesitate to rouse the Marchonian Guards to her aid should she see any suspicious activity.

It certainly wasn't foolproof.

And still, she hadn't been expecting the *fool*.

Who should stride through the last set of doors now but Thibaut?

Thibaut, decked out in green to match his gloves, a glibly placed hat upon his brow, smile wide and carefree. He was in the company of a rather raggedy-haired gentleman, but that was neither here nor there.

Seeing Thibaut always put warmth in her chest, whether she wanted it—was prepared for it—or not. Sometimes, that warmth was like a hot meal, hearty and comforting. Sometimes, it was like a shot of hard liquor, burning on its way down. And sometimes—this time—it was like the sun on a heavily humid day: an uncomfortable addition to an already-uncomfortable situation.

Thibaut's very presence was a threat, if for no other reason than he was always an uncertainty—a vector for chaos.

Weaving through the crowd, she took him by the elbow. "You've got to be joking."

He turned immediately, a protest clearly on his lips, but he thought better of it. He might not be certain, yet, that it was his friend beneath all that black leather—if "friend," indeed, was the proper word—but he clearly suspected. "Isn't the customary greeting 'How may I be of aid?'" he asked, arching an eyebrow.

"What are you doing here?" she asked.

He nodded toward the shaggy man. "Earning a living, same as you."

She looked more closely at the man he was escorting. His expression was far too stunned for her liking. "Come here," she said, quirking a finger at him, putting the exact amount of vibrato in her voice that the mask suggested. She tempered the tone she wanted to use—put a graciousness where her gruffness would usually be.

The nobleman obeyed.

Thibaut was unbothered. "This is Lord Vedansh Basu. Keeper of the—"

"The Chief Magistrate requested that the Basus stay home this evening," she pointed out.

The lord opened his mouth to speak, but Thibaut kept control of the conversation. "His sons have been *detained*," he assured her, though there was a particular quirk to the last word she could not decipher.

"They're under house arrest," Lord Basu said.

She did not like the tremor in his tone.

Nor the lay of his mustache. She examined the lord closely. It was clear he was in disguise—not a poor one, to be sure, but there were tells. Given the way he shifted from foot to foot, it seemed more a boyish ruse to escape a watchful guardianship than it did an attempt at political subterfuge or clandestine murder. And yet . . .

Basu. Even if he wasn't Vedansh Basu, there had to be a reason he'd chosen that alias.

And how had he managed to get this far?

"Identification, if you please, Lord Basu."

The man pulled out a metal billfold and presented it to her with a slightly shaky hand. Inside were the usual enchanted papers nobles carried to assert themselves, complete with photograph and seal. "Your hand, please."

She expected some sudden fumble—an attempt to switch the papers—but instead the man simply laid a bare palm on the enchanted fibers and voilà, the papers glowed green, indicating a verified match.

This wasn't right. Despite the sepia tone of the photograph and the shagginess of this noble's hair, all it took was a little scrutiny to realize this couldn't be the same man.

The magic was *wrong*.

"You are not Vedansh Basu," she said frankly.

"His papers say otherwise," Thibaut protested.

"Exactly."

She only had one option here—to detain both the supposed Basu and Thibaut until she was sure the deadly threat had passed. She was tempted to call Tray over, to leave them in his capable hands while she sustained her vigil. But Thibaut was both slippery and *her* intelligence asset. She felt responsible for him on a personal level. And Basu . . .

She'd nearly convinced herself the potential victim had to be a foreign dignitary, but here was a *Basu*.

If she took him to a holding cell or the palace dungeon, would she be delivering the target straight into his assailant's grasp? If they truly meant to frame her, the tale of death in a dungeon by the hands of an infuriated Regulator wouldn't be a difficult one to weave.

But where else could she take them? To keep them safe?

She snapped her fingers as an idea came to her. "Follow me, gentlemen."

"But, dear Regulator—"

She bowed, waving her arms in an easy, inviting gesture. "Please, messieurs." It felt so unnatural, but Motomori insisted.

And the young lord followed.

Thibaut looked as though he half intended to walk the other direction, to leave his employer's side, and Krona hoped she wouldn't have to press him with the mask. A little extra persuasiveness was one thing, but she didn't want to weigh on Thibaut's mind. Their relationship was already tenuous and conditional. If he thought she'd manipulated him with something like hypnosis, he might never confide in her again.

Indeed, she wouldn't blame him.

But, at the last moment, he sighed deeply and took up Lord Basu's arm.

⊱─◈─◇─◈─⊰

"Master sommelier, I have use of your wine cellar."

Thibaut openly reveled in the sights and smells of the kitchen, delighted to glimpse the fine food being prepared for the performance's intermission.

The sommelier, on the other hand, didn't appear half so keen to see them in his domain. He was a tall, lanky man with a hooked nose upon which a pair of small spectacles sat. "Oh, Mastrex Regulator, I'm afraid that's impossible," he said, faux disappointment heavy in his tone—as though he would *love* to comply, you see, if only. "Each bottle has been carefully curated by me, personally, and the conditions within the cellar must be kept just so in order to maintain the vintages properly. Thus, only *I* ever enter the cellar. Additional bodies would increase the temperature, which we work hard to maintain, and—"

And time to see if Motomori's influence was really as terrifyingly thorough as she remembered it to be.

The mask told her exactly how to pitch her voice and move her body. How to grab and maintain her subject's attention, how to capture their focus. "May I see your hand, please?"

"My hand?" He held both out, displaying they were empty.

Abruptly, she grabbed one of his wrists, tugging him forward, pulling him temporarily off-balance. According to Motomori, sudden jolts opened the subconscious, left it amenable to suggestion as it naturally searched for extra information that would help the individual re-achieve their equilibrium.

"The best way to protect your wine—and your position here—is to turn it over to my supervision for the evening. Retrieve whatever bottles you need now. Any losses incurred by an *excess of body heat* will be covered by the city-state. Do you understand?"

"Yes." There was a strange hiss in his *yes*. Like the air was slowly leaking out of his lungs. He appeared both alarmed and relaxed at the same time.

"Give me the key."

He dutifully pulled it from his pocket, handed it over. She unlocked the wrought-iron gate that opened onto a set of stairs leading down to the cellar door proper.

"Retrieve your required bottles, then return to this exact spot."

He nodded, complied. Each opening of the cellar door let cool air waft up to greet them in the stove-warmed kitchen.

When he was finished, standing precisely where he'd been before, she said, "Now repeat after me: I will not return to the cellar until midnight."

"I will not return to the cellar until midnight."

"At that time, I may restore it as I like."

"At that time, I may restore it as I like."

She could feel the mask's influence like a sick pit in her stomach. Molding the world, making it her own. Bending this man's subconscious instincts to her own will. Not quite like the Thalo but dangerously, nauseatingly akin.

With that, she clapped her hands in front of his nose, and he shook his head, blinked rapidly, his subconscious having been startled again.

"Very good," she told him. "You are dismissed."

He turned on the spot like a little clockwork automation and stomped away.

"All right, you two," she grumbled. "In."

Grinning openly, Thibaut skipped through the open wrought-iron gate to the heavy, inner wooden door and flung it wide. He breathed deeply, filling his lungs with the scent of cold sandstone, aged barrels, and dusty bottles. "You have excellent taste in interrogation rooms, Mastrex Regulator," he said cheerily, fully understanding why she'd brought them here.

"In-interrogation?" the supposed Basu stammered.

With a hand at the small of his back, she nudged him down the steps. "After you, *Lord Basu*."

Inside the cellar, at its center, was a small table boasting a lit oil lamp—clearly a modest tasting station for the sommelier. It sported a single chair, which Thibaut gestured for his companion to take—perhaps thinking it gracious to offer his employer the only available seat—but the young man clearly took it the wrong way.

"Oh, no. *You* sit in the interrogation chair."

Thibaut shrugged. "If you insist." He blithely sat, immediately throwing his boots up on the small table.

The lord's eyes nearly popped out of his head. He slapped Thibaut's shoulder. "Show some respect! Do you really—"

He chattered on for a minute more, and Krona made no attempt to stop him as she secured the cellar door behind her. She was certain Thibaut's flippant airs were because he was confident it was Krona beneath the helm, and for half a moment she wished she were someone else, simply so she could see that self-satisfied smirk leave his face when she revealed him to be wrong.

Wasting no time, she brandished the suspect papers as she approached the table. "Where did you get these?" she demanded.

"They're my father's," the young man quickly blurted. "I'm Mandip Basu. It's an enchantment gone wrong. Simple mistake."

"Malfunctioning enchantments are to be turned over to the Regulators upon discovery," she snapped at him. "Lord Basu or no, I could arrest you for possession, never mind its improper use."

"That you could," Thibaut said evenly. "But, dear Regulator, all you have here is a young man looking for a bit of fun and bending a few rules. Surely, that doesn't denote—"

"Thibaut, *shut up.*" She was in no mood. "More trouble has been caused in this world by young men looking for a bit of fun than anything else, I swear to the gods. You have no idea what the two of you have walked into." She pointed firmly at Thibaut. "What you have *led* him into."

"Me?" he asked incredulously. "How is this on *me*? In what way am I responsible for the comings and goings of anyone on palace grounds?"

"This whole business was difficult enough to deal with without having to concern myself with your proximity to the matter."

"*What* whole business?"

"No. No, I do not have time to deal with you." She took out her manacles, snapping one cuff to Thibaut's wrist, who simply raised an eyebrow at her—and the other to Mandip's wrist, who looked rather stunned.

Neither had enough gumption to so much as protest, let alone fight back.

Or perhaps producing the manacles had proven how serious she was.

"The two of you will *stay here* until I retrieve you."

"If you think shackling me and locking me away in one of the finest wine cellars in the entire Valley is going to keep me in your good graces, Mistress, well, then—"

"*You must assure me I am right,*" she finished for him. "Thibaut. Please. No theatrics, no jokes. Not now."

The slickness left his voice, his expression sobered. "Mistress?"

"If I don't come back for you by midnight, the sommelier will let you out. Find Tray. He knows you; he'll uncuff you."

"Why wouldn't *you* be back for us?"

She turned toward the stairs, stomped up them.

"Krona!" he shouted after. He rarely used her given name. "Why wouldn't *you* be back?"

She almost stopped. Almost thought twice about locking the pair of them away. What if *this* was what the assassins wanted? Was the young Basu a sitting duck down there?

No, there was no way anyone could anticipate she'd lock him in a wine cellar. And if she'd been followed, she was sure she'd know. She might not always be able to see a Thalo plain as day, but she could sense them, detect a shimmer where others couldn't. No one was trailing her; she was positive.

But was that in and of itself suspicious? How did they intend to frame her if they failed to keep track of her?

She huffed at herself.

She couldn't second-guess every course of action. Mandip wasn't supposed to be here, in this cellar, and therefore no one would look for him in this cellar. She would both threaten and buy the silence of the kitchen staff.

These two would be safe. They had to be.

20

THALO CHILD

Less Than Two Years Ago

"Anything?" Hintosep called from her end of the long reading table.

"Nothing," Thalo Child called back.

The pair of them had been in the antiquarium for *hours* now. Thalo Child was sure it had to be approaching dawn. And still they'd not come across a single account of anyone actually observing a varg entering the Valley from the outside. Stacks of books lay scattered all around them, some opened, some bookmarked, all now completely out of order. The antiquarians would not be pleased.

"And if anyone were to see a varg arriving, it would be a Guardian," she said firmly. "*I* would have seen it. I sat on the rim for centuries. The varger numbers, their correlation with the people of the Valley, the beasts' magical properties, their obsession with humans and humans alone . . . I'm all but convinced."

"Convinced of what?"

"They don't come from outside the Valley, and they aren't born in the Valley. They're created. A by-product."

"A by-product?"

She didn't elaborate; instead, she stared into the distance, thumbed thoughtfully at her chin. "The real question is, does He know?"

"Does who know?"

"The Savior."

Thalo Child gasped. "The Savior knows *everything*. How could He not know?"

"The Savior is just a man, fallible as anyone."

Thalo Child shot to his feet as his blood surged, warming his face and neck and hands with fear and shame. "Don't *say* that. Don't let Him hear you say that!" His respect and reverence for someone such as Hintosep was only supplanted by his respect and reverence for the Savior.

To hear such disrespect fall from her lips, of all lips—

"He's not here," she said, tone tired—*bored*, even, "you don't have to be afraid of Him."

"He's *everywhere*," the child countered.

"Then why is His hold on me *slipping*?"

He didn't know what she meant.

How could the great Hintosep, of all people, sit there and say such blasphemous things? She who had His favor, she who was of divine reincarnation, she who was the only one who had the privilege to choose her station and how she protected the Valley at any given time?

She looked at him squarely, raised her chin with a challenge thinning her lips. "Come here," she bade, curling a finger at him with the perfunctory swiftness of someone who is used to being instantly obeyed.

And obey he did.

He left his end of the long table, attempting to stride confidently, fearing this was some kind of test to see if his loyalty ran as deep as it should.

When he stood before her, she appraised him without leaving her chair. She pushed the book in front of her aside and leaned her elbows heavily on the tabletop, peering at him with intensity. "You do not remember how you came to live in this castle," she said.

It was not a question, but he answered anyway. "No."

"You do not remember the first Thalo arms that cradled you."

"No."

She nodded, glanced away. "They were mine."

He blinked, uncertain. He didn't know what to do with that information, didn't know how to feel about it. She'd acted as Harvester? *His* Harvester?

She slid the book back to her, began reading again. "When the time comes, mine will also be the arms that ferry you from the keep."

"What . . . what are you talking about?"

She raised one hand, held her fingers outstretched toward him. Still, she did not look at him, but he knew what she wanted. "Are you to take—"

"Give," she said frankly. "I want to give you a secret."

"Whose secret?"

"Our secret. Yours and mine."

"I cannot keep secrets from Gerome," he said quickly, taking a hasty step back, out of her reach. She must know how easily his Possessor could peel back the layers of his mind, no matter how keen Thalo Child was to stop him.

"I will bury this secret for you," she explained, gaze still cast away. "He will not be able to undo the mindlock."

"Why must—"

She looked up sharply. "*Come. Here.*"

Something was deeply wrong. He felt it in his gut. This was not a test—this was *subversion*. "Why must I keep a secret from Gerome? He is my Possessor; I belong to him. To the Eye."

"You belong with your family."

Her words were twisted, something no Thalo would say, something no faithful servant of the gods and the Savior would say. Why was she doing this? What had happened to Hintosep? This could not be the same woman that the Possessors spoke of with such reverence. The one person left who had been with the Savior *from the beginning.*

"I will not betray Gerome," he said softly.

"Child, this world is about to come to an end. And you must be prepared."

"What?" he gasped softly. "How can you . . . How can you say that? The world of the Savior has always been. The world of the Savior always will be."

"Come here. The sooner I bestow this on you, the sooner I can make you forget you were ever distressed at all."

He took another step back. "No."

"*No?*"

He slid backward once more as she rose to her feet.

"No," he breathed.

"Gerome has done his work well," she sighed. "The Eye is effective. Just like the Cage. You would have been a Possessor, for certain."

"*Would* have?"

"If I'm successful, I'll see you come into your power in a whole new way." She rounded the table, took strong strides toward him.

Thalo Child bolted.

He ran away from her as fast as his little legs could carry him. He ran for the antiquarium's entrance, only to find the crystalline wall perfectly intact—sturdy and impassable. Turning his back to it, pressing his shoulders tight against it, he searched for another means of escape. He could weave his way through the shelves, perhaps outrun her, but not forever, and to what end?

Though she followed, she did not give chase. She knew better than he did the ins and outs of the horn-shaped hall. Knew there was nowhere for him to go.

But he could not resign himself to her manipulation. Not yet.

As she calmly strode toward the crystal door, he ran at her, past her, darting around shelves just beyond her reach before sprinting for his only hope of salvation.

He ran to the Fallen, God of Secrets.

Above him, the ceiling rose higher and higher. He wished his hopes matched.

He wished drawing closer to the dead god made him feel like he had half a chance of keeping his mind his own. But even as he made it to the far end of the antiquarium and threw himself to his knees beneath the massive opalescent casing, he knew all entreaties were futile.

A dead god's body might still possess power, but it possessed no will. There was no pity to be found, no sanctuary to claim.

The giant deity hung—bound and stoic—in their sarcophagus, arms outstretched, each meaty finger tipped with a blackened claw. They were dressed in ceremonial armor made for them by Nature, the materials all organic and grown on the damp underside of dead logs, like fungus—bits of it billowy and meaty just like the furls of oyster mushrooms and turkey tail. The colors were very unlike mushrooms, however, from raven purple to still-waters aqua to phthalocyanine blue.

Phthalocyanine blue.

Phthalo blue.

The blue from which the Thalo's name had originated. The blue taken from the Fallen's eyes after the god had plucked the five still-seeing orbs from their own skull. The blue which became the first pigments in the first power-absorbing lines, etched in skin, in flesh.

From his knees, Thalo Child fell forward onto his hands. "Please," he begged, though if he were begging the god or the former Guardian, he did not know. Perhaps both. "I haven't even earned a name."

Heavy footfalls landed loudly behind him. He knew if she wanted to, Hintosep could approach without so much as a whisper of a sound. "You should not have to earn that which was stolen from you," she said, tone sympathetic.

Hintosep's lines came straight from the pigment in the god's eyes. She was *that* old, that important. That powerful. How could she not kneel down beside Thalo Child in awe and reverence? How could she be the one whispering these confusing things into his ear?

"Haven't I been good to the babe you gave me? Haven't I been a faithful Child? Surely, someone else . . . someone else . . ."

Someone else, what?

He didn't even know what she was doing, why she wanted to share a secret with him. A secret he must keep from Gerome. All he knew was this felt very wrong. He just wanted to keep his head down and earn his name and perhaps aspire to the priesthood, but no higher. He realized now he was made to follow—not just in his youth but always.

His name could not belong to someone powerful. His former incarnation could not have been something special, someone important.

These were things he truly did not want to be.

She crouched down behind him, pulled him up by his shoulders, cradled him firmly against her chest. "I do not relish these things I do," she whispered to him, tone rich and dark. "I think you're happy here. You don't know not to be. But I promised her."

"I don't know what you're talking about," he sobbed. As tears blurred his vision, he gazed upward at the Fallen once more.

Thalo Child knew the people of the Valley did not know Secrets. They knew Time, and Nature, and Knowledge, and Emotion. But not Secrets.

"I need their loyalty," she said. "And you and your babe are how I get it."

He lunged away from her, but her arms tightened like clamps around him. It was no use struggling, trying to push her away. She was dressed for action and alert, despite the hour. He was still just a child, and one in his thin nightclothes, no less. Groggy and weepy from lack of sleep to start with.

She held one palm up near his head—more of a soothing gesture than one required for her to perform whatever magics she needed.

Slowly, he felt realizations dawn in his mind as information percolated through his system, gently dripping from her stash of secrets into his. He couldn't fully comprehend what it all meant—there were faces, and maps, and an unfamiliar blond woman cooing down at a baby in her arms. Next to her was another, much shorter woman with brown hair who seemed overjoyed, but soon a pale man—also blond, and who looked like he might be sick at any moment—approached them.

Whatever this scene was, Thalo Child realized he was watching it through Hintosep's eyes. It was a memory, though he could not say how old. None of the people in it took notice of the Thalo peering at them.

Gerome didn't know any of this. Hintosep didn't want Gerome to know any of this.

"I don't . . . I don't want to be a pawn," Thalo Child said, trying to keep the sob from his tone. "I don't want to betray Gerome. I want to be good and earn my name and—"

"Child, you shouldn't have to earn a name when the one first bestowed on you was stolen," she said again, and this time the words truly struck.

He blinked, baffled. "What?"

"You do not yet know where our infants come from," she said, dismissive.

"I know where babies come from," he said defensively. All Thalo children were well versed in the human life cycle by the time they were eight.

"That's not what I meant. You know that babies are born and brought here, but you don't understand what that *means*. You know how babies are *made*, not where they *come from*. You have no concept of *parents*. Just Possessors.

"The Harvesters harvest more than the Sacrifices. They go into your homes, test each infant during the time tax, and find the babies who can wield secrets— the rarest of inborn magics. They do not harvest them all, but they take many. And your parents . . . I wish we simply made them forget their children. But that would mean tracking down everyone who ever knew a Thalo's mother was with child. Instead, we steal their ability to see their baby's chest rise and fall, to feel their heart beating, or hear their mewling cries."

"Stop it," he pleaded. "Please!" The confusion and fear made him hiccup, and Thalo Child covered his face with both hands.

More twisted knowledge wormed its way inside him. His charge—the infant she'd left in his care. He knew now: the baby was different. The baby had power, yes, but the baby . . .

The baby wasn't a Thalo.

Zhur power did not lie in secrets.

No one else knew this. Only Hintosep knew this.

"You understand this is a rare thing I'm doing, yes? A mindlock," she said soothingly. "It is not a ritual I can perform often. Sealing a secret inside so that it is not gone but *entirely hidden*—even from a Possessor—is no small feat."

"Then why do it? Why must I have this? Surely, it would be better not to tell me at all."

"Oh, small one, believe me, there are many things I could let slip to you that I instead keep tucked in my own mind for now. But you will need this information—especially the complete map of the keep—when the time comes. And I don't know when I'll get another chance to bestow it."

She was planning something. Something awful, terrible. Something that would shake the very foundations of the keep and put them all in great danger. Of this, he was certain. But only for a fleeting moment.

The torrent of secrets ended, and right behind them came a dark, imposing monolith. A wall. A void. Thick and dense and somehow an empty, yawing *nothingness* all at once.

"It may be years again before you remember this moment," she said. "A single year must feel like an eternity for one so young as you. When you live as long as I have, everything feels like it happens very slowly and very quickly at the same time. A year is nothing, and yet there are so many."

Thalo Child felt very sleepy all of a sudden, as though his mind was forgetting how to stay conscious, stay awake.

"Rest," she whispered into the crown of his hair, rocking him slightly. "You've been of great help and will need to help me further still."

Just like that, she put him to sleep as readily as she'd made sure his babe would stay asleep, and Thalo Child feared no more.

21

MANDIP

Thibaut finally sobered, his cockiness faltering just as the door closed, his boots slipping off the table. He looked down at his manacled wrist, then followed the chain up to Mandip's arm and back again.

"Well?" Mandip asked incredulously. "Now what?"

The other man appeared at a loss for all of half a moment, clearly searching for his footing. "Now . . . now we take this grand opportunity to inspect one of the most prized wine collections in the entire Valley." He sprang to his feet and swiped up the lantern, briskly sweeping over to the nearest rack.

Mandip had no choice but to follow, lest he be *yanked*. He'd never been restrained before, and the metal cuff was heavier than he would have imagined.

Holding up the lamp, Thibaut examined the brass plates affixed to the shelf space, which proclaimed the vintage of each set of bottles. Here and there were gaps in the rack, where a bottle had been lovingly pulled—retrieved from this treasury to complement the perfect occasion.

The pair of them moved from the rack to a row of casks, then to another rack, admiring the collection as thoroughly as they would any assemblage of superb art.

"You don't seem at all perturbed that we've been locked away." Where Mandip was jittery and uncertain, Thibaut was calm and self-composed. "*Or* chained."

"I find my confinement tends to be fleeting," he said casually. "Though it does seem the Regulators truly wanted to keep you away from the Rotunda tonight."

"They claimed there was a threat of some kind . . ."

Abruptly, Thibaut turned, holding the lamp up to see Mandip's face better. "A threat to . . ."

"My personage."

Thibaut's gaze narrowed; he frowned and lowered the light. "As in a *violent* threat?"

"Perhaps."

"I was joking, earlier, about your bodily integrity being at risk. By the gods, here I thought you'd simply escaped overprotective parents or some such. If the Regulators say there is a threat, there is a threat."

"It was a messenger from the Chief Magistrate, actually, who—"

"Oh, yes, because *he's* known to overreact, being so unfamiliar with the likes of threats. Egads, and here with the watch incident, I thought you had an ample sense of self-preservation."

"Our family has received threats before. Usually, they're *specific*. This was vague enough that I deduced it to be a political ploy invented to—"

"You deduced," Thibaut scoffed, turning away toward the nearest rack. "You deduced nothing and chose the most inappropriate time to grow a sense of adventure. And now we're here, in gods know what kind of danger. I enjoy thrills, you see, but not *danger*. No one in their right mind enjoys danger. Well, lucky for us my Mistress Regulator friend was here to catch us blundering into whatever we're blundering into." He set the lantern down on the end of an upturned barrel. "I daresay I'm saddened to be deprived of Juliet's performance, but since we're here in this makeshift cell for what could be the rest of the evening, I suggest we enjoy it."

"In what way?"

Thibaut stopped near the rear wall, sizing up a rack of dusty reds. "We took the opportunity to inspect; now we take the opportunity to raid."

"*Are you out of your gourd?*" Mandip batted down Thibaut's reaching hand. "Any one of these bottles is worth more than your life. Perhaps my life. We will *hang* if we so much as crack a seal or let a drop past our lips."

"Nonsense. This is the *Rotunda's* wine cellar. Not the Grand Marquises' exclusive collection. Its vintages are meant to be shared with those attending performances. Guests."

"One minute you're bemoaning the air of danger, the next you're planning more trouble."

Thibaut selected a bottle, his green gloves leaving distinct impressions in the dust, the coat of it was so thick. "From Grand Marchionesses Sabrina and Tatianna's inauguration year."

"You're mad."

Thibaut pointed the bottle at him. "And you are infuriating. Bold and cowardly at distinctly inopportune times."

"I could—and do—say the same of *you*."

"Come, let's look for an opener. Likely the sommelier keeps one on him rather than stashed down here, but our only alternative is to snap the neck."

Mandip felt the blood drain from his face. "You wouldn't."

"Find me the appropriate tool and I won't have to." He tucked the bottle under his arm and scooped up the lamp once again.

As Thibaut whisked the light this way and that, casting strange, unnerving shadows across the many nooks and crannies of the cellar, Mandip wondered how long the oil would last. If they truly were trapped in here until midnight, how many hours would they spend locked in the dark?

He silently added candles to his list of tools he was searching for.

As the manacles didn't allow their wrists to be more than a foot and a half apart at any given time, they were stuck searching the same area. Alas, Mandip saw neither vintner's tools nor a sommelier's. No extra taps, or corkscrews, glasses, or stirring wands.

But his hopes rose when he spotted a small nook with a pyramid of stacked candles. "At least we won't have to suffer the dark."

Thibaut suddenly pulled up short, yanking Mandip back the way they'd come. "Look at this bottle," he said, making sure to haul the young lord to his side. "It's been palmed often—look how clean it is compared to the others. Someone's favorite? That they've never opened?"

"A pet vintage," Mandip proposed.

"Perhaps, or . . ." He proceeded to jostle the bottle, to pull it forward, but then pushed it up so that its neck pointed at an awkward angle on the rack.

Something *clicked*.

A selection of wines on their right jolted forward, making both men jump back.

A cool breeze whipped into Mandip's face from nowhere, carrying with it the scent of aged dust, lampblack, and pomade.

With caution, Thibaut reached out toward the affected rack. Finding a seam, he pulled.

The rack swung outward.

"A secret passage!" Mandip declared. "It's a wonder the sommelier didn't warn your Regulator about it."

"She didn't exactly give him a chance, now, did she? Shhhh, listen."

The light sound of chatter, tuning instruments, and the occasional muffled *bangs* seeped from the dark.

"I think this might lead to the stage," Thibaut said, inching his way in. "Oh, how quaint; it's an actors' cozy."

"Are you suggesting there's a way for just anyone working the stage to help themselves to the contents of the Rotunda's wine collection?"

"Oh, no, not just any actor would be allowed in a cozy. This would be someplace clandestine for a Grand Marquex to meet a theatrical paramour, perhaps. I wonder if anyone working tonight knows about it."

"Juliet might," Mandip admitted. "She was very familiar with most aspects of the palace I showed her. Rightfully, our roles should have been reversed."

Thibaut paused, looked thoughtful. "But she was the one that requested a tour, you say?"

"Yes. And I'm now under the impression she asked for me by name, to be her guide."

"And this was before you and I even met?"

"Yes."

"It can't simply be the Charbon concern, then. Her interest, I mean. Seems she targeted you first, and I was just a pleasant surprise."

"Targeted? What a harsh word for a lady's pointed curiosity."

"*Pointed*, indeed. And I would not be so quick to dismiss anything La Maupin takes an interest in as simple *curiosity*. Come." He stalked forward.

Mandip resisted. "But—"

Thibaut turned, raised a wry eyebrow, and grinned. "This might be an excellent way to still see Juliet perform while keeping your not-so-well-coiffed head from becoming a target. Our discovery of the cozy has officially demoted the *danger* to *thrill*."

The passage beyond was very dark and perhaps long—it was difficult to tell. It was winding, for sure. "Wait!" Mandip pulled Thibaut back, made for the nook with the candles, scooping up all but one.

"You're expecting several days' journey?" Thibaut quipped.

"I'm expecting the rest of the evening not to go as planned."

Thibaut made an appreciative face, nodding lightly. "Fair enough."

22

KRONA

After secluding the troublemaker and the young noble—hopefully out of harm's reach—the new tension in Krona's body did not wane. There was too much at stake and too many unknowns. The venue was too large, the pool of possible victims too vast.

Returning to her post, she did her best to narrow the problem, to not only look for things out of the ordinary—possible threats—but specifically telltale signs of the Thalo's presence. The rest of her detail was more than qualified to pinpoint typical pressures, but only she (for reasons still unknown) could detect the Blue Woman and her ilk.

Even as the last of the guests arrived and the theater doors closed, she paced the lobby and its offshoots like a caged animal certain a predator was near but unable to pick up its trail.

Would anything she did make a difference? If the target was in the delegation from Winsrouen, would they simply be killed in their lodgings instead of the Rotunda? If instead the target was a set of young, noble Lutadorian twins, was their home truly any safer than the palace?

How could she even hope to be one step ahead of an adversary that would so blatantly alert her to the plan?

There was a brief fanfare as the Grand Marquises were led by a heavy detail of Marchonian Guards across the glass bridge and into the Rotunda. The entrance to their bespoke balcony seats lay near the end of said bridge, preventing them from having to wander down into the theater lobby.

Krona caught only a quick glimpse of one of the Grand Marquises as the procession passed above her position. As they were identical, it was difficult to tell which. A curling gray beard and mustache cascaded over a barreled chest swathed in yellows and golds, with various metals touting various accomplishments pinned to the front in military fashion. On his hip—contrasting sharply to the pomp and order of the march—was a small child dressed in pink. The Second Grand Marquis's youngest daughter.

The girl looked down and over her shoulder as they passed, catching Krona in her sights for a moment before offering a small, bewildered wave.

Krona waved back.

Within moments, the procession was gone.

And Krona's attention was stolen away by a light shimmering of blue mist.

For a brief moment, Krona connected the two: the mist and the Second Grand Marquis.

But the mist wasn't on the skywalk, nowhere near the little girl in pink. Instead, it was below, on the ground level with Krona, curling around one arm of the theater's half-moon, passing many of the entrances to the auditorium, headed toward the end of the lobby.

Determined yet cautious, Krona followed.

Wearing a mask beneath her helm meant Krona had kept her reverb bead stashed in her cheek the entire time rather than dangling near her lips. Making sure her tone was even, she alerted the others that she was in pursuit and asked Tray to come to her position. Even if he couldn't detect the mist, perhaps the two of them could nevertheless trap it at the end of the hall.

"Currently on level three; meet you there," he confirmed.

She continued forward, maintaining a strict distance between herself and the mist, not wanting to lose its shimmer in the enchanted light, and keenly aware of how easily it could slip by her should she let the Thalo puppet know too soon that she'd spotted it.

Beyond the house doors, she heard the orchestra strike up in the pit.

▷━┼━◆▷━━○━◁◆━┼━◁

Thibaut, for all of his showboating, was worried about Krona.

But, ever the pragmatist, he realized there was nothing he could do for her.

Except, perhaps, stay out of trouble.

Which he fully intended to do.

Truly.

With the lordling stumbling behind him, Thibaut blithely walked ahead, pretending not to feel or care about the tug on his wrist.

He'd been chained by Krona before. Bound, gagged. Led along by a leash behind her horse. Perhaps another man might take affront, as not one of these instances of bondage had been the fun kind. But Thibaut understood that everything Krona did, she did with a purpose, and that purpose was never cruelty. He wouldn't go so far as to say it never amused her to see him squirm, but she would not be one to seal him away behind lock and key unless she thought it a true precaution.

So, this actors' cozy was really a godsend for the both of them, now, wasn't it? It would allow him to access the stage without ever sticking his neck out where it didn't belong. He could keep the young Basu occupied—amused, even—while she went about the hard work of keeping everyone safe.

Safe from *what*, he wished he knew. Some object of enchanted evil or other. He wished she'd confided in him, but he understood.

He did.

Priceless wine bottle still in hand, he touched the box in his pocket, wondering when he'd get a chance to give it to her.

As he and Mandip, the pair of them, hit what was surely the midpoint in the cozy's passage—given it was occupied by a small, ornate table, two matching chairs, a wall-mounted candelabra, and a velveted settee—Thibaut heard the band begin to play.

"Hurry, or we'll miss the opening performances," he prompted Mandip, giving a completely unnecessary yank on their joint tether.

><+>-0-<+>-<

When the mist reached the end of the lobby, Krona stopped at the last door to the auditorium, barring the shimmer's escape into the house. There was nowhere for the Thalo to go from there, not without coming within arm's length of her.

She suppressed a smirk of triumph.

It was strange how different she felt—how confident—from when she'd first truly confronted a mist like this, on Vault Hill during the Charbon-Gatwood concern. Simply knowing what she was up against changed her footing dramatically.

That is, until a section of the wall abruptly slid aside, revealing a darkened passageway, and the shimmering mist slipped inside.

Krona didn't have time to curse at herself, but she realized she should have been prepared for such trickery. Theaters throughout the Valley were known for their trapdoors and false walls. Why wouldn't one of the grandest theaters in all of Lutador sport the same?

Oh, no you don't, Krona swore, springing forward even as the hidden door began to slip closed again. She barely scraped inside, the horns on her helm catching against the inner wall as she attempted to avoid colliding with the disguised door as it heavily slid back into place.

Immediately, darkness fell all around her. There was no light at all with which to catch a full-bodied person, let alone a glimmer of mist. She held perfectly still, listening, shallowing her breathing so that it wouldn't rattle inside the enclosed space of her helm. She tried to pick up the patter of footsteps, but all she could hear was the music.

How many passages like this did the theater hold? Why hadn't Captain Veratas shown her such entrances—unless, perhaps, zhe didn't know about them?

She turned, ran her gloved hands over the door behind her, looking for a way to open it again.

"Krona? I'm here; where are you?" asked Tray, via the shell in her ear.

"There's a secret door," she whispered. "On the right, at the end. I didn't see how it was triggered from the outside, but—"

"You're on the other side," Tray deduced.

"Right." There were no obvious protrusions. No kickplates, no levers or buttons. "I'm not sure I can open it from here."

"Where are you? Where does it lead?"

She listened more closely. "Backstage, perhaps? I'll continue pursuit. Grab Sasha and see if you can meet me on the other side. Use the performers' entrance."

"Yes, Captain."

"Hurry. I don't like this."

"Should I alert the Marchonians?"

"Not yet. I don't want to cause a scene if we don't have to."

>—+—‹›—O—‹›—+—‹

The air in the cozy passage was remarkably fresh. Often, hidden storage spaces smelled of mold or old cheese. *Ask me how I know*, Thibaut quipped to himself. It was also noticeably clean, the floor swept and the walls freshly lime-washed within the past few years. Which meant it was currently in use. He wondered which Grand Marquis was having the clandestine affair. Could be either, as neither man was exactly known for his small appetites when it came to the excesses and privileges of both their station and wealth.

Suddenly, Mandip stopped in his tracks, pulling up short enough that it whipped Thibaut around when the chain went taut, sending the lamp's glow bouncing wildly in the dark space.

"Shhh," Mandip said quickly, glancing behind. "Footsteps."

Thibaut strained his ears, listening. He heard nothing out of the ordinary.

"Must be out on the stage," he whispered. "These hidden chambers, they amplify and muffle sounds in unusual turns."

"No, I don't think . . ." Mandip trailed off, then turned wide, brown eyes under arched brows on Thibaut. "Perhaps we should go back. Mayhaps the Regulator was right and I *am* in danger."

"Then shouldn't we proceed on? Toward the stage? Surely, there's safety in numbers."

"You're right," Mandip conceded, waving impatiently for Thibaut to move on. "You're right."

⊱━◆◦◆━⊰

Krona wished she had a light vial with her. She lifted her helm's visor, let her eyes adjust without the treated glass to warp her vision.

Her ears caught wisps of conversation. Distorted echoes that lost all form and meaning and direction by the time they reached her ears. It was impossible to tell if they came from the auditorium, stage, or elsewhere.

The passage kept turning, bowing in a wide arc. It was narrow and cold. A passing whiff of old lavender perfume caught in her nose, made her sniff dryly. After a few minutes of slow going—dragging her palm along one wall to follow it—she began to make out the corners of the hall, to see the seams where floor met wall met ceiling.

But still no figure. No mist.

She hoped her brief conversation with Tray hadn't dangerously delayed her. For all she knew, this tunnel could deliver the Thalo assassin directly to their target's seat. Seconds might make the difference.

With her eyes better accustomed, she picked up her pace, risked alerting her quarry with her footfalls. Though they'd used their reverb beads, if the mist was close, it might have overheard her speaking with Tray anyway. Whoever it was might very well know she was following already.

As the tunnel continued on and on, she let her steps come faster and faster.

The Thalo's powers were such that the cloaked individual could be running and she might not hear. They could have ducked around *behind her* and she might not have sensed it.

But they could not wrest control of her mind and wield her to their own ends. She took what comfort she could in the knowledge.

She nearly collided bodily with the wall when the passage took a sudden, sharp turn. She'd been headed in the same direction for so long, always curving the same way, that she could not say where she was relative to the stage anymore. She might have passed it, might still be approaching it.

Either way, she had no other choice but to press on.

⊱━◆◦◆━⊰

"Ah, here we are!" Thibaut announced, having clearly reached the end of the hidden passage. "We'll have you among people again in no time, milor."

Thibaut blew out the oil lamp and, though it took some effort, convinced Mandip to abandon his stock of extra candles.

Once through the hidden cozy—its exit simply concealed on the outside by dark, blank paneling much like the dark, blank paneling around it—Thibaut was struck by a contrast. The bright luxuriousness of the palace here became the dark, bare bones of a backstage. Pulleys, ropes, sandbags, and levers went this way and that. Curtains separated parts of the backstage from the front stage, and the smell of sawdust and fresh paint permeated everything.

A potbellied, balding man in a sweat-stained tunic, which clung to him like wet paper rather than cloth, rounded a strip of curtain, and the three of them narrowly avoided running into one another.

"Oi!" the man exclaimed. "You gentlemen shouldn't be back here. I know it seems like the perfect place for an illicit affair, but we's got work to do and—" A thought occurred to him. "Oooh. You's with Julie, ain't you?"

"I believe so, yes," said Mandip, blinking slowly, painfully, in response to "you's" and "ain't."

Thibaut frowned, suspicious of the stranger's accuracy. "How did you guess?"

The man matched Thibaut's frown. "You match 'er description of the personage she 'ad me send a carriage fer. Sent a man out to meet yer, but 'e said you disappeared."

"We were . . . detained," Mandip said, sounding tired.

Which was understandable, Thibaut thought. That single word had done a lot of heavy lifting this evening.

"Come with me," the stagehand grunted, yanking on a rope, freeing it from its mooring and sending a sandbag plummeting within inches of Mandip's feet. A curtain lifted in response, revealing a set of bare wooden stairs.

The man didn't so much as bat an eye at their obvious restraints.

Ever the gracious escort, Thibaut bowed and gestured for Mandip to lead the way—though it was difficult to navigate stairs in anything resembling a normal fashion, given their bound state. The noble mounted them like he was attempting stilts or the high wire.

As Thibaut was about to follow, something brushed past him and he heard a giggle. It was dark backstage but not so dark as to conceal someone. But he was sure he'd felt a body and seen none.

To his right, a parental "Come here!" emanated from nowhere and everywhere. Then a distinct "Shhhh."

But no one was there.

He'd heard of theater echoes: imprints of actor's performances captured by the scraps of enchanted wood some smarmy set designers nabbed from maskmakers' filings. Supposedly, it was bad luck to build a set without at least a sliver of enchanted wood, without the chance to capture a performance forever. But that was just superstition.

Wasn't it?

"Thibaut!"

He shook off the strange moment and hurried after Mandip.

>-+-◆>--O--◆+-◄

As Krona hurried on, an oppressive feeling settled over her. As though she'd missed or forgotten something. As though at some point, she'd held the answers she was looking for in her grasp but had dropped them in favor of straws or phantoms.

Every step forward started to feel like the wrong direction. Like it was leading her away from where she needed to be. She considered turning around, letting the mist go.

In her ear, Tray kept asking her where she was. And all she could tell him was "Still in the passage."

Then, blessedly, a door.

The hall ended, and a clear *door* marked the terminus. It was notably door-shaped, made of rich, red wood with a brass handle and no obvious lock. It was also closed, with no one standing between her and it, but light—and *music*—seeped out from beneath.

>-+-◆>--O--◆+-◄

Their seats were *above* the stage—a private box but at the wrong angle, looking down on the performers. Mandip couldn't decide if they were wonderful because they were so close or terrible because none of the other nobles could see them up here. None of the people in the know knew they were La Maupin's special guests. And since most nobles didn't just want nice things, they wanted other people to see them having nice things, Mandip was at a loss.

"Turn off your high-society brain for a moment," Thibaut said, slumping against the velvet cushions of the loveseat they shared. "Enjoy it—the decadence of privacy, the luxury of secrecy. You don't have to sit up straight—nay, we must lean forward, look down, if we want to enjoy the show. Pick your nose, muss your hair. Dare to *not* look bored." He took a swig from the wine bottle, which the stagehand had oh so graciously helped them open.

"You really are a pretender, aren't you?" Mandip asked with sincerity.

"Dear boy, would you be paying me if I wasn't?"

The performances were already in full swing, of course. As they'd taken their seats, the First Grand Marquis's daughters—eleven and six respectively—

went about introducing the audience to their ponies. With the first *clop-clop* of hooves, it was clear that these "ponies" were more like *asses*, in that they were grown men dressed up as animals.

It was a bit of a laugh before the main performance, to butter up the crowd and endear them to the scenes to come.

Eventually, the children and their make-believe ponies scrambled off stage, the lamps dimmed, the orchestra gave a few fluttering notes to signal a small interlude before sputtering out into restless quiet.

Thibaut tried to feel purely excited, but he couldn't shake the odd encounter at the bottom of the stairs. It was as though he could feel important events swirling around him, just at the edge of his knowing, his seeing.

Below, the sweaty man who'd led them to their seats darted out on stage, no less damp but much more refined in his makeup and costume. He wore a noble's garb of grays and browns, but his were covered over in reflective surfaces, glitter and sequins, pips of glass and exceptionally thin discs of metal. He spoke boldly to the house audience, projecting his voice far, making a flamboyant sign of the Valley and welcoming them all to this night's performance.

Everyone clapped heartily as he announced the next act.

Scanning the crowd, Thibaut squinted, trying to see what he could of the main house. Their height and the glaring stage lights meant that the true box seats were hidden from view, which was likely where the representatives from each city-state were seated. After a moment, he sat back, relaxing into his seat despite how his own knees blocked his view. Thibaut was here for one act and one act only.

A few more jaunty players took the stage and left—a juggler, a ventriloquist—before a hush fell over the auditorium. Thibaut finally leaned forward once again, joining Mandip, who seemed to be enjoying his new perspective on life. The noble leaned on the railing with both arms, head in hands, a giant smile gracing his lips.

There came a soft rustling, a tinkle, from stage left. The lighting changed—new lamps lit, others dimmed—and then, out came La Maupin in stunning splendor.

>-+-◇>-○-<◇+-<

Krona only hesitated for a moment before letting one hand fall on the brass handle and the other on the hilt of her saber. The music coming through the door sounded . . . small? As though it all emanated from a single point instead of many instruments.

With a deep breath, she pushed forward, telling herself she was prepared for nearly every possible scenario, any possible scene.

The light from several gas lamps hit her forcefully as she exited, making her eyes hurt after so long in the dark. She blinked rapidly, trying to assess where she was as quickly as possible.

It appeared to be a bedroom. Grandiose, lavish. With everything soft covered in satin, all plush and overstuffed. At any other time, Krona would have marveled at the sheer amount of gilding in the room—every hard surface that could be covered in gold or pearl inlay had been. Even the merrily playing jewelry box. Likewise, the air was thoroughly adorned—perfumed through by the many, *many* vases of white lilies scattered across the various filigree-and-glass tables. It was like walking into a life-size jewelry box—a place for precious, garish things.

But all of these details slid in and out of her mind like water through a sieve, leaving nothing but two figures and their muffled struggle.

A blue-shrouded individual crouched over a prone form sprawled out on the grand, canopied bed. The hooded figure raised one hand—the other perhaps clutched around their victim's throat, it was difficult to tell from Krona's angle at the door—and in their fist they held a long syringe, one far more massive than she usually encountered as a Regulator but clearly meant to interact with enchantment.

Krona's body reacted before her mind could. She darted forward, lunging onto the plush mattress, intending to wrestle the needle—poised like a knife— away from the attacker.

The distance Krona had to cover was a hair too far, a breath too wide. The needle was already descending, plunging. The needle struck, and the pinned figure thrashed, their limbs seizing and flailing upward for one grotesque moment before they fell still. Stiff.

Krona's arms fell around the hooded figure and she reeled backward, pulling them off-balance. They did not struggle.

With a feral cry, Krona yanked their hood back and was both somehow entirely unsurprised and completely stunned to see the Blue Woman staring back at her.

>-+-<>-O-<>+-<

Juliet Maupin's gown was the most exquisite treasure Thibaut had ever laid eyes on.

How it didn't cut her to ribbons or weigh her down like an anvil, he could not say.

She was draped in stained glass. Bits of black wire suspended the panes, while creating joints and movement, mimicking the lead that usually held the different sections of glass together in a window or lamp. The colors were soft on her torso, pale greens and yellows and heather purple, but as her skirt broadened, the hues became bold. The foamy greens turned to blazing leaves, and the daisy yellows edged golden. The violets led down into shards of magenta and then into the deep cherry red that was close to the same color as a Regulator's typical faceplate.

Bits of coterie imagery had been painted on the panels. Though Thibaut couldn't make them out in detail, all five gods appeared to be represented. Twins Time and Nature with their wings; Knowledge in feir twisted state, like a wizened tree; Emotion, a patch of glittering brightness, as though too difficult to look directly at, like a sunburst, just suggesting a human form within; and a dark shroud with an open maw where a face should be—the Unknown God.

Short and round as La Maupin was, her presence was such that she projected immense height. She was the focus of everyone's rapt attention, as was only good and proper.

As she stepped onto a small dais center stage, Thibaut held his breath.

All the world stilled as a single tonkori player plucked the strings of their instrument. As the strumming became more rhythmic, a metal flute joined in.

Juliet's voice was bright and big the moment she began. Appropriately, the piece she sang contained musical stylings from all over the Valley. The instrumentals accompanying her were just as varied. Thibaut had never heard such an arrangement before. Haunting, beautiful, worthy of both the audience and the performer—he wondered who its composer was.

He took in a sharp breath as, suddenly, Juliet began to dance, adding in a rhythmic stomping to her song, jingling the dress to mimic traditional Marrakevian bells underscored with a Xyoparian beat. Likely, Juliet had arranged the music herself. Her talents were wide, her skills sublime.

He could not have been more of a La Maupin fanatic. She did things to his heart and soul.

When the song finished, and Juliet raised her fist and chin into the air on the final note, a collective wave of breath was released. Every audience member had their air stolen by the moment, only to have it return in a collective reckoning.

And that was only the first song.

A sudden, communal roar rang out—but not from the audience.

Thibaut's heart clenched in a new way. A startled way.

The roar was not a raucous sound of appreciation or awe or reverence.

This was a cry of pain. Of loss.

Of grief incarnate.

23

KRONA

"It is done," the Blue Woman said. "It is *done*, and only I can save you."

Krona's gaze darted to the other figure—now limp, placid, and devoid of life, arms and legs outstretched across the fine bedding.

She expected the victim's face to shock her—to be surprised or appalled by their identity. But she couldn't tell who it was, for their face was shrouded. Covered in a mask.

A death mask.

An *enchanted* mask?

The mask had been carved in the likeness of a serpent, mouth open, fangs and forked tongue bared. It looked almost comical from this angle, the proportions all wrong for a snake's head. From between the arches of the snake's brow stood the syringe, imbedded deep and standing tall, the needle piercing the victim's brain as fatally as any blade.

Then, suddenly—through an open window and muffled by the walls and eking through every crack beneath seemingly every door—Krona heard a great, collective cry. A *roaring*. Many voices, twisted and made rough with *agony*.

It was a death cry. A cry ripped from a plethora of throats all experiencing the final heartbeats and last breath of one man at once.

Which could only mean one thing.

Krona let go of the Blue Woman and fumbled across the bedding to the dead person—the dead *man*, she knew—fully knowing what face would stare blankly back at her when she ripped the mask and murder weapon away, but needing to see nonetheless. She pulled the whole mess of wood and glass and metal free in one vicious yank, and made no effort to suppress the gasp that was punched from her lungs when her eyes confirmed what she already feared.

The First Grand Marquis.

Dead. His graying ringlets fanned about his head in a messy halo, his lips parted and his pale eyes blank.

But, more disturbingly, on his forehead—a mark. Forming right before her eyes, bubbling up like a blister on the skin, raged and misshapen, but an *enchanter's mark* for certain.

"Fast. Good. Fast is good. On some, it takes days to appear," the Blue Woman said flatly, as though speaking of nothing more troublesome than the frequency of rainstorms.

Krona reeled back, stepping clumsily off the bed—overbalanced by her helm and unsteady from the whirlwind in her mind and the cries of the Marchonian Guard.

Gods, the Marchonian Guard.

They were in a frenzy, had been triggered into a blood rage. They'd go on a rampage soon, searching for the murderer, ready to remove anything or anyone who got in their way.

More people would die tonight.

She had to evacuate the dignitaries—*everyone.* Everyone needed to *get out.*

"What have you done?" she cried, turning on the Blue Woman.

"What I had to. I can't refuse an order, not yet. I told you to stay away." She slid off the bed, offered her hand to Krona. "Come with me."

"Why the fuck would I come with you?" She drew her saber, the *shing* of sliding metal on metal a grounding, focusing sound. "I'm keeping you here until the Marchonian Guards come. Until they *kill you.* That's the only way to get them to stop. They won't rest until the assassin *dies.* Until everyone in their path dies, if that's what it takes."

"Then you should hand yourself over to them," she replied flatly. With that, her form shimmered, dissipated, and she faded away like the ghost she was.

Krona's face contorted beneath her helm—beneath Motomori's mask—

The mask!

"Show yourself!" Krona commanded, determined to wrest back any control she could, attempting to press the woman with Motomori's abilities.

The Blue Woman *laughed*, but there was no joy in it.

There came a tremendous *bang* through the bedchambers. Like someone ramming a door.

Exactly like someone ramming a door. Perhaps the door to the bedroom's antechamber.

"As though the piddling power of a *mask* could compel me," the woman said. "Please, we have to get out of here." Then she raised her voice, threw it outward. "Death to tyrants!" she yelled. "Long live the empire of Winsrouen!"

A *crack* sliced through the air. The door was splintering.

A million thoughts swarmed through Krona's mind, a million questions. How did she get the First Grand Marquis alone? How did she know of the secret passage to his chambers? Why the mask? Why the needle?

But there was no time to voice any of these.

Her pure anger pushed out all else. She seethed, swiping her blade through the air, striking nothing.

"*I told you* you would take the fall for this," the woman said. "And even though I have framed a thousand people for a thousand misdeeds, I'd *like* to tell you you're not so special, but that's not true. I need you."

The voice seemed to come from behind her now. Krona spun. "Face me, you coward!"

"Coward? I've been called a lot of things in my time, but never coward."

More splintering, shouting—*raging* from the Marchonian Guards.

The memory of the guards ripping that horse apart came back to her, struck her viscerally. She remembered the blood and the entrails, joints pulling free and muscle exposed. They'd descended on that poor animal and its master like a pack of wild dogs, and that had been over nothing more than a broken bone.

"*Come with me,*" the Blue Woman urged, shimmering into existence for half a moment, hand outstretched. "You are no good to anyone if they kill you."

Krona brandished her saber, intending to cut that hand off at the wrist.

The woman disappeared again. "I can fool your eyes but little else," she said impatiently. "We cannot compel each other. Not through magical means. You *need* to come with me. Not *trust* me; I won't ask you for that yet. But know this: I can give you magic. I can *return* your magic."

"What the fuck are you talking about?"

Another *bang*—this time clearly the sound of a door failing, *falling.*

"You only have two options: let them strike you down here, now, or follow me. I cannot see all of your secrets the same as I can others'. You are immune to me, to most of my magic. And you are only beginning to understand how powerful this makes you. What this means. Let me show you."

Enraged voices clamored from no more than a room away.

The slightly open window threw itself wide. A moment later, the Blue Woman let herself be seen again, crouching on the seal, once again holding out her hand for Krona to take.

Krona knew that if she was seen fleeing from the scene, it would confirm her guilt in the minds of all Marchonian Guards. From Captain Veratas on down. But if she was found in the First Grand Marquis's chambers, it would not only confirm the same but lead to her instant execution.

There was no way to hold the Blue Woman accountable without also playing right into her hands.

Letting a ragged half curse, half cry rip from her throat, Krona sheathed her weapon, lowered her visor, and slapped her palm into the woman's hand, allowing herself to be led through the window and out into the night.

24

MANDIP

Someone in the audience shrieked as the roar continued, on and on, interspersed with grunting, like that of wild animals.

Audience members began to rise to their feet before a voice Mandip recognized as the Captain of the Marchonian Guard rang out. "Everyone remain where you are! My most illustrious gentlefolk, for your own safety, do not leave the confines of the auditorium."

The original shriek now became a scream—high-pitched, panicked, and blood-curdling.

Below their seats, Juliet twirled on the stage, leaping down from her pedestal and rushing—as best she could—back behind the curtain. The panes of her dress clinked wildly, like windchimes in a violent storm.

Next to Mandip, Thibaut leapt up. "Come on," he said with a shove, half-drained wine bottle forgotten.

Mandip was at a loss. "What?"

"*Down.* We need to see to Juliet's safety."

"*Her* safety? Do you—do you have any idea what's just happened?"

"Not a clue." Thibaut attempted to clamber over him to reach the rickety stairs. "But I suspect it has something to do with why we were locked up with the wine."

Mandip managed to get a hold of him, to halt him. "That cry is half the Marchonian Guard being whipped into a frenzy," he hissed. "Something has happened to one of the Grand Marquises. Given the honorable Veratas's remarkably even tone, I'd say it was the First, as zhur charge is the Second. We should not move from this spot. Here we'll be safe. Out there—"

"And does *Juliet* know what's happening?"

"I daresay she strikes me as a woman who knows how to take care of herself."

"And I daresay that just because someone can see to their own safety, that doesn't mean they need to be the only one who cares about it." With that, he vaulted over Mandip's legs and thew himself at the stairs, making the whole contraption—their seats, their box—seesaw back and forth perilously.

And what am I? Chopped liver? Mandip groused.

His instincts and training told him to stay put. He knew what to do when the Marchonian Guards were riled: stay out of their way. That was the only rule. Everyone currently in the theater should just be thankful that whatever had caused the First's guards to fly into a rage had happened—apparently— elsewhere.

But, seeing as how he and Thibaut were still quite irritatingly *chained together*, he didn't have much choice in the matter, lest he wish to wrestle with the determined man atop this rickety platform, so perilously placed as it was above the decidedly hard and unyielding surface of the stage.

Together, they awkwardly bounded downward.

Despite Captain Veratas's calm orders, mayhem had quickly broken out in the theater. People of all ranks were rushing to the exits, and the Sublime Protectors had all gathered in a defensive formation around their charges.

Beyond, it seemed the main doors had already been barred. A wash of nobles banged their fists and pounded their shoulders against the heavy wood, despite Veratas's continued calls for calm.

As they reached the bottom of the stairs, a stagehand ran past them with a lit lantern held high.

"We need to get out of here," Thibaut said directly into Mandip's ear. "We've been locked in for our protection, to be sure, but all it'll take is one frantic usher knocking over a stage light to start a fire that will fry us all to a crisp."

"One worry at a time!" Mandip insisted.

"I'm afraid that's not how worries work. Come on—to Juliet!"

Thibaut took his hand—better not to tug each other's arms from their sockets—and just as he turned to run off, flitting around aimlessly backstage, who should appear but the very songstress they were to search for?

Rather than her resplendent stained-glass dress, she now wore something entirely indecent. A tight bodice with long sleeves and a high collar enveloped her torso, black and perhaps made of crushed velvet, but it was difficult to tell in this light. Her skirt, by contrast, was nearly as poufy as the pink fabric contraption she'd been wearing when they met, yet this one—black as well—ended scandalously above her knees, leaving her legs bare and her thick-soled boots brazenly apparent.

"Good heavens," Mandip muttered, throwing one hand over his eyes for a moment.

"How did you manage such a quick wardrobe change?" Thibaut asked.

"As though I weren't prepared for just such a frenzy?" she quipped.

Disturbingly, Mandip couldn't tell if she was truly joking.

"Why, my dear lord Basu, you did make it after all," she noted happily, as though panicked screams weren't echoing out all around them. "How did you enjoy my performance? I admit, I didn't get to present my full set, but alas, my mistress has always been impatient. I'm sure you're both dying to get away from this tense atmosphere. Please, follow me."

Mandip was keenly aware that half of her words were candidates for deep suspicion and her tone was distressingly chipper, yet the cognitive dissonance this created had him stumbling along after her as soon as Thibaut set the two of them in motion.

He did, luckily, notice she was leading them back exactly the way they'd come.

"No, not into the cozy! The cellar is locked; we'll be trapped just the same."

"Well, that would never do," she agreed. She glared in the direction of the hidden door for a moment, clearly irritated to have a hitch in her plan. "How are you boys at climbing?" she asked.

"Like this?" Mandip asked incredulously, raising his fist to show off their shackles.

"We can still manage," Thibaut assured her.

Mandip wasn't as hopeful.

"This way, then," she said.

They wove in and out of various set pieces hidden by various curtains, all waiting for cues this evening that would never come. People of all shapes and sizes ran around them in disarray, each with a purpose all their own. The ground wasn't shaking, but the floor sure was, what with all of the hidden compartments and hollow sections and people's heavy stomping as they fled this way and that.

Juliet led them to a ladder that looked even more rickety than the cobbled-together stairs, but Mandip had decided there was no use in protesting and had simply thrown himself into fleeing for the time being.

He did spare a moment before mounting the first rung—behind Juliet (gods help him, he was staring straight up her skirt into her bloomers) and in front of Thibaut—to be grateful Adhar had elected to stay home. He wasn't sure what he'd be doing if he had to worry where his brother was in all this chaos.

Their going was slow. Juliet reached the top well before the two men had so much as sighted the halfway mark, and she tapped her foot impatiently at the top, staring out over the stage's rigging into whatever she could see of the audience.

When Mandip neared, she reached down for him, helping haul him to the top with surprising strength for her size. "Watch your balance," she instructed, before turning and hurrying away across the narrow platform.

The rigging swayed. Why did everything on a stage have to sway?

Now pulling Thibaut in tow, both men stumbled after her, each keeping their free hand on the narrow railing the platform offered, but clearly equally skeptical about this whole upward endeavor.

Glancing down, Mandip spotted two Regulators, clearly searching for something or someone. Thibaut noticed them a moment after and looked like he might call out to them, but thought better of it.

Juliet left them no time to hem and haw. They had to follow or be left behind.

"Where does this lead?" Mandip asked after a few minutes and small leaps to several more shaky platforms.

"The roof," she called casually.

"*The roof?*"

"Does repeating it incredulously make it easier to comprehend?" she snarked.

"Pray tell, what awaits us on the roof?"

"Freedom."

25

KRONA

Krona sprinted hand in hand with her enemy. Away from the window, away from the First Grand Marquis's chambers, away from the murderous Marchonians and all hope of explaining herself.

Within moments, the guards were at that very window, shouting at her—roaring more like great beasts than people instructing her to halt.

They'd seen her uniform. They would know, now, to blame a Regulator.

Pulling the reverb bead under her tongue, she thought to warn her team but wasn't sure just yet if communicating with them would place them in further danger.

Beside her, the Blue Woman still seemed visible, but Krona couldn't be sure. Wherever this woman got her power, she seemed to be able to wield it with great skill and precision. It was entirely possible Krona could see her and the Marchonians could not.

At first, Krona was disoriented. She couldn't tell where on the palace grounds they'd emerged. All of the thoroughfares were well lit with gas lamps on high, but the hidden passageway had completely turned her around. She tried to get her bearings as they fled, but it wasn't until she set eyes on the unusual shape of the Rotunda itself that she fully realized just how far the tunnel had taken her.

It was two rooftops away, and she and the woman were, understandably, not running toward it but rather parallel to it for the moment, working their way not toward the front gates but to some other destination.

All around them, constabulary of all ranks burst out of buildings and either ran toward the wailing Marchonians or made to secure the entrances and exits to the palace complex. Krona nearly ran headlong into a Watchperson who seemed to be completely unaware of her presence.

This was her chance, Krona realized. She could not use Motomori's influence on a whole host of Marchonians at once—and she had no idea how the berzerking frenzy would affect Motomori's capabilities, regardless—but this? One calm individual? That she could handle.

She tried to stop them, looping an arm through theirs, thinking that if she could gain an ally in the moment, it might buy her sanctuary, at the very least. Time to think. But when she yanked on their arm, they pulled up short as though running into something invisible. Their expression was a monument to shock, and they whirled on the spot, swinging a single fist wildly.

That was when Krona realized she could no longer be seen. She was now invisible, just like the Blue Woman.

The Thalo's magic had struck again.

It was Krona's turn to startle when, with a definitive tug, the Blue Woman pulled Krona back into a run. "If only I could steal the secret of wakefulness from you, this would be much easier," she grumbled. "Dallying like this will only cause both of us problems."

Bewildered, Krona simply followed, De-Lia's mask bouncing at her side.

She tried not to think about how badly she'd failed, how thoroughly she'd underestimated the Blue Woman's ability to move about unhindered and unseen.

A powerful, important man was dead, and the Lutador that saw the sun rise tomorrow would not be the same one that had seen it set this evening.

The entire palace complex was in an uproar now. All of the security she'd had the Chief Magistrate put on high alert was out in full show searching for *her*, intent on capturing *her*.

No, not you, she said to herself. *A Regulator. All they saw was a Regulator. They'll have no way of knowing it was you they saw.*

Minutes flew by as the pair of them dodged lawpersons in all manner of uniform. Krona thought once more to attempt communication but was unable to keep that intent secret from the Blue Woman. The Thalo puppet pulled her into an ornately sculpted set of bushes. More footsteps were rushing their way, and even if she'd somehow shrouded Krona with her magic, she clearly wasn't going to give the Regulator any extra chances to undermine her escape.

Several Marchonians ran by, but before the pair could extricate themselves from the foliage, three new figures abruptly dropped down from seemingly nowhere, right on the other side of the topiaries. One made a remarkably graceful landing, as though they'd leapt from that exact spot time and time again. The other two were decidedly less prepared for the impact, both letting out great *oofs* and half crumbling, half tumbling like dolls with no control of their limbs.

They were all dressed differently but each rather flashy in their own way.

The Blue Woman surprised Krona by jumping out of her hiding spot, almost as though she'd forgotten Krona entirely, and with clearly no mind to conceal herself. "Juliet!" she called.

The first figure whirled. "Hintosep!"

They ran at one another, arms outstretched. Their embrace was quick but fiercely tight, with the familiarity of family.

"You were to meet me at the basket," the Blue Woman—*Hintosep*—said to the new young woman, who appeared to be none other than the famous songstress, La Maupin.

Krona's stomach flipped over when she realized the two other figures were the very same men she'd locked away in a wine cellar not so long ago. "Saints and swill, what are you two doing here?" she cursed through clenched teeth, keeping herself confined to the bushes.

Now that she was no longer the Blue Woman's primary focus, Krona considered trying to escape again, to flee for help. But she couldn't simply leave Thibaut with an assassin.

Hintosep nodded toward the men. "I thought we were to collect him later."

Juliet shrugged. "Seems he's more enterprising than I gave him credit for."

Too much was happening all at once. Hintosep and Juliet spoke as though nothing was wrong, as though the Blue Woman hadn't just murdered the head of a sovereign city-state. Krona wanted to grab both women and shake them, as though that might wake Krona herself from this nightmare.

"No time to dawdle," Hintosep said.

"Boys!" Juliet called, gesturing for them to follow.

Thibaut and Mandip looked just as confused as Krona.

"We don't need the other one," Hintosep said.

"Seems someone cuffed them together, so we don't really have the option of either-or at the moment," Juliet explained.

"Mistress Hirvath?" Hintosep bade.

Feeling much like a trapped rat that had no option but to scurry through the maze, Krona braced herself and emerged from the topiaries.

"Krona?" Thibaut exclaimed before visibly relaxing, as though he'd found his evening's savior. "Thank the gods. Perhaps you can tell us what's happening and get us the hells out of—"

Angry shouts grew close.

"Sorry to disappoint," Krona said, trudging up beside him and earnestly taking his unbound arm. She was sure he thought she'd be the one to get him out of this pickle rather than cement him inside it. "I'm just as tied up as you."

"This way, everyone," Hintosep said, running on, knowing they had no real choice but to follow.

There was no more time to pause, to think, to ask questions or attempt an explanation. They hurried in the opposite direction of the main gates, into the gardens, out past the bright halos of the gas lamps. Toward, it seemed, the cliffs.

The sheer, unfeeling, ungiving cliffs. The cliffs whose very existence protected one side of the complex from potential assault, at whose base lay the Praan River.

"You can't expect to scale the bluffs," Krona said.

"Of course not," Hintosep said. "Who has the strength to climb all that way? We're jumping."

"*Jumping?*" Lord Basu squeaked.

"See, there you go again," said Juliet.

"We'd never survive!" he countered.

"That's exactly what we hope the guards believe," Juliet explained.

Krona spared a glance behind them, noting the number of torches now raised in pursuit to ward off the night. If that light reached their small party, how many people would it illuminate? Would Thibaut and Lord Basu and Juliet be marked as regicidal as well?

Overhead, the sky rumbled. The wind picked up.

The rampart on the cliff's edge was easily accessible but patrolled. A pair of palace guards—not Marchonians—stood with lanterns raised and arms at the ready, clearly looking for an assassin on the run. More guards ran along the wall, heading in the party's direction.

Hintosep focused on the nearest guard, moving right into their space, hand outstretched toward their head. "Sleep," she commanded.

Instinctually, Krona turned on the second. She pushed with Motomori, her tone strong and commanding. "Drop your weapon."

The first guard collapsed in a heap, apparently having gone unconscious on the spot. The second one, after throwing aside their sword, was gently encouraged to lie down next to the first.

Juliet braced herself on the wall's ledge, leaning far over to peer down.

"Is it there?" Hintosep asked.

"It's there," she confirmed. With that, she heaved herself over the side.

"Juliet!" Thibaut cried in horror, lunging after her. Mandip was yanked along with him.

"Up and over, gentlemen," Hintosep instructed.

"W-wait. *Wait,*" Basu stuttered.

But Thibaut had already climbed onto the stones, was ready to fling himself over. "Come *on,*" he shouted, grabbing the lord just above the manacle and boosting him up beside him.

There was still no telltale *splash* of Juliet hitting the water.

Was the fall just that far, or—?

"Here we go!" Thibaut yelled. The two men leapt.

"You next, Regulator," Hintosep insisted.

Krona was crouched beside the two guards, double-checking their vitals, making sure she hadn't pushed too far and Hintosep hadn't stolen more than the first guard's wakefulness.

The first fat drops of rain splattered onto the stonework, then the guards' faces. A flash in the clouds brightened the ramparts for half a second before plunging them back into relative darkness. A growl of thunder followed.

"Quickly!" Hintosep called. "To beat the rain!"

Krona wanted to know how jumping into a river qualified as beating the rain, but even as she approached the ledge, she was sure it wasn't water she'd be hitting at the end of her leap.

After all, there were still no splashes.

"Krona!" Thibaut called from below. And, she judged, not that far below.

But the darkness and the wind and the new rain blurred cliff and river and all else together. She thought she saw figures—shadows—but was unsure.

"Jump, Regulator, or so help me—"

She didn't need any more encouraging. With a protective hand on De-Lia's mask, Krona vaulted off the cliff.

26

THALO CHILD

One and a Half Years Ago

The metal rattle was old, dented. It caught the candlelight in the nursery with a dulled, matte sheen. Little fingerprints dappled its top, and larger fingerprints covered its handle.

Thalo Child's infant was clearly getting too old for such nonsense toys.

"No!" zhe cried when he shook it in front of zhur face. "Outside," zhe demanded, dark cheeks rounded, puffed out. Zhe stamped zhur small foot and shook zhur black curls from side to side.

"It's not time for outside," Thalo Child said with a put-upon sigh. "You used to love the rattle."

"No rattle," zhe said, snatching it from his fingers, holding it up and away from him—clearly thinking it out of his reach.

"Babe," he said warningly. "Little one . . ."

"No!" zhe said again, shaking the rattle firmly once in zhur tight little fist, as though zhe meant to dash it to the ground.

But instead of throwing it, zhe gripped tighter, gritting zhur baby teeth, squinting hard at the object, pursing zhur tiny mouth and clearly focusing all zhur baby will on the offensive thing in a picture of pure infantile fury.

After a moment, zhe unclenched, softening again from head to toe, entire demeanor shifting into something more relaxed. "No more rattle," zhe said softly, handing back the toy.

Thalo Child was shocked to find a lump of granite in his palm where the tin rattle should be.

At first, he thought his senses had fooled him. That his infant had been able to switch the rattle and rock when he wasn't looking. But the stone matched the rattle's shape perfectly, as though carved into its exact likeness, dents and all.

"Where did you . . . How—"

The baby giggled, clearly ever so pleased with the stunned look on his face.

"Where did you get this?" he asked firmly, holding it up between them.

Scrunching up zhur nose, zhe wrapped zhur chubby fingers around the granite.

A moment later, cool tin replaced the stone in his fist.

Stunned, he dropped the rattle.

It had been transmuted. Right in the palm of his hand.

That was a power no Thalo possessed.

"Outside?" zhe asked again, much less petulantly than before.

"Outside," he agreed. "And we will have a *talk*."

He knew interrogating his babe would prove little more than useless, but he also knew he had to try, and he couldn't do it in the nursery. Quickly, he bundled zhim up in zhur outside clothes, with a thick ram's-hide cloak and fur-lined moccasins that had been sealed with beeswax—every stitch of it dyed blue, of course.

The eldest of the Nameless eyed him warily as he went about preparing for the outing, feir pale gaze tracking him the whole time, a curl of suspicion on feir lips.

"You seem harried," fey said as he scooped up his infant and made for the nursery door.

"Zhe is restless and wishes to go out into a courtyard. I don't want to risk zhim upsetting the other babies."

He felt a small probe at his mind, looking for secrets. He mentally batted it down and glared at fer. "I'm not so young anymore," he snapped. "Do not treat me like one of your charges."

"Apologies. I only wish for the infant's well-being."

"Zhe is fine."

"Of course."

He made to leave again.

"Don't be long," fey called after.

A warning, he was sure.

⊱──⊱♦◯♦──⊰

Thalo Child's infant absolutely adored the snow. As soon as they were outside, zhe wriggled in his arms, impatient to play in the fresh early-morning dusting. The courtyard was empty, as expected. Mealtime was soon. The two of them had a few minutes to themselves, at least, before those who loved to eat their porridge in the crisp cold ("Good for the constitution!" he could hear the cook say) made their way with their steaming bowls out into the communal space.

A terror now that zhe could walk, the little one immediately zoomed away, scream-giggling as zhe ran between the cold-hardy bushes and over the tread-resistant moss that covered the cobblestones. Thalo Child took up a bench where he could see zhim clearly, no matter which direction zhe darted. As the freezing marble met his backside, his body clenched, his spine straightened, and his hands turned into fists deep in his pockets—a visceral and automatic reaction that made him clutch the handle of the tin-that-had-been-stone that rested at his left side.

For a little while, he simply watched his infant play. To zhim, everything was new and wonderful, and each discovery—of a fallen leaf, a strange insect—apparently required the loudest possible exclamation of excitement zhe could muster.

He wondered when he'd stopped being . . . like *that*. Exuberant. Unashamed or afraid of an extreme display of enthusiasm, or fear, or anger, or sorrow.

When had he become so subdued? Before the Ritual that bound him to Gerome, he was sure.

He'd *learned* to be submissive. To ask questions, but not the *wrong* questions. To seek Gerome's guidance before decisions, and his approval after all actions. None of it had come naturally to Thalo Child. Not in the beginning, anyway.

But he'd learned. Because he'd seen what had happened to those who could not learn or learned too late.

What kinds of *penalties* they'd faced.

Secret's penalty had always been the worst to Thalo Child. Perhaps because he saw so many examples of it roaming the halls of the keep. Time's penalty might mean an early death, but Secret's meant no life. It meant the draining of all personhood.

It meant becoming a Mindless.

He hoped his infant would learn quickly.

"Little one, come here, please," he called, and zhe obeyed.

Three more Thalo entered the courtyard—priests—as the infant toddled over to his bench. They took up a different corner, well away from the pair, so Thalo Child did not fret.

Not too much, anyway.

Still, he covertly drew the rattle from his pocket. "That trick you showed me earlier, can you do it again?" he asked.

Zhe nodded, smile wide. He passed zhim the toy, and zhe shook it enthusiastically, but nothing happened. Perhaps zhe didn't truly understand what he was asking.

Perhaps my mind was playing tricks on me.

His eyes darted nervously to the priests.

Hopefully, no one else is playing tricks on me.

The trio's attention was on their breakfast. They didn't appear to find a young Nameless and an infant out on their own too curious.

Suddenly, his babe thrust the rattle back into his hands. He was disappointed to find it still tin.

He cast around him for a different object. Maybe he truly hadn't seen what he'd thought he'd seen. Maybe he hadn't felt what he'd thought he'd felt. Perhaps the rattle's density, and weight, and temperature, and entire *nature of being* hadn't actually shifted at his infant's touch.

There were a few stray pebbles at his feet, but a rock wouldn't do. He wanted something more complex.

Settling on a leaf from the nearest bush, he held it out on the flat of his palm. "With this? Can you change this?"

Zhe picked it up carefully, just by the stem, showing zhur chubby fingers had more dexterity than he would have given them credit for. Still simply delighting in the world, zhe whipped zhur wrist back and forth, making the leaf flutter and flap like a bird's wing.

And when zhe held still again, there was no longer a leaf in zhur hand but a leaf-shaped crystal.

Thalo Child gasped and yanked it from the baby's hands, afraid the priests would see. Startled, zhe looked like zhe was about to cry—tears began to brim in the corners of zhur eyes. Clearly, he'd simply alarmed zhim, not hurt or scared zhim, but still, Thalo Child immediately felt bad and scooped the young one into his arms, hugging tight and petting at zhur hair. "You did well," he mumbled. "Very good."

His heart was pounding fast and heavy in his chest.

This was not the magic of the Thalo. This was not the magic of the keep's artifacts, nor the watered-down magic of the city-states' enchantments.

A distant memory tickled at his consciousness. Something someone had locked away. As though he'd known these things about his infant, then been forced to forget.

Yes, yes. At some point, he'd been shown the truth, then had it taken away.

His charge wasn't a Thalo.

Impossible, he thought. *Impossible. What in the Valley is going on?*

27

MANDIP

It was their sprint over the palace rooftops that cinched it for Mandip: Juliet Maupin was far more than what she seemed. That she would know about the actors' cozy made sense; it wasn't difficult to imagine one of the Grand Marquises trying to covertly woo her into his bed. But that she would know how to exit the Rotunda via a bit of ventilation onto the sloping ceramic tiles that clad its roof? Not so much.

Even before the three of them ran across a glass bridge to the palace proper—then up and over and around the various slopes and vaults that made up a topography most definitely not designed to be traversed—he considered plopping himself down and refusing to flee, because he couldn't shake the feeling that she wasn't leading them away from the ruckus so much as toward something.

Something complicated.

And, though he felt very ungentlemanly thinking it, perhaps something *sinister*.

Running into the Regulator and the mysterious woman in blue confirmed his fears: rather than escaping, he and Thibaut had darted smack into the thick of it.

He wasn't sure what exactly had befallen the First Grand Marquis, but it wasn't anything *pleasant*. The grievous roaring had yet to stop, and he couldn't help but suspect this woman—Hintosep—had something to do with it.

He was well aware of what the rampaging Marchonians would do to him if he were caught with their quarry. They may very well serve him one day, but on this night, if he stepped in their way, he would be just another obstacle. Something to be removed from their path—violently, if necessary.

So, when the group continued to bolt—away from the well-lit cobbles, away from the guards, away from the bystanders—he bolted as well. Of course, being chained to Thibaut had figured in to his compliance. Perhaps if it had just been the two of them with Juliet and the new woman, it would have been easy to convince his escort not to go with them. But the presence of the Regulator changed things. He could see how Thibaut shifted, immediately deferring to the figure in black.

Now here he was on some kind of platform—or basket? The woman had said "basket," and it did indeed possess woven sides of reed and thick grasses, with a floor of solid planks—helping to catch the Regulator as their boots hit the bottom and they pitched forward, off-balance.

"We've got you. *We've got you*," Thibaut whispered hastily.

There came a thump behind Mandip, and then a rustling all around and overhead. La Maupin and Hintosep moved a sheet, or perhaps a tarp, up, around, and over the group. Covering them.

Shielding them?

"Do not move," Hintosep ordered. "Do not make a sound. So help me, I will gut you if you breathe too loudly. Do you understand me?"

No one answered.

"Good."

The rain fell all the harder, each drop thudding dully against the tarp. Glancing around, Mandip noticed that the basket was plenty large enough for the five of them and then perhaps a handful more besides. Something easily spotted as unnatural and human-made, even in the dark. How stretching a tarp over the top was supposed to actually hide them, he couldn't divine.

He closed his eyes, waiting for the inevitable shout of rage and recognition from above. He felt like a child playing a (deadly) game of hide-and-seek, pretending that if he could not see the seekers, then they could not see him.

The voices of their pursuers grew louder, and then there came a flickering glow through the tarp, like several lanterns or torches being thrust over the wall at once. Someone cursed as the rain doused their fire.

"There's no one! Just rocks."

"Are you sure? They could be clinging—"

"No place for them to hide."

"I want a detail to stay on the wall!" came Captain Veratas's familiar voice. "The rest of you, follow me. Find me that villain! Dead or alive."

Most of the light receded. The rest slowly dimmed as the detail on the wall ran off to scan the rest of the cliff.

How they'd gone undetected, Mandip could not fathom.

And still, no one in their ragtag party dared breathe easily.

Juliet and Hintosep handed off their bits of tarp to Thibaut and the Regulator—neither protested, though it was clear the Regulator wanted to argue—before dealing with some kind of winch-and-pully system. Slowly, they lowered the basket toward the water.

Mandip kept himself quiet until they touched down on the river's surface—until the basket became a boat, the tarp became a sail, and the songstress and the mysterious woman became sailors. There were two oars in the craft, but they remained stowed for the moment, as Hintosep let the current take them where it willed.

The wind picked up, propelling them south, downriver, at a clip. Luckily, the rain had fizzled out by then, and there was no more threat to his attire or Thibaut's fine velvet. But that was neither here nor there in the grand scheme of things.

Steeling himself, Mandip stalked up to Hintosep, who now sat poised at the tiller, pulling his shoulders back and summoning all of his noble authority. Thibaut begrudgingly followed. "Madame, I demand to know who you are, what happened to the First Grand Marquis, and why you have subsequently kidnapped myself and my companion."

She gazed right past him and addressed Juliet at the bow. "Is he going to be a problem?"

"Oh, I don't think so," La Maupin replied. "He may be a bit fussy, but no need to put him under." Her eyes, in turn, darted toward the Regulator. "What about her?"

The Regulator was pacing like a caged cat.

"She's considering trying to commandeer the boat," Hintosep said casually.

The Regulator stopped marching, whirled, and ripped off her helm, revealing a terrifying mask beneath. It depicted a demonic grin and only covered the bottom half of her face. In turn, she yanked a glass shell from her ear and pulled a thread with a bead on the end out from under the mask. "Would you stay *the fuck* out of my head?" she shouted.

"Not as long as you keep thinking about pushing me overboard. Really, Mistress Hirvath, I tell you."

Mandip would not be so easily dissuaded. "I'll have you know, my detainment verges on treason, so if—"

Juliet cut him off with a very loud, overly dramatic sigh.

He fell quiet, but only for a moment, until an understanding suddenly struck him. "If it's ransom you're after," he said, "they won't pay it. Not my parents, not the palace."

Now La Maupin let out a great, gleeful bark of a laugh. "Oh, Mandip . . ."

"No need to be so dramatic, my lord," said Hintosep. "We're not after time vials, though we are interested in *treasure*. My explanations can wait until the palace lights are dimly behind us," said Hintosep. "Nothing is simple, and I'd much prefer it if we were somewhere more secure before dividing my attention. Perhaps for the time being—Mistress Hirvath? You can busy yourself setting the gentlemen free and explaining to Lord Basu who I am."

"I have no idea who you are," the Regulator spat. "Not really."

"*What* I am, then."

Mistress Hirvath did, at the very least, seem to think uncuffing them was a fair idea. Grabbing the chain suspended between them, she yanked both men to the bow as Juliet retreated to Hintosep's side, then bade them sit, huddled together. With her brows pinched in frustration—and that terrible, grinning maw of a mask still covering her face—she crouched down to fiddle with the locks.

"We are on your side and at your service, Mistress," Mandip whispered to her. "Whatever you need from me and my companion in order to right this situation, I assure you, you have it."

"Thank you," she said with a huff. "If only it were that easy."

Once she'd released Mandip's wrist, she turned her attention to Thibaut, and her expression changed. The familiarity between the two of them was palpable, both fondness and exasperation coloring her tone when she spoke again. "You remember the invisible forces in Gatwood's cellar? The ones we barely escaped?"

Thibaut rubbed his freed wrist. Mandip had no doubt they'd both be sporting cuff burns in the daylight. "Of course," the escort said.

The Regulator nodded over her shoulder at Hintosep. "She's one of them."

What followed then was a series of descriptions and explanations that Mandip found not only preposterous but downright ludicrous. The Regulator sounded absolutely *mad,* and if it hadn't been for the way Thibaut was nodding along—taking in every word as though it was writ in the scrolls themselves—Mandip might have said as much.

"And that woman over there killed the First Grand Marquis, before my eyes," she concluded, capping off her tale of blasphemous wonders with the truth as Mandip had feared it.

Mandip gritted his teeth, staring at the woman managing the boat's helm, turning over their options in his head. They couldn't let her escape. They couldn't let her get away with this. Especially since Mandip had no idea what she intended to do with them in the end. "Should we not, the three of us, attempt to overpower her?" he suggested, tone low and conspiratorial.

"No, you should not," Hintosep called.

"I told you," the Regulator grumbled, "she can read your thoughts. She will always know our minds—perhaps even before we do."

"We can't simply give up and let her take us—wherever she's taking us," he spluttered.

Thibaut turned to him, with a frustratingly patronizing set to his lips, and gently peeled away his fake mustache, then removed the wig and fluffed out his hair. "Your determination is commendable," he said. "But if my mistress says there's nothing to be done now, we must wait for her signal. She will tell us when the time is right to rebel." With a wink, Thibaut raised his chin and his voice. "Did you get that one?" he called to Hintosep. "We're going to rebel; just you wait!"

Mandip couldn't be sure in the darkness, but he thought the woman rolled her eyes.

Suddenly, the Regulator reached out, settling a gloved hand on the side of Thibaut's face. He turned startled eyes on her, and she reclaimed her hand. "I'm just . . . glad you're all right," she said hurriedly, before looking away sheepishly, her body following soon after. She spun and stood, walking away.

"What was that?" he asked Thibaut, raising an eyebrow at him.

Absently, Thibaut himself let his gloved fingers trace the ghost of her touch. "I don't rightly know."

28

KRONA

Krona had taken off her ear shell and pocketed her reverb bead as soon as they were free of the palace grounds, largely to halt the constant pleas for her to answer. There was nothing she could say just yet—no reassurances she could give—that would either end her team's worry or assure her own safety. Until she had a better understanding of the situation, their loyalty to her could only spell danger.

But she missed their voices. The shell and bead were her connection to backup, to support, to people she knew would come to her aid and follow her instructions without question.

At least she had Thibaut, even if she'd prefer he was far away, safe and sound in his bed.

Cradling his face had been impulsive. She was just . . . overwhelmed by everything that had happened this evening. Juliet and Hintosep had clearly been after Mandip, but it seemed Thibaut was an accidental acquirement, and she hoped that meant he would be safe from whatever ill-fated Thalo plans had yet to come to fruition.

Leaving the two men to coo over each other at the bow, she once again stalked up to Hintosep. "Why did you bother to warn me in the first place?" she asked, her patience wearing thin.

"I told you to stay away," Hintosep said calmly, gaze fixed ahead on the waters.

"You could have told me the target was a Grand Marquis," Krona countered, moving closer, forcing the woman to look at her. "You could have told me *you'd* be the assassin. You could have just *not* killed—"

Most people would have been intimidated by a Regulator invading their personal space, but not Hintosep. She stood her ground and stared sternly at Krona. "No. The point of warning you wasn't to save the Grand Marquis; the point was to save *you*. And to keep him away," she added, with a nod at the young lord. "Now I have to rethink our next steps."

"Why do you care what happens to me?" Krona asked.

"Because I need you. And we can help each other. Your resistance to my magic points to Kairopathy, and I have a theory as to how we can make you stronger—immune to many more of my abilities."

"Why . . . why would you want that? To strengthen my resistance? You won't even stay out of my head of your own accord."

"I'm hoping we can be allies, not enemies."

Krona scoffed, disgusted. "You've attacked Lutador at its heart, and you think I want to ally with you?"

"What are you going to do instead?" Hintosep challenged. "Arrest me? No, you won't so much as *attempt* to arrest me, because—besides the futility of it—you realize all of this"—she made a sweeping, encompassing gesture—"is beyond any law you know of or adhere to. Yes, I killed a man. An important man. I've done it before and I have every intent to do it again."

"Then, in the spirit of cooperation, at least tell me *why*," Krona demanded.

"Would it help if I told you he was a terrible person?"

"As though murder is permissible if it happens to bad people? You think I have the constitution and moral leanings of a child?"

Hintosep seemed to take this as a fair point. "I killed him because he was going to be assassinated either way. Doing it myself ensured I had more control over the situation and was there in case you disobeyed my direction, *which you did*. If anyone else from my order had volunteered for the deed, you'd be dead by the hands of the Marchonian Guard this very hour."

"You mentioned next steps. What are they?"

"Mandip has guessed it already."

Basu sat up straighter at the mention of his name. Krona had told him of Hintosep's ability to peer into his mind, but she understood how shocked and violating it felt. "A heist at the Treasury," he said. "All of this for common thievery? Robbery. You killed a man to open a vault?"

"Of course not. I killed a man to start a war. One of the more favorable side effects is that it also allows us access to a vault. All of this is for a much larger picture. A greater purpose. The heist is only a small but necessary step."

"A step toward *what*?" Krona asked, still trying to process Hintosep's casual mention of war—*war!* "Speak plainly; I've had enough cryptic nonsense for a lifetime."

"Rescue," Juliet said, her voice thick. "We're rescuing my brother."

"Rescuing all of Arkensyre, if we can manage," Hintosep said, handing off the helm to Juliet. "Hard to port, my dear. Rocks up ahead."

Juliet guided the boat accordingly.

"This is going to sound complicated," Hintosep went on, "but I promise you it's all very straightforward. The one I serve, He's called the Savior. My clan—the Order of the Thalo—may take its name from the creator, but it is the Savior who directs us. And He always has, ever since before our work passed into the myth of bedtime stories and night terrors. He twists everything to His liking. Everything.

"If you were given a directive you could not refuse—and I mean *could not*, despite it being a command you disagreed with at its core—you would do your best to work within those orders for the best possible outcome of all the terrible outcomes, wouldn't you?" she asked Krona.

"Of course."

"That's what tonight was. That's why I killed the First Grand Marquis. This is exactly the sort of thing the Savior does with impunity: orders people to their death. Dreg, commoner, public servant, noble. Heads of state. *Children.* They're all the same to Him. Sacrifices for the greater good, He claims. He cares deeply about Arkensyre—of this I'm certain. But He's lost sight of how to care for it and its people. This conflict with Winsrouen? He's fanning the flames on purpose. *He* ordered the Grand Marquis's assassination and you framed as a traitor. In this mess I saw an opportunity to claim you for my side, and so I volunteered to put the man to death myself. If I hadn't, he would still be dead by another's hand and—as I said—you would've already been seized and sentenced—if not reduced to a bloody smear on the Grand Marquis's bedroom wall. If we're lucky, the Savior will not be able to uncover that I've helped you for a while still. That is the long and short of it," she finished.

"So, you've betrayed this *Savior* because you disagree with his war?" Krona asked.

"Yes."

Yes. A perfectly noble answer.

And Krona didn't buy it for a second. Still, in the moment, she didn't know what her next actions should be. After the initial frenzy at the palace, all the constabulary would regroup, and their numbers would be counted. Krona doubted anyone besides herself would be missing. And yet, was that really enough to frame her? The sight of a Regulator fleeing and her absence from a roll call?

She began pacing the boat, fiddling with her reverb bead, trying to decide if she should reestablish contact with her detail or not.

Hours passed. And still, she paced. Occasionally, Mandip would attempt to draw her into another ill-advised planning session, and Thibaut would shush him or distract him—often with a peck on the cheek or lips, which made Krona turn away and vehemently self-deny the surge of jealousy it ignited in her gut.

La Maupin was the most carefree of the lot, perfectly content with her position at the stern. "Relax," she bade Krona. "Fretting will get you nowhere."

And yet fret she did.

"Where are we going?" she asked Hintosep.

"Someplace safe. Mirthhouse. My old home."

Eventually, the Thalo woman steered them toward shore. At first, Krona thought they were headed for a rocky outcropping, but the sheer, solid face of it proved to be an illusion. The dark mouth of a cave appeared, hidden by some enchantment Krona could not name.

As they entered and the starry sky was exchanged for dense blankness, she shivered. Her chill was inside and out. Her adrenaline from their escape had long since ebbed away, and now she felt drained and hollow.

She hadn't been able to stop the assassination. If anything, her own arrogance, her own self-importance had made the situation worse.

She needed rest, sustenance. Renewed focus, so that she could puzzle out the complexities of the situation and figure out exactly what to do next. It didn't help, for instance, that she felt responsible for Thibaut and Mandip's safety. She needed to keep at least one eye on the two men, lest their captors try to separate them from her.

"Up, up," she bade the both of them, wanting them on their feet and by her side.

"No one's separating anyone," Hintosep assured her. "Not tonight. And no, Regulator, I will not stop probing your secrets until I'm sure you pose no threat to myself or Juliet."

"You'd earn my compliance more quickly by staying out of my mind."

"I'm hoping to earn your trust by admitting to my capabilities rather than hiding them," she said. "And if you want me to stop accessing your thoughts, then stop treating them as though they're clandestine."

"They're my *thoughts*; of course they're clandestine."

"Not so. Take Thibaut here"—it was too dark in the cave to make out more than vague shapes, but Krona imagined Hintosep nodding in his direction—"I only get whispers from him. There are only a few direct thoughts he'd rather we not all know. Or, to be more specific, there are many things he'd rather *you* not know, Regulator, but as for the rest of us . . . For a man who apparently trades in secrets, his thoughts are remarkably open and thus inaccessible to me."

Thibaut, surprisingly, said nothing. But Krona could feel him cringing next to her in the dark.

"A Thalo's power lies in secrets," Hintosep continued, "and must follow the rules of secrets. Ah! Here we are."

The boat skidded onto a shallow embankment on a bend in the underground river. Immediately, Hintosep pushed by Krona and the men, leaping into the ankle-deep waters of the shoreline to tie the boat to a post before proceeding up the shore to several waiting shapes. One by one, she lit large wax candles, each as large as Krona's helm, set around the site in natural stone candelabrums. They'd all been used frequently, the wax having run down in great, tearing globs for what could have been decades or centuries.

At the rear of the cave was an inexplicably ornate wooden cabinet, wholly at odds with the barren rock around it. And in the center of the space lay a well-used fire pit complete with roasting spit. Above the pit in the cave's ceiling was a deep crack, which Krona assumed facilitated ventilation.

This was not a hideout, though—no Mirthhouse, whatever that was, that was clear. It was a liminal space, an area of transition—between the water and the land but also what had been and what would be. Krona had no more time to ponder. No more time to pace. No more time to hope she'd instantly find her way out of all this, instantly stumble upon a plan or a solution.

"Settle," Juliet said, laying a hand on Krona's shoulder, which she quickly shrugged off. But the songstress simply smiled. "I know that look," she said. "It might be half-hidden behind that carved grimace, but it's uncertainty and fear. Your back is to a corner, and your sense of duty and honor would have you bite off our helping hands rather than listen to our reasons."

"You're not wrong," she conceded.

"That mask compels people, does it not? I saw you use it on the cliffside, during the escape."

"Yes."

"Well, here, then." Juliet held up her wrists, as though for cuffing. "Why don't you compel me into your service until you're satisfied with Hintosep's explanations? I've never played the part before, but I'd make a fine hostage, I assure you."

Krona balked at the suggestion, ready to snap at the songstress to put her hands down when Hintosep called, "Regulators don't use bodies as bargaining chips."

The repeated insistence that she knew Krona's mind—perhaps even better than Krona herself—finally tipped a scale. Something in Krona snapped, had her acting on instinct, snarling as she drew her saber and lashed out at Juliet.

It was Thibaut who made a distressed sound of surprise. Mandip stumbled away, and Krona spun Juliet, yanking the smaller woman against her chest with her free hand, brandishing her blade beneath her chin to keep the singer in place. The bewildered Juliet did not scream, though she pulled stiff in Krona's grip.

Krona let the steel nestle against her skin, let her feel the sharpness of its well-honed edge.

Krona's heart pounded in her chest. This felt so different from capturing a suspect—so *wrong*. But that wrongness was what had allowed her to act without thinking. If foresight was her downfall in Hintosep's presence, then she wouldn't plan; she'd only *do*.

On shore, Hintosep froze.

Both men stood more alert, shuffling from foot to foot, clearly thrown off by the sudden violence. "Mistress, what are you doing?" Thibaut whispered, harried.

"Untie the boat, Thibaut."

"But, Krona—"

"Now!"

Jumping at the harshness in her order, he leapt to comply.

Krona tried to ease her own nerves by reminding herself all evidence pointed toward La Maupin being Hintosep's co-conspirator rather than someone simply under the Thalo's thrall. Which meant there was no reason to treat her with kid gloves.

Krona would trade Juliet's safety for Thibaut and Mandip's. For a swift escape. "Stay where you are, Thalo. As long as you do not follow us, La Maupin will be fine."

Hintosep held up her hands placatingly. "Mistress Regulator, I understand your need to resist, but this performance is entirely unnecessary. Where will you go?"

Juliet squirmed in Krona's grip, testing her boundaries.

"Relax," Krona whispered to her, putting Motomori's abilities to work. The woman's curls were perfumed and set softly against Krona's cheekbone where it peeked above the mask. "Don't fight me."

Juliet slackened.

"You can't go home," Hintosep said. "The Nightswatch will already be at your apartment. The Chief Magistrate himself will likely barge through the door, work his way past your mother—"

Krona surged forward threateningly, her grip tightening on Juliet as she flicked her saber tip forward to point it at the Thalo woman. "If anyone so much as lays a finger on her—"

"Your mother is fine. Will *remain* fine. I promise you."

"You say that like someone who often trades in loved ones' safety."

"That's because I do. And it works, every time. The thing you must accept in this moment," Hintosep continued, "is that I know far more—about everything and everyone—than you do. As I was saying, they'll be breaking down the door to that shrine of a bedroom any minute now. You know what they'll find inside. Contraband. Illegal enchantments. Your files on the mark epidemic. Which may very well lead them to conclude that not only are you responsible for the assassination but the epidemic as well. There are plenty of clues to suggest you've been behind it. Locally, at least. Illegal experimentation: with masks, with echoes. And it won't be difficult for them to deduce a motive—a *why*—will it?" She gestured to where De-Lia's mask hung at Krona's hip. "The Grand Marquis's method of demise will likely cinch their conviction that you are the culprit. This is what made you such an easy mark: you laid out all the 'evidence' yourself. We didn't have to hand you a length of rope to hang yourself; you wove one all on your own."

Krona thought of the Penalty Block then. Of Jemiss crying out and the way the sunlight glinted off the fresh bloodstains.

"There is nowhere in Lutador you can step foot without the entirety of the constabulary raining down on your head," Hintosep went on. "You are free to risk capture and death, if you think they'll give you a chance to speak. But you know they won't believe your story of a Thalo puppet assassin, and even if they did, you know I'll evade them. With ease. You have few options, my dear. And I don't believe myself too conceited in thinking you'd rather not go down in history as a regicide *and* the murderer of beloved La Maupin."

Krona had envisioned herself next to the prisoners paying their penalty. She'd been both too arrogant and too cowardly to join them. Too arrogant and cowardly to free them.

So, fate or the gods had conspired to make sure she paid her debts regardless.

Perhaps the gods would take pity on her if she went back and confessed her crimes. If she told the truth about the assassination and the events leading up to it. Even if no one believed her—not her colleagues, the Chief Magistrate, or the Marchonians—divinity would know the right of it.

Maybe that was the best she could hope for.

Freeing herself from the Thalo woman's influence would at least give her the chance to think clearly.

"Thibaut?" Krona barked. "The rope?"

"Getting there," he insisted, fumbling with the tie on the boat's cleat.

His gloves were slipping, his hands trembling. In the next moment, Mandip was at his side, trying to help, but it was all taking too long.

Dragging Juliet backward with her, toward the tether, Krona raised her blade. Thibaut ducked out of the way, pulling Mandip back just before she swung her saber and severed the line in two. "Push off!" she ordered.

Thibaut dutifully vaulted into the shallow water, began pushing the boat off its beaching.

"Mistress Hirvath, please," Hintosep insisted, taking an imploring step forward. "Let us call a truce for the span of a few hours. Then, if you still wish to kidnap the singer and steal my boat, you can go with my blessing."

Krona had seen the Thalo puppets control people, even if they could only do it briefly. She'd seen Hintosep kill a man in cold blood. The fact that the Blue Woman's face fell as the boat floated free, the fact that she did not hide herself from them and take action as an invisible force, gave Krona pause. If nothing else, it suggested she truly cared about La Maupin's safety. And about gaining Krona's attentive ear.

Perhaps her talk of allyship had possessed a grain of truth.

Hintosep looked at a loss, as though she'd been sure Krona's curiosity or need to seek the truth would override all other considerations in the moment. She clearly hadn't imagined the Regulator would simply try to strand her on shore.

Feeling slightly smug, Krona turned her back on the woman, sheathed her saber, and gently helped Juliet sit in the bottom of the boat. "Stay," she ordered. The craft rocked as Thibaut jumped back in, and Krona took up an oar, tossing it to him before scooping up the second for herself.

She had no idea how close Hintosep had to be to read her secrets—if proximity was even a factor. But she had to hope they could row themselves far enough away to formulate a plan without—

Hintosep's voice echoed harshly in the cave. "I might know how to bring back your sister!"

Krona tensed. Anger rose like bile in her throat.

She and Hintosep both knew De-Lia was Krona's weak spot. Hells, Thibaut knew it. She wouldn't be surprised if the dithering lordling and the flashy little performer knew it as well.

It was an easy play. A sure advantage.

A low blow.

She shoved her feelings down, gritted her teeth, and dunked the oar in the water. "'Might' isn't good enough!"

"It's all I have. It's more than you have now."

Even if Hintosep was merely using her love for her sister to trick her into staying, could she really risk turning her back on an opportunity? This was De-Lia's *life*, after all. It wasn't something to be bargained with, but nor was it something Krona could simply dismiss.

Krona struggled with herself, for what both felt like an eternity and not nearly long enough. "Answer me one thing," Krona demanded. "And then I'll agree to a truce. For the course of one hour, no more."

"What? Anything."

"Did you kill Melanie Dupont?"

29

KRONA

It was the talk of masks and marks that had made Krona wonder. Why had Hintosep chosen a needle—not just to the brain but through enchanted wood—as her method of assassination when there were numerous other ways to kill the Grand Marquis that would have indicated a Regulator—even Krona specifically—was the assassin? Krona was sure this meant she knew where the pandemic originated. And how Melanie had received her mark in the first place.

"You've seen the pictures, then?" Hintosep asked carefully.

Krona unbuttoned part of her uniform, near her neck, and drew forth the photographs of Melanie's body prone in the snow. "You mean these pictures?"

Hintosep couldn't possibly see the photograph's details, not from her vantage on the shore and in such bad lighting, but she squinted as though scrutinizing them anyway. "Good, then they've done their job," she said firmly.

"Which was what?"

"To stop people like your Chief Magistrate of Justice and many of my colleagues from looking for her."

"You're telling me she's alive?"

"Very much so."

Krona wanted to believe her. It would make everything so much easier if she could. But she was absolutely certain that Hintosep was the type of person to say whatever she thought necessary—to lie straight-faced, through her teeth—to get to her goal.

"Now, will you come ashore and converse like a civilized human being?"

Krona bristled. "For someone who wants my ear, you clearly have no qualms with throwing out casual insults. Of the five of us, I believe it's only you who's murdered someone and started a war."

"I take no pride in it and it gave me no pleasure."

"I'm sure it would comfort the Grand Marquis to hear that," Krona snapped. "You speak of war so casually, like it's nothing. The Valley has been in relative peace for nearly a century."

"The key word being 'relative,'" Hintosep said. "You have no idea what little violences are visited on all of Arkensyre, every day."

"So, why not immerse us in large violences, then?" Krona asked indignantly.

"Just like the assassination, the war is coming whether I want it to or not. But this isn't the end of my part; it's the beginning. The Savior placed the dominos, and they have been tipping over since the Introdus. I plan to scatter them."

"You make this Savior sound like a god," Thibaut said.

"Next closest thing," Hintosep said. "Never be surprised when the man who cut you off at the knees starts to look like a giant."

Krona held her ground, waiting for Hintosep to give her something substantial. She'd levied vague reasons and promises at them so far—nothing of real sinew for Krona to sink her teeth into. She was a Regulator; she needed hard evidence of either the woman's claims or intentions before she dare give up the high ground.

"Proof?" Hintosep asked. "The fact that you're still alive should be proof enough, but I understand you're a more object-oriented person." Swiftly, she stalked over to the cabinet and flung the doors wide, revealing an assortment of weaponry. "Take your pick," she said with a sweeping gesture. "Arm yourself as you please. This should be enough to earn me your ear for at least the rest of the evening, don't you think?"

Even at her distance, Krona could see a small selection of swords—from cutlasses to nodachi to rapiers and falchions—hung beside a handful of quint-barrels, flintlocks, and small knives.

It would be a fine gesture, were her enemy's weapons of like kind—but Hintosep's true armaments were her inborn powers.

"There are enchantments, too," Hintosep sad, tugging open a drawer. "If those are more to your liking."

She couldn't trust Hintosep, but perhaps it made more sense to keep her close than to lose sight of her. Which meant only Krona's pride was still keeping her on the water. "Thibaut?"

"Bring the boat back in, I know," he sighed. The underlying, weary *make up your mind* in his tone was not lost on her.

Mandip had crouched next to Juliet, seemed exceptionally concerned by the dazed look on her face.

Krona released Juliet from Motomori's hold with a swift word and a snap of her fingers. In an instant, the songstress was on her feet again—much to Mandip's surprise—having lost her over-the-top cheer and replaced it with an air of indignation. "I haven't been manhandled that roughly since wearing teal instead of black to meet the Winsrouen High Supplicants. And that was by a pack of *dogs*."

Ignoring her, Krona jumped over the side to help Thibaut haul the craft up the shore again, retying it in place. After, she slogged through the water to stand opposite Hintosep, maintaining a good distance between them as she carefully removed Motomori's mask and secured it next to De-Lia's on her belt.

"You have my attention."

"Thank you. Grab whatever you think you'll need—including rations. There are dried fruits and meat. Water as well. We need to keep moving. The Marchonian Guards will not cease searching, even if they conclude you've died jumping into the river. They won't be satisfied without a body. We should appreciate the respite while we can, even if it's only for a handful of minutes."

"We aren't staying here, then?" Thibaut asked, wringing out the cuffs of his trousers as he came to stand beside her, sounding far too eager for Krona's tastes. She glared at him, but he merely gave an apologetic shrug in return. "I'm in *velvet*, mistress. Caves and velvet aren't exactly the best of friends."

"I presume that also applies to velvet and the forest," Juliet said, joining them, leading Mandip by the hand. "Alas."

"Forest? How far do you intend to take us?" Mandip asked cautiously.

"Many miles yet," Hintosep said.

The cabinet's drawers housed a plethora of objects Krona had never seen before. Small globes that could fit in one hand and gave off the faintest glow; what could have been a teacup with a distinct and deliberate looking chip in its rim, except there was a hole sculpted into its bottom that no self-respecting teacup would possess; linked glass tetrahedrons; a clock with no face and six hands; and a device that at first glance appeared to be a lighter—with a bulbous reserve of fuel at the bottom and shiny brass components on top—but when Krona moved to strike a flame, Hintosep quickly covered her hand, stilling the Regulator.

"I wouldn't," she said.

"I've never seen these designs before," Krona said. Which meant they were clearly developed illegally, via unholy attempts at engineering. "What are they?"

"Weapons," Juliet said simply, reaching around Krona to grab a falchion and its scabbard from their nesting.

"Mostly defensive," Hintosep said quickly. "They make good use of the Fallen's magic."

"The Fallen?" Mandip asked.

"You call them the Unknown. They were the God of Secrets."

"Were?"

"They've been dead for quite some time."

Krona lost her breath.

Everyone but Juliet and Hintosep paused.

The reverberations of the women's movements around the cave struck harsh and unnatural. Just like Hintosep's words.

The Unknown . . . was *dead*?

Krona could hardly conceive of such a thing.

"But they're a *god*," Thibaut eventually said incredulously. "You can't . . . Gods can *die*?"

"Yes."

"*How?* Surely, not of *old age*."

"No. They were killed."

A chill of tingles radiated down Krona's spine. "How do you kill a *god*?"

"Not easily."

"But the Thalo wouldn't let that happen," Mandip said. "The creator might hate humanity, but it loves its children."

Hintosep gave a heavy sigh. The kind common to someone who knows they have a long road ahead. "You need to understand that much of your known origins are myth," she said.

Krona pocketed several of the mysterious enchantments, not intending to use them but instead take them to the den for safekeeping if—*when*—she got the chance.

"*Where* is this safe haven of yours, exactly?" Mandip asked, reaching for a rapier, apparently surprised when no one stopped him from arming himself.

"Mirthhouse is in the mountains. But I fear before we arrive, some of us will have to loop back to Lutador proper for an important task at the Treasury." She looked at him pointedly. "I don't think it'll be too difficult to guess which category you belong to."

Krona noted him rubbing nervously at his forearm. "I will not help you rob Lutador's people of their time vials."

"Excellent, then we should have no quarrel with one another. We're not after time vials at the Treasury; we'll be looking for something much more valuable: an enchantment I secreted away when the building was being built."

"A half a dozen centuries ago?" Thibaut scoffed.

The look she leveled at him was unamused. "Yes."

"Lutador doesn't keep enchantments in the Treasury," Mandip protested. "Other than time vials, I mean. Everything else belongs on Vault Hill."

"Ah, but that's where you're wrong. There are plenty of enchantments in the Treasury. The difference is they're not part of the hoard."

". . . They're part of the infrastructure," Mandip said slowly, catching on.

Hintosep nodded. "We're not stealing any of the treasure. We're stealing a piece of the Treasury itself."

30

THALO CHILD

One and a Half Years Ago

As Thalo Child grew, he gathered secrets. Rarely on purpose, rarely because he wanted to. Was it like this for everyone? Did secrets accumulate like snowdrifts inside each person? Most of them seemed small: a secret smile shared between friends; someone caught crying unawares; a little white lie; an extra helping of sweets. A simple defiance, a slight rebellion.

Many of these secrets seemed to fade from his consciousness as fast as he gathered them. What was forgetting except keeping a secret from oneself, after all? But a few he had to shove down, away. Deep into his subconscious. He could never let his mind wander in their direction, lest Gerome realize Thalo Child had something of *real* importance to hide.

Specifically, he lived each day terrified Gerome would look inside his mind and see the truth about his charge—that zhe had powers beyond a Thalo. Powers no person should have.

He'd told his infant never to show zhur trick to anyone else, but young ones are fundamentally unpredictable. Zhe did not know to fear Gerome just yet, and so Thalo Child feared him doubly for zhim.

He realized now how long he'd mistaken his own fear for awe and respect.

><>O<><

He regularly helped Gerome with the Sacrifices these days.

Too regularly, he realized.

The first time Thalo Child had helped Gerome, his Possessor had said that twenty Sacrifices was rare, that the Savior had only requested so many at one other point in Gerome's life.

But, since then, Thalo Child had seen to a party of that size three times over.

The Savior was drawing more and more time for Himself. Hoarding more and more years. But why? Thalo Child thought He should logically be content with the thousands He'd already drawn, that He wouldn't need any more Sacrifices until another age had passed, at least.

But they kept coming.

Now Thalo Child stood shivering on the rampart, waiting for the next batch to arrive. The mountain winds were especially harsh today—rabid, fierce, and clawing as though they meant to tear him apart. He startled slightly when Gerome reached out for him, drawing him under his arm, keeping him close. His Possessor still towered over him, despite the inches Thalo Child had gained these last few years, but he at least came up to his shoulder now. The child risked a glance up, searching for a reason Gerome had chosen to show affection, but there was no special expression on Gerome's face; he looked blankly ahead beneath his curtain of sapphire beads, waiting for the Sacrifices to arrive.

Gerome radiated warmth, and soon Thalo Child stopped shivering.

Something clicked in the child's mind then. A small hint of a memory, the last time he'd been held close by someone larger than him. It had been Hintosep. She'd taken him to the library to see the God of Secrets and to search for . . .

To search for . . .

As he grasped for the memory, he felt Gerome stiffen beside him but paid it no mind until he was unceremoniously shoved away from his Possessor's warmth.

With a desperate sort of clawing, Gerome fumbled at the front of Thalo Child's cloak, yanked him near as the Possessor fell to his knees on the rampart so that the two of them were more of a height. Instinctually, the child leaned back as the Possessor leaned forward with a snarl.

"*What is this in your mind?*" Gerome demanded.

Terror hit Thalo Child full-force, making his thoughts spring clear and open. *No, please, no.* He thought Gerome had found his secret about his babe, which meant zhe would be taken from him. That perhaps zhe would end up banished, or a Sacrifice, or experimented upon.

Thalo Child's heart thudded in his chest and he forced himself to keep his hands down, away from Gerome's white-knuckled grip on his clothes. He forced himself not to outwardly panic.

"This—this *wall*. Who would—" Gerome cut himself off, clearly having come to the conclusion on his own. "Why would she . . . Me. She wants to hide something from me, specifically." He took Thalo Child by the shoulders and shook him. "What is it? Did she show you the Cage? Tell you of its location? That must be it."

Thalo Child was wholly confused.

Who *she* was seemed clear. He'd just been thinking of Hintosep, trying to recall . . . something. But it had not been about the Cage, he was sure. He had no real concept of the Cage; it was simply an abstraction, an artifact he'd heard of and knew Gerome desired, but—

He clamped down on his thoughts about the artifact, made them as clandestine as possible.

Made Gerome *chase* them.

He realized Gerome's desire had clouded his judgment. Instead of looking at Thalo Child's real secrets, he'd made assumptions and, in those assumptions, mistakes. Mistakes Thalo Child could use to protect his charge.

He wasn't sure what kind of wall Hintosep had put in his mind, but he didn't care at the moment. He would twist it to his own advantage.

He put the Cage out of his mind. The fact that he knew nothing about it meant Gerome would only look harder when he found nothing. Thalo Child could tell by the determination on his Possessor's face that Gerome was sure this was it: the location of the information he'd long craved was *here*.

As Gerome delved, bits of *his* secrets brushed against Thalo Child's awareness. The ecstasy he'd felt in the Cage, the way he'd fetishized his own loss of control. In the Cage, he had no expectations placed upon him, no responsibilities to fulfill. Those in Gerome's cohort hadn't understood. They'd fought the Cage, thinking it took their freedom, when in reality it *gave* them freedom. It had meant freedom from demand and thought. Freedom from having to make even the smallest of decisions.

When the stress of the world became too much, when the Savior's demands became too burdensome, Gerome longed for the simplicity of the Cage. He'd give anything—*anything*—to have even fleeting moments of that pure freedom *back*.

If Gerome knew Thalo Child could see this intimate secret, he didn't seem to care.

"Where is it?" the Possessor mumbled. "Just a glimpse, just a—"

The doors at the end of the parapet opened. Harvesters marched through with their prizes.

Gerome cut himself off, shooting to his feet, remembering their purpose here.

⊱──◈──◉──◈──⊰

From then on, the wall in Thalo Child's mind was all Gerome cared about. He picked at it constantly, whenever he was in Thalo Child's presence. His Possessor clearly thought Thalo Child couldn't sense it, didn't know he was there, but the child could feel him prodding, even when his back was turned.

And Thalo Child was glad for it.

Gerome slid past *his* secrets to worry over what Hintosep had hidden.

His charge would remain safe for now.

31

KRONA

The cave system was wet, its passageways well-worn but narrow. Both men slipped several times; their fine shoes were made for slick floors but not dampened cave slime. Krona kept her helm off—the better to see Hintosep's single torchlight—and had to keep her weapons sheathed and holstered in order to use both hands to guide the helm's horns through some of the narrowest corridors.

Most of the way, they had to work forward in single file. Hintosep led, of course, and though Krona wanted to keep the Thalo woman close—it was easier to demand answers if she could hiss directly into her ear, after all—she ultimately chose to bring up the rear. That way, she could keep an eye on everyone, at the very least. Mandip followed right behind Hintosep, with Thibaut taking up the middle and Juliet just behind him.

Krona couldn't shake the distress brought on by the assertion that the Unknown was dead. Gods didn't just *die.* She wasn't sure she'd ever thought too hard about whether or not gods *could* die. The other four had endured, trapped on the Valley rim, from the beginning of Arkensyre's creation until this very moment. The idea that the Unknown wasn't with them was nothing new. But the idea that they were simply *nowhere?* Defeated? Departed?

It nauseated Krona. It made it difficult to ask her questions. To say much of anything at all.

She'd known from the start that she wouldn't like any of Hintosep's answers, but now she wondered what other gruesome things the woman would say about the world. What ideals she might uproot or twist, what wrongs she might insist were necessary or right.

Several times, Juliet turned on her heel and walked expertly backward along the path, grinning in the dark at Krona, apparently thrilled to be there, in diametric opposition to Krona's sour mood.

"I don't know if Thibaut has had a chance to tell you," the songstress said now, "but I came to see you at your den yesterday."

"I was out," Krona grumbled.

Juliet didn't reply immediately. Perhaps she was waiting for Krona to elaborate or to inquire as to the purpose of the songstress's visit. Krona had no intention of doing either.

"I have great respect for what happened on your Gatwood concern, with Louis Charbon's mask," Juliet continued, immediately raising Krona's hackles once more. "I have a stake in Charbon's atrocities," she said, voice now gone somber. Suddenly, she ducked to one side, narrowly avoiding a rocky outcropping behind her head, moving smoothly backward as she did. Obviously, this was not her first time traversing this cave. "And I feel it's my responsibility to aid the victim's families, if I can," she continued. "But there was one corpse—made by Gatwood's hand—that was never publicly identified. I was hoping, perhaps, that you'd uncovered their identity, so that I might bring aid to their relations as well."

The tightness of the passageway made their conversation seem muffled, intimate. The darkness beyond Hintosep's torchlight was like a thick blanket, wrapping them all in what could have been a warm bubble, if not for the distrust permeating the atmosphere.

"What kind of aid?" Krona asked, trying to keep her tone even, though her question came out clipped regardless. "The families don't need to be harassed by a celebrity for the sake of a philanthropic piece in the papers."

"Oh, no, I daresay none of the families know why they receive gifts of time vials, or that they're from me. That's not why I do it. I do it because . . ." She pursed her lips, let out a deep breath. "I simply must. It's a personal conviction."

"Ah, yes, a *personal conviction*," Krona sneered. "What could Charbon mean to you? I myself was not yet a woman when he was hanged; why would someone so young as you have any kind of stake in his ugly legacy? You're sure you're not simply after a bit of gruesome gossip?" Sometimes, nobles enjoyed wallowing in stories of the sordid sins of Lutador's underbelly.

"Mistress Regulator, I'm insulted," Juliet said firmly. "Many famous artisans pick a point of charity to pursue as a way of giving back to the world. I have prospered while others have died." She spun on her heel, smoothly continuing on with her back to Krona once more. "And Louis Charbon is the reason."

Her last, whispered sentence struck Krona as particularly alarming. Ominous, even. Again, allowing herself to move on instinct so as not to rouse Hintosep's abilities, Krona snatched Juliet by the shoulder, halting her in her tracks, spinning her back around. "What does that mean?" she asked, bending close to the smaller woman's face, searching her eyes in the dimness. "Why are you wrapped up in all this? You mentioned a brother, yes, but how does someone like you end up in cahoots with someone like her?" She nodded past Juliet, and they both knew who she meant.

"Sometimes, the best secrets are gotten from the shadows, and sometimes, they're gotten from the spotlight," Hintosep answered for La Maupin, stopping in her tracks and bringing the others to a halt as well.

"You'd be surprised what people have admitted to me simply because they wanted to impress," Juliet agreed. She didn't cower back from Krona. She held her ground, despite her stature.

"You are very good at answering my questions without actually answering my questions," Krona called to Hintosep.

"Call it the nature of my upbringing," Hintosep said, clearly some kind of dark joke. "You have never raised a child, but trust me when I say it does no good to answer each of their *whys* and *hows* with an in-depth dissertation on the topic. When describing the world to a child, you answer piecemeal, in ways they can understand."

"So, we're just children to you?" Krona spat, making no secret of the fact that she hated Hintosep's patronizing.

"Yes," the woman said firmly. "Figuratively *and* literally. I have seen centuries pass. *Ages* pass. You are but a moment to me."

"Where did you get your time?" Mandip asked.

"Where do you think?"

They all knew it was theoretically possible to keep cashing out more and more time, adding years and years onto the end of one's life if they had access to as much bottled time as they liked. But it should see them bedridden. It should see them stretching out what would have been their very last natural year.

Hintosep did not look on the edge of death. Quite the opposite. For her claim to be true, that had to mean injected time didn't behave the way they'd all been told it behaved.

Krona hadn't realized they'd all gone quiet again until Hintosep broke through the silence. "See? Piecemeal. There's no way you could process the entirety of all your missed truths at once."

"I think that's just your excuse," Krona countered. "A way to string us along—keep us beholden to you."

"Think what you will." She sighed deeply. "Why did I have to pick someone so stubborn as you?"

That, oddly enough, felt like a compliment.

"We should keep moving," Juliet said. "We'll never make it to camp if we keep stutter-stopping like this. And there were boats on the water. The cloaking enchantment on the river entrance won't have worked if someone saw us pass through. The secret will be secret no more."

"Always so pragmatic," Hintosep said fondly, and Krona thought it an odd thing to say about someone who exuded frivolity and fancy. With that, the Blue Woman turned and strode away.

Krona realized she was still holding on to Juliet like a predator with claws in its prey, but Juliet wasn't looking at her with fear. There was clearly admiration and something even . . . *warmer* in her gaze. Krona swiftly let go.

She glanced up to see Thibaut staring at her—at them, really—a slightly hurt but otherwise unreadable expression on his face. When he caught her looking, he quickly turned away, taking Mandip by the arm and urging him onward behind Hintosep. The moment confused Krona, but she tried not to think about it. There were too many confusing things happening as it was; she didn't need one more.

Krona and Juliet both stood too close to one another for a moment more, before something broke the thread between them and they rushed to catch up with the others.

"Come along, dears," Hintosep called, voice echoing, indicating the passageway must be widening ahead. They continued to navigate the cavern system for a long while still, the flare of her torch highlighting glittering crystals and wet surfaces alike.

By the time they were out of the caves, into the woods, and midway up the slopes of the rim's encroaching mountains, it was the wee hours of the morn and everyone was exhausted. "Just a little farther and we'll make camp," Hintosep assured them. "There's shelter and a supply cache—bedding, gear for hunting."

The trees were thick, hiding the decline down to the river. Krona wondered if they were too far away now to see the waters regardless.

Thibaut seemed to be the most drained of the lot of them. He was certainly not used to long, impromptu treks, and Krona wasn't sure how much vigorous activity he usually saw—outside of a bedroom, anyway.

"You certainly are well prepared, madame," Thibaut huffed, pausing for a moment to rest, leaning against the closest tree. "It must have taken an age to arrange for this night." Krona wondered why he insisted on talking when he could barely catch his breath. She stopped beside him and put a hand on his shoulder, which he patted gently to indicate he was fine.

"Luckily, it's not all in service to one assassination," Hintosep said, graciously stopping as well. "Being a Thalo of certain rank means near-constant travel. Parties of six or so are the usual size. Once in a while, a few more or a few less, depending on the task."

"How many of you are there?" Krona asked. "In all?"

"Approximately ten thousand."

"And yet thousands of leaders are not dropping dead every day."

"The hands we play are usually more subtle," Hintosep said, not at all thrown by the glib remark. "But the Savior has grown impatient with subtlety lately. Its effectiveness is not as certain as a swift, deadly blow to the top. Arkensyre's societies keep progressing too quickly, and He wants to put a harsh and decisive stop to it."

"Progressing too quickly?" Mandip asked with a shake of the head. "What does that mean?"

"You wouldn't understand," she said dismissively, but then added, "It's the railway. The new steam engines your city-states are designing. It . . . goes against Knowledge."

"We've had steam-power technology for decades," Mandip scoffed, clearly offended at the mere suggestion that the entire Valley could be engaged in a penalty-worthy blasphemy. "Steam pumps keep many of the mines dry—silver, coal."

Hintosep laughed—a private chuckle to herself. "It's amazing that you by-passed coal engines entirely, actually."

Krona kept silent while Mandip continued to argue in favor of Arkensyre's innocence, but the strange use of "bypassed" was not lost on her.

Having recovered himself, Thibaut assured them they could all carry on. Krona tried not to feel an odd way about Juliet grabbing Thibaut's hand and dragging him alongside her on their renewed trek.

Mandip continued to chatter on about divinely compliant progress for some time, only occasionally shot down by something scathing from Hintosep. But as they approached the camp, the Thalo pulled up short, shushed him, and threw out a halting arm. "Wait. I see fire ahead."

Krona saw nothing.

"Damn it," Hintosep cursed. "The camp is already occupied. We'll have to keep moving." She pivoted to the left. "This way. Take each step with caution. Keep as quiet as you can. I can hide myself from my fellow Thalo, but it would be a chal-lenge to hide the rest of you effectively if we need to run. There may be a lookout. Be ready if we meet them."

There were other Thalo puppets in these woods. The knowledge roused Krona's awareness, swept the early-morning cobwebs from her mind. She put a hand on the hilt of her saber, sinking into her training.

They could be ambushed by invisible attackers at any moment.

Each step they took was careful, guarded. The party followed Hintosep's movements precisely, keeping vigilant.

They hadn't gotten far when a twig snapped to their right.

In the next moment, Hintosep vanished.

32

THALO CHILD

One Year Ago

Thalo Child had gotten used to Hintosep coming to him for aid in various tasks around the keep. He still had no idea why he'd been singled out—or, he supposed, if he really *had* been singled out. Perhaps she had helpers like him throughout the Thalo's realm, each belonging to a different Possessor, each involved in different work.

But when one is expected to be a master of secrets one day, it becomes difficult to sit in ignorance, to abide silence. Especially when he knew she'd locked something away in his mind—hidden it behind a wall strong enough to keep Gerome out, which meant it was strong enough to keep *everyone* out, all but the Savior Himself.

She'd come for him at night, once again, long after the rest of his cohort was asleep. His infant slumbered through the night these days and was in the nursery with the other babes, so no need to steal the secret of wakefulness from zhur little mind.

The halls were eerily quiet in this part of the keep, deep beneath the Savior's own chambers, at the heart of the stronghold. There weren't even any Mindless about, cleaning or seeing to the upkeep of the old stones. Thalo Child knew better than to trust that the shadows were truly empty, but if he could not ask his questions now, then when? It could be years still before he earned his name and was afforded the freedom to leave the keep.

He watched the edges of her pale-blue cape billow across the floor for several minutes as he followed, trying to dredge up enough courage to let the words passed his lips. "Why did you assign me an infant before I was of age?"

Her stride did not falter. "Because I swore to protect you," she said over her shoulder, the edges of her long white hair sweeping like a silk curtain across the small of her back. Some of it had been arranged in delicate plaits—fine, wispy braids. "The both of you. Having the pair of you invested in each other has made that easier. *Will* make it easier, in the time to come."

That he or his infant would need any extra-special protection made little sense. "To whom did you swear this?"

"I swore it to zhur mother . . . and your father, though he did not know it."

"Mother? Father?" These were foreign words.

"Someone who would have been like a Possessor to your babe. Someone else who would have been like a Possessor *to you*."

"I don't understand."

"I know, Child," she said sadly. "I know."

He continued to trail dutifully behind as she strode toward a staircase that twisted down, down. They were almost directly at the center of the keep now, the most protected part of Thalo Child's encapsulated world. The air was thick, as it lacked the same circulation the high towers and walkways naturally received. There was something old and oppressive about it—a sense of stillness in a stale, solid sort of way.

At the bottom of the staircase, they approached a large archway, a darkened maw of an entrance, past which Thalo Child could make out nothing but blackness.

There, Hintosep paused. "The dark keeps them quiet," she explained softly. "Subdued."

Them?

She hadn't enlightened him as to what their task was this evening, and, truly, he'd been so wrapped up in the mystery of why she'd selected him as a helper to ask after details.

She held one finger up to her lips, signaling for quiet, before heading beneath the archway. Thalo Child had no choice but to follow.

Here, the air changed again. Instead of thick, it was crisp, like after a rain—though it rarely rained on the ice field—cut through with a sharpness. But not the sharpness of static electricity, like the air in the Time Tower when he aided Gerome with the Sacrifices. This was more like the metallic sharpness of blood, though less organic.

The fine hairs on his arms stood on end as soon as they crossed the threshold into the darkened room.

As they entered, Hintosep pulled a lever, and a series of heavy clicks rattled overhead, indicating long chains and pullies were working unseen. Suddenly, lights sprang up across the ceiling, each a bright flame shining down, spotlighting a glittering, reflective *something* beneath.

Each something was a bottle. An exceptionally large bottle—many larger than Thalo Child himself, despite his recent growth spurt.

The bottles were full of *varger*.

Monsters had been living beneath his feet all this time, and he'd never known.

Rows upon rows of them graced the elongated room, each set upon—and bolted to—a three-foot-tall dais, which gave the space the impression of a gallery, like the one at the front of the halls that lead into the Savior's sacred rooms. The magically fortified bottles looked like sculptures. He supposed they were, in a way.

Thalo Child knew it was customary, in most city-states, to stuff vaporous varger into enchanted jars small enough to hold in the palm of one's hand. But here, each varg had its own spacious (relatively speaking) glass cage, grand and opalescent in the dim light. Some of the enchanted glass was etched with additional markings that were plated over in enchanted metals—sigils of some kind—and there were no obvious lids or stoppers, though every bottle had a seam frosted over in a layer of thick salt.

Each cage was its own work of art, possessed of its own shape, which seemed to dictate the state of the varg within. The more bulbous or geometric the glass, the more obviously vaporous and restless the creature. But several had been sculpted to be the shape of a varg—their stances crouched and poised for attack—and the mist inside had somewhat materialized to fit into that shape, as though finding comfort in the echo of solidity.

And still there were others shaped like different creatures. Birds, mammals, marsupials, reptiles. A crocodile from Xyopar. A giant sloth from Asgar-Skan. A great Winsrouen brown bear, a Marrakevian firebird, and a thin-legged Luta-dorian stag. Each trapped varg filled out its prison, letting the ghost of its essence seep into the form, even as the cloud of it clearly vibrated with nervous energy.

Interestingly, the monsters in the animal vessels were notably calmer than the varger in the geometric ones.

As Thalo Child strolled down the line, taking in each cage beneath its spotlight, he tried to keep his expression stoic, cool. He did not want Hintosep to see how disturbed he was, how each bulging eye and grotesque tongue made his throat run dry and his blood run cold. After all, he was a teenager now. He was still a child in title but could no longer share his youthful fears and hope to be comforted as one. He was expected to be mature. To have some solidity to his backbone.

Still, he pulled up short and sucked in a sharp breath when he came to the last bottle in the row. The eeriest cage of all.

It was in the shape of a person. Just like the other animal vessels, the varg inside had seen fit to mold itself to the form of the glass, filling in every gap, down to the fingers and toes. Its eyes settled perfectly into the space where the eye sockets should lie—though there was nothing in the contour of the glass that should have told the varg that was where eyes went. And its *teeth*—its terrible grin spread wide across the jaw. That, coupled with the lidless eyes, gave the humanoid face a wild, manic, *murderous* look.

But behind that murderous look was . . . contentment? This varg was the mellowest of them all—barely shifting, never flinching or gnashing. Thalo Child had no doubt it was ravenous and would gleefully tear him to shreds the moment it was offered freedom, but it made no attempt to get at him through the glass. Its gaze did not track him with hunger or rage.

"Why does it make such a difference?" he asked. "The bottle's shape?"

She didn't answer.

Instead of indulging his curiosity, Hintosep was rummaging in a cabinet on the other side of the room. All along the perimeter were cupboards and tables—surfaces covered in flasks and pipets, spiraled glass tubes, trays, syringes, thin metal implements he had no name for. And needles. Many needles.

Clearly, experiments on varger had been performed there, and these cages were their own kind of trial.

"Why do we . . . Why are they here?" he asked, trailing up beside her.

"Each varg you see before you has behaved most uncharacteristically," she said lightly—almost flippantly, as though she had not just shown him a secret lab at the very core of a secret keep.

"Uncharacteristically?"

"They attached themselves to a person. They didn't eat them. Instead, they seemed to . . . *bond* with them."

"How? Why?"

She was quiet for a long moment. "That's why we brought them here. To find out."

"And have you?"

She didn't answer.

"You *have*," he stated firmly, the implication hitting him hard, nearly taking his breath away. "You've learned something—"

"It's still only a hunch. One I'm trying to confirm."

Suddenly, he noticed an archway next to him in the back wall, with a long, thick curtain draping down, covering another entrance. It had sprung from the shadows, clearly secreted away by an illusion, only visible to his untrained eye now that he was on top of it.

"What's back there?" he asked, not really expecting an answer.

"That's where the Artifacts reside when not in use."

"You mean, the Eye?" He shuddered.

"The Eye, the Teeth, the Song. All seven of them. Well, six now."

"That's where the Cage used to rest?"

She side-eyed him, but nodded. "Yes."

"But no more?"

"No more. Now if I could just—Ah-ha!" She came out of the cupboard with a heavy tool—a wrench for thick bolts. "Come," she said, waggling a finger at him as she moved between the pedestals, leading him to a bottle in the shape of a great cat—a panther or a jaguar, perhaps. Like those molded to the likeness of actual varger, the cat held a prowling pose. Always stalking, perpetually on the hunt.

In fact, all the cages shaped like predators appeared as though about to spring. Even the prey animals—the stag, a ram, even a Grand Falls eel—were poised for conflict, the kind they might have with another of their own species, over territory or a potential mate.

But not the human. The human's posture was placid—straight-backed, stance firm, hands hanging loosely at its sides.

The varg inside the glass cat-eyed them as they approached, its green mist colored through with vague streaks of purple.

"Help me get this down," Hintosep said, immediately working open the bolts that kept the great cat's glass paws pinned in place.

Thalo Child's heart leapt into his throat. "W-why?"

"I have use of this varg."

"Will no one notice it's gone?"

"I've already taken care of that," she said dismissively.

It frightened him, how flippantly she said it. Full Thalo were not to use their magic against each other. Gerome used his to guide his children, but this was different. Whichever priests or Named Ones toiled in this lab should have been secure in the knowledge that their knowledge was *secure*. That their own thoughts would not be made a secret from themselves.

Few Thalo could so much as brush against the abilities Hintosep had mastered. She was ancient, she was powerful, and above all, she was *trusted*. She'd been the Savior's right hand during the Great Introdus and thus named the first Guardian and given her post on the Valley rim. As the years progressed—as whispers and rumor had it—she'd grown weary of the Guardianship and had been given free rein to flit from rank to rank as she pleased, acting as Harvester one day, Orchestrator another.

And then there had been her stint as a Possessor, and when she'd given up that position, she'd hidden one of the great artifacts, the Cage, and that was that.

How long had she felt free enough to enter the minds of other Thalo and manipulate their secrets?

He recognized that this was not the first time he'd had this feeling around her. This bone-deep, visceral *fear*. There'd been another, over a year ago at this point, he was sure. But as he reached for the memory, it eluded him. His own retrieval *fought* him.

The wall.

Thalo Child swallowed the anxiety and panic that rose in his throat as he probed at the vacancy in his mind. He was not surprised by the wall, of course, but for some reason, it hadn't *concerned* him until now. It had been useful, and he hadn't felt as though he'd been missing anything. He'd let Gerome probe at it for him, but now that he tried himself, his breath caught and he felt voids open in his mind, chest, and feet.

There was a place in himself he could not go, and only now did he feel the full force of its wrongness.

"Why are you taking this varg?" he ventured, trying not to gasp for breath, to show how distressed he'd suddenly become. "What are you going to do with it?"

"Solve a riddle," she said cryptically.

Once the bolts were free of the metal ties, the varg quivered in its confines. It began to press at the glass, back and forth, trying to rock its prison—perhaps intending to tip it over, to shatter it. The glass was unbreakable by nonmagical means, but the monster didn't know that.

Thalo Child's hand shot out to steady the bottle, and the varg turned its insubstantial self inside out, sharp teeth gnashing, eyes darting. It lunged at Thalo Child, mouthing and licking at his fingers through the glass.

Startled, the child reared back, tripping on his own robes.

Hintosep caught him before he could fall. "Steady," she said. Her hand on his shoulder sent frigid spikes of revulsion through him. "I need you to help me place it on a cart."

"Where are you taking it?" he demanded again, subtly skirting away from her touch.

"You ask too many questions these days," she said. But instead of sounding irritated, as Gerome often did when Thalo Child pressed too far, she sounded . . . proud? "Come now. Lift."

He positioned himself at the cat's front paws, while she saw to its rear. Luckily, he'd sprouted recently. He'd never be as tall as Gerome, but he and Hintosep were nearly of a height. His limbs had lost their gangly quality, filling out with muscle. He had the strength to be of true help.

With a gentle, well-timed heave, the pair of them were able to easily lift the sculpted prison from its pedestal and place it on the floor.

Inside the bottle, the varg bristled, and even the most subdued of the others were roused to excitement by the pure novelty of *shift* and *change* in their environment.

After retrieving a small trolley—clearly built for just this kind of transport—they moved the great cat once more, hefting it onto the trolley's bed before leaving the lab without a glance back.

Hintosep pulled another lever, and the gallery was plunged into darkness once more.

The trolley's small wheels squeaked—one occasionally spinning, awkwardly, in the wrong direction—as it trundled across the uneven pavestones of the floor. Thalo Child wondered how they were to manage the staircases—of which there were many—but when they came to the first set of stairs, Hintosep pulled thin sheets of a dark-colored metal from the folds inside her robe. Each sheet was cut in the shape of a wing, about as big as a raven's, and when she curled them in on themselves, they sprang back as if alive.

Pairs of them—six in all, when she was through—fluttered, at her direction, to the sides of the trolley and attached themselves to the bed with little metal talons. At Hintosep's command, they lifted the trolley free of the stone, following her up the staircase with it suspended between them, keeping the cat bottle perfectly level and evenly balanced. The trolley wheels spun anemically beneath, loose on their small axles.

Thalo Child had never seen such an enchantment before and wondered, out loud, why such wings were not used everywhere—in place of such menial inventions like *the wheel*.

"There are two primary kinds of enchantments: solid-state and consumable," Hintosep explained as they rose through the keep's levels, still meeting no one along the way. "Solid-state enchantments, like the varger bottles, take incredible amounts of energy to create but none to maintain. Consumables, like these wings, need a constant input of energy, or else they are themselves consumed and need to be remade. These will last me until I reach the ramparts but no longer." They reached the top of the stairs, and the wings continued to keep the cart aloft.

This was new information—a new concept for Thalo Child, which felt odd. Surely, he was old enough to know such things about enchantments. It sparked his curiosity, pushing aside his fear for a moment. "Two *primary*?" he prompted, hoping to learn more.

"Many enchantments, like death masks, have aspects of both," she said as they continued to climb through the keep's levels. "The knowledge is perpetually contained in a solid state, but accessing and utilizing the knowledge takes energy, consumed from the wearer. All magic is like this, in some way."

All magic? "But what about *our* magic?" he asked. "Secret magic. It's given to us by the gods, and we absorb energy through our lines on Ritual Way, so does that mean—"

She stiffened at the word "gods." "It is *created* by our bodies and *maintained* by our bodies," she said firmly, with an edge that warned him not to argue. "All existence is the movement of energy from one place to another."

Her words seemed to confirm what he'd just said, but her tone . . . "We absorb god energy on Ritual Way," he said slowly.

She took a deep breath, but no words came.

"Don't we?" he pressed. "That's what our lines are *for*, aren't they?"

His many lines he'd received *early*, received *all at once*, the pain he'd endured—it had all been for a reason. Had been part of the natural process of being a Thalo. Wasn't it?

"I had not intended to have this conversation with you until—"

She pulled up short and stopped speaking as Thalo Child's mind was still tilting, still trying to piece together what she was saying. It took him a moment to realize why she'd cut herself off.

There, at the end of the corridor, dark hair draping like a cascade of black ink over his shoulders, eyes shrouded behind a curtain of aquamarine, was Gerome.

33

THALO CHILD

Gerome had clearly been waiting for them, for this moment. Ever since he'd found the wall in Thalo Child's mind, he'd been biding his time for a confrontation with Hintosep. And he'd followed them here and decided now was his chance.

"What in the Valley could you be doing with one of the test varger?" he asked, striding steadily toward them, his tone coiled and ready, like a tightly wound spring or a snake about to strike.

Thalo Child was already behind Hintosep and the jaguar-shaped bottle, but he moved now so that they blocked Gerome's line of sight, hiding himself the best he could.

"The Savior has need of it. *Why* is not your concern," Hintosep said, drawing herself up to her full height as Gerome came to stand before her, clearly hoping the Possessor's fear and respect of the Savior would force him to back down, to stop his interrogation before it had really begun. After all, he would not dare question the Savior's motives, would not ask Him to His face such things.

But the Savior's involvement in this was a lie.

And if Gerome's biting smile was anything to go by, all three of them knew it.

Up until that moment, Thalo Child had *suspected* but pushed the idea from his mind as subversive and insidious. This was *Hintosep,* the servant the Savior prized above all others. He had to believe that whatever she did, she did with His goals in mind and His blessing.

"How many times have you played that card to great effect, I wonder?" Gerome asked, voice silken and low. The Possessor projected satisfaction with his every move—with the line of his shoulders and tilt of his head and curl of his scarred lips. "Has it ever failed you, before now?"

He leaned in, sneering at her for a moment, the beads of his headdress tinkling lightly, before he walked around her to the jar. Without fear, he dragged his fingertips lightly over the jaguar's back—ignoring the way the ethereal varg vibrated inside—striding toward Thalo Child, whose gaze immediately fell to his own slippered feet.

"I have been probing minds throughout the keep," Gerome announced, rounding behind Thalo Child and striding back up the other side of the jar without touching or acknowledging him. "There is an unusual number of priests, Mindful, and Mindless with lost moments and fractured memories. Someone of distinct power has been fiddling with their gray matter, which I don't have to tell you"—he stood before her once more—"is an offense of the *highest order.* I know what the Savior would do to the rest of us if we'd repeatedly committed such a heinous act, but I have no idea what He'd do to *you,* His favorite, His most *loyal.*"

Thalo Child's heart raced in his chest, and his blood pounded out stuttering drums in his ears. Physically, he stood behind the two of them—and perhaps he'd be lucky enough to be considered piddling, unworthy of involvement—but he knew, truly, that he was *between* them. If they didn't think him inconsequential, then they'd think him a pawn. Someone of his age and station could only ever be a piece to be maneuvered in whatever terrible game of push-and-pull the two of them were playing.

He kept his head lowered but glanced up to see what Hintosep would do—if her spine remained straight or if she'd slackened under the rarity of a direct challenge.

She stood as fixed and certain as ever—as the mountains to which the keep clung.

"You've been planning something," Gerome said. "On your own, without the Orchestrators' or the Savior's approval."

"You have no proof of that."

"Don't I?"

Thalo Child wasn't sure if Gerome was bluffing. Were the walls he claimed he'd found enough to condemn someone like Hintosep, whose judgment was only second to the Savior's own?

"What is this? A vie for more power? Is all you wield not enough? Would you be a usurper? Do you think anyone would ever accept you in His place?"

"I'm not after His place. Or His power."

"What do you want, then? What are you hoping to achieve?"

She stayed silent. The two of them stared at each other for a long moment, no doubt throwing up internal walls and reaching out with probing tendrils, trying to find the cracks in the other's mental fortitude.

Gerome gave up first, sighing dramatically, crestfallen. "What stings the most is you did not think to include me. To confide in me. Instead, you've taken one of my children as though he belonged to you, to the Cage. He belongs to the Eye. And I know what you hid from me in his mind."

Hintosep's exterior did not crack. She did not miss a beat or bat an eye. "Oh?"

"The location of the Cage. You're using this child as both backup plan and errand boy. A small minion whose brain can be used as a convenient lockbox for whatever you need stored, in case something should happen to you."

When she did not contradict him, Thalo Child went cold. He felt suddenly brittle, like a piggy bank waiting to be smashed so that its valuable contents could be retrieved.

"You wonder why I no longer confide in you," she said, "yet you see me performing a perfectly inconsequential chore and draw the wrong conclusions. You've made up a conspiracy where there is none."

"Well, then, I look forward to being thoroughly admonished for my doubts when I ask the Savior myself."

He bowed condescendingly, then turned and strode away.

He'd called Hintosep's bluff, and she had no choice but to acknowledge that. "Who do you think the Savior will believe?" she called. "One wayward Possessor, or me?"

Gerome stopped. "Your confidence in your standing is not surprising. But clearly, you are not confident enough to let me go to Him unopposed." When he faced them again, there was a smirk on his lips.

"And if your concern was truly for the Savior, you would not bother to confront me first," she countered.

"There are things we both want here."

"A bargain? You believe I mean to undermine the Savior's will, but instead of alerting Him, you wish to strike a deal?" She scoffed, disgusted. "I did not raise you to be so—"

"You raised me to look up to you, to rely on you, to trust you!" he shouted, his self-satisfaction dissolving into hot fury in the blink of an eye. "And then you left me. Which ultimately taught me to rely only on myself, first and foremost."

"That is the way of things here!" she shouted back. "We do not have *families* like the people of the Valley. We all play our parts and then move on. The Savior is our only constant. His word, His wisdom."

"I belonged to *you*," he roared.

"You belonged to the Cage," she spat back. Her demeanor shifted, then, as a realization clearly struck her. "You still do."

Gerome drew a sharp breath, clearly ready to yell either a denial or more accusations, but faltered before he could form the words.

Watching Hintosep shift her regard for Gerome was both fascinating and unsettling. She purposefully softened her voice, her body language, her gaze. She took soft steps in his direction and held out her hand cautiously, like Thalo Child did whenever he tried to befriend the birds in the courtyards.

Gerome let her come but did not surge forward to seek her touch as Thalo Child had witnessed him do in the past.

"How can you call yourself a Possessor when you yourself are still possessed?" she asked, tone melodious and soothing. Sympathetic, not patronizing.

Before she could touch his cheek, Gerome caught her hand, but not violently. "You want this varg," he said evenly, "this child—my silence. I want the Cage."

Thalo Child's stomach was in knots. He'd known it would come to this: his life, given in trade. His Possessor did not care for him, yet he accused Hintosep of abandonment.

He held his breath while the adults stared at each other, deciding his fate. If Hintosep decided Thalo Child was ultimately unimportant to her, how would his life under Gerome change? Would his Possessor resent him for not proving valuable enough to net him the Cage? On the other hand, he had no concept of what would happen if he officially belonged to Hintosep.

The entirety of his life hung in the balance, yet was nothing but a passing thought to the people who controlled it.

"Fine," Hintosep conceded. "I will get you the Cage, but you have to give me time to formulate a plan. It's not simply sitting on a shelf somewhere. I wanted it out of everyone's reach—including mine."

Gerome scowled skeptically.

"Please," she said, her tone a prostration, "you of all people know that I don't do anything by half measures. This is not a ploy. I'll get you what you want. But I need *time*."

"One year."

"Only one?"

"A flash in the pan for both of us but generous by any standards," he said coldly. "If I am not in possession of the Cage in one year's time, I tell the Savior of your devilry, and the boy . . ." He glanced past her, made eye contact with Thalo Child. ". . . becomes a Mindless."

Thalo Child met his Possessor's gaze as steadily as he could, though he felt his lips tremble and his eyebrows bow, and could not prevent a pit of despair and betrayal from forming in his belly.

"On the other hand," Gerome continued, "after you've honored our agreement and delivered my prize, I will turn over the varg, and the child, and you can continue on with"—he let go of her and waved dismissively—"whatever this is. Do we have a deal?"

Thalo Child surged forward before Hintosep could answer. "Wait!"

They both turned to him, expressions surprised. He even let himself hope the glint in Hintosep's eye was one of *pride*. "And my infant," he said, steeling his spine. "If I am to belong to Hintosep, I wish to take my charge as well." With zhur strange powers, zhe would not be safe without him to watch over zhim, he was sure.

Gerome smiled at him. There was fondness there, but also cruelty. His teeth looked particularly sharp beneath his veil of jewels. "And the babe," he agreed. "Do we have a deal?"

"One year?" she clarified.

"One year," Gerome agreed. "But I'll hope for less."

They did not shake on it. Instead, Gerome made a sweeping, gracious bow, gesturing for her to be on her way without further impediment.

Hintosep looked to Thalo Child. "One year," she said, her tone a promise.

He nodded his understanding, and his Possessor moved to his side. "We'll put the creature back where it belongs. Don't let us keep you."

She took it as the dismissal it was.

With terror in his heart and Gerome's hand on his shoulder, Thalo Child watched Hintosep turn her back and walk away. "One year, but I'll hope for less," Gerome repeated, hissing in Thalo Child's ear, "and so should you."

34

KRONA

Hintosep was still present, Krona was sure. But her torch had been doused, and in the misty haze of the predawn forest, not even a blue shimmer was left to mark where she lay.

Krona, Thibaut, Mandip, and Juliet all instinctually drew in to one another, shoulder to shoulder, back to back, drawing their weapons—all but Thibaut, who'd apparently left the cave grotto empty-handed.

The undergrowth was only thick in patches, but there were enough trees and downed logs to hide approaching attackers—even those *without* supernatural magics.

Collectively, they held their breath, ears straining for more twigs snapping or ruffled foliage. Seeing nothing in the murky shadows, Krona knelt in the damp soil and dead leaves, thinking to put her ear to the ground, only to stop short.

A clear set of animal prints—fresh and four-legged—marred the mud. "Tracks," she whispered harshly, trailing her gloved fingers over them, suppressing the shiver that rode up her spine when the touch confirmed her fears. She snapped upright. "Those weren't made by Thalo," she said, sweeping her gaze wide. "It's a varg."

Why aren't we dead yet?

"A varg?" Mandip squeaked. "As in teeth and claws and—"

Thibaut smacked a hand over his companion's mouth. "Do you *want* it to disembowel you?" he hissed.

The varg tracks were so fresh, and that snapping had sounded so close, the monster should have easily noticed them. Krona could only speculate as to why they were still breathing. Perhaps the party was downwind, or the varg was distracted. Perhaps it had eaten recently—the prints were fully fleshed and well fatted.

Her palms immediately went sweaty in her gloves, and her vision began to tunnel. She'd gotten better at handling her vargerangaphobia since facing the bottle-barker with De-Lia at Melanie's wedding, but it still bested her in the field.

Moving deliberately, she handed Thibaut her helm and untied De-Lia's mask from her belt.

Please, Lia, please work with me. If there was ever a time she needed the knowledge De-Lia had preserved for her, it was now.

"When I say," she whispered, "you all *run*."

"Where?" Mandip demanded.

"We have to get to that camp," Juliet said.

"How will that help?"

"There's a protective barrier," Hintosep said, making them all jump, her voice hard and sure. "The varg won't be able to make it through."

Krona looped the leather strap of the mask around her neck, let the balsa settle against her clavicle as she loaded her quintbarrel, eyes darting in the dark, looking for the faintest flicker of movement.

The prints had revealed the beast's gait—a trot, unhurried. It was not far.

She prayed it was alone.

She took several deep, calming breaths, drinking deeply of the wet forest air before holding her breath and releasing it slowly.

You can do this. If it's just one, you can do this.

And with that, she put on the mask.

De-Lia's echo was there in an instant, so familiar and yet so foreign. Despite the night, light exploded behind Krona's eyes, illuminating not the forest but an insistent memory. The urge to sink inside it, to let the echo have her body for just a little while, came as it always did, but this time she fought it off immediately. Quickly, she tried to contain the echo, putting up mental walls, trying to herd it into a secluded corner of her psyche.

The echo beat itself against those walls, and they bowed. Bowed in a way that no other echo of its magnitude would have been able to force them to bow. Soon, it knocked each wall down, battling even as Krona threw new walls up.

She took more deep breaths, refusing to let frustration set in, refusing to let the echo cow her.

It had been a long night. It had been a long week. It had been a long three years. But Krona dug in to herself, pulling forth every last ounce of energy and fortitude she could muster, knowing that afterward, the effects of wearing the mask might hit her like any other mask-wielder: she'd drop like a stone. At least they'd all still be alive—

If she could manage this. Just once.

She heard a growl, out in the gloom.

The varg had finally caught their scent.

Krona shrank the space in her mind, making the walled pocket around the echo tighter. It tried to swell, and she clamped down. Sweat broke out across her brow and lip—whether from the phobia taking hold of her limbs or the battle inside her psyche, she could not say.

She wasn't in control of the mask yet, but the others couldn't wait. "Run," she said, voice low. "Go, now!"

Their dashing footsteps would draw the varg's attention. It would zero in on its prey so quickly, so easily.

De-Lia! she screamed in her mind, taking on the firm tone of a scolding parent, of their maman. *No!*

A ripple of hesitancy went through the echo.

Krona snatched her chance, fortifying her walls and snapping all escape routes shut. She threw the mental equivalent of chains and girders around the echo's prison, supporting the structure as best she could.

The influence of the echo—the personality, the will, the memories—receded. The knowledge—De-Lia's sharpshooting—flooded to the fore.

She'd done it! She'd contained De-Lia's echo.

But it was an uneasy containment. The edges of De-Lia's mental prison vibrated; thin fingers from the echo occasionally breached the seams before being snapped off and pushed back. The echo was *not* settled, and Krona knew she would not have access to De-Lia's quintbarrel-related abilities for long.

She needed to locate the varg and put it down. *Now.*

⊱──━─◦─━──⊰

When Krona said "Run," Thibaut ran. With his mistress's helm beneath one arm and Mandip's hand clutched in his other fist, the two of them stumble-ran through the brambles and between the trees. Juliet was already ahead of them, suddenly holding up a crystalline flower in the palm of her hand. It glowed ever so faintly—clearly enchanted, but not enough to see by. Just enough to be a beacon of direction. Hintosep was both somewhere and nowhere, and Thibaut figured if there was one person in the Valley who could be wholly counted on to be perfectly fine at the end of this ordeal, it was likely the Thalo.

"Where is the camp?" Mandip asked. "I still don't see the fire."

Juliet's legs were far shorter than the men's, but she took charge, leading with certainty. "This way!" She held the flower out in front of her, at the ready. "Hintosep will have to breach the border first. The camp's security will listen to a Thalo and a Thalo alone."

With both of his hands occupied, Thibaut could not defend himself against low-hanging branches, and though he did his best to duck, several lashed at his face and caught on his clothes. They yanked and tore at what was once his wedding garb. He tried not to think about what it meant, tried not to regret putting the outfit on for the Pentaétos celebration instead of leaving it safely in the closet at the Creek Side Inn. On the other hand, he could not stop himself from wishing he'd donned something much more practical in terms of footwear; his dress boots were bound to be in tatters come daylight, whether a varg used them as a chew toy or not.

Suddenly, a figure appeared before the rushing trio. Hintosep. "There," she said, pointing at a small clearing, perhaps two dozen feet across.

Thibaut saw nothing special except a break in the trees but had confidence the Thalo saw far more than he did.

They closed in on it in no time.

"Juliet?" Hintosep asked.

"Ready!" she replied.

Hintosep drew her sword and leapt past the perimeter, vanishing once more as she did, though this time she appeared to be swallowed up by something instead of falling out of his perception.

Juliet never slowed. "Do exactly as I say," she ordered. "Jump, now!"

Moving on blind faith, Thibaut vaulted over the same patch of ground she did, watching her get swallowed into nothingness moments before he felt a slight tingle trail over his entire body. Mandip jumped behind him, and an instant after, they were all three standing in what appeared to be a different clearing entirely.

A roaring blaze of a campfire occupied the center. Various cooking accoutrements and bedding were alternately neatly arranged and lightly strewn about the site. The camp smelled of smoke and bacon, and a half-eaten pig stood skewered on a roasting spit near a tall boulder, which two individuals—dressed head to toe in blue, their visible skin tattooed with equally blue swirls—had clearly been sitting upon only seconds before. Now they were on their feet, and a third individual stood with what looked like washing in hand over a bucket.

Hintosep's arrival had clearly startled them, but it hadn't alarmed them the way the chain of three perfectly average Lutadorian citizens did.

One of the Thalo by the fire gasped. "Hintosep?" They and their nearest companion sank down in genuflection.

But the Thalo doing the washing was not fooled. They stood abruptly and grabbed a nearby scabbard, registering faster than their companions that this was a conflict from the outset. They were closest to the trio and clearly had aim to strike down the civilian intruders swiftly.

Hintosep ran by, aiming for the other two, and shouted "Disarm!" as she went—an order apparently meant for Juliet.

The songstress skidded to a halt, lifting the crystal flower above her head. "Cling to me!" she ordered Mandip and Thibaut. "Keep as close as possible, lest you lose a limb."

Thibaut tossed Krona's helm aside and threw his arms around her waist; Mandip's flew around her shoulders.

"Tighter!" she ordered, and Thibaut slid down to clutch at her legs like a small child.

The Thalo pulled their sword and charged—hands still wet, the front of their robes sodden.

Juliet held perfectly steady, statuesque and resilient in the face of a raging enemy. She activated the enchantment silently, and it let out a mighty, whooshing gust, which nearly took Thibaut's hat, though he snatched it at the last moment. But the brim hit the edge of the enchantment's influence just as the Thalo's sword struck *down*.

Both the brim and the sword *grew vines*.

Long tendrils of greenery erupted across the entire surface of the magic-affected area, looking for all the world like curling worms for how fast they grew and writhed.

Shocked, Thibaut threw the hat away, and as it passed the Thalo's feet, the entire thing burst into plant life.

Juliet shook with the force of the magic, her muscles straining, teeth gritting.

The vines on the Thalo's sword wound up the pommel, then around their wrist, squeezing until Thibaut heard bones grind and snap. They dropped their newly verdant weapon, clutching their injured arm to their chest and cursing.

In the next moment, the vines all withered and turned to ash, leaving everything they'd touched crumpled or bent but otherwise without a hint of enchanted interference. Juliet grunted and slumped, the flower falling—dull and insignificant-looking—to the ground. Her body quaked as though she'd been out in the cold for too long, and as both Mandip and Thibaut moved to help her gently into a kneeling position, Thibaut noted that her skin felt clammy and feverish.

The Thalo stumbled back. Though their hand was broken, they would not give up so easily.

Thibaut quickly turned to Mandip. "Was all that swordplay just for show? Go! I'll stay with her."

"I'll stay with *you*, my dear," Juliet countered. "In a fair fight, I could take you down in two swings." She said it with both sincerity and a wink, despite her state.

Mandip, for his part, did not shy away from the fray. He was on his feet before Thibaut had gotten the last syllable of "swordplay" past his lips, drawing his weapon and surging forward.

But, of course, the Thalo puppet chose that moment to vanish before their eyes.

>·—·◦·—·◦·—·<

Krona didn't need to follow the low growl. As the others dashed away, their footsteps rustled the underbrush, drawing the varg's attention, letting it pinpoint Krona's location. It stalked forward with heavy footfalls, sliding between the trees with a rattling of quills. Its rancid smell wafted over Krona, even from a distance, even with her face shielded by De-Lia's jaguar mask.

Then her gaze caught it. There it was, a single beast that had slipped past the Borderswatch.

She didn't have to wait long for it to reveal its type. The creature flickered, disappearing one instant only to reappear yards to her right.

"Jumper," she breathed, rotating the barrel on her quint to bring the silver needle in line.

She sighted it with her needle gun but did not take the shot. De-Lia's gifted knowledge reminded her to have patience, even when a split second could mean the difference between getting to keep her jugular or losing it to a slime-slicked set of incisors.

The best time to take down a jumper was not after it had appeared, but right after it jumped. She knew to look for an unnatural wavering in the air, like a heat mirage shimmering off of desert sands. Such a phenomenon would flash before her eyes, happen only an instant before the jumper reappeared—but it should be enough.

If De-Lia were truly here, it would be enough.

The monster took two stalking steps forward before hunching down, preparing for a pounce. As it took to the air, it also jumped—disappearing for a split second.

Krona turned on the spot, swinging her body in an arc, hoping the darkness wouldn't be her downfall.

There. On the left. An unnatural sheen in the air.

On borrowed instinct, she pulled the trigger.

The dense shape of the beast flashed back into existence, still mid-leap, and was met a moment later by the *thunk* of a silver needle hitting home.

It made a whimpering screech, and Krona dodged to the side as the varg fumbled its landing and fell hard, with the needle sticking out of its shoulder and pinning it magically to the spot as surely as a javelin.

She'd done it! But Krona didn't let herself revel in the reality of her success, not yet. She'd overcome her phobia and the echo, yes, but celebrating was for safety.

Fingers shaking, she moved to load another silver needle—better to be sure the beast could not move than to rely on hope.

As she raised her quintbarrel once more, something just beyond the jumper caught her eye and stole her breath.

This varg wasn't alone.

She saw the mimic only because it opened its jaws—the rest of it was still perfectly camouflaged as it leapt over its fallen packmate.

Krona shot without thinking.

The shock of a sudden second varg made her lose control of both the echo and her footing. She tumbled backward as she tried to dodge the oncoming predator, her heels slipping out from under her, sliding against the freshly wetted muck of the forest floor.

The mimic landed just beyond her, skidding through the underbrush, the silver needle having done little more than infuriate it.

Mimics needed bronze.

But first she had to put distance between herself and its teeth.

Her heart beat in her throat, and every jarring movement as she struggled to her feet punched extra air from her lungs. Despite the enchanted stones in her bracers, despite De-Lia's expertise, the fear came roaring to the front.

And the echo—

Fuck, *the echo.*

Its tendrils shattered the edges of its mental prison, sending shards through Krona's psyche, making her head swim and her vision blur.

Luckily, she and the echo wanted the same thing in this moment. De-Lia's will was focused on neutralizing the varger but, unfortunately, wanted to take control of Krona's body to do it. While Krona wanted to run away—to gain distance—the echo wanted her to spin and confront the beast head-on. The echo twisted her ankles, her knees, her hips. It made her right side go numb with the sudden force, and she nearly dropped her quintbarrel.

She fell hard again and bit back a sob of frustration.

Part of her wanted to stay down. Between the struggle in her mind and the teeth at her back and the fear in her chest and her failure at the palace, what was the point of fighting? She could not give herself to the echo—it would take too long for it to settle in her mind to the point where it could save her life anyway, where it could stop the varg. But she could no longer contain it. It would take just as much time to try to control it again as it would for it to fully control her.

This tug-of-war with herself ultimately left her vulnerable. More vulnerable than if she'd simply run with the others.

And now she wasn't even sure where they'd gone.

Quickly, she thrust her neck in the direction they'd sped, certain she would see no sign—

But there was a flicker between the trees.

Something had changed; she saw the campfire now. A clear blaze—a beacon.

Hintosep and Juliet had both believed the camp a safe haven. A place varger could not enter.

It gave her the hope she needed.

"De-Lia!" she shouted at the confused echo, at herself. "We have to run!"

If she could get it to listen to her, to recognize her as her sister, to understand her distress—

The mimic growled behind her, its footfalls newly pronounced.

The echo let go of her body, and Krona was off like a shot. That orange flicker meant everything. It was her only way out.

▷·◁◈▷·○·◁◈·▷·◁

Mandip swatted his rapier through the air, hitting nothing.

Thibaut dove for the Thalo's fallen sword. The vines that had sprung forth from the enchantment had mangled it just the same as centuries beneath ancient tree roots. Clutching it to his chest, he scrambled back to Juliet's side.

He'd taken one weapon, but Thibaut knew a Thalo puppet didn't need a blade to defeat their foe.

He could vaguely recall a hand with blue tattoos reaching out for him, once. That hand had made him remember his wife, of another time when they'd run from the authorities. It made him relive a warped reiteration of that moment, and he'd retraced those past steps in his mind, unwittingly playing out a bastardized version with his body.

That had led to his and Krona's capture, which ultimately planted them in that cellar with Gatwood and his goons.

If these people so much as *nearly* touched you, they could take hold of you. They could turn Mandip in an instant, making him think he was in a fencing match while in reality forcing him to skewer his companions right through.

In the moment, there was no way for Mandip to know that a brush with such a hand would be a brush with madness. All the young lord could do was swing wildly enough to keep the Thalo at a distance.

Beyond Mandip's adulterated dance, Hintosep fought with ferocity. These were her brethren, and still she did not hold back.

Suddenly, a cloud of dirt burst in Mandip's face, stopping his rapid spin. He spluttered and stumbled, pawing at his eyes with his free hand, blinded by the grit the invisible Thalo had thrown. His sword tip drooped, his arm going slack.

Thibaut didn't know what to do. Juliet still shuddered beside him, near-boneless, and he couldn't see Mandip's adversary to run into the fray and help, even though he wanted to.

He was built for clandestine meetings and sly manipulations, not these kinds of hostilities. Direct confrontation was Krona's domain, not his.

Oh, gods, Krona.

They'd simply left her with the varg. At a monster's mercy. The others must think her well suited to the task, but *he* knew. He knew what facing a varg could mean for her.

At a loss, he cried out for the Thalo woman. "Hintosep!"

His call must have been suitably distressed. The woman's attention snapped over her shoulder, taking in Mandip's predicament in an instant. Without missing a parry, she flung her free hand in the lordling's direction.

Her magic itself could not be seen, but its effects were instant. Suddenly, the attacking Thalo was made visible again, their own powers countered.

Blinking rapidly, still wiping at his face, Mandip was stunned to see his adversary so close, right in front of him.

He took the advantage without thinking, thrusting his weapon forward, eyes going wide when the blade sank into flesh.

The Thalo's brows raised in shock, matching Mandip's expression save for the obvious additional pain.

After a slight hesitation, Mandip stood his ground and threw his body weight behind his pommel, sliding the sword deeper, making sure it hit home. A moment later, he seemed to come back to himself, to realize what had just happened, and he let go of the weapon altogether, taking stiff strides in reverse.

The Thalo clutched at the sword lodged deep in their abdomen, pulled slightly as though to take it out, only to collapse to their knees.

Thibaut looked away, looked for Hintosep again, only to realize all three of the other Thalo had shrouded themselves.

The three Lutadites were exposed. At any moment, their lives could end, and they'd never see it coming.

Mandip stared blankly as the Thalo before him slowly slumped over and went still. The lordling's breaths came high and shallow, and he was flushed and trembling.

Minutes later (or perhaps only moments; Thibaut's head was whirling) someone on the other side of the camp cried out in pain. It might have been Hintosep. He hated that he couldn't tell.

Then, to his left, a new shout ripped through the night. Krona came bounding across the barrier, a dark shape at her heels.

⊱┈◈┈◯┈◈┈⊰

Krona aimed for the fire, propelling her entire body forward as though she meant to throw herself into the flames. As she ran, she spun her barrel to the proper needle, keeping the shot at the ready, though she dared not stop to fire. When she broke out of the trees and into a clearing, a flood of tingles washed over her. And though she couldn't be sure it *wasn't* from hyperventilating, its line through her body felt distinct, as though she'd crossed a threshold.

Was she through? Was she safe?

She chanced it, turning on her heel.

The mimic was right behind her. It leapt—massive paws splayed, belly exposed, teeth gnashing—and she raised her quintbarrel. The monster landed against an invisible barrier with a yowl of surprise.

It was just as Hintosep had said; the camp's enchantments could deflect a varg attack.

But there was nothing about the magic that forced the creature away or made it bounce back. Instead, it slid down to its hind legs, keeping its forepaws extended, trying to dig its claws into the wall it could feel but couldn't see.

She stood there for a long few moments, stunned by the unusual view of such a beast. Behind Krona, someone made a ghastly, gurgling sound. She nearly turned once more, to defend against a new assailant, but then Hintosep materialized at her side and a body slumped at her feet. "Shoot!" Hintosep commanded.

With no help from De-Lia, Krona shot the varg point-blank as it scrabbled at the barrier. The needle caught the creature under its right forelimb, deadening the arm. She went to reload, but the echo wrenched her off-balance.

Krona seethed. She wasn't used to this kind of bodily hijacking, of losing her autonomy to an echo. When she wielded a mask, she was supposed to be in control. She was supposed to be steady and calculating. This was what she was good at, what gave her the right to carry her Regulator coin *despite* her failings with a quintbarrel.

But *this* echo took away her ability to think properly, to plan. It forced her to be impulsive because she couldn't count on self-rule from one moment to the next.

Angry at De-Lia in a way she hadn't allowed herself to be angry for many years, Krona tore the mask from her face, tore the echo from her mind. She wanted to *hurt* the echo, to punish it for nearly costing her her life. And, unthinking, her attention was drawn once more to the flames.

She threw the mask as hard as she could, aiming for the heart of the coals.

It hit the fire before she'd fully come back to herself. Before she could register what she'd done.

Guilt and regret took hold of her before she could even move her feet.

But someone else was already there. Sprinting, reaching into the fire without regard for their own safety.

Thibaut.

He hissed as the flames licked at his leather gloves, but did not hesitate to use his hands instead of looking for a tool. Swiftly, he tossed the mask into the dirt. The edges had begun to smolder, and smoke curled from the eyelets.

Krona prayed she'd only damaged the surface.

Biting her lip and holding back sudden tears—tears of frustration and exhaustion and shame—she finished her fight with the varg, putting two more needles into its hide before being satisfied it was pinned.

Next to her, Hintosep was bloodied. Her blood, someone else's blood. The bodies of three people in blue robes lay scattered around a ruined campsite. Juliet looked drained and frail, and both men looked sick to their stomachs.

This night had been long, and awful, and all any of them wanted was sleep.

35

MANDIP

Mandip had never killed anyone before. He'd never imagined he'd have to.

Dead eyes stared up at him from the Thalo on the ground, and hot blood was quickly drying on his hands. While he'd silently listened to Krona's insistence that Thalo puppets were real and, in turn, Hintosep's insistence that they were simply human, he hadn't really accepted the notion until now.

This body before him did not have claws like in the stories, or visible fangs, or knives protruding from their skull. Their blood was just as red as his, and their form just as substantial.

This was no terror conjured up by a cruel creator.

It was just a person.

And he'd killed them.

As his stomach soured and threatened to spill, he took short, sharp breaths through his mouth and tried to justify it in his mind. *They were attacking you; it was self-defense.*

It wasn't *self-defense*, he chided himself. *This was their camp. You invaded it. You* attacked. *You needed their sanctuary and you killed them for it.*

"We only beat them unscathed because they were unprepared," Hintosep said, kneeling next to another body—one of the two she'd killed. "They thought they were safe. Untouchable." She pushed a lock of dark hair back from the body's brow before turning to Thibaut. "Help me move them." She nodded near the rock. "Over there."

"We have to keep them inside the camp?" Mandip asked.

"You'd rather set them outside the perimeter and wake up to a horde of scavengers and mutilated forms? No? Thought not. Besides, there could be more varger about. No need to attract them."

Mandip turned to the varg half draped against the perimeter. It was breathing steadily but lay otherwise still. He'd never seen one this close before but knew enough about them to identify this as a mimic, what with the way its quills looked like pine needles and twigs and knots of brambles and bark. Drop this same varg in a desert, and it would blend in with the sand and stones just as easily.

The Regulator scooped up her mask from where it lay in the dirt, and wouldn't meet anyone's gaze. "Do we have to keep looking at it?" she asked, meaning the varg.

Hintosep waved a hand near the perimeter, and the circle of it went dark, like a curtain. "The enchantment is buried," she said, pointing at the ground. "Do not cross the line of it unless I say. I've changed the frequency again, and it will not let you back through if you leave."

Mandip was curious how it worked, as he was privileged to many types of enchantments the common people would never see, and still, this was far outside what he thought was possible—think of the military applications! And even though he had no idea what *frequency* meant in this context, he was too rattled and too tired to formulate his questions.

After tending to the bodies, they cleaned themselves and the rest of the camp, ate the remainder of the wild pig, and settled uncomfortably into the available bedding laid out around the fire. Thibaut removed his tattered jacket and pants, exchanging them for some of the linens from the Thalo's washing. The group's mood was somber and subdued, and despite being so tired, sleep was as elusive as conversation. Even Juliet, who was still chipper in the face of her enchantment-induced illness, could only muster so much good humor.

Mandip kept seeing the shock on the Thalo's face as he drove his blade into their body. Shock he'd felt in his own features—in all his muscles and down his spine. It felt so unlike impaling straw practice dummies with a rapier, unlike the whipping touch of an epee or foil. He'd felt their muscles *split*, had heard their viscera yield and tear.

His hands still shook and bile still threatened to leave his belly, and yet he could not stop reliving the moment over and over, as though by repeating it, he could change it. Change it into *what*, he wasn't sure. If he had not killed the Thalo, likely they would have killed him.

At some point, the moment dimmed, blurred, and sleep finally overcame all else.

In the morning, Hintosep woke him before the others—before the sun had even penetrated the forest canopy. The air smelled damp, and crisp, and green. "You were troubled last night," she said.

"I made no secret of it," he insisted.

"Oh, but you did." She ordered him to his feet. "You're coming with me." He was instantly suspicious. "Where?"

"We're building a pyre. We killed them; we should see to them."

Together, they carried the bodies away, exiting the opposite side of the camp from the pinned varg so as to avoid riling it. There was a smaller clearing not too far from camp, and there they constructed the base of what would be a poor excuse for a funerary fire, but they made do with what they had. For a long while, they gathered dead wood in silence.

Mandip did not recognize this as an opportunity to flee. At the very least, he knew an attempt to escape would not end in death—Hintosep needed him alive for her heist; that was obvious. So, it was not a fear of reprisal that kept his footfalls even and pointed in whichever direction Hintosep guided him.

Instead, he felt a *duty* to see this task through, and he didn't know what that meant. Surely, he couldn't be expected to owe the *Thalo* anything. Even having just learned they were real, and people at that, they were fundamentally enemies of Lutador. In fact, his duty to his city-state and his fallen Grand Marquis dictated he should be attacking Hintosep—the assassin—at this very moment instead of helping her.

Beyond his loyalty to his city-state was a different sense of responsibility. *This* was not a game. This was not the maneuvering of political pawns. This was not idle intrigue at court or a calculated display of influence.

This was life and death.

"It's all life and death," Hintosep said suddenly.

Mandip dropped an armful of grayed branches on their growing pile. "What?"

"The political maneuvering and what you think of as *idle* intrigue. None of it's a game. These small turns have little influence on your daily life, but they mean life or death for many beyond the palace walls.

"You don't simply command that kind of power with a blade in your hand. You, as a potential Grand Marquis, would command that kind of power with a pen. With a *word*. Nearly every decision you'd make—about trade, infra-structure, worship—would inevitably draw a line between those two worlds for someone." She shook her head, disgust written in every line of her face. "Collateral damage. I'm so *sick* of collateral damage. Did you truly think you'd never kill anyone simply because you'd never tear out their guts yourself?"

For a moment, he was left speechless.

"Forgive me," Hintosep said, staring at the limp forms, her voice quivering. "As you can see, I am not immune to leaving collateral damage in my wake."

"They were Thalo—"

"They were good people. Indoctrinated to a certain worldview but not evil. I'd known them each since they were children, and they—" Her voice broke; she covered her mouth with her hand and turned so Mandip could not see her face. He gave her a moment to compose herself. "I thought I'd made peace with my decision," she said quietly. "I knew where it would lead."

When she faced him again, she was the hardened woman from the night before. Inscrutable and unwavering. "Help me lift them. This is not a proper send-off—not our way. But it'll have to do. We certainly can't take them to the salt pool, and we can't leave them here to rot."

▷━◆▷━◦━◁◆━◁

Once the conflagration had consumed all three Thalo, Hintosep hummed a low hymn, one Mandip did not know, so he stood by in silence. In Lutador, bodies were burned in crematoriums, not out in the open like this, and he found the scent especially disturbing. It was like any other meat that had fallen into the flames of a cooking fire, and that realization sickened him.

"Return to the others," she instructed after a time. "My fellows here surely laid game traps in the usual places. I'll check them to see if we have breakfast or must leave on empty stomachs."

Mandip wasn't sure his belly could manage meat at the moment but made no argument.

When he reached camp again and stepped across the perimeter, he was met with a shout.

"Wait, milor, don't—"

But he was already through. "What?"

Everyone else was awake. Juliet sat relaxed and idle, but Thibaut and the Regulator were on their feet, standing right at the edge of the enchanted space.

Thibaut threw up his hands, clearly frustrated. "She made it sound like we could go freely, but she's trapped us in," he said.

Mandip immediately tried to step back out and was repelled as though trying to unsuccessfully press through a well-pinned stage curtain.

"We're fine," Juliet insisted in her singsong way, seemingly back to herself this morning with no lingering effects from the flower enchantment—a germination salt crystal, she'd explained last night.

"What if there are more varger out there and she never makes it back to release us?" Captain Hirvath asked.

"You think Thalo never have to deal with varger?" She waved at the camp. "Hintosep did this for us. To save *us*, not herself. She wouldn't have so much as disturbed these people, let alone killed them, if we hadn't been her first concern."

Mandip believed Hintosep's grief at the pyre had been genuine, and her outpouring hit him differently now. It hadn't been a do-or-die situation for *her*. She'd been made to choose—safety and secrecy for the Lutadites, or the lives of three people she'd known since their youth.

Krona looked skeptical. She considered Juliet for a moment, then asked, "What is your game in all this, La Maupin?"

"I told you, she's helping me rescue my brother."

"Rescue him from what?"

She pointed to where the bodies had previously lain. "From the fate of those poor sods."

"He's in the Order of the Thalo? How?"

"Snatched from the cradle. My family was made to mourn him as though he was dead."

Hintosep eventually came back with two large hares in hand, their feet dangling, blood dripping into the dirt.

She tossed them down at Mandip's feet. "Get to skinning if you want to eat."

"Not a good idea," Krona said, taking in Mandip's sour expression. "He's more likely to pierce the intestines and spoil the meat than so much as pull away a clean strip of skin."

Mandip scoffed. "I *have* been hunting before." After the pyre this morning, he had no interest in eating the rabbits, let alone skinning them. But he wouldn't let them think him incompetent in areas he was fully capable.

"Which included breaking down and preparing your kill for supper?" she asked. "Or did you leave those bits to the servants and the cooks?"

He glared at her.

"I don't know why you're so offended, milor," Thibaut said. "Doesn't seem like the kind of activity you'd be jumping to get into, regardless of know-how. I'll do it," he offered.

"*You* know how?" Krona asked.

"Believe it or not, I'm not entirely helpless."

"That wasn't a yes."

Thibaut scooped up the limp conies. "Pass me a knife and find out for yourself, mistress."

"You'll have to take off your gloves," Krona said softly, unsheathing her dagger. Her tone had dipped, strangely, into *considerate*.

"Once in a while, my skin does see the sun," Thibaut assured her, his hand resting over hers on the dagger's hilt for an unnaturally long moment.

Their eyes met, and Mandip looked away. There was an intimacy there he didn't feel privy to. Something that went beyond the heated fumbling and messy kisses he and Thibaut had shared.

Juliet looked up from where she was attempting to darn her skirt, and her gaze darted between the others. To break the tension, her lips seemed to move of their own accord:

The hunter's blade knows not what it cuts
But sinews and tethers and furs and guts
The life beneath means naught but the hunt
Even though the heart beats hot and blunt

Thibaut cleared his throat and stepped away from Krona.

Hintosep quirked an eyebrow at Juliet. "That little talent of yours is devastatingly annoying sometimes."

Juliet shrugged.

Krona seemed satisfied and went to tend to her equipment. Only Mandip watched Thibaut as he went to work.

Thibaut pulled a fire-blackened stone from around the fire pit and flipped it fired-side up, depositing the hares there. When he removed his gloves, Mandip caught sight of dozens and dozens of thin, raised scars. But more curious than that was the way he stared at the rabbits, as though they were a puzzle he'd never encountered before. He turned one over and over, clearly trying to decide where to begin.

Mandip strolled over to his side, and as though he was harried by the young noble's presence, Thibaut immediately pointed the knife at the creature's belly. Gently, before he could make a beginner's mistake and ruin their breakfast, Mandip put his hand over Thibaut's. "What are you doing?"

"About to butcher this rabbit?"

"In the most unkind sense of the word, it looks like. You said you knew what you were doing."

Thibaut leaned in and curled a finger at Mandip. With raised eyebrows—though it was no surprise, really—he said, "I lied."

"Why?"

He shrugged. "Second nature. I'm quite used to bullshitting my way through any situation. Just comes naturally. Usually, I figure it out—whatever it is—well enough to get by."

Mandip scrutinized him for a moment. The slight blush in his cheeks, the way he would not meet Mandip's gaze. "Were you trying to impress her?"

"What? Of course not. Besides, she knows all my tricks. Likely it was a fifty-fifty shot on whether or not she'd believe me anyway."

"And knowing you as she does, she simply let you?"

He shrugged. "We trust each other. Far more than we probably should. Even when we definitely shouldn't."

"Well, you'll lose the hide and spoil the meat that way. Let's find some rope—we need to hang them by their feet."

"So, *you do* know how to process your hunt?"

"Silver spoons do tend to be accompanied by silver knives," he said with a wink.

⊷⊶

After the rabbits had been properly butchered, they were lightly seasoned from the camp's stash of goodies and placed over the fire for roasting. The group was mostly silent until after they'd divvied up the portions of cooked meat and began filling their bellies.

Mandip kept thinking about the varg. Up until now, he'd had no experience with them, and still he'd only had a glimpse. He kept glancing in the direction of the one pinned near their camp, but the border was still opaque. "Are varger so violent all the time or—"

"Yes," Captain Hirvath said sternly, picking sinew from between her teeth.

"Strange thing for you to say," Hintosep pointed out, "seeing as how your sister kept one as a pet. Monkeyflower, wasn't it?"

The Regulator drew in a sharp breath.

"Don't forget, I'm not the only Thalo who's been watching you. You were tracked all through the Gatwood concern. Well before, even. On the streets, in the vaults . . . to his apartment." Hintosep gestured at Thibaut. "And your sister had been of note to us ever since she found that varg of hers as a child. There are exceptions to everything in this world, and reasons for those exceptions. And via those exceptions, we can learn the true way of things."

Captain Hirvath looked unimpressed. "Oh? Enlighten us."

"For example, I believe your sister's encounter is a key clue that will help us understand the beasts."

"What's there to understand? They hunt, they kill, they hunt, they kill. They come from beyond the Valley, sent by the creator with only one purpose: to destroy us."

"A tidy bit of propaganda."

"As though I haven't seen them tear out throats and stomachs with my own two eyes?" the Regulator demanded.

"I'm not denying they're killers. I'm denying the simplicity of your explanation for *why* they kill."

"To eat, like any other creature."

"No. I don't think so."

"All you have are hypotheses, then?"

"All I have are thousands of years of observation and some newly acquired research. I was told they are monsters from beyond the Valley, same as you. But

I have reason to believe this is just one of the many lies I've been told by the Savior. Of course, in this instance, I'm not even sure He Himself knows it a lie. Regardless, I'm ready to move on to the experimental phase. Thus my interest in you—your immunities, your affinities. How's that vargerangaphobia of yours, Mistress Hirvath?"

"Under control. Mostly," she said softly, avoiding eye contact.

Mandip looked between them, unable to read the situation, unable to tell if the Regulator was lying or not.

"Good," Hintosep said, a false kind of brightness in her tone. "Because our experiments will require us to get rather cozy with a beast or two."

"Oh, *that* sounds promising. You didn't save me from the Marchonian Guards simply because you knew I was innocent and could be an ally, but because you expect me to play lab assistant."

"Lab *rat*, actually."

The Regulator looked taken aback. She had no counter-comment.

"That's how I intend to increase your power," Hintosep said. "In order to understand my theories about where varger come from, and how that relates to you specifically, you'll also need to understand far more about what's been done to humanity." With a stick, she drew a five-pointed pinwheel in the dirt beside the campfire. Between each line she wrote the name of a god, starting with Emotion, then Knowledge, Nature, and Time, but when she came to the space that should have been reserved for the Unknown, she wrote *Secrets*.

"Five gods, five magics, all interrelated. Yes?"

The others all nodded.

"So, why would the creator's monsters reflect the gods and their gifts?" With a wave of her hand, the dark curtain disappeared, leaving the surrounding forest fully visible—including the fallen varg. "Five types of varger, each with abilities that correspond to the five types of magic." She turned to Krona. "What were the types you faced last night? Which is *that*?"

"Mimic," Krona said, suddenly extremely interested in her coney shank. "The one out in the woods is a jumper."

Mandip had never seen a fully fleshed and fully controlled varg up close before. He stared at it from a distance, until Hintosep noticed and encouraged him over. "Go on."

With the hesitation of a child who's not sure if the permission granted is genuine, he stood and took the handful of strides required to draw him up close to the beast. It seemed reasonably subdued, as though sleeping, and Mandip wondered if the camp's perimeter also shielded them from the varg's nose.

He'd been an equestrian all his life, and this creature was easily the size of a quarter horse. But lying curled up as it was, from only a few feet away it looked no more ferocious than the average bush, it so perfectly blended with its environment.

As he stared, Hintosep continued. "Mimics can camouflage themselves in any natural setting. Jumpers ignore the constraints of time and space . . ."

Krona's armor rattled, and Mandip turned in time to see her glance up sharply. "Love eaters target strong emotions. The pack leaders are much more intelligent—they retain more knowledge."

"And mirrors know every *secret* move before you make it," Hintosep finished. "When you know what the final gift is, it becomes easy to see, doesn't it? Though there are many things I still do not know, there are a few things of which I am certain. Varger are not monsters from beyond the Valley. They can't traverse the border; they're trapped inside just like everything else. No one has ever found any pups or broods, because they do not procreate like any other creature, and yet they proliferate. No matter how many are captured, no matter how many are bottled, there are always more. And after all these many years, I have come to one foundational assumption—one that you will help me test."

"And what's that?"

"That varger are born of people."

Mandip resisted the information, even though he knew deep down that he had no right to be skeptical. Still, incredulous confusion threatened to push a sardonic laugh from his chest, but he bit it back. Thibaut, on the other hand, had no such reservations, and let loose a bark of derision—the kind that could only come from someone who had no firm footing in the conversation to begin with. Thibaut was surely skilled at many things, and certainly crafty in his own way, but enchantment expert he was not.

"Just as all magic is born of people," Hintosep said firmly, ignoring him. "It all springs from the same origin. It may come from the gods, but it *resides* in people. Most of what you've been taught about magic is carefully curated, if not an out-and-out lie."

"That's nonsense," Mandip said. "Raw enchanted materials have magic in them straight from the ground. I've been to the mines. I've seen the enchanted forests. I've *held*—"

"I'm sure you have," Hintosep cut him off. "You need to forget what you think you know, realize that most every enchantment you've encountered is the result of sleight of hand. The materials do not absorb God Power on the rim. It is purposefully placed into the materials after it is harvested."

"Harvested from where?"

"Haven't you been listening, milor?" Thibaut asked, still clearly amused by what he thought was a joke or, at the very least, an obvious lie. "Magic is harvested from people."

36

THALO CHILD

Nine Months Ago

Gerome's command quickly turned cruel. It wasn't overt enough to draw notice from the priests—mostly small slights in more public areas of the keep, and larger indignities in private. Gerome started to use the Eye's influence on him at random, manipulating Thalo Child's emotions without warning. He made him burst out laughing during a silent call to worship, and sob in the middle of breakfast.

Those minor humiliations Thalo Child could take—and if it hadn't been for Hintosep's deal, he would have thought Gerome was testing him; he would have thought it a lesson or an exercise that would help him become a stronger Named One in the end.

The true malice lay in his efforts to keep Thalo Child from seeing his charge. There were days where the Possessor would stroll up to him, pluck Thalo Infant from his grasp, and stroll away with zhim. Others where Gerome would order him to return Thalo Infant to the nursery because of an "important task," only to relegate Thalo Child to hours cleaning the privy.

Thalo Child tried to convince himself that his Possessor was only toying with him. That the moments he was separated from Thalo Infant were meant to worry him, nothing more. Gerome wouldn't hurt the babe once he took zhim out of Thalo Child's sight. Of course not.

Of course not.

Even knowing the separation pangs were just that, he could not keep himself from obsessively fearing for the infant's safety while they were parted.

⊱┈┅•◦○◦•┅┈⊰

One afternoon, a few months after Gerome's deal with Hintosep, the Possessor and Thalo Child trod a familiar path, out onto the rampart, but instead of stopping halfway to wait for the Harvesters to bring in new Sacrifices, Gerome hurried on without a pause, toward the door that led . . . led *away*.

Surprised by this turn, Thalo Child stumbled, but he quickly recovered. When they reached the door—sturdy wood with iron studs—Gerome pushed through without explanation.

A dangerously narrow open-air staircase met them on the other side. Just like the rampart, it soared above the natural slope of the mountain, and a fall in either direction would be deadly. Thalo Child wondered how the wind hadn't claimed any of the Sacrifices he'd tended to—seeing as how it howled with ferocity even now, threatening to take him off his feet before he'd even attempted to leave the landing—until Gerome stepped onto the staircase and his robes fell straight and calm.

Of course. The staircase was enchanted with a protective barrier. Invisible, and, he assumed, likely to give out should anyone attempt a crossing without a knowledgeable Thalo to manage it.

Thalo Child followed cautiously but confidently. The stairs alighted on a narrow path that wound around an outcropping, shielding its true length and destination from view. It too was guarded from the elements, though it appeared exposed.

The path twisted for a long way, following the natural flow of the stone at a smooth-yet-steep downward slope.

There were several times Thalo Child wished to stop—not to catch his breath but to simply look out over the Severnyy Ice Field and what little he could see of the curling Valley to the west.

Eventually, they came to a lowered drawbridge, and on the other side stood a carriage house. Nothing but forest and road lay beyond.

Real, open, winding *road*.

Thalo Child could not hold his tongue any longer. "We're leaving the keep?" His voice broke at the end in a combination of pubescent cracking and sudden fear. He'd never been outside the keep. No one his age had ever been outside the keep, as far as he knew.

It made him instantly wary of what Gerome had planned. He wanted to believe his Possessor wouldn't dare harm him, at least not before Hintosep either succeeded or failed to retrieve the Cage. But he'd come to understand that he truly knew little of Gerome's motives and reasons. His Possessor seemed both extremely measured and overly impulsive in contradictory turns. Perhaps Gerome's suspicion of Hintosep's plans for Thalo Child had won out over his desire for the Cage. Perhaps he thought getting rid of Thalo Child was the most practical way to stop her and prove his loyalty to the Savior.

"Your feet are not made of lead," Gerome said impatiently.

Thalo Child raised his foot to move from the last step onto the waiting road, calculating what his chances would be in the mountains if he decided to run. Could he escape Gerome? If he fled, what would be his charge's fate? Sure, he had helped Hintosep, but zhe was innocent, had done nothing. Was Gerome so depraved as to hurt a young one purely out of revenge?

Gerome was a Possessor. His whole life was devoted to raising and training young Thalo, a noble endeavor, a righteous and humbling calling.

It also afforded him easy and automatic power. Young children were trusting; Thalo Child had seen proof of that in his infant, in the way zhe had taken to him right away, with no proof of his ability to care for or to be kind to zhim.

They were brought horses and supplies by several Thalo manning the bridge and carriage house. "It is several days' travel to where we're going," Gerome informed him as he mounted his steed.

The shock of such a simple statement went straight to his lungs, made them stutter. "But Thalo Infant, my obligations—" *Your obligations,* he wanted to add. Gerome did occasionally leave his cohort with another Possessor for a short time but never without warning. Was it possible the others had been told and Gerome had kept him in the dark on purpose?

The idea only served to stoke his fears.

"Everything's been taken care of," Gerome said, in what Thalo Child used to think of as a reassuring tone.

"I don't know how to ride," Thalo Child pointed out. He'd never seen more than an illustration of a horse, let alone touched the real beast before.

"Your horse will follow mine. All you need to do is not fall off."

>-+-+>-O-<+-+-<

Horseback riding, Thalo Child decided, was not fun in the least. His entire body ached, especially his thighs, hips, and back. But he didn't complain, and he didn't hesitate to dismount and climb back up on the horse every time he was ordered. The horse he'd been given was indeed a patient, gentle soul, and he was thankful for its demeanor every time he burdened its back.

Day turned to night turned to day turned to night. They camped under the stars, which Thalo Child thought might have been pleasant with different company.

Early afternoon on their third day, Gerome signaled they were near their destination. "The village is just a ways ahead. We'll stop outside, off the beaten path."

They crested a hill and Gerome pulled his horse to a halt. "We'll put up camp here."

They tied the horses, set up their perimeter, and prepared a slight meal in awkward silence.

"Now what?" Thalo Child ventured once they'd eaten.

"Now we wait until we are summoned."

He said no more than that. Thankfully, not too much longer passed before Gerome received whatever signal he'd been waiting for. Thalo Child didn't notice any change, but his Possessor was soon snapping his fingers and ordering him to prepare for a small hike.

Together, the two of them trudged out of their protective, climate-controlled circle and through a fresh, light powdering of snow. All around, the mountains were a twist of steep slopes topped with rocky outcroppings, sheer and sharp. They had to make their way between two ridges before they came upon a clearing. Around the clearing, ancient, warped trees with trunks as broad as the carriage house rose into the pale sky, their branches wide and their needles long and sharp. The woody scent of cones mixed with damp stone and a slight edge of sulfur in the air, giving the mountains a distinct smell, not wildly different from the scents of the keep.

They pulled up short as they alighted upon a herd of caribou nosing their way through the snow to get at something underneath. The creatures were large, with antlers as wide as Thalo Child was tall, all covered over in velvet. Each wore a harness of small brass bells. The creatures were intimidating but fascinating. Thalo Child longed to approach one, to see if a deer would allow him to touch it, but Gerome spotted the herdmaster, and the two of them hurried on.

The way dipped down into another clearing with a small stream trickling through it—fed by ice runoff high in the glacier regions. To one side of the stream, at the rear of the clearing, lay a massive circle of the broad-trunked trees, nestled right up against a bare-stone cliff. Some of the trees even appeared to climb up the rock, coiling and branching up it like grasping fingers in the way the keep grasped at the mountains. Thalo Child had never seen such trees before, curving out in strange ways, bulbous and shiny, as though polished. The wood was a lovely warm reddish.

"There it is," Gerome said with a nod, face still remarkably pale even after their strenuous trudge.

"What?"

"The village," he said. "Those trees—the village is inside."

He pictured the homes like little fairy holds, carved right into the wood.

"Come. The Harvesters are expecting us. You must stay close to me. I will hide us from the villagers' sight, but in order to do that, I must be aware of your position at all times. Understand?"

"Yes, Possessor."

"Good."

Soon, they found a well-trodden, narrow road and entered the circle of trees. The reality of the village was different but no less wondrous than Thalo Child had imagined.

The trees themselves had been trained to grow around and up the cliff. They encircled small stone cottages with dramatically pitched roofs, in the traditional Marrakevian style. The stones of the walls had been laid in an almost-haphazard way, giving each building a lean and a swirl. There weren't many, perhaps a dozen, and most of the houses rested directly against a tree or the cliff. In the village center—more of a communal circle than anything—lay a heap of fire windows, which glowed with everlasting warmth. It was at least ten degrees warmer inside the gathering of trees than out, and Thalo Child guessed it never froze inside.

A zigzagging staircase wound up the cliff face, cut directly into the stone. This led to a series of stacked caves, which appeared to shelter a small market and various vendors.

Thalo Child noted there were more people milling about than could possibly live there. It must have been a hub, a small trading post between the vast stretches of wilderness and secluded trappers and hunters.

Everywhere he looked, there were carvings and adornments formed right out of the natural environment. Branches and roots had been manipulated to grow into topiaries representing various animals—one in the shape of a caribou had horns sprouting leaves and berries. There were surprise reliefs that could only be viewed in the stone when someone stood at the correct angle. And bells. So many brass bells and ornaments. From huge temple-style bells to small chimes. Even the Marrakevian clothes sported bells at the collars, wrists, and ankles.

It was wondrous and lifted Thalo Child's spirits. Clearly, he'd been wrong to fear Gerome, that this outing was some kind of ruse to be rid of him. Why would he bring him to such a fascinating place before dispatching him for good?

"This way," Gerome indicated, deftly dodging a woman with her arms full of wrapped goods. She aimed right for him, completely oblivious to his presence. As she hurried past Thalo Child, her eyes looked his way, but her gaze fell right through him. He pulled his cloak tight around him at the last moment so that she would not brush up against it.

"They truly can't see us?" He'd known this was a skill he'd learn one day—to hide himself from the world while standing smack-dab in the middle of it—but he'd never witnessed its usage, as far as he knew, anyway.

"They cannot see us, hear us, or feel the lightest of our touches unless we want them to."

Thalo Child looked down at himself, then up at Gerome. As far as he could tell, nothing had changed about the two of them.

"It is a projected secret," Gerome explained, making for a cottage near the cliff. "I've created a blind spot around us, and their minds fill in the gaps. It is not us that change but the perception of our existence in space and time. This is why I must know where you are. If I cannot place you, I cannot protect you."

They approached a cottage nestled in the gnarled, raised roots of one of the great trees. There were so many bells encircling the door—hung from the low-dipping eaves, attached to little hooks in the stone cladding, and strung across the threshold—Thalo Child wondered how they could possibly enter without being noticed, altered perceptions or no.

Gerome simply *knocked*.

A Thalo—a Harvester, given their robes—opened the door and beckoned them inside with a small bow of respect for the Possessor.

They entered into a small room that clearly served as both kitchen and primary living space. It was cozy and smelled of ginger, and Thalo Child's attention was immediately drawn to the large cast-iron pot hanging over the fire. Two doors sat next to each other at the rear of the room, and given the overall size of the cottage, Thalo Child suspected they led to the only other rooms in the house.

The Harvester guided them to one. "Please wait here. The taxing has just commenced."

The door opened into a dyeing room filled with hanging, twisted fibers drying on racks and dangling from the ceiling. The strong scent of wet yak hair and fermented berries hit Thalo Child hard, and he immediately covered his nose with his sleeve. The colors, though, were brilliant—vibrant purple and deep maroon and grieving red. Tubs of dyes and alcohol were stacked in the various corners, and several stained washbasins took up most of the floor, though they were pushed to the side.

A single large chest caught Thalo Child's eye—stylistically out of place as it was amongst the Marrakevians' belongings. It bore symbols he often saw around the keep, and he knew it must belong to the Harvesters.

"Come, stand away from the door," Gerome said, waving him closer once the Harvester had left, standing near a stack of undyed spools of off-white yak wool. "They will need all the room we can give them. This is not a ritual I usually invade upon, but Hintosep sees fit to keep thrusting responsibility on you early, so I don't see why I shouldn't do the same."

At the mention of Hintosep, Thalo Child tensed again, but he did as he was told. They settled in together to wait.

"Harvesters do more than just bring us Sacrifices," Gerome explained. "They are as important as the Orchestrators and the Guardians to keeping Arkensyre

Valley in stable working order. Every time an infant pays the time tax, the Harvesters are on hand."

"Why?"

"To ensure magic is only used by the citizenry in the proper way. The safest way. Their lives *depend* on simplicity and conformity, and all Thalo—via our own positions within the order—provide that for them."

After several more minutes, a high-pitched yawing noise started in the next room, then quickly rose in volume as whatever was making the sound headed their way. The door opened, and in rushed five Harvesters, including the one that had let them into the cottage—in their arms was an infant, bawling and bare.

Each Harvester moved with deliberation, and Thalo Child pushed even closer to Gerome as they swept about the cramped space, each gathering tools or cloth or unlocking the chest Thalo Child had noted earlier.

"The adults who care for him and the time-tax taker are in the next room," Gerome explained, nodding at the baby. "They will have each been trapped inside a secret memory for the moment, in order to subdue them. It will afford the Harvesters perhaps fifteen minutes, which is all they will need."

Once prepared, the Harvesters gathered around the baby. With the longest, finest-tipped needle Thalo Child had ever seen, one pricked the babe between the ribs, pushing in the needle's full length before pulling on the plunger. The infant's whines did not falter or increase.

As with the excessive taking of time from the Sacrifices, it was not immediately obvious that anything had entered the barrel. The baby held remarkably still as a test sample of his pneuma was extracted.

Once the barrel was a quarter full, the Harvester with the needle moved quickly, injecting the pneuma into a bottle of blue liquid held out by one of their comrades. The second Harvester let the bottle's contents settle for a moment before shaking it vigorously and holding it up to the lamp light. After a moment, something solidified inside—wafer-thin and shiny, like flecks of gold. The Harvester turned to the others and silently shook their head.

"Not a Thalo," Gerome explained. "The baby is a would-be Physiopath, so he will remain here, and we will transform him into a typical citizen of Arkensyre."

Immediately, each Harvester took a pudgy limb, with the fifth managing the baby's head. They pulled the child taut between them in a way that strained the small body, made the baby's wails all the sharper.

"They're hurting him," Thalo Child said, turning to Gerome with a plea in his eyes.

But the gaze he met was steely. Unmoved. "They will hurt him more before this is over."

The Harvester at the head revealed a contraption from deep in their robes. A hooded katar—a long, thick dagger with an H-shaped grip and a sweeping wrist guard. It was ornate, with silver reliefs depicting geometric patterns and various inlays of lapis lazuli.

Thalo Child's chest tightened.

The Harvester's arm swooped beneath the small body and drove the weapon upward, punching through the baby's back, making the tiny thing's spine bow. His shriek of pain pierced Thalo Child's ears, but before the teenager could look away, the weapon pierced the baby's sternum, and a great crack of light appeared around the wound where there should have been blood. The Harvester pulled on the katar's handle, and the blade scissored open into three prongs just as the other Harvesters let out a conjoined "Heave!" and pulled on the baby's limbs, *rending the child in two.*

With a cry of heartbreak, Thalo Child turned his head and shut his eyes, cringing, trying to pull away from Gerome, to escape this awful scene, but his Possessor's grip only hardened. "You must witness it all," he growled.

What was left to see? Surely, the baby was dead, and they'd killed him for some depraved reason, not out of any *need,* despite Gerome's insistence.

But even as Thalo Child kept his eyes screwed shut, the infant's wailing went on. He could not be certain the dead never screamed, but this cry of agony could only belong to the living.

"Look," Gerome said, shaking him. "*Look.*"

A burst of air and heat and light erupted in the room. Suddenly, a great pressure swamped in all around them, and Thalo Child's ears threatened to pop. He felt more than heard a feral roar—it seemed to move *through* him—and only dared crack one eye.

The baby was in fact still whole, though he was beet red, his small face scrunched in pain and his mouth open, revealing pink gums, curling tongue, and a raw throat. His body still shone bright where blood should have been, and as the triple-pronged weapon closed and withdrew, it dragged with it a viscous substance, something both clearly of this world and not. Not ethereal and yet not physical—an in-between state that appeared to link the mystical and the mundane.

"Pneumoplasm," Gerome said.

As they had with the test needle, the Harvester moved quickly to secure the substance they'd captured with the katar. It tried to cling to the baby, reaching tendrils back his way, trying to flow like water.

The rest of the Harvesters let go of the baby's limbs, one of them cradling the child and holding him close to their chest, shushing softly even as the infant writhed in obvious agony, tears streaming down its ruddy face, the light leaving him, but thankfully, there was still no blood in its place.

The large chest was brought over to the katar wielder, and its lid opened to reveal five boxes, each of a different color and construction. Different symbols littered each cube, and instead of opening one, the Harvester thrust the katar into the top of the last box in the row just as firmly and fiercely as they'd thrust that same blade into the screaming babe. No light shone this time, but the weapon and its harvest passed through the solid-looking top as smoothly as if it were softened butter.

The baby's cries continued to escalate, the raw intensity of its screeching the most distressing sound Thalo Child had ever heard. There must have been some kind of protective barrier around the cottage—soundproofing. That was the only explanation for why no other villagers had yet stormed into the house seeking the child's tormentors.

"Rob it of wakefulness," Thalo Child pleaded with Gerome. "Make it sleep. *At least* let him sleep."

"There is a process. We are here to observe, for you to learn."

Once the plasm had been secured and the weapon cleaned and put away, all five Harvesters surrounded the infant once more. They pressed in close, cooing and chittering. The baby clearly found no comfort, confusion and panic now coloring the cries of pain.

Thalo Child half expected them to come at the boy savagely—to rip him apart with their bare hands—for what else could they possibly do to this tiny, helpless person that they had not already done?

Each lay a blue-tinted hand on his tiny bald head, covering even his eyes, nose, and mouth. It muffled his screams in the most disturbing way, and Thalo Child's knees went weak, his stomach turned over. If they meant to smother the babe, Thalo Child couldn't be here. He *could not*. He angled his whole body away from the scene, but Gerome drew him viciously back.

The group began to mumble, a discordant sound at first, one that rose in pitch and eventually coalesced in tempo, becoming a chant. The baby's body sagged and his sounds died away.

"It is a mindlock," Gerome explained softly, bending close. "Like the one you bear but more—it is also an emotivelock, a soullock. A ritual that can only be performed with no fewer than five Thalo. It is a lock so firm, so deep, it cannot be detected, penetrated, or removed. Ever. Not by those with the best of recalls, not by a Thalo. Not even by the Savior. And the process must be correct, every time, lest the child experience a fracturing of self. The trauma the Harvesters have inflicted on him is bone-deep. It is enough to split a mind, to make it fail. They have harmed him—this ordeal will take years off his life just as surely as the tax—and now they do what they can to heal him so he can live a normal life."

A normal life? *Normal?* What was *normal* after having one's essence ripped away? What was a word like "normal" supposed to describe after such trauma and pain?

"Each citizen of Arkensyre is a Sacrifice in this way," Gerome continued. "All magic in enchantments comes from this source: pneumoplasm drawn from infants, people. *All* people, except those children born with the ability to wield Secrets. And even then, not all of them are chosen for the Order of the Thalo. Those that are, they—*we* get to keep our pneumoplasm and thus our magic. We are allowed to train it, hone it."

"But the lines?"

"Our tattooed lines are representations of achievement. Hallmarks of progress. Symbols that bind us all in a rite of passage. They are important to our unity, but they are not where our power comes from."

Thalo Child looked at his own hands, his arms. He brushed his fingertips against his chest, remembering the needles in his legs, his back, laying the ink. If Gerome was telling him the truth, he'd neither earned nor needed these lines, and forcing him to receive them all at once was nothing more than cruel showmanship.

No, that was—

"How do you find them all?" he demanded, trying to keep his voice from wavering. Maybe Gerome's words were the lie and Ritual Way was real. Maybe he could prove it. "All the babies in all the Valley, everywhere? How can you be sure?" It seemed impossible to locate every single person ever born.

"We do miss one, occasionally. A small family living in the wilds, far from civilization. Or a tax cheat. But the babies who haven't been properly processed make themselves known sooner or later. Most children believe they can do magic, and most adults treat children as far below their notice, so they never prove too hard to find or the surrounding memories too difficult to blur. The Valley rim and the god-border assure none can ever truly outrun the Thalo."

The Harvesters packed up their equipment, and the one holding the babe returned the now-dazed-looking child to his caretakers in the next room, none of whom would ever be the wiser that he'd been gone or tortured at all. The infant appeared entirely unblemished.

As the others went about their business, leaving Gerome and Thalo Child alone in the dye room once more, Gerome bent down to whisper in Thalo Child's ear, his breath hot and intense. "If you disobey me," he warned, "*betray me*—I will do this to your infant."

Thalo Child went cold, and he took a giant, instinctual step back. Gerome let him go, but their eyes met, and Gerome's gaze was predatory in a way Thalo Child had never witnessed before.

"I will take away zhur magic," the Possessor confirmed, and each word had *teeth*. "I will put them through the ritual with the katar. And *I will leave zhim with the trauma*."

Humiliation, horror, fear, and sadness all swamped through Thalo Child at once, forcing him to bite back on a sob, lest *humiliation* win out over all.

The fact that Gerome felt the need to threaten him this way—with the safety of an innocent—shamed and horrified him in equal turns. What did Gerome have to fear from Hintosep that would force him to do this? What did that mean for Thalo Child? Perhaps *he* did not fear Hintosep *enough*.

But behind all that was the sadness. Grief was the foundational emotion of the moment. Where once he'd had hope and pride and felt a connection with his Possessor, now there was nothing but this resentment and coldness. Perhaps the relationship he thought he'd had had always been a false construction, something one-directional. But now no semblance of that remained. The love was gone, and with it, the last remnants of his childhood.

"What do you belong to?" Gerome asked.

"The Eye of Gerome," he mumbled.

"*Who* do you belong to?"

"You."

"That's right." Gerome patted his head condescendingly as he brushed by, exiting the room, simply expecting Thalo Child to follow, as he always did. "Good boy."

37

KRONA

"I believe, during that ceremony, when pneuma is ripped from an infant, something else inside them tears away as well," Hintosep said, tossing the bones she'd gnawed bare into the firepit. "Something ephemeral, initially undetectable. Something that should belong to another realm when separated from us— perhaps it's part of the spark of our soul that extinguishes when we die."

Krona didn't trust Hintosep, and she wanted to consider every word that dripped from her lips a lie. She wanted the world to be as it had been explained to her when she was young. There was an order to things and a reason to things. But she'd seen too much to deny that what the Thalo woman said must hold some truths. De-Lia, while under Gatwood's control, had written a letter to Krona, and even she'd said she feared the needles could take more than the city-states claimed.

"Whatever it is," Hintosep continued, wiping off her hands and standing, "it flies away but is just tangible enough to remain trapped within the Valley, just as we are. It is violently torn from a child, infantile itself, and is immediately trapped on a plane it was never meant to experience in such a raw fashion. It hurts, and it festers, and it *hungers*. Hungers to return to the body it belongs to."

"And you believe that—whatever it is—becomes a varg?" Mandip asked, bewildered.

"There's one varg for every person in the Valley," Hintosep continued. "Or, nearly every person, I should say. There's one for every person who's paid the time tax. One for every person who's had their magic stolen.

"Just being near a human—especially one who's missing that varg-shaped piece of themselves—must drive them into a frenzy, and they express that need to dig and rejoin the only way they know how. With teeth and claws and blood and death."

"A bottle-barker doesn't devour you from the outside," Krona said. "It tries to get *in*."

"Exactly."

"But Monkeyflower . . ." Krona could barely force her tongue to form the name; her mouth felt dry, her cheeks thick. "Monkeyflower behaved atypically around De-Lia."

Even as she said it, Krona amassed an understanding. Rather than puzzle pieces falling into place, it felt like a swarm gathering in her mind—one bee of information buzzing around her skull becoming two in an instant, then four, then eight. Until the swarm filled her brain like a hive, making her insides vibrate with the force of a terrible deduction.

If a varg came from a person, and that varg tried to eat everyone that crossed its path—making meals of all those vessels it did *not* belong to—then it stood to reason that a varg would behave differently when it found its point of origin.

Krona dropped her head into her hands. Took a shaky breath.

"Monkeyflower *was* De-Lia," she croaked.

"I believe so, yes."

Krona had half hoped Hintosep would tell her she was being ridiculous. She wanted her to laugh, *Of course that monster wasn't De-Lia; whatever gave you that idea?*

De-Lia hadn't simply befriended a strange varg. It was *her* varg. Part of her. A part of her come home.

"Over the centuries, there have been a handful of cases like your sister's. That I'm aware of, at least. I think just being near its true host is enough stop a varg's ravenous tearing. They become docile. They might not feel whole, but they're no longer in such pain."

Monkeyflower may have been soothed by her body's presence, but she was still disjointed and beastly and hungering. Still ready to turn her teeth on the next human she encountered. When separated from De-Lia's side, in her worldly pain and confusion, she had killed their father.

Had Monkeyflower sensed the gnawing hole inside *him*? Was she trying to burrow down through his throat? She must have wanted to fill the space. Stopper him up like a cork in a wine bottle.

If they are human—some scared, pained, beastly part of us—then they are not conscious of it, Krona realized. They acted on instinct and feeling, not reasoning.

"Can they be rejoined?" she asked "Varg and human?"

"That's what I'm hoping you'll help me find out. I believe their drive to burrow means it's possible—that, like time taken by the tax, these pieces of lost souls can be returned to their owners.

"Time made it obvious, actually. So obvious, I should have realized centuries ago—all magic is transpositional. If it comes from people, then it can be returned to people. Time, everyone knows, can be returned. Now think of how death masks work. You remove knowledge from a person and put it into a vessel. Just like taking time and putting it into a vial."

"So, it would stand to reason knowledge can be taken from a death mask and put back in a brain," Krona said, adding firmly, "Melanie."

Hintosep nodded. "Melanie."

"That's what this epidemic really is, then?" Krona asked. "These people with similar scars are trying to accomplish what Melanie Dupont accomplished: transferring knowledge from a mask into herself?"

"If you knew what Melanie went through to get Master Belladino's knowledge, I don't think you'd call it an accomplishment. *She* certainly wouldn't."

"You speak as though you know her well."

"I do. But that is beside the point."

"What happened to her?" Krona demanded.

"She hid in a Marrakevian village for some time before someone dubious and close to the family uncovered her secret and spread rumor of it. Various people of various social ranks have tried to recreate her transfer. Many have failed. Not all have."

"So, you aren't the only one who's come to the realization that magic can be returned."

"No. That's another thing I'm sure the Savior is hoping this war will accomplish: stamping out such experiments and understandings. Relegating them back into the realm of myth and scary stories, where He believes they belong. It's easier to straight-up murder people when state-sanctioned fighting is going on. That's how this epidemic will stop."

Mandip suddenly stood and hissed, holding his left arm as though he'd dropped a hot iron onto his sleeve.

Hintosep didn't appear surprised. "Ah, sooner than I expected," she said, standing herself.

"Nevertheless," Juliet said jovially, hopping up to join them, "that's our cue."

38

KRONA

"Mandip has been summoned, and so have we," Hintosep said. "When a Grand Marquis dies, there's protocol. Preparation. Rites. I'd planned on escorting Mistress Hirvath a little farther before heading back into Lutador to tail you and Juliet, but I think if we leave now, we can at least meet with one of my scouts before splitting up."

"Tail us?" Mandip asked. "Where?"

"On your very grim date to the Treasury."

"*Date?*"

"This is why you weren't supposed to be at the theater, silly," Juliet said, striding by and bopping him on the nose with the tip of her finger. "You spoiled the plan's beautiful natural flow."

"But you *invited* me."

"You were already expecting to go whether I invited you or not. The invitation was for Thibaut's sake, because, dear Basu, you were supposed to be *single* when we met. But there I go and run into you before our arranged meeting, and you've already got someone on your arm. So, when I invited you, I expected Captain Hirvath would have you on lockdown and you'd be a no-show. I wanted Thibaut along because I thought it would either give me a chance to cement our little throuple or to pay him to step aside and let me have you. But, ta-da, you appeared regardless. Late—and in handcuffs, I might add. So, I never got to have my chat with Thibaut, and you were never kept safely away from the night's proceedings.

"In a perfect world, I would have swept you off your feet—you thinking you were sweeping me off mine, of course—and then I'd subtly express to you my lifelong desire to lay eyes on the inaugural jewels. As a performer of the highest caliber, I've of course already seen many court jewels—from Xyopar to Marrakev—but sadly, no one's ever been able to get me in to see the Lutadorian inaugural jewels because Lutadorian security is *just that much more advanced*."

She laid it on thick, her play-acting heavy, and Mandip rolled his eyes.

"You wouldn't know that I know about your little, hmm, imbedded enchantment there, and yet—ah-ha!—a Grand Marquis has just died. Very sad, but you'll
be called in to open the vaults for the funerary accoutrements. It's a rare *ceremonial* opening, so any noble twin with a watch that matches yours is required to
be in attendance to hide the true identity of the Treasury's Repository Key. What
a coincidence; it's the perfect opportunity to impress the *acclaimed* La Maupin."

"You believe I put so little value on my responsibilities as to use them to entice a woman I've just met? *And* under such morose circumstances?"

Both Thibaut and Juliet gave him the most uncouth of stares.

"You *are* the type to snap away another child's toys just so *fey* can't play with
them," Thibaut pointed out.

"So, yes," Juliet said plainly. "But you went and cocked it all up, so now all my
brilliant wooing and finessing skills are going to total waste, and you'll just have
to be in on the scheme because I never got the chance to really con you at all."

"And you think I'll help you rob Lutador *why*, exactly?"

"It's not something they'll miss. And because we asked," Hintosep grumbled. "And if you're thinking of arguing, just remember you are as susceptible to
blackmail and bargaining as anyone else. Juliet prefers a lighter touch, but a day
or two with your brother missing . . ."

"I think we should all agree that if we're to work together, family-based
threats are off the table," Krona warned.

Hintosep side-eyed her, then sighed deeply and tried a different tactic. "You'll
help us because we all want the same thing," she said firmly. "For ourselves and
the citizens of the Valley to live their lives in peace, free from tyranny and violence. From the moment you enter this world, tyranny and violence are what
meets you, no matter if you are born to be the next Grand Marquis or to live
your life as a Dreg. This is what I've been trying to tell you; even the privileges
in your system are a lie. The very stratification of your society is orchestrated,
created to bolster itself, to get the people at the top to continue to mete out extra
injustices to the bottom so that you don't realize you're all fighting over crumbs.
The king of the rats is still a rat, and the cats will laugh when they eat him just
the same."

It all sounded so noble. But Krona knew, no matter how noble a cause, there
was always something personal about it for anyone leading the charge.

What was personal about this for Hintosep?

"I know enough about you and your brother to know you both take govern-
ing seriously," Hintosep said to Mandip. "You might be sheltered, but you are
not hard of heart."

"A moment ago, I was an alleged flippant playboy. Now I'm a serious statesman?"

"You are a young man who thought he knew his path but are not so married to your station and worldview that it cannot change."

"Well, that's cryptic."

"It's honest," she countered. "I think you will help us because of everything you've seen and heard here. Now come on. We have a lot of ground to cover before night catches us again."

They cleaned up the camp as best they could. Once again, Krona attached De-Lia's mask to her belt, gently petting over the slightly scorched edges in apology first. Thank the gods Thibaut had known her mind better than she had in the moment. If the jaguar had actually burned, if Krona had destroyed her last gift from De-Lia—

She shuddered, feeling sick just from the phantom loss.

As they prepared to leave, her glances kept returning to where the varg slept—pinned right next to the perimeter enchantment.

"What do you plan to do with the varger?" she asked Hintosep.

"I wasn't planning to do anything with them," she replied with a shrug.

"It's irresponsible to leave them," Krona said. "Even if they stay pinned, that means they'll starve, grow insubstantial. A vaporous varg is even more of a threat than a solid one." Krona could not abide the risk. "I'll contact someone I trust to retrieve the pair."

"And alert them to our present location?" Hintosep asked suspiciously.

"If you want me to cooperate, you will let me tend to the beasts' disposal."

Hintosep considered for a long moment. "You will tell them of the varger, nothing more."

Krona nodded. "Nothing more."

She had no interest in betraying Hintosep—not in this moment, anyway.

She'd never tried using a reverb bead at this distance before. It was likely she was out of range, and her call would be for naught. "Hello?" she tried, regardless, after retrieving the bead and ear shell from where she'd stashed them in her pouch. "Hello? Is anyone there?" A strange hissing and clicking was followed by deep hum that could have been distorted words. "Hello?"

"Krona?"

"Tray?" The connection was weak; he sounded distant, with an unnatural reverberation in his voice, as though he were speaking from the end of a long, echoing hall.

"And Royu."

She'd seen them both just the day before, but her heart fluttered as though she'd been separated from them for years. It was good to hear their voices.

"Thank the gods you're alive," Tray said, genuine relief in his voice. "Where are you? What happened? The Marchonian Guards are saying—"

"I know. I know. I need you to listen to me. There're two pinned varger . . ."

She gave them the location, as precisely as she could. She knew they'd both pore over her words ad nauseam after, looking for a hidden message, some further context for the assassination's circumstances, but she gave them nothing of value. She trusted them both implicitly, and she trusted them to do their jobs with loyalty and honor. Which meant, even if they believed her innocent, they would report that she'd made contact. It was the right thing to do, and she did not blame them.

"They look well fed, but don't let them sit out for too long," she warned. She knew she should cut the conversation short. This was a natural place to end it. But she couldn't let Tray go without asking, "How's my maman?"

"How do you think? The Chief Magistrate had to cordon off your apartment; they've claimed everything there for the city-state's investigation—"

"*Where is she?*"

"I helped her move in with the Iyendars. The Chief Magistrate doesn't believe you're responsible—said you warned him something was going to happen. I made him swear Acel would get anything and everything she asked for. She's well taken care of, I promise you."

Krona breathed a sigh of relief. "You're a good man, Tray. A good friend." *You were always there for us, for our family. For De-Lia.*

"You know I'd never abandon her," he said earnestly. "I'd never abandon *you*. Krona, come to the den and we'll—"

She tore her earpiece away. His pleading wouldn't work; it would only hurt. She'd told him what she needed to say, heard what she needed to hear.

When the Regulators or the Borderswatch came to retrieve the varger, they'd look for clues at the campsite as well. Their ragtag group would need to make sure they were mindful of their tracks.

➤━◆◇━○━◇◆━◄

Their day's travel was much like their night's travel, with everyone moving swiftly, utilizing game trails while on the lookout for both varger and Thalo agents alike. They moved higher and higher up the rim, and the altitude meant the climate subtly shifted, becoming colder as the air grew thinner. Thibaut threw his ragged velvet back over his borrowed blues. Krona donned even her helm to keep the wind from nipping at her ears and nose. Morning turned to afternoon to evening, and then, out of nowhere, a strange birdcall—obviously not of bird origin at all, if Krona was being honest—rang out.

Hintosep answered back with a similarly faux chittering.

A figure came out from between the trees, stepping onto the path before them. The person wore long, heavy skirts to match the cold, and a thick scarf and hood. She pulled the scarf back to reveal rosy cheeks, mouse-brown hair, and a scarred forehead sans ferronnière.

"Melanie?" Krona asked, taking off her helm to make sure it was no trick of the light.

The apprentice healer. The unlucky bride. The would-be murder victim Krona had sent away, hoping the woman could find some semblance of peace with her new family.

The body she'd seen sprawled in a photograph.

Those versions of Melanie seemed no more than shadows of who she was now. She carried herself taller than she had before—shoulders back, chin high. No longer the mousey-yet-defiant young lady, she was now a rugged woman of the world. She'd donned what looked like a heavy bow and quiver on her back, and the cloak and boots she wore were hard-worn.

Krona was inexplicably overcome. She dropped her helm and rushed at the other woman, throwing her arms around her as though she were a long-lost sister.

Exactly like a long-lost sister. She embraced her as she would have embraced De-Lia.

The relief was overwhelming. Krona held her crushingly close before pulling away just to study her face, to put her palms on her cheeks and kiss that stupid mark on her forehead. She knew she should be embarrassed about this sudden outpouring for a woman she'd only met a handful of times, and eventually wrangled her emotions back into their usual tight knot in her chest.

"I'm sorry, I'm sorry," she said quickly, trying to take a step back to recover some of her forfeited dignity.

Melanie would have had every right to push Krona away and demand decorum, but instead she smiled a sad smile and set her hands over Krona's, holding them in place. "Please. I've seen few friendly faces from my old life in the last three years. There's nothing to be ashamed of."

"I thought you were dead."

"I'm sorry. I had to disappear. More completely this time."

Krona whirled to face Hintosep. "Why didn't you tell me we were to meet Melanie?"

"Out of the blue, you asked me if I'd killed her," she replied. "You would have been more suspicious of my denial if I'd added *In fact, I'm taking you to her*. It would have seemed coincidental to you." She smiled at Melanie. "In truth, I had no way of knowing she'd be sent out as today's scout, but you've been wrapped up in each other's fates for years now, so it's only fitting the world brought you together again sooner rather than later.

"And here is where we part, for now," Hintosep concluded. "Juliet and I must return young Basu to his duties before he is too sorely missed. Melanie will take you the rest of the way to the safe house."

"This isn't like the campsite, is it?" Krona asked. "Should we be on our guard for wandering Thalo?"

"No. None of my people have been to Mirthhouse in over a century, and none would have reason to return."

"And where will you go, Master Thibaut?" Juliet asked sweetly.

"I get a choice?" he asked, clearly surprised.

"He stays with me," Krona said quickly, heart stuttering at the thought of him being taken away. Not for an instant did she believe she'd get Thibaut back in the same condition he was in now—and perhaps not at all—if she let him go off on this heist scheme.

"Seems I *don't* get a choice," he corrected himself, but without ire. That might have even been a blush dusting his cheeks.

"Fine by me," Hintosep said.

"But . . ." Mandip looked torn.

"Oh, I'll see you again, milor," Thibaut said. "You can count on it. After all, I haven't been paid for escorting you to the Rotunda, and I charge double when there's threat to life and limb." He gave Mandip a quick embrace, then turned to Juliet. "My lady," he said, taking her hand and kissing it. "Meeting you has been a great adventure."

This parting felt strange. They'd all been suddenly thrust together and now had a shared secret unlike any other. And yet Krona didn't know what awaited her and Thibaut if they followed Melanie. She didn't know if Basu's part in all this was nearing its conclusion, or if his trials had just begun.

If he was elected to serve in the dead man's place, what then?

"In my absence, don't be idle," Hintosep told her, glancing at De-Lia's mask. "I don't believe in coincidences; your sister unwittingly did something to call her varg to her, I'm sure. I'm working on a way to locate yours—what city-state it's in, at the very least—but we'll need more than that if we're to figure out how to re-merge the two of you. The echo's memories should hold the key. Look into your sister's past and decipher what happened."

"I'm only doing this for her," Krona said, making her stance clear, retrieving her horned helm and slipping it back into place. "For the chance to bring her back. You'll get what you need when I'm satisfied you can truly help me. Are we clear?"

"Crystal."

39

KRONA

Something had finally gone right. Melanie and Sebastian were alive. It was a small win in the grand scheme of wars and hidden magic, but it meant everything to Krona. They were not long parted from the others before she could no longer contain her questions.

"Where have you been?" Krona asked. "You seem different."

"We spent a little over a year and a half with Sebastian's great-aunt before we were forced to flee with Hintosep. If she hadn't come for us, I don't know what we would have done. The villagers, they . . . Half of them were eager to have one of these for their own." She touched her forehead. "And the other half were ready to burn us at the stake for blasphemy. It didn't help that Great-Aunt Umara had been toeing that line for decades before we came along."

"How do you mean?" Thibaut asked.

"She's a soothsayer. Fortune-teller."

"Ah."

"Yes. *Ah*. Hers are parlor tricks, mostly. Gallium spoons and the like. She's a lovely person, mostly brought comfort to the grieving. Sebastian was terribly disappointed to find out her tricks were not true magic. He'd hoped she'd . . ." Melanie unexpectedly trailed off.

". . . Be able to help you with your enchanter's mark?" Krona ventured.

Melanie let out a heavy sigh. "It wasn't just my magic troubles we hoped she could help with but *his* as well. We've kept it all a secret for so long, it feels strange to simply tell someone everything we've been through. Let me start from the beginning. Maybe I can make it sound like a fairy tale instead of a horror story if I tell it right. There once was a great healer named Master Belladino . . ."

They hiked as Melanie's story went on. Thankfully, the sharp nip in the air did not get any colder, and the path wasn't too rugged. They wound through the forest at a clip.

"I gave birth," Melanie said, now past the portions of her tale that had involved Lutadorian mass murderers. "Zhe was healthy; we were happy. The requisite months passed, the tax taker came, and not long after, our child died. Or so we were made to believe."

Even though Krona already knew how the story ended, her heart still sank, still went out to Melanie. Losing a loved one suddenly, inexplicably, was a great torture.

"Why would someone take your child and convince you zhe was dead?" Thibaut asked.

"Hintosep said the Thalo search for children with certain abilities and snatch them away in order to grow their own ranks. Their magic makes the snatching easy to cover; an infant dying suddenly is much more common than an infant gone missing.

"When I sent you that letter," she said to Krona, "I was desperate, didn't know who else to turn to. Hintosep had not yet come to us. We were alone, isolated. The community had already come to suspect we were different, and then we tried to insist that our baby had been kidnapped and replaced. That the body we burned wasn't zhurs. And eventually . . . the mob came for us. Torches and pitchforks, just like in the storybooks.

"One villager had already successfully transferred a mark. Two more were unsuccessful. One died. The other . . . I think the needle transferred the echo to them instead of the knowledge."

"Ah," Krona said, struck by an understanding.

"What, *ah*?" Thibaut asked.

"I've encountered several victims of this unsuccessful transference. One man seemed to insist his face was not his face. It might have been an echo speaking."

"The echo—the echo was *conscious*? In a body? Out of a mask?" Thibaut asked, aghast.

Krona's hand moved to the jaguar of its own accord. If . . . if that man had—No. She squashed her train of thought. "The man was not well. It was no reincarnation."

Melanie looked pained to hear that Krona had met such a soul. "The information got out, spread," she conceded. "Hintosep has been finding the survivors—the successes—bringing them to the safe house if they can be . . . convinced." She let out a put-upon sigh. "This is precisely what I didn't want to happen. Why I left Gatwood's mentorship in the first place. He wanted to enchant others, and I knew it was dangerous."

Krona wondered how much Melanie knew about the assassination—if anything. Did she know the method of execution? Did she realize Hintosep had used her very story to help frame Krona at the behest of the Savior?

She kept silent. She didn't want to interrogate Melanie, to spoil the swift comradery they'd formed. There would be plenty of time for those kinds of inquiries later, if the safe house was as advertised.

"May I ask what it was?" Thibaut pressed. "If you burned a body but it wasn't your baby, what was it?"

"A suckling pig."

Krona and Thibaut shared a look, recalling the wild pig they'd finished off after *finishing off* the cooks in a different fashion.

"They kidnapped our child *and replaced zhim with a pig*," she emphasized. "And we didn't notice. They could make us see what they wanted us to see. That there are people out there who not only can do that but are *willing* to do that? Disgusting."

Melanie's tone and expression were hard, but there was still a freeness about her. Krona thought it a marvel that, with all that had happened to her and her family, the young healer hadn't given up on the world. She might have retreated into hiding, but clearly that was only a temporary situation in her mind. She seemed like someone who was preparing, biding her time.

"Emotion blessed you with an intersex child, then?" Krona asked, trying to add some hope, some lightness into the conversation.

Melanie's expression softened. "Yes. And zhe looked so much like Sebastian from the moment zhe was born. We are so ready to see if that still holds true today. Hintosep is going to rescue zhim along with Juliet's brother."

⊱─◈─○─◈─⊰

Well after Melanie had concluded her tale of magic, mystery, and attempted murder, the three of them came to a cliff with a not-quite-a-creek, not-quite-a-river below, and sixty-foot-high sheer bluffs on the other side.

"There it is," Melanie said, pointing across the way.

Sitting up on a crag on the opposite side of the water, perhaps one hundred and fifty feet away, were the clear burnt-out remains of a mansion. The ruins were old, but the climate had preserved them well. The winds nearer the border here were cold and dry, yet none too harsh, which had allowed several of the main timbers and most of one wall to remain.

"That's the safe house?" Thibaut asked skeptically.

"Safer than it looks," Melanie said. "Which is the point."

It was a treacherous, scrabbling climb, first down one side, across the creek, and then up the other.

"How exactly does one get supplies in and out, given the—all—you know, *this*?" Thibaut asked as they went.

"There-there is . . . an easier . . . entrance," Melanie tried to explain between heavy breaths. "A door. In the bottom . . . of the cliff . . . beneath . . ." She pointed below the mansion. "But only Hintosep . . . can open it."

Melanie was the fastest climber, having obviously made her way up and down these stones several times before. Krona was perfectly capable, but her armor slowed her down considerably. Thibaut, though physically fit, surely had been nowhere near this particular activity since childhood. When Krona made it to the top, she reached down for Thibaut, taking him by the hand and pulling him to his feet, though slightly off-balance.

He swayed forward, and she steadied him. Their hands were still entwined, and now their bodies were close. Her heart fluttered—distinctly not from exertion but something else—and she was grateful for the blankness of her helm's faceplate.

His hand tensed in hers before letting go, and that was the only indication she had that their proximity had affected him at all.

The door to this burnt-out husk of a house was, remarkably, still standing— frame and all. As they stepped up to it, light snowflakes started to fall, and Krona watched them land on the charred wood and melt away in an instant— like the wood was *warm*.

Melanie withdrew an object from her pocket that looked like a key but was clearly more. She swept it up and down the door in a distinct pattern before inserting it into the lock. With a hearty shove, she pushed the door inward.

What met them on the other side was not, in fact, a charred ruin. A well-lit, well-walled, well-functioning intact mansion lay beyond.

Krona immediately removed her helm to better take it all in.

The entryway was stuffed with evidence of many lodgers—boots and gloves and cloaks choked the narrow, muddy foyer. Beyond, the grand room they stepped into was decorated like an old hunting lodge. It *smelled* like an old hunting lodge, too—like woodsmoke and musty pelts. Antlers formed the chandelier, and a massive stone fireplace made from river rock consumed the center space, creating a delimitation between what appeared to be a communal living space— full of many hide-upholstered chairs and a thick bearskin rug over an old wooden floor—and perhaps a kitchen and dining room beyond. The ceiling was over two stories tall, and off the great room were dozens of doors and hallways that led left and right into the mansion's wings. Twin staircases on either side of the fireplace led to a second-story balcony lined with still more doors and hallways beyond.

On the fireplace's mantel sat a stuffed pheasant and an ornamental weapon of some kind—a katar, by the looks of it.

"This place can fit more people than the inn," Thibaut gasped.

A handful of people sat in the living room, two playing Marquises and Marauders and two quietly discussing something scribbled in a notebook.

Though she should have expected them, Krona was surprised to realize they were none other than Melanie's family.

"I'm back," Melanie said briskly, "and look who I brought."

"My stars, it's the Regulator," said Melanie's mother, Dawn-Lyn. She, who'd seemed so standoffish when hosting the Regulators in her one-room cabin, now jumped to her feet—nearly knocking over the game board—to greet Krona as if she were her long-lost daughter.

"And—*Thibaut*," said Sebastian, Melanie's groom, who Krona had not previously made formal acquaintance with. The older woman of Xyoparian descent next to him graciously took the notebook they'd been poring over, allowing him to rush to the foyer as well. "We weren't expecting you," he said with a grin, clapping Thibaut on the shoulder.

"That appears to be the general consensus wherever I show my face," Thibaut joked.

"How's the inn?"

"Runs well enough without me there; don't worry."

Several people wandered down from one of the balconies but only gave the new arrivals a passing nod before going about their own business.

Melanie and Sebastian introduced the pair to the older woman, Sebastian's great-aunt Umara who sported a long, graying braid and an assortment of colorful shawls, and her Marrakevian gentleman friend, Boyra-Tam.

"You said we were expecting a new recruit; why didn't you say it was Mistress Hirvath?" Dawn-Lyn asked her daughter.

"Hintosep told me not to tell anyone."

"Ah, that means she's got plans for you," Umara said, tapping her nose knowingly, tossing Krona a wink. "The woman does like to prevaricate and tergiversate."

"I suppose that means you have things to discuss, then?" Sebastian asked Melanie. "More or less in private?"

"If you please," she said warmly, standing up on tiptoe to give her husband a kiss on the cheek.

"I'll redirect the curious," he promised her before waving the others out of the room.

Melanie bade Krona and Thibaut sit while she raided the kitchen for a bit of food and spot of drink to offer the new guests.

No, not guests, Krona realized. Dawn-Lyn had said "recruit."

"Looks like enough space to house a small army," Krona noted, gratefully accepting a mug of cider wine after setting her helm on a nearby chair. "How many people are currently staying here?"

"Near fifty," Melanie said proudly. "Gathering more bit by bit. And this is just one of a handful of safe houses Hintosep has scattered throughout Arkensyre. We"—she made a gesture between the three of them—"aren't the only people whose lives have been touched by the Thalo. Such people are everywhere—all over the Valley. Hintosep's collecting who she can."

"Who she thinks she can *use*, you mean," Krona said into her mug.

"And now she's collected us," Thibaut said. "I wasn't aware *conscription* lay at the end of our little trek through the woods."

"It's not like that," Melanie said. "No one is kept here against their will."

"But they certainly don't get to keep any memories of the place if they choose to leave, do they?" Krona challenged.

"Hard to keep a mansion full of resistance fighters a secret otherwise," Melanie said.

"And what, exactly, are you fighting? How? What's she planning?"

"Right now? The rescue. After? Not sure yet. But we're prepared to follow Hintosep's marching orders. She intends to lead us against the Valley's oppressors."

Krona held her tongue, but even though Melanie was vague about the details, to her it sounded like Hintosep had sleeper cells planted in all the city-states, just waiting for a call to action. Like a bandit horde.

Or a terrorist group.

Melanie took another sip of her cider before her eyes widened and she said, "I'm sorry; you must be exhausted. We can talk more in the morning. There's a private room all set up for you on the second floor, but we . . . we weren't expecting anyone else, Monsieur Thibaut. I'm sure we can find a place for you—"

"It's fine; he'll stay with me," Krona said—eager to have someplace she and Thibaut could talk in private—consciously catching the implications only after the dismissal rolled off her tongue. She was too tired to be embarrassed, however. Embarrassment could fuck right off. "For now," she clarified. "Temporarily."

"Of course."

They finished their drinks and followed Melanie as she carried a lit candle out of the great room, through the kitchen, and to a flight of log steps. Along the way, she pointed out rooms that were genuinely burnt out and in tatters. The barrier provided a seal that kept the working bits of the mansion insulated. "The barrier conforms to the usable space. Helps add to the illusion, should someone stumble upon us. They can still access much of the ruined part of the building without being aware there's more beyond."

Melanie continued to chatter as they mounted the steps. Halfway up, two people sidled out of a nearby doorway and stopped to greet the three of them once they'd alighted on the upper landing. Though the pair smiled warmly and made casual introductions, Melanie suddenly went quiet, buttoning up until the two had moved on. The young healer watched them go, making sure they were out of earshot before speaking up again.

"I trust that you'll keep Hintosep's plans for you hush-hush for now?" she asked, continuing to lead Krona and Thibaut down the hall. The question sounded innocent enough—light, casual. But there was a seriousness beneath it. A worry.

"She doesn't want everyone to know the details, in case something goes wrong," Krona said frankly.

Melanie nodded, stopping in front of a worn door and handing Krona the candle. She turned the knob and gestured inside, rushing the two of them in so she could say more without prying ears.

The door opened into a modest room with a single window, a vaulted ceiling, dresser, and an ornate-if-old changing screen.

Krona noted there was only one bed.

"It's not that she doesn't trust everyone here at Mirthhouse," Melanie said quickly, once the door latched. "It's that she is not one to overpromise if she's not sure she can deliver. This is why she's so easy to follow. When she says something can be done, I know that means *it can be done*. We all know it. You see, if Hintosep can merge you and your varg, and the results are auspicious . . ."

"Then there will be more," Krona said.

Melanie nodded. "None of us know how to track down our own varger, however. That's part of why you're a special case."

"The test case."

"Yes."

"We can be counted on to be discreet," Krona assured her.

Melanie gestured at the thin mattress. "Sorry about the bed," she apologized, opening the door again, "but there are extra linens and several quilts. I also wasn't sure if you'd come prepared to stay, so there are changes of clothes—trousers, skirts, nightshirts, what have you—in the dresser there."

"Thank you," Krona said, trying not to rush Melanie out, though she was twitching to settle in. "Good night. It really is good to see you again. To see you well."

"Same, mistress. Thibaut. Good night."

"Good night."

Krona closed the door swiftly and threw the latch. She braced her back against it with a huff.

"Couldn't wait to get me alone?" Thibaut teased, turning round and round in the center of the threadbare throw rug that covered the uneven floorboards.

She tossed her helm on the bed before brandishing the candle and swiftly searching the room, looking for seams and hidden doors and cracks big enough to press an ear to. "I wanted to talk to you away from everyone else. Yes, even Melanie," she said, lifting the mattress to glance under it before letting it plop down heavily again. "Did you notice how *enamored* she is of Hintosep? Ready to fight for her. Which likely means they all are."

"You're worried she's controlling them?"

"Or . . . or something. Her explanations, about pneuma and stolen magic . . ." They'd triggered something in Krona—an old memory. Perhaps a memory that wasn't even hers, something she should have completely forgotten, one she'd touched while in a mask. For a moment, she seemed to leave her body as her mind tried to follow the thread, to find the reverberation of a similar notion nested somewhere deep in her subconscious.

Thibaut nodded sagely, throwing back the drapes from the window and peering out. "She sounded like Charbon," Thibaut said darkly, warningly, his entire demeanor shifting. It was the first time Krona had detected that particular *protective* degree of heat in his tone. He'd heard Charbon speak with her lips, after all. He remembered far better than she what had gone on while she wore Charbon's mask.

At least she wasn't the only one to recognize the parallels.

"How do we know we're not just repeating his mistakes?" Krona asked. "Going round and round with the likes of Thalo puppets as they do their damndest to convince us the world works differently, convincing us we're the special few who know the truth, just to tear our lives apart?"

"She already did it to you," Thibaut pointed out. "You can't go home." His gaze remained distant, focused on something outside, under the rays of the soon-setting sun.

Satisfied the room was clear of potential peepholes, Krona began to divest, scattering the pieces of her heavy armor here and there. When she removed her belt and satchel, she took special care to untie both masks and lay them side by side on the dresser top. "Hintosep wants me to put on the mask," she said, stroking the jaguar's muzzle. "She's giving me every reason to indulge myself."

"You think it's a trap? She'll play into your obsession, and then what?" He turned away from the window, eyes darting uncomfortably when he realized she'd stripped down to her undergarments—thin, black linen trousers and an undershirt to match. She'd left her chest bound for the moment.

"I don't know," she admitted. "I can't tell what's the truth and what's a lie. At least she can't control me like the Thalo puppets can control . . ." She trailed off, recognizing she was about to walk them into a painful memory.

"Me?" he asked coldly.

She winced, remembering the Gatwood concern and the way the valet's goons, with the help of Thalo magic, had beguiled Thibaut—trapping him in a memory, forcing him to relive a secret in order to lead both he and Krona into a trap.

"Anyone. Everyone," she clarified. "*That* I'm sure of: my immunity. Bits of truth seem to be how these Thalo seed their lies. How they dress them up to make them feel real. At no point can we count on what she tells us. About magic, about her motivations. And yet nothing can be dismissed outright. She's made us dependent on her version of the world. We can't go back to what we knew before, yet we have no one else to turn to for verification. It's all a trap, whether calculated or not."

"Do you think the Savior really exists? He feels a bit like a phantom." Thibaut changed his tone, lifting up both hands to wriggle them at her like a spook. "A dark master that controls all from the shaaaaadooooows."

She huffed out a small laugh but made no open speculation.

"We should rest," he said. "You need to sleep."

She pulled her helm off the bed by one of its horns, staring briefly into the gold of the faceplate before setting it where neither of them would trip on it. "We need to figure out what's really going on here."

"And as long as we're bunking together, we can be alone to talk about it any time you'd like," he pointed out—sans innuendo, even, which had to be a struggle. "So, how shall we do this? Given the narrowness of this cot here, am I spooning you, or are you spooning me?"

She scoffed openly. "As though I'd let you share a mattress with me. I do have some dignity left."

"Will you at least let me curl up on the foot of the bed? Like a dog? Even a pet is allowed to lay at his master's feet."

"You have a very strange habit of insisting I have you on a leash," she said frankly, determined not to rise to his bait. "Feels like a fetish at this point."

"Do my fetishes interest you?" he asked with a sly raise of one eyebrow.

She bit her lip, staring him down. "No."

"Liar," he purred.

"Cretin," she shot back, grabbing a pillow from the cot and tossing it into his stomach.

He caught it with an exaggerated *oof.* "Fine, fine. I'll take one of those quilts our healer friend mentioned and make myself a cozy little nest on the floor right here."

"Why don't you get out of that ridiculous outfit first? It's ruined anyway."

"Ridic—" He looked down at himself, clearly having forgotten what he was wearing. Green velvet, perfectly matched to his gloves, over secondhand blues. All of his cockiness suddenly dissipated. "Right. Right." The pillow fell from his fingers, and he moved toward the dresser—pulling out a nightshirt and trousers—then the changing screen, dragging his feet the whole way.

"Do you remember when we first met?" he asked once he was out of sight, tone somber.

"What kind of silly question is that? Of course I remember. I arrested you."

"And you made me a deal."

"I made you a deal," she agreed.

"You wouldn't look for my . . . my *accomplice* if I agreed to inform for you."

Sitting down on the bed, she narrowed her gaze at the changing screen, as though she might divine the reason for this odd change in the conversation by tracing the wavy lines of its wind motif. "Why this particular stroll down memory lane?"

⊱────✦────⊰

Thibaut looked at the tatters of his wedding attire and, though devastated, thought they'd met a fitting end. The marriage had ended in shreds; why not the clothes?

"Why this particular stroll?" she asks, he thought as he pulled out the jewelry box he'd kept on his person for what felt like weeks now, its casing a tad scuffed. *Why?* Because there was still a shred of guilt in his heart. Something keeping him from taking a leap—a leap he desperately wanted to take.

He and Krona danced around these feelings. They talked about it, teased about it, but had never acted on it.

"My accomplice—her name was Venessa."

"You said that name in the alley. When the Thalo—"

"I know. She . . . she was my wife."

Krona knew he'd been married before, but he didn't think she'd guessed this particular fact, that the person he'd been guarding all these years was his spouse.

Her voice was thick when she replied. "Oh, Thibaut . . . I'm so sorry."

The way she apologized—the weight of her "sorry"—clearly meant she assumed Venessa was dead.

He let her assume. People always *assumed.*

Perhaps he should be grateful—they were kind enough to think she'd died, that the two of them wouldn't have parted on purpose.

There was a *romanticism* in the assumption that he liked. Being a dashing widower with a tragic backstory was titillating. Losing the love of one's life to misfortune suggested an impassioned soul marred by the grand cruelty of the uncontrollable universe. It made him seem more dynamic, more gallant, more sympathetic.

In reality, she'd left him.

Because of Krona.

And there was nothing romantic about *that*.

"I could marry a thief," Venessa had said when she left, *"but I could never love a rat."*

He'd never intended to tell Krona who his accomplice had been, but now things had changed. Their *lives* had changed at the Rotunda—the assassination had shifted everything. Krona couldn't go back on their deal and decide to track Venessa down after all, because Krona couldn't *go back*. And if he stayed with her, here, their deal was null and void anyway. An informant needed someone to inform *on* as much as they needed someone to inform *to*.

The change meant they were closer; the two of them had been caught in one another's orbit for years, but now they were about to be in one another's *pockets*.

He'd made a promise to himself long ago—when he'd started to feel the way he felt about Krona—that he would never let himself fall into her. She'd forced his hand to save Venessa, turned him into the very thing his wife scorned the most. Krona was the reason she was gone, and in many ways he still loved Venessa despite everything.

To want Krona was to betray Venessa all over again.

A fleeting dalliance was one thing, but to fall in new love with the woman who'd cost him his first love—

And yet, as the years passed and he'd realized Venessa wasn't coming back either way—whether he denied his feelings for Krona or not—his promise to himself had come to feel needlessly self-flagellating.

He looked at the box, at the gift he'd gotten for Krona. It was both practical and pretty, enchanted but not obviously so. Something about it had seemed so very *her* when he'd bartered for it.

If he gave it to her, it would become very *them*.

He looked again at the rags.

For years, he'd hoped Venessa would reconsider. He'd hoped she'd get curious and come knocking on their apartment door to see if he still lived there. He'd glimpsed her once or twice in a crowded market and had given her space, hoping she'd choose to say hello, but she'd said nothing. Their eyes had met and she'd swiftly looked away.

She'd made her choice.

He didn't *owe* her this distance between himself and Krona. He didn't owe her anything anymore.

Maybe he owed himself a chance.

▷—◁▷—○—◁▷—◁

Krona slipped under the blankets before Thibaut finished changing. When he came out again, overly tight gray trousers clung to his legs, and the nightshirt hung loose and open about his frame. But it was his eyes that caught her attention—red-rimmed.

"The suit matched the gloves she gave you," she said, letting him know she understood. "And now the suit is ruined. I'm sorry, really."

He shrugged and waved it off. "Part of a past life." He held the rags in a bundle.

"But it was important to you."

"Yes. And now you know."

He trusted her enough to share such things. He trusted her enough to stay with her—to follow her into the unknown when he could have argued and gone back to the city.

He shut the bundle in the top of the dresser, closing the drawer with a hardened touch, as though he were signaling some sort of finality. When he turned around again, he was holding a box between both hands. The kind that jewelry came in.

She sat up against the narrow headboard, bunching the covers up to her chest. She hoped he wasn't about to do something trite.

"I've been looking for the right time to give this to you," he said, uncharacteristically sheepish. "Bloodied and battered in the woods didn't feel like the ideal circumstances, but now I'm not sure ideal circumstances are in the cards for us."

"Thibaut—"

Krona had seen him with clients before. Just brief glimpses, nothing drawn out. He was a character with them, not himself. True, he put on a façade for her as well, but it was a thin veneer. She liked to think he was mostly genuine with her and wouldn't try to dazzle her with the same flashy tricks he used on the wealthy who paid him. She might once in a while wear a pair of earrings or a meager chain around her neck, but such trinkets were typically of little consequence to her.

"Now, I know what you're thinking," he said. "I do. But before you protest"—he covered the small space in a single stride and held out the box insistently—"just open it."

Trying to be gracious instead of gruff, she took it with a nod and carefully flipped open the box's hinged lid. "Oh," she gasped softly, completely caught off guard by the contents. Nested inside was a four-ringed silver knuckleduster. Peering closely, she was just able to make out an enchanter's mark on the grip in amongst the attractive art deco engravings that gave it a bit of style.

She took it out of the box and slid the rings over her fist, clutching the grip. It felt good in her hand. Solid.

"I saw it and thought of you," he said, suddenly very interested in a knot in the floorboard near his foot. He licked his lips, then glanced up through his lashes. "Of course, I'm always thinking about you."

Her breath caught in her chest. This felt like more than a casual gift. More than their customary bit of banter, where they flirted—with both impropriety and each other. His voice was smooth and sincere. The present itself spoke to how well he knew her, and the heated look in his eye sent a thrill through her core.

Her gaze kept falling on his mouth, tracking every quirk of his lips and flick of his tongue. Heat crept into her cheeks when he politely cleared his throat and she realized she hadn't said anything yet. "It's—it's beautiful," she stuttered. "It's wonderful. Thank you. Where did you get it? Is this something Hintosep had in her enchantments stash?"

"No. No, I've had it for a while now. Happened to have it on me when we all—" He made a fluid gesture across his body, like a bird taking off and flying away. "Fellow who traded me for it swore up and down it was enchanted, and that you could break a time vial with it—smash unsmashable enchanted glass. Might not be, though," he added quickly, nervously. "Enchanted, I mean. Should have been noticed by scanning spheres at the Rotunda if it was, so"—he shrugged—"I don't know."

"Thank you, sincerely." She admired the way the rings curved over the backs of her fingers, just like one might admire a gemstone ring. An unusual impulse overtook her, and she brought the knuckleduster to her lips, let them lightly peck its engraved surface.

She hadn't meant it to be suggestive, but the way Thibaut stiffened in surprise made her blush all the harder. She swiftly dropped both hands into her lap and hoped, not for the first time, that her dark complexion would save her from him noticing any extra ruddiness in her cheeks.

Thibaut's complexion, on the other hand, wasn't nearly so kind. His cheeks, and even the tips of his ears, were pink, peeking out from the ruggedly disheveled curls of his blond hair—not heated from embarrassment, it seemed, but an entirely more impassioned response. His eyes had gone dark, pupils blown wide in the low candlelight.

When he moved, it was slow and deliberate, gaze locked on hers, giving her plenty of time to snap the tension, to break the spell if she so desired. He crawled onto the bed, knees hitting first before he prowled up her body to hover over her, face inches away.

She wetted her lips in anticipation, sitting up a little straighter.

But instead of going in for a kiss, he lifted her hand lightly—the one fitted with the knuckleduster—and kissed it like he'd kiss a noble lady's hand, except that his mouth fell onto the silver, right where her own lips had graced it.

"So, it's safe to say you like it, then, mistress?" he asked, voice breathy, gaze lingering on her hand in his.

"Very much," she answered just as quietly. Carefully, she twisted her wrist out of his grasp, cupped his chin, and ran her thumb over his bottom lip. "It's perfect."

His smile was boyish and entirely too charming.

She quickly matched it, unable to remember the last time she'd smiled so easily.

As she leaned in for the kiss they both so clearly wanted, Thibaut suddenly pulled back. "Well, good night, mistress," he said cheerily, and hopped off the bed.

She sat there stunned, hand still outstretched, and let out a surprised scoff as he began arranging himself, the quilt, and an extra pillow on the floor.

Then she smiled all the wider.

Bastard couldn't help himself. He had to be a tease.

She turned on her side to watch him for a few moments more, letting him play out his casual farce with her lips twisted in what she hoped was a good feign of disapproval.

When he planted himself facedown in the pillow, lying still as a dead log, she said casually, "Thibaut?"

"Hmm?"

She threw back the covers beside her in invitation. "Get up here."

He sprang up lightning-quick, pillow in hand, and she laughed at him. Smoothly, like silk, he slid onto the mattress next to her, his body radiating heat.

She wanted to roll over and hold him, so she did. She pressed her face into his neck and simply breathed him in, just as she'd wanted to many times before. Lightly, her lips graced his throat, and he shuddered, hand alighting on her hip, bunching in her underthings.

"Krona," he whispered, dropping "mistress," at least for the time being, along with all other pretenses of formality and society's definition of propriety.

She kissed her way up his neck, then rolled over him farther, so that she was now the one hovering, looking down, her fine braids cascading around them. He brushed several behind her ear. "Finally," he said softly.

"Finally," she agreed, sinking into a kiss—tasting him for the first time, trusting him fully with her heart and her pleasure, not worrying about tomorrow, simply existing in the here and now, with him.

40

THALO CHILD

Six Months Ago

The next time Thalo Child saw Hintosep, he *hoped*, even though it had only been a few months. *Maybe it's time. Maybe she's done it.* Maybe Gerome would cast aside his threats. Maybe Thalo Child could leave with his charge, unaccosted.

But instead of walking toward him with a purpose, Hintosep strode right past him, her gaze never meeting his, her chin not even dipping in acknowledgment. She looked right through him, as though he wasn't there at all.

He wondered if retrieving the Cage had proved too difficult a task. It was possible she'd given up—not just on the varg but on him, on Thalo Infant. She could have deemed the two of them no longer worth her time.

He watched her go with a knot in his chest, feeling as though a similar knot had just been tied around his wrists.

⊱━◈━○━◈━⊰

Hintosep's thoughts are too occupied with her mantra to notice anything else. *Ever the servant*, she reminds herself, clearing her mind of all else. *Ever the servant, ever the servant.*

She walks like an automation toward the Savior's hideaway—a small antechamber He's cordoned off to use as a private place of relaxation, on the lower levels near the springs. When she enters, she immediately kneels, head bowed in respect.

"Is it done?" He asks, tone maddeningly paternal.

The chamber is warm, heated not just by the springs but by half a dozen braziers as well, their fires low, the coals glowing a mesmerizing orange red. He sits upon a well-padded lounge, leaning over the armrest to reach a Marquises and Marauders board set upon an end table. It is a two-player game, but He will not invite her to play a match.

As in real life, the Savior only plays against Himself.

She glances up from her position on the floor. Like this, He looks imposing but not glamorous. Not to her, anyway. Perhaps that is because His face is uncovered and she can see Him for the man He simply is. Only *she* is allowed to glimpse His true face. He trusts her that much.

She trusts Him not at all.

"I helped place the charges myself," she says evenly. "The mines in Winsrouen's Altum arm will collapse. Asgar-Skan will take the blame."

"Good. Presuming that goes to plan, we must make sure to remove our northern obstacles next." Fingers flicking through the air above the board, He circles several pieces before picking one and maneuvering it to a new position. "I cannot decide how to draw in the other two city-states. Winsrouen's border nations are easily prodded, but Marrakev, Lutador—they consider themselves neutral."

"They need proper motivation, is all," she says, standing. "Personal stakes. A city-state is called to action just as a person is called. For money, for love . . . or for revenge."

He sighs. "If only we hadn't allowed Lutador to become quite *so* prosperous, dangling extra resources in front of them might have worked. And, alas, I don't see how love could be of any use in this situation. But revenge—"

She tenses.

"—that sounds promising. Tell me more. What great wrong do you imagine will have the city-state rushing to reprisal?"

Before answering, she mentally spits out another line of her mantra, *Ever the servant, ever the servant,* using it to drown out her feelings, to push back any other thoughts that threaten to rise up and expose her.

This conversation is too close to home. But she cannot avoid the subject.

"Assassination," she suggests curtly.

"Direct. Bold."

"And undeniable. Not so easily swept aside by a new treaty and a few talks."

"And who would you like to kill?" He makes it sound like a gift, like He's asking what kind of treat she wants, as He's happy to provide.

Yes, that's the question, who?

She's surprised to realize she *knows* who.

Everything clicks into place in that moment. She sees the future laid bare before her. She can imagine each step perfectly. They'd been building the pyre of war for a long time, but now she can pinpoint the exact spark that will ignite the conflict.

And that very spark could open doors and send the Savior *away.*

"One of the Grand Marquises. It needs to be a blow at the very top."

"Excellent," He says with pride. "See to it."

She bows, turns on her heel, but He quickly speaks up again.

"Oh, before you go: what of that Regulator? Weren't we going to do something about her?"

Hintosep scrambles to align her thoughts. "Since her sister's death, she's—"

He looks up pointedly, brown eyes blazing, gaze sharp despite His many, many, many, *many* years. And yet, there is something tired about it. "The pair of them were supposed to be turned, utilized, and killed. You still have not explained, to my satisfaction, why Gatwood only went after the one."

Carefully, she closes her mind. She cannot let Him see the real reason they failed to ensnare the younger Hirvath—simply that they *could not*.

"The sisters were not as close as we thought. It was difficult to coordinate them. Gatwood had time and opportunity for the eldest. We had a timeline—one *you* set—and worked with what we were able."

He glares for a moment, then goes back to His game, swiping at one piece with another, knocking it over violently, so that it is swept from the board and bounds along the stone floor, eventually rolling over and over, until it is stopped by Hintosep's boot.

She does not bend to retrieve it. She does not allow her breathing or heart rate to change.

"Let's use the assassination to be rid of her, then," He says firmly. "Figure out a way for her to be caught in some crossfire. Or, better yet, hanged for the deed itself."

"That can be arranged," she assures Him, purposefully feeling no feelings, making herself a blank slate inside so that He cannot sniff out her secret.

"The point of this war is containment," He reminds her. "The people's ambitions need to be reset, just as sometimes the climates need to be reset. There needs to be enough violence and heartache that they conclude what should already be obvious: that Knowledge's commandment is there for a reason. That it is their ill-advised advancements, this railway, that has caused so much pain."

"I understand."

"I want this all out of the way before the next Awakening. The gods are difficult enough to manage during peacetime."

"Of course."

Without another word, He holds out His hand toward her, palm up. She knows what's expected of her. She swipes the game piece from the floor and brings it to Him, setting it carefully in His palm.

Only then does He move, posture shifting. He sets the piece next to the board, takes her hand in His. It's a gentle touch. Familial, though the two of them are not bound by blood or twined lineage. "Are you well?" He asks with genuine interest, and His sincerity pierces like a knife. There are warmth and love in His voice, in this gesture.

He has never raised a hand to her. Never been spiteful or threatening. Has never tried to strike fear in her heart, or used cruel words to wound her spirit.

But He has ruined her just the same.

"I'm worried," she confesses, skewing the specifics of her thoughts. "War is messy. There are too many variables. No matter how careful we are, how well we plan, we cannot control everything."

"I can control much," He assures her. "I will oversee many of the battles myself, personally."

"You will leave the keep, then?" she asks, strangling the eagerness out of her voice.

This is it. *This* is what she's been waiting for, as she's been scouring the Valley for her soldiers and allies. She needs Him to go. Needs Him to lay His hands on the outside world and neglect the treasures here.

"Yes," He says with a soft smile. "You forget, I thrive in war."

41

MANDIP

Climbing *back* into the family estate with a very beautiful and very famous woman in tow was much easier than Mandip expected. Yes, security met them almost immediately but said nothing of their dirt-ravaged clothes, the branch scratches on their cheeks and forearms, or their strange method of arrival—on foot and unaccompanied.

Or seemingly unaccompanied. He could not see her, but Mandip knew Hintosep lurked nearby.

"See, what did I tell you?" Juliet whispered, pulling him down by the shoulder so she could get at his ear while they marched between two sets of grounds guards. "A whirlwind affair is an easy cover: so readily accepted, so conveniently dismissed. And if it is fleeting and I am gone by tomorrow, people will say, 'That's how performers are,' and think nothing of it."

"It's amazing how similar you and Monsieur Thibaut are," Mandip said. "Both brazen. Both shameless."

"Being shameless lets us take advantage of other people's prudishness. Which—surely you've noted—is a quite effective strategy."

Security walked them into the receiving room. Mandip insisted they be shown into the house proper—he wasn't a guest or an intruder, after all—but Rajnish, who'd been in service to the Basu family for years, made him stay put. "If you came home, we were instructed to bring you here."

"*If?*"

Juliet let out an overly loud, clearly forced laugh. "Darling, don't you see, they feared we'd eloped to Asgar-Skan!"

"They feared you'd been murdered the night the First Grand Marquis was assassinated," Rajnish corrected.

The bottom dropped out of Mandip's stomach.

Rajnish bowed stiffly before leaving them, a stern frown plastered to his lips. He closed the room's door with a firm snap, and Mandip was more than a little alarmed to hear the lock turn.

"They thought I was dead," Mandip said as soon as he was sure Rajnish was out of earshot. Juliet opened her mouth to speak and raised her hand to make a gesture—likely to bat away his concern like it was as inconsequential as a fly—but he quickly reiterated, "*Dead*," and she thought better of it. She sidled over to the nearest chair and plopped down into it, skirts puffing up around her.

He felt hollow. Ashamed.

Mandip couldn't look her in the eye, so instead he looked at the art—the Jugendstil sculptures on the glass shelves near the door, and the dark oil paintings on the rear wall. But he saw none of it.

In their place he saw a face with blue tattoos and a surprised O of a mouth. He felt the heft of a sword in his hand and the sickening jolt it had made when it slid into the Thalo puppet's body.

No, I'm not dead, he imagined telling his parents, *I was off killing someone else.*

He'd worried his family, and that was shameful. He felt guilty for it, having hurt them like that. But he felt worse about where he'd really been. What he'd really done.

What he was about to do.

Maybe he couldn't go through with it after all. He'd been tasked with helping to protect the treasure in the vaults by becoming a Key, and he'd justified this upcoming heist by telling himself he wasn't breaking any vow or betraying his city-state. The treasure would not be touched. The incident would do no real harm, but it might do a spot of good.

But was that true?

After a few minutes, Mandip composed himself, swallowing that conflict down, pushing it away. Instead, he turned to a lighter subject that had been troubling him. Finding Juliet's eyes, finally able to make contact again, he bade her, "Tell me truthfully: did you hire Thibaut to steal my watch and take me to that Regulator den?"

"No! Running into you like that was simply good fortune. Perhaps something arranged by Time herself. I was quite confident in my ability to beguile you during our arranged palace tour—until the moment of our meeting, that is. *Then* my confidence began to waver—which hardly ever happens, mind you—and I began to fear the plan would go awry. Which it did, of course, but in a very different fashion."

"Was our first meeting really so off-putting? I mean"—he smiled to himself, thinking of the way Thibaut had fallen on his arse—"yes, it wasn't the most genteel of introductions, but all in all, I didn't think it went that poorly."

"If I'm honest, it's because you seemed far more enamored of Thibaut than me, despite your grumblings. But, in turn, since Thibaut is a fan of my music, it was easy to see how I could still string one along with the other, so I didn't lose all hope. And look where we are now—co-conspirators!"

Mandip winced. "Do you need to declare it quite so loudly?"

She grinned wide and said, "Sorry," in a tone that smacked of no remorse.

The door rattled. A key turned in the lock. Mandip was surprised when it wasn't his mother or father who walked in but Adhar.

"Where have you been?" his brother demanded, but not unkindly. His voice was low, furtive.

"You're the one who helped me sneak out, and now you're here to give me a talking-to?"

"You were supposed to sneak out for the *night*, not days on end," Adhar said. "Look, I'm on your side, I'd assumed you had your reasons, but . . . I had no idea where you'd gone, or if you even knew about the assassination. Do you?"

"I do."

"Did you know it was a Regulator working for Winsrouen that killed the First Grand Marquis? Or that the Second has vowed reprisal?" He ran a hand over his face. "Lutador's domestic leadership is in shambles after losing its head of state, and now our head of foreign affairs is readying for war. This is no time for—" He waved pointedly between Mandip and Juliet. "Gods, Mandip, I thought you were supposed to be the responsible one."

"I am," he insisted. "I received the Treasury summons, just like you, and returned for the Repository's opening. I haven't shirked any duties. What *should* I have been doing after the assassination, in your opinion? Seeing as how I hold no office."

"Not worrying your family, for one."

"Please don't blame Mandip," Juliet said, rising and moving to Mandip's side, taking his hand and standing close—displaying an uncomfortable level of intimacy in front of Adhar that Mandip attempted to relax into. "I asked him to come with me on a jaunt through the countryside. We knew there'd been a disturbance at the Rotunda, but how could we have known . . ." She bit her lip and fluttered her eyelashes as though holding back tears.

Adhar's exasperation eased, and his upbringing kicked in. "Pardon me, dear lady, I've been exceedingly rude."

They exchanged formal introductions.

"I'm sorry for my behavior, but you must understand, the entire Winsrouen delegation has been detained," Adhar went on. "Not escorted home as they should have been, mind you, because the Second Grand Marquis has lost all reason. I fear he means to execute them. Publicly."

Mandip went cold. "But does he have proof any of them had a hand in it? The representatives themselves could be innocent."

They *were* innocent.

"He doesn't seem to be in the investigative mood. Diplomacy should be his first concern, not revenge. But here we are."

Not only had Hintosep assassinated the Grand Marquis and framed the Regulator for dealing the blow, she'd framed an entire *nation* for ordering it. She'd doomed the Winsrouen delegation.

She'd said the Savior meant to start a war.

He was apparently going to get one.

It was just like what she'd said about framing Captain Hirvath—Winsrouen had been pressing its luck with its allies, trying to force expansion, trying to redraw its borders. All the city-state's threats and posturing made it easy to blame.

Twin chimes rang out in the room, and both Adhar and Mandip pulled out their watches. A set of the hands had moved, proclaiming the Treasury opening would be tomorrow.

"Looks like you arrived home just in time," Adhar said, and Mandip tried not to read suspicion into his tone. "I suggest you clean up and show your guest to her room."

"I could never impose," Juliet said quickly. "I have a hotel—"

"Nonsense, you must stay with us," Adhar asserted.

"Oh, well, if you insist."

⊱─━⊱⊰━─⊰

Mandip showed Juliet to their guest quarters, a lavish set of rooms decorated in a silver-and-teal motif. He promised to send for her things at her previous lodgings.

"You had attendants before—bodyguards. They don't wonder where you've gone?" he asked.

"Oh, no, I disappear on them all the time. I leave them a special sign so they know I've gone of my own accord and haven't been kidnapped, but that's just between us," she said with a wink, leaping onto the bed despite the dirt on her clothes. "Oh, this is lovely."

Mandip tentatively set himself down on the corner of the bed, keeping a respectful distance, though Juliet was definitely not the sort to care about such things. "Hintosep," he said softly glancing around suspiciously, "is she here with us?"

"In the room now? No, she's gone off to rifle through your family's less-securely stowed enchantments."

His eyes found every cranny in the room, studying it for any movement. "How can you be sure?"

"Because she told me," Juliet said. "She doesn't hide herself from me. Ever."

Mandip wished he felt as confident about the assertion as Juliet. "Tell me about her," he bade. If they were truly alone, this might be his only chance to delve into Juliet's honest thoughts. "You sincerely believe everything she says? About dead gods and a secret organization and myths and magic and—"

"Yes," Juliet said emphatically. "All of it. I saw far too much of the world far too soon to maintain any doubts. You saw what she can do; how would you explain it?"

He couldn't. "But if what she says is true, then the whole world is based on lies."

"Is this not something we accept daily, regardless?" she asked. "Are there not obvious lies we pretend not to see, or readily convince ourselves we don't see, for the sake of order? Like your ancestor's papers, perhaps?"

"If there were doubts about Absolon's writ, I would not be here today," he said firmly. "Don't you think the nobility of the time would have had every reason not to accept my family into their ranks?"

"On the contrary, I think they had every reason not to raise a fuss. Because here's the truth: if you start looking too closely at one writ, you'll start people looking too closely at *all* the writs. I wonder how many people who wield power might have family histories similar to yours. Perhaps they can count themselves among the crème de la crème for more generations, perhaps the con goes further back, but still: how many stray bristles would it take to bring down an entire class? To sew doubt? Spread uncertainty and unrest? It was a good-enough forgery to fool most, and that's all that was required. Calling out your ancestor would have led to retaliation. Accepting him let them all sail right along."

"Are all musicians this cynical?"

"Cynical?" she gasped, taken aback. "I'll have you know there is nothing mocking or pessimistic about my outlook on life. I face the world with a hearty dose of realism and a heart full of hope. Noting problems is how one fixes them. Understanding the world is beautiful but could be better is how one *progresses*. It's *stagnation* and *neglect* I can't abide. *Cynical?* Tosh. I'll have you know I am the very picture of optimism. That Regulator, on the other hand . . ."

"She had to watch her sister bleed out, as the papers told it."

This seemed to strike an unnerving chord with Juliet. She pursed her lips, nodded. "Well, then, that makes two of us," she said, her demeanor souring. She rolled away from him, clutched at one of the pillows, and curled around it.

He knew a dismissal when he received it, and decided not to ask after what she meant. "I'll let you rest, and call for you at dinner."

"Thank you."

Mandip had a difficult time sleeping in his own bed that night. His parents had berated him and showered affection on him in turn, utterly disappointed in his behavior but happy to have him home and whole. They'd been nothing but gracious toward Juliet, and he would have expected no less.

It was a nagging dread that kept him awake. Uncertainty plagued his every thought. He'd never been an overly anxious man, but tonight anxiety made his limbs feel like lead, and his heart thump heavily, and his palms sweat, and his mouth go dry.

He'd asked Juliet for details of the heist and now wished she'd simply left him in the dark. She wouldn't tell him everything, apparently still worried he might disrupt the plan, but with a heavy sigh she had admitted, "You weren't even supposed to know about the heist, remember? You were supposed to be my charming escort and completely none the wiser. When the time came and we needed you to act, Hintosep was going to commandeer your mind for a few minutes, nothing more. But now I suppose it's best for you to act out your part of your own free will. Do you know about the glass golems in the treasury's hall of mirrors? What am I asking; of course you do. Well, you'll need to neutralize one for us. Beyond that, don't worry. Do your part at the Treasury just as you would otherwise, and everything will turn out fine."

42

MANDIP

"*'Don't worry,'* she says," Mandip huffed under his breath, sitting on a bench, wrists weighed down by glass shackles between his splayed knees. "*'Everything will turn out fine,'* she says."

Everything had *not* been fine. Everything had *not* gone to plan and now here he was—alone, gods knew what had happened to Hintosep—waiting in the Treasury lobby to be interrogated by Commander Anthousa of the Spriggans, the one person who knew, definitively, that he was the Key.

Though few people ever saw it, the lobby was as grand as could be, with a beautifully tiled mosaic floor, its pattern that of interlocking mandalas framing a sun at the lobby's center. Below lay the hall of mirrors and the various vaults, including the one that held the official funerary accoutrements required for a sitting Grand Marquis's death rites.

He was alone in the lobby. The Spriggans didn't fear he would run—there was nowhere to run *to*.

The Treasury lay at the center of a Borderswatch outpost several hours away from Lutador proper, surrounded by a moat—which required a drawbridge to cross—and a vast moment-minefield.

The building itself was imposing yet squat. Only a single story stood above-ground, having been carved out of a lone granite outcrop. Its outermost walls were thick, and nearly everything inside was composed of enchanted glass and metal.

The entire facility *reeked* of time. It was a difficult scent to place, but there was no denying it had a smell. Something similar to the freshness of washed crystalware mixed with the history of old tomes. It was the sharpness of the new mixed with the dullness of the ancient. A heady combination that now made Mandip's temples throb.

Commander Anthousa's *clop-clop-clopp*ing boots announced her before she appeared around a corner. When she came into view, the lobby's gaslights caught the enchanted-glass outer coating on her armor, sending sharp darts of refracted light across his vision. He winced away from it.

Glass armor might seem counterintuitive to the uninitiated, but the Spriggan uniform was a trap in and of itself. Should anyone attempt to strike the petite commander and crack this particular kind of glass, the enchantment would trigger, instantly aging the attacker centuries in a moment. They'd disintegrate—shrivel into nothing but dust to be blown away by the wind.

The same would happen should he try to break free of his glass cuffs.

Mandip tried not to think too hard about how many vials full of time it took to create even one set of armor, one pair of manacles.

"Milor," she addressed him, still giving him a proper bow despite holding him prisoner. Her wheat-colored hair was curly on top and undercut on the sides, and her cheeks were soft and round. But her eyes were dark and piercing, her stare indicating she would give him little leeway, regardless of his station.

"Commander," he acknowledged, nodding back. "Where's my brother?"

"He'll be with you soon enough. I saw no reason to detain him, given his absence from the incident. Was I wrong to do so?"

Mandip sat up straighter. "No, no. And . . . and Juliet? La Maupin?"

She tilted her head thoughtfully, then began pacing with her hands braced at her sides, armor shining, lips pursed, as though considering her words carefully. "Did she know about the minefield?"

In his mind's eye he saw Juliet—done up with all the dramatic flair he'd come to expect, in her low-cut, sunny-yellow dress that complemented her stoutness as much as it evoked titillating scandal—after all, high collars were still all the rage for feminine wear.

She'd looked back at him as she'd skipped off the path, all smiles, her camphor glass jewelry iridescent in the midday sun—the effect aided by a handful of imbedded opals in her ear cuffs and the glass cuckoo-clock pendant that dangled from around her neck.

Mandip could do nothing as she'd sprinted across the expanse of grass—*directly into the minefield*—skirts pulled up to her shins as she bounded like a carefree child on a summer's day.

Alarms had rung out across the complex—bells struck by the watchtower guards who had seen her, as well as something high-pitched clearly activated by enchantment.

It had only been a few seconds more before her foot found one of the moment-mines, compressing the trigger and shattering the glass tube within.

And that had been after. After the golems—

Mandip swallowed harshly, throat gone dry. He was sure Juliet had to have known—had to have her reasons. "I don't know," he said. "I didn't mention it."

"What did you mention?" the commander asked, tone merely curious, though Mandip knew there was nothing academic about her probing.

Sighing, he leaned forward, dragging his wrists upward to press the heels of his palms into his eyes. The glass was so heavy. He needed to buy time to convince her he was innocent here. "I—I don't know. I don't remember."

"Well, you must have told her something; why else would she have accompanied you here?"

Why else, indeed?

He'd told Adhar it had been for love. He'd had to tell him something, after all. As a watch-wielder but not the official Key, Adhar had been required to attend the public opening of the Treasury vault. And while guests were not unheard-of in such instances, it was surely a shock that Mandip would invite anyone along.

It was so easy to play the besotted fool. Juliet made it easy. She was charming, quick-witted, talented, wondrous.

"Milor?" the commander prompted.

"She wanted to see the inaugural jewels," he said, remembering the lie Juliet had intended to use on him. "I saw no reason to deny her. She does love pretty things."

"You didn't think that perhaps her—how can I graciously put this—*impulsive personality* might be an issue at such a somber event?"

It was true; Juliet had delighted in creating a hubbub before they'd even entered the Treasury. But it was all in service to a cause.

⇒⚬⬥⚬⬥⚬⬦⚬⬅

When he, Adhar, Juliet, and the invisible Hintosep arrived, many of the other potential Keys were already in place—some with guests of their own—everyone decked out in finery appropriate for the occasion. The mood was solemn, and enchanted opals abounded. Once the group was complete, they alighted on the long, black-graveled path that led through the minefield and to the Treasury proper.

As they marched—a detail of Spriggans keeping them all at a steady pace—Juliet did her best to divert Mandip's cognizance away from his own nerves. Internally, he'd been a mess ever since they'd left home and was finding it more and more difficult to keep himself together. Fidgeting, biting his lip, he tried to think about anything other than the fact that he was about to engage in robbery, but was failing miserably.

Despite the somber processional, Juliet kept ahold of her chipperness. Several of the noble's guests had clearly been surprised—and delighted—to find La Maupin in their midst, and the songstress knew how to direct a throng's attention as much as she could draw it—which she took great amusement in demonstrating purely for Mandip's benefit. She saw a small wildflower growing at the edge of the path and made a point of stopping to look at it. The rest of the group stopped as well, until the Spriggans ordered them onward. She complimented Adhar's waistcoat, told him it made him look otherworldly ("otherworldly," what thing to say about a waistcoat!), and had demanded, "Don't you think so?" of everyone marching near her until they'd all voiced their agreement.

"Oh, what's that?" she asked in awe, pointing at nothing in the sky. The next instant, she dropped both her gaze and hand as everyone else—save Adhar and the Spriggans—shielded their eyes against the sun and frantically searched the clouds for whatever La Maupin had noticed.

She immediately smirked at Mandip.

"You're incorrigible," he whispered in good humor, walking onward while the group still stared, slack-jawed, at nothing.

"I think you like it," she said, matching his stride and threading her arm through his.

Mandip was beginning to understand how being readily noticed offered similar protection as going unnoticed all together.

"Are the two of you quite finished?" Adhar asked.

Mandip could tell when his brother was sincerely put off and when he was being stern because he thought it was expected of him. This was definitely an instance of the latter.

But, with his nerves at least temporarily quelled, Juliet halted her teasing and they entered the Treasury in formal ranks, a procession full of dignified tradition.

There, things began to go awry.

>⁃⬩⬥⬩⃝⬩⬦⬩⃔

"La Maupin is no more impulsive than half the nobles who were here."

"So, she didn't run into the minefield on impulse, then?" the commander countered.

"Juliet is *not* a *threat*," he said firmly. "What we *should* be discussing is the golems." Burly eight-foot forms composed of bulbous, rough-hewn glass boulders—milky blue and opaque—battered each other in his memory. Atop their shoulders sat wooden mimicries of heads, the faces stylized and monstrous. Nobles' panicked screams and a rush of bodies had knocked him off his feet. "Why wasn't I informed the protocol had changed?"

"We did our best. Orders arrived from the Second Grand Marquis just this morning. He's . . . He's got the constabulary increasing security everywhere, all over the city-state, no matter if the measures are within reason or not. Why did *you* attack my Spriggans?"

"It was . . . an accident."

"An accident," she said evenly.

It was, and it wasn't.

"If you'd told me I wouldn't have any control over the extra golems, I might have acted more quickly." If he could put even a little of the blame on her shoulders, maybe he could create enough doubt for her to let him go. "Instead, I did the only thing I could think of, and that was fight back."

Mirrors smashed in his mind. A noblewoman shrieked.

"I hope," he said, drawing out an authoritative tone, "that you have in custody whoever was managing the reins of those rogue golems. Yes, I said *rogue*. There is a reason that I, as the Key, have control of each vault's golem, and that's because I am trained to rein them in if they are accidentally activated."

The commander looked skeptical, but Mandip barreled on. "The golems are there to prevent unauthorized persons from entering any given vault, and I am there as a safeguard so that a curious noble who gets too close or—or a visiting Grand Marquex themself—does not get pummeled by a mindless glass *troll*."

"So, you're blaming this all on an accidental triggering?" she prompted.

"Well, *I* certainly didn't see anything amiss in the vault itself, did you?"

Mandip's heart was hammering itself against his rib cage, despite his steady, even breaths. He could hear it beating in his own ears and hoped Commander Anthousa couldn't see it fluttering in his pulse point.

It was an out-and-out lie. All of it.

And, gods, if Hintosep hadn't been fuck-it-all invisible, he wouldn't have a lying leg to stand on.

><+>-0-<+><

After entering the lobby, they were separated into their twin-sets, and ferried—along with any guests and an accompanying set of Spriggans—down to the mirror maze via hand-operated lifts. The elevator cage was large—built to accommodate carts and carts of time vials at once. Mirrors lined the rear wall, and, catching his own reflection and his already-harried expression, Mandip had taken a deep breath.

And so it begins, Mandip thought, turning to face the front of the lift. *Mirrors. Mirrors, mirrors everywhere.*

When one of the Spriggans threw a lever, closing the gate, the mirrors on the rear wall swung around to become the door, closing off the lobby.

And Mandip nearly jumped out of his skin.

Hintosep was standing right behind him.

Everyone else, including Juliet, looked at him like he'd lost his mind.

Hintosep, for her part, smirked. He hadn't pegged her for a sense of humor, but clearly she'd given him a scare on purpose.

Eyes forward, lordling, she said, though her lips did not move.

The elevator's weight-and-pulley system started with a jolt.

He tried to look at nothing in the mirror. Or everything—except Hintosep. He failed miserably, his gaze repeatedly catching on hers. Deliberately, he moved his stare, fixing it on Juliet instead. At least then Mandip could blame his nerves on *infatuation* if anyone asked.

But now his nervousness had flared again. His palms grew sweaty and his mouth went dry.

When the elevator stopped, they were far, far below the surface, with stories' worth of bedrock settled over their heads. Swiftly, the elevator's mirror wall rotated behind them once more, revealing an entire hallway clad just the same.

The mirrors were lined with nickel and framed in enchanted wood, all ceiling-lit by lamps in gold sconces that reminded Mandip of curling spider legs—as though a host of arachnids hovered above their heads, waiting to drop down.

Next came a dance he knew well.

The mirrors were an intricate, twirling maze, made to separate parties from one another, constantly creating new paths. The maze served two purposes—to confuse potential intruders, yes, but it also allowed the Spriggans to view every-one inside from all angles, to observe them carefully and to see them from every aspect in detail.

One by one, Mandip was separated from the party members, and they from each other. The only person who never left his side was Hintosep.

The maze itself recognized Mandip as the Key, guiding him toward panels where enchanted locks that resonated with the metal in his arm lay.

No need to play coy, Hintosep whispered to him—inside his mind—when he tried to covertly open the first lock. *You forget, I was here when this maze was constructed. I know its layout and its locks intimately. It's simply* access *I cannot gain on my own.*

Reflections of himself and Hintosep flashed across his vision again and again as the mirrors twirled. Once in a while, they were privy to a glimpse of Adhar or Juliet, but most terrifying were the flickers of Spriggan armor, reminding Man-dip that they were always on guard, always watching, and above all, *trusting him* to do his duty.

Eventually, the mirrors spilled him out at the vault they were after—the one housing the funerary accoutrements.

And there, waiting for them, not one golem, as he'd expected, but five. Five milky-blue monsters, ready to smash their way through any unauthorized skulls, each created through the melding of a *Teleoteur* and *Kairoteur's* skills. They might have been beautiful if they weren't so deadly.

The usual golem was placed directly next to the vault door, and the others stood in a cluster, a ways off and to the side, clearly only recently moved away from their own assigned vault doors. Theoretically, this left several of the other vaults vulnerable, but he supposed—given the unprecedented circumstances under which the First Grand Marquis had died, perhaps unprecedented security measures had been ordered for this particular vault opening.

Which was something Hintosep clearly hadn't anticipated. She raised an eyebrow at him, and he gave her a reassuring nod in return.

He'd been surprised by the additions but not worried. Neutralizing one golem wasn't that difficult. How hard could five be?

Turns out, *very.*

The vault's door was clear, the glass of it thick, yet it did not distort the shapes beyond. Inside lay the jewels, censers, and funerary robes they'd come to fetch for the obsequies.

The final lock was physical rather than enchanted—workable only by a Spriggan who knew the combination. Everything in the repository was designed to need more than one hand—for *safety.*

Once the maze had guided all of the nobles into place, the ceremony began.

"First Grand Marquis Salvadorio the Third has passed," a Spriggan said, raising both their hands in rite as they approached the vault. "Survived by Second Grand Marquis Luscious-Komas."

Everyone bowed their heads, and Mandip slipped one hand into his watch pocket. His part in this wasn't over. A small twitch of his thumb across the crown of his watch set time in motion—literally.

The items inside each vault were perfectly preserved—*perfectly,* because time did not touch them.

To create a perpetual pause inside the vault, time had to be constantly siphoned away, bled into the surrounding repository halls, which meant time moved more quickly in this building than anywhere else in the Valley. In a single day of work, the guards aged two. The building would decay twice as fast as it otherwise would, and the enchanted security measures needed twice the maintenance. But that was all deemed worth keeping Lutador's prize treasures in pristine condition.

After a moment of silence, the Spriggan spun the lock on the vault door, then drew the thick slab of it outward.

Mandip immediately looked for a cage-like object within—that was what Hintosep had said they were after—but he saw nothing that fit such a description.

Inside, red banners with depictions of the gods rose up and up—the ceiling itself was at least twenty feet high and narrowed at the top, giving the room a yawing funnel of a feeling. The same spider-like sconces he'd noted earlier lined the walls about two-thirds of the way up. The funerary robes hung on a polished wooden stand with the sleeves spread wide so that every detail could be admired, and the top-down lighting gave them a mystical aura. They were made of yellow silk harvested from wild golden orb spiders that lived in Asgar-Skan. The First Grand Marquis's body would wear them while he was put on display at the palace coterie for five days and five nights. Nearby were jeweled censers, a red mourning hood for the Second Grand Marquis to wear for the same week-long duration, and an overly large hourglass that jointly housed the sand of Lutador's first-ever Grand Marquises—twinned in death as they were in life—along with several other flashy items of gold and silver meant to inspire a sense of grandiosity.

No cage.

A small chill slithered down his spine as he considered for the first time that Hintosep might have lied about what she meant to steal.

The attending Spriggans all marched inside, and Hintosep brushed past Mandip to follow.

Hand still on his watch, he held his breath and subtly flexed his forearm, feeling the enchanted metal grow hot underneath his skin. He felt the jolt of the golems coming awake as Hintosep stepped over the vault's threshold, triggering the protective enchantment.

Twisting the air in his fist, he grabbed hold of the enchantment's invisible reins tied to his person.

Only someone entering a vault in Spriggan armor could leave the vault alive. Trapped within the wood and glass of the golem was a warrior's skill—a recorded pattern of offense and attack. The golems weren't conscious and contained no echoes. Every move was preordained, a pattern recorded into the wood and released via a flood of time. The golems were made to perform only one task: seek and destroy.

His control was meant to be a safeguard. But it was a weak point. One Hintosep had easily figured out how to exploit.

Except, when he'd taken hold of the golems' reins, only *one* heeded him. The four extra jerked and jostled, no matter how hard he willed them to be still.

The pieces of the hulking forms scraped together as they came alive, sounding more like rocks grinding than glass clanking.

And their shifting did not go unnoticed. The tension outside the vault rose suddenly. Intensely. One of the nobles shrieked, and the entire group moved back—but they were hemmed in by the mirrors.

Mandip looked to Juliet in horror, shaking his head, trying to tell her with his eyes that he couldn't stop them, he couldn't keep them from doing what they were made to do: enter the vault and kill the invader.

Hintosep might have been invisible to human senses, but she could not hide herself from the magic.

The Spriggans outside the vault tried to decipher who'd stepped out of line, who'd activated the golems, but whoever had control did not try to bridle the glass sentries. They herded the nobles away from the statues—whose boulder-like fists came up and swung open.

Juliet bit her lip, her eyes darting, clearly looking for a way to reclaim control, while Adhar tried to do the gentlemanly thing and guide her away.

Someone else grabbed for Mandip, tried to tug him aside, but he tugged back and simply succeeded in being tipped to the floor as feet scrambled around him.

Mandip's heart raced; his breath came painfully fast. How was this all falling apart? Juliet had made it seem so clean, so simple, and yet—

The four golems turned toward the vault door, their thick legs taking bone-rattling steps toward it.

Just as one of the Spriggans inside the vault came to see what the commotion was—funerary cloak in hand—Mandip did the only thing he could think to do. He let his golem *go*.

The golem roared fully to life, its milky-blue body shimmering in the dim light, like oil-slicked water.

It took a step forward, the bulk of it jerking like a clockwork. Close as it was to the open vault, it slid its hulking form into the open doorway, slamming into the Spriggan with the funerary cloak—who went sprawling. The Spriggan's armor cracked, a flash like a spike of sunlight hurtling up out of the wound. It targeted the attacker, as designed, but the golem wasn't flesh and blood; time could not touch it the same. It did not disintegrate. An enchantment aging centuries in a moment meant little.

Unfortunately, the cloak did not fare so well. Its strings broke, frayed, and unraveled, until there was nothing left.

Once the golem's bulk completely filled the vault door, Mandip pulled it to a halt, willing it to go dormant again. Just in time for its fellows to reach it—to try to move *through* it. Again and again, the brainless forms bumped and battered themselves against each other, but their glass was made of sterner stuff than the armor. It was the same as varger bottles and time vials. It could not be broken through blunt force.

Mandip, at the very least, had successfully created a roadblock. A stopper. A wall to keep Hintosep safe.

⊰•⟡•⊱

"I did what I had to in order to protect everyone from those rampaging monstrosities," Mandip told the commander. "I don't know who was in charge of their reins, but whoever it was was *too slow* to respond. *They* are responsible for whatever was lost today."

"That doesn't explain why your guest threw herself into the minefield."

"I don't understand why you're so fixated on that. Of all the—"

"Because it *makes no sense*," the commander hissed.

"Maybe she was scared," he offered.

Once the chaos had been tempered, the nobles evacuated, the golems subdued, and the accoutrements—those unmolested—obtained, only then, back in the lobby, had Mandip realized Hintosep had not made it out of the mirror maze with them.

He wasn't even sure at this point if she'd made it out of the vault.

For all he knew, she was trapped inside, with time now paused again. Stuck in a moment.

Just like Juliet.

He wished he could give Commander Anthousa a better explanation, but he couldn't fathom it himself: why Juliet had done what she'd done.

She'd run. Simply taken off. Even after the fiasco with the golems, Mandip was sure, now, that her strange attempt at escape was why he had ended up sitting here in glass manacles. It was the only thing that had happened here today that, on the whole of it, could hardly be interpreted as anything but suspicious.

She'd darted from the lobby, and the Spriggans had darted after, followed by the curious nobles who'd made it as far as the lobby windows but daren't step out of line themselves.

Mandip had watched, in horror, as she fled the path, leading the Spriggans on a not-so-merry chase into the minefield.

Like the vault, the mines siphoned time away once triggered. When she'd stepped on one, she'd been trapped in a bubble, drawn unnaturally to a halt. Not only did her body snag on something invisible, but the wind stopped whipping at her clothes, leaving seemingly sculpted ripples in the fabric. Her hair and glass jewelry streamed out behind her, frozen and preposterous. She'd looked like an elaborate life-size doll, positioned at the whims of a fanciful child.

Spriggans had rushed at her from several directions, bobbing and weaving through the grass as they followed routes they knew to be safe.

As they'd approached her, stepping into the extra time sloughing away from her position, they began to move strangely—extraordinarily quickly. The group had been too close in the vaults for Mandip to observe the effects of the time displacement there—being caught in it himself—but here it was on full display.

The discordance in the Spriggans' movements compared to Juliet's had created a conflict between Mandip's eyes and mind—a dissonance that made him blink rapidly and eventually look away. The inharmony was disturbing in a way he'd never experienced before. He'd turned from the scene just as the first guard reached her, pushing into that frozen moment and stalling in time themself.

All the sentries had had to do was align themselves properly and wait for the enchantment to give out. To Juliet, it would seem as though they'd appeared next to her out of thin air, apprehending her before she'd even had a chance to note she was being chased.

Now Mandip was at a loss, and his insides roiled with worry. He didn't know where Hintosep was, and once Juliet thawed from her time-freeze, she would be arrested and imprisoned.

"A woman like that? La Maupin, *scared*?" The commander shook her head, not buying it. "It makes no sense," she muttered again.

Mandip held out his hands imploringly, giving her a slight shrug. "That's just Juliet for you."

43

MANDIP

It was clear Commander Anthousa was wholly unimpressed by his testimony. He had no doubt his time as Key was over. They would sever him from his enchantments, just as he'd feared when he thought he'd lost the watch.

As promised, when she was done questioning him, Adhar was allowed to see him. His brother came rushing in, looking him over as though he'd feared Mandip would be missing limbs already. At this point, it was obvious, at least to his twin, that he was the Key.

"They told me they have to keep you in the Treasury jail until they can cross examine La Maupin," Adhar told him. "Gods damn it, Mandip, what has she got you wrapped up in?"

"I'm—I'm not *wrapped up*—"

"At least tell me you haven't done something rash like gone and proposed to her already."

Mandip furrowed his brow. "What, no, I—"

With a grunt of frustration, Adhar began to pace—rather reminiscent of how the commander had paced, actually. "I wanted to tell you yesterday, when you came home. But she was there, and I . . . And now you may or may not still be *imprisoned* when I leave, so I best tell you now or it'll be a shock."

"What are you talking about?" He reached out to try and stop his brother's pacing. "Look at me. Adhar?"

Shaking his head, clearly irritated and upset, Adhar paused, faced him. "I've been ordered to deploy with a Borderswatch unit."

"What? When?"

Adhar looked at him with an openly fearful gaze. "The Second Grand Marquis won't declare war until the official mourning period is over," he said gruffly. "But then . . ."

War. *War* was on the horizon.

Mandip could hardly envision it. War was a terrible artifact of days gone by, something epic and unreal. War happened *then*; it didn't happen *now*. A thing he'd only ever encountered in abstract terms. The idea that huge swaths of people would march across the land just to kill a stranger whose hand they would have gladly shaken on any other day seemed absurd.

And the idea that his brother—that Adhar would be one of those people marching, that he might take a stranger's life just as swiftly as a stranger would take his—Mandip didn't want to think on it. To even consider it.

The foundation of their lives had been shaken, and the stately task of retrieving the funerary paraphernalia only served to drive the matter home.

Mandip's brow furrowed. "But the election? We need a pair of Grand Marquises. Why would you be sent away when everyone knows we'll be nominated?"

Adhar's gaze shifted. "If he declares a state of emergency, he can put off the elections for a year."

Given their conversation only a few days earlier, about Adhar's private ambitions, Mandip had to ask, but he did so carefully. "Do you *want* to go?"

"If you'd asked me before the assassination, I would have said yes. But now it's . . . it's . . ."

"Real."

"Yes."

Real.

Adhar would be sent off to war. And Mandip . . .

Gods, what would happen to him now?

How had this gone so sideways?

The commander returned to the lobby. "Milor Basu? Adhar. Your carriage is here."

Adhar drew himself up to his full height, the remnants of fear flaking away from him. "Thank you." He set a hand in Mandip's hair, then let it slide to his cheek. "I'll talk to the Chief Magistrate. To Ma and Baba. I'm sure they can clean this up."

"But not before you . . ."

"I don't know," he said sadly.

Mandip watched his brother go with a hollowness in his chest—a nauseous kind of void. As Commander Anthousa led Adhar away, he found himself wanting to call out, to beg him to come back, to beg for a hug, some larger, less formal show of affection.

If Adhar was sent away and the position of Key was taken from him, what did Mandip have left?

He nearly leapt off the bench when a disembodied voice next to him said, "I'll admit that was quick thinking. Blocking the door. But you could have at least maintained your composure. How do you expect to head inter-city-state espionage when you can't even remain at ease during one little heist?"

"Saints and swill," he said, grasping at his chest, looking around to make sure no Spriggans had noted his odd behavior.

Hintosep was very near, and he could hear her voice perfectly clearly, but she was imperceivable otherwise. "You got out."

"I did."

"Juliet's been detained."

"Don't worry about her," she said dismissively. "She can handle a night or two in the Spriggans' care."

"You're just going to leave her?"

"For now. It would raise far too many eyebrows if I retrieved her. Regardless of my abilities, I can't go around hiding every inconvenient memory. Sometimes, it's easier to let Nature take his course."

"Nature take his course?" he asked incredulously. "She'll be locked away! As will I, I might add."

"For a handful of hours more, perhaps, before they realize all they have on their hands is a silly celebrity who mistakenly thought her glamour and fame meant she could walk through a minefield unscathed just because she felt like it. Juliet knows what she's doing. It's not like she's never been arrested before."

"It was a ruse, wasn't it? She was a distraction."

"Yes. I am the secrecy and she is the spectacle; you must have realized that's how we operate by now." She suddenly revealed herself—only to him, he was sure—and gestured at the center mandala on the lobby floor. "There's an emergency tunnel in each of the repository vaults, to prevent any one of the Spriggans becoming accidentally trapped inside. The door to each can only be opened from the inside, and only when the primary vault door is closed. And they all lead *there*, to a disguised hatch. Alarms automatically trigger if the hatch is opened. We needed a reason for the alarms to go off that had nothing to do with me. Seeing as how I can shield myself, I was able to open the hatch and close it again without anyone being the wiser. If I'd been sans decoy, however, they might have taken a closer look at the hatch or at the remaining contents of the recently opened vault."

"How did she know when to run into the minefield?"

Hintosep stuck out her tongue. Resting on the tip of it was a small sphere of glass: a reverb bead, just like the Regulators used. "Those ear cuffs of hers are for more than glamor," she said, tucking the bead back into her cheek.

"Did you at least get what you were after?" he asked.

"Indeed," she said, pulling a blue bundle bigger than Mandip's head from beneath her cloak. She set it on the bench between them. "It's not leaving my side until I can deliver it."

He eyed the bundle carefully, trying to discern from the bumps and valleys in the fabric what might lie beneath. "Can I see it?"

She folded back the layers of blue until the object lay bare. He was surprised to see one of the spider-like sconces that had been present nearly every which way he'd looked in the Treasury. But this one was special?

"All that for a *light fixture?*"

She regarded him sharply, and he withered under her stare. "You play dumb quite often. I'm not sure it suits you."

He took a deep breath. "Fine. This is the Cage?"

"Yes. A rather wicked contraption made to bend the wearer to its controller's will. It takes away the ability to choose even the smallest action for one's self. When to eat, when to speak. Even when to blink."

"That's horrible."

"It is," she agreed. "Which is why I hid it here in the first place and had all the sconces made to match. Easy camouflage." She immediately wrapped it up again and stood. "I thank you for your aid, Lord Basu," she said gruffly.

Despite her thanks, he felt trivial—strangely useless. "Adhar was always going to be the Second," he grumbled.

"What was that?"

"You mentioned inter-city-state espionage. I wouldn't be involved, anyway. Adhar's the one that thrives on foreign affairs. I'm to oversee the domestic. Or I *was*. Surely, they'll find me not at fault here, won't they?" He set his jaw. "Anyway, doesn't matter. They're sending Adhar away, you know. He'll be on the front lines because of you."

"Because of the Savior," she corrected.

"Hmm," he acknowledged with a half-hearted nod.

He could feel Hintosep sizing him up, trying to decide if he was still useful or if it was time to cut loose her noble-shaped baggage. "I think it's time to set you back into your life as you know it."

She reached out her hand, and Mandip knew what was coming. He'd be made to forget all this. She wouldn't even necessarily need to replace it with anything. The people around him could easily convince him that the haze in his mind was caused by drug, or drink, or hormones—the stress of having flighty Juliet fly in and abruptly out of his life. If he forgot what he now knew about the Thalo, he'd have no reason to contradict them.

He jerked away from her hand, spinning off the bench, putting what distance between them he could without drawing a guard's attention. "Wait. Please. I can still be of help. Take me with you. I want to go with you."

Clearly, she believed him, but that might not matter. Her schemes were her own. "You're meant to be the next First Grand Marquis," she said reasonably. "That is the role the Savior has picked for you. His framed assassin disappearing is just a happy outcome; no need to question the circumstances. But if you or Adhar were to vanish? You are one man, and things happen, so perhaps it would mean nothing to Him, or perhaps He'd start to see a pattern."

She kept coming for him, menacing forward, and he shuffled away, staying out of arm's reach. "You've been right about me," he said. "I've been naïve and sheltered, but I do truly care about Lutador. Service requires sacrifice. If you take my memory, I've sacrificed nothing, not really. Let me come with you, if only for a time. The elections might not be for a year, and I want to *do* something. In the long run, I'll be a better Grand Marquis if I *still remember*." She paused, and he saw his opening. "Then you'll have an ally in the office. One who knows of the Savior's manipulations. We can still help each other."

"You make a clean argument," she said. "But how will your renewed disappearance be explained?"

He shrugged. "It was easy enough to blame Juliet the first time. Who would second-guess a man in love?"

44

KRONA

Krona woke up that first morning at the safe house with Thibaut curled into her side and his head on her stomach. He'd wriggled like a snake in his sleep, tossing and turning, curling and uncurling, all the while clearly sleeping well instead of fitfully. Instead of irritating, she found it endearing, and as she came fully awake, with morning light streaming through the small window, she absently ran her fingers through his hair.

She pretended for a moment that everything was right in the world. That no one had been assassinated. That De-Lia was still alive. That she went about her days content and focused, coming home at the end of work to find Thibaut waiting for her.

The fantasy was both impossible and inappropriate, but no one needed to know about it.

When Thibaut's breathing changed, she pulled her hand away. He sniffled and raised his head, blinking sleepily at her. "Is this a dream?" he asked, groggy.

"You tell me," she said, pulling him in for a gentle good-morning kiss, which he returned with a pleasant hum. When he tried to deepen it—presumably in order to tantalize her into a second rendition of last night's showing—she playfully pushed him away.

He rolled over and, clearly having forgotten how narrow the bed was, promptly fell heavily onto the floor, dragging the blankets with him.

She certainly hadn't meant for that to happen, but she snickered at the sight of him flailing nonetheless.

"Watch that first step," he warned, fighting his way out of the tangle of sheets.

A sharp knock at the door startled them both. "Everything all right in there?" came a stranger's voice.

Krona had forgotten about the mansion full of other people. "Yes, fine, thanks."

"There's breakfast downstairs if you're so inclined," the voice called back.

"Thank you!" Thibaut answered in his best now-go-away-please voice.

They both dressed quickly, helping to straighten each other's garments when they were finished but making no mention of their sleeping arrangements from the night before—which was just fine for Krona. She didn't want to have to define exactly what they were to each other just yet.

"Will you help me with De-Lia's mask? Like you did with Charbon?"

"If I recall correctly, your sister didn't like me much."

"Facing her can't be any worse than facing a killer."

"Clearly, you've never had in-laws before." The joke hit off-kilter, the layers of implication behind it unintentional. He cleared his throat and quickly added, "Of course I'll help you."

⊱•◦◦◦•⊰

The next few days were a whirlwind of new faces and deep dives into her and her sister's shared past.

Krona got to know the other people in the mansion and the tales of how Hintosep had brought them here. There was Master Clive, a blacksmith whose wife—a tax taker—had mysteriously disappeared. They found her body three weeks later in the river. "Undertaker said she went for a swim and drowned. But she was deathly afraid of the river. Had never gone near the thing. Kept digging until I got too close to the truth—one of her tax sessions had gone awry. Must have glimpsed something she shouldn't have. Hintosep got to me before I wound up in the river too."

An actuary had glimpsed records being removed from a Xyoparian municipal office, and a lesser noble from Winsrouen had somehow failed to have his memories taken after Thalo had interfered during an important political discussion. A pair of bakers—Anita and Samia—proudly declared themselves the village kooks. "We saw the Thalo sabotage supplies meant for the iron mines," Anita explained. "No one believed us."

"We'd been telling people about the mind-control drugs the government has been putting in our wells for *years*," Samia said indignantly, "and no one believed us about that, either. They only see what they want to see."

After she spoke to them, Sebastian gently pulled Krona aside. "There are no mind-control drugs," he clarified. "The two of them are blatant conspiracy theorists. They aren't bad people, but I wouldn't go to them if you're looking for facts."

"And yet they were right about the Thalo sabotage, weren't they?"

"It's the cleverest weapon in the Thalo arsenal, I think," he said. "It's not their magic that makes them truly dangerous; it's how they twist us in on ourselves. They take people whose opinions we already dismiss and tell them the truth. They make reality unreal by letting it fall from the lips of the unreliable."

The unreliable. Like men who claimed to murder at the behest of their god.

Like a Regulator assassin working for Winsrouen.

There were at least a few professionally trained warriors as well. A set of three Borderswatchpersons, all from the same Marrakevian outpost, an exhibition boxer from Asgar-Skan, and a former bouncer who'd done a fair bit of hand-to-hand fighting for a living; she had not one but *three* enchanter's-mark scars.

The group trained every day out in the forest, taking a plethora of weaponry, from bows to axes to enchantments, and everyone participated, no matter their background. Krona watched them from afar and was easily convinced that she was indeed looking at the bedrock of a guerilla force.

Her daily routine at the safe house was very different from the rest of the residents. Every afternoon, Krona put on De-Lia's mask and didn't come up to clear her mind until well after sundown. Thibaut was there the whole time, jotting down anything of note she said, anything she wouldn't be able to remember once the echo left her. She'd been asked to indulge in her obsession, been given a reason to spend hour after hour losing herself in her sister's memories. And it felt so *right* when she was there. It was like being sound asleep and enwrapped in a pleasant dream, while wakefulness only brought sadness and worry.

It could have easily become a trap—a world Krona sank into and never left. But Thibaut always drew her back out again, with a gentle voice and light touches and a soothing presence.

Krona had to walk the fine line between letting De-Lia run rampant and having full control over the echo. She was used to letting De-Lia's echo wander through whatever memories it wanted, but now Krona needed to search for something specific. She had to know what De-Lia had done in the days leading up to her discovery of Monkeyflower.

Trying to lock the echo away in order to control it had never really worked for Krona and wouldn't work now. She had to approach it differently, like someone offering a hand instead of a leash.

"*Hello, De-Lia,*" she silently greeted each time she settled beneath the jaguar.

Her sister's echo came on strong, as it always did. Instead of sinking herself away, letting it play in her mind however it would, Krona held herself firm and conscious. She shoved back with a firm *no* when the echo attempted to alight in certain parts of her brain. She kept it from wandering into private corners and sneaking into her limbic system to appeal to her emotions.

She thought of how she'd soothed De-Lia during her sleepwalking. How she'd been able to guide her back to bed.

Shhh, De-Lia. Quiet. Sleep. Please sleep. Come on, it's bedtime.

De-Lia's echo seemed to take heed of that. There was a sort of curious tilt in Krona's mind, like her sister had gently turned an ear in her direction to hear more.

When the sisters were little, there'd been a hymn their parents had sung to them. Maman and Papa had harmonized so well, and when he'd died . . . the song had died too.

Krona used it, whispering it in her head, humming it just for the echo, imagining the harmonies, imagining her voice was *their voices*, imagining the memory into life.

> *Time tumbles down, but She never trips*
> *She passes us all, dear, through our mind slips*
> *Slips . . .*
> *Slips . . .*
> *Slips . . .*

> *What would we be, without her hand?*
> *Bones before birth, dust before death*
> *Wed before maidens, memory before sand*

> *Rise before sleep, dusk before noon*
> *Exist before our parents*
> *And enter the world too soon*

> *Time tumbles down, but She never trips*
> *She passes us all, dear, through our mind slips*
> *Slips . . .*
> *Slips . . .*
> *Slips . . .*

Slip De-Lia did. Not away, but into a more placid state, as though sleepy.

In this state, Krona was able to search De-Lia's memories, looking for anything unusual.

Carefully, she bypassed memories of Monkeyflower herself, unwilling to confront that specter even in memory. Instead, she shuffled back. Back. Before the cave and the sparkle of gold that had drawn De-Lia to the creature.

And that's how she found the ritual.

Eerie, bloody.

Incomprehensible.

⊱──◆──◇──◆──◇──⊰

A memory from childhood is a hazy, painted thing. Impressionistic rather than realistic. Everything is large and loud. Shadows are deeper and somehow have lives of their own. Light is in everything and everywhere until it is gone—never seeping slowly, but whisked away suddenly by the tilt of day to night.

It is out of such eyes that Krona peered, tucked in one of little De-Lia's recollections.

Evening had fallen, and the darkness was like a blanket, save for its chill. A candlelight in a cloister window drew her attention and then her feet, her tiny, bare toes tickling through soft grass as she approached the white-stoned building.

Through the pane of warped glass I saw three people, came De-Lia's voice, the echo narrating its own memory. *Nature's priest stood in the center of what I was sure was a circle of salt, what with the particular way the candlelight caught in the granular crystals. Their sibling, Time's priest, strode around the circle, painting shapes on the floor with a wide brush dipped in tar-black stain.*

The third person was a priest of the Unknown—shrouded completely in dark purple, from head to toe. They were chanting, deep in their throat. It was a reverberating, breathy sort of invocation—both ominous and heart-lifting. Devastating and exciting.

I found myself echoing the tones, as though pulled into a trance.

De-Lia was still so small, standing on tiptoe to observe the eerie scene.

Nature's priest wore a metal crown with a coppery sheen. When Time's priest had finished marking the floor, they turned to Nature's and swiped the brush over their robes, creating a large symbol Krona had never seen before. An inverted five-pointed figure, reminiscent of both a pentagram and a person, surrounded by a circle made of circles and interlocking triangles, the symbols each evoking a compass rose.

Krona dug deep into De-Lia, pushing at her, trying to get her to reveal if she'd ever seen the symbol before or again.

De-Lia had searched for it, in the Hall of Records, but to no avail.

Next, Time's priest brought their twin the bowl of paint, and Nature's dipped both palms in. Their hands came up oily and putrid-looking, and they placed palmprints on either side of their neck, one on their forehead, and one on their chin.

As fascinated as young De-Lia was, none of this seemed shocking to her. It was interesting and clearly secret, and she'd felt extremely clever for having stumbled—quite by accident—upon the scene. But nothing felt forbidden or truly foreign until the priest of the Unknown—one of those *always* shrouded—pulled back their hood, revealing a face that was, most peculiarly, *blue.*

Krona found herself thankful that, at the very least, it wasn't Hintosep beneath the hood.

And now De-Lia's echo bucked, strained—tried to turn the memory, to seep into another day, another time. Krona could tell it wanted to avoid what came next—something that had disturbed her in the moment, as a child.

The echo began to chant, *Not the blood. Not the blood.*

Krona did her best to soothe her, to cradle the echo, to remind it that it was right here, with her, that this was all in the past.

People think too much of blood, the echo said, voice a pained whine. *That somehow the properties of blood make us different, that someone's blood can hold them above someone of another blood. But blood is what binds us. What makes us the same. We all need it. We can all lose it. There is no better blood, no worse blood. If one must define what is "good blood" and what is "bad blood," let it be by this: blood is good when it is on the inside.*

Blood is bad when it is on the outside.

The blood—

Krona cooed and shushed her. "This is important," she insisted. "Please, I need to know what you saw. Please. Please." She couldn't tell the echo it was important because Krona was trying to save her—save De-Lia.

After all, the echo didn't know it was dead.

But it responded to Krona's "Please." It stopped twisting, stopped trying to stretch itself thin and slip away.

In the memory, the blue-lined priest of the Unknown drew a knife from beneath the folds of their burqa and approached Nature's priest. Carefully, they drew the blade's tip through the paint smears on Nature's priest's hands, creating red, weeping lines. Deep enough to drip but shallow enough to heal.

The bloodied priest walked the salt lines, leaving the minerals red and caked in their wake.

Krona was enwrapped, trying to decipher what she was seeing, trying to line up the strange ritual with what she knew now about magic's true properties.

But then child-De-Lia's attention snapped away from the salt. She locked eyes with Time's priest.

She'd been spotted.

Krona could not blame her for running.

Terrified, the little girl slipped on stones, then grass, fleeing as though her life depended on it.

Running.

I'm running now. I was running then. I'm running always.

Running as the cloister door opened and light spilled into the courtyard. Running as sharp cries chased me to the lime-washed coterie walls. Running as heavy footfalls fell quicker and faster than mine, swiftly closing in from behind.

Running even as something cold and invisible wound its way around my shoulders.

And still, I refused to stop.

So close to home and yet so far.

As those icy fingers took hold of me, I wondered if the gods were angry with me. I'd trodden somewhere I wasn't allowed to tread and seen something I wasn't supposed to see. And now my punishment: a cold, quick end.

Still, I struggled. Still, I pushed forward.

Still, I tried to make sense of the ritual I'd seen.

This is it, Krona thought, hurting for her sister, wishing she hadn't been forced into . . . whatever this was. This unnatural ritual that had called her varg and ultimately killed their father.

De-Lia was pulled against a chest she could not see. There was nothing around her, nothing near her—or so her eyes proclaimed. Krona knew better; she understood. A great hiss of a voice whispered in De-Lia's ear, "I want you to remember this. I *should* take it from you. But I'm curious to see what such an inquisitive child might do."

The icy fingers and cold form retreated.

The memory began to fade.

"Wait, that can't be all there is," Krona protested. She'd thought she'd found it, the memory that would help her find the varg, the ritual that had called the creature. But if that was all . . .

But the echo wasn't trying to retreat again. It slipped into the next memory, one deeply entwined with the first.

And, for a moment, Krona was horrified.

De-Lia hadn't been sucked into a ritual.

She'd recreated it, all by herself.

For days after, the little girl could not sleep. She'd made it home without being followed, but still, she waited for repercussions. For a punishment.

When none came, her worry returned to curiosity.

The whole event sat sour with me. Something about it was so wrong, but I thought perhaps if I could reenact it, I could make the sourness go away, because then I'd see how it was all reasonable and good and not as blasphemous as it felt at all.

It was a child's logic.

We mimicked adults, the good and the bad, trying to understand.

I wasn't sure how to go about my reenactment until Papa brought home salt from

Marrakev. Special salt, he said, mined from the salterns on Lake Konets. It was an expensive gift for Maman, but I didn't realize that. All I heard was special, and I knew I needed something special for the ritual I was to perform.

As soon as she had the salt, she gathered the other things she needed—a knife, the ink, the candles—and found a place to draw her runes: the old, dilapidated barn on Tray's family farm. She chose to perform the ritual in the middle of the day, too afraid to work it in the dark.

I wanted to share it with you, Krona.

A small jolt of shock went through Krona. Did the echo truly understand who she was speaking to? That Krona was there with her? No, that seemed too much of a stretch—beyond the awareness she could sense. Charbon's echo had understood what it was, but if De-Lia's echo had any consciousness, it was only a fraction of whatever that had been.

I did, truly, the echo went on, *but I was embarrassed, afraid, and greedy all at once. It was my strange discovery, my burden, and my pride. It was the first real secret I kept from you.*

It was the beginning of the end, in that regard. Ever after, each secret was worse—another wound in our relationship. Another wedge that drove us further apart, no matter how firmly we tried to stick ourselves together.

I'm sorry, Krona. I'm so sorry.

Little De-Lia cut everything with that single blade: the wax seal on the salt container; the barn's floorboards, into which she'd etched the runes before applying ink; her palms, from which she drew fresh blood, letting it well up and drop on the salt circle.

The whole while, she chanted. The rhythm and key had been playing over and over in her mind since the incident, and she knew she had not missed a word or soured a note. When she was finished with the staging, she walked the circle, over and over, chanting louder and louder.

Feeling sillier and sillier as she progressed.

But then, Krona felt it just as De-Lia had felt it: a shock through her entire body, her soul. A yanking snag, like she was caught on a fishing hook.

De-Lia *screamed.*

And Krona screamed back.

45

THALO CHILD

When his Possessor led him and Thalo Infant to Gerome's own quarters, Thalo Child knew the time had come. Even before Gerome warned him, "She's here," he knew what the day's meeting held in store.

They paused outside the door. "Give the infant to me," Gerome instructed.

Thalo Child hesitated, but all it took was a simple eyebrow raise—just visible beneath the headdress he wore—for him to comply. Zhe was old enough that zhe'd toddled zhur way there on zhur own two feet, holding Thalo Child's hand. Slowly, he passed zhur little hand off to Gerome, who swooped over Thalo Infant, raising zhim into his arms.

"Good," Gerome said. "Come."

Gerome's rooms were tight and sparse. A place for sleeping and little else. A narrow closet of black stone held his robes, and a simple table to match held a metal stand that branched like a tree. Atop each branch was one of Gerome's many headdresses, all of his veils and half-helms and crowns, each with its own beauty, each with its own sinister aura. His bed was more like a coffin, what with its high sides and stone covering that extended out just over his pillow.

The space was claustrophobic, the walls sharply angled, and the floor split into narrow sections. The ceiling was high, stretching up and up in a way that only served to make the walls feel like they were drawing nearer—closing in.

In one darkened corner sat the jaguar bottle, the varg inside vibrating with anticipation. In another stood Hintosep, exuding eagerness just the same.

"Show it to me," Gerome demanded without greeting.

"You do not want this back in the keep," she said as she held out a bundle, a final plea. "I lost so many children to it. So many potential Thalo simply went mad instead of—"

"What happens to the children hasn't concerned you for many years," Gerome snapped. He clutched Thalo Infant all the tighter. "Put it on the table. Unwrap it. I need to verify you've brought me the real thing."

With a reluctant sigh, she unwound the bundle. The thing she placed looked more like a giant, dead insect than a cage. A thick, curving "spine" would have been the body, and many eerie, jointed legs sprang from it—too many to be a spider, too few to be a centipede.

It reminded Thalo Child of the chair they strapped Sacrifices into in order to drain them of all their time.

Gerome picked it up swiftly, snatching it from the table like it might disappear—was only an illusion. He turned it over and over in his grasp. Thalo Infant reached for it, curious, and he yanked it out of zhur reach. "No," he snapped, making tears well in the toddler's eyes.

Seemingly satisfied, he set it down again, letting the back of it lay against the stone, the "legs" of it upturned and curled, just like a dead spider. At the end of each tip was a small set of pincers, clearly made to dig in and hold strong.

Thalo Child looked at Gerome's face more closely than he'd allowed himself in near a decade. He took in the scars above his lips, on his cheeks and temples, and was easily able to match them to legs on the contraption.

The Cage surrounded and burrowed into the wearer.

Gerome caressed the joints of one leg, his eyes rolling back and fluttering closed in an uncomfortable display of ecstasy.

"Would you like me to help you put it on?" Hintosep asked, voice warm, tone innocent.

"You'd like that, wouldn't you?" he sneered. "Me, under your complete control once again."

"You can't both wear it and command it," she said gently. "It needs a Possessor to wield it."

"This is the greatest teaching tool ever devised, by gods or otherwise. I don't intend to wear it; I intend to use it."

Hintosep didn't seem shaken, but Thalo Child feared she'd miscalculated. Her face fell, just slightly. It might have been imperceptible on anyone else, but on Hintosep, who remained stoic in the face of so much, it worried Thalo Child to his bones.

"This is why you agreed, isn't it?" Gerome asked, clearly reveling in his turnabout. "You thought you'd lock me away in a prison of my own choosing, and then what?" He searched her eyes, genuinely looking for an explanation, wanting to know why he'd been cut off from her—her guidance, her plans. Why she'd clearly intended to put him in the Cage and *leave him there.*

When she didn't answer, his face contorted. Pure rage, the likes of which Thalo Child had never seen on him, blasted forth as Gerome yelled, *"And then what?"*

Hintosep did not back down. Thalo Child thought anyone should have rightfully recoiled—*he* had—as spittle and ire both erupted from Gerome, spewing the potential for violence into the air, making the tension in the room thick with yet-to-be-unleashed blows.

Poor little Thalo Infant was leaning away from him, pushing at his shoulder, terrified.

"You have what you wanted," she said, voice even. "Now give me the children."

Gerome hiked Thalo Infant higher on his hip, turning away from her. "I don't see why the infant should go with you. Zhe belongs here. You're already robbing one Thalo Child of his rightful path and name; why should I let you rip that from another?"

"We had a deal: the Cage, for your silence, the varg, the boy, *and* the infant."

"Getting quite a lot, aren't you? Hardly a fair deal."

"You thought it was fair enough when we made it."

"Take the boy and the varg. The infant stays with me."

"Then I'm taking the Cage," she said defiantly, rushing to grab it.

His hand descended like a claw on top of hers. "Then I'll go to the Savior. Which do you need more, the baby or my discretion?"

There was no frustration evident in the lines of her body, but Thalo Child was sure her feelings had to mirror his own. He clenched his jaw and thinned his lips and rolled his neck. Every minute look that passed between the two full Thalo put a cold pit in his stomach.

Hintosep considered her options for only a moment.

"Fine," she conceded, ripping her hand out from under his.

No.

That cold pit became a void. A whirlpool, draining away all of Thalo Child's hope.

He wanted her to fight for them. She'd gone through all this trouble to bring Gerome the Cage; he should have to *pay* properly. She was *Hintosep*—she could *make* him. She was Hintosep; she could do anything.

Anything.

Couldn't she?

He'd thought of her as all-powerful, but if she couldn't even save a toddler from inevitable cruelty, what good was she?

"Thalo Child," she said, "come to me."

She held out her hand, and he backed away. "No."

"No?"

"I wish to stay."

Gerome hadn't ordered him to do it. He hadn't so much as suggested it, let alone asked for it. But Thalo Child had understood since the moment he saw the katar in that cottage what was expected of him. To go with Hintosep was to *betray* Gerome—his Possessor had made that clear. If Thalo Child went with her, Gerome would be sure to exact his revenge on Thalo Infant, as promised.

He'd thought Hintosep would still rescue them in the end. That her sheer power would overcome whatever designs Gerome put on their lives.

But no. She'd barely protested.

Thalo Child knew that if he himself had any honor, any potential as a named Thalo, he would put himself between Gerome and the baby. This was the right thing to do.

Gerome's smile of approval was *wicked*. "You wouldn't *force* the boy, would you?" he asked, only barely reeling in his gloating tone.

Thalo Child tried to pretend he'd made this decision without coercion—knowing Hintosep was about to look in his mind—but a simple glance from her old eyes revealed the truth.

"You *threatened* him."

"So what if I did?" Gerome's complete candor and lack of remorse should not have surprised Thalo Child, but it did. "I showed him exactly what he and the infant have been spared by being chosen for our order."

"He's coming with me," she said definitively.

"No," Gerome said. "He made a choice. Take him and I *will* alert the Savior, so help me."

"We *had* a *deal*."

"You had a *plan*. I'm sorry it's gone so awry," he said sarcastically. "Take your varg, my silence, and let us put this behind us."

For a moment, Thalo Child felt Hintosep in his mind, a brief flash of certainty while Gerome's attention was drawn—covetously—back to the Cage.

She had planned for Gerome's duplicity, had suspected he wouldn't give her all that she wanted. *We will be back for zhim*, she assured him. *The varg is only the first step. We will return.*

Then she must return for him as well. He couldn't risk Gerome's wrath. Thalo Infant was fragile, trusting. Zhe needed a protector.

"I'm staying with my Possessor," Thalo Child asserted, though every syllable felt like rough glass in his mouth. "I wish to be everything an unnamed should be."

"Humble?" Gerome asked, his H harsh. "Obedient?" he demanded, T sharp.

"Everything," he confirmed.

"You heard the boy," Gerome gloated. "He belongs to the Eye. I expect you not to trouble him ever again."

In reward, Gerome passed the toddler to Thalo Child, who took his charge in both arms, holding zhim tight against his chest.

"You are wise beyond your years," Gerome praised.

"Yes," Hintosep agreed. "He is."

46

KRONA

Krona lay on their narrow bed, submerged in De-Lia's memories, searching for details that would explain what the dark ritual was for and why De-Lia had been able to replicate it to any effect. Thibaut's hand in hers was her only tether—the way she kept firmly ahold of the outside world. Somewhere in the distance she could hear the scratching of lead on paper as Thibaut jotted down notes with his free hand.

Krona screamed when De-Lia screamed and could feel her body thrash. So deep in the echo's memories, she couldn't tell if their screams simply rattled in her skull or had managed to escape from her lips.

Either way, Thibaut clutched her hand all the tighter.

I must have passed out, the echo said. *I came to licking the blood from my fingers, cringing at the sharp taste of salt. Tray's mother found me lapping at my hands like a small woodland creature. She should have been horrified. If she was, she didn't show it. She simply brought me a clean rag and told me never to go near the barn again.*

A year later, the structure fell over. Do you remember, Krona? So rotted out, they burned the lot of it, erasing my transgressions along with the decay.

The question was rhetorical, asked of a presence the echo didn't know was there. De-Lia's echo was a ghost to Krona and she was a ghost to it and the veil between their worlds was both opaque and gauzy thin.

Suddenly, there was a tug on Krona's arm—in the real world, the here and now of the safe house. Thibaut's hands squeezed hers like a vise, and in the distance, he called out for her to *come up, come up, mistress.*

In the finite world of the echo's memories, it was difficult to tell how much time had passed. Sometimes, it seemed like she'd been under for days, sometimes only minutes. This session had felt lightning quick.

She sat up with a gasp, as though she'd been holding her breath underwater. Her temples throbbed with the effort of being in the mask—of keeping just enough of a barrier up to prevent the echo from taking hold of her body.

Immediately, she realized Thibaut's voice hadn't been the only one calling out.

"They're back!" came a shout from outside on the landing, echoed by a farther-off "They're back!" perhaps from the great room.

Krona tried to stand, but Thibaut—still holding her hand—eased her back down and handed her a waiting glass of water. "Drink first. You'll never forgive me if you get a migraine."

She gave him a tired smile and downed the whole glass in one go.

Tying De-Lia's mask to her belt where it belonged, Krona followed Thibaut out of the room and to the landing's railing. Juliet's blond head appeared below for a brief moment, followed by Mandip's black mop, and the smile Thibaut turned on Krona was beaming.

But the joy was short-lived.

They joined a group of the others—anyone who wasn't out training—in the great room, where Hintosep was unburdening herself from the long journey with a distracted flair, tossing her gloves and her cape about as though deep in her own mind, clearly calculating, reorienting.

Juliet—still fully laden herself—gathered up the errant pieces and set them where they belonged, on hooks and mats near the door. Her expression was lax, her face missing its usual glow. She looked tired, disappointed.

Melanie and Sebastian were two of the last people to file in. They both looked around eagerly, as though expecting someone else. After a moment, Melanie's eyes began to water. "Where is zhe?"

Coming back to herself, Hintosep put both hands on Melanie's shoulder, looking her square in the eye. "We knew Gerome might renege. We anticipated this."

Sebastian's lip trembled, and his eyes grew hard. "But you said—"

"I said we would rescue your baby, and we will," she said, voice strong and commanding. "It is better to cede some ground to the enemy than alert them to your larger plans. He gave up the very tool we need to remount our efforts for the children. That is a win that I could not jeopardize in the moment. Do you understand?"

Sebastian nodded.

Hintosep looked up, found Krona in the crowd. "I'd hoped we'd have more time to get you settled, but you are my plan B. If I can't get the children out via bargain, then it'll have to be by force."

Quietly, with the dour, humble expression of some coterie novice, Juliet finished hanging up both her and Hintosep's things, and made her way through the crowd with her head hung low.

Thibaut tried to stop her with a gentle touch of the shoulder as she went by, but Mandip stopped him, shook his head.

Juliet's face pinched and she hurried on, clearly looking to escape to a place of privacy before her tears fell.

"She truly thought this was it," Mandip explained. "She was ready to have him back."

Melanie and Sebastian were surrounded by friends and loved ones offering condolences and vows of support. Krona understood their pain—she missed De-Lia terribly, would gladly do anything to get her back. Only, their suffering had to be worse; they knew their child was alive and where zhe was, and yet zhe was out of reach.

The others all seemed too intimidated to approach Hintosep. She wasn't a comrade to them; she was a leader. Or something more. What with her powers, she probably held an aura of divinity for many of the people here, but Krona was undaunted. She went to Hintosep's side, followed closely by Thibaut.

"The sooner we can get you ready," Hintosep said quietly, "get you your powers, the better." She straightened her spine and asked firmly, "Have you learned anything?"

Krona appreciated her directness. "I think so, yes."

"And?"

"And I'm still waiting on evidence that offering me hope for De-Lia wasn't just a twisted ploy."

"Fair enough." She turned to the hooks by the door, pulled a cloak from one and tossed it at Krona. "Put this on and follow me."

Krona threw it around her shoulders, and Thibaut—not waiting for an invitation—wrangled a jacket from a nearby coat stand, heedless of who it belonged to, and quickly tugged on a pair of boots. Together, they followed Hintosep, not out the front door but toward the kitchen and to the pantry, of all things.

It was enormous, of course, as far as pantries went. Plenty large enough to hold enough food for all the people that could theoretically occupy the mansion. As it was, the shelves were well stocked with preserves of all kind, rice aplenty, and dried meats.

"Step inside," Hintosep bade.

"Don't tell me this is that special entrance Melanie told us about," Thibaut said.

"Indeed it is," she confirmed.

The entire inside of the pantry was on a pulley system. It was a giant dumbwaiter, which sank into the cliffside and let them out in a room at the bottom, which opened up onto a thin supply road that skirted the river's edge. The door to the road was locked via enchantment, and only Hintosep could wield the key.

"Luckily, we didn't return from the keep completely empty-handed," Hintosep said, locking the door behind her.

Out here, the river roared, the sound a constant white noise they all had to shout over to hear one another.

"I didn't want to bring it into the house," Hintosep shouted. "Just to be safe."

They walked the supply road a short way until they came upon a shallow cave—deep enough to shelter a cache of supply crates but not deep enough for any sort of animal to attempt to make it a permanent home.

There, nestled inside—a jaguar. A huge, glimmering glass cat, with teeth and claws and eyes within.

Krona froze in her tracks—her stop so jarring, Thibaut ran into her. She was instantly transported back—not to the horrible, bloody day she'd met Monkeyflower but to the day she'd picked up and read De-Lia's accursed diary. Where she'd learned of the strange relationship De-Lia had shared with a varg. The way her sister had described the beast—the metallic glint of the needles in its hide, the way it had stalked out of the shadows—echoed how Krona saw this creature now.

She turned and tried to barrel over Thibaut to get away.

He caught her, held her.

Krona knew this wasn't *her* varg. Hintosep said she had a way of tracking down *that* creature, but Krona had never suspected—"That's Monkeyflower, isn't it?"

"That's what we need to confirm. If it is, then theoretically, I can use it to figure out where in the Valley *yours* is.

"A Thalo Orchestrator watched De-Lia play with the monster in the fields. They observed the strange bond between girl and beast, and once the trauma of your childhood had played itself out, they took Monkeyflower away for study."

Krona forced herself to glance over her shoulder. Save the shape of its prison, this bottle-barker looked like any other, and Krona was loath to get near. She may have confronted the guilt that had haunted her since childhood, but she had failed to conquer her phobia. Utkin, her healer, had tried everything in recent years, and still . . .

Still her heart beat unnaturally fast, even with yards upon yards of clear space between her and the creature—with it secure, with everyone safe.

"Give me the mask," Hintosep said. "We need to see if the creature responds to it."

Krona's hand flew to the wood at her hip, clutching the mask tight. Even now, the idea of handing it over to anyone else, even briefly, made her hackles raise.

"Give it here. You have no idea what I traded to get this varg," Hintosep said with a huff. "How I managed to get it here without the Savior knowing."

"I'll do it myself," Krona said defiantly.

"Can you?" Hintosep challenged.

Taking a deep, shaky breath—suppressing her anxiety and letting her vision tunnel so that she was far, far removed from the moment—she pushed away from Thibaut, standing unsteadily under her own willpower.

With everything inside her screaming for her to run away, she stepped toward the cave, putting one foot in front of the other.

It watched her come, vibrating in its strange cage, reminding Krona of the bottle-barker that had seeped into her throat and attempted to eat her from the inside.

She stared at the varg, and it stared back. But there was no recognition in its eyes, no indication it had any thoughts—not even thoughts of hunger or attack, let alone anything complex and human. There was nothing innate to confirm to Krona that, somehow, this beast was really a broken-off bit of her sister.

"I think you killed my papa," she whispered.

She held up De-Lia's mask, and the creature went still. Lightly, she touched the wood to the glass.

And the varg began to *glow*.

Faint enough that it would have been unnoticeable in the full light of day, but there in the dimness of the shallow cave, it made the glass glimmer and the rock shine.

The bottle-barker bunched itself up in the jaguar's head, trying to meet with the mask, trying to get into it or bond with it. This wasn't like when the vapors tried to eat someone. This was gentle. Loving. Like the varg wanted to embrace the mask.

Terrified as she was, Krona felt like crying—not out of fear but recognition. Out of love and loss and loneliness.

This *was* Monkeyflower.

And she was De-Lia.

"This is why I said I might know how to help you resurrect your sister," Hintosep said. "If we can rejoin you and your varg, then who knows what other pieces we might be able to bring together? You have her varg, her echo; you know where to find her sand."

"And her blood," Krona said, voice choked. They'd stowed the blood pen that had killed De-Lia away on Vault Hill, still blood-encrusted. That was likely where the journal had been taken, after the raid on her apartment. "I know where I can get her blood. And her words."

"The more you can gather, the better. But we need to take this one step at a time. We've wandered into a realm of magic that's only theoretical at this point. You'll need to be patient. You'll need to do as I say. Agreed?"

Krona took a steadying breath. "Agreed."

"How . . . how are they the same? The bottle and the mask?" Thibaut asked.

"I can only guess that, being a part of De-Lia herself, the two of them share a resonance. Something about jaguars was appealing to her. She had an affinity or a fondness for them. Or"—she shook her head, like she was just making it all up as she went along—"maybe the incidental shape of the monster's cage created some kind of tie, and De-Lia subconsciously chose a jaguar mask for herself in response." She shrugged. "Who knows. Either way, it's only further proof in my eyes that we have the right varg and can move on to the next stage: a conjuration."

"What's that?"

"Think of it as a precursor to enchantment. Using objects with certain properties, one can channel their inborn magic in ways they cannot achieve with skill alone. We Thalo only occasionally use such things; mostly, they're more trouble than they're worth, since they require long lists of typically rare ingredients."

"I think . . . I think that's what De-Lia did before Monkeyflower appeared," Thibaut said. "She saw someone performing a ritual and recreated it." He quickly laid out a few of the specifics he'd gathered from Krona's mumblings while she'd been in the mask.

"That does sound like a conjuration. Peculiar. She shouldn't have had any magic to channel, so how was she able to cast it successfully? Unless . . ." She gestured at Krona. "Unless whatever band of Harvesters left you with a drop or two were messy with your sister as well."

"But De-Lia didn't have any resistance to Thalo magic."

"If she wasn't a Kairopath, she wouldn't. The continuum of power has its own way of balancing itself. Remember the pinwheel I drew for you? The two types of magics flanking yours are your weakness and your immunity, while the two opposite you on the wheel are your additional affinities. Immunities run clockwise, while the weaknesses run counterclockwise; secrets are vulnerable to time, time is vulnerable to nature, nature is vulnerable to knowledge, knowledge is vulnerable to emotion, and emotion is vulnerable to secrets."

"So, it's Physiopaths I need to be wary of," Krona said, half a joke.

"Yes," Hintosep answered, in all seriousness. "And I think . . . I think your sister might have been one."

"Could that be why I've had such a hard time with her echo?"

"Could be any number of factors, but that's my suspicion, yes. That and her relation to you."

"Seems unfair that Goddess Time's weakness should be her brother," Thibaut said thoughtfully, staring at the jaguar bottle. After a beat, he looked at Krona. "But it tracks. De-Lia always was your weak spot."

From her pocket Hintosep drew a syringe like those the tax takers used. "Go back to the door and wait for me," she ordered, before venturing into the cave herself.

"What are you going to do?"

"Now that we're certain we have the right varg, I need a sample for the conjuration."

"You mean you have to open the bottle?"

"Yes. I don't want you close, in case something goes wrong."

⊱•◈•⊰

"We'll do the conjuration in here, where the map is," Hintosep said when they emerged in the kitchen once again. "I need everyone out! I need the room!" she yelled, clearly knowing the command would reach all corners of the safe house without any extra effort. "But get me Melanie, Sebastian. Get me Juliet!"

The three of them made their way to the other side of the kitchen, which adjoined the long dining room just off the back of the mansion, boasting tall, fogged windows that looked out on the mountainous landscape.

The dining table itself was a transformative thing, with sections to be removed and added as needed, depending on the number of diners. What Krona hadn't realized, however, was that the table leaves were double-sided. Hintosep made quick work of rearranging the sections and flipping them over to reveal a giant, etched map of the entire Arkensyre Valley.

Hintosep went about preparing for her ritual as the others filed in. A buzz of anticipation undercut the idle chatter in the room, and though everyone gave Hintosep room to work, they each strained to note every move she made.

She took a knife from her belt and a clean dishcloth from the kitchen, and handed both to Krona. "I need your blood," she said frankly. "From where is up to you."

Thibaut gave Krona subtle side-eye as she rolled up her sleeve.

Blood magic, blood magic—Charbon was obsessed with blood magic.

She raised an eyebrow at him and shook her head before drawing the blade across the back of her forearm, letting him know she understood his concern, but also as if to say, *So, what am I supposed to do about it?* She could refuse, but then what?

She dabbed up the blood with the dishcloth, held both at the ready for Hintosep.

In a large copper bowl, Hintosep mixed dried herbs, enchanted salt, silver shavings, a swallow's tongue, and what Krona was only half certain was a glob of compost from the heap out near the vegetable garden.

"Like recognizes like," Hintosep explained as she worked. "Usually, we use this conjuration to find undeclared children. I've never tried it on varger before, but if I'm right and they are essence of human, then I don't see why it shouldn't work just as well."

Fresh water went into the concoction, and Hintosep stirred and stirred until the mixture was a thin soup, chanting under her breath the whole time before reaching in with her bare hands and splattering the map repeatedly, making everyone rear back lest they get caught in the spatter. "The chanting helps to center the mind," she said, "to direct the power precisely."

Without wiping her hand, she raised the syringe. "Now the line to be tracked," she said, ejecting its essence into the bowl. The small wisp of varg circled the bottom like it was searching for a drain. "A line of relation," she said, taking the bloodied cloth from Krona and tossing it on top of the vapors. "And a line by which to trace," she finished, before spitting into the concoction herself.

Krona frowned at her.

"What?" Hintosep asked. "I said conjurations were crude."

She drew the cloth through the murky substance, drenching it thoroughly, before taking the dirty thing to the tabletop, sweeping it over every last inch of the engraved map.

As soon as she slopped the cloth back into the bowl, a small, bright purple fairy light flickered over their exact location, indicating Monkeyflower as clear as day. A moment later, seven other lights appeared as well.

Hintosep didn't bother to hide her smug satisfaction. "Red for parentage," she said, gesturing at two spots in Xyopar that sat in a cluster of aqua—directly over what Krona knew to be Xyopar's version of Vault Hill. "Aqua for grand-parentage, and . . ." She pointed firmly at a blue flame in Marrakev, near the rim. "Blue for siblings. No gold. Seems your sister didn't have any secret children, at the very least."

Instead of the cobalt blue catching her eye, Krona's gaze stuck fast on the red. Twin dots, her maman and papa's varger.

Part of her papa still existed.

She didn't know what to do with that information or how to feel. But she definitely felt *a way* about it—cold and empty, but also grateful, strangely. He had died when she was so young, but a part of him had lived on. As a bottle-barker, if she was reading the clues correctly. As a lost piece longing for a body that no longer was.

As she stared at it, she subconsciously reached for it, as though touching the light might in some way connect her to her past, to her father.

But the light disappeared a moment later.

"Crude, complicated, and weak," Hintosep said. "But there we have it." She took the dagger and thrust its tip into the table, exactly where the cobalt light had been. "Your varg. Now put on the mask and walk me through De-Lia's ritual."

47

KRONA

"Ah, that's it," a voice said in the distance. *"The lake; I should have known."*

Krona stayed under in the mask. She knew, in a far-off way, that the voice belonged to Hintosep, and Hintosep needed her to finish rewatching the memories. Thibaut had taken notes aplenty, but he was there once more, holding her hand and ushering her through. Slowly, she waded through the images, slogging her way to the barn, jumping when Tray's mother came in, even though she knew it was going to happen.

"Yes, the salt," Hintosep confirmed.

"Come back to me, mistress," Thibaut said soothingly. *"Come back."*

"As I suspected, a conjuration. Performed with salt from Konets, no less."

With her head still firmly planted against her pillow, Krona pulled off the mask and rubbed at her strained eyes, spots swimming in her vision. They'd gone to her and Thibaut's room, and it felt strange to have a third person there with them, invading their space. "What's so special about Lake Konets?"

"Bodies," Hintosep said, standing at the foot of the bed.

"Ah, lovely!" Thibaut exclaimed, letting go of Krona's hand and standing—moving from where he'd been knelt beside her on the bed—distaste writ clear across the twist of his lips.

"During our trouble on the way here," Hintosep reminded them, "I mentioned to Mandip that a pyre was not the proper way to see to a Thalo's funeral. It's our custom to sink our bodies—bare—into the lake. There are centuries' and centuries' worth of corpses at the bottom. The salt there must have been infused with remnants of secret magic—enchanted through natural means instead of forced ones."

"Oh, so, enchanted materials *do* come from mines," Thibaut said.

Hintosep gave him a sharp look.

"What? Just trying to keep up with your oh-so-helpful explanations."

"Magic comes from people; it can go all over the place after that," she said, voice even, not rising to his challenge. "Case in point. It appears the conjuration De-Lia performed was for the creation of a temporary beacon. Consuming the conjuration materials—blood, salt, and ink—drew her varg in. Now that we have the location of your varg, Krona, we can mimic De-Lia's conjuration and set you and the creature on the path toward finding one another."

With De-Lia's mask in her lap, Krona sat up. "And what happens then?"

"Then we tether you and the beast together so we can reverse the ritual that ripped the varg from you in the first place, and hope that stitches you whole."

Krona looked to Thibaut. He blanched, handing her the requisite glass of water before piping up. "Say it all works. The varger types display magical abilities, so clearly you expect a remerging will return some of one's lost power. Can we expect my mistress here to be spitting in Time's eye and reversing the hands of the clock, or . . . what?"

"Are you familiar with the phases of matter?" Hintosep asked.

Thibaut put his hands on his hips and shrugged. "Sure. Solid, liquid, gas," he ticked off.

"Yes, very good. I believe magic should be described similarly, as having phases. Think of its original phase as its solid state, magic as it resides in a newborn body. Its liquid equivalent, then, is when it is removed from its origins and put into its corresponding materials—sands, metals, salts, woods, and gems. In other words, we can think of it as 'liquid' when it's most malleable, when it's imbued into substances that are then formed into enchanted objects. Its gaseous state is what you've observed in Melanie, and what happens when time is returned. By then, magic has become a wisp of itself; little more than the elemental power of time, emotion, knowledge, secrets, and nature remain.

"But matter has a fourth state," she said. "Don't look so crestfallen; it's not your fault you didn't know. We Thalo have access to more knowledge. There's solid, liquid, gas, and *plasma*—lightning being the quintessential example."

"Then the plasma equivalent state of magic . . ." Krona prompted.

"Is purely my theory," she said with a sly smile, rounding the bed to Krona's side. "But I think it's what we'll find when you and your varg rejoin. And, like lightning, I believe it will be *powerful*." She winked at Thibaut. "Your mistress might not be able to turn back the hands of Time, but she will be a force unlike the Valley has ever experienced." She patted Krona's shoulder, moved toward the door. "Rest up. We don't want your varg to wander too far from where we spotted it before we turn you into a beacon. Luckily, I have salt from Konets, in a locket. It's sentimental but worth sacrificing for you. Shouldn't be more than a day's hike or two, once we're over the border and into Marrakev, to get to your monster, so I say we set out in the morning. Sound good to you?"

Krona clutched at her chest. So soon. She thought she'd have more time to grapple with the idea of being tethered to a varg. Of having to meet the beast face-to-face out in the open.

"Yeah," she said, uncertainty making her voice shake.

"Good," Hintosep said, leaving with a nod to Thibaut.

Once she was gone, Thibaut wasted no time weighing in on the matter. "I don't think you should do this."

Krona sighed, put upon. "Oh, Thibaut, why must you?"

"Why must I what? Always be the voice of reason?"

"This is how I get De-Lia back."

"Is it? Isn't this the kind of nonsense Charbon was promised? That he could save the people he cared about if he just did what the Thalo asked of him?"

"This is different," she asserted, though it sounded like a weak excuse, even to her. "She didn't deserve to die that way."

"*Lots* of people don't deserve their fate," Thibaut said emphatically. "I just want—" he started, but cut himself off.

"*What?*" she asked harshly. "Please, tell me, Thibaut. What do *you* want? What you want seems to be the only thing ever at the forefront of your mind."

"I want you to be all right," he said softly, eyebrows and hands raising slightly, as if he were at a loss. "These things, this magic—we don't really know anything about it. Except it's dangerous. Except that it bewitched and killed De-Lia. The more you seek these secrets, the more I fear you invite death down on your head."

"I'm not giving up on her," she said, looking into the empty maw of the mask, running her fingers over the jaguar's nose.

"She's dead," he said, not unkindly. "That's usually when it's okay to give up on people." He knelt before her, put a tentative hand on her sword wrist. She didn't shake it off. "I would be remiss in my duties as a friend and a lover if I did not show my concern. It is folly to seek life for the dead over preserving the life of the living, is it not? There is a whole world out here that you've shunned these past few years. A whole Valley full of people. You have friends; you have . . . you have me."

She leaned down, brought their faces close, but did not set the mask aside. "The curtain has been pulled back. I cannot unsee what I have seen. If there is a chance, then I must take it."

He stayed close, searched her eyes. "But why? It's not just the injustice of it. It's not just that she's your sister. It's not even to make the pain go away. So, what is it? Why are you hellbent on throwing yourself—nearly literally—to the wolves?"

Krona clenched her jaw, pulled away, averted her gaze. "She was the better of the two of us."

"That's not true. The two of you were different people, no better than—"

She cut him off with a glare. "I'm not done. After our papa died, our maman became a different person. Withdrawn. So, it often felt like the only one I could look to was De-Lia. She was the one who forged paths, plowed the ground, and I followed in her wake. But I never really knew her. Not in the way some sisters share. There was guidance but no closeness.

"I spent our shared existence idolizing her, longing to be her. Instead of getting to *know* her. I had nearly twenty-five years to learn to love her as I should have, but instead . . ." She flicked her chin toward the jaguar. "I gave it up in exchange for a petty rivalry, jealousy, and a stupid mask whose echo I can't even properly control.

"Yes, she deserves justice. But she also deserved a sister who acted like one. If I can still find a way to give that to her, I will."

Thibaut nodded, as though accepting not her reasoning but that he could not change her mind. He stood then, moved to sit beside her on the bed—near but not touching.

He didn't deserve this, she realized. He wasn't built for this—these dilemmas, this angst. He should have gone back to the city. She should have *let* him. Back to his run-down apartment, back to his nice clothes and fake smiles and good food and soft beds.

He was a fool, and she was weak, and if life had any logic to it, their inability to go their own ways would destroy them both.

><+>+O+<+><

Krona was distracted all through dinner. Thankfully, the dining table had been thoroughly cleaned and rearranged, but every time she looked at the polished wood, she saw those little fairy lights. It was all too much—the thought of facing a varg so exposed, the idea of not just touching but tethering herself to a monster. She could guess what that entailed—not ropes or manacles but needles. They were the only weapons that worked against varger.

They'd need silver. Silver was for jumpers.

Thibaut's gift would serve her well. Enchanted or not, the silver would prove out.

Her discussion with Thibaut had done nothing to calm her nerves, but it did solidify her decision. No matter how dangerous it seemed, how ill advised, she had to take the risk.

She couldn't live with herself if she didn't.

When the sun began to set, almost everyone went outside to sit around the fire pit and enjoy their home-brewed mead. The safe house had beehives, and a small vineyard, and a vegetable garden—all kept from freezing due to some enchantments Hintosep had buried.

Krona sneaked away before anyone could pour her a mug, however. She wanted time to sit with her decision. To integrate what it meant.

To continue to justify it to herself, if she was honest.

There was a music room just down the hall from the kitchen. She'd noticed it days before but hadn't given herself permission to explore until now. There was a piano, but it was missing keys. A drum, but its skin was broken through. A bent horn of some kind was propped in the far corner, and a harp occupied the center of the space, surrounded by pillows. It appeared to have all its strings, so Krona approached.

Sitting with her legs tucked under her, she plucked at the harp absently, enjoying the light notes, the thrumming of each string.

"Do you play?" came a soothing voice from the door.

Krona looked up to see Juliet standing in the doorway, leaning casually into the room. Her performer's finery had long been done away with, but even her traveling clothes had seemed majestic. Now even that had been replaced with a milkmaid's shift, and though Krona was sure Juliet could wear a miller's sack and look regal, it seemed unfair. Someone who carried themselves with such self-assuredness deserved all the flamboyant skirts and embroidered regalia she desired.

Give Krona a sturdy set of leathers and she was happy. Or a heavy skirt, sure—she was comfortable in either. She knew Juliet, likewise, wanted to be blanketed in silks and lace.

The opera singer and the thief were two peas in a pod that way.

"No," Krona said quickly, dropping her hands like she was a small child fiddling with a forbidden trinket. "I always wanted to learn to play . . . something. Not necessarily the harp. I considered the cello for a while. Was urged to pick it up, actually, but I . . ." She let that train of thought drop. "It's just . . . to be able to fill the air with music seems like such a small happiness, a thing I could carry with me wherever."

Juliet smiled. Her tears from earlier had dried. "It is. A happiness." She eased into the room, leaving the door ajar. "Lucky for you, I am well versed in a cornucopia of instruments. I could teach you a little, if you like."

"Yes?"

Juliet chuckled at Krona's hesitancy, moving to her. "We'll start with a scale. Lay your hands on the strings."

Krona did so, but Juliet quirked her lips immediately, as though she'd done it wrong.

"May I?" the singer asked, sliding in against Krona's side. She was so small compared to Krona; she couldn't reach around to guide both of the Regulator's hands at once, so she placed them each in turn. She leaned in, whispering near Krona's ear as she instructed. "Good, keep your shoulders square."

Juliet smelled nice. Clean. Krona wondered where she'd procured the perfumed soap. Her cleanliness was scented through with lemon.

"Look, look here," Juliet said, fitting one hand over Krona's on the strings. "You strum like this, yes, and there. That's a B-flat. Then like this. C. Good. D—Oh, dear, this poor thing is in need of a good tuning . . ."

Her hands were tiny compared to Krona's. Palms petite but fingers long and nimble—made for something like stretching between keys on a piano or bending around the neck of a lute. Flexible but not as strong as Krona's. Juliet might know how to wield a sword, but could she keep her grip on it in the long run?

The pads of her fingers were string-callused. Entirely different kinds of calluses from the kind Krona's training had left her with.

Krona was too focused on Juliet's hands to fully heed their guidance. She fumbled on the E.

"That's all right," Juliet said delicately. "Try again, like this. There you go." She rubbed her thumb encouragingly over Krona's knuckles.

The gesture stirred something in her that only Thibaut had stirred in a long while.

Startled by her own reaction, Krona released the harp, reclaimed her hands. "Everything all right, mistress?"

Krona could feel her face flushing. Juliet's breath was sweet over Krona's cheek, and her body pressed just so against her side—soft and warm. The Regulator's breath hitched and her heart thumped in her throat.

Juliet was too perceptive for her own good. She smiled sweetly, her lips holding a knowing, sly quirk. "Music also has a way of bringing people together," she said softly.

The singer let her chin rest on Krona's shoulder, and she delicately moved one braid away from the Regulator's neck.

"Juliet," Krona said swiftly. She meant it to be a warning, a caution, but it came out unexpectedly needy.

"You seem like you need some tender company."

Krona tilted her chin down, her gaze finding Juliet's as the other woman looked up through her lashes. Krona didn't say anything, but her chest constricted. Yes, she could stand a bit of tenderness. She hadn't been tender with *herself* in a long time; that was certain.

But at least there was one person she'd allowed close lately. And he'd been soft with her. Gentle. Patient. He'd even been patient with her today, while pleading with her not to take such risks.

Krona parted her lips to say Thibaut's name.

In the same moment, Juliet surged forward to kiss her.

Not so long before, Krona might have simply sunk into it. She might have allowed her mind to turn off and accept a brief moment of pleasure. Especially since the kiss was entirely too deep and too sweet, and Krona didn't feel like she deserved it.

But when her eyes fluttered closed, all she saw was Thibaut. She wanted to be kissed, yes, to share herself, yes—but only with him.

There was nothing wrong with being the kind to flit from flower to flower, but she was the single-minded sort.

She pulled away, biting her own lip. "Juliet . . ."

"Please, call me Nadine," she corrected lightly. "Juliet is for the stage, for the public. Not for . . ."

"Nadine?" Krona said, trying it out on her tongue.

"Just for this," Juliet told her. "Not on the road, just . . . for intimate moments."

The name ruffled something in the back of Krona's mind, pricked at her senses, at her training. She'd known of another Nadine. Who'd owned that name?

A floorboard squeaked in the hall. They both turned toward the open doorway. No one stood there, but Krona could make out footsteps retreating, toward the kitchen.

"Someone saw us," she noted.

"So, let them see," Juliet said, leaning in to kiss her again. Krona pulled back before she could make contact. The singer's brow furrowed.

"I'm very flattered," Krona said sincerely. "But . . ."

Juliet immediately looked taken aback. "I'm sorry. I don't usually read these things wrong. Is it me? Or . . . women in general?"

"No, I do. Like you, I mean. And women. Both," she added with a blush. "I like both. That's not it." Juliet's kiss had been nice, and Krona didn't want to embarrass her. For some reason, she struggled to find the words to explain.

Luckily, Juliet was perceptive. "Ah. You're flattered . . . but someone else has your heart."

Krona sighed in relief. "Yes. I'm sorry."

"Don't be," Juliet said reassuringly. "Alas, I shall mourn what a lovely time we could have had. But I do understand." She strummed the harp casually. "And if you'd like to learn, I promise my offer to teach you wasn't just a ploy to get in your trousers."

"Thank you," Krona said graciously. "But for now, I really think I should go see who was spying on us." Krona didn't like that whoever it was hadn't made their presence known. Parts of the house were technically still dilapidated, which could make them difficult to defend. Everyone else was supposed to be outside.

It could have been *anyone*.

"Ever vigilant," Juliet said with admiration, sending Krona off with a nod.

Moving with the practiced caution of a Regulator in pursuit, Krona looked left and right as she entered the hallway. Seeing no one and nothing obviously out of place, she moved toward the kitchen. Halfway there, a door on her left hung open, revealing the caved-in roof over the top of a bare four-poster bed. Assured the space was empty, she closed it off. No sense relinquishing warmth to an unusable room.

A clattering of porcelain came from the kitchen.

Hurrying onward, she found Thibaut rinsing off the plates and teacups they'd used earlier in a bucket of well water plopped on the counter. His linen undershirt was tucked into his high-waisted breeches, the sleeves rolled up past his elbows to keep them dry. His green gloves lay on the countertop, out of the water's way.

"It's just you," she sighed with relief. She'd nearly convinced herself someone malevolent was prowling through the house.

"Well, hello to you, too," he said, not turning around.

"I was with Juliet, and I was just making sure—"

"Yes, I know you were with Juliet," he said sharply.

She ran a hand over her eyes, took a deep breath. Then she strolled slowly to his side, leaned against the lip of the counter. "You saw?" she asked lightly, trying to keep all hints of emotion from her voice.

"Yes, *I saw*," Thibaut said, still not looking up from the pile of dishes. Brandishing a rag, he wiped one saucer dry with a flourish. "And I heard what she asked you to call her. *Nadine*. Well, I can certainly see why she took a different name for the stage. Nadine is a sweet little child's name—or perhaps a sweet old lady's—it certainly doesn't belong on someone with such a sheer force of will and undeniable presence. She's like a whirlwind"—there were a bite and a bend to his tone—"just *ripping through*—"

Krona scowled.

"Thibaut."

"*What?*"

She spun him around, plucked the dish from his fingers, then the rag, placing them on the counter before taking his damp hands in hers. His hands—his bare hands. She knew he hid them because of the scars, but they were beautiful, and now she kissed them, because she could. Because she was allowed to. Because she wanted to.

"Don't be stupid," she said, fully understanding why he was in such a huff. He flitted about so much, it was hard to imagine him possessive, but clearly, he was hurt. "I told her I was flattered," she said carefully, "but my heart belongs to someone else."

"Oh," he said flatly, all the angry bravado going out of him.

"Oh," she agreed. "So, why don't you dry off these hands, come to bed, and make love to me. You can still pretend to be in a jealous rage, if you like," she added with a wink, releasing him and walking away, toward their shared room.

A sharp clattering of dishes followed as he attempted to clean up mid-mess before hurrying after. She went slowly, and when he caught up to her, he threw his arms around her waist, whispering titillating promises in her ear.

As they passed the room with the harp, they heard Juliet strumming, her soft voice letting out a breathy melody that Krona had never heard before. Perhaps the woman had composed it right then and there. Mesmerized, they both paused to listen:

> *And there's a hunger in her bones, for books and blanks and tomes*
> *And all the other ways in which to know*
> *How to keep the gentle closeness of this skin*
>
> *But the pain of knowing never, the sounds of falls and drying heather*
> *Secrets of the veins beneath, just blue*
> *While sky turns gray and the mountain sighs*
>
> *He sees her perched atop the cliff, 'ere sand and slate tumble, shift*
> *Catch her, is his only thought o' breath*
> *And yet she slips and soars from his grip*

Thibaut tightened his hold on Krona, keeping her close in counterpoint to the lyrics. He kissed her temple soundly, and they moved on, letting Juliet's voice drift after.

> *She is more than has ever been, the sparkling one, diamond sheen*
> *He is left alone . . . bereft*
> *While sky turns pink and the mountain a-lights.*

48

KRONA

The only other people Hintosep invited on the mission to Marrakev's rim were Juliet and Melanie. "Juliet's a crack shot with a bow," she reassured Krona. "We'll need her. And I'm sure you're well aware of Melanie's healing abilities. Hopefully, we *won't* need her to apply anything more than simple first aid, but better safe than sorry."

That morning, before they left, Krona and Thibaut spent their time wrapped together in bedsheets.

"Why don't you leave De-Lia's mask here, with me?" he suggested, trying to sound casual about a topic they both knew was anything but.

"But what if—what if I need it?"

"You won't be using your quintbarrel," he pointed out. "It'll be more of a distraction than a help."

Anxiety rose in Krona's chest. Since its creation, she'd never gone more than a few hours without its presence, but to leave it was to acknowledge that she was truly on the right path. Moving toward a solution, toward helping reconstruct De-Lia, rather than wallowing in her death.

"Um. Yeah. Yes. All right."

"I'll keep it safe," he promised. "You just keep you safe, agreed?"

"Agreed."

Their small party of four set out with only the briefest good-byes, assuring everyone they'd be back soon. Mandip was at Thibaut's side when they left, and Krona tried not to let her own jealous monster loose in her mind.

＞┝◆▷•○•◁◀┥＜

Every morning and every evening, Hintosep performed the same conjuration she had in the dining room, only with a small leather map of only Marrakev. Hintosep helped Krona perform the beacon ritual—which had her consuming salt and blood and ink—and as they stalked closer and closer to their prey, their prey stalked back.

Southern Marrakev was colder than most of northern Lutador, but the safe house was at a high-enough altitude that the summer climates of the two felt comparable. Hintosep set up a small barrier around their camp every night—much smaller than the one they'd stolen from the other Thalo when on the run—which kept them warm and protected.

On their fifth morning in the wilds, the four of them left camp before sunrise, using the map conjuration to confirm Krona's varg was close. They *would* meet it today.

Krona wore her bracers, her leathers, and the silver knuckleduster Thibaut had given her, but no other armor. Hintosep carried Krona's quintbarrel in one hand and the katar from Mirthhouse's mantel in the other. Juliet's quiver was stuffed with arrows, the heads plated with all the necessary metallic types, though she'd also overstocked on silver. Melanie had her own hunting bow for protection, but more important, she carried her medical bag, knowing there would be blood at the end of this, especially if everything went according to plan.

Mist rolled through the trees, and everything smelled bright and cold. Each small snap of a twig or flutter of a bird's wings sounded like thunder, the world was so quiet.

As they followed the beacon's pull, Krona pictured her varg approaching her like a bouncing puppy—like any other gutter dog looking to play with a friendly human. *Yes, just a dog,* she thought, trying to fool herself, to trick her phobia. *Just a good dog.*

Never mind they were much more like bears and stalked like wolves. Never mind that they smelled like death and sounded unholy.

As the four of them walked, the silence grew in Krona's ears. Until the *thu-thud, thu-thud* of her own heartbeat in her ears began to feel external, like drumbeats.

Thu-thud. Thu-thud.

Thu-thud, thu-thud.

Thu-thud-thu-thud-thu-thud.

Thudthudthudthud—

It wasn't just her heart. Something was drawing closer, running toward them.

The heavy footfalls belonged to a sizable creature.

"Get ready," Krona said. "It might not be alone."

There came the delicate *zing* of metal sliding on metal as Juliet drew an arrow from her quiver. Melanie stayed close to her side.

Krona gestured for the three of them to give her space. If it was her varg, then she needed it to zero in on her as soon as possible. When De-Lia had met

Monkeyflower, she'd been alone, with no one else about to draw its ire or re-mind it of its pain. In an ideal world, Krona would have done this by herself, but Hintosep needed to wield the katar, and someone had to bind Krona to the varg to begin with.

"Don't shoot it until I have it," Krona said. "Not unless you need to."

The pounding grew louder and louder, and Krona could feel the beacon-pull in her chest strobing wildly.

When the creature burst through the trees twelve paces away, she was ready, but instead of leaping—either through the air or through time—the beast skidded to a halt, clearly sensing something unusual about its prey.

Its body was thick and muscular, its shoulders high and haunches low. The pads of its feet were large enough to cover Krona's entire face, and she knew one powerful blow to the chest from its muzzle or paws could be enough to make a heart fail its beating.

As soon as she laid eyes on it, Krona felt naked. She'd purposefully left all of her usual touchstones behind: De-Lia's mask, her helm, her saber. Luckily, the enchanted stones in Krona's bracers were able to bolster her courage and resolve just enough to overpower her phobia—to let her hold her ground and keep her vision focused. Though an undercurrent of pure fear sizzled through her body, she took half a breath to really *look* at the varg.

To look at the tortured, fractured piece of herself.

She expected an instant connection, to *know* herself, but there was nothing different about this varg—not the way it looked, not the way it felt—that would have, at any other time, told her it was special. Its sores and lesions festered just the same, its spines rattled warningly, and its back arched in a hulking, threatening curve.

But then she found its eyes. Met its gaze.

Its irises were golden—a far cry from her deep brown. Its pupils were slitted, and the whites near-yellow and heavily veined. Its eyes weren't human, and there was nothing obviously human behind them. But there *was* kinship. She didn't know how to describe it, or where the realization physically settled into her—her heart, her core, or her spine. If she hadn't searched its gaze, she never would have seen the flash of it.

And that's all there was. A flash.

The varg shook its head, breaking their eye contact. It bared its fangs, and its tongue curled out of its mouth as it roared, sending spittle everywhere.

It pawed at the ground once, twice, then charged.

At least it still had Krona dead in its sights rather than one of the others.

It jumped before its forepaws hit the ground again, vanishing.

A spike of fear shot through Krona's chest, stealing her air, but she didn't move. She needed it to come to her. To jump to her.

Hold your ground, hold your ground, hold your—

It materialized in front of her, mid-leap, and her knees gave out, driving her to the forest floor. She covered her head as it sailed over the top of her, sliding in the dirt beyond. Instinctually, she searched for a weapon. A rock, a stick, anything to fight back with, even though her conscious mind knew it wouldn't make a difference.

No. No. Stop it. You can't fight it. You're not supposed to fight.

Yelling, she stood and ripped the bracers from her arms. The threads of emotion—the resolve and the courage granted by the enchanted stones—tore out of her like razor wire. She knew as long as she had the false emotion, she would struggle against the varg. They would force her to stand her ground, to battle her phobia and fight the creature.

But she didn't *want* to fight it.

She needed to embrace it.

Krona whirled to face it as the monster howled. It lunged at her, paws out-stretched.

She froze—not out of willpower but out of sheer terror.

It landed against her chest with an awful force, punching the air from her lungs and propelling her to the ground again. Pain shot up her spine as she landed on a sharp rock, and several loud *cracks* told her something on her body had popped if not broken. The creature's claws raked her shoulders, slicing soundly. The pain made her grit her teeth, but she did not fight back.

Suddenly, the varg paused.

It seemed confused. One moment it was lunging at her face, snapping its jaws, and the next it pulled back as if to study her.

It didn't know what to do with the sensations that had come over it. It was clearly disoriented. It felt better—better than it ever had, and that was cause for confusion.

Unfortunately, Krona was sure they were both about to feel *a lot* worse.

She grabbed its snout with both hands. The silver knuckleduster Thibaut had given her helped form a magical sort of muzzle over its jaws. In surprise, it reared up, dragging Krona with it, wrenching its head from side to side, trying to throw her off.

"Shoot it now!" Krona yelled.

"I can't get a clean shot!" Juliet shouted.

The quintbarrel went off—a needle whizzed by Krona's ear.

Shit.

Unable to shake her, the varg changed tactics. It slammed her back into the dirt, pounding her body against the forest floor again and again until her grip finally gave out and she was left sprawled on her back.

Once it was free, it was wary. It tried to scramble away. Screaming nonsense, Krona rolled over and onto all fours.

Confused, it tried to run by her, back into the woods.

Without thinking, she jumped onto its back as it passed. Burying one silver-covered fist in its nape, she *pulled*, like she was trying to control an angry house-cat. Once again, it tried to dislodge her, ramming its side into a tree, then another. When that failed, it stopped and reared up, bracing itself against a thick tree trunk—just like the mimic at the camp's barrier. Its claws scraped at the bark, pulling away long curls of wood. Krona struggled not to fall.

She fisted its nape all the tighter, ignoring the way its quills sliced her hand. She tucked herself tight against the creature, squeezing its back with her thighs, throwing out her other arm so she could cling to its paw where it was lodged firmly in the trunk.

"Now! Shoot it! Before it jumps!"

Thunk.

Krona shrieked.

The silver arrow pierced the back of her left hand, sliding between her delicate bones and bursting out her palm and into the varg's paw. The force of Juliet's shot plunged it farther still, sinking the arrowhead into the tree, tying all three together on the shaft.

"Another!" Hintosep ordered.

Krona wrestled her other arm from where it was pinned between her chest and the sharp quills, reaching out to frantically grasp the varg's right foreleg, providing Juliet with what she hoped was another obvious target.

A moment later, the mirrored pain in her right hand was her answer.

Gritting her teeth against the pain, Krona waited for the varg to still. The silver sliding through her tendons was no different to her than if the arrows had been plated with iron or gold—the wounds were just as torturous—but the varg responded as they'd all hoped. It growled and bucked but was much more immobilized than Krona herself.

"Shh, shh," she whispered. "I know it hurts. But it'll all be over soon." Whether she was talking to it or herself didn't matter, and the irony was not lost on her.

"Are you sure it's the right one?" Melanie shouted.

"Yes! Do it now!" Krona demanded. "Please!"

Great stomping rushed up behind her.

Krona buried her face in the varg's spines, tensing. She felt something slice through her spine *before* the katar's blade did—something icy, sharp, yet slithering and fluid. Only an instant separated the sensation from the definitive sting of metal. She jerked, and her skin tingled all over—head to toe—from panic. A horrifying flash of déjà vu took hold of her, and she convulsed, as though her body remembered having suffered this exact trauma before when her mind did not.

The blade sank deeper and deeper, all in one swift move. An instant later, she could only feel burning pain above the blade, and absolutely nothing below. Her legs went limp.

Her spine had been severed.

Her vision blurred; her head whirled.

Behind her, Hintosep did something with the katar, and Krona and the varg both jolted.

It's okay, Hintosep gritted out. Krona couldn't tell if the voice was in her ear or in her head. *You can pass out if you'd like.*

She would. She would have liked to, very much.

The katar *twisted.*

Hintosep *yanked.*

A sucking sort of vortex ate at Krona's insides—not painful, but unnatural, as though she were being mixed together, swirled like paint. The vortex tugged on her stomach muscles from the inside, drawing her belly back tight, toward her spine, compressing her organs and making her blood roar in her veins.

The sucking pulled on the varg as well, pulling it *back,* pulling it *tight.* Its quills dug into Krona's flesh—her face and hands and arms. The fluids of its sores smeared over her skin and clothes. Its awful smell, pungent before, now became tangible and thick as its source was pushed *into* her nose. She could *taste* it.

Krona reeled back, trying to escape, recalling the way the bottle-barker at Melanie's wedding had burned her throat, trying to eat her from the inside out. Just like her freezing before the jumper, her reaction was visceral and beyond her control. She choked, gagged, struggled against the creature she couldn't let go of—that was actively becoming part of her.

Beneath her, the varg *thinned,* lost mass.

The metal blade left her, and suddenly the feeling in her lower extremities returned. The damage to her spine had been undone, and as the coldness drew away as well, the varg pressed farther *in.*

It rolled its now-flattened head, its body thin as a bearskin rug, and tried to bite at the bark and at Krona herself. But there was nothing it could do. Truly, Krona didn't think it wanted to stop whatever was happening; it was panicking on the same instinctual level she was, resisting, no matter the outcome.

Its skull pressed into hers; her teeth went through the back and met *its* teeth at the front. For one gruesome moment, its fangs were her fangs.

There was a warped *snap*—like a bowed leather belt being pulled taut—and then she gasped. A giant, yawing silence made her ears pop, and all the air in the vicinity seemed to be pulled into her lungs at once.

The world stopped.

The pause of it all seemed to have its own waves and ripples.

And then everything *shook* as energy blasted out of Krona, and she felt like she was being welded together, every cell being tethered to another with molten metal.

It was hot and furious and over before it felt like it had begun.

Krona stilled. She shut her eyes and panted heavily, unable to move or think.

As the varg was pulled into her, its mass had diminished, and instead of clinging to the back of a huge beast, eventually there had been nothing between Krona and the tree. Her legs no longer wrapped around thick haunches, her hands no longer clung to spiny paws, and her face butted up against rough bark instead of sores. Now she dangled, unable to reach the ground, held up and pinned to the tree by nothing more than the arrows in her hands.

At the periphery of her awareness, someone called her name. Fingertips touched her cheek. Leverage was applied to the arrows. Wood splintered. Her body sagged farther, but strong arms caught her, lowered her to the ground.

Then hands on her forehead, sliding to her temples. Pressing. Pressing *hard*. She whimpered.

No more. It was over. No more.

"What are you doing?" Melanie asked frantically.

"Walling away what I can of the trauma. It's not the same as when the tax is taken—thank the gods—not as psyche-shattering. She doesn't feel as broken as a baby does after. She'll be all right."

The pain in Krona's body didn't change, but it felt like someone had poured a soothing balm on her soul. She wasn't completely at ease—she was exhausted, utterly drained, barely able to keep her eyes open—but she wasn't the fractured mess of shock and suffering she'd been the moment before.

"Did it work?" she croaked. Krona could feel something new inside her, a part not yet settled. Like an echo not yet fully contained, but instead of just her mind, it was everywhere. It throbbed in her fingertips and tingled in her teeth and pushed at the backs of her eyes.

"You remerged," Hintosep said. "But we won't know if it gave you any of your power back until you try to use it." She gently touched Krona's wrist. "Try. Try speeding up the healing on your hands."

"Wait," Melanie broke in, grabbing Krona's shoulder. "Don't. Not until I can clean and stitch them."

Hintosep's brows knitted together.

"She only controls time, doesn't she?" Melanie asked. "Time can't pretend her wounds are stitched if they never were. The katar made magical wounds that were healed by magical means, but the arrows are just arrows. She might end up with gaping holes, or a systemic infection in mere moments instead of days, if she doesn't get real medical attention." She stood, withdrew. "Let me do what I do best."

Her footsteps pounded off across the ground, and then Krona felt like she was spinning. Spinning down and away. Away, into the dark.

49

KRONA

Krona woke up with a shout when disinfectant hit her palms. The other women had managed to drag her back to camp and now had her laid out on a bedroll while Melanie tended to her wounds.

Their camp was only a handful of strides across. In the center was their fire pit, and their supplies and bedrolls were all kept at close quarters.

"You're all right, you're all right," Hintosep assured her, clearly worried Krona, while disoriented, might start swinging. She and Juliet held Krona down while the healer did her expert work, first dabbing each laceration clean, absorbing the excess blood, before prepping the edges of the skin with iodine.

"I'm good. I'm awake," Krona reassured them.

Hintosep pulled Juliet up, and the two of them went to start the campfire and prepare their rations while Melanie performed her work.

"Do you want to sit up?" Melanie asked. "I can get at your shoulder better. You really sunk your claws into you, didn't you?" she quipped.

"Always knew I was my own worst enemy." It was only half a joke.

Melanie mixed some kind of bitter-smelling poultice with a mortar and pestle and applied it to each open wound before pulling out her suture kit. "What shall we sew up first?" she asked.

Krona held out her right hand.

Melanie gently tested for broken bones. "A fracture here," she said, pressing, making Krona hiss. "This one, snapped. And I think the arrow tore a ligament in your middle finger. We'll need to keep this immobilized. If you really can hasten your healing, that might save some flexibility that might otherwise have been lost. Though I doubt these will be wounds forgotten." A moment later, the needle tugged firmly through Krona's palm. Melanie's stitches were precise and smooth, she didn't wriggle the needle any more than necessary, and when she trimmed the knots, they were tight, set low, and didn't fray.

"Over," Melanie commanded, moving on to the back of Krona's hand to show the exit wound the same treatment. "You sit for sutures remarkably well," she noted.

"Been stitched a fair few times is all," Krona said.

"What's it like?" Melanie asked carefully. "Having a varg inside you?"

"I don't know. What's it like having a baby inside you?"

"It's like having a new wriggly organ with a mind of its own. One that's especially fond of squeezing all your other organs."

Krona snorted. "This isn't like that."

"I'd hope not. Pregnancy already lasts nine months and should definitely last no more. Certainly not *forever*."

"This is more like a . . . a brightness in me. Like the soft light of dawn." It was an easy awareness of herself that felt like floating, or flying, or maybe drifting in a pond. If her sense of self had been a musical instrument, then she was finally in tune.

"That sounds lovely," Melanie said.

It really was.

⊱┈•◦❖◦•┈⊰

She awoke again in the middle of the night. It must have been the wee hours of the morning; the fire had burned out and the other three were asleep. Rubbing lightly at the fresh dressings Melanie had wound around her hands, she took the quiet moment to see if she could, in fact, do anything about her own wounds.

She focused on the palm of her left hand, not daring to remove the bandage, just navigating her body by feel. She focused on the pain, on telling it to *hurry up and go away*.

A terrible itching followed, bad enough that she had to bite her lip and hold her other hand tight to her stomach to keep from scratching at it and crying out. The sensation was maddening, but it was in fact a sensation. Something new. Something she'd *willed* to happen.

Even if she'd had more than starlight to investigate by, she did not yet dare to look, unsure if she'd done more harm than good.

But she'd done *something*, and that was cause for at least some sort of celebration.

⊱┈•◦❖◦•┈⊰

She tried little else on their way back to the mansion, wanting the security of the safe house and its surroundings before testing anything that might draw unwanted attention or create undue problems.

Everyone was relieved to have them all back safe and sound, but it was Thibaut who rushed at Krona right inside the door, who threw his arms around her shoulders and refused to let go for a long moment.

"How do you feel?" he asked when he pulled back. "You did it, didn't you? You found it."

"We did," she said, trying to give him a reassuring smile. "And I feel . . . I feel good."

She did—it wasn't a lie. But what she felt encompassed more than "good," in a way that defied Krona's words. Perhaps Juliet would be able to describe it if she herself ever remerged.

"And . . . can you . . ."

He asked quietly, like the conversation was private.

She looked to Hintosep.

"This way," the Thalo woman said, gesturing for Krona to follow her to her first-floor offices—a place for strategizing, planning. There, a large desk was matched by a large table nearly the size of the one in the dining hall. The space was all business, echoing the warmth and ruggedness of the rest of the mansion in its decorating, but nothing overtly personal sat anywhere in the open, and Krona could only guess that was by design.

Thibaut was the only person, aside from the hunting party, to be invited inside.

"Let's see," Krona said brightly—excitedly—moving toward the bank of windows that lined the far wall, hoping for better light.

She unwrapped her left hand, finally laying eyes on what she'd been able to achieve back at camp. Krona had been the subject of many stitchings in the past and knew what her skin should look like a few days after a treated wound. This looked like it had been shut well over a week, perhaps going on two. Injuries in the palms and soles tended to take longer to heal than on other parts of the body—there was no way her wound's progression was natural.

Removing the bandages from her right hand, she compared the two. Yes, her left was definitely further along.

She turned, holding out both hands palm-up. Melanie was on her in an instant, taking both hands in hers, looking them over.

"Someone's been playing already," the healer said.

"Couldn't help myself," Krona admitted.

"Well, go on, then," Hintosep prompted. "Let's see you work."

Closing her eyes, she willed her right palm to move forward faster. *Progress, progress, progress.*

The display might not have been as dramatic as it could have been, seeing as how her wounds weren't gaping—Melanie was too good a healer for that—but it was still effective. Juliet and Thibaut both gasped as her body did its natural work, only in fast-forward. The irritating itching flared again, and she struggled to keep her hand open.

"Wait." Melanie stopped her after a moment. "Not too far. The stitches need to be removed. Let me."

Krona was grateful for the interruption. The ability itself was wonderful, but she'd rather not use it any more than she had to.

Opening her eyes again, she was happy to see Hintosep had an approving sort of twist to her lips.

Thibaut, on the other hand, looked like he'd just witnessed something holy. Divine.

As Melanie retrieved her bag and began to work on the stitches, Krona shook her head at him. "Don't give me that," she said.

"What?" he asked, blinking as though she'd startled him out of a reverie.

"It's not a miracle," she said softly. "It's just magic."

⊱──◦──⊰

The instant the healer had dubbed her free to go, Thibaut had grabbed her newly healed hand and dragged her up to their room—leaving Hintosep to spread the news of their success however she liked. He'd kissed Krona silly before they even managed to shut the door behind them. Each touch of his lips sent an extra zing down her spine. It seemed like she could feel *more* than before, like her nerves were primed for the lightest brush.

His fervor did not diminish as he pulled her farther into the room.

"Did you think I was going to die?" she teased.

"I thought you might," he said between kisses. "I didn't know what would happen, Krona. That's just it. Hintosep won't tell us anything, nothing of substance. You could have come back in pieces, and I doubt I ever would have gotten the full story out of her."

"She's not that bad."

"Isn't she?"

Hintosep had promised her power, and now she felt it simmering beneath the surface. Finally, the Thalo woman had done something to earn real trust.

Krona shoved Thibaut toward the bed, slipped off her bracers, and began undoing her blouse. Her eyes tracked around the room for a moment, searching subconsciously for a familiar splash of yellow. When they failed to find it, she paused. "Where's De-Lia?"

"Now?" He waved at the state of his trousers. "You're going to ask about the mask *now*?"

She raised an expectant eyebrow at him.

"It's in the dresser." He thumbed over at the bureau. "It's fine. Didn't so much as see daylight while you were gone."

Which meant he didn't know if it was still there.

She quickly sidestepped him, hurrying over to see for herself. Gods damn it all, she barely knew most of the people beneath this roof, and any number of them could have taken an interest in the mask for any number of reasons.

Yanking the top drawer open, seeing it was empty, she slammed it shut again. Then the next, and the next, growing more panicked by the moment. "Where is it?" she demanded.

"It's in the bottom." He leapt to his feet again. "With the other one. Relax. Why are you—"

"Relax?" she demanded, whirling on him. "De-Lia's mask is the most important thing to me in the entire world, and you—"

He bent to set his hand over hers before she could yank open the last drawer. "I thought you trusted me," he said sadly.

Her heart broke a little. He'd been so happy to have her back—she'd been happy to be back—and now she'd spoiled the moment. "I should," she said. "I mean, I do. I *do*." Her lip trembled, and she bit it, brows bowing as she tried to apologize with her gaze alone, because she couldn't trust her voice not to break.

"Then what is it?" he asked earnestly.

"I don't trust *myself*."

"Oh, Krona." He wrapped his arms around her, and she let her forehead fall to his chest.

"I know how to be loyal. I know how to be duty-bound. I don't know how to do things just for me. Any moment of happiness I get feels selfish if she's not at the forefront of my mind. I don't . . . I don't want to lose myself, and I don't want to lose her. But I don't know how to balance both."

"Well, seems you're well on your way to conquering step one."

She pulled back, wiped at a damp eye. "Which is what?"

"Letting someone else in," he said with a smile. "You don't have to go it alone."

50

MANDIP

While the ladies had been away, Thibaut and Mandip had gotten reacquainted on friendlier but less salacious terms. "Made a slight fool of myself in front of my mistress, dear Captain Hirvath, and I can't very well go around acting the jealous clown and then turn straight about and start snogging you again, can I?" Thibaut had teased. "Though in truth, I don't think she's one to begrudge me my gainful employment."

"You, sir, are assuming I still have any interest in employing you further," Mandip shot back.

"Further, harder, faster. I think you're still interested in employing me any number of ways."

Mandip crossed his arms, unimpressed. "That was a failed stretch of an innuendo and you know it."

The other safe house residents had accepted Mandip into their fold, though mostly begrudgingly, for the sheer fact that he was nobility and therefore his motives suspect. He didn't blame them.

He wanted to pretend that his brief stint in the Spriggans' jailhouse had somehow changed him. That he was a rougher sort now. And perhaps it *had* changed him, a little, what with the new direction of his civics-oriented thoughts these days. But his parents had helped him and Juliet clear of that mess, and even though he'd lost so much, he knew it all could have gone far worse.

The negotiations that had seen him set free had included removing the enchantments from his person, his connection to the Treasury. Despite there being absolutely no evidence of any wrongdoing on his or Juliet's part, the incident had spooked the Spriggans enough that they decided they needed a new Key.

An anyone-but-me Key, he thought sardonically to himself.

And yet, he was still a high-standing noble twin. With a possible appointment to the palace waiting in his future. So, no matter how much he felt he'd sacrificed to stand amongst them, he was sure all the people here could see right through him. Many of Mirthhouse's residents were life-beaten in ways he could barely envision. Wind-scarred and sun-hardened and dirt-stained. Difficult trials had brought them here; they hadn't simply been swept up in it all like he had.

He mostly tried to blend in. He gave everyone space and pretended he couldn't hear the suspicious whispers behind his back.

But when he heard Thibaut's and Juliet's voices seeping through a closed door only a few days after Krona's miraculous remerger with her varg, he didn't pull his usual turnabout and walk the other way. Instead, he inched toward the door, curious as to why they were speaking in such conspiratorial tones.

"And this is where Gerome's keeping them," said Juliet.

"Are they always together, or is there a chance we'll need to split up?" asked Thibaut.

"I think he suspects I'll try something again soon," came Hintosep's voice. "Likely he'll have them close until I show my face again."

Yet another heist being planned without him. Only this time, they were stealing children. He and Juliet hadn't accompanied Hintosep to the keep when she'd made her bargain, what with their being harangued by the city-state, but Juliet had detailed the Thalo's plan to him once they'd been released.

This time, Hintosep had included Thibaut—of all people—but hadn't thought to invite *him,* and Mandip refused to simply let the offense stand.

Straightening his jacket and squaring his shoulders, he barged into the room, unsurprised to see Thibaut, Juliet, Hintosep, Melanie, Sebastian, *and* Krona all crowded around a map that extended across the full expanse of a table, which itself sat on an intricate red rug surrounded by various planning paraphernalia like notebooks, more maps, a compass, and a star chart.

This was some kind of war room.

"So," he said loudly, by way of announcing himself, "when do we storm the castle and make off with the children?" he demanded.

"We? Why in the Valley would you assume such a plan included you?" Hintosep asked. "This is supposed to be a private meeting, by the way."

"Why wouldn't it include me?" he asked. "I'm handy with a sword, I travel well, and am ready and willing to run head-on into danger. I asked to come back with you because I want to fight. I mean it. I want to do some good in this world, so let me. I want in."

"I already have too many bodies to keep track of as it is," Hintosep said dismissively.

"If it helps," Sebastian spoke up, "I won't be joining you."

Hintosep frowned at him. "Why not?"

"Melanie and I agreed: one of us should go, and one of us should stay here, just in case. And you may need a healer."

"I need people I can count on."

"You can count on me," Mandip promised.

Hintosep considered for a moment, and the others stayed quiet. "Fine," she conceded. "Get in here and close the door." He shut it behind him with a firm *click,* then strode confidently into the room, but she stopped him before he came too close to the table. "First off, this isn't your world where you can demand things, lead the charge, and expect to be heaped with accolades at the end of the day. You will take my orders and follow my instructions to a T. The moment you become more of a hindrance than a help, that is where we leave you."

"Understood." He squeezed himself in between Thibaut and Juliet, both of whom, in contrast to Hintosep, seemed happy to have him.

The map laid out before them was in fact a cross-section of Hintosep's home, the Thalo keep. Seven main floors with perhaps a dozen more offset levels and a handful of towers and tunnels presented a maze of a stronghold.

"There's only one primary entrance and exit, here." Hintosep drew a sweeping line with her finger across a great, bowing rampart that stretched over a craggy ravine and led to a thin, winding road beyond. "It creates a bottleneck that would prevent any armies from being able to mount an effective direct attack on the keep. But it's how we'll go in. Through the front door, like nothing is amiss.

"It'll be difficult, I'm not used to tracking the precise position of so many people at once, but I should be able to shroud you all long enough to get you in unnoticed. From there, my plan is to distract Gerome. To separate him from the children long enough for you to nab the two of them. He'll suspect I'm up to something, but his imagination is limited; he'd never think I'd bring outsiders into the keep. But if he realizes the children are gone, he'll raise the alarm. It's getting back out again that may prove difficult. Luckily, we have a secret weapon." She nodded at Krona. "No one will see a Kairopath coming. As such, Krona, once we're inside, you and I may need to clear the way for the others in order to make our escape."

They would travel on horseback to the terminus of the Severnyy Ice Field, and from there their small fellowship would make a trek—hopefully undetected—to the gates of the keep.

"It'll be a hard journey, but I want to set out tomorrow, first light," Hintosep said. "I fear Gerome means to put one of the two children in the Cage. The longer we dally, the greater they suffer. I need everyone to pitch in, gather the supplies we'll need. And, Krona?"

"Keep testing my limits," she replied.

"Right. I'm sorry we don't have more time for you to train, to be more confident, but I dare not leave them at the keep in the interim. Even as new as your abilities are, they give us great advantages."

In the days since she'd been back, Krona had been getting to know herself again far afield of the mansion, where she could practice in private. She'd been mum so far—at least publicly—on what the rest of her skill set entailed, and Mandip had been dying to catch a glimpse. If nothing else, at least this mission would afford him the opportunity.

When the meeting broke, Thibaut and Juliet instantly swept Mandip away for grunt work. Packing their provisions and prepping their gear and making sure all their weaponry was clean and sharp. He was out back with Clive, the blacksmith and fletcher, and had just about finished making sure Juliet's stock of plated arrows was well rounded when the songstress herself came to retrieve him.

"Follow me," she whispered in his ear, pulling him away.

There was a sly twinkle in her eye that made Mandip feel like he was sneaking out of his bedroom window all over again. "Where are we going?"

She hooked her arm through his, led him away from the back of the mansion and into the stand of trees out past the vegetable garden. It was a sunny day. Warm. It hadn't snowed, even lightly, for a few nights, and the ground was clear and dry. Not far into the grove, they found Thibaut leaning against a thick trunk with a closed, eggshell-white parasol in hand, which just happened to match the eggshell-white of Juliet's dress.

"Hintosep might have been reading your mind a little during our meeting," Juliet said. "Don't balk—she wanted to make sure there were no secret motives underlying your insistence. Instead, she noted your desire to see Captain Hirvath in action. And so, off we go."

Thibaut took up Juliet's other arm, opening the parasol and holding it over her head as the three of them stepped out from beneath the shelter of the grove and began trudging up the hillside, toward what Mandip suspected had once been sheep pastures.

"I thought she wanted to practice alone," Mandip said, his one, weak attempt at a protest.

"She can't very well remain camera-shy forever," Juliet said. "What happens if she gets performance anxiety when we're neck-deep in Thalo?"

"Not going to happen," Thibaut said confidently. "If there's one thing I'm confident in, it's Krona's ability to shine in a fight. You, my dear, simply have voyeuristic tendencies and are shameless enough to spy on my mistress, which I should really put a stop to."

The tease was obvious, though the words themselves were no less galling for it.

Juliet's eyes went wide, and she scoffed as though truly wounded. "Did you hear that, Mandip? Are you really going to let him speak to your betrothed that way?"

Mandip half stumbled over his own feet. "Betrothed?" he asked.

"You know that's what Adhar is surely telling everyone," she said. "It's the only way your disappearance can be logically explained. You must have decided to marry the wild woman after all." She patted his arm. "Don't worry, love; I'm more than happy to add you to my list of paramours. But answer me one thing, if you will. Call it a wedding present."

Mandip's mind had stalled out. "I . . . er . . ."

"Why did you come back with us? Really?" she barreled on. "I know it's not just because you feared for your memories."

Ah. Well. As it turned out, there was a rumble of new aspiration in his chest. He'd wanted to effect change for the better, and Hintosep had shown him a radical way forward. "What ignites a true revolution?" he asked. "Trying to grab the reins of the system as it stands—play by its rules to gain its power—or bucking the system outright? If the point is to stop the manipulation of Arkensyre's destiny, then one cannot play into that manipulation for long; otherwise, we'd succumb to it. So, I thought trying to change my path now made more sense than trying to change my path later. My power as Grand Marquis would come from the very structure we're trying to bury, which means it should really hold no power at all."

"You've become quite the philosopher in these short weeks," Thibaut said. "I know Winsrouen had itself a pair of philosopher kings once, but I don't think we've ever had a philosopher Marquis."

"Nor should we," Mandip said. "That's the point. If it's always been the Savior deciding, then no more kings. No more Marquises."

"Now you've got it," Juliet said, only a hint of smugness in her tone. "Forget philosopher; I think we have a budding anarchist on our hands."

51

KRONA

Jumping should be easy, Krona thought. After all, that was the ability her varg had mastered innately. She'd been hesitant to try it so far—sending oneself across an expanse of time and space, however short, was daunting. Despite her misgivings, maybe she'd get lucky and retain the monster's level of skill.

She'd strolled even farther from the mansion than usual, up into the sloping lower hills of the mountains. She kept the safe house in sight but ventured far enough that she came across the remains of an old stone wall, low enough that it was probably meant to pen in sheep and nothing more.

She rubbed her hands together—still tender but fully healed—and gave herself a pep talk.

Early on, she'd realized she could create lenses that let her peer forward and backward in time across whatever part of the landscape she pointed them at. The lenses were insubstantial and small at first—no bigger than a compact— but she worked up to the size of a window, then a door.

Peering backward was as simple as thought, but she fought hard to look forward. She'd thought, logically, that being able to see the future was the best way to win any war—know what your opponent was going to do before they did it, and ta-da. She'd soon realized, however, that looking into the future was not only immensely difficult but also a fool's errand. Even peering forward for no more than a few seconds was migraine-inducing and worthless. The future was a blur of possibilities, constantly shifting as choices and circumstances created new avenues of potential. There was no set future, no inevitable. There were snippets of what *could be* there to see, nothing more.

One day, when she was more skilled, she hoped she'd be able to untangle the mess of probability enough to at least plan for possible outcomes. But that day was far off, if it even existed at all.

Knowing the future was not set in stone lifted an unexpected weight from her shoulders. Choices mattered, and there was no such thing as a foregone conclusion.

There was one thing the forward-looking lenses were good for, though.

Intuitively, she'd connected them to the varg's ability to jump. Recreating the ability was instinctual, but it turned out controlling it was a whole different matter.

Now she formed a lens, one that gazed no more than a few seconds into the future, and pointed it at a nearby destination: a patch of grass on the other side of the low-built stone wall.

Tentatively, she pressed her hands to it and *pushed.*

The lens immediately warped and twisted, pulling her forward, yanking her off her feet, and propelling her through a sudden tear in reality—a hole, swirling around her, tunneling to that point in time and space.

It spat her out again, with enough forward momentum to send her sprawling—but not before an unfortunate bird flew directly into her path. By the squawk of it, and the flurry of black, she was sure it was a crow. It hit her in the left shoulder, with enough force to bruise. It flapped and clawed but flew off before she smacked into the ground face-first.

She wasn't prepared for the raucous laughter that followed. Pushing herself up, she saw Thibaut, Juliet, and Mandip walking arm-in-arm toward her. Juliet projected the air of a wealthy woman out on a stroll, while Thibaut and Mandip looked like some unfairly handsome farmhands she'd just happened to pick up along the way.

"I told you I wanted to train alone," Krona grumbled, not fully displeased at their presence but thinking she should make a show of it regardless.

"If you've been falling on your face this whole time, I can see why," Thibaut said.

"You just witnessed my first jump," she said, fighting off embarrassment but feeling cheeky enough to give them a facetious half bow.

"Well, then, that wasn't bad at all, was it?" Juliet said. "Come now, try again. We came for a show."

Resigning herself to an audience, she repositioned herself and made a new lens, pushing through for another attempt. And another. And another. She fell again and again, over and over, feeling very much like how a fledgling must feel being kicked out of its nest before it was ready to fly. The others whooped and hollered encouragements like they were the only three spectators at a sporting match, which she found lifted her spirits. She siphoned their energy and wove it into her own determination. But, alas, it made her landings no nimbler.

Eventually, she tired of tossing herself to the ground and simply stayed down. The others flopped beside her, and they all stared at the clouds for a gentle moment before Krona shot up, propping herself on her elbows to exclaim, "Your dress!"

Juliet sat up as well. "What?" She looked around, almost as though she expected the dress to be gone. "What is it?"

"The *dirt.*"

"Ah, tosh," Juliet dismissed, lying back down. "What's the point in looking pristine if it means you can't join in the fun?"

"Here, mistress." Mandip fished in his pocket for a moment, then passed something to Juliet, who passed it to Thibaut, who handed it to Krona. "You can use it to practice time things on. I don't need it anymore."

Tentatively, she took it. Recognized it—his pocket watch. "This belongs to the Treasury, not you," she said.

"You're welcome to try and give it back," he said listlessly, raising his left arm and rolling up his sleeve to bare a long scar, pink in its newness. "But as you can see, I am no longer the Key to the Treasury. I've been released from my duties and am lucky to still have all my limbs. That watch you have there is no more remarkable than the one my brother holds. A stand-in for the one that meant something. This one is merely a symbol of what I've done—the responsibilities given me by Lutador that were revoked, but only because I chose to shun them first." He grinned sadly at everyone, his expression lopsided. "I've made my choice. And I believe it's the right one. But who knows? I don't suppose you can tell me? Now that you're . . . more *you*?"

"Unfortunately, it doesn't work like that."

"Not a prognosticator, then?" Thibaut asked. "Can't tell us if we'll all end up rich and happy in the long run?"

"Rich? Doubtful. Happy?" She subtly slipped her hand into his. "We can only hope."

"Access to time still doesn't mean access to certainty, then?" Juliet asked.

"Alas, no."

"Shame."

"I wonder what I am," Mandip mused absently. "Everyone here must wonder about themselves, don't you think? What magics we were born with. Which kind of wings were clipped. I thought I always knew myself. Turns out I knew very little."

"What with the number of broken hearts you must have left scattered all over Lutador, surely you're an Emotiopath," Juliet teased.

He scoffed. "Especially now that we're getting married."

"Who's getting married?" Melanie asked as she and Sebastian crested the hill—taking the words right out of Krona's mouth.

Juliet and Mandip spoke at the same time—

"It's just a jest," he insisted.

"Mandip and I. Come." Juliet sat up for a moment, patting at the grass around her. "Come gaze at the clouds with us. A calm before the storm, if you will."

They sat around chatting long after the sun began to dip itself below the rim. There was a gentle unity in it, an ebb and flow of ease that reminded Krona of a less-structured version of her detail. She missed them—Tray, Royu, Sasha, Tabitha, and even Gorvin.

And, of course, De-Lia.

With a start, she realized she hadn't thought about De-Lia all day. In fact, the jaguar mask wasn't even on her—it was back in the bedroom, on top of the dresser. For an instant, a panic-laced guilt coursed through her, but it was soon subdued by the chatter of those around her. She hadn't forgotten De-Lia, after all; she'd simply been in the moment, connected to the world. She'd been living her life. Which, she realized, was something De-Lia would have wanted her to do.

When they finally returned to the mansion, had their supper, double-checked their supplies, and sent themselves to bed, Krona felt freer, lighter, than she had in a long time. It was the freedom of letting go of a worry, of a deep, unfair demand on her soul.

She wasn't giving up on De-Lia by not obsessing over her. After all, she was closer to understanding the possibilities of life and death than she ever had been before. All she was giving up on was the fixation, the all-consuming guilt that had led her here.

She wondered if a similar sort of guilt or worry drove Melanie, Sebastian, and Juliet. What kind of weight would be lifted off their hearts once their loved ones were safe and sound? What bits of themselves would return to the world? Parts that they'd cut away or buried.

After putting on her nightclothes, she picked up the jaguar mask and traced it with her fingertips. The form of it was so familiar, she was sure if she had any talent with an awl, she could carve an identical one purely from memory.

Just like it hadn't accompanied her on her quest for her varg, so too would it stay safely tucked away while she and the others went on their rescue mission. It was better that way. For her sake and its.

Gently, she set it in the bottom drawer, and closed it snugly. "Sleep now, De-Lia," she whispered, and began to sing softly:

What would we be, without her hand?
Bones before birth, dust before death
Wed before maidens, memory before sand

Thibaut, already in bed, surprised her by picking up the next verse. She'd never heard him sing before, and while he was no La Maupin, it was beautiful, simply because his voice was his.

> *Rise before sleep, dusk before noon*
> *Exist before our parents*
> *And enter the world too soon*

"Or too late," she said, slipping under the covers next to him.
"It's never too late," he assured her.

52

THALO CHILD

Naming ceremonies were always joyous for all in attendance. Only, this one carried a special sting. Two of the children from Thalo Child's cohort were to be given proper names, revealed to be embodiments of great Thalo from times gone by.

The naming itself was private—a special ritual performed only by the Savior Himself—but the processional—lively and celebratory, like a parade—was for all. Nearly everyone in the keep followed those to be named on a winding journey through multiple levels of their home. They were boisterous, full of song and shouts of glee. Members of the Order were, as a general rule, stoic, calm, and centered. Thoughtfulness and deliberateness were considered virtues; rowdiness and impulsiveness were weaknesses. Once in a while, though, as with the feasts that followed the taking of Sacrifices, the Thalo were encouraged to let loose and indulge in some off-the-cuff expressions of delight.

Thalo Child walked along some two-thirds of the way behind the named, striding arm in arm at the end of a chain that consisted of four others near his age who belonged to the Eye. One teenager would occasionally skip or jump off cue, throwing the others all off step, jostling the line and eliciting barks of laughter and good-natured ribbing.

Thalo Child was mid-laugh when Gerome swooped up beside him and whispered in his ear, "After the naming, come to my quarters. We have much to discuss," before striding on. He and the other Possessors kept a careful eye on the procession, making sure none of the celebrations got out of hand.

For weeks now, Gerome had remained in a good mood—self-satisfied, triumphant. The little cuts and cruelties he'd visited upon Thalo Child disappeared. In fact, his regard for Thalo Child seemed to turn itself inside out. Instead of disdained, he felt valued. He'd made what Gerome had deemed the right choice, and was rewarded with renewed favor.

Still, Thalo Child's stomach dropped, fearing what time alone with Gerome might now entail.

He tried to keep up his smile, but the joy was gone.

Once the procession had arrived at its destination and the crowd had dispersed, Thalo Child took his time snaking his way back toward Gerome's rooms. He'd lost sight of his Possessor as the celebration went on and had no way of knowing if Gerome had ducked out early or stayed until the newly named had re-emerged.

When he reached the dreaded door, he rapped lightly. A drowsy "Come in" bade him enter.

Thalo Child was not prepared for the sight that greeted him.

In the middle of the small room, next to the table that bore the headdress-tree, Gerome sat on the floor in the lotus position, eyes closed, black hair cascading over his shoulders like oil, chest bared—thin and pale, ribs prominent.

Around his head was the Cage.

The spine of it curled over the back of his skull, and the legs reached around his temples and cheeks and chin to prod at the corresponding scars.

Thalo Child froze in the doorway. He didn't know what to do, what was expected of him.

"I said come in," Gerome repeated, maintaining his pose, keeping his eyes closed.

"You said you didn't mean to wear it," Thalo Child blurted as he closed the door behind him.

"I don't," Gerome said flatly. "There is no life to it," he said, opening his eyes, piercing Thalo Child with his cold stare.

Looking more closely, Thalo Child could see that he was right. While the legs aligned with Gerome's scars, they did not penetrate his skin. There was a husk-like quality to the Cage, as though some golden creature had just shed its exoskeleton and slunk away.

Carefully, Gerome removed it, peeling back the legs, opening them like he was prying open a death-stiffened hand. "The artifact's very nature means I cannot subject myself to its power," he explained. "It is pure control. To be subjected to it is to relinquish any sense of will. One cannot be in control and have no control simultaneously." He stood and set it on the table.

It was rare to see Gerome without anything covering his forehead or dangling before his eyes. Without a headdress, he seemed less himself. Diminished.

"I've learned all the lessons it could teach me. No matter how I miss it, I cannot go back to the days that were easy. The days I simply wore the Cage and turned off my mind and let my body do Hintosep's bidding. It is time to fit the Cage on another."

He flexed his hand and the Cage flexed, each of its twelve legs fluttering as though attached to his fingers by puppet strings.

Thalo Child jumped back. He was already terrified of the Eye as it was. "Please," he said, voice small, throat gone dry, "I promised to be good."

For a moment, Gerome looked confused, as though unable to parse out what Thalo Child's promise had to do with the moment. But then his lip curled in a knowing smile. He let the silence hang, thick with the unknown, as he chose a new headdress from his stand—one made of platinum and diamonds. Slicking his hair down, he lowered it into place.

"You misunderstand," he finally said, eyes now hidden beneath the low brim. "Your time with Hintosep taught you more about true duty than I ever could have on my own. You don't need the Cage. It is a force best used on the willful. One in denial of their place. That is not you.

"I asked you here because if I am to become the Possessor of the Cage, I can no longer rightfully lay claim to the Eye. I will need an apprentice. You will no longer *belong* to the Eye. You will wield it."

Thalo Child knew in his heart that he was no Possessor—reincarnated or otherwise. He couldn't visit torture upon children—for no matter what Gerome said, Thalo Child knew that was all the artifacts did: torture. They broke a person down, made them malleable. "I can't," he choked out.

Gerome obviously expected a different response but read Thalo Child's denial generously. "Of course not. Not yet. You're still growing into yourself, becoming who you have always been. I will help you. And once you are named, once your full power as a Possessor is revealed, I will hand over the Eye, and the Cage will be Possessed once more."

Thalo Child wished he knew more curse words. He wished he knew how to firmly tell Gerome *no* without his Possessor flying into a rage.

"I understand," Gerome said fondly, taking a single stride to stand in front of Thalo Child. "The future is intimidating. The responsibility? Daunting." He set a hand on Thalo Child's cheek, and it took everything in Thalo Child's power not to recoil. "But I am here, no matter—"

The Possessor cut himself off, tilted his head back, peering out from beneath his headdress with a deep frown, as though he'd just noticed a terrible smudge on Thalo Child's nose.

The boy didn't realize what had changed until it was too late.

Gerome was no longer distracted by his lust for the Cage. He had it now and could turn his mind to other things.

Like Thalo Child's secrets.

"Your infant has abilities you don't understand."

Thalo Child was sure his heart stopped. It felt like a stone in his chest—thick and solid and perfectly useless.

"Zhe is . . . a Physiopath. That—Why?"

Gerome looked even more confused than Thalo Child had been when he'd first seen his charge turn zhur rattle to stone.

"Zhe should have had zhur magic taken and stayed with zhur parents," Gerome continued. "Zhe should have continued on as a perfectly normal citizen of Arkensyre. Zhe never should have come here. Why would Hintosep want to raise a Physiopath as a Cryptopath?" He thought for a long moment, hand leaving Thalo Child's cheek so he could tap one manicured nail against his own bottom lip. "Ah, but she didn't, did she? The babe was supposed to be long gone by now. Which means—"

He lashed out, grabbing Thalo Child by the chin, fingers digging into the meat of his cheeks as he forced the child's head this way and that to examine him. "She did not choose you at random to care for zhim."

He laughed then—a brutal guffaw of a thing. "I should have known. Her time spent as an Orchestrator served her well. She is pulling many strings I see, manipulating players not just here in the keep but well beyond. She took the babe when she shouldn't have, in order to get something she wanted. From who, I wonder. A Harvester? Or the baby's parents?"

Gerome let Thalo Child go, baring his teeth in a gleeful smile, clapping his hands. "I've destroyed even more than I meant to, I think. How delightful. Whoever you are, child, whoever she took you from, whoever she thought you'd be—none of that matters now. She abandoned you, just as she abandoned me. She has made us more kindred than we ever were before."

Thalo Child kept silent but made no secret of how he felt. Inside, he screamed denials. He didn't want to be like Gerome. He didn't want to be a Possessor.

He didn't want any of this.

Hintosep had promised him she'd try again. That she'd be back for the babe if he'd gone with her.

But he'd stayed.

And perhaps she'd lied.

He looked to the Cage, understanding for the first time what the appeal was. To be left bereft of decision, to simply *be* while the world worked around you, to let go of responsibility and pressure—to not even have to think about what expression to wear on your own face at any given moment—would be a bliss.

"What is she truly after?" Gerome mused to himself. "And what terrible troubles can we meet her with?"

53

MANDIP

Fog swirled around the mansion's low foundations, streaming up and around the illusion's charred beams without a hint of artifice. Mandip admired the craftmanship of the enchantment as they marched away, waving to Sebastian—the lone individual there to see them off.

Mandip had watched (while pretending not to) Melanie and Sebastian's tearful good-bye. They'd held each other, foreheads rested against one another's, as they mumbled promises and reassurances. Watching them separate had been like watching a whole rip itself in half.

What was worse was realizing that the reason they'd decided to part was because of how dangerous it was to walk straight into the Thalo keep. They knew this mission might fail—catastrophically—and if that happened, they wanted at least one of them to still be alive to try again.

❧

To call the journey difficult would be to call their dash from the Palace Rotunda a breeze. It was arduous, excruciating. The mountains that built toward Marrakev's rim were not like the mountains of Lutador. These were sheer things, twice as tall, with snowcaps that never melted and winds that never ceased. They made the days' travel pure hardship and the nights mostly miserable—even with Thalo enchantments to help protect them.

Though the environment was unforgiving, it was also undeniably beautiful. Below spread a lush valley basin, narrower overall than any other city-state in Arkensyre but filled with trees and high plateaus. They crossed gorge after gorge flush with running water, where the ice melt of centuries had worn great rivulets into the stone. Cold-weather lichen clung to trunks and dangled from tree branches like celebratory streamers. Snowbirds wound strings of moss, vines, and even horsehairs plucked from their steeds into large hanging nests that housed dozens and dozens of ice-colored avians.

White stags with black spots occasionally wandered close to their camps, as did slinking snow ferrets, white foxes, and graying wolves. Hintosep swore there were snow leopards about, but the cats were far too stealthy to let themselves be spotted.

The air was crisp. So cold that it stung the nose and cut sharply through any scents. The smell of their campfires, the dirt kicked up by their horses' hooves—even the scent of the horses themselves—couldn't compete with the piercing frigidness that closed the pores and stung the nostrils.

The horses had been procured from who knew where. These were not the sleek sort of thoroughbreds Mandip was used to riding but instead tough-built, stocky workhorses. Hintosep's was rugged and clearly familiar with her as a rider, but Mandip wouldn't be surprised to learn that his steed had been nabbed from in front of some poor workman's cart.

Not long into their Marrakevian trek, they all began to don their heaviest cloaks and thickest furs. Most were typical blacks, grays, and woodland browns, but of course Hintosep's was cobalt blue, and Juliet had brought a wardrobe's worth, varying between bloodred, snow white, and shimmering leafy green.

They were mostly quiet as they rode, cautiously watching and listening for any signs of trouble. Captain Hirvath's armor rattled in her saddlebag occasionally, reminding them of the conflict to come. They stopped often for Hintosep to scout ahead, as she was concerned a Thalo detail might spot their approach to the keep, give away that she wasn't alone. Only then, during these rests, did the others gather around to chat or to help Krona practice her abilities. Hintosep's good-bye bidding to Captain Hirvath was always the same: "Keep jumping. It may turn out to be your most vital skill."

And so, jump she did.

"Right-o!" Juliet called out, five days into their journey. "You almost landed on your feet with that one!"

Krona, who'd managed to land on her hands and knees—keeping her face from becoming too acquainted with the forest floor, at the very least—gave Juliet a gruff "Thanks" before hauling herself upright and trying again.

Watching the Regulator disappear and reappear repeatedly was still mind-bending. She said she created "lenses"—some kind of doorway, it seemed—to thrust herself through, but no one else had the ability to see them. To Mandip, one moment she was simply there, then for several beats she was gone, and then, miraculously, there she was again, on the other side of their temporary camp.

They'd picked a spot with heavy tree cover, but through the branches they could see sweeping vistas and large knots of ancient trees, which were actually small, primeval villages protected by living walls.

"At least she hasn't run into a tree for a while," Melanie commented under her breath, giving Thibaut a face—lips pursed, nose scrunched—which he returned in kind.

Their collective tension rose as they neared the northernmost end of the Valley, where the basin of it curved around to the east and plunged into a long, expansive fissure covered in glacial ice—the Severnyy Ice Field. Hintosep pointed to a tall bit of mountain range near the rim—snow-encased and craggy—where the Thalo keep lay. They couldn't see it from their angle of approach, and even if they could, it would only look like more mountain from their distance. It was meant to blend in, to defy detection by mere magicless mortals.

The horses they had to leave well before they left the last vestiges of civilization behind, and the final two days they had to spend entirely on foot. Captain Hirvath exchanged her furs for her armor, and suddenly everything felt far too real. The sword at Mandip's side wasn't for show; the arrows in Juliet's quiver weren't for hunting.

They were venturing into enemy territory with a purpose, hoping Hintosep could hide them, hoping Krona's powers gave her the depth of immunity Hintosep claimed.

"Everything will be simpler if you follow my instructions precisely," Hintosep warned them as they approached what she described as a carriage house—as the first guarded station on their way to the keep's grand doors. "You will walk ahead of me when possible, not behind. I need to be able to note your positions in order to shield you. Keep together and in the same order. You will be invisible to each other as well. Do not speak until we are well past the guards here. I can hide your voices, but it is one more thing that will require attention, energy. Trying to shield this many people at once is already difficult enough. I need you to walk swiftly, with confidence, but do not run, or I might lose you. I need to approach normally. I will be given the benefit of the doubt, but it's still best my behavior appear as usual. Understand?"

Mandip immediately grabbed hold of Juliet's hand, who gave him a wink and continued the chain, taking Melanie's hand, who took Thibaut's, who took Krona's.

Hintosep nodded in approval. "Good." With a snap of her fingers, everyone around Mandip vanished except for Hintosep. "Follow the road," she instructed. "There's only one way you can go, and that's up. You can't get lost." She urged them forward. "Go."

Krona led the line. When Mandip was tugged forward by Juliet's invisible grip, he let his feet follow.

It was undeniably strange to stride up the middle of the road, toward the carriage house, feeling utterly exposed. He tried not to make a sound of protest, not to yank back on Juliet's arm, when a figure in blue—another Thalo, plain as day, stepped out near them, a metal staff in hand. The person's eyes—framed by deep-blue swirls—tracked well past their approaching line and back to where Hintosep trailed behind them.

They passed the Thalo easily and within arm's reach. Not only could Mandip make out the whites of their eyes but the freckles on their nose and the dimples in their cheeks. He held his breath as they went by, worried one errant puff of wind would give them away, sending the guard into an attack.

He drew level with the Thalo, noting the way their gloved hands tightened around the staff, and the runes on the shaft began to glow. Slowly, their eyes shifted in Mandip's direction. He could have sworn their stare locked onto his, that it was over.

But in an instant, their focus snapped back to Hintosep, and the Thalo let her pass with a sweeping bow of acknowledgment, clearly humbling themself before her, recognizing that she wasn't just anyone returning to the keep but someone of great import.

He didn't know if anyone else in their party had asked Hintosep what part she played in the Thalo's hierarchy, or if there even *was* a hierarchy beyond the Savior's supreme seating. He'd suspected she was an elite magic-user and fighter, what with the way she'd taken out her former comrades at that first camp and the fact that she'd been assigned the vital role of assassin. He'd thought, perhaps, she might be considered on par with Krona—a top-ranking member of the constabulary. But now he got the sense that she was far *more*; no one bowed *like that* to a Regulator.

They passed a handful more guards at close proximity before finding themselves alone, trailing up a winding, precariously narrow path. Harsh winds beat repeatedly against their necks and shoulders, but something seemed to be protecting their legs, and he wondered if there was an invisible barrier that made the trek slightly less dangerous than it seemed.

A number of small obstacles, clearly meant to confuse and deter anyone who might unwittingly find themselves on this path (however unlikely that was) met them as they traveled, including an invisible bit of trail that Krona barreled over without a second thought, dragging everyone with her.

But when they came around a corner and finally laid their eyes on the keep proper for the first time, even Krona stopped and gasped.

Mandip had seen the maps, the drawings. He already had a sense of what to expect, but seeing it in person, in all its grandeur, had no equal. There was no way to convey, by sketch or photograph, just how magnificent the stronghold was.

"It's supposed to be a monument to the gods," Hintosep said from behind them. "A place of strength and wonder to house the Valley's protectors and guides."

"And yet, somehow, blasphemous and grotesque in its sprawl," Mandip said, echoing Thibaut's words from the night at the Rotunda, suddenly feeling their meaning deep in his bones, truly understanding Thibaut's point about the dual awe and ugliness of excess for the first time.

They continued on, through the gates at the end of the sweeping ramparts, past two more guards at the entrance, and then—

Through the front doors. Like they belonged. Just as Hintosep said.

He realized now that her power had to be enormous. The Order of the Thalo could manipulate all of the Valley from this very place, and yet there she was, all on her own, walking outsiders in—bringing *enemies* in—beneath the noses of people whose capacity to keep them out otherwise was nearly absolute.

Mandip was used to vaulted ceilings, to detailed craftsmanship and an abundance of art and sculpture for art and sculpture's sake. When resources were plentiful, buildings became more than four walls and a roof. They were built not just to house something but to invoke certain feelings in the visitor.

And this place was clearly constructed to invoke power and terror. There was an omnipotence to the space, the walls made one feel pinned in, and the high ceilings and long corridors made one feel constantly as though a watchful eye could be anywhere, spying on them at any time. The lighting was low, sconces and windows both few and far between. He stepped lightly, fearing the echoing of his boots against the stones would sound as loud as timpani.

As soon as they entered, Hintosep had taken the lead without a word. They passed few Thalo in the halls—winding as they were—and Mandip wondered how many people occupied the keep versus how many it could accommodate. It seemed a city in and of itself, and yet it was far from bustling.

He knew Hintosep was leading them through all the areas she thought she might find Gerome, and the trail was dizzying. He wasn't sure, what with all the switchbacks and stairways and seemingly endless halls, that he'd be able to find his way back to the entrance if asked.

Eventually, they rounded a corner deep within the keep—so deep, he could smell the hot springs—and there, striding toward them, were three others. One was a tall, thin man with pale skin, long, slick black hair, and a half-helm over his eyes. Trailing just a step behind him was a teenager a few years Mandip's junior, who carried a dark-skinned toddler on his hip.

Melanie gasped softly, Juliet squeezed Mandip's hand all the harder, and he understood.

These were the children they were after.

54

THALO CHILD

The sense of relief that washed over Thalo Child at the sight of Hintosep was sudden and unexpected. He'd been struggling to cultivate resentment toward her, like he'd wanted to—too great, still, was his despair. He didn't want any of the "greatness" Gerome had offered him, and he didn't want to see a Possessor's artifact ever again, let alone wield one, and only Gerome's suspicion that Thalo Child and Thalo Infant had been given special attention by Hintosep *for a reason* gave him hope his fate was not yet set.

If she'd had a purpose for him—not just as a helper but something more—then she would not give up as easily as it appeared. Her assurances had to be genuine.

And now, here she was again, so soon.

"I believe there's something wrong with the Cage," she said to Gerome by way of greeting, ignoring Thalo Child and his charge all together. "Have you used it yet?"

"No," Gerome replied flatly.

"Where is it?"

"Back in its proper home, on its pedestal in the reliquary."

"Excellent. Leave the children and take me to it."

"One Who Belongs to the Eye does not leave my side these days, and the infant does not leave his."

"They are not Possessors; they are forbidden from entering the reliquary."

"I think we can make an exception. The boy is my apprentice."

"Your apprentice? He is not yet named; how can you know he will be a Possessor?"

"*Because I will it,*" he snapped between clenched teeth.

She had Gerome's temper teetering on a knife point. He was done being questioned by her and clearly had no patience for the way she spoke down to him. Thalo Child knew his Possessor thought he had Hintosep over a barrel—had already deemed himself the winner of their back-and-forth, whatever the game was—and couldn't stand the fact that she still met him with the same demandingness as ever.

He wanted her to defer—to acknowledge him as her equal if not her better. But she behaved as though nothing had changed. As though she *hadn't* been outmaneuvered.

And Gerome couldn't let that stand. "If you wish to go to the reliquary, we will *all* go to the reliquary."

"Fine," Hintosep said, glancing over her shoulder, as though she expected someone to walk up behind her. "We will all go."

>-+→-○-+→-+-<

Thalo Child personally had no desire to enter the reliquary. He did not need to traverse the winding steps down into the keep's bowels and once more expose himself to the gallery of bottled varger that guarded the reliquary's entrance.

He paused just outside the darkened maw of the lab's archway as the adults confidently strode inside. Though the entrance was wide, there was still only one way in, one way out—one way *up*, back into the rest of the keep—and instinct told him he didn't want to be cornered in such a place. Especially not with Thalo Infant.

His charge could feel the change in the atmosphere, the pure foreboding in this place, just as he could, and hid zhur face against his shoulder. He rubbed the toddler's back to soothe zhim, wishing there was someone here who could soothe him the same in return.

With a deep breath, he stepped them both inside.

The varger were even more jittery when the spotlights came on than the first time Thalo Child had been subjected to this place, and the gallery itself was just as macabre. Even the monsters who seemed settled in their shapes now made the large glass bottles vibrate upon their pedestals. They snapped and swirled, and Thalo Infant quietly shook from fear.

For every step forward, Thalo Child wished he could take two steps back. This seemed like a terrible place to bring the Cage and an even worse place to allow an infant.

The way the varger moved in their sculpted prisons disturbed and refracted the overhead lighting, sending odd shadows and bursts of color across the floor, their faces, and the shafts of the pedestals. It made the room itself—the very stones— look like a writhing, breathing creature. The flashes were harsh and threatening, the shadows fleeting but ominous.

Hintosep paused just outside the rear arch to the reliquary, hand outstretched for the concealing curtain. "Leave the children here," she instructed. "You may no longer recognize my authority, but surely you still bend to the Savior's."

"Why so keen to adhere to His rules *now*?" Gerome asked. "You've already stolen a varg specimen without His consent. Tell me again why that bottle-barker was so important? I've forgotten."

She glared at him.

"You can't fault me for being curious," he said lightly. He gestured her forward. "After you."

The reliquary was far larger than Thalo Child expected, given only seven artifacts were kept there when not in use: the Eye, the Song, the Wing, the Teeth, the Rage, the Fruit, and now of course the Cage. And he'd expected the inside to be a thorough mirroring of most of the rest of the keep: stark, cold. All stone and rough edges. Instead, it had a softness to it, and there was plenty of light inside to see by.

Thin, gauzy fabrics of pinks and purples and deep reds hung from a high ceiling, delineating smaller spaces in the large room. Soft, seemingly natural light filtered down from skylights above, though Thalo Child knew it couldn't be sunlight, since they were deep in the keep and it was approaching evening.

Still, the skylights didn't illuminate every corner. There were still plenty of shadows to give Thalo Child a sudden start—a problem only made worse by how easily the dangling fabrics fluttered in the slightest air currents.

Thalo Infant clung to him, and Thalo Child hoisted zhim higher, onto his shoulder. The toddler kept looking behind them, reaching out for some reason, and Thalo Child couldn't keep zhim still.

Hintosep and Gerome walked in front of him, moving through the room with purpose, each step certain and direct, leaving Thalo Child only moments to scurry by and take in the details of this forbidden place. Near the back of the cavernous room, the curtains of fluttering fabric became denser, truly obscuring what lay beyond. The light from the nearest skylight was just so that as they approached, Thalo Child distinctly caught sight of kneeling human shapes and yelped in surprise.

"They're just carvings," Hintosep reassured him, pulling back the last of the curtains to reveal a low wall of statues, each stooped in a strenuous position, their faces set in hard expressions as they jointly lifted a massive marble slab. "This is what we're here for."

The wall sat upon a low dais with shallow steps leading up to it. Atop the slab held aloft by the tortured-looking figures were seven golden pedestals, each with a seating designed to perfectly cushion the unique form of each artifact. Currently present were most, excepting primarily the Fruit and the Song, which were presumably currently in use by their Possessors.

The Eye had been removed from the top of Gerome's staff and sat inertly in its place of honor, looking almost unimpressive next to the Wing—the gold-plated arm of some leathery-hide creature, the flaps of the wing veiny, the three-toed tip of the arm clawed and menacing. But none of the artifacts sent dread down Thalo Child's spine quite like the Cage.

The Cage, which *wasn't* there.

Hintosep approached the empty seat, swiping her hand across it.

Gerome stopped short at the bottom of the steps. "What's so wrong with the Cage that you had to hurry back so soon after delivering it?" he asked, his tone betraying a snobbish kind of *knowing*.

She turned and examined him. "Neither of us are ignorant of the other's intent, so I suggest we drop the charade."

"Excellent idea," said someone from the shadows.

Under the circumstances, any new voice would have made Thalo Child jump out of his skin, but *that* voice? Every nerve ending in his system flared, and despair swamped him. His entire being jolted with panic, as though he'd just missed a stair in the dark, and he felt like he was both falling and spinning, unable to make it stop. He wanted to run and scream but found himself stiff and rooted to the spot.

They were caught.

One moment the Savior wasn't, and then He was. He stood less than a stone's throw away and had surely been watching them the entire time.

Thalo Child had only ever glimpsed the Savior from a distance. He'd never been this close, had never seen the carefully embroidered patterns in His robes or the details of the carvings on His mask. He'd never felt the raw power of His presence before, and the very air seemed to thicken with it.

Hintosep whirled to face the Savior. She bared her teeth at Gerome, an accusation on her lips, but the Savior interrupted her.

"Oh, my dear child, Gerome didn't have to tell me anything. You really thought you could keep me out of your mind? That your skills were enough to rival *mine*?

"I didn't want to believe it—these little snippets of subterfuge I sensed wafting away from you. I told myself, *repeatedly*, that I must be mistaken. That what seemed like a plan to undermine me must really be something else. I *couldn't* believe it, not unless I saw your betrayal with my own eyes. And *here* you *are*." As He spoke, the Savior's voice grew from calm yet belittling to heated and enraged. He clearly spat His words through clenched teeth behind the mask. "And not even alone, I might add."

With a wave of His hand, like He was clearing the air of a cloud of incense, an entire *crowd* of people appeared. Thalo Child wasn't just shocked to see five strangers instantly revealed but also all five of the Grand Orchestrators, each masked so he could not tell who was who. They moved on the strangers, crowding them into one wall, away from the exit.

That was why Thalo Infant had been reaching out. Zhe'd known the whole time that people were behind them. Young children's brains, being undeveloped, often had a way of bypassing things like shrouds, a way of being impervious to the mature manipulations of secrets.

The strangers huddled close together, but not like a group of frightened Sacrifices brought in by Harvesters. This group had *weapons* and set themselves shoulder to shoulder in a defensive line.

One wore distinct, imposing armor and clutched a saber in one fist and a silver knuckleduster in the other.

"Why would you want to hurt me like this?" the Savior continued, disappointment heavy in His tone. His concern bordered less on angry, more on tired. "After everything I've given you? Time, power, freedom—anything and everything you've ever asked of me, I've given to you."

"I also asked for *honesty*," she shot back.

"I've been as honest as I could be. As I knew how to be. I've been like a parent to you, a father—"

"*I had parents*," she shouted. "And *he* had parents." She waved wildly at Thalo Child. "How many parents have you killed? How many children have you taken? How many families and souls have you ripped apart all so that you can hide atop this mountain and toy with the entire population of the Valley like they're dolls in your giant playhouse?"

"You know that's not why I do it," the Savior said, striding around, weaving through the hangings, coming in and out of the soft light, His gaze slipping from Hintosep, to the strangers, to Gerome, to the Grand Orchestrators—but never falling on Thalo Child. "I take no pleasure in all this, but it must be done. You forget what humanity can do when it has access to power it doesn't understand. How dangerous people can be to themselves, to the planet. It's better this way. *We agreed* it was better this way."

"You've been *slipping*," Hintosep hissed between clenched teeth. "I remember what you tried to hide from me."

He fell silent, stopped His pacing. At first, Thalo Child thought her statement had simply given the Savior pause but quickly realized He must be probing Hintosep's mind, looking for which wall (Thalo Child knew there must be many) had fallen.

Hintosep seemed to grasp what He was doing a moment too late. She was skilled enough to feel everyone else's probing, but His was a perfect infiltration.

She tried to fight back, resisting with all her will, obviously straining to close off parts of herself as He speared through her defenses.

This was not like watching her spar with Gerome, where she'd clearly held the upper hand, though Gerome's abilities hadn't lagged too far behind. The Savior ripped her *down*, cleanly and smoothly making her drop to her knees within seconds. He yanked further on her mind and she half toppled, half slid down the steps to crouch at Gerome's sandaled feet.

He pulled her further still, and she jerked headfirst across the floor, as though she had a fishhook in her mind. The Savior guided her toward the exit curtain, as though He meant to shove her out of the reliquary.

Hintosep stopped herself just short, rearing against His raw hold on her secrets. She clenched her teeth and screamed behind them—either out of defiance or pain—it was the most rattled Thalo Child had ever seen her, the weakest, the most human, and he felt defeated. He swiftly set Thalo Infant on zhur feet and went to Hintosep, kneeling down next to her, taking her hand.

"Stop it," he pleaded with the Savior. "Whatever you're doing to her, please stop."

The Savior let out a long-suffering sigh. "Gerome. The children, if you please."

Gerome strode swiftly, happy to comply. As he approached, hand outstretched to pull Thalo Child up, Hintosep looked to Thalo Child and tried to give him a reassuring smile despite her clenched teeth—one that made him want to cry. He could not fathom how there could be anything reassuring in this situation at all. "It is time," she whispered, reaching out, her straining fingers grazing his cheek just as Gerome tore him away.

The wall inside his mind *crumbled*.

A whirlwind of information fluttered to the fore of his consciousness, temporarily blinding him to everything else in the room.

A name. He had a name. Hintosep had given it to him, or—no, simply told him of it.

Avellino.

Half the things in his mind made little sense; he didn't understand why she'd told him what she'd told him. But he did know her true purpose here. Her plan.

Thalo Child struggled against Gerome, but the Possessor dug his fingers into Thalo Child's arms and shook him with a vengeance, stomping over to grab Thalo Infant as well. Terrified, Thalo Infant tried to get away, darting around Gerome's legs, trying to reach the exit. But zhe was no match for the Possessor. He caught zhim by the arm, and when zhe began to cry, Gerome—cold and uncaring—slapped the toddler across the mouth before wrenching zhim up by zhur hair.

"Abby!" shouted one of the strangers, breaking formation, dashing forward.

One of the Grand Orchestrators moved to intercept the woman, and Gerome turned, a sneer on his lips, glancing in the commotion's direction for half a moment.

It was all the time Hintosep needed.

She *sprang*.

She lunged straight for Gerome, throwing herself bodily at him. Hintosep—ever poised and controlled—turned *savage*. Wild in a way Thalo Child had never observed anyone turn wild, not even an infant in the deepest throes of a tantrum.

They were so near the reliquary's exit that her leap thrust the three of them—Thalo Child, Gerome, and Hintosep—through the dark curtain. It flapped once, in a harsh *snap*, before they were swallowed up by the varger lab beyond.

Behind them, the reliquary erupted into the sounds of motion and chaos.

In the gallery, the bottles rattled with barely contained, monstrous glee.

Hintosep struck the Possessor with her full weight, hands outstretched and pointed at his head. Looking to defend himself, Gerome let go of Thalo Child, who pitched to the floor. In the reliquary, metal clashed, the Savior shouted.

Scrambling away from Hintosep and Gerome, pressing his back into one of the pillars supporting a bottle-barker, Thalo Child reached for Thalo Infant, who'd followed them through the curtain and was already crawling into his arms. When he caught sight of what Hintosep was doing to Gerome, he covered the toddler's eyes.

Gerome, in his attempt to get away, had stumbled backward into the shadows, down one row of bottle-barkers, though he didn't get far. Hintosep was wild and unrelenting. She clawed the half-helm from his face, tossing it aside to get at her prey. The stark lighting of the gallery made Gerome's skin even more sallow, his features even more drawn, and Hintosep's white hair reflected the vapor colors refracting the nearest spotlight.

Diving in, she latched on to his throat with her *teeth*.

A great spurt of blood sprayed away from his neck as she wrenched her head back, tearing at his jugular. It splattered up her face and over the nearest bottles, painting everything a terrible crimson.

They both fell to the floor as Gerome let out a strangled gurgle instead of a scream.

The two of them were tangled together in each other's clothes—his robes catching and snagging on the grommets and studs of her armor—twisted and caught even as they tried to kick themselves apart. Both of his hands flew to his throat, trying to staunch the flow, while hers wrenched at their garments, trying to tear her way out of the knot they'd created.

The glass and stone in the room rattled like they were at the mercy of an earthquake. The creatures howled and gnashed and reveled in the viciousness.

Blood. So much blood. On Gerome's neck, chest, and fingers, under his head and pooling on the floor. Most grotesquely, on Hintosep's chin and cheeks, down the front of her robes, and across her teeth. Soon, it was in her hair and on her boots and under her nails. Gerome's pale skin looked like he'd been bathed in it.

Moments later, four of the Grand Orchestrators came bursting into the gallery, flying toward Hintosep and Gerome, descending upon her, attempting to subdue her. They tried to slip inside her mind and control her, but the sheer power of her will forced them back, sent them physically skidding across the floor.

But they pushed forward, through it, like fighting against a violent wind, and one soon reached her, throwing themselves atop her, then the next, and the next. The first screamed, clutching their head, wrenching themself away, putting just enough distance between themself and Hintosep to regain control of their own mind.

One of the strangers—the one in flashy armor—stepped backward through the curtain, engaged in combat with the remaining Grand Orchestrator, whose right side was covered in yet more blood. Something *thunk*ed and the Grand Orchestrator jerked, cried out—an arrow had torn through the dark fabric, lodging in their shoulder.

Thalo Child felt sick. The image of Hintosep's teeth in Gerome's neck—pulling out *chunks* of Gerome's neck—would not leave his inner eye, and the gory scene was only growing worse as Hintosep continued to flail rabidly beneath the horde of her fellows.

He snapped his eyes shut.

Footsteps. Then the Savior shouting.

Thalo Child had to move; he had to escape. This was no longer about him and his charge—truly, it had never been.

Holding Thalo Infant close, Thalo Child kept low, crawling away—toward the exit—trying to shut out the bedlam as they went. He wove through the pillars as hurried steps drew near, then retreated—as the sounds of fighting, clashing, and snarling swamped together.

Suddenly, there were boots before him. He glanced up into the face of a man not much older than himself, just on the other side of adulthood. He carried a sword, and Thalo Child instinctually shied back.

The stranger held out a hurried hand. "Come with me," he implored. "Come on; we've come to rescue you."

Hoisting his charge up from the floor, Thalo Child took the man's hand. He tried to place him, to integrate his face into the new information Hintosep had allowed him to access—the memory of all she'd told him so long ago, beneath the body of the Fallen.

"Are you the Kairopath?" he asked.

55

MANDIP

As soon as he realized exactly what filled the darkened space, Mandip was sure they'd lost—even before they'd been revealed and Hintosep had fallen. He'd never been to the slaughterhouses before, but he imagined cattle led to a butchering would be lined up as they were, brought carefully into such a room, single file, then trapped with no hope of escape. Dozens and dozens of varger filled the space, all encased in bizarre glass statues, all starving and long without a meal.

The Thalo were vulnerable to Krona's magic, but she was vulnerable to the very presence of a varg. He knew she'd fought her own bare-handed to get her magic, but this was something else entirely. The aisles between the pedestals were little wider than a single person, which meant they each had to take extra care not to bump into anyone or anything. Should anything wobble unexpectedly, or a Thalo bump into a protrusion they could not see, the jig was up.

But the jig was already up.

Now he wasn't sure there'd even been a proverbial jig to start with.

Once they'd passed the varger into the reliquary, the Savior had revealed them with little bravado, wiping away Hintosep's influence like it was nothing.

Instinctually, the group had created a wall, shoulder to shoulder, ready to brute-force their way to freedom if necessary.

Mandip thought both Juliet and Melanie had shown amazing restraint, being this close to their loved ones that they'd missed for so long. If it had been his brother who'd been held here in this terrible place for years, he wasn't sure he'd have been able to keep himself from pouncing the moment he saw him.

So, he couldn't blame Melanie at all for crying out and trying to reach her baby when Gerome handled zhim so *brutally*.

Her shout of *"Abby"* had cracked through the air like the sting of a whip. As Melanie bolted for her child, one of the hooded figures barreled to her side, reaching out for her, but instead of wielding a weapon or a closed fist, the figure grabbed the front of her face, clutching her cheeks tightly in their bare, blue-tattooed hand.

Melanie instantly went limp, held up only by the violent, crushing grip of the offending fingers.

Krona had leapt into action only a moment after Melanie, and she reached Melanie seconds after the Thalo did, hacking through the Thalo's arm like it was nothing. The masked assailant screamed, but it failed to rival the screams and barks emanating from the adjoining room—the confusion around Hintosep.

Thibaut caught Melanie before she could hit the ground, and Juliet sprang over him, an arrow in hand instead of nocked in her bow. She drove it at the Thalo's chest, who deflected it and instantly shrouded themself, becoming a ghost.

A ghost to all but Krona. She fought with the air, swinging her sword at nothing while clearly being deflected by *something*. Even in the chaos, Mandip wished he could see their faces—wished he could pinpoint the moment when they realized they couldn't hide from her.

Mandip had spared a glance for the Savior then. He stood solid, hands folded before him, face inscrutable behind his mask. He seemed to be vibrating with barely contained fury. And yet he did not interfere.

Perhaps he was too used to keeping his hands clean. Too used to others simply following orders and solving his problems.

When the flood of violence spilled from the reliquary back into the room of bottles, Mandip made it his mission to wrangle the children. He ran past the flailing bodies, bypassed the blood slick, and dodged beneath Krona's sword arm, eyes darting frantically down each row.

When he found them, he flailed at the two of them like a madman, encouraging them up, babbling, hardly paying attention to the pair or his own words, too focused on getting them to move so that they could all *run*.

But in the next moment, Mandip found himself completely and utterly alone.

Between one breath and the next, everyone vanished. Even knowing about the Thalo's power had not prepared him for how complete the illusion was.

All of the sounds cut off; all of the motion disappeared. There was no one.

Not even the blood remained.

A hand took his.

He looked down, still saw nothing.

"Are you the Kairopath?" asked a voice that sounded very distant—a scream that reached him as a whisper. He could only assume it was Juliet's brother.

"No, the Regulator!" he replied, feeling like he was shouting into the void. Regardless, he kept his voice raised, unsure if the boy was similarly afflicted by the sudden disappearances.

"The *what?*"

"The woman with the horns. The horns, on her helm!"

The hand tugged on his, as though the boy expected them to be of one mind, and then jerked suddenly when he didn't move.

"I can't see them!" he tried to explain.

"Then keep hold of me," the child instructed, and this time when he yanked, Mandip followed. "Don't let them touch you!" the boy warned, pulling him around a pillar and then around what seemed like nothingness but was likely an invisible adversary.

Mandip knew the Thalo could control people for a short burst, stick them in a secret memory and make them commit nearly any act or make them fall unconscious. He couldn't imagine what these particular ones would do to him if they got a hand on him.

The boy changed directions again, tugging him at a sharp right angle, whirling him around until he bumped into something else. Mandip raised his sword, unsure how to defend against an enemy he couldn't detect. A hand found his cheek, and he tried not to panic-swing, for fear of hitting the children.

"It's me!" came Juliet's voice, just as distant. "Closer. This way."

He shuffled a few more steps forward and suddenly the world was back, if distorted. There were figures all around, ethereal, hazy, and jumpy but recognizable, as though two realities were competing for his eyes.

Krona had created some kind of field in which she could disrupt the Thalo's ability to play with their minds—similar yet different to how the Savior had disrupted Hintosep's—but it only worked so well, and clearly only in close proximity to her.

One Thalo lay dead. They'd lost a hand and ultimately their head. Krona's saber hadn't cut clean through, but it was enough.

Their weakness hadn't been Krona's powers so much as their own arrogance. Just like the Thalo in the camp, they'd presumed they had the upper hand and had botched the chance to take the threat seriously. It was a failure of imagination that killed them.

From here on out, Mandip doubted they'd get so lucky.

Now there was no one between them and the exit. No one keeping them from leaving this eerie gallery behind.

Instead, their enemies all lay between them and Hintosep.

Even with clear freedom before them, they all hesitated.

"Go!" Hintosep shouted, fighting her fellow Thalo on the floor but clearly resigned to losing. "Avellino, guide them!"

The child let go of Mandip's hand, walking backward toward the arch. Thibaut followed, carrying the unconscious Melanie bridal-style in his arms.

A Grand Orchestrator's attention was suddenly divided—they moved to spring toward the door, but the Savior stepped through the shredded curtain and shouted them down. "Others will deal with them. I want her *contained!*"

"Go!" Hintosep cried again.

"No, we can't leave her!" Mandip protested.

I'm a hindrance, Hintosep said directly into his mind. *Not a help.*

He wasn't prepared to simply abandon her. She was a traitor to these people, and no matter the civilization, traitors never met happy ends. She was asking them to do something incredibly cruel. And for what?

Follow Avellino. I knew it would come to this. I did. I've made my peace. Trust the boy and go.

Everything in him raged to ignore her—to be the hero, to go against orders, to do what *he* knew was best. But she'd brought him because she trusted him. He'd promised to accept her orders. Promised to follow, to squash his own arrogance and be a good soldier like he'd insisted he could.

Krona put a hand on his shoulder, shoved him toward the exit. "You and Juliet need to guard the others," she ordered. "Protect the children. I'll take care of this."

This was what Krona had just gone through all hells for—to be the one that could face these people head on.

He nodded and rushed out the arch, ready for whoever or whatever might meet them as they mounted the stairs.

56

KRONA

Krona knew the only reason that first Thalo had fallen so easily was because she'd taken them by surprise. The Savior wouldn't make the same mistake.

He was her target now.

Perhaps it was madness to simply go for the head of the snake. He'd presumably had thousands of years to hone his skills, and she was a mere infant by comparison. Even if his magic was vulnerable to hers, she would not delude herself: this wouldn't be an even fight.

She reasserted her grip on the knuckleduster and pointed the tip of her saber at the Savior. Somehow, in all this bloody mess, he still remained untouched.

Hintosep still writhed under her former allies. They all tried to hold her down on top of the bleeding man, but she kept heaving upward, creating a grotesque mimicry of breath, like the lungs of some demon beast.

If she was trying to say anything to Krona covertly, her words were lost. A Thalo could no longer speak inside Krona's mind.

Curling her lip inside her helm, letting Hintosep's feral fury feed her own, she rushed at the Savior, ready to have his head.

He turned to her with a curious tilt of the head, apparently interested by the fact that she hadn't taken the opportunity to flee. He stood his ground, let her come; even as her muscles coiled to bring the blade to him, he barely moved.

At the last moment, he held up his hand, a casual gesture for her to halt.

She had no intention of stopping.

And then it struck her.

She'd expected an attempt at manipulating her awareness; what she hadn't expected was to have her *emotions* squeezed.

The giddiness that smashed into her was unbearable in its completeness. She let out a coarse, awful *laugh*, her whole body gone loose with it. It sounded so distorted in her ears, and her true emotions fought with the false ones, feeding her fear on top of the unmoored humor. Both feelings made her woozy, unsteady, and her saber slipped from her fingers simply because she was wheezing and shaking so much.

It was worse than the panic that accompanied her phobia, and the enchanted stones in her bracers did nothing to counteract it.

Confused and scared, she dropped to the floor and scrabbled for her sword before crawling away from him, back toward the exit.

She'd been wrong. So very wrong. She wasn't an infant compared to him; she was an amoeba. She knew he had to be a Thalo—*had to be*—and yet he possessed Emotion's powers as well.

Which meant—

The Savior closed his fist, and the bones in Krona's back *shifted*.

Pain radiated up her spine as parts of her reconfigured themselves, as he bent and twisted her shoulder blades, pulling spurs off them, up through skin to cut through her leathers. Two long ones grew up and over her shoulders themselves, sharp and bloody and living, over the top of her pauldrons, curling back around to aim at her jugular.

They stopped just short as he let out a frustrated growl.

Krona turned, saw Hintosep had clawed herself over to him, had him by the leg.

This was Krona's one chance. She had to run. There was no way she could fight him.

No way she could save Hintosep.

With tears streaming down her cheeks beneath her helm—wrenched out of her by the pain of the bone growths—she dragged herself to her feet, holding her weapons close, and hobbled toward the archway.

"Krona!" Hintosep shouted.

She made herself turn around again.

"Set them free!" Hintosep demanded.

She could only mean one thing.

Krona looked to the knuckleduster. Supposedly, it could break enchanted glass.

Without hesitation, she wrenched her fist back and punched the nearest bottle—a fierce-looking wolf. A great smashing rumble—like thunder mixed with glass shattering—rolled through the gallery as Krona's silver made contact with one of the enchantments, cracking it.

The glass splintered up the wolf's leg, and the varg within punched itself at the seam, pounding again and again at the breakage until the very smallest bit of vapor began to seep out.

Krona looked to Hintosep, who nodded with approval.

An emptiness threatened to steal Krona's air as she realized Hintosep had resigned herself to not only staying behind but being eaten alive by a bottle-barker.

The very least Krona could do was make it quick.

Still reeling from the pain, she threw herself at the next bottle, and the next, smashing into each with a fury, crying out in pain—of the body, the mind, and the soul—as she released monster after monster. She shook with the wrongness of it, could taste the foulness of it on her tongue and in the back of her throat. She was condemning Hintosep to die in the most horrible way imaginable.

Maybe, at the very least, she'd take the Savior with her.

With six bottles cracked, Krona half sprinted, half stumbled through the archway and to the stairwell. The others were gone; no one was in sight. She had no one to help her and no one to guide her, but she had to keep going. She had to run.

When she reached the top of the stairs, the sounds of a clash drew her attention. She followed them to another staircase and swiftly ran to the next level. The landing dumped her out into a wide hall. There, maybe thirty paces away, Mandip, Juliet, Thibaut, and even the boy—Avellino—were doing their best to stave off a wave of Thalo that had found them. A few bodies already lined the floor, and Juliet's dress was covered in blood from a wound in her shoulder.

Thibaut was closest to the still-unconscious Melanie and her child, using a sword to beat back a Thalo about his size.

Krona stumbled on the landing, trying to go to him. She could feel blood dripping down her back, beneath her armor, from where the spurs had ripped through her. Aching, grimacing, she forced herself upright.

Just as she stood, Thibaut lost sight of the Thalo in front of him. They shielded themselves from view, and he swung in the wrong direction, missed. They put out a foot and tripped him, made him go sprawling. Frantically, he rolled onto his back, trying to defend himself from the blow he could not see but knew was coming.

He couldn't see it, but Krona could. She could see the long knife in the Thalo's hands; she could see their triumphant face as they stood over him. Their arm coiled. She expected them to thrust *down*, but they clearly had another thought.

Instead of skewering him, they stooped, lightly brushing a fingertip over Thibaut's temple.

Thibaut's grip on his own weapon changed. He twirled the blade around, holding it to his own throat, ready to *slice*.

Everything seemed to slow, to still. Krona's vision narrowed to where the sharp metal kissed his skin.

His arm jerked, and Krona erupted.

Her roar of denial was beastly, formed of pure despair.

So much had been taken from her. Her station, her home, her sister, her maman. *Not* Thibaut too. Not when they'd only just begun to really see each other. To really know each other. She would not stand for one more person she loved losing their life—not like this. Not to brutality, while not even in control of his own hand.

Krona's cry was a feral rejection of the reality she saw before her. Not a *no* but a primal scream that started from behind clenched teeth, only to be ripped from her throat—thrust forward with the same force of will she would have thrust herself forward if there hadn't been such a gulf between them. She lifted her foot to run—*run*—to try to reach him, even knowing she could never move fast enough.

There was a split second between the blade moving and her stomach dropping, but it wasn't enough to do anything. There was too much distance, impossible to cover, even though it seemed no distance at all in the grand scheme of things. Nothing but her denial, her wish to stop this, could traverse such a distance so fast.

But she wouldn't accept defeat. She *would not* be helpless.

As her cry rose, *something else* ripped itself from her body. A flash of brilliant orange, tangerine, and gold. A blinding light engulfed her. She *burned*, utterly incandescent with rage, fear, and magic.

Krona was a pyre of power, consumed in a force as sudden and intense as her hopelessness.

Not just force, not just energy. Substance, form. She was a pillar of something akin to fire before there was a *rushing*, something barreling forward with a force—like a storm front, moving swifter than sound, quicker than lightning.

She felt threads sliding through her—like an emotion stone being torn away—only these didn't hurt. They were silken, smooth, almost soft, but draining—they drew all of her energy with them, away.

As the last wisp left her body, as the final threads slipped out of her fingertips and her heart and her eyes, there was a rush of wind—like all the air being sucked from her pores instead of her lungs—she fell to her knees, slumping forward. Devoid of strength.

She didn't have time to think, to see, to consider.

It all happened so fast.

This great burst of *something* shot straight at Thibaut and his attacker, pouring over the floor, morphing as it went, like a conflagration but more fluid. It slipped between Thibaut and the blade, throwing the sword away and the Thalo *back* just as a fine line of blood began to appear at Thibaut's throat.

This did *not* look like her time magic.

It was as though her will had left her body behind, stronger without the cumbersome nature of flesh to hold it back.

On her knees, on the edge of the stairs with barely enough strength to keep her from toppling over, her ears started to ring. After a moment—mere heartbeats—someone yelled and ran to her—Juliet? They were saying something but seemed to be talking to Krona through a layer of water, muffled and distorted.

The energy continued, whisking around not just the Thalo Thibaut had been fighting but the others as well, taking on form as it went, swelling in size. It adopted the shape of the living, of a creature. An amalgamation of animals settled into one silhouette: a pair of twisted ram's horns settled atop a distinctly horse-like head that was armored, like a lizard. Around its neck lay a thick mane, like that of the southernmost great cats. The fur trailed down the horse-lizard's back, terminating in an elephant's tail. Two sets of wings, like those on a gull, sprouted from blades near its spine. And its legs—

Korna shuddered at its legs. There were eight of them, and each hoof blazed with energy—bright and flickering, more like starlight than fire.

Smoke curled from its nostrils, and its eyes—four of them—were shining, their gaze severe.

But what was most surprising was the *sound* it made. Nothing so predictable as a roar or shriek. Not a neigh or bark.

It made *music*.

It sounded like chimes. Like flutes. Not the high-pitched fluttering of metal and bells but the soulful reverberation of wooden pipes.

It was the music she'd been searching for her whole life. The music that was inside her, waiting to burst out.

And it *charged*.

The chiming creature bore down on the Thalo with a vengeance, stamping and twisting, ravaging the Thalo both physically and with the relativity of time. After a stunning, violent few minutes, each Thalo collapsed, clutching at their throats, voices hoarse, faces gaunt.

Dying of thirst, Krona realized.

The creature had made them suffer weeks in a moment—made them experience time without the resources necessary to live.

One Thalo fell into a seizure, and Krona looked away, crawling across the floor to Thibaut.

His hands were shaking, and he touched the cut on his throat tentatively, the pads of his gloves coming away bloody, confirming what he feared: he really had been about to kill himself at the Thalo's order.

Krona scooted nearer and threw an arm around him. He leaned his forehead against hers. For what felt like a long time, they breathed heavily together, rocking together, neither fully comprehending what in the Valley had just happened.

When the last of the Thalo lay dead, the ethereal creature returned, trotting back to Krona's side. As it approached, it shrank, obviously well aware of her discomfort around large creatures. When it reached her, it was no bigger than a mastiff, and its eight legs had become four, and its four eyes had become two. A mad crackling of energy no longer surrounded it. Now it took on an almost-innocent air.

She held out her hand, and it nuzzled her palm.

"I've never . . . I don't know what this is," Juliet said. "Hintosep never said anything like this would happen. I don't understand it."

"I do," Krona said softly.

"What is it?" Juliet asked. "Where did it come from?"

Krona swallowed, finding it hard to explain. "It came from me. It's . . . me. The part of me that was the varg."

"You can disentangle it again," Mandip said, breathing heavily, sword dangling at his side.

"You can *summon* it," Juliet said with a mix of awe and excitement. "This is it. Your *lightning*. But why doesn't it *look* like a varg anymore?"

"Because we're still connected," Krona said. She could feel the threads between them—thousands and thousands of them. This wasn't the creature ripped from her; it was still tethered. Grounded. "This is what it looks like healthy. Happy."

"How did you do it?" Mandip asked.

Krona blinked; her tongue fumbled. "I—I don't know. It was like . . . like I had to project myself beyond myself. I just couldn't—" She turned to look at Thibaut. "I couldn't let my own limits contain me. Not with all I had to lose."

Thibaut's gaze met hers, and the kiss they fell into was desperate and heady but brief. They both knew there was no time to revel in their relief.

Shaky, Krona rose to her feet, helping Thibaut scoop up Melanie. The varg—if she could still call it that—helped her stand, and she petted its nose affectionately. Her phobia lay dormant, completely untriggered by the creature's new form.

"Gods, what happened to your back?" Thibaut asked. "What are—"

"A gift from the Savior," she said bitterly. "I'll be fine."

Avellino, sounding nervous, said, "We need to go. There will be others soon. And we still have to retrieve the minds."

"Minds?"

"What Hintosep brought you to get."

"We came for you," Juliet said.

"Yes," he said, "and no."

It was the sort of answer Krona had come to expect from a Thalo—even an adolescent one.

"You look shaky," Mandip said to Krona. "Can you walk?"

"I think so. I'll be okay. I think the summoning . . . I'm exhausted. But I can make it. Let's go."

As they went, Juliet's brother explained the Savior's ability to make Mindless—people whose will and identity he'd been able to pluck from their bodies and make a secret even to themselves. "It is the harshest punishment one can face," the boy said. "An ability given to the Savior by the Fallen."

The fifth penalty, Krona realized. The Unknown's penalty.

Mindlessness.

"Is that what happened to Melanie?" Thibaut asked, tone filled with quiet dread.

"No," Avellino assured him. "It is a power only the Savior possesses, and it is not a quick process."

The varg barreled ahead of them as a Thalo appeared around the next corner. It took down the puppet with ease—and the next, and the next. When they ran into one with a baby at their hip, Juliet's brother ran ahead and put himself between the Thalo and the varg. "Not fer," he said, and Krona ached at the plea in his voice.

It was a voice that was used to having no agency, to scraping out what little favors he could.

It spoke of a decent person in an indecent place.

As much as that realization pained her, it was the sight of another child that truly twisted the invisible knife in her gut. She willed the varg back, and as the Thalo Avellino had protected went screaming off down an adjoining corridor—forcing the group to hurry on—Krona made herself ask, "How many children are there?"

Of course there were more. Why hadn't she anticipated that?

"I'm not sure, exactly," he said. "Once we belong to an artifact, we don't often see those who are not in our cohort. But there are hundreds of Nameless, for certain."

Hintosep hadn't simply failed to mention the other children; that much was obvious. She'd focused on these *specific* children because they were important to those she'd recruited. There was no sense in trying to rescue more now, but Krona tucked the information away for later.

"Here," Avellino said, suddenly stopping in front of a wall that looked like any other wall. "They're in here."

"In where?" Mandip demanded.

"Here," he reiterated, slapping the stone. "This is why she always intended to bring a Kairopath. She couldn't reach them on her own. No one can. The Savior buried the most important minds and made them impossible to retrieve without tearing down part of the keep itself. The compartment they're stored in is completely enclosed."

"She needed a jumper," Krona realized. "Shit."

The varg nuzzled her side, and she let it send comforting waves into her as she approached the wall. Krona knew she should have trusted her instincts. Hintosep only told people what she wanted them to know when she wanted them to know it, and of course there'd been more to the plan. Of course she'd had a specific reason for needing Krona to rejoin with her varg before storming the keep. She wanted to be angry at Hintosep for keeping her in the dark, but she also knew why Hintosep had done what she'd done: if none of them knew what she was up to, then it wasn't a secret any of the Thalo could glean from their minds.

"I don't know. I've only ever jumped someplace I could *see*. And that's never exactly ended well." She could end up jumping herself straight into a mass of bricks. Would she even have any time to change course if her attempt went badly?

"And you'll need to take me," the boy added.

"Why?"

"Because there are more minds inside than you could possibly carry, and we're only after four. She told me how to identify them."

"I can't even guarantee I can jump myself in. And I've never tried with someone else."

He looked just as skeptical as she did. "It's Hintosep's plan, not mine," he said. "Plan A was for her to bring you here alone, but then when Gerome got the Cage and we stayed . . . she must have decided getting everything at once—us and the minds—was still a solid Plan B. But now she's not even here, and she . . . There was a wall . . . I'd forgotten . . ."

"We're on Plan C," Krona acknowledged. "Understood." She sheathed her sword and rubbed her hands together, shuddering at the prospect of landing under tons of brick and mortar but unable to think of a different plan. If this was the very reason Hintosep had been so dogged in bringing her and her varg together—important enough that it still had to be done, whether Hintosep was there to see it through or not—then Krona was willing to try. "All right. Hold tight to me," she instructed.

Avellino stepped away from the toddler, handing zhim over to Juliet, who looked at him with a pride he couldn't yet understand, before putting his arms around Krona's waist. "Ready?" she asked.

He nodded.

Krona waved her hands in front of her, attempting to draw out a lens like she had many times before.

Nothing happened.

She tried again.

Still nothing.

Worry bubbled up in her throat. Was she too tired? Too anxious?

The varg gently butted into her side.

Oh.

Without *it,* she had no magic. In this state, devoid of her varg, she was perhaps even weaker than before. Her abilities were entirely wrapped up in the part of her that used to be monstrous. She had to figure out how to remerge with it, and quickly.

It had taken a violent ceremony to force it back into her body in the first place. She had neither the tools, time, nor the willpower to go through such a thing again.

Trying to put herself at ease, she remembered that the varg wanted to be with her. It wanted to be joined, entwined. It was a part of her and would always feel most comfortable when it was within the whole.

She opened herself up, imagining she was a flower welcoming a bee. She lightly petted the varg, sending it soothing thoughts of strength and unity.

Slowly, it brightened, losing its substantial state and reverting back into energy, into that first pillar of light. Soon, that brightness shifted up her hand, through her palm, and into her body, the sense of starlight resettling in her very being, filling her with a sparkle and warmth and song.

Immediately, she felt more energized, more certain of herself and her capabilities.

"Let's try this again," she said, as Avellino clung to her more tightly. "Ready? Three. Two. One. *Jump.*"

⊱━◆─○─◆━⊰

They did not meet stone, or sand, or even a terrifying pit of nothing. Krona's lens had shown her true; she'd willed it to show her deep behind the wall, to the pocket of air—the small sanctuary—she trusted was there. She looked, she felt, she focused, and in they went.

Soon after, they were plunged into complete darkness but had fared no worse, landing firmly on their feet. Krona pulled a light vial from her pouch and crushed it, releasing its glow.

The chamber they'd jumped into was no bigger than a cell back at her

Regulator den and was completely sealed on all sides. The boy had been right; the only other way to get to this room was to dig—an endeavor that would be neither subtle, easy, nor quick. Impossible to hide from someone like the Savior.

That also meant their air was limited and they'd have to be quick.

A large marble chest occupied one end of the chamber, and she and the boy made quick work of the heavy slab of a lid, pushing it over far enough that they could reach in. Chunks of isometric crystal, each encased in a glass box of appropriate size and shape—none any bigger than Krona's closed fist—filled the entire casket.

Emboldened, Krona thrust her arm in elbow deep, making the small boxes shift and roil like a pot of boiling water as she turned them over and over.

"These are minds?" she asked. The boxes and crystals made a tinkling sound as she sifted through them, like little bells.

"When the Savior creates a Mindless, He doesn't *erase* who they are—He can't do that," Avellino explained. "He simply takes their will and stores it elsewhere. Here. In halite." He held one up. "See the inclusions, the color? That is a sense of self made solid."

"Whose minds are you looking for?" she asked, holding up a particularly pretty smoky gray-and-purple crystal. "Specifically?"

"The minds of the gods."

The box slipped from her fingers, clattering back onto the pile.

"They'll have a metallic sheen," he went on, voice thick, clearly aware of how gut-wrenching and preposterous it sounded. "Gold, copper, and two of them silvery—though one is more matte, like nickel."

"Are you saying the Savior . . . He made the gods *Mindless*? How is that even—"

"I don't know," he said swiftly, lip trembling. "Please don't ask. She didn't tell me. I don't know."

The gods were trapped on the Valley rim, past the magical border, in a place no one could reach them. How could they be maintaining the magical barrier if they were *Mindless*?

Krona swallowed her shock and focused on the task. There would be plenty of time to contemplate that horror once they'd escaped the keep.

Not to mention the terrible question of what exactly they were supposed to do with the gods' minds once they found them.

"Ah-ha!" the boy exclaimed, pulling a long chunk with golden veins into the light. He handed it to her, and she made a basket from her cloak, folding it over to wrap the mind tight.

Not long after, she found the second crystal. The third and fourth came soon after.

"There's not a fifth?"

"No." His gaze looked distant, like he was searching inside himself for an explanation. "I don't think the Savior ever got a chance to make the Fallen into a Mindless."

"Who are the rest?" she asked before they replaced the slab and prepared to jump away again.

"Some are servants in the keep. But there are too many here. The rest, I don't know," he said sadly. "She didn't tell me."

Just like she hadn't mentioned the other children; Hintosep only bothered with the ones she thought mattered.

Krona tried not to resent her for it.

Having gotten what they came for, Krona jumped them back out again, only to be met with far-off shouting.

The others were immediately at their side—anxious.

"The Eldest must have alerted someone," said Avellino. "If the priests and guards know you're here, then we can't leave via the ramparts."

"How else do we get out?" Juliet asked. "Which way now?"

"I . . ."

"*Which way,* child?" Krona demanded

"I . . . I might know one," Avellino admitted, clearly reluctant. "I believe many have tried to escape before. They were not met with a pleasant end, but I can think of no other way."

"When you say 'unpleasant' . . ." Thibaut prompted.

"All that's left of them is ash."

57

THALO CHILD

The only way out was up. Through Ritual Way.

Would the overexposure to direct God Power burn them alive? Leaving nothing but a white splash of ashen remains?

Or had Ritual Way's danger also been an overstatement? Another lie to keep the young ones in line? Another exaggeration to keep them from exploring the crevasses that lay beyond?

What if it was the truth, though?

Still, he saw no other choice. "This way," he said, dashing for the stairs that led up, up—high into the keep.

It was a long slog, made more difficult while carrying a toddler, who he'd taken back from the young blond lady—Juliet; he'd been trying to pick up their names as they went—but they managed, finally skidding around the bend to behold the tall, black door that disappeared into the shadowed depths of the incredibly high ceiling. Its inverted triangles and vertical gold bar stood stoic and ominous at the opposite end of the hall.

He warned them of the danger—how the door could channel lightning if they tried to open it without the proper key. "Our only chance is not to use a key at all," he said.

The Kairopath—Krona—took him at his word. "I don't know if I can get us all through at once."

"No time to try like the present!" the blond woman said, clearly eager to be done with this place.

"I don't want to risk leaving half of someone behind," the Kairopath said. "Two at a time. I think I can manage that."

"Avellino and Abby first, then," Juliet said.

Krona nodded, taking hold of his shoulder before he was even ready and pushing him through in a jump.

On the other side, all lay quiet.

It was just as he remembered it from those years before, when he'd inducted the six-year-olds into Gerome's care. He hadn't been back since—despite giving him so many lines, Gerome hadn't blessed him with a chance to absorb any extra power. Now, as he trod beneath the hazed, purple, crackling sky, he wasn't sure he believed what Gerome had said—about the lines being a symbol and nothing more. His skin prickled here, the fine hairs rising, *reaching*.

The Kairopath retrieved the others in quick succession, ordering Thalo Child to keep leading the way as soon as Thibaut's boots met stone.

As he rushed past the altars, Thalo Child tried not to look at the scorch marks that littered the Way's walls. He knew almost nothing in the keep was as it seemed. None of it worked the way he'd once been told. The older Thalo lied to the children so that when the children were eventually told the truth, they'd feel special—part of the inner circle that *knew* things. It was all a well-balanced system, an orchestrated cycle that shaped their reality into whatever the Savior wanted it to be.

Even knowing what he knew now, Thalo Child still cringed as they moved toward the narrow crack in the rear of the fissure. Gerome might have blurred the line between what was true and what was false in his world, but Thalo Child knew for certain that there were *dangers* there, regardless.

Lightning flashed overhead, and his charge cringed, zhur chubby hands twisting the shoulder of his robe into a tight knot. He rubbed zhur back as he rushed onward, hoping they'd all find safety soon.

"Through here," he said, coming to the fissure where the ash caked as thick as snow. Supposedly, failed, would-be-Thalo who were instead destined to become Mindless tried to flee through here, unsuccessfully. This ash was all that was left of them. Supposedly.

The gap *was* narrow. Perhaps easy enough for him to fit through, were he still a scrawny twelve-year-old, but he wasn't slight of build anymore, and he was by far the gangliest of the group.

"Looks treacherous," said Krona. "What's back there?"

He told her honestly, "I don't know." In truth, it could be a dead end.

But if Ritual Way was not a source of great power, then the ash was all theatrics. A warning, nothing more. There'd only be a need to warn Thalo off if something of great importance—like freedom—lay beyond.

"How am I supposed to get Melanie through?" Thibaut asked, gently setting the unconscious woman down. "Can you jump her to the other side?"

Krona made a swirling motion with her hands, then moved her palm as though redirecting the light from a candle. "I can't see the end, and the passage is dangerously narrow. We'll have to do the best we can."

The natural passage was tight—so much so that Thalo Child had to place Thalo Infant on zhur own two feet and Krona had to abandon her horned helm. Mandip and Thibaut managed Melanie, moving slowly, carefully, protecting her from protruding rocks at every turn. The way was winding, and the open sky crackled above the entire way. It smelled of sulfur here, like it did in the hot springs sometimes.

Thalo Child kept praying and praying for an end, though he knew the path could terminate just as easily in a solid wall as freedom.

Thankfully, it widened, but instead of spilling them out on the mountainside, it ended at another door, like the ones that led into the courtyards in the keep. It seemed to be built into the mouth of what might have been a natural cave.

"What's in there?" Mandip asked.

"I have no idea."

Krona tried the handle. It was locked, but locks were no match for their Kairopath. Since they had no other option but to move forward, she jumped them through, one by one, into an area of pure darkness. Once they were all inside, Krona smashed another light vial and used it to search for an alternate means of illumination. She found a lever imbedded in the wall and threw it. A string of dim, yellow lamps turned on overhead. Only, the light was strange—unwavering. When Thalo Child looked closely at the lamps, he could see clearly that they weren't gas. There wasn't even a flame.

But there was a strange buzzing.

"What powers these? Enchantment?" he asked.

"Not like I've ever seen. Not like a light vial."

The lamps revealed a curving path through rough, blackened walls. It was a lava tube, and clearly portions had been hand-carved to widen the way. The floor had been padded with black sand, and their steps made no sound as they advanced.

Around only the second bend, they came across a vast chamber that not only contrasted starkly with the lava tube but mirrored the reliquary in that it had a *softness* to it. Similar thin, gauzy fabrics of pinks and purples and reds hung from the ceiling of the large room. Veined marble tiles replaced the sand. A rectangular reflecting pool—the water deep and black, perfectly still—lay in the center of the room, and they carefully skirted it.

Those same buzzing lights that illuminated the lava tube illuminated the chamber, their glow an odd yellow.

Just beyond the far end of the reflecting pool lay a tall dais bearing a massive marble slab, easily a dozen feet long and four feet wide.

Atop it lay what, from a distance, looked like a long mound covered in rime frost.

"What in the Valley?"

The world seemed to yaw beneath Thalo Child's feet.

"No. Please—no."

Not another one.

No.

Please.

He rushed to the slab, his hands falling on the mound, accidentally breaking away the tips of the frost-like layer. Their fragility shocked him, and he pulled back, gaze frantically roaming the shards from one end to the other. The air suddenly had a saline quality to it, and Thalo Child realized the small white spikes were salt crystals, not frost.

Setting his jaw, settling an internal argument with himself, he began brushing his palms through them all, snapping them on purpose and wiping the remains away like so much dust.

Beneath the thin, white crystals were larger ones. More substantial and clear, cleaving together to form a shape. For a brief moment he thought it was a stylized glass coffin, as he realized there was a body inside.

But not just any body. One unnaturally large.

The outer casing looked like a fractured starburst, and the body was a deep, eggplant purple.

His hands finally alighted over the upturned face, scrubbing furiously. He knew what he would see, but he didn't want it to be true. He didn't want this to be real.

He drew in a sharp breath when the salt was gone, despair overwhelming him. His limbs became weak, useless, and he could barely prop himself up on the slab.

The crystal-encased head was a bare skull—a *bird* skull—with a sturdy horn that curled back in on itself atop the long, sharp beak. From the eye sockets grew clusters of amethyst crystals, and the beak and horn looked as though they'd been carved with swirling filigree.

As the others approached, he knelt down next to the form, tremors wracking him—the adrenaline ebbing and flowing through his system making him unsteady. He left one hand tentatively covering the amethysts, as though he meant to close zhur eyes—eyes that weren't there. "I've never seen zhur face before," he said. "I've seen zhim depicted a thousand times, in a thousand ways, but . . . Zhe was supposed to be so bright, you couldn't look at zhim. But zhur light . . . zhur light is *gone.*"

His mind had refused to name the body until that moment. He'd been guarding himself, but now his world was shattered.

That was two dead gods.

Two.

How long ago had Emotion joined the Fallen?

The silence that fell over them was thick with shock. Thalo Child's throat went tight and hot, and his vision blurred as tears filled his eyes.

Krona fell to her knees beside him.

This was too many losses, too many revelations.

Behind them, something gurgled and water splashed.

The Kairopath stiffened, whirled. But Thalo Child couldn't look. He didn't want to face something new. He wanted to sit there next to the corpse of a dead god like he was just some penitent statue and sleep.

Or perish.

Metal clattered against stone as Krona hoisted herself up, gasping in clear discomfort as her leathers pulled at the bony protrusions that had curled out of her back and over her shoulder like morbid additions to her armor.

"Find an exit!" she shouted, rushing away, toward the reflecting pool.

Taking in a hot, shaky breath, Thalo Child steeled himself and turned.

A creature had crawled out of the pool, water sloughing off of its hide, repelled by a row of thick, scaly armor down its spine—the only protection for its otherwise naked, mammalian skin. The long black claws of its forelimbs clacked against the floor as it pulled itself onto the dry tile, its belly dragging. More and more of it uncoiled out of the water, revealing fifteen feet of a pale, veiny body, followed by a long, thick tail. It walked with a menacing sway, so low to the floor, it nearly slithered. No eyes graced its pointed skull, but a giant set of yellowed rodent's teeth jutted from its lipless face. It opened its jaws to hiss, revealing a black, forked tongue and a throat lined with razors.

It seemed some giant, abominable amalgamation of monitor lizard and mole rat.

This was no creature found in the Valley.

Gods, where had this come from?

Grief suddenly became secondary to his fear for his charge's life.

Thalo Child swept Thalo Infant into his arms, darting behind the slab as the others frantically searched for an exit.

"There's no other way out!" Juliet shouted.

Krona didn't look like she could endure another fight. The Savior had mangled her body, and that magical entity had ripped itself out of her and sifted itself back in. Mandip slid beside her, sword at the ready. "I'll hold it off," he insisted. "See if you can *make* us a way out."

She sheathed her sword and stiffly began searching, holding her arms in front of her, turning on the spot.

The creature lunged, and Thalo Child dared not look. He ducked behind the dead god as the animal shrieked in pain—meeting Mandip's blade. All he could think about was how perfectly Thalo Infant would fit down the monster's throat, how easily it could take those inner teeth and peel the skin from his charge. He couldn't let that happen.

"This way!" Krona yelled. "I can see out. To the mountainside. Thibaut!"

"Coming!"

Squeals, splashing. Thalo Child peeked out to see that Mandip had battled the thing back partially into the pool. He'd landed a blow to its snout and slit its tongue, but the claws on its forelegs were no laughing matter.

"Shit!" Krona cursed, attempting something and failing. "I have to go through. I can't just make a door for you—I have to go or it doesn't work."

"Then *go*," Juliet insisted, nocking an arrow. "Take Thibaut and Melanie first. Come back for us." She let the arrow loose, hitting the monster's side. It reeled upward, then lunged at her, striking like a snake. She rolled out of the way, dodging artfully.

Thalo Child whipped back behind the slab again, shaking.

It felt like an eternity until Krona's voice cut through the creature's hissing once again. She called for him, and he stood. Moving with a purpose, she stomped over to him and grabbed his shoulder, but he resisted. "The god first."

Her face ran through a gamut of feelings in the breadth of a second, from denial to curiosity, to desperation, to resignation. He wasn't sure it had even crossed her mind to take Emotion, but he couldn't imagine leaving zhim.

Frantically, her gaze darted to the monster, then to the god. "You'll have to help me."

"Stay close," he told Thalo Child, setting zhim down. "Hold on to my robes."

Together, they tried heaving the crystal form from the slab, but it was heavier than anticipated. "We need more hands," Krona panted. "Juliet!"

The blond woman vaulted over to them, twirling to loose another arrow before stowing her bow. Krona tugged at the body's shoulders while the other two pushed at its feet. It scraped over the stone of the slab with a mind-bleeding grind of a high-pitched sound. Krona was just able to keep her grip on it when the back end slid off, smashing against the ground, breaking the tiles but leaving the crystal intact. She dragged it backward to where she needed to make the jump.

A moment later, she, the body, and Juliet were gone.

Now it was just Thalo Child, Thalo Infant, and Mandip.

The creature was bleeding profusely from many gashes, but so was Mandip. Its claws had caught his stomach, not tearing down to organs but deep enough that he pressed his free hand to his belly while still battling it *back*.

When Krona jumped into the cave again, she stumbled, fell on her hands and knees. Thalo Child helped her up, and she hissed through her teeth, then barked at him, "Hold on to the baby," before calling for Mandip.

Mandip skidded backward, leaping away from another swipe as he realized her shout was his cue to flee. He turned, ran, and Krona looked away from him to make her jumping lens.

But the monster wasn't finished. It reached out, struck down, catching a single thick claw in the back of Mandip's calf. He went down in a flash, losing his grip on his sword as his belly smacked the tiles. All the air was clearly punched from his lungs, and he couldn't even cry for help as that single claw dragged him across the floor, toward the pool.

"Mandip!" Thalo Child shouted.

It was too late. Before Krona could even look back again, the three of them had already jumped.

⊱━•⊰━●━⊱•━⊰

The outside air was extra frigid after the somewhat-humid cave. It stung Thalo Child's lungs, burned his nose. Krona didn't land them on their feet; instead, they tumbled through, and she landed partially on her new growths. She snarled in pain, but ultimately, the stumble didn't seem to matter. In the next moment, before anyone could say anything to her, she was up and jumping back inside, frantic to save Mandip.

Thalo Child stared blankly at the rough mountainside from which they'd emerged. There was nothing to indicate what kind of horrors lay on the other side. Luckily, they'd happened upon what appeared to be an animal trail, the snow packed down from bighorn sheep hooves.

Next to him lay Emotion.

Everyone waited with bated breath, staring at the jump spot. The wind whistled through nearby trees, blowing swirls of loose snow off the mountain crags and into the growing darkness.

After a minute, Juliet came over and draped the cloak she'd been wearing over Thalo Infant like a blanket.

Time ticked on. The silence stretched, began to feel oppressive.

It was Thibaut who finally approached the rock, holding out his hands, swiping over it like he might actually discover a secret entrance.

"They can't be gone," Juliet whispered, voice carrying cleanly through the crisp air.

"No, they can't," Thibaut agreed.

An instant after, two figures burst through, out of nothing, knocking into Thibaut, slamming him into the ground.

It might have been comical if Mandip hadn't looked so limp in Krona's grasp.

He was still conscious but soaked to the bone and gasping for breath. Clearly, the beast had nearly had him. All three of them rose shakily to their feet, but Krona was still in fighting mode—they weren't safe yet.

"Quickly, before he freezes," Krona said, wrestling Mandip out of his jacket. "Get his clothes off. I'll see if there's a safe place to light a campfire down in that stand of trees."

She handed him to Thibaut, who went to work stripping him down.

"Is this . . . payback?" Mandip asked weakly, shivering profoundly, leaning heavily against Thibaut even as the other man tried to remove his clothes.

"Payback?" Thibaut asked.

"For the strip search."

A relieved smile spread over Thibaut's face. "If you're well enough to make jokes, I think you'll live."

58

KRONA

He did live. Mandip needed a fair few bandages and had to suffer through Krona's inexpert attempts to stitch his stomach, but he lived.

They were able to retrieve their supplies and their steeds, and set out for the safe house, traveling as quickly as they could. They made a sled for the strange body they'd found, dragging it with them every step of the way.

Their second night retreating, Krona watched with careful interest as Juliet approached Avellino. She looked nervous, abashed, like she didn't know how to talk to her brother now that they were reunited.

The boy had just tried to wake Melanie, to no avail. Krona was sure they could care for her if her unconsciousness persisted, but the prospect was daunting.

The songstress sat herself down next to her brother, who was holding Melanie's child, and they both stared into the fire silently for a while. It looked like there was a torrent's worth of words building up behind Juliet's teeth, but she was holding them back.

Krona pretended to be preoccupied with cleaning her armor—what was left of it—to hide her eavesdropping. Thibaut and Mandip were already asleep, snuggled in their bedrolls on either side of Melanie, keeping her safe.

"Melanie is Abby's mother, you know," Juliet said eventually.

"Abby?"

Juliet gently stroked Thalo Infant's hair, and zhe didn't shy away. "This is Abby. And you—you're—"

"Avellino," he said, clearly feeling disconnected from the name, even though he knew it belonged to him. "One is supposed to earn a name," he said. "And yet, Hintosep told me this one was bestowed on me at birth by my parents. A mother. A father."

"Yes," Juliet said, tears welling in her eyes. "Avellino. And I'm Nadine." She put a palm on the side of his face, fingers shaking like she was doing everything in her power to restrain herself. "I'm your sister."

"Nadine," he said slowly.

Only a few paces away from them, Krona froze for a moment before her grip violently tightened on her breastplate.

Avellino and Nadine.

The realization cut through Krona like a knife—she'd heard those names together before. "*Gabrielle*," she said, the third child's name punched from her chest.

Juliet turned to her, nodding, face now red and wet but unashamed. "We lost our older sister, just as you did."

"Nadine *Charbon*?" Krona asked. "You are Louis Charbon's *children*?"

The boy looked more confused than ever. That name meant nothing to him. But it meant so many terrible things to Krona.

Louis Charbon had thought his infant son was dead. Without that catalyst, he never would have committed his murders—and the boy had been alive the whole time.

Her disdain for the Savior only grew.

>-+->-O-+-+-<

When they finally reached the mansion, it was to a mixed reception. They'd brought back the children and proven they could infiltrate the Thalo's keep. But they'd lost Hintosep. And discovered an atrocity beyond measure: dead gods, Mindless gods. On top of that, they received news that Lutador's army was on the march, which meant Adhar had likely left the city.

They took Emotion to the war room, laid zhim out on the table, unsure yet of what to do with the body.

As soon as Sebastian set eyes on his baby, he'd scooped zhim up and held zhim close, crying in relief—and crying in despair. He had his child, but his wife . . .

Thibaut carried Melanie to her room, with Sebastian and Abby trailing behind.

"I want to try again," Avellino said to Krona and Juliet. He'd tried to wake her every time they'd made camp, and had yet to have even a hint of success. But Krona nodded, and the three of them followed after.

Thibaut lay Melanie down on her bed, on top of the duvet. Sebastian sat down beside her, and the toddler crawled on zhur knees to look into Melanie's face, as zhe had done every night. Krona had rarely ever seen a little one with such a penetrative stare. Zhe was fixated on Melanie, entirely focused. Zhur little hands went out to explore her face—her temple, her nose, her lips, her scar.

Avellino stepped up beside the sleeping woman, flexing his fingers, clearly nervous yet determined.

The first time he'd tried this, Thalo Child had noticed that as he'd swept back the curls from her forehead—noting the strange scar—Thalo Infant had crouched down, peering at her in an odd way.

"Do you know her?" he'd asked.

Zhe'd turned to him with forlorn, confused eyes and nodded, and a faint memory had tickled the back of Thalo Child's mind, almost like déjà vu. There had been another young one, and another face in their mind; a comforting smile, a secret memory.

A mother. He couldn't recall how or when—almost like it had been walled away—but he'd seen someone else's memory of their mother.

Hintosep had once said that it was dangerous to take the secret of wakefulness from someone, and he could see why. If he couldn't decipher a way to undo what had been done, Thalo Infant's mother would sleep like this forever.

Every time he tried, he was afraid of making it worse, of damaging her mind. He had only just begun to train in this kind of manipulation—Gerome having had him practice on the Sacrifices—and while he knew he was an adept Thalo for his age, he could not claim to have skills to rival a Grand Orchestrator's.

Now, as she lay in a comforting bed, surrounded by those who loved her, he touched her mind with his, looking for a small bit of self separate from the rest. Navigating through a personhood was like navigating through a storm on a dark night. Thalo Child had no access to anything but her secrets. There were vast voids in her sense of self that, make no mistake, were vibrant and full but were simply off-limits to him. Her secrets pelted him like harsh rain, coming out of nowhere and slipping off him before he could so much as see what they contained. He'd become quite good at seeing a secret when someone was holding it close or at the front of their mind—in a special place of importance. But here, in the world of the unconscious, there was nothing to distinguish one secret from another, nothing to distinguish what was secret because she'd made it secret, and what was a secret that had been forced upon her.

Thalo Infant twisted zhur fists gently in Melanie's hair, clinging.

He wanted to do this for zhim. He wanted to bring her back for his charge.

He stood there for long minutes, everyone growing nervous around him in the silence, praying, waiting. Guilt started to bubble up in his chest as he kept searching and searching, hoping for some differential in the downpour of secrets.

If he could not wake her, she *would not* wake. Her body would fail to follow its natural cycles, to send the right signals and—

"Sleeping and waking, it's the natural order of things," he whispered. "Something Nature would help govern."

He wasn't sure why he hadn't thought of it before. It was a long shot, but if Thalo Infant could turn a rattle to stone, then zhur capabilities already possessed some depth. Maybe zhe could do something to help.

Or maybe Thalo Child was grasping at straws; he didn't know. He took one of Thalo Infant's hands, held it to his own forehead. "Can you *feel* how awake I am?"

"Yes," Thalo Infant said curiously.

"How about your father?" he asked, gesturing to Sebastian, who leaned in so his child could touch his face. "Can you feel his wakefulness?"

"Yes."

He moved zhur hand to the woman's forehead. "Can you *feel* how asleep she is?"

"Yes. I can feel it."

"How about you?" he asked, putting Thalo Infant's hand on zhur own cheek. "Do you feel like me or like her?"

"Like you," zhe giggled, perhaps thinking this a game.

"Good." He moved both of their hands back to Melanie's face. "Concentrate on the difference. Why she feels different. Can you find it?"

Thalo Infant scrunched zhur nose, clearly concentrating hard. Thalo Child let himself slip back into the rain, under the deluge.

This was a far cry from transmutation, and Thalo Infant was so young.

You can do it. I know you can.

Thalo Child kept searching, pelted left and right by useless secrets. He caught one or two—found things like how she would sometimes purposefully come back empty-handed from hunting, still too new to the concept to not feel guilty every time she felled a deer—but not the one he so desperately searched for.

And then, deep in the night-like void, he saw a flash of red. A droplet, streaming down an invisible shape, before reappearing high and then dripping down again, over and over.

"Found it!" Thalo Infant declared.

Thalo Child almost didn't dare hope, even as he mentally swooped toward the red drop. He could see it—he could see Thalo Infant manipulating a portion of Melanie, lighting it up like a beacon. And it was, in fact, a secret.

He didn't let himself get excited until he took hold of it with his magic, scraping at the red, trying to turn it clear like the rest of the rain.

But it didn't turn clear. It disappeared entirely.

Thalo Infant leaned forward and pressed zhur lips daintily to the scar on Melanie's forehead. "Wake up now."

And wake she did. Thalo Child expected her to gasp and flail—like a drowning person coming finally up for air. Instead, she blinked softly, stretched, like she'd just awoken from an easy night's sleep.

Her eyes focused and immediately saw nothing but Thalo Infant. Without a word, she scooped zhim into her arms and began to cry.

"It's okay; you're awake now," the toddler said.

A small knot tied itself in Thalo Child's chest. Had someone cried for him like this, once? Had his parents—his sister—missed him this fiercely? He looked to Juliet, who stood in the doorway, staring at him with a small tremble in her lip.

Sebastian leaned over Melanie, running the back of one finger down her arm, and she turned to him, roping him into a hug with one arm slung around his neck and the other still around Thalo Infant. She kissed them both profusely, and Thalo Infant giggled the whole time.

⊳—⊷⊶○⊷⊶⊲

Krona and Thibaut staggered up to their room, hand in hand. They were both silent but clearly deep in their own heads.

Inside, Krona opened the drawer with the mask in it and gazed at it for a long while, not touching, just looking. Hintosep had given her hints as to how De-Lia might be brought back, but nothing of substance, and now she was gone. The next steps Krona would have to work out on her own.

She glanced over to where Thibaut was readying himself for bed.

No, not on her own. She didn't have to do any of it by herself.

Carefully, she took the gods' minds from her satchel and deposited them next to De-Lia's mask. They'd need a safer place to store them, but this would do for one night.

Thibaut helped her undress. The places where her new bone growths had torn through her skin had healed, and the bones themselves were tough, living, and pain-free. They made sleeping on her back nearly impossible, but so far she'd managed.

She had yet to see what they looked like in a mirror.

"Hey," Thibaut said gently once she was nearly naked. "All right?"

She bit her lip, dipped her head noncommittally.

He seemed to understand what was bothering her. "You look even more the warrior," he said, voice a low rumble. "I think perhaps they suit you."

She felt her lip twitch in a light smile, but it wasn't one that reached her eyes.

He moved up behind her and slid his bare fingers over her right shoulder, beneath the swoop of the bones, caressing her skin but keeping clear of the spurs. He leaned near her neck, nosing up the column of her throat until his hot breath fell on her ear. "Can I touch them?" he whispered.

After a deep breath of consideration, she nodded.

He took one fingertip and ran it from the tip of the thickest bone down the curve of it to where it connected to her back.

She shivered, surprised she could feel it. The touch was distant, less like a touch of skin and more like the touch of teeth.

He petted the others just the same, growing bolder as he went. Eventually, he dipped down to kiss between her shoulder blades, and that was when she led him to bed.

After they'd indulged, Krona lay on her front, awake in the dark, thinking about crystalized minds, dead gods, and revenge. And what Avellino had said.

When they'd made their temporary shrine for the god's body, she'd asked Avellino what they were meant to do from there. What Hintosep's plan had been.

He'd stared into the amethyst skull, as though he might will Emotion to rise.

"There's only one way to liberate the Valley," he'd said, voice firm. "And that's to free the gods."

She'd nodded her understanding, whispering to herself, "The few that remain."

EPILOGUE

As the varger seeped into the room, Hintosep stopped struggling. The masked Grand Orchestrators saw their chance and fell on her with all their might, pushing her down until her head cracked against the floor—until her cheek was smearing against a puddle of Gerome's blood.

He lay still next to her. She couldn't tell if he was dead.

She suddenly laughed like Krona had, but not because anyone had manipulated her into it. It was a reaction fully contradictory to what she felt. The Savior had shown His true stripes. He commanded more than just natural power. How had He gotten it? What kind of awful experiments and magical distortions had allowed Him to turn Himself into an abomination?

Perhaps that was why He was slipping. Why His walls were crumbling and His time injections weren't stretching as far as they should.

It didn't matter now. Not with their deaths so close.

The vapors curled toward them. Krona had released a half a dozen. This would be over quickly.

But as they dove for the knot of Thalo, the Savior stretched out His hands. The varger hit an invisible wall—not stopping but slowing. Advancing like molasses.

Hintosep despaired.

Of course. Of course.

He'd shown He could manipulate the form of a living thing, like Nature. That He could spin emotions as well as manipulate secrets.

Of course He had command over Time's realm as well.

"Yes," He said, clearly reading her thoughts. Thoughts she hadn't even bothered to try to hide. "I have power over Knowledge as well." He knelt before her, keeping His robes just out of stain's way. "I have more power than any god," He declared darkly. "I truly *am* the Thalo."

She closed her punch-swollen eyes. Let her body go lax.

Either by His hand or her own exhaustion, her consciousness was taken from her.

When Hintosep woke, it was dark. She couldn't tell where she was, but it was cold—drafty—and there was a gentle *drip drip drip* of a nearby leak. Blood still caked her hair and face and clothes. She was leaning against a stone wall, hands in her lap, temple pressed against bare, gray bricks. The base of her skull throbbed, and as she lifted one hand to touch the spot, she realized she was chained.

In the far corner of the small space, someone struck a match, lit a candle on a wall sconce.

The Savior.

"What happened to Gerome?" she asked.

"He's no longer your concern." He stepped forward, holding something behind His back. "I must say, this is a lot of trouble for a pair of children and one Kairopath."

"Yes," she said firmly, emptying her mind of everything else—of all the things He had yet to find. "But an important pair of children, and a powerful Kairopath."

He sneered at her. "She fell in an instant against me. I don't know what you thought she could accomplish."

Hintosep watched Him approach with trepidation. She knew what would come next. She'd be made a Mindless. He'd take everything she was and lock it away.

"Oh, no, my dear," He said. "I have a much more fitting punishment for you."

She blinked at Him, unsure what He could mean.

"You've proven to me that you've forgotten many lessons. You're rash, arrogant, untrustworthy. You've favored personal ambitions over the greater plan to protect the Valley. Clearly, you need to be reeducated."

From behind His back He revealed the Cage. He held it up and out, and the legs flexed and opened, then rapidly shut again, jerking in the Savior's grasp like it could launch itself from His hands. "You were so helpful, bringing it back to us," He said. "I think it's only fitting that you wear it."

It was a creature grasping in the dark, searching for prey, for something to envelop. It wasn't alive but looked alive. Looked desperate. Hungry.

Her chest constricted; her breath wouldn't come. Not that. To have will but be unable to wield it—to be trapped in one's own body, forced to act out the puppetry of another. No. She'd rather die. She'd rather be a Mindless. "Please," she sobbed. "Absolon, please, no, I beg you."

"Yes, and I'm sure you'll keep begging," He said, stalking closer, taking a strand of her hair—white now stained red—and tucking it affectionally behind her ear. "For long years to come."

She wriggled backward as He bore down on her, trying to sink into the wall—to disappear into the stone.

Its sharp little feet with their sharp little claws flinched and clenched, eager to dig into her skin, world-toughened as it was.

"Now, now," He chided her, tone amused and patronizing. "It'll only hurt a little."

She tried to struggle more, to kick out when He came near, but it was not the reach of her chains that restrained her—held her perfectly still—but the strength of His stolen magics.

He did not bend her bones or morph them, the way He had with Krona. Instead, small vines erupted from the cracks in the walls, shooting toward her like a volley of worms with the crushing strength of giant Asgar-Skanian pythons. They bound her into position, with her head bowed, ready to accept the Cage as though it were a diadem and this was a coronation instead of retribution.

Her breathing became labored as she struggled still, committed to fighting until her will was taken from her limbs. She would not give Him the satisfaction of seeing her defeat herself before He delivered His final blow.

The Cage's hinges creaked as its legs splayed as wide as they could, and Absolon slipped it around the back of her skull with ease.

She screamed at Him then, pulling forth the most monstrous sound from the depths of her lungs, spitting out one last powerful denial before the legs snapped closed around her face.

As the claws latched themselves into her skin—sinking into her upper lip and her cheeks and her jaw and her temples—she instantly fell silent, her scream cut short as surely as if her head had been severed from her neck.

The claws drilled themselves deeper, and the pain made her want to thrash, but her body no longer heeded her. Everything from her arms to her legs to her spine to her fingers to her very eyelids no longer took orders from her but from the Cage's Possessor: Absolon Himself.

She went limp, like a ragdoll.

"There," He said. "Isn't that better?"

Hintosep wanted to grit her teeth and claw at His face and spit in His eye, but she did nothing.

She knew better than to keep willing herself to move or to speak. She'd been the Cage's Possessor for millennia. She knew the more one resisted, the more one fought to keep control, the quicker one lost their mind.

The only way to stay sane was to submit to the cage—not the artifact but the real cage in which she now found herself trapped. The cage of her own body.

"Smile, dear," He commanded.

The metal legs around her lips pulled taut, but it was the magic inherent in the enchantment that forced her to comply. It commanded her face to give Him an unnaturally wide, toothy grin.

"Wonderful," He said curtly, directing the vines to pull her into a resting position against the wall before retreating entirely.

Without another word or silent command, He turned and walked away.

Leaving her just as she was.

Painfully broad grin and all.

She knew better—she did—but she still couldn't suppress her instinct to fight, struggle, and deny. She tried to shout at Him, to kick her feet and demand He wait, demand He at least slacken her jaw and release her cheeks.

Already, little tremors wracked her lips from the unnatural strain.

But no matter how much she screamed in her head and willed herself to move, she remained still, dead-limbed and glassy-eyed, with nothing but her autonomic functions to indicate she was still among the living.

He snuffed the candle and left the cell, leaving her alone in darkness with nothing but impotent thoughts of revenge.

APPENDIX:
PERIODIC CIRCLE OF ELEMENTS

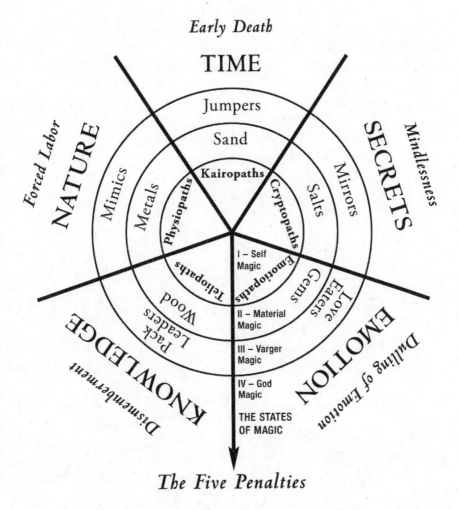

Early Death

TIME

Forced Labor

NATURE

Mindlessness

SECRETS

Jumpers

Sand

Kairopaths

Mimics

Metals

Physiopaths

Cryptopaths

Salts

Mirrors

Teliopaths

Wood

Pack Leaders

Emotiopaths

Gems

Eaters

Love

I – Self Magic

II – Material Magic

III – Varger Magic

IV – God Magic

THE STATES OF MAGIC

Dismemberment

KNOWLEDGE

EMOTION

Dulling of Emotion

The Five Penalties

ACKNOWLEDGMENTS

Big thanks to everyone who helped make *The Cage of Dark Hours* a reality, including but not limited to my agent, DongWon Song; my editor, Will Hinton; cover artist Reiko Murakami; mapmaker Jennifer Hanover; as well as Devi Pillai, Oliver Dougherty, Richard Shealy, and everyone in the design, production, audio, marketing, and publicity departments.

I'd also like to thank the members of my writing group (the MFBS), my family, and last but not least my husband, Alex, for supporting me with kind words, big hugs, and honest critiques (not to mention drawing up my Periodic Circle of Elements).

Fun additional fact: Juliet is, in both name and personality, a tribute to a real opera singer known as La Maupin, Julie d'Aubigny.